Hodder M. Westropp

The Travellers Art Companion to the Museums and Ancient Remains of Italy, Greece and Egypt by Hodder M. Westropp

Hodder M. Westropp

The Travellers Art Companion to the Museums and Ancient Remains of Italy, Greece and Egypt by Hodder M. Westropp

ISBN/EAN: 9783742808332

Manufactured in Europe, USA, Canada, Australia, Japa

Cover: Foto ©Andreas Hilbeck / pixelio.de

Manufactured and distributed by brebook publishing software
(www.brebook.com)

Hodder M. Westropp

The Travellers Art Companion to the Museums and Ancient Remains of Italy, Greece and Egypt by Hodder M. Westropp

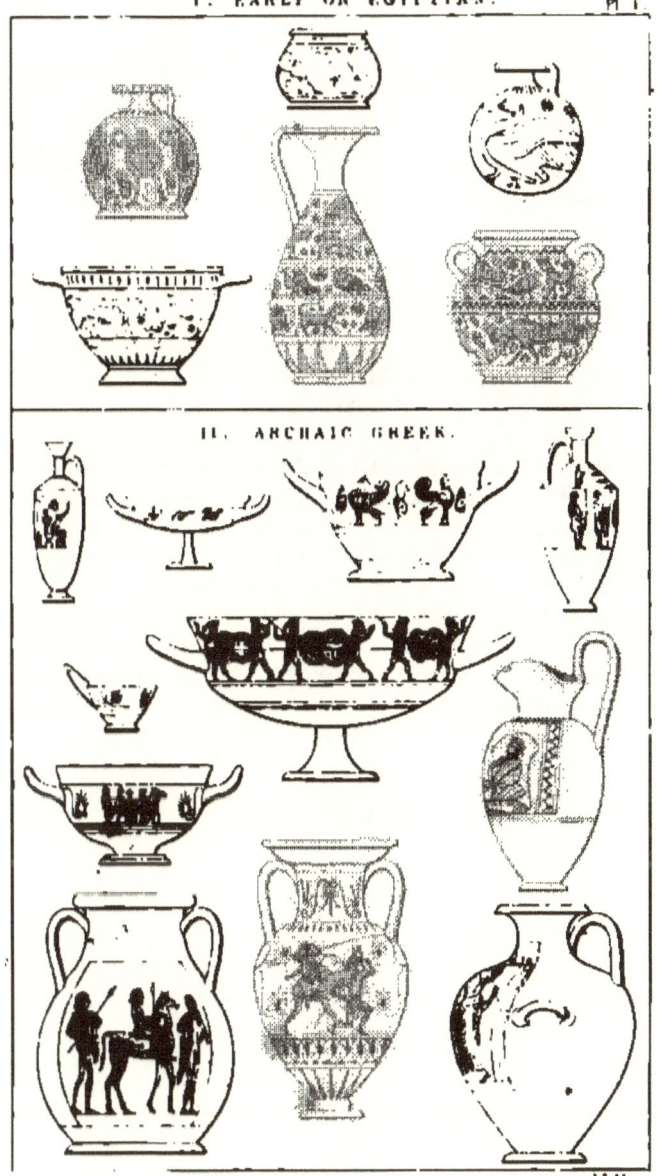

II. ARCHAIC GREEK.

J Jobbins

PREFACE.

Visiting the ancient countries of Egypt, Greece, and Italy, being the chief object of travelling at the present day, and the consequent interest taken in the remains of the former grandeur, magnificence, and high civilization of those countries, has made Archæology one of the most important and most interesting studies of the present day. Egypt, Greece, and Italy, were the fountain heads of our civilization and the sources of our knowledge; to them we can trace, link by link, the origin of all that is ornamental, graceful, and beautiful, in our architecture, sculpture, and in the arts of design. Remains, evincing the perfection they have reached in those arts, and attesting the stages of development which have been passed through leading to that culminating point of excellence, are still objects of the greatest interest in those countries. An intimate knowledge, therefore, of the original state and former perfection, and also of the present state of these remains, has been a matter of the deepest interest to many. Each country has found ardent investigators in its history and antiquities. The ruins of Egypt have yielded an endless amount of historical information to the ardent researches and zeal of Young, Champollion, Rosellini, Wilkinson, Dunson, Lepsius, Birch. The temples and Cyclopean remains of Greece have been accurately drawn and described by Chandler, Stuart, Dodwell, Müller, Leake, Falkener, Wordsworth, Penrose. The remains of ancient art in Italy have been always a favourite

theme of writers of different countries, English, French, German,
as well as of Italian writers. Braun, Cramer, Dennis, Fergusson,
Lanzi, Micali, Inghirami, Canina, have written largely on those
subjects.

The works of these authors, treating of the various subjects of
ancient art, are for the most part not only voluminous and very
costly, but also difficult to be procured. The present work has,
therefore, been compiled to supply a want often felt when travelling
in Greece, Italy, or Egypt; a work which would afford concise
general information on the objects of antiquity so frequently met
with in these countries. Its chief object has been to condense,
within the smallest possible compass, the essence of the information
contained in the writings of authors who are considered as authorities on these subjects

We have adopted the following division in this work :—

ARCHITECTURE	Egyptian, Grecian, Etruscan, Roman,	Walls, houses, temples, altars, columns, obelisks, pyramids, theatres, amphitheatres, mausolechia, hippodromes, stadia, baths, public roads, bridges, gates, aqueducts, tombs.
SCULPTURE.	Egyptian, Grecian, Etruscan, Roman,	Statues. Busts. Bas-reliefs.
PAINTING	Egyptian, Grecian, Etruscan, Roman,	Frescoes, painted sculpture, painted vases, mosaics.
GLYPTIC ART	Egyptian, Grecian, Etruscan, Roman.	Engraved stones, in intaglio and cameo.
INSCRIPTIONS	Egyptian, Grecian, Etruscan, Roman,	Material, alphabets, languages, abbreviations.

To avoid notes of reference, appended is a list of the works and writers consulted, and whose words are frequently quoted and introduced.

Bunsen's *Egypt.*

Lepsius' *Egypt.*

Wilkinson's *Ancient Egyptians.*

Sharpe's *Egypt.*

Müller's *Ancient Art* (Leitch's translation).

Fergusson's *Handbook of Architecture.*

Dennis' *Etruria.*

Flaxman's *Lectures.*

Westmacott's *Handbook of Sculpture.*

Gell's *Pompeiana.*

Winkelman.

Canina's *Roma Antica.*

Vitruvius.

Smith's *Dictionary of Antiquities.*

———— *Classical Dictionary.*

Gwilt's *Encyclopædia of Architecture.*

Rawlinson's *Herodotus.*

Wornum's *Epochs of Painting.*

Birch's *Ancient Pottery.*

C. W. King's *Antique Gems.*

———— *Natural History of Precious Stones.*

Vaux's *British Museum.*

To the kindness of Mr. Samuel Sharpe we are much indebted for the use of several woodcuts from his "History of Egypt."

H. M. W.

TABLE OF CONTENTS.

SCULPTURE.

MYTHOLOGY OF SCULPTURE.

PAINTING.

PAINTED VASES.

Second Division.

GLYPTOGRAPHY, OR ENGRAVED STONES.

LIST OF ILLUSTRATIONS.

SEPARATE PLATES.

HANDBOOK OF ARCHÆOLOGY.

MONUMENTS OF ARCHITECTURE.

EACH nation has its rules, its proportions, and its particular tastes, having always in view the same end—solidity, regularity, and convenience. The architecture of a people is an important part of their history. It is the external and enduring form of their public life: it is an index of their state of knowledge and social progress. The influence of climates and public institutions was particularly displayed in the productions of architecture. The material also afforded by the country must necessarily have an important influence on the architecture of a people. In our West, temples open to the sky would be as little suited to its climate as to our habits. Scenic representations formed more a part of the national customs of the Greeks and Romans than with us; and lastly, the art of war, such as it was among the ancients, imposed other principles on military architecture.

SECTION I.—WALLS—MORTAR—BRICKS.

WALLS: *Egyptian.*—The walls of inclosure of the Egyptian towns are generally constructed of crude bricks, dried in the sun. Their dimensions are various; the mud of the Nile supplied the material, which, however, required straw to prevent the bricks cracking. Sometimes they bear short hieroglyphic inscriptions enclosed in an oval, which is the stamp of the king under whose reign they were made. Burnt bricks were not used in Egypt, and when found they are known to be of a Roman time. Large and massive stones were used in the construction of the temples. Calcareous stone was generally employed in the walls of buildings. The only works of

B

Egyptian architecture known are temples, palaces, pyramids, walls of inclosure, quays, and other public constructions; private constructions, houses, &c., have disappeared in the lapse of time, either because they were built of clay or brick, or of some other as perishable material. The pyramidal or sloping line was a characteristic feature of the Egyptian style in temples and other buildings—the chief object of which was solidity. Another feature was the road moulding, with lines cut obliquely on it, on the angles formed by the faces of the wall. The walls were surmounted by a projecting cornice. The solidity of Egyptian masonry is well known: it is the result of the good choice of materials, of its extraordinary size, and of the care bestowed on the building. It has been frequently remarked, that in the courses the neighbouring stones were attached to one another by plugs of wood, dove-tailed at each end, and imbedded in the stones. The Greeks and Romans employed bronze and iron for the same purpose. There is no appearance that metallic cramps were ever used among the Egyptians.

MASONRY.

A   The reticulated work (opus reticulatum).
B   The uncertain (opus incertum).
C   The isodomum.
D   The pseudisodomum.
E   Emplecton (emplecton).
F   The section of bonds iron.
G   The isodomum (on a larger scale).

Grecian.—At first the Greeks built their walls of rough stones of large proportions; the interstices were filled up with smaller stones; remains of similar walls can be seen at Tiryns. At Mycenæ,

Corinth, Eretria, and Cadyanda in Lycia, the most ancient walls are of irregular polygons, carefully cut, and well joined together. When Grecian architecture arrived at perfection, it adopted three different kinds of masonry:—the *isodomum*; courses of stone of the same height, and in general very long: the *pseudo-isodomum*; courses of stone of irregular height: the *emplecton*, for extraordinary thickness. The two faces of the wall were built with cut stone, and the intervening space was filled with rough stones imbedded in mortar, and, at certain distances, stones (διατόνοι) long enough to extend to both sides, consolidated this kind of construction.

Italian.—In Italy the stages of the development of masonry are not very different from those followed in Greece. The following division of the relative antiquity of the different styles of masonry in ancient walls seems to be approved of by the best authorities, and may answer for the description of walls both in Greece and Italy, for the sequence of styles was similar in both countries. First, the *Cyclopean*, composed of unhewn masses, rudely piled up, with

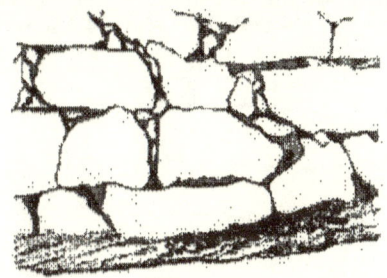

CYCLOPEAN WALLS.

no further adjustment than the insertion of small blocks in the interstices, and so described by Pausanias. Of this rudest style of masonry few specimens now exist; the most celebrated one is the citadel of Tiryns. The second style, which we would call the *Polygonal*, though generally called the Pelasgian, is a natural and obvious improvement of the former. The improvement consists in fitting the sides of the polygonal blocks to each other, so that exteriorly the walls may present a smooth and solid surface. What goes far to prove the high antiquity of this polygonal masonry is the primitive style of its gateways, and the absence of the arch in

B 2

connection with it; and also that it is found as a substruction under walls built in the horizontal style, which is of later origin, as in the walls of Cosa. This style is prevalent at Mycenæ, and also to

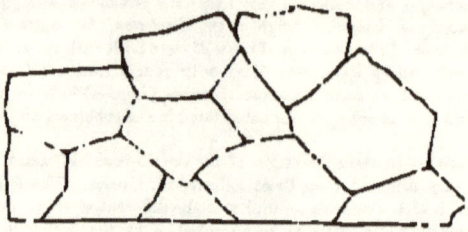

POLYGONAL WALLS.

be seen in the walls of Cadyanda in Lycia. It is also to be met with in the Etruscan cities of Cosa and Saturnia. Similar polygonal masonry is to be found in the walls of Alatri and Arpino. In the

WALLS OF COSA.

third style, which we shall call the *Irregular Horizontal*, by some called Etruscan, and also Hellenic, from its being the prevalent style in Etruria and in Greece, the blocks are laid in horizontal courses, with more or less irregularity; and the joints, sometimes accurately fitted, are either perpendicular or oblique. Cement was not employed in any of these walls: the massiveness of the parts rendered it unnecessary. An approximation to this style is visible

IRREGULAR HORIZONTAL.

at Mycenæ, but is seen in perfection in the cities of Etruria, many of which still retain their ancient walls; we may name Fiesole, Volterra, Cortona, Populonia, Roselle, and others.* To this may be

* Some attribute the adoption of these different styles of masonry to constructive necessity, and affirm that the character of the masonry is determined by the material, limestone splitting readily into polygonal forms, and travertine having a horizontal cleavage. This theory is however contradicted by the walls of Saturnia, for they are polygonal and built of travertine.

If I may be allowed to hazard a conjecture, I would say, that in the art of building, as in every other art, there is a progress from the rudest state to perfection; each separate style of masonry is the result or necessary consequence of that progress and gradual development in the art of building in any country, and not peculiar to any particular race; each style marking the stage of development in the art. As in sculpture there are three different styles; the first, rigid, hard, and rude, which was the first beginning of art; the second, when there was more regard to proportion and beauty; and lastly, the third or perfect style—so in masonry, the first or primitive style was but a piling up of rough blocks which might be suggested to any people; the second style may be considered an improvement of the former; the third style, a still greater improvement, when the masonry was brought to its most perfect state. Specimens of polygonal and horizontal masonry,

added a fourth style, which is the final improvement on the irregular
horizontal, and is composed of regular horizontal courses of cut
stone, such as was used in the flourishing period of Greece, and
similar to that now in universal use. This may be distinguished as
the *Regular Horizontal*; these different styles are not, however, of

REGULAR HORIZONTAL.

the same period or age in all countries, but they mark the stages of
development of the art of masonry in the country in which they are
found.

Roman. — At first the Romans imitated the Etruscans their masters,
and were ever borrowing of their neighbours, not only civil and
religious institutions, but even the sterner arts of war. In the
same manner in their architecture and fortification : in the Sabine
country they seemed to have copied the style of the Sabines, in
Latium, of the Latins, in Etruria of the Etruscans. Afterwards they
adopted two kinds of construction : the *incertum*, or antiquum, composed of small rough pieces placed irregularly, and imbedded in a

---

with a similar sequence of styles, are found in Peru and in the central parts of
America (Missouri), where they cannot be said to be of either Pelasgic or Etruscan
origin. According to Mr. Fergusson, examples occur in Peru of every intermediate
gradation between the polygonal walls of the house of Manco Capac and the regular
horizontal masonry of the Temples, precisely corresponding with the gradual progress of art in Latium, or any European country where the Cyclopean or Pelasgic
style of building has been found.

large quantity of mortar: and the *reticulatum*, composed of stones, cut and squared, but joined so that the line of the joining formed a diagonal, which gave to the walls the appearance of net-work. Vitruvius says, that this mode of building was the most common in his time; several examples of it still remain: one may be seen in that part of the walls of Rome called the Muro Torto. The Greeks gave it the name of *dictyotheton*, synonymous with net; they also communicated to the Romans their *emplecton*. Another structure of which the Romans made great use, and which was one of the most durable of all, was that composed of flat tiles. Caninn distinguishes five species of Roman masonry: (1) when the blocks of stone are laid in alternate courses, lengthwise in one course and crosswise in the next: this is the most common. (2) When the stones in each course are laid alternately along and across; this construction was usual when the walls were to be faced with slabs of marble. (3) When they were laid entirely longthwise; (4), entirely crosswise. (5) When the courses are alternately higher and lower than each other, as in the temple of Vesta, over the Tiber. The earliest instances of Roman masonry are to be found in the Carcer Mamortinus, the Cloaca Maxima, and the Servian walls. They are constructed of massive quadrangular hewn stones, placed together without cement.

MORTAR.—The perfection of that of the ancients has passed into a proverb. The Egyptians never employed it in their great constructions; but other monuments preserve traces of it: the pyramids were formerly covered with a coating which supposes its use. That plaster, lime, bitumen were employed in the arts, is attested by numerous examples. The Greeks and Etruscans were also acquainted with it, evidences of which are to be seen in a reservoir at Sparta, built of stones, cemented together; and in the sepulchral vaults of Tarquinii, which are plastered with stucco, covered with paintings. Necessity must have made the use of mortar familiar to every people. Time, which has hardened it, has caused it to be considered more perfect than the modern. Its extreme hardness may probably be accounted for by merely referring to the circumstance that the long exposure which it has undergone, in considerable masses, has given it the opportunity of slowly acquiring the carbonic acid from the air, upon which its hardness and durability depend. The chief excellence of the mortar of the ancients lay in their knowledge of the art of mixing lime with sand, more or less earthy. So scrupulous were the ancient masons in the mixing and blending of mortar, that the Greeks kept ten men constantly employed for a long space of

time in beating the mortar with wooden slaves, which rendered it
of such prodigious hardness, that Vitruvius tells us that slabs of
plaster cut from the ancient walls served to make tables.

BRICKS.—The ancients both baked their bricks and dried them in
the sun. The Egyptians used sun-dried bricks in the large walls
which inclosed their temples, and in the constructions about their
tombs. Pyramids were sometimes built of bricks, which consisted
of clay and chopped straw. In some of the paintings in Egyptian
tombs, slaves are represented mixing and tempering the clay, and
turning the bricks out of the mould. They are sometimes found
stamped with the oval of the king in whose reign they were
made. They are about sixteen inches long, seven wide, and five
thick. Burnt bricks were not used in Egypt until the Roman
period.

It has been supposed that the Greeks did not employ bricks until
after their subjugation by the Romans, as none of the works executed
prior to that period, the ruins of which still exist, exhibit any signs
of brick-work: yet there are Greek buildings mentioned by Vitruvius, as built of brick. Vitruvius (lib. ii. cap. 8) mentions the
walls of Athens, towards Mounts Hymettus and Pentelicus, and the
cells of the temples of Jupiter and Hercules. The Greek name for
bricks were didoron, pentadoron, tetradoron, from the Greek
δῶρον, a handbreadth. The didoron was a foot long and half a
foot wide. The pentadoron was five dora wide, and the tetradoron
four dora wide on each side. All these bricks were also made half
the size, to break the joint of the work; and the long bricks were
laid in one course, and the short in the course above them.
Vitruvius says, the pentadora were used in public works; and the
tetradora in private. The Romans, according to Pliny, began to
use bricks about the decline of the republic; but a brick building,
called Temple of the god Rediculus, still remains, which is said to
have been built on the occasion of the retreat of Hannibal. This
building is, however, now supposed to be a tomb and an imperial
structure, probably of the time of the Antonines. The Roman brick
used in the buildings on the Palatine hill, in the baths of Caracalla,
and in various remains of Roman buildings in England, is more like
a tile than a brick, being very thin compared with its length and
breadth. The dimensions of Roman bricks vary, being 7½ inches
square and 1½ thick; 16½ inches square, 2½ thick, and 1 foot
10 inches square, and 2½ thick; the colour is red. The terms used
by the Romans for bricks dried in the sun, were lateres crudi; and
for bricks burnt in the kiln, lateres cocli, or coctiles. Though

Augustus boasted that he found Rome brick and left it marble, brick continued to be generally used in the Roman buildings erected in the times of the later Roman emperors.

Section II.—HOUSES.

THE ancients acted differently from the moderns in this essential part of social customs. It does not seem that they ever occupied themselves in adorning towns by private buildings; public monuments had alone this privilege, and the honours decreed to citizens who had them built or repaired at their own expense, turned towards them their attention and the employment of their fortune rather than towards domestic habitations. The degree of comfort exhibited in the arrangement of their houses is a very important characteristic of a nation's degree of civilization, and we may mark the progress of this civilization in its successive stages from a rude condition to a high state of perfection by studying the architecture of a people as shown in their ordinary dwellings.

Egyptian.—Egyptian houses were built of crude brick, stuccoed and painted with all the combinations of bright colour in which the Egyptians delighted; and a highly decorated mansion had numerous courts and architectural details derived from temples. Over the door was sometimes a sentence, as "a good house," or the name of a king, under whom the owner probably held some office. The plans varied according to the caprice of the builders. In some houses the ground plan consisted of a number of chambers on three sides of a court, which was often planted with trees. Others were laid out in chambers round a central area, similar to the Roman impluvium, and paved with stone, or containing a few trees, a tank, or a fountain, in its centre. The houses in most of the Egyptian towns are destroyed, leaving few traces of their plans; but sufficient remains of some at Thebes and other places to enable us, with the help of the sculptures, to ascertain their form and appearance.

Greek.—The Greeks, according to Vitruvius, and probably the rich Greeks, divided their house into two apartments distinct one from the other, that of the men—andronitis, and that of the women—gynæconitis or gynæcum. A porter guarded the entrance of the house, which was generally a long corridor leading to the apartments, a Hermes, or a statue of Apollo Agyieus, or an altar to that god, adorned the entrance; at the end of this corridor was the peristyle of the andronitis, which was a space open to the sky in the centre, and surrounded on all four sides by porticoes, which were used for conversation and for exercise. Round the peristyle were arranged rooms used as banqueting rooms, music rooms, sitting, sleeping rooms, picture galleries, and libraries. A door from this peristyle opened into a passage leading to the gynæceum, which was at first in the upper story, when the andronitis was on the ground floor; afterwards it occupied, adjoining the latter, the most distant part of the house. Greek habits condemned women to habitual seclusion. A large hall was destined for their usual employments, surrounded by their slaves; at the further end of this hall or peristyle was the πρωστας or vestibule, on the right and left of which were two bedchambers, the θαλαμος and αμφιθαλαμος, the former was the principal bedchamber of the house. A dining-room, and the other rooms necessary for domestic purposes lay contiguous. Some smaller buildings, next the house, were destined for strangers. It seems that Greek houses had but one story; the pavement was a very hard cement, the roof was a platform surrounded by a balustrade. The light was admitted more through the upper part of the house than through the sides.

Roman.—The Romans, who lived in a common apartment with their women, adopted for their houses a different distribution from that of the Greeks: they were divided into two parts, one intended for public resort, the other for the private service of the family. The door, ostium, led through the vestibule, or prothyrum, where the porter, ostiarius, usually had his seat, into the atrium or cavædium, a kind of portico built in the shape of a parallelogram, according to the proportions of the different orders of architecture. It was roofed over, but with an opening in the centre, called compluvium, towards which the roof sloped, so as to throw the rain water into a cistern in the floor, called impluvium. The atrium was the most important part of the Roman house, it was used as a reception hall. Here the wealthy Roman exhibited to his numerous clients and flatterers all his wealth and magnificence. The atrium of M. Scaurus was celebrated for the richness of its marble columns and the beauty of its decorations. Vitruvius distinguishes five species of atria: I. The Tuscanicum, or Tuscan atrium, the oldest and simplest of all. It was merely an apartment, the roof of which was supported by four beams crossing each other at right angles, the included space forming the compluvium. It was styled Tuscan from the Tuscans, from whom the Romans adopted it. II. The tetrastyle, or four-pillared atrium, resembled the Tuscan, except that the girders or main beams of the roof were supported by pillars placed at the four angles of the impluvium, III. The Corinthian atrium differed from the tetrastyle only in the number of pillars and size of the impluvium. IV. The atrium displuviatum

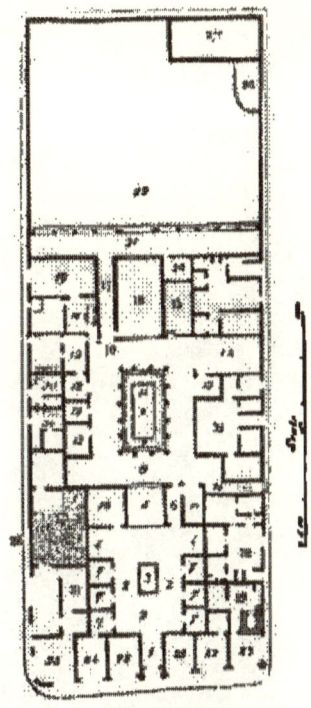

HOUSE OF PANSA.

1. Prothyrum.
2. Tuscan Atrium.
3. Impluvium.
4. Ala.
5. Open Tablinum.
6. Fauces.
7. Apartments.
8. Peristyle.
9. Open court.
10. Private entrance to Peristyle.
11. Basin.
12. Bedchambers.
13. Library.
14. Triclinium.

15. Winter area.
16. Large Summer area.
17. Fauces from Peristyle to garden.
18. Kitchen.
19. Servant's hall.
20. Cabinet.
21. Portico.
22. Garden.
23, 24. Shops.
25-29. Baking establishments.
26. Entrance to Peristyle from side street.
27. Reservoir.
28. Tank.

had its roof inclined the contrary way, so as to throw the water off to the outside of the house instead of carrying it into the impluvium. V. The atrium testudinatum was roofed all over, without any vacancy or compluvium. At the further end of the atrium was

RESTORED ATRIUM OF HOUSE AT POMPEII.

the tablinum, where the family archives were kept. It was separated from the cavædium by an aulæum or curtain, like a drop-scene. In summer the tablinum was used as a dining room. Near the tablinum were two small open rooms (alæ), and in a corner of the

atrium was the lararium, or small private chapel. By the side of
the tablinum was a corridor (fauces) which led to the private
apartments—the first of which to be mentioned is the peristyle.
It resembled the atrium, being in fact a court open to the sky in
the middle, and surrounded by a colonnade, but it was larger in its
dimensions. The centre of the court was often decorated with
shrubs and flowers, and was then called xystus. The other rooms,
besides the bedchambers, the smaller ones for the women (cubicula),
others with an alcove (thalami) for the master of the house, for his
daughters, were the triclinium, or dining room, so named from the
three beds, κλιναι, which encompassed the table on three sides,
leaving the fourth open to the attendants. The œci, from οικος, a
house, were spacious halls or saloons borrowed from the Greeks.
They were used for more extensive banquets; the œci, like the

TRICLINIUM.

atria, were divided into tetrastyle and Corinthian; the pinacotheca
or picture gallery, and the bibliotheca or library. The exedra was
either a seat intended to contain a number of persons, or a spacious
hall for conversation. In the furthest corner of the house was the
culina or kitchen. The floors of the higher order of Roman houses
were generally covered with stone, marble, or mosaic. The houses
at Pompeii contain specimens of floors in mosaic, exhibiting exquisite taste in the variety of ornament elaborated in them. The

walls of the rooms were sometimes lined with thin slabs of marble; they were also painted in fresco. Their decorative paintings generally represented mythological subjects, dancing figures, landscapes, and ornamentation in boundless variety. Windows (fenestræ) were seldom used in Roman houses. The atria and peristyles being always open to the sky, and the adjoining rooms receiving their light from them, prevented the necessity of windows; windows were only required when there was an upper story. Roman life, as at the present day, being so much out of doors, windows were seldom wanted.

The house of Lepidus was at first considered the finest in Rome; the thresholds of the doors were of Numidian marble; but he was soon surpassed by others in splendour and magnificence, especially by Lucullus. At Athens the houses of Themistocles, of Aristides, differed but little from those of the poorest citizen. The Romans had many stories to their houses; to prevent the inconveniences which would result, Augustus restricted their height to seventy feet, which Trajan reduced to sixty.

It was in their villas or country houses that the Romans displayed a boundless luxury; objects of art and the productions of the most distant nations were collected there in addition to the profusion of other ornaments. Lucullus erected several magnificent villas near Naples and Tusculum, which he decorated with the most costly paintings and statues, in which he lived in a style of magnificence and luxury which appears to have astonished even the most wealthy of his contemporaries. The emperors Nero and Adrian also built magnificent villas, which the arts of Greece and the luxury of the East contributed to adorn. It was in the villas of the emperors, or of the most wealthy citizens, that the most beautiful productions of ancient art have been found.

A Roman villa, according to the rule laid down by Vitruvius, and the younger Pliny's description of his Laurentine villa, had its atrium next the door or porch at the entrance. Opposite the centre of the peristyle was a cavædium, after which came the triclinium, on every side of which were either folding doors or large windows, affording a vista through the apartments, and views of the surrounding scenery and distant mountains. Near this were several apartments, including bedchambers and a library. Attached to the villa were baths, halls for exercise, gardens (xystus), and every arrangement which could conduce to the pleasure and amusement of a wealthy Roman. The suburban villa of Diomedes at Pompeii presents a somewhat different arrangement to that of Pliny's Laurentine villa.

SECTION III.—TEMPLES.

TEMPLES are sacred edifices destined to the worship of the divinity. All nations have raised them, and the piety which founded them hastened the progress of architecture by the desire to render these edifices more worthy of their destination. The Egyptians have surpassed all nations in the extent and magnificence of these public monuments; they had ancient temples when the oracle of Delphi dwelt in a cabin of laurels, and the Jupiter of Dodona had but an old oak for an abode.

Egyptian.—The temple, properly so called, or the cella, or adytum, was in the form of a square, or an oblong square. It was there that the god dwelt, represented by his living symbol, which superstitious minds have taken for the divinity itself. The religious rituals prescribed in all its minutiæ the order of the service of the priests towards these sacred animals, the representatives of the god, chosen and pointed out according to exterior signs prescribed by the ritual. The adytum, or σηκος, the principal part of the temple, is always the most ancient part, and bears the name of the king who had it built and dedicated. The plans of the different temples of Egypt display a great diversity, but evince a certain uniformity in the principal parts. An Egyptian temple, as Mr. Fergusson remarks, is an aggregation of parts around a small but sacred centre, which have been gradually elaborated during several centuries. The larger temples were generally approached by an avenue of sphinxes, and a pair of obelisks was placed in front of the pylons. We extract the following description of the temple known as the Rhamesson, from Mr. Fergusson's "Handbook," as affording an accurate general description of an Egyptian temple. The whole temple was built by Rhameses the Great, in the fifteenth century, B.C. Its façade is formed by two great pylons, or pyramidal masses of masonry, which are the most appropriate and most imposing part of the structure externally. Between these is the entrance doorway (propylon), leading almost invariably into a great square court-yard, with porticoes, always on two, and sometimes on three sides. This leads to an inner court, smaller, but far more splendid, than the first. On the two sides of this court, through which the central passage leads, are square piers with colossi in front, and on the right and left are double ranges of circular columns, which are continued also behind the square piers fronting the entrance. Passing

through this, we come to a hypostyle hall of great beauty, formed
by two ranges of larger columns in the centre, and three rows of
smaller ones on each side. These hypostyle halls almost always
accompany the larger Egyptian temples of the great age. They
derive their name from having an upper range of columns, or what
in Gothic architecture, would be called a clerestory, through which
the light is admitted to the central portion of the hall. Although
some are more extensive than this, the arrangement of all is nearly

ENTRANCE TO EGYPTIAN TEMPLE.

similar. They possess two ranges of columns in the centre, so tall
as to equal the height of the side columns, together with that of
the attic which is placed on them. These are generally of different
orders; the central pillars having a bell-shaped capital, the under
side of which is perfectly illuminated from the mode in which the
light is introduced: while in the side pillars the capital was narrower at the top than at the bottom, apparently for the sake of
allowing its ornaments to be seen. Beyond this are always several
smaller apartments, in this instance supposed to be nine in number,
but they are so ruined that it is difficult to be quite certain what
their arrangement was. These seem to have been rather suited to
the residences of the king or priests, than to the purposes of a
temple, as we understand the word. Indeed, palace-temple, or
temple-palace, would be a more appropriate term for these buildings
than to call them simply temples. They do not seem to have been
appropriated to the worship of any particular god, but rather for the

great ceremonials of royalty, of kingly sacrifice to the gods for the people, and of worship of the king by the people. He seems to have been regarded, if not as a god, at least as the representative of the gods on earth. Though the Rhamesion is so grand from its dimensions, and so beautiful from its designs, it is far surpassed, in every respect, by the palace-temple at Karnak, which is, perhaps, the noblest effort of architectural magnificence ever produced by the hand of man. Its principal dimensions are 1,200 feet in length, by about 360 feet in width, and it covers, therefore, about 430,000 square feet. The following description is from Sir G. Wilkinson. The principal entrance of the grand temple is on the north-west side, or that facing the river. From a raised platform commences an avenue of Crio-sphinxes leading to the front propyla before which stood two granite statues of a Pharaoh. One of these towers retains a great part of its original height, but has lost its summit and cornice. Passing through the pylon* of these towers, you arrive at a large open court, or area, 275 feet, by 320 feet, with a covered corridor on either side, and a double line of columns down the centre. Other propylæa terminate this area, with a small vestibule before the pylon, and form the front of the grand hall of assembly, the lintel stones of whose doorway were 40 foot 10 inches in length. The grand hall measures 170 feet, by 329 feet, supported by a central avenue of twelve massive columns, 62 feet high (without the plinth or abacus), and 11 feet 6 inches in diameter; besides 122 of smaller, or, rather, less gigantic dimensions, 42 feet 6 inches in height, and 28 feet in circumference, distributed in seven lines on either side of the former. The twelve central columns were originally fourteen, but the northernmost have been enclosed within the front towers or propyla, apparently in the time of Sethi or Osiroi, himself, the founder of the hall. The two at the other end were also partly built into the projecting wall of the doorway. Attached to this doorway are two other towers, closing the inner extremity of the hall; beyond which are two obelisks, one standing on its original site, the other having been thrown down and broken by human violence. Similar, but smaller, propyla succeed to this court, of which they form the inner side. The next court contains two obelisks of larger dimensions, the one now standing being 92 feet high, and 8 feet square, surrounded by a peristyle of Osiride figures. Passing between two dilapidated propyla, you enter another smaller area, ornamented in a similar manner, succeeded by a vestibule, in front of the granite gateway of the towers which form the façade of

* Sir G. Wilkinson terms the pyramidal towers, pro-pyla; and the entrance gateway the pylon. Mr. Fergusson seems to reverse this.

the court before the sanctuary. This sanctuary is of red granite, divided into two apartments, and surrounded by numerous chambers of small dimensions, ranging from 20 feet by 16 feet, to

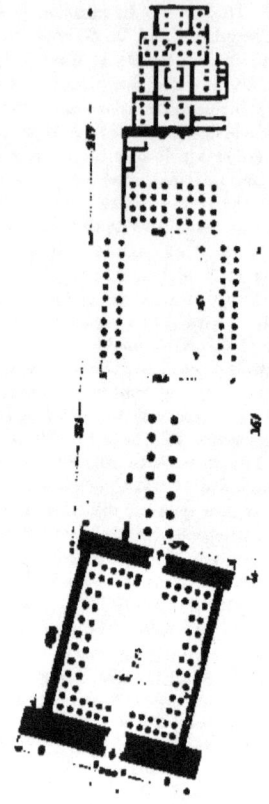

GROUND-PLAN OF LUXOR.

16 feet by 8 feet. The sanctuary, which was the original part of this great group, was built by Osirtasen, the great monarch of the twelfth dynasty. Behind this a palace, or temple, was erected by

Thotmes III., considered by Mr. Fergusson as one of the most singular buildings in Egypt. The hall is 140 feet long, by 55 feet in width, internally, and the roof supported by two rows of massive square columns, and two of circular pillars of most exceptional form, the capital being reversed. Like almost all Egyptian halls it was lighted from the roof.

A dromos, or avenue of sphinxes lead from Karnak to the temple of Luxor, in front of which were two obelisks covered with hieroglyphics, remarkable for admirable execution. One of these has been carried to Paris. Immediately in front of the propylon are two sitting statues of Rameses II. Behind these tower two enormous pylons, the façades of which are covered with bas-reliefs, representing the wars and victories of king Rameses. Within there was a court, 190 feet by 170 feet, surrounded by a peristyle consisting of two rows of columns. This was built at a different angle from the rest of the building, being turned so as to face Karnak. Beyond this was once a great hypostyle hall, of which the central colonnade alone remains. To this succeeds a court of 155 feet by 109 feet, surrounded by a peristyle, terminating in a portico of thirty-two columns. Still further back were smaller halls and numerous apartments, evidently meant for the king's residence, rather than for a temple, or place exclusively devoted to worship. Like the palaces, of Nineveh, the Egyptian temples were, doubtless, palace-temples; for the sovereigns of Assyria and Egypt combined the offices and duties of priest and king. The irregularity of this temple has led to the conjecture that the whole was not built at once, according to a general plan, but that it was the work of successive ages. The southern end was built by Amunoph III.; the great court, the pylons, statues, and obelisks, were added by Rameses the Great.

The temples of Apollinopolis Magna (Edfou), and of Tentyra (Dendora), being of a later age, differ considerably in plan and arrangement from the elder palace-temples, for they are more essentially temples. They are also remarkable for their dimensions and richness of decoration. The large temple at Edfou is built on the grandest scale, and like most Egyptian temples, is covered with paintings and sculpture, representing mythological and regal personages. It was erected in the age of the Ptolemies. The columns of this temple are remarkable for their elegance and variety, being formed on the type of the different plants and flowers of the country. It has the usual façade of an Egyptian temple, the two large and massive pylons with a gateway in the centre. Within there is a court, 140 feet by 161 feet, surrounded by a colonnade on three sides, and rising by easy steps, the whole width of the court, to the front or portico, which in Ptolemaic temples takes the place of the great hypostyle halls of the Pharaohs.   It is lighted from the front

PALACE OF EDFOU.

over low screens placed between each of the pillars, a peculiarity scarcely ever found in temples of earlier date.   Within this is an inner and smaller porch, which leads through two passages to a dark and mysterious sanctuary. The temple of Dendera, was dedicated to the goddess Athor, the Egyptian Venus. It was built in a

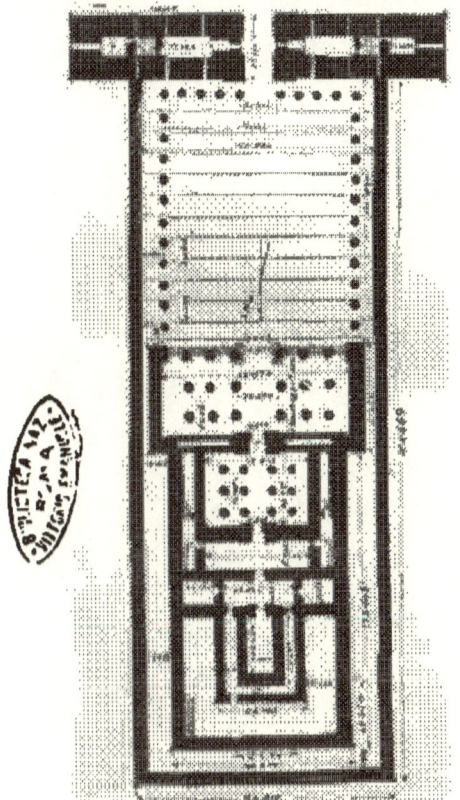

PLAN OF THE TEMPLE OF EDFOU.

Roman or Ptolemaic period, and consequently in the decline of Egyptian art. It is a large and massive building, overcharged with hieroglyphic sculpture and ornament, evincing in its profusion and gracelessness the decadence of the Egyptian style. It has no fore-court, nor propylons. Its columns terminate in a capital representing the head of the goddess Athor, repeated four times, surmounted by a quadrangular pylon.

TEMPLE OF DENDERA

Grecian.— Temples in Greece were very numerous. Cities erected them to their tutelary deities: Athens to Minerva, Ephesus to Diana, &c., and the inhabitants of the country to the rustic

divinities. The temples of the Greeks never equalled those of
Egypt in extent, size was not the object with the Greeks. Their
genius was shown more in the exquisite perfection of architectural
design and sculpturesque ornament employed in their religious
creations. All within the sacred fence, περίβολος, which enclosed
the temple properly so called, the habitations of the priests, and
ground sometimes of considerable extent, was styled the Hieron
(ἱερὸν), and also τέμενος. The naos, cella or temple, properly so
called, was generally in the shape of a parallelogram. Sometimes a
court, surrounded by a portico or colonnade, was placed before it,
as at the temple of Isis, at Pompeii, and at the temple of Serapis, at
Pozzuoli. A portico surrounded the cella, the extent of which
depended on the construction of the temple. It was there that the
people assembled, the priests alone had the right of entering the

TEMPLE OF JUPITER AT ÆGINA RESTORED.

cella; the Peribolos, or court, surrounded by a wall which separated it from the rest of the sacred grounds, added still more to the
extent of space; it was generally adorned with statues, altars, and
other monuments, sometimes even with small temples. The temples of the tutelary divinities were, in general, on the highest point
of the town: those of Mercury on the lower grounds; the temples
of Mars, Venus, Vulcan, Æsculapius, outside and near the gates;
the best situations were chosen, and the oracles were also consulted
for this purpose. According to Vitruvius, the entrance of the
temples looked towards the west, so that those who came to make
their sacrifices were turned to the east, whence the statue of the

gul seemed to come; most of the temples, however, still extant in Attica, Ionia, Sicily, have their entrance towards the east. The anterior part, before the entrance of the cella, was called the pronaos, or προδρομος, the vestibule; the posterior part, if there was any, the posticum. The opisthodomos was the chamber behind the cella, which sometimes served as a place in which the treasures of the temple were kept. Above the entablature of the columns arose at both fronts, a pediment or triangular termination of the roof, called Aetos and Aetoma by the Greeks, which was generally adorned with statues and bas-reliefs. The front was always adorned with an equal number of columns—of four (tetrastyle), of six (hexastyle), of eight (octastyle), of ten (decastyle). On the sides the columns were generally in an unequal number, and as the length of the temple was generally the double of the breadth, there were thirteen columns on the side of the front of six, seventeen for that of eight, counting both the columns at the angles, which is to be seen in the smaller temple at Pæstum, in that of Concord, at Agrigentum, and in the Parthenon, at Athens (see p. 26). The statue of the god to which the temple was consecrated, was the most sacred object in it, and the work of the most skilful artists. The eastern part of the cella, or σηκος, was assigned to it, and it always faced the entrance. The place where the statue stood was called ἑδος, and was generally surrounded by a balustrade. Private persons might place, at their own expense, either in the naos, or in the pronaos, statues of other gods and heroes. Sacrifices were made to them also, and the altars were dedicated to the principal divinity, and the other gods adored in the same temple; θεοι συνναοι. The altar of sacrifices was placed before the statue of the principal divinity. Sometimes many altars were to seen in the same cella. The interior walls were covered with paintings, representing the myth of the god, or the actions of heroes. The rich offerings, the spoils carried off from the enemy, which were consecrated to the gods by kings, towns, generals, and private persons, were deposited in the treasury of the temple, frequently placed in the opisthodomos. Sometimes, also, the public treasure was deposited in the temple. Around the temple was a platform of three ascending steps, which formed a basis or substructure, on which the colonnade was placed, this was termed the stylobate, and also stereobate. These structures present the most beautiful models of ancient architecture; the Doric order characterizes the most ancient, the Corinthian the most beautiful.

Among Grecian temples, the most ancient existing specimen of the Doric order is the temple at Corinth. Its massive proportions, the simplicity of its forms, the character of its workmanship, and

the coarseness of the material, are sufficient indications of its antiquity. The latest date that can be ascribed to this temple is the
middle of the seventh century, B.C. Seven columns alone remain of it.
Next in age to this is the temple of Ægina. The temple of Jupiter
Panhellenius, at Ægina, was of the Doric order, and was hexastyle,
peripteral, and hypæthral. It is remarkable for the traces of
painting on its architectual decorations, and the archaic sculpture of
its pediments. The style of its architecture indicates the middle of
the sixth century, B.C. The next in order of time and style is
the Doric temple of Theseus at Athens. It is of a rectangular
form, peripteral, and hexastyle. This temple, remarkable for
its exact proportions, and for being perhaps the best preserved
monument of antiquity, probably furnished the model of the Parthenon. As Mr. Fergusson remarks, it constitutes a link between
the archaic and the perfect age of Grecian art. Of all the great
temples, (we again quote Mr. Fergusson), the best and most celebrated
is the Parthenon, the only octastyle Doric temple in Greece, and, in
its own class, the most beautiful building in the world. It was
constructed by two architects, Callicrates and Ictinus, in the time
and by the order of Pericles, and was adorned by Phidias with those
inimitable sculptures, fragments of which are now in the British
Museum. It was erected about 448, B.C. The length is about 230 feet
and breadth 100 feet. Its plan is peripteral octastyle. Besides the
outer columns there is an inner pronaos hexastyle. The naos
was hypæthral, and 98 feet long and 63 feet wide. At the
further end of this was the chrys-elephantine statue of Minerva, by
Phidias. Behind was the opisthodomus or treasury of the temple.
The sculptures of the pediment, the metopes, the bas-reliefs of the
frieze, were the productions of the school of Phidias, and the most
perfect examples of sculpture executed. After this comes the
temple of Jupiter at Olympia, famous for its size and beauty. Its
site can alone be identified at the present day. To the same age
belong the temple of Apollo Epicurius at Bassæ, its frieze, probably
the work of the scholars of Phidias, is now in the British Museum;
the temple of Minerva at Sunium, and the greater temple at
Rhamnus.

Sicily and Magna Græcia, colonies of Greece, afford a number of
examples of Grecian temples. In Sicily, the earliest example is
that of Selinus. The style of its sculpture indicates a very early
date, about the middle of the seventh century, B.C. At Agrigentum
there are three Doric temples, and one remarkable for its gigantic
dimensions. At Segesta is a temple in an excellent state of preservation. Pæstum, in Magna Græcia, presents a magnificent group of

temples. Of these the earliest is the temple of Neptune, supposed
to be coeval with the earliest period of Grecian emigration to the
south of Italy. It is hexastyle and hypæthral. Solidity combined
with simplicity and grace distinguishes it from the other buildings.

The other temples, the basilica, and the temple of Ceres, betray the influence of a later or Roman style. At Metapontum are the ruins of a Doric temple, of which fifteen columns with the architrave are still standing.

The earliest Ionic temple of which remains are yet visible is supposed to be that dedicated to Juno at Samos. At Teos, a town in Ionia, there is a very beautiful Ionic temple dedicated to Bacchus. It is now in ruins. The celebrated temple of Diana at Ephesus is said to have been Ionic. Even its site is now unknown. Of Ionic temples in Greece, the oldest example probably was the temple on the Ilissus, now destroyed, dating from about 488 B.C. Of all examples of this order, the most perfect and the most exquisite is the Erectheum at Athens. It was a double temple, of which the eastern division was consecrated to Minerva Polias, and the western, including the northern and southern porticoes, was sacred to Pandrosus, the deified daughter of Cecrops. The eastern portico, or entrance to the temple of Athena Polias, consisted of six Ionic columns. The northern portico, or pronaos of the Pandroseum, had four Ionic columns in front, and one in each flank. The southern portico, or Cecropium, which was a portion of the Pandroseum, had its roof supported by six caryatides. Within its sacred enclosure were preserved the holiest objects of Athenian veneration—the olive of Minerva and the fountain of Neptune. Its sculptured ornaments exhibit the most perfect finish and delicacy in their execution.

Though of Grecian origin, there are few examples of the Corinthian order among Greek temples. The temple of Jupiter Olympius at Athens may be considered as the sole example of that order in Greece. It is, however, of a Roman period, having been commenced by the Roman architect Cossurius and completed by Hadrian. It was a magnificent structure, and of vast dimensions, measuring in its length 354 feet, and in its breadth 171 feet.

Etruscan.—According to Vitruvius, there were two classes of temples in Etruria. The first circular, and dedicated to one god; the other rectangular, with three cells, sacred to three deities. Mr. Ferguson believes the original Etruscan circular temple to have been a mere circular cell with a porch. In the opinion of Muller, Vitruvius took his rules of an Etruscan temple from that of Ceres, in the Circus Maximus, dedicated in the year of Rome 261, which was of a rectangular form, and divided in two parts in its length, the outward for the portico, and the inner for the temple, which was divided into three cells. There are no remains at the present day of an Etruscan temple—supposed to be in consequence of their

being principally constructed of wood. The temple of Jupiter
Capitolinus at Rome was evidently, from the description of Dionysius,
as there are no traces of it at the present day, built in the Etruscan
style. According to Dionysius, it had three equal cellæ (σηκοι)
within the walls, having common sides: that of Jupiter in the
middle, on one side that of Juno, and on the other that of Minerva,
all under the same roof. It was commenced by Tarquinius Priscus
and finished by Tarquinius Superbus. Burnt down in the wars of
Sylla and Marius, it was restored by the former according to the
original plan, upon the same foundations. It occupied the site of
the church of the Ara Cœli.

Roman.—Rome, the disciple of Greece, imitated it in general, in
the construction of its temples, and what has been said of the
temples of the Greeks can be almost entirely applied to those of the
Romans. "From the Greeks they borrowed the rectangular peri-
stylar temple, with its columns and horizontal architraves, though
they seldom if ever used it in its perfect purity, the cellæ of the
Greek temples not being sufficient for their purposes. The principal
Etruscan temples were square in plan, and the inner half occupied
by one or more cells, to the sides and back of which the porticos
never extended. The Roman rectangular temple is a mixture of
these two; it is generally, like the Greek examples, longer than its
breadth, but the colonnade never entirely surrounds the building.
Sometimes it extends to the two sides as well as the front, but more
generally the cella occupies the whole of the inner part, though
frequently ornamented by a false peristyle of three-quarter columns
attached to its walls. Besides this, the Romans borrowed from the
Etruscans a circular form of temple unknown to the Greeks, but
which to their tomb-building predecessors must have been not only
a familiar but a favourite form. As used by the Romans it was
generally encircled by a peristyle of columns, though it is not clear
that the Etruscans so used it. Perhaps this is an improvement
adopted from the Greeks in an Etruscan form. In early times these
circular temples were dedicated to Vesta or Cybele." (Fergusson)
The Romans differed essentially from the Greeks in the arrangement of the columns placed on the sides. The Romans, in fact,
counted not the columns, but the intercolumniations, and Vitruvius
informs us that on each side they placed double the number on
the front, so that a Roman temple which had six or eight columns on
the front, had eleven or fifteen on each side. The temple of Fortuna
Virilis at Rome has four columns in front and seven on the sides,
thus the number of intercolumniations of the sides was double that of

the front. But exceptions are to be found to this rule. The statue of the god was also the principal object in the temple, an altar was raised before it. Some temples had many statues and many altars. The temples of the Romans contained paintings also; in the year of Rome 450 (304 B.C.), Fabius ornamented the temple of the goddess Salus with them, which acquired for him the surname of Pictor, preserved by his descendants. Paintings carried off from the temples of Greece were sometimes placed in those of Rome. The national style of temple architecture of the Romans, with few exceptions, was the Corinthian; that of Greece and its Italian colonies, the Doric.

It has been observed that there is perhaps nothing that strikes the inquirer into the architectural history of the Imperial city more than the extreme insignificance of her temples as compared with the other buildings of Rome itself, and with some temples found in the provinces. The only temple which remains at all worthy of such a capital is the Pantheon. All others are now mere fragments. The finest example of a temple of the Corinthian order at Rome is that which is now styled the temple of Minerva Chalcidica. Its three remaining columns are frequent models of the Corinthian order. It was octastyle in front. The height of the pillars was 48 feet, and that of the entablature 12 feet 6 inches. The temple of Vespasian, at the foot of the Capitol, formerly styled the temple of Jupiter Tonans, has only three columns left standing. These Corinthian columns, only slightly inferior in size to those of the temple of Minerva, belonged to a building about 85 feet long and 70 feet wide. This was hexastyle and peripteral. The temple of Saturn, near this, presents a portico of eight Ionic columns, six of which are in front and two in the flanks. The temple of Mars Ultor, erected by Augustus, formerly considered to be a portion of the Forum of Nerva, has only three columns remaining. It is of the Corinthian order. Its cella terminates in an apse—an early instance of what became afterwards a charac-teristic of all places of worship. The temple of Antoninus and Faustina, in the Corinthian order of a much later period, affords an example of a pseudo-peripteral temple. Of this class is also the small Ionic temple of Fortuna Virilis. It is the purest specimen of that order in Rome. Of the Composite order, though a Roman invention, there are no examples among Roman temples. The other temples at Rome, the existing remains of which are but few, are the temple of Concord, the temple of Venus and Rome, the temple of Minerva Medica, the temple of Æsculapius, the temple of Remus.

Of circular temples the Pantheon is the most famous. It has

been admitted to be the finest temple of the ancient world. It was dedicated by Agrippa to all the gods. It is a circular building, with a portico in front composed of sixteen Corinthian columns, eight columns of these are in front, and the remaining eight are arranged behind them. The interior of the temple is circular, covered with a dome, one of the features for which modern architecture is indebted to the Romans. The internal diameter is 142 feet. The height from the pavement to the summit is 143 feet. A remarkable feature in this building is the central opening of the top, about 26 feet in diameter,

TEMPLE OF THE SIBYL AT TIVOLI.

to admit light into the interior. The temples of Vesta and of the Sibyl at Tivoli were circular peripteral. The circular cella of the temple of Vesta is surrounded by a peristyle of twenty Corinthian columns. The entablature and ancient roof have disappeared. It is supposed to have been originally covered by a dome, which rested on the circular wall of the cella. The temple at Tivoli is supposed to have been also dedicated to Vesta. Its cella was surrounded by a peristyle of eighteen Corinthian pillars, ten of which remain. It is 21½ feet in diameter.

The examples of Roman architecture exhibited in the temples of Palmyra and Baalbec are not to be surpassed for extent and magnificence. The buildings of Palmyra, whose ruins yet remain, were evidently built at very different times, but the prevalence of the Corinthian order must make them rank as Roman structures. The temple of the Sun, the chief building among the ruins, is in an enclosed space 660 feet square. This court was bounded by a wall having a row of pilasters in each face. In the midst of this court are the mighty ruins which formed the temple, exhibiting an amazing assemblage of columns, sculptured profusely with those decorations which constitute the distinctive features of the Roman Ionic and Corinthian orders.

The temples of Baalbec form a most magnificent temple group. They consist of three structures: a temple of the sun, or great temple, a smaller temple, and a very beautiful circular temple. The great temple which was decastyle peripteral, had in its front a court nearly 400 feet square, which was approached by an hexagonal court with a portico of twelve Corinthian columns. The terrace on which the temple stands is formed of stones of enormous magnitude; at the north-west angle are three stones, two of which are 60 feet, and the third 62 feet 9 inches in length. They are 13 feet in height, and about 12 feet thick. Close to this is the smaller temple, it is octastyle peripteral. It is remarkable for the beauty and proportions of its portico. In plan it somewhat resembles a Roman basilica. The circular temple is of the Corinthian order, with niches on the exterior of the cella, and decorated with twelve columns.

The Maison Carrée, at Nismes is also a Roman temple. It is a pseudo-peripteral Corinthian temple, for the side columns are half imbedded in the walls of the cella. It has a hexastyle portico in front, and eleven columns along each flank. The columns of the back-front are also encased in the walls of the building. There are no windows, and, consequently, it must have been hypæthral. It has been recently shown to have been erected to M. Aurelius and L. Verus. There is also a Roman temple at Evora in Portugal, in excellent preservation. The portico is hexastyle Corinthian.

Among the Greeks and Romans the simplest form of the rectangular temple was the apteral or *άστυλος*, without any columns; the next was that in which the two side walls were carried out from the naos to form a porch at one or both extremities of the building. These projecting walls were terminated on the front, or on both faces of the building, by pilasters, which, thus situated, were called antæ; and hence this kind of temple was said to be *in antis ἐν παραστάσι*. It had two columns between the antæ. When columns were placed at one extremity of the building, in advance of the line joining the antæ, the temple was *prostyle, πρόστυλος*. It had four columns in front. If columns were placed in a similar way at both extremities of the building, it was said to be amphiprostyle, *ἀμφιπρόστυλος*. A temple having columns entirely surrounding the

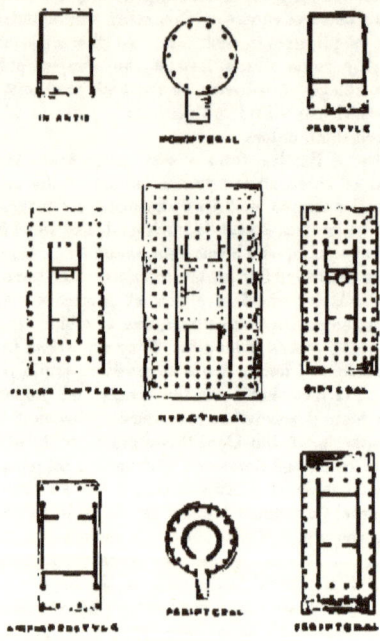

IN ANTIS

MONOPTERAL

PROSTYLE

PSEUDO DIPTERAL

HYPÆTHRAL

DIPTERAL

AMPHIPROSTYLE

PERIPTERAL

PSEUDOPTERAL

PLAN OF TEMPLES.

walls was called *periptoral, περίπτερος, ἀμφικίων*. A temple was of the kind called *dipteral, δίπτερος*, when it had two ranges of columns, one within the other, and which entirely surrounded the naos. When there were two rows of columns in front and in rear, and only a single row on each flank, the temple was said to be *pseudodipteral, ψευδοδίπτερος*. When a temple had a range of columns in front, and the side columns were engaged in the wall of the cella instead of standing out at a distance from it, this arrangement was termed *pseudo peripteral.* It was invented by the Roman architects of a late period for the purpose of increasing the cella without enlarging the whole building. A temple was called *hypæthral, ύπαιθρος,* open above, when the cella was in part exposed to the air. Hypæthral temples, being those of the greatest magnitude, had generally a double range of columns surrounding the naos on the exterior, and contained in their interior two tiers or ranges of columns, placed one above the other, as in the temple at Pæstum. The walks round the exterior of the temple were called *pteromata.* The names given to the temples, according to the number of columns in the front, were the following:

τετράστυλος, tetrastyle, when there were four columns in front.

ἑξάστυλος, hexastyle, when there were six.

ὀκτάστυλος, octastyle, when there were eight.

δεκάστυλος, decastyle, when there were ten.

Vitruvius gives the following set of terms applied to the temples according to their intercolumniations:

πυκνόστυλος, pycnostyle, or thick set with columns; the inter-columniation was a diameter and a half. This was adopted in the temple of Venus, in the forum of Cæsar.

Σύστυλος, systyle, the intercolumniation was two diameters. An example of this was to be seen in the temple of Fortuna Equestris. Vitruvius considers both these arrangements faulty.

Εὔστυλος, eustyle, the intercolumniation was two diameters and a quarter. This Vitruvius considers not only convenient but also preferable for its beauty and strength. There is no example of this style in Rome.

Διάστυλος, diastyle, the distance between the columns was three diameters.

Ἀραιόστυλος, aræostyle, when the distances between the columns were greater than they ought to be. In consequence of the excessive length, the architrave or epistyle was obliged to be of wood. The temples in Rome built in this style were the temples of Ceres, near the Circus Maximus, the temple of Hercules, erected by Pompey, and that of Jupiter Capitolinus.

Several of the most celebrated Greek temples are peripteral, such as the temple of the Nemean Jupiter, near Argos; of Concord, at

Agrigentum ; of Theseus, at Athens. The Parthenon, the most perfect and the most majestic temple in the world was peripteral and octastyle ; it had eight columns on the front, and seventeen on each flank. The Grecian peripteral was larger than the Roman by two columns. According to Vitruvius, the examples of the peripteral form in Rome were the temple of Jupiter Stator, by Hermodus, and the temple of Honor and Virtue. The dipteral and pseudo dipteral forms of temples were only used in the grander and more expensive edifices, and, consequently, few of them were erected. The celebrated temple of Diana at Ephesus, built by Ctesiphon, and the Doric temple of Quirinus at Rome were dipteral. The temple of Diana, in Magnesia, built by Hermogenes of Alabanda, and that of Apollo by Moncathes were pseudo dipteral. According to Vitruvius, no example of this form of temple is to be found in Rome.

The Greeks and Romans built temples of a circular form also ; this invention does not ascend very high in the history of the art, as it is of a late date. These buildings were covered with a dome, the height of which was nearly equal to the semidiameter of the entire edifice. The temples were either monopteral or peripteral, that is, formed of a circular row of columns without walls, or with a wall surrounded by columns distant from this wall by the breadth of an intercolumniation. The Phillippeion, or Rotunda of Philip, at Olympia, was peripteral ; such were also the temples of Vesta at Rome, and that of the Sibyl at Tivoli. This kind of round temples was usually dedicated to Vesta, Diana, or Hercules. Another form, of which we have the chief example in the Pantheon, consists of a circular cella surmounted by a dome, without a peristyle, but with an advanced portico, presenting eight columns in front, surmounted by a pediment. There was an ascent of two steps, and, in general, the temples of the ancients were surrounded by steps which served as a basement.

The temples received their light in different ways : the circular monopteral, formed of columns without walls, received it naturally ; the peripteral through windows made in the wall or in the dome. The rectangular temples received their light according to their dimensions : the smaller temples, generally through the door alone. The large temples received their light from on high through windows. As to the temples with a cella open to the sky, or hypæthral, ὕπαιθρον, according to the general acceptation of the word, no specimen of it remains.

The best solution of the difficulty with regard to the manner in which hypæthral temples were lighted, seems to be the suggestion of Mr. Fergusson, of a clerestory, similar internally to that found in all

the great Egyptian temples, but externally requiring such a change
of arrangements as was necessary to adapt it to a sloping instead of
a flat roof. This seems to have been effected by counter-sinking it
into the roof, so as to make it, in fact, three ridges in those parts
where the light was admitted, though the regular slope of the roof
was retained between these openings, so that neither the ridge nor
the continuity of the lines of the roof was interfered with. This
would effect all that was required, and in the most beautiful manner,
besides that it agrees with all the remains of Greek temples that
now exist, as well as with the descriptions that have been handed
down to us from antiquity. This arrangement agrees perfectly with
all the existing remains of the Parthenon, as well as with all the
accounts we have of this celebrated temple. The same system
applies even more easily to the great hexastyle at Pæstum.

A peculiar feature in Greek temples of the best period, and of
which the most remarkable instance is to be found in the Parthenon,
must not be omitted here, which is the systematic deviation from
ordinary rectilinear construction, which has for its object the
correction of certain optical illusions arising from the influence
produced upon one another by lines which have different directions,
and by contrasting masses of light and shade. Almost all lines
which are straight and level in ordinary architecture are here
delicate curves; and those lines which are usually perpendicular
have here a slight inclination backwards or forwards, as the case
may be. This peculiarity may be very palpably remarked in the
steps of the Parthenon, which rise very perceptibly in the middle,
and give to the whole pavement a convex character. The rise is
about 3 inches in 100 feet at the fronts, and 4 inches in the flanks.
This refinement in the construction of Greek temples was first
noticed by Mr. Pennethorne, and afterwards more fully elucidated
and developed by Mr. Penrose.

We must also notice here the practice adopted by the Greek
architects of colouring the architectural decorations of the temples.
It cannot admit of a doubt, however repugnant to our cherished
notions of the purity of Greek taste, that the Greeks adopted the
practice of colouring the architectural decorations of their temples.
The mouldings of the cornice and ceiling were brought into prominence by the aid of lively colouring. The capitals of the antæ, the
mouldings of the podiments, were severally adorned with the
designs usually distinguished as the Fret, mæander, ogg and dart.
The tryglyphs were also painted blue. Some even believe they have
discovered traces of paint on the marble columns; but it has been
proved that these traces are not results of painting, but natural

oxidation. The Greeks, however, made a careful distinction with
regard to the material on which they painted. The old tufa temples
were coloured, because the material required colour; the marble
temples were white, because marble needs no colour. Colouring in
marble temples was confined to the mouldings, tryglyphs, and other
ornaments alone. The marble columns were never coloured. In
later times among the Romans, the practice of colouring buildings
seems to have degenerated into a mere taste for gaudy colours.
Pliny and Vitruvius both repeatedly deplore the corrupt taste of
their own times. In Pompeii we have several examples of painted
temples. The material, however, painted is always stucco or
plaster.

Section IV.—ALTARS.

Their shape is greatly diversified and depends on their destination,
either for the purpose of making libations, or for the sacrifices of
living animals, or, in fine, for placing vases, or offerings on them.
Votive altars are often remarkable for their simplicity, being made
of a single stone, more or less ornamented, and bearing an inscription
indicating the reasons and period of their consecration, with the
name of the divinity and that of the devotee who had erected it.
Many have been discovered belonging to the Greeks and Romans;
they must not, however, be confounded with the pedestals of statuary
dedicated in the same way by the zeal and piety of private
individuals. The votive inscriptions bear great resemblance to one
another in these two kinds of monuments; but the remains of the
soldering of the statues which they bore, or the holes which served
to fix them, can be observed in the pedestals.

Egyptian.—Egyptian altars are generally in green basalt and in
granite, and made of a single stone. An altar in the British Museum
shows the trench for carrying off the libation. An altar was usually
erected before a tomb for presenting the offerings.

Grecian.—Grecian altars, at first of wood, afterwards of stone, and
sometimes of metal, are in general remarkable for the taste exhibited
in their execution. These altars were of three kinds: those dedicated to the heavenly gods (βωμοι) were often structures of considerable height; those of demigods and heroes were low and near
the ground (ἐσχάραι); and those of the infernal deities (if such may
be called altars) were trenches sunk in the ground (βόθροι λασκος).
They may again be divided into three classes: those for burnt

ALTARS.

offerings (ἔμπυρα); those on which no fire was used, which were meant for offerings of fruit, cakes, etc., (ἄπυρα); and those on which fire might be used to consume vegetable productions, but upon which no blood was to be spilt (ἀναίμακτα); when dedicated to either of the latter classes it was often nothing more than a raised hearth or stop. Each temple usually had two altars; one in the open air before it, for burnt offerings, another before the statue of the god to whom the building was sacred. Altars were often erected where there was no temple. The altars placed in the temples were of different forms, square, circular, or triangular, of brick or of stone; they never were too high, so as to conceal the statue of the god. The altars destined for libations were hollow, the others solid. They were often made of marble, and elegantly sculptured; they were ornamented with olive leaves for Minerva, myrtle for Venus, with pines for Pan. Sculptors afterwards imitated these ornaments, and the difference of the leaves, of the flowers, or fruits which composed them, indicated the god to whom they were consecrated. Greek altars exhibit Greek dedicatory inscriptions.

Roman.—What has been said of the Grecian altars can be, in general, applied to the Roman altars. We must, however, distinguish between *altare* and *ara*. The former, as is indicated by the syllable *alt*, signifying high, was an elevated structure, used only for burnt offerings, and dedicated to none but heavenly gods; the latter might belong either to the heavenly or infernal gods, or to heroes. Latin inscriptions mark the Roman altars; we must not, however, forget that the Romans employed only Grecian artists, and the taste of the latter predominates in all their works. The instruments and vessels of sacrifice often occur upon these altars as ornaments:—1. The securis, or axe, with which the victims were slain. 2. The scoospiter, or culter, with which the sacrifices were cut to pieces. 3. Preferioulum, or ewer, which contained the wine for libation. 4. The patera, or bowl, into which the wine was poured before it was thrown upon the altar. They were also ornamented with heads of victims, roses, bas-reliefs, the subject of which was relative to the sacrifices.

SECTION V.—COLUMNS.—OBELISKS.

COLUMNS: A column is a cylindrical pillar, which serves either for the support or ornament of a building, and is composed of the *shaft*, or body of the column, of a head, or *capital*, and of a foot, or *base*. At first they were made of wood, and afterwards of stone and marble. Columns at first were but supports, but taste and the progress of the arts ornamented them afterwards, and the difference of the ornaments, and of the proportions which were given to the different parts of the column, constitute the different classic orders, which have been reduced to five:—Greek orders—Doric, Ionic, and Corinthian. Roman orders—Tuscan, Roman, or Composite. Specimens of almost all those orders remain.

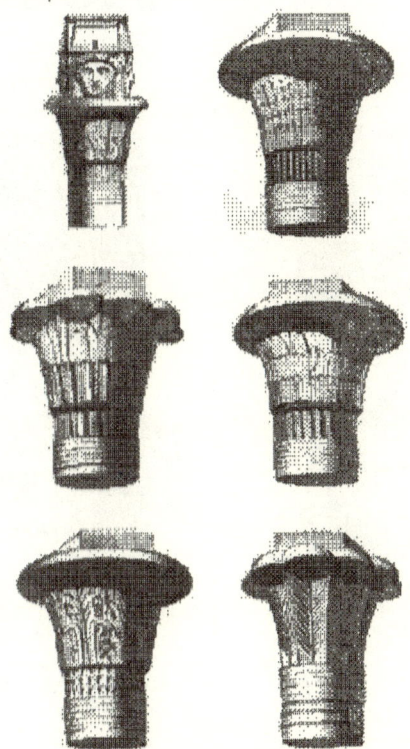

CAPITALS OF EGYPTIAN COLUMNS.

Egyptian.—The form of the genuine Egyptian column, anterior to the influence of the Greeks, is greatly diversified. The simplest

form, such as is found in the earliest constructed porticoes, was that
of a plain square pier, such as would be suggested by a prop or support in mines, or as would be used in quarries.   The second stage in

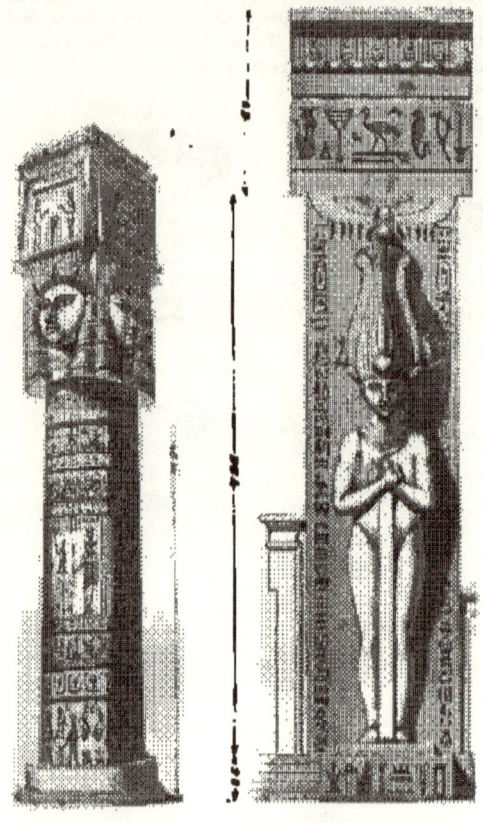

PILLAR, DENDERA.   OSIRIDE PILLAR.

the development of the column was the octagon form, produced by
cutting off the angles of the square, with an abacus surmounting it.
By further cutting off the angles of the octagon, it was gradually

converted into a polygonal shape, such as is seen in the tombs of Beni-Hassan. The want, however, of room, and a place for sculpturing and painting hieroglyphical inscriptions and mythological figures, led at a later period to the necessity of adopting a round form of shaft, such as was used in the temples of Karnak and Luxor. These were always covered with sculpture and hieroglyphics. Their proportions varied greatly. Those columns destined to support large masses, are of a very large diameter in proportion to their height. Their capitals were in endless variety. Some capitals in the shape of the calyx of a lotos, or of a bell shape, are of extraordinary elegance and richness. On others we have the papyrus plant, with its stem and leaves, and the palm branch, with its leaves and fruit. According to Herodotus the pillars were in imitation of palm trees. Indeed, the imitation of natural objects may be traced in every part of Egyptian columns. One of the most curious capitals is that on the pillars of the portico of Dendera. It is quadrangular, with the head of Athor on each side, surmounted by another quadrangular member, each face of which contains a temple doorway. The square pillar, with a colossus in front of it, commonly called Caryatide, has been styled an Osiride pillar by Sir G. Wilkinson, as the colossus attached to the pillar was the figure of the king, in the form of Osiris.

Grecian.—The three main portions of the column are :—

I. Spira, the Base. It gives the column, besides a broader foundation, a sort of girding at the lower end of the shaft; it is therefore suitable for slender and more developed forms of columns, whereas the Doric columns of the early period ascend immediately from the pavement. Its divisions are :—

A. In the Attic order:—1. plinth; 2. torus; 3. scotia, or trochilus; 4. a second upper torus.

B. The Ionic:—1. plinth; 2. trochilus; 3. an upper trochilus; 4. torus; in which are not included the separating and preparatory fillets.

II. Scapus, the Shaft. It is generally fluted, and the column gains in apparent height by means of the vertical stripes, and also in beauty by the more lively play of light and shade. The external surface of the column is by this means divided either into mere channels or flutings, or into flutings and fillets. In the shaft we observe, in the later Doric and other columns, the ἔντασις, or swell.

III. Capitulum.   Capital.

A. The Doric, divided into:—1. hypotrachelium, neck, with
the grooves or channels as a separation from the shaft ;
2. echinus with the annuli or rings (originally, per-

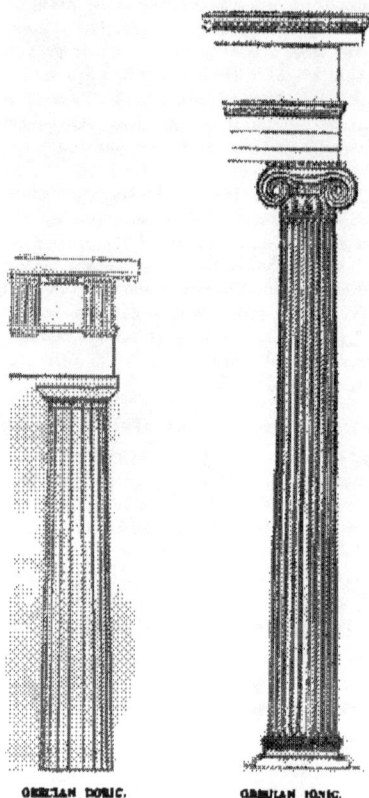

GRECIAN DORIC.   GRECIAN IONIC.

haps, hoops of metal around the wooden capital); 3.
plinthus s. abacus (in Roman edifices with a cymatium.)

B. The Ionic :—1. hypotrachelium (only in the richer form);

2. echinus with an astragalus losbius beneath (a torus above it in the richer kind) ; 3. canalis, the canal, and the volutes with the oculi and axes on two sides, on the two others the pulvini, cushions, with the baltei, straps ; 4. abacus and cymatium.

C. The Corinthian. Two main parts :—1. calathus, the vase or bell of the capital, the ornaments of which rise in three rows : a. eight acanthus leaves ; b. eight acanthus leaves with stalks (cauliculi) between ; four volutes and four scrolls (helices) with acanthus buds and leaves : 2. abacus consisting of cymatium and sima, or otherwise composed with projecting angles, and at the curved parts enriched with flowers.

CORINTHIAN CAPITAL.
TEMPLE AT TIVOLI.

The most ancient order among the Greeks was the Doric. It is a column in its simplest suggested form. From its resemblance to

the pillars at Beni Hassan some wish to argue its Egyptian origin.
It was short and massive, such as would be used in ancient and
primitive constructions: yet it combines a noble simplicity with
much grandeur. The Doric was at first very thick and very low: it
was but four diameters of the base in height: afterwards it was
made a little higher; such are the columns of the two temples at
Pæstum. Later it was given five diameters and a half—this reform
was made about the time of Pericles; those of the propylæa at
Athens have nearly six; and lastly, the columns were given six
lower diameters and a half, as at the temple of the Nemean Jupiter,
between Argos and Corinth.

GRECIAN CORINTHIAN CAPITALS.

TOWER OF THE WINDS.   MONUMENT OF LYSICRATES.

The *Ionic* order combines simplicity and gracefulness, and is
much more slender than the Doric. Its chief characteristic feature
is the volute or spiral scroll. In some instances, as in the Erectheum
at Athens, there is a hypotrachelium separated from the shaft by an
astragal moulding, ornamented with the anthemion, or honeysuckle
pattern. The shaft rests on a base. At first its height was eight
diameters. The columns of the Erectheum at Athens are about nine.

Authors differ with regard to the earliest known example, some giving the temple of Artemis at Ephesus, others the temple of Juno at Samos. The principal examples of the Grecian Ionic are in the temples of Minerva Polias, of Erecthous, the aqueduct of

CARYATIDE.

Hadrian, and the small temple on the Ilissus. at Athens; in the temple of Minerva Polias at Prione; of Bacchus at Teos : of Apollo Didymæus at Miletus.

The *Corinthian* column, properly so called, is more a Roman than

a Grecian order, and was only introduced into Greece on the decline of art. According to Mr. Fergusson, the most typical specimen we know of the Grecian Corinthian is that of the choragic monument of Lysicrates (see p. 44). Its capital is formed of a row of acanthus leaves overlapping one another, and rising from a sort of calyx. It is surmounted at each corner by a scroll volute, the intervening space being filled up with scrolls and the anthemion. Its base and shaft partake of the Ionic. Another Athenian example is that of the Tower of the Winds (see p. 44). The capital is in the form of a calyx, with a row of acanthus leaves close to the bell, and without any volutes. This column has no base. The Corinthian columns of the temple of Jupiter Olympius at Athens belong to the Roman order.

Caryatides. Another form of column only used in connection with the Ionic order, is the so-called caryatide (see p. 45); a draped matronal figure supporting a cornice. According to Vitruvius, these figures represent the captive women of Carya, a city of the Peloponnesus. The most famous examples of these are in the temple of Erectheus, at Athens. Others bear baskets on their heads, and are supposed to represent Canephoræ, who assisted in the Panathenaic procession. Another form of support are the Telamones, or giants, sustaining a projection of the roof of the great temple at Agrigentum.

TELAMONES.

Roman: Doric.—This was considered by the Romans as an improvement on the simpler and severer Grecian Doric. The shaft of the Roman Doric was terminated like the Tuscan, but is distinguished from the Tuscan by the triglyphs in the frieze. It had also a base; an example of the Roman Doric may be seen in the lower columns of the Theatre of Marcellus, at Rome.

Ionic.—This modification of the Ionic was, like all Roman modifirations, for the worse. The change consisted in turning all the volutes angularly, making them mere horns, as Mr. Fergusson remarks, and destroying all the meaning and all the grace of the order.

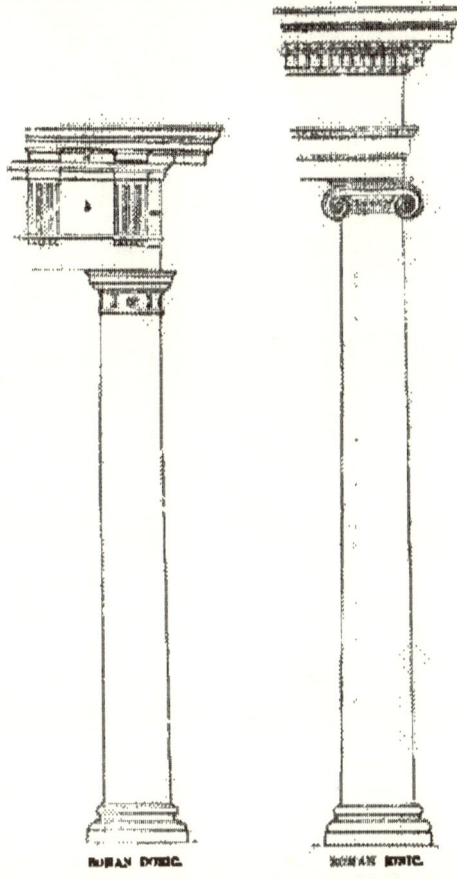

ROMAN DORIC.　　ROMAN IONIC.

It has an Attic base. The only remaining examples of the Roman Ionic are the temple of Saturn, in the Forum, and the temple of Fortuna Virilis.

The Corinthian column surpasses all others in elegance and magnificence.   It is, except in its capital, of the same proportion as the

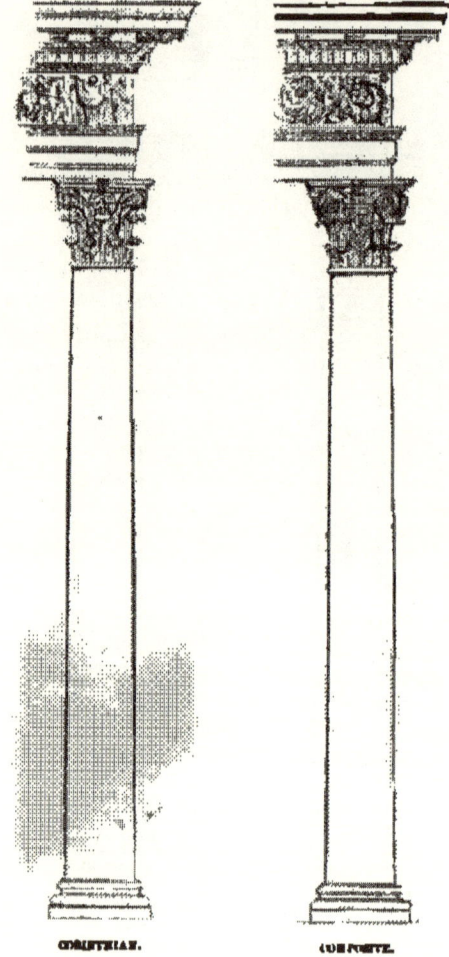

CORINTHIAN.   CORINTH.

Ionic: but the additional height of its capital makes it taller and more graceful; the Ionic capital being but one-third of the diameter of the shaft in height, whilst that of the Corinthian is equal to the thickness of the shaft. The capital is composed of two rows of acanthus leaves, eight in each row, and the upper row is placed between and over the divisions of the lower row. Four spiral volutes in each face rise out of two bunches of the acanthus leaf, and two of them are connected at the angles. They support an abacus, the face of which forms the segment of a circle. The capital rests on an astragal, which serves as a base, and which terminates the shaft of the column. The flutings of the shaft are twenty-four, and divided by fillets. It has an Attic base. The invention of the capital is ascribed to Callimachus, who, seeing a small basket covered with a tile, placed in the centre of an acanthus plant, which grew on the grave of a young lady of Corinth, was so struck with its beauty that he executed a capital in imitation of it. The best examples are to be sought for rather in Rome than Greece. The most correct examples of the orders that remain are to be found in the Stoa, the arch of Adrian, at Athens; the Pantheon of Agrippa, and the three columns of Jupiter Stator, or as now styled, Minerva Chalcidica, in the Forum, at Rome.

Composite.—The Composite order is a Roman invention, and as its name imports, a compound of others, the Corinthian and Ionic. The capital was composed of the Corinthian acanthus leaves, surmounted by the Ionic volutes. Though considered an improvement on the order out of which it grew, it never came into general use. The principal examples of the order in Rome are in the temple of Bacchus, the arches of Septimius Severus, and of Titus; and in the baths of Diocletian.

Etruscan.—The Tuscan order belongs properly to the Etruscans. The height of the Tuscan column, the capital and base included was equal to a third of the width of the temple. The lower diameter was one-seventh of the height, and the diminution of the shaft was,

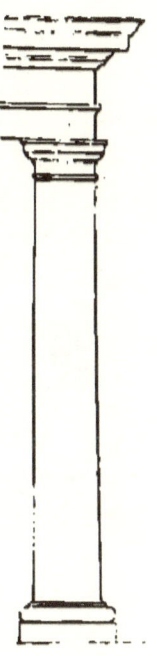

TUSCAN.

E

about a fourth of the diameter. The height of the capital was half a
diameter. Such are the proportions given by Vitruvius, after the
Tuscan temple of Ceres, at Rome. No examples of it remain to the
present day. It was thought to be found in the amphitheatre of
Verona, but the proportions differ sensibly from the primitive Tuscan which is spoken of here. It is probable the Tuscan is only a
simplification of the Doric,
of which there are so many
remains. The only remaining
examples of this order of a
Roman period are the lower
columns of the Coliseum,
which are Tuscan, and not
Doric, as the entablature
wants the distinguishing feature of that style, the try-
glyph.

Monumental.—They are of
large proportions, and have
been erected in honour of an
emperor or military chief.
Of this kind there are several
still remaining.

The column of Trajan, in
his Forum at Rome, erected
about A.D. 115, was dedicated
to Trajan by the Roman
senate and people in com-
memoration of Trajan's two
Dacian conquests. It is of
the Doric order, and is composed of thirty-four blocks of
Carrara marble. The shaft
is covered with bas reliefs,
which go round the whole
from the bottom to the top in
twenty-three spirals. They
represent the exploits of
Trajan in both his Dacian
expeditions. There is a spiral

COLUMN OF TRAJAN.

staircase within, which winds thirteen times round, and contains 184
steps. The height from the base to the summit of the capital is

124 feet. A bronze gilt statue of Trajan formerly surmounted the whole. The column of Marcus Aurelius, commonly known as the Antonine Column, was erected to him by the senate in commemoration of his victories in Germany over the Marcomanni. The bas reliefs represent these victories. The column is formed of twenty-eight blocks of white marble. It is 88½ feet high, including the base and capital. This style of column was called columna cochlis. The column or pillar, so called, of Pompey, at Alexandria in Egypt,

POMPEY'S PILLAR.

a later inscription announces to have been erected by a Roman prefect in honour of the Emperor Diocletian. It is 88 feet 6 inches high, and its shaft is of a single piece. The capital announces the decline of the arts.

There is also the column of Phocas in the Roman Forum, erected in A.D. 608, by Smaragdus the Exarch to the Emperor Phocas. It is in the Corinthian style.

Naval, or Columna Rostrata.—In the Capitol at Rome is a plain column of marble, in bas relief, with three prows of ships on each side, and part of an inscription in obsolete Latin; it is supposed to be the column which was erected by C. Duilius after his first naval victory over the Carthaginians. B.C. 492. It is mentioned by Pliny.

Milliary, also called Lapides.—Milliary columns were erected along the roads throughout the Roman dominions. Augustus erected a column in the Forum, which was called the Milliarium Aureum, from which it is supposed the distances on all the roads of Italy were marked. Some remains of it still exist close to the arch of Septimius Severus. On these pillars were generally inscribed— 1. The name of the town from which the distance was reckoned; 2. The number of miles expressed in figures, with MP (milliarium passuum) prefixed; 3. The name of the constructor of the roads, and of the emperor in whose honour the work was dedicated. On the balustrade of the Capitol at Rome are two of these milliary columns. One marked the first mile on the Appian way. It was found beyond the modern Porta San Sebastiano, about one Roman mile from the site of the ancient Porta Capena. It has the names of Vespasian and Nerva inscribed on it. The other was erected at the seventh mile on the same road. A column found at Saquoney, in Burgundy, on the road from Langres to Lyons, bears this inscription—AND. MP XXII ab Andematuno milliarium passuum vigesimum secundum. Andematum being the ancient name of Langres. In some parts of Gaul the distances were marked in leagues, as in the following inscription—AB. AVG. SVESS. LEVG VII ab Augusto Suessonum leugæ septem. Augusto Suessonum is the ancient name of Soissons. The date of this column was about the time of Caracalla.

Obelisks.—Obelisks were in Egypt commemorative pillars. They are made of a single block of stone, cut into a quadrilateral form, the width diminishing gradually from the base to the top of the shaft, which terminates in a small pyramid (pyramidion). They were placed on a plain square pedestal, but larger than the obelisk itself. Obelisks are of Egyptian origin. The Romans and the moderns have imitated them, but they never equalled their models. The word ὀβελίσκος is a diminutive of ὀβελός, a needle.

Egyptian.—Egyptian obelisks are generally made of red granite of Syene. There are some, however, of smaller dimensions made of sandstone and basalt. They were generally placed in pairs at the entrances of public edifices, on each side of the propyla. The shaft was commonly ten diameters in height, and a fourth narrower at the top than at the base. Of the two which were before the palace of Luxor at Thebes, one is 72 feet high, and 6 feet 2 inches wide at the base; the other is 77 feet high, and 7 feet 8 inches wide. Each face is adorned with hieroglyphical inscriptions in intaglio, and the summit is terminated by a pyramid, the four sides of which represent religious scenes, also accompanied by inscriptions. The corners of the obelisks are sharp and well cut, but their faces are not perfectly plane, and their slight convexity is a proof of the attention the Egyptians paid to the construction of their monuments. If their faces were plane they would appear concave to the eye; the convexity compensates for this optical illusion. The hieroglyphical inscriptions are in a perpendicular line, sometimes there is but one in the middle of the breadth of the face, and often there are three. The inscription was a commemoration by the king who had the temple or palace built before which the obelisk was placed. It contained a record stating the honours and titles which the king who erected, enlarged, or gave rich presents to a temple, had received in return from the priesthood, and setting forth, for instance, that Ramexes was the lord of an obedient people, and the beloved of Amun. Such is the subject of the inscription which is in the middle of each face of the obelisk; and though the name of the same king and the same events are repeated on the four sides, there exists in the four texts, when compared, some difference, either in the invocation to the particular divinities or in the titles of the king. Every obelisk had, in its original form, but a single inscription on each face, and of the same period of the king who had erected it; but a king who came after him, adding a court, a portico, or colonnade to the temple or palace, had another inscription relative to his addition, with his name engraved on the original obelisk; thus, every obelisk adorned with many inscriptions is of several periods. The pyramidion which terminates them generally represents in its sculptures the king who erected the obelisk making different offerings to the principal deity of the temple, and to other divinities. Sometimes also the offering is of the obelisk itself. The short inscriptions of the pyramidion bear the oval of the king and the name of the divinity. By these ovals can be known the names of the kings who erected the obelisks still existing, whether in Egypt or elsewhere. The largest obelisk known is that of St. John Lateran, Rome. It was brought from Heliopolis by the emperor Constantine, and was afterwards erected in the Circus Maximus by his son Constantius. The height of the shaft is 105 feet 7 inches. The sides are of unequal breadth at the base, two measure 9 feet 8½ inches, the other two only 9 feet. It bears the name of Thotmes III., in the central, and that of Thotmes IV. in the lateral lines, kings of the eighteenth dynasty, in the fifteenth

century, B.C. The two obelisks at Luxor were erected by the king
Rameses II., of the nineteenth dynasty, 1311 B.C. (Wilkinson). One
of these has been taken to Paris. The obelisk of Heliopolis bears the
name of Osirtasen I., 2020 B.C. (Wilkinson), and is consequently the
most ancient. It is about 62 feet high. The obelisks at Alexandria,
called Cleopatra's Needles, are supposed to have been brought from
Heliopolis. They bear the name of Thotmes III. In the lateral

OBELISK AT HELIOPOLIS.

lines are the ovals of Rameses the Great. They are of red granite of
Syene. One is still standing, the other has been thrown down. The
standing obelisk is about 70 feet high, with a diameter at its base of
7 feet 7 inches. The obelisk of the Piazza del Popolo claims greater
interest, as it once stood before the temple of the Sun at Heliopolis.
Lepsius attributes it to Menepthah. It was removed to Rome by
Augustus. There are several other Egyptian obelisks in Rome.
Nothing can afford a greater idea of the skill of the Egyptians, and
of their wonderful knowledge of mechanism, than the erection of
these monoliths.

Greek.—The Greeks never made obelisks out of Egypt. The Macedonian kings, or Ptolemies, who reigned in that country, from Alexander to Augustus, erected, terminated, or enlarged many monuments, but always according to Egyptian rules. Egyptian artists executed obelisks for their Greek princes, but they did not depart, no more than in the other monuments, from their ancient customs. The Egyptian style and proportions are always to be recognized, and the inscriptions are also traced in hieroglyphics. The obelisk found at Philæ was erected in honour of Ptolemy Energetes II. and of Cleopatra, his sister, or Cleopatra, his wife, and placed on a base

CLEOPATRA'S NEEDLE.

bearing a Greek inscription relating the reason and occasion of this monument. It was removed from Philæ by Belzoni, and has been now erected at Kingston Hall, Dorset, by Mr. Bankes. It is very far from equalling the Pharaonic obelisks in dimensions, it being only 22 feet high.

Roman.—After the Romans had made of Egypt a Roman province, they carried away some of its obelisks. Augustus was the first who

conceived the idea of transporting these immense blocks to Rome
he was imitated by Caligula, Constantine, and others. They were
generally erected in some circus. Thirteen remain at the present
day at Rome, some of which are of the time of the Roman domination in Egypt. The Romans had obelisks made in honour of their
princes, but the material and the workmanship of the inscriptions
cause them to be easily distinguished from the more ancient obelisks.
The Barberini obelisk, on the Monte Pincio, is of this number;
it bears the names of Adrian, of Sabina his wife, and of Antinous
his favourite. The obelisk of the Piazza Navona, from the style of
its hieroglyphics, is supposed to be a Roman work of the time of
Domitian. The obelisk at Benevento is another, on which can be
read the names of Vespasian and Domitian. The name of Santus
Rufus can be read on the Albani obelisk, now at Munich, and as
there are two Roman prefects of Egypt known of that name, it was
therefore these magistrates, who had executed in that country these
monuments in honour of the reigning emperors, and then had them
sent to Rome. The Romans also attempted to make obelisks at
Rome, such is the obelisk of the Trinita de Monti, which formerly
stood in the Circus of Sallust. It is a bad copy of that of the Porta
del Popolo. The Roman emperors in the east had also some
Egyptian obelisks transported to Constantinople. Fragments of
two of these monuments have been found in Sicily, at Catania, one
of them has eight sides, but it is probably not a genuine Egyptian
work. The use of the obelisk as a gnomon, and the erection of it
on a high base in the centre of an open space, were only introduced
on the removal of single obelisks to Rome.

Section VI.—PYRAMIDS.

In the earliest ages the tumulus, or mound of earth, was the simplest
form of sepulture for heroes and kings. The pyramid of stone was
afterwards adopted by nations as the most lasting form of sepulture
for their kings. Many ancient nations have raised pyramids. The
form of the pyramid is well known. There is, however, this difference in the form, that some pyramids are raised with steps, others
with inclined plane surfaces. The most celebrated are those of
Egypt; the Etruscans have also erected some, and the Romans
imitated them. Some suppose the word πυραμις to be derived from
πυρ, fire; others from the Egyptian " pehram," " the sacred place;"
the Greeks, adopting the native name, and adding a termination of
their own, it was converted into the Greek word Pyramis. Accord-

ing to Lanci, it is derived from 'pi-ram;' pi, being the Coptic article: the word 'ram,' besides being a Semitic, is also a Coptic word, with the sense of 'height.' (Nott and Gliddon, 583)[*]

Egyptian.—All antiquity has admired the pyramids of the environs of Memphis. They are distinctly mentioned by the oldest

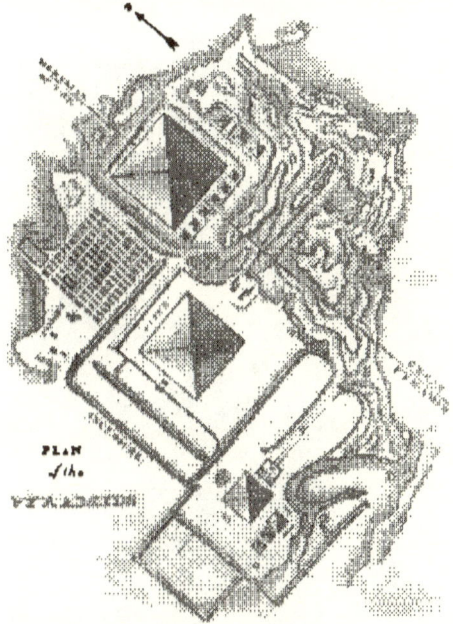

PLAN OF PYRAMIDS.

Greek historian, Herodotus; and the three largest are ascribed by him to Cheops, Chephren, and Mycerinus, three Pharaohs who

[*] Mr. Kenrick gives a more obvious and judicious derivation; according to him it is probably Greek on the following authority : "Etym. M. πυραμις, ἡ δια πυρος και μελιτος, ωσπερ εισαμος, ἡ δια σησαμου και μελιτος." The πυραμις was a pointed cake used in Bacchic rites. That the name, he adds, of the mathematical solid was derived from an object of common life, and not vice versa, may be argued from analogy : σφαιρα was a handball ; κυβος, a die for gaming ; κωνος, a boy's top ; κυλινδρος, a husbandman's or gardener's roller.

succeeded each other. There has been much discussion with regard
to their destination, but at the present day there are no further
doubts on the subject—the pyramids were tombs. The faces of the
three pyramids stand exactly opposite to the four cardinal points.

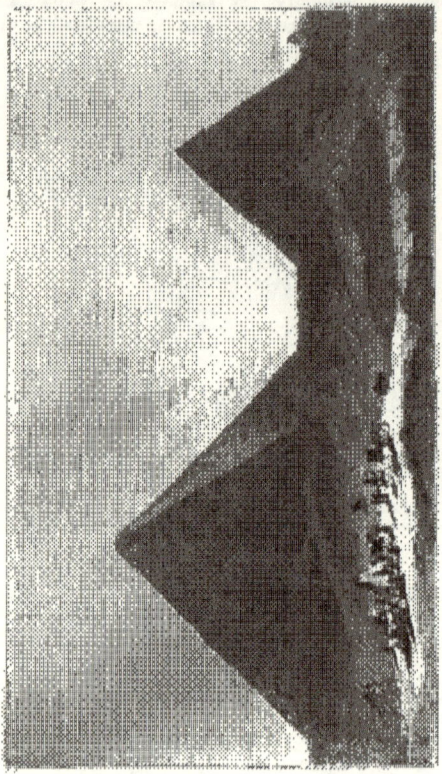

THE PYRAMIDS OF GIZEH

They are built of calcareous stone, partly from the neighbouring
hills. Granite was also employed for some portion of the outer
part. The principal chamber in one of them is of granite. It was
there that the sarcophagus of the owner of the tomb was found, in
which his mummy was formerly enclosed. Many chambers and

passages in different directions have been discovered in those which have been entered. The entrance of the pyramid was carefully concealed by an interior casing. In the interior the passages communicated sometimes with wells and deep subterranean passages excavated in the rock on which the pyramid was erected. It seems that some of them were covered over with stucco or marble, and that religious and historical subjects, and hieroglyphical inscriptions, were sculptured on them, but no trace of them remains at the present day. The environs of Memphis not having, like those of Thebes, high mountains in which they could excavate the tombs of the kings, those factitious mountains were raised, and this explains their real destination. The larger pyramid at Memphis, called that of Cheops, rises in a series of platforms, each smaller than the one on which it rests, thus presenting the appearance of steps. Of these steps there are 203. The length of each face, when entire, was 756 feet. Its present base is 732 feet. Its perpendicular height, when entire, was 480. The present height 460 feet. It covered an area of about 571,530 square feet, or 13½ acres. To form an idea of the great pyramid, the reader has only to suppose the vast square of Lincoln's Inn Fields, the dimensions of which are the exact base of the great pyramid, wholly filled up from side to side, and gradually rising, in a pyramidal form, to a height exceeding that of St. Paul's, by at least one third. The solid contents of the pyramid have been calculated at 85,000,000 cubic feet. The entrance to the great

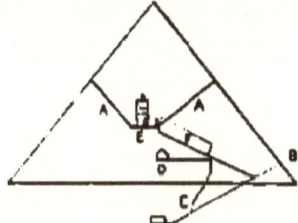

SECTION OF PYRAMID.

A Air channel.	D. Queen's chamber.
B Entrance.	E. King's chamber.
C Well.	F Great gallery.

pyramid is in the north face, about 47 feet from the base. From the entrance a passage, 4 feet high, leads downwards at an inclination of 26°: this passage leads to another, which has an ascending inclination of 27°, at the top of which is the entrance to the great gallery.

From this point a horizontal passage leads into what is called the queen's chamber, which is small, and roofed by long blocks, resting against each other, and forming an angle; its height is about 20 feet. At the end of the great gallery, which is 132 feet long, 26½ high, and nearly 7 wide, and is a continuation in the same line of the former ascending passage, is another horizontal passage, which leads to the king's chamber. Here was discovered a sarcophagus of red granite; the cover and contents have been carried away; it is entirely plain, and without hieroglyphics. Above the king's chamber are other small chambers, which, according to Sir G. Wilkinson, were for the sole purpose of relieving the pressure on the king's chamber. Here was discovered the oval containing the name of the founder, Shofo (Suphis). Another has been discovered in a small tomb near the pyramid.[*] The second pyramid, generally attributed to Chephren, is smaller in size, and its style of masonry inferior to that of the larger pyramid. It stands on higher ground than the great pyramid. It was probably built by Shafre, whose oval has been found in one of the tombs near the great pyramid. The length of its base is 690 feet, and its height 446 feet. It retains a portion of the smooth casing with which all the pyramids were once covered. The passages in this pyramid lead only to one main chamber, in which is a sarcophagus sunk in the floor. This pyramid had two entrances. It was opened by Belzoni. The third pyramid, that of Mycerinus, is about 203 feet high, and its base 333 feet long. The outer layers or casing were of granite, many of which still continue in their original position at the lower parts. The chamber has a flat roof, formed of stones placed one against the other. The name of Mencheres, its founder, was discovered by Colonel Vyse on a wooden coffin, which was found in this chamber, now in the British Museum. It was opened by Colonel Vyse. This pyramid is built in stages or stories, to which a sloping face has been afterwards added. It has suggested a theory to Dr. Lepsius. Near the great pyramid are three smaller ones. The centre one is stated by Herodotus to have been erected by the daughter of Cheops. Besides the pyramids of Gizeh (Memphis) there are several other pyramids at Abooseer, Sakkára and Dashoor. The largest pyramid of Sakkára has its degrees or stories stripped of their triangular exterior. It measures about 137 paces square. In the opinion of Mr. Fergusson, its outline, the disposition of its chambers, and the

---

[*] Sir G. Wilkinson is of opinion that the Great Pyramid was built by two kings (Shofo and Nou-Shofo, who reigned together, and that the funereal chambers were, one for each king, rather than, as generally supposed, for the king and and queen.

hieroglyphics found in its interior, all seem to point to an imitation of the old form of mausolea, by some king of a far more modern date. Two brick pyramids are found at Dashoor. It is supposed they were originally cased with stone.

According to Lepsius, the height of these royal monuments corresponded with the length of the monarch's reign under whom it was erected. We here quote his words:—" It occurred to me that the whole building had proceeded from a small pyramid, which had been erected in stages of about 40 feet high, and then first increased and heightened simultaneously on all sides, by super-imposed coverings of stones from 15 to 20 feet in breadth, till at length the great steps were filled up so as to form one common flat side, giving the usual pyramidal form to the whole. This gradual growth

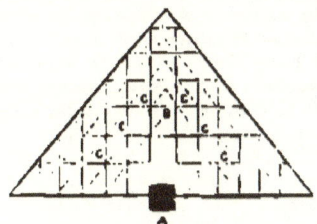

PYRAMID ACCORDING TO LEPSIUS.

A Sepulchral chamber.
B, C, D Sizes of pyramid according to length of reign.

explains the enormous magnitude of particular pyramids, besides so many other smaller ones. Each king began the building of his pyramid as soon as he ascended the throne; he only designed a small one, to insure himself a complete tomb, even were he destined to be but a few years upon the throne. But with the advancing years of his reign, he increased it by successive layers till he thought that he was near the termination of his life. If he died during the erection, then the external covering was alone completed, and the monument of death finally remained proportionate to the duration of the life of the king." Mr. Bartlett, in his pleasing work on Egypt, has advanced an objection which is somewhat fatal to this theory; his words are, " it appears inconsistent with the construction of the great pyramid of Cheops, since the existence of a series of interior passages and chambers, and even air passages communicating with the exterior, seems to argue a regular design for the construction of the entire monument." It would be more natural to suppose that their relative sizes were in accordance with the rank and popular estimation of the deceased.

Small pyramids in stone were also made in Egypt. They are generally of a single block, and are about 1 or 2 feet in height. They bear on their four faces inscriptions and figures, or scenes analogous to those on the sepulchral tablets found in tombs, both being destined for the same purpose. They were dedicated to the dead. They were found more frequently in the environs of Memphis and in Lower Egypt than in Upper Egypt. There are several in the British Museum.

Etruscan.—The Etruscans also erected pyramids. According to Pliny, the tomb of king Porsena was a monument in rectangular masonry, each side of which was 300 feet wide, 50 high, and within the square of the basement was an inextricable labyrinth. On that square basement stood five pyramids, four at the angles and one in the centre, each being 70 feet wide at its base, and 150 high, and all so terminating above as to support a brazen circle and a petasus, from which were hung by chains certain bells, which, when stirred by the wind, resounded afar off.

Greek.—Pyramids of remote antiquity are also found in Greece. The best preserved of these pyramids is that of Erasinus, near Argos. The masonry of this edifice is of an intermediate style between the polygonal and irregular horizontal, consisting of large irregular blocks, with a tendency, however, to quadrangular forms

PYRAMID OF ERASINUS, NEAR ARGOS.

and horizontal courses; the inequalities being, as usual, filled up with smaller pieces. It is supposed to be a monument of the same primitive school of art as the Gate of the Lions, and the Royal Sepulchres of Mycenæ.

Roman.—There is only one Roman pyramid. It is the tomb of

Caius Cestius, who was one of seven epulones, appointed to prepare the banquets for the gods at public solemnities, in the time of Augustus. It is close to the Porta San Paolo, Rome. It is 114 feet high and 90 feet broad at the base. It is built of brick and tufa, covered with slabs of white marble. In its interior is a chamber adorned with paintings. The Pope, Alexander VII., had it restored.

SECTION VII.—THEATRES.—AMPHITHEATRES.—CIRCI, HIP-PODROMES.—NAUMACHIE.—BATHS, OR THERMÆ.—TRIUMPHAL ARCHES.—FORA.

THEATRES. —After the temples the theatres were, among the Greeks and Romans, the most necessary public edifices. Connected with the worship of the gods scenic representations were not considered profane; the public also assembled in the theatre on certain solemn occasions. They were generally consecrated to Bacchus, because he was considered the inventor of comedy; at least it is supposed to have taken its origin in the solemn procession in honour of that god. Sometimes the theatre was built in the temple itself of Bacchus. The enormous extent of many of them, and the prodigious solidity of their construction, are attested by the numerous remains of such edifices which have been explored, not only in Greece and Italy, but also in Asia Minor.

Egypt.—No traces remain which would allow us to attribute the use of theatres to the Egyptians. The solemnities and pomps of religious ceremonies were festivals more suited to the gloomy and religious mind of the Egyptians.

Greek.—The Greeks, to whom we are indebted for the invention of the drama, constructed the first theatres; cabins of branches of trees, destined to shelter the actor from the sun, were soon replaced by wooden scaffolds, in the towns especially; and lastly, by stone edifices, remarkable for size and magnificence. The first great theatre of Athens, that of Dionysus, situated near a temple of the God, was excavated, in the time of Themistocles, on the side of the Acropolis, which looks towards Mount Hymettus. Those of Ægina, Epidaurus, and Megalopolis, surpassed all others by their extent and magnificence. The Greeks of Asia Minor followed the example of the Greeks of Europe and of Sicily. The theatre at Ephesus must have been the largest ever erected. Its diameter was 660 feet; allowing fifteen inches for each person, it would accommodate 50,700 spectators. The general arrangement was, in their being constructed on the slope of a hill. That the seats of the spectators might be more solidly fixed, the side seats rested on strong masonry, which was connected with the stage. The building itself may be divided in two parts—the κοῖλον,—in Latin cavea, the part for the audience; and that devoted to the business of the play, which is again subdivided into the ὀρχήστρα, and σκηνή, the orchestra and stage. The κοῖλον was bounded by two concentric circular arcs,

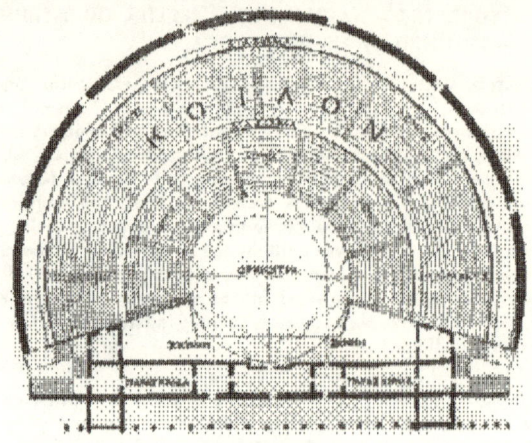

one of which separated it from the orchestra, the other formed its extreme outer limit. The Romans seldom suffered the arc to exceed a semicircle. The Greeks commonly used a larger arc. It was composed of a succession of seats, divided into two or more flights by διαζώματα, or præcinctiones, a sort of landing which ran round the whole, and facilitated the access from one part to another. These were again subdivided into κερκίδες, cunei, or wedges, by stairs κλίμακες, converging to the centre of the orchestra, and leading from the bottom to the top of the building. When the theatres were large, there were commonly intermediate staircases, to facilitate the ascent to the upper and broader portion of these cunei. The lowest seats, of course, were the best, and were reserved for the judges (agonothetes), the magistrates, and those who, by their own or their ancestors' services, had acquired a right (προεδρία) to have places reserved for them. Behind these were the young men, ephebi, and behind them again, the citizens and the rest of the people. At Athens women were not admitted to scenic representations. The rich brought cushions and carpets with them.

The orchestra (ὀρχήστρα) was a circular level space, extending in front of the spectators, and somewhat below the lowest row of benches. But it was not a complete circle, one segment of it being appropriated to the stage. The orchestra was the place for the chorus, where it performed its evolutions and dances, for which purpose it was covered with boards. In the centre of the circle of the orchestra was the thymele (θυμέλη), that is, the altar of Dionysius, which was, of course, nearer to the stage than to the seats of the spectators, the distance from which was precisely the length of a radius of the circle. The chorus generally arranged itself in the space between the thymele and the stage. The thymele itself was of a square form, and was used for various purposes, according to the nature of the different plays, such as a funeral monument, an altar. It was made of boards, and surrounded on all sides with steps. On these steps, sometimes, the chorus ascended; the coryphæus, or leader of the chorus, then mounted the upper portion of the thymele, which was on a level with the σκηνή. According to Millin, it served as a tribune, when popular assemblies were held in the theatre.

The stage (σκηνή) was elevated ten or twelve feet above the orchestra; the wall which supported it was called ὑποσκήνιον, and was relieved by statues, pillars, and other architectural ornaments. The stage itself was a broad, shallow platform, called by the Greeks λογεῖον or προσκήνιον; by the Romans pulpitum. Strictly speaking, the προσκήνιον was the entire space from the scena to the orchestra; the λογεῖον, the narrow portion opposite the centre of the scene, where the actors stood and spoke. The backside of the stage was closed by a wall called the σκηνή or scena. It represented a suitable background, or the locality in which the action was going on. The παρασκήνια were rooms behind the stage, where the actors retired to dress, and where the decorations and machines were kept. In the Roman theatre this part of the building was called the postscenium. In the front of the stage was a recess in the floor, meant to contain a curtain (aulæa), which was drawn up previous to the performance, to conceal the scene. A flight of steps, called κλιμακτῆρες, led up from the thymele to the stage, for the use of the characters of the play, who, when they were supposed to come from a distance, often entered by the orchestra. There was a flight of steps concealed under the seats of the spectators, called Charon's staircase (χαρωνι κλιμακες), by which ghosts entered, and proceeded up the thymele to the stage.

As the theatres of the ancients were never covered, a large awning (velarium) was extended over the theatre, of a purple colour, and sometimes highly ornamented; it was attached to poles placed in the orchestra and on the walls. In hot weather the enclosure was refreshed by jets of perfumed water, thrown up in the finest rain. To increase the resonance of the voice, brazen vases (ηχεια), resembling bells, were placed in different parts of the theatre, under the seats of the spectators. Vitruvius relates that Lucius Mummius carried off vases of this kind from the theatre of Corinth, and dedicated them in the temple of Juno.

Etruscan.—The Etruscans were exceedingly fond of scenic representations. They were connected with religious practices, and were intermingled with music and dance. We have historical evidence that Rome derived her theatrical exhibitions from Etruria. Livy tells us that the ludi scenici were introduced into Rome in the year 390, in order to appease the wrath of the gods for a pestilence then devastating the city; and that "ludiones" were sent for from Etruria, who acted to the sound of the pipe, in the Tuscan fashion. He adds that they were also called "histriones," bister, in the Etruscan tongue, being equivalent to ludio, in Latin. There is strong ground for the presumption that the edifices the Etruscans used were copied by the Romans. Remains of theatres are found at Falleri, Ferento, Fiesole. They are, however, now proved to be of a Roman period.

Roman.—In the Roman theatre the construction of the orchestra and stage was different from that of the Greeks. By the construction peculiar to the Roman theatre, the stage was brought nearer to the audience (the arc not exceeding a semicircle), and made considerably deeper than in the Greek theatre. The length of the stage was twice the diameter of the orchestra. The Roman orchestra contained no thymele. The back of the stage, or proscenium, was adorned with niches, and columns, and friezes of great richness, as may be seen in some of the theatres of Asia Minor, and in the larger theatre at Pompeii, which belong to the Roman period. On the whole, however, the construction of a Roman theatre resembled that of a Greek one. The Senate, and other distinguished persons, occupied circular ranges of seats within the orchestra; the prætor had a somewhat higher seat. The space between the orchestra and the first præcinctio, usually consisting of fourteen seats, was reserved for the equestrian order, tribunes, etc. Above them were the seats of the plebeians. Soldiers were separated from the citizens. Women were appointed by Augustus to sit in the portico, which encompassed the whole. Behind the scenes were the postscenium, or retiring-room, and porticoes, to which, in case of sudden showers, the people retreated from the theatre. The earliest theatres at Rome were temporary buildings of wood. A magnificent wooden theatre, built by M. Amilius Scaurus, in his edileship, B. C. 58, is described by Pliny. In 55 B. C., Cn. Pompey built the first stone theatre at Rome, near the Campus Martius. A temple of Venus Victrix, to whom he dedicated the whole building, was erected at the highest part of the cavea. The next permanent theatre was built by Augustus, and named after his favourite, the

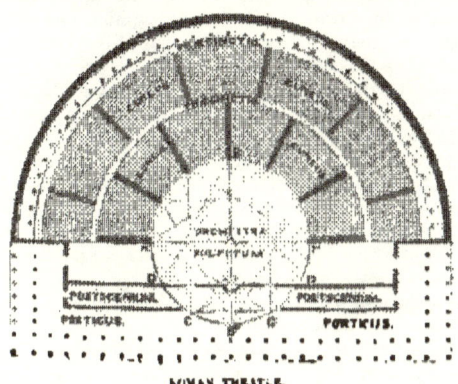

ROMAN THEATRE.

young Marcellus, son of his sister Octavia. Vitruvius is generally reported to have been the architect of this building, which would contain 30,000 persons. From marks still visible in the large theatre at Pompeii, the place reserved for each spectator was about 13 inches. This theatre contained 5,000. The theatre of Pompey, at Rome, contained 40,000. The theatre of Scaurus is said to have contained 80,000. The Romans surpassed the Greeks in the grandeur and magnificence of their buildings. They built them in almost all their towns. Remains of them are found in almost every country where the Romans carried their rule. One of the most striking Roman provincial theatres is that of Orange, in the south of France.

AMPHITHEATRES: *Etruscan.*—Romains of amphitheatres are found in several cities of Etruria. The amphitheatre of Sutri is considered to be peculiarly Etruscan in its mode of construction. The Romans copied these edifices from the Etruscans. We have historical evidence, also, that the gladiatorial combats of the Romans had an Etruscan origin.

Roman.—Amphitheatres were peculiar to the Romans. Caius Scribonius Curio built the first edifice of this kind. It was composed of two theatres of wood, placed on pivots, so that they could be turned round, spectators and all, and placed face to face, thus forming a double theatre, or amphitheatre (ἀμφι. on both sides, θεατρον, a theatre.) Statilius Taurus, the friend of Augustus, B.C. 30, erected a more durable amphitheatre of stone, in the Campus Martius. Ever since, this kind of edifice was erected in numbers, in almost all the towns of the Roman Empire. The form of the amphitheatre generally adopted was that of an ellipsis, with a series of arcaded concentric walls, separating corridors, which have constructions with staircases and radiating passages between them. It enclosed an open space called the arena, from its being strewed with the finest sand, on the level of the surface of the ground on which the structure was raised. It was here that were given the combats of gladiators and wild beasts, which were enclosed in cells (carceres) on the same level as the arena. From the innermost concentric wall, which surrounded the arena, and which was of sufficient height, about fifteen feet, to guard the spectators against any danger from the wild beasts, an inclined plane rose upwards over the intermediate walls, staircases, and corridors, to a gallery, or galleries, over the outermost corridors. The inner and upper part of the inclined plane was covered with a graduated series of benches. On the top of the first concentric wall or parapet (the podium), was a broad præcinctio, or platform, which ran immediately round the arena. This was set apart for the senators, magistrates, and other persons of distinction. Here the magistrates brought their curule seats, or bisellii, and here was the suggestus, a covered seat appropriated to the Emperor. The person who exhibited the games (editor) had his seat here also. Above the podium were the gradus, or seats of the other spectators, which were divided into stories, called mæniana. The first mænianum was appropriated to the equestrian order. Then, after a horizontal space, termed a præcinctio, and forming a continued landing place from the several staircases which opened on to it, succeeded the second mænianum, where were the seats called popularia, for the third class of spectators, or the populace. The doors which opened from the staircases and corridors on to the several landing places, were designated by the very appropriate name of vomitoria. Behind the second mænianum was the second praecinctio; above which was the third mænianum, where there were only wooden benches for the pullati, or common people. The open gallery at the top was the only part of the amphitheatre in which women were permitted to witness the games. The seats of the maenians did not run in unbroken lines round the whole building, but were divided into portions called cunei (from their wedgelike shape), by short flights of stairs, which facilitated the access to the seats. The whole of the interior was called the cavea. A contrivance, by which the spectators were protected from the overpowering heat of the sun, must not be omitted. It was called Velum, or Velarium. This was a vast extent of canvas, which was supported by masts fixed into the outer wall. Projecting stones are still to be seen at the top of the Colosseum and other amphitheatres, which were evidently connected with this contrivance. Sailors were employed for the purpose of straining the canvas. We learn from Lucretius that this covering was coloured, and Dio mentions a purple awning, in the middle of which was a figure of Nero driving his chariot, and stars of gold placed round him.

The most famous amphitheatre was the Colosseum or Amphitheatrum Flavium, at Rome. This amphitheatre was begun by Vespasian in A.D. 72, and dedicated by Titus in his eighth consulate, A.D. 80. It was completed by Domitian. At the dedication of the building 5,000 wild beasts were slaughtered in the arena, and the games in honour of the event lasted for nearly 100 days. It was the scene of gladiatorial spectacles for nearly 400 years. The amphitheatre is, as usual, elliptical. The wall which surrounds the whole consists of three rows of arches, one above the other, with columns between each arch. In each row there are eighty arches: still higher was a fourth row of pilasters, with forty square windows, but without arches. The Tuscan, Ionic, and Corinthian orders were successively employed in the three rows; and the pilasters of the fourth or upper row were also Corinthian. It was terminated by an entablature. The entrances were by eighty arches in the outer wall, which opened into the first arcade: from thence the people might pass by as many arches into the second, where they found at intervals staircases leading to the seats. The immense crowds which frequented this amphitheatre could enter and depart in a short time, and with little confusion. The arches were all numbered on the outside, from 1. to LXXX. Between XXXVIII. and XXXIX. is an arch a little wider than the rest, without a number,

and with no cornice over it, which is supposed to have served as the
private entrance from the palace of Titus, on the Esquiline Hill.
The height of the outer wall is 157 English feet. The major axis
of the building, including the thickness of the walls, is 584 feet;

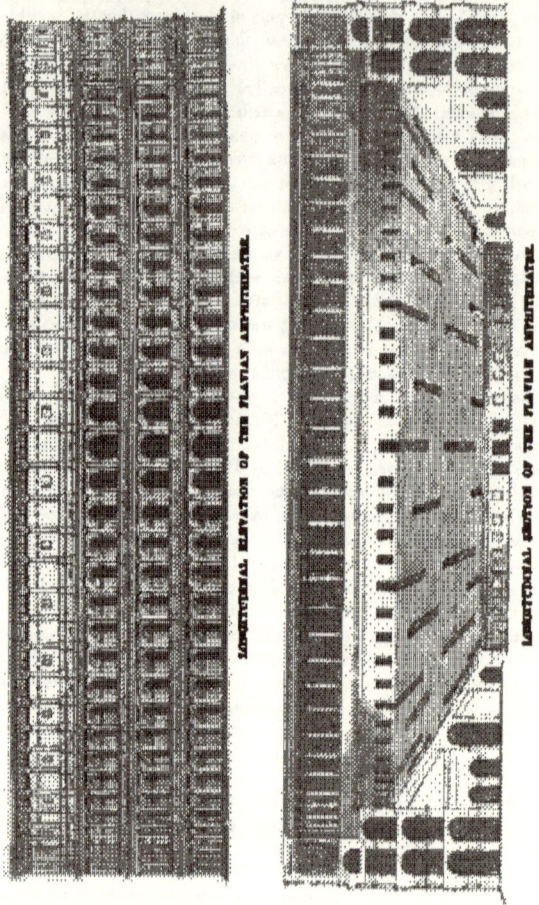

LONGITUDINAL ELEVATION OF THE FLAVIAN AMPHITHEATRE.

LONGITUDINAL SECTION OF THE FLAVIAN AMPHITHEATRE.

the minor axis 486 feet. The length of the arena is 278 feet; the width 177 feet. It covers nearly six acres of ground. According to P. Victor, 87,000 persons would be accommodated in the seats,

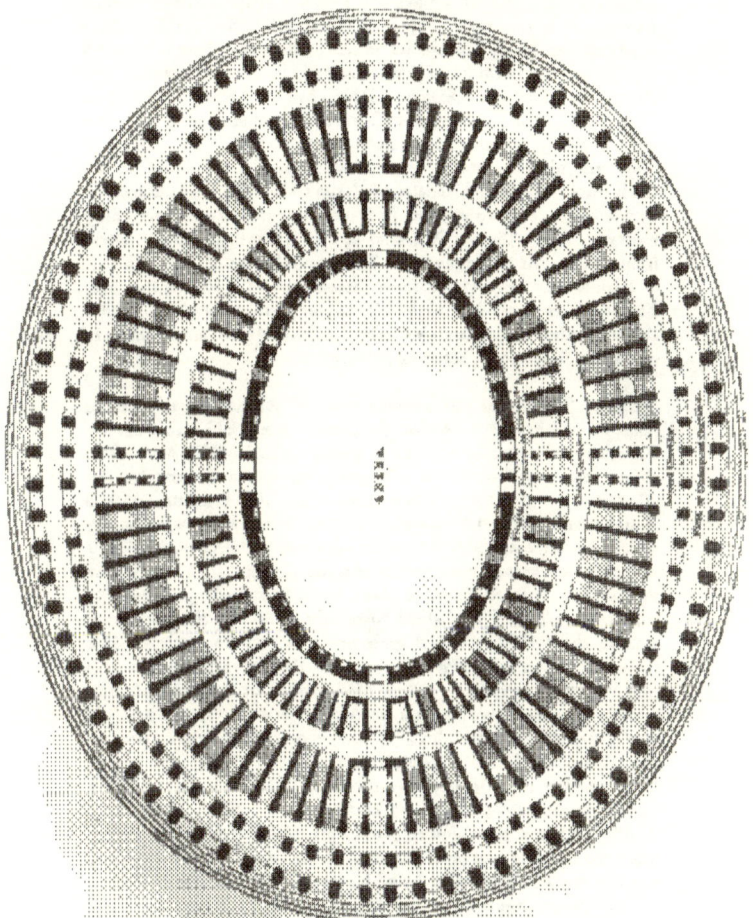

GROUND-PLAN OF THE FLAVIAN AMPHITHEATRE.

and some consider it probable that 20,000 more could have found places above.

As a delight in the bloody scenes of the arena was peculiarly a Roman feature, and an enjoyment so much indulged in by Roman soldiery, it is natural to expect that we should find amphitheatres wherever we find a Roman settlement. Remains of amphitheatres are to be met with at Verona, Pæstum, Pompeii, Pozzuoli, and Capua, in Italy; at Nismes, Arles, Frejus, Saintes, Antun, in France; at Pola, in Istria; at Syracuse, Catania, and some other cities of Sicily; even in the remotest parts of Britain and Germany. They are all constructed on the same general principles as the Colosseum. The amphitheatre of Verona was built about the same period as the Colosseum, and is interesting from its interior being nearly perfect. The amphitheatre at Pola derives its chief interest from its exterior being perfect. The amphitheatre of Pola and that of Nismes have nearly the same dimensions—436 feet by 346 feet. That of Pola is 97 feet high. In the amphitheatres of Capua and Pozzuoli the arena contains many substructures and chambers which are found in no other amphitheatre.

CIRCI.—The circus was another kind of building peculiar to the Romans. At first it was a place for chariot-races and horse-races; it was afterwards used for combats of gladiators and wild beasts. The circus was of an oblong form, straight at one end and curved at the other, the length being about three times the breadth. At the straight end were the *carceres*; in the centre was the *ostia*, by which the horsemen and the chariots entered. On each side of this were six apertures, or *carceres*, where the chariots stood before they started. A little in front of these were two small pedestals, to which was attached a chalked rope (alba linea) for the purpose of making the start fair. The space enclosed by the seats was called the *area*. Running down the centre of the area was the *spina* (so called from the central position of the spine in the human body), round which the chariots ran, keeping it always on the left. It was a brick wall 4 feet high, at each end of which was a *meta*, or goal, round which the chariots turned, and on which were placed three wooden cylinders, with an oval ornament at the top. An obelisk sometimes adorned the middle of the spina. There were also little pillars, on which eggs were placed to mark the number of times the chariots had gone round. At the curved end of the circus was the Porta Triumphalis, by which it is supposed the conqueror at the games went out. Seats (gradus, sedilia) were arranged round the area, with similar divisions, as in the amphitheatre. Each curia had its particular place assigned to it, as well as the senators and knights. The emperor's seat, or pulvinar, was placed near the carceres, where the emperor would have the best view of the start and of the arrival at the goal. The Circus Maximus of Rome was built in the reign of Tarquinius Priscus. It was enlarged by Cæsar, and embellished by Augustus and Tiberius. Cæsar separated the area from the seats by a euripus, or ditch, in order that the spectators might not be exposed to the attacks of the animals, which sometimes broke down the barriers. According to Dionysius, this circus was 3½ stadia long, and about 4 plethra (about 400 feet) wide. It contained 150,000 people. Pliny makes it only 3 stadia long, and 1 wide, containing 200,000. Each computation is, however, supposed to have reference to different periods. The remains of a circus outside the walls of Rome have afforded means of studying the general arrangements of this class of building. It was formerly named the Circus of Caracalla, but inscriptions have been discovered, recording that it was erected in honour of Romulus, the son of Maxentius, A.D. 311. Its length is 1,580 feet,

CIRCUS OF ROMULUS.

and its breadth 260 feet. It is calculated that it could have contained 20,000 spectators. The next circus, in point of antiquity, to the Circus Maximus was that of Flaminius, built by the consul of that name, U.C. 531, but this has entirely disappeared. The other circi at Rome were the Circus Agonalis, or Alexandri, built by the Emperor Alexander Severus, the exact form of which may be traced in the Piazza Navona. The length was about 750 feet. The circus of Flora was situated in the space between the Quirinal and Pincian hills, now partly occupied by the Piazza Barberini. The circus of Sallust, called Circus Apollinaris was situated in the depression between the Quirinal and Pincian hills. Slight vestiges of it may still be traced. The circus of Nero stood partly on the site of the Basilica of St. Peter. It was destroyed by Constantine when he built the old church, A.D. 324.

NAUMACHIÆ.—Naumachiæ were mock naval engagements. This kind of spectacle was enjoyed by the Romans. The Naumachiæ generally took place in the circi and amphitheatres. Subterranean canals brought in the water requisite for the entertainment; there were other canals for the purpose of letting it off. These two operations were performed in the presence of the spectators, and in a few minutes. Some of the emperors erected buildings on purpose, which were called Naumachiæ. Two of the largest were built by Cæsar and Augustus. Suetonius, speaking of the former, says a lake was dug in the form of a sholl, in which ships, representing the Tyrian and Egyptian fleets, engaged, with a vast number of men on board. It was filled up after Cæsar's death. The naumachia of Augustus was on the other side of the Tiber, and was 1,800 feet in length, and 200 feet in width, so that thirty ships could engage in it. Domitian also constructed one, and erected a building of stone round it, with seats for the spectators. It was on the site of the present Piazza di Spagna. The Emperor Claudius changed the lake Fucinus into a naumachia, placing seats round about it for the spectators. In the sea-fight 19,000 combatants were engaged, and there were fifty ships on each side. The combatants were usually captives or criminals condemned to death. Heliogabalus, upon one occasion, filled the euripus with wine, and had naval exhibitions performed in it. P. Victor mentions ten naumachiæ.

HIPPODROMES.—Hippodromes were used for chariot and horse races. They were peculiar to the Greeks. The general form of the hippodrome was an oblong, with a semicircular end, and with the right side some what longer than the left. At the other end was the starting-place, in the form of the prow of a ship. Along the sides of this were stalls for the chariots which were to run. When the cord fell, the contending chariots formed into a line, and started. At the further end was the goal they were bound to reach, which was placed in such a manner that but one chariot at a time could pass near it. The Greeks generally managed that the seats of the spectators on one side should be on the slope of a hill. Music accompanied these games. The judges were seated where the race ended. The Greek hippodrome was much wider than the Roman circus. The hippodrome of Olympia was 4 stadia long, and 1 wide. There were two at Constantinople, and the remains of others have been found in Greece, Syria, and Egypt. Hadrian, who erected several structures in imitation of Greek and Egyptian buildings, introduced a hippodrome into his villa, near Tibur.

STADIA.—The stadium was also peculiar to the Greeks; it was generally appropriated to foot races and gymnastic exercises. The stadium of Athens was on the south side of the Ilissus. According to

Pausanias, it was a hill rising from the Ilissus, of a semicircular form in the upper part, and extending thence in two parallel right lines to the bank of the river. The spectators were seated on the turf until Herodes Atticus constructed Pentelic marble steps, and otherwise completed and adorned the stadium. It is supposed to have been capable of holding 40,000 spectators. Extensive ruins of stadia still remain at Sicyon, Delos, and Delphi.

BATHS.—BALNEÆ.—THERMÆ.—The Greek name is βαλανειον, of which the Roman balneum is only a slight variation, and generally signified a private bath. The bath was in general use among the Greeks, but we have little knowledge of the construction of their baths. The public baths of the Romans were generally called *Thermæ*, which literally means " warm waters." In the time of Scipio Africanus, the Roman baths were very simple ; it was not until the age of Agrippa, and the emperors after Augustus, that they were built and finished in a style of luxury almost incredible. The public baths were opened at sunrise, and closed at sunset. The price of a bath was a quadrans, the smallest piece of coined money. The usual hour for the bath amongst the Romans was the ninth in winter, and the eighth in summer.

The most complete kind of baths were composed of the following separate rooms or halls :

I. The *Apodyterium* of the Greeks, the *Spoliatorium* of the Romans, where the bathers undressed. Slaves, called *capsarii*, were stationed here, who took care of the clothes.

II. The Λουτρον of the Greeks, the frigidarium of the Romans, where cold baths were taken.

III. The tepidarium was a temperate hall, which was merely heated with warm air of an agreeable temperature, in order to prepare the body for the great heat of the vapour and warm baths, and, upon returning, to obviate the danger of a too sudden transition to the open air.

IV. Concamerata sudatio, or sudatorium, the vapour bath, was of a circular form,* and was surmounted by a cupola. In the centre of this cupola was an opening, from which a bronze shield (clipeus) was suspended. This regulated the temperature of the apartment. In the centre of the room was a vase (labrum) for washing the hands and face. In this room was the laconicum, a kind of stove, which served to heat the room.

* At Pompeii it is a semicircular niche in the caldarium.

V. The Caldarium, called also the balneum, calida lavatio, was the hot-water bath. In the centre of this was the basin or bath (lavacrum, it is also termed labrum): around this was a platform (schola) or space for the accommodation of those who were waiting for their turn to enter the bath.[*] As a further accommodation, a seat (pulvinar) was generally added.

VI. The Elæothesium, or unctuarium: in this were kept the oils and perfumes, which were used on coming out of the baths, as well as before entering them; this was generally next the apodyterium.

VII. The hypocaustum, or subterranean furnace, which distributed heat everywhere where it was required, and in different degrees.

In some of the larger baths there was a large hall called a Piscina, which contained a reservoir for swimming. Separate baths were assigned to the women, generally on the same principle as those for the men, but on a smaller scale.

The Thermæ of Imperial Rome were not alone baths on the grandest scale of refinement and luxury; they also included promenades, planted with trees, and covered alleys in which the idle took the fresh air. There were stadia where athletes wrestled and exercised themselves; there were numerous galleries, magnificent pinacothecæ, in which painters exhibited their paintings, sculptors, their statues; libraries also, and halls for conversation (exedræ), where wise men came to read, philosophers to discuss, orators and poets to recite their prose and verse. Such were the baths of Caracalla.[*] There were not less than sixteen hundred rooms for baths, all separate, and adorned with precious marbles. They were approached by a royal road, and were surrounded by porticoes; the emperor himself had a palace in it, and a private bath. Many master-pieces have been discovered here. The Hercules of Glycon, the Flora and the Toro Farnese were found in its ruins. Baths of granite and basalt, with other treasures have been discovered within its walls. Next to the Colosseum no ruins afford a greater idea of the magnificence of the structures of Imperial Rome. Size, grandeur, and solidity, with, however, a want of taste in the ornamentation and minor details, were the chief characteristic features of Roman architecture. Diocletian erected baths on the Quirinal, and Titus on the Esquiline. They are inferior, however, in size and magnificence to those of Caracalla. The baths of Titus are remarkable for the exquisite frescoes which were painted on its walls, and have been imitated by Raphael. Agrippa also erected baths. Remains of them have been found in the rear of the Pantheon. The site of the baths of Nero is uncertain. The baths of Pompeii are built on a smaller scale, such as would be suited to a provincial town. The Romans carried the luxurious practice of bathing into their remotest provinces. Remains of Roman baths are found in several parts of France and England.

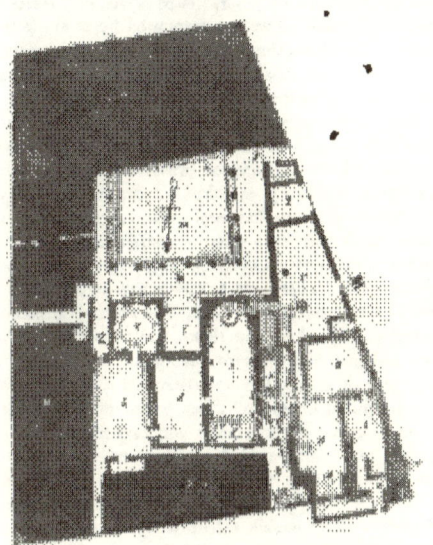

PLAN OF BATHS, POMPEII.

MAN'S BATHS		*k* Reservoir for cold water.
a *o* *p* Entrances.		*l* Room for attendants.
b Apodyterium.		*m* Court or vestibule to the baths.
c Frigidarium.		*n* Colonnade.
d Tepidarium.		
e Caldarium.		**WOMEN'S BATHS**
f Lavacrum.		*u* Entrance.
g Labrum.		*t* Apodyterium.
Apartments for stokers.		*s* Tepidarium.
i Furnace.		*u* Caldarium.
j Furnace.		*y* Labrum. *r* Court.

TRIUMPHAL ARCHES.—Triumphal arches were structures peculiar to the Romans. They generally consisted of arches erected at the entrance of cities, across streets, bridges, and public roads, in honour of victorious generals or emperors, or in commemoration of some remarkable event. At Rome they were generally placed in the way along which the triumphal procession passed to the Capitol. Sometinues temporary arches were erected during the triumph, and the more durable afterwards. The more simple structures had but a single arch, decorated with Corinthian columns, such as the arch of Titus at Rome; that of Verona has two arches, and seems to have served as gates to the town. In those with three arches, the two lateral arches are smaller than the middle one; such is that of Constantine at Rome. The arches of this kind were surmounted by a very lofty attic, which bore inscriptions, sometimes bas-reliefs, and also supported triumphal cars, equestrian statues. Its archivolts were ornamented with victories bearing palms. The bas-reliefs represented the arms of the conquered enemies, trophies of every kind, and even the monuments of art which had adorned the triumphal procession. When the conqueror in the triumphal procession passed under the middle arch, a figure of victory, attached by cords, placed a crown on his head. When a triumphal arch was erected as a monument of gratitude, or in commemoration of some event, and not in honour of a conqueror, no remains of trophies or military symbols are to be found on them. There are a number of triumphal arches still remaining. The principal are:—1. The arch of Drusus is considered the oldest triumphal arch in Rome, and is ascribed to Nero Claudius Drusus, father of the emperor Claudius. 2. The arch of Titus, the most elegant of all the triumphal arches, was erected by the senate and the people in honour of Titus, to commemorate the conquest of Jerusalem. Some of the vessels and ornaments which belonged to the temple at Jerusalem, and which were carried in the triumphal procession, appear on one of the bas-reliefs in the interior of the arch. On the opposite bas-relief the emperor is represented in a car, drawn by four horses, attended by senators, and crowned with laurel. 3. The arch of Septimius Severus. This arch was erected in honour of Septimius and his two sons, Caracalla and Geta, to commemorate two triumphs over the Parthians (a.d. 205). On the summit stood a car, drawn by six horses abreast, containing the statues of the emperor and his sons, as represented on coins. This arch stands at the foot of the Capitol. It is of white marble, and consists of one large arch, with a smaller one on each side, with a lateral communication from one to the other. It is ornamented with eight fluted composite pillars, and has bas-reliefs on each front. 4. The arch of Constantine was erected by the senate in honour of Constantine's victory over Maxentius. This, the largest and most imposing of the arches in Rome, consists of one large arch, with a smaller one on each side, and is ornamented with eight Corinthian columns, surmounted by statues of Dacian captives. The bas-reliefs with which it is decorated, are supposed to have come from an arch of Trajan, which stood in his forum. It stands at the foot of the Palatine hill, near the Colosseum, and was built in the Via Triumphalis. 5. The arch of Janus was probably not a triumphal arch. There is no certainty with regard to the date or purpose of this arch. Of arches built to commemorate remarkable events, we may notice, in particular, that of Trajan on the mole at Ancona.

ARCH OF TRAJAN AT BENEVENTO.

It was erected by the senate and people to Trajan, for having, at his own expense, constructed the mole, and having thus rendered the port safer to navigators. Another arch erected by Trajan at Beneventum, when he repaired the Via Appia, is not only remark-

able for its excellent preservation, but also as affording, perhaps,
the best specimen of Roman workmanship existing. It is a single
arch of Parian marble, and entire with the exception of part of the
cornice; both its sides are adorned with four Corinthian pillars
raised on high pedestals. The frieze and panels, as well as the
interior of the arch, are covered with rich sculpture, representing
Trajan's achievements and his apotheosis. The figures are in alto
relievo and exquisitely executed. Triumphal arches have been
erected in several parts of the Roman empire. Many are to be
found in various parts of Italy, at Aquino, Aosta, Susa, Rimini, Pola
in Istria, several in the south of France, of which the most remarkable are those of Orange, Nismes, Saint Chamas, Saintes, the latter
two are built on bridges. They also are met with in Macedonia,
Athens, Syria, and in Barbary: in Egypt also, at Antinoe, there is
a gate which is considered a triumphal arch.

FORA.—An important feature in a Roman city or town is the
Forum. The Greeks had also a forum, or αγορα, where the citizens
collected, but it differed from the Roman, in being of a square form.

RESTORATION OF THE ROMAN FORUM.

Vitruvius laid down rules for the plan of a Roman forum. According to him it should be of an oblong form, the breadth being about
two-thirds of the length. Adjoining the forum should be situated

the basilica, and around it the public buildings, temples, porticoes, and shops. The basilica was a court of justice, it was also used as an exchange. Vitruvius directs that it should be placed in the warmest side of the forum, so that the merchants might assemble there in winter, without being inconvenienced by the cold. It was of an oblong form, and was generally divided into three parts, consisting of a central nave (media porticus), and two side aisles, each separated from the centre by a single row of columns. At the end of the central aisle was the tribunal; on each side of which were small chambers which served as offices for the judges or merchants. A peculiarity of the basilica was its semicircular and vaulted end (apsis), which has been adopted in the Christian basilica. According to Vitruvius, the treasury, prisons, and curia should also adjoin the forum. The curia was the council-house, where the senate and chief magistrates met to consult and deliberate. The Roman forum was destined for the transaction of public business. Here the comitia were held, here the orators harangued, and through it the triumphal processions passed on their way to the Capitol. The forum of Trajan and other Roman emperors were intended more as embellishments of the city, than for the transaction of business. There were other fora in Rome, but which were only market-places, such as the forum boarium, the cattle market; forum olitorium, the vegetable market; forum piscatorium, the fish market. The forum at Pompeii illustrates the plan laid down by Vitruvius, it is of an oblong form; at one end are the curia, prisons and treasury, at the other end the temple of Jupiter, at the sides are the basilica, the temples of Venus and Mercury, a granary, a chalcidicum, and the whole was surrounded by porticoes.

Section VIII.—PUBLIC AND MILITARY ROADS—BRIDGES —GATEWAYS—AQUEDUCTS.

PUBLIC AND MILITARY ROADS.— Frequent intercourse between different nations led to the necessity of finding means of communication, and thus recourse was had to the plan of laying down and constructing roads. All nations constructed them with more or less solidity and perfection. Roads and pathways have been constructed in Egypt with much care; but it seems that the Greeks did not give that attention to the laying down of public roads which would have rendered them useful and convenient. The public roads are among the things which Strabo mentions as having been neglected by the Greeks: no people equalled the Romans in this kind of public constructions, which were mainly formed to facilitate military movements. The invention of paved roads was borrowed from the Carthaginians by the Romans.

ROMAN ROADS.—Rome was the central point to which all roads converged, by numerous branches which thus united the most remote provinces. In the early ages of the republic, the construction and superintendence of the roads were committed to the consors. Augustus gave particular care to the construction of roads; he established messengers and, later, couriers. The Romans laid out their roads in a straight line, and avoided all winding by filling up valleys, lowering elevations, tunnelling rocks and mountains, and building bridges. Two trenches (sulci), in the first place indicated the breadth of the road, the loose earth between the trenches was then removed, and this excavation as far as the solid ground (gremium) was filled with materials to the height fixed on for the road. Some Roman roads were near twenty feet over the solid ground. The lowest course, the statumen, was composed of small stones; the second, called the rudus, was a mass of broken stones cemented with lime; the third, the nucleus, was composed of a mixture of lime, clay, fragments of brick and pottery beaten together, on this was placed the fourth course, the summum dorsum, composed of a pavimentum of flat stones, selected for their hardness, cut into irregular polygons, and sometimes into rectangular slabs. When the fourth course, or pavement, was not put on, the surface was a mixture of pounded gravel and lime. The ordinary breadth of the principal Roman roads was sixty feet. It was divided into three parts, the middle, somewhat larger, was paved and slightly curved; the two lateral parts were covered with gravel; some roads, however, were only fifteen feet wide. Footpaths (margines, umbones) were raised upon each side and strowed with gravel. On the principal roads there were frequently to be seen temples, arches of triumph, villas, and especially sepulchral monuments, which recalled to the passers by the memory of illustrious men, or of memorable events.

We shall now mention the principal military roads, which were the means of communication between Rome and the provinces.

I. The Via Appia, or Regina Viarum, was commenced B.C. 312, by Appius Claudius Cæcus, the censor. It commenced at the Porta Capena, passed through Aricia, Tres Tabernæ, Appii Forum, Terracina, Fundi, Formiæ, Minturnæ, Sinuessa, Casilium, and terminated at Capua; it was afterwards prolonged through Calatia and Candium to Beneventum, and thence, through Venusia, Tarentum, and Asia, to Brundusium; this extension being made, it is said, by Trajan. It became not only the great line of communication with Southern Italy, but with Greece, and with the most remote eastern possessions of Rome. At Brundusium there was was a magnificent port, which was the principal point of communication with Greece. This road was famous for the number, beauty, and richness of the sepulchral monuments with which its sides were lined. A number of them, extending for over eight miles beyond the tomb of Cæcilia Metella, have been lately discovered and brought to light by the energy and skill of the late Commendatore Canina.

II. Via Latina. This road is said to have issued from the Porta Capena. It also led to Beneventum, but kept more inland than the Via Appia. It passed through Anagnia, Frusino, Aquinum, Venafrum, Casinum, and joined the Via Appia at Beneventum. It was formed in the time of Augustus, under the direction of Messala. Several tombs, painted with great eleganco and taste, have been lately discovered on this road, about two miles from Rome.

III. Via Labicana. It commenced at the Porta Esquilina, it passed Labicum, and joined the Via Latina about thirty miles from Rome.

IV. Via Prænestina, formerly Via Gabina, began at the Porta Esquilina. It passed Gabii and Præneste, and then merged in the Via Latina below Anagnia.

V. Via Tiburtina, so called from its leading to Tibur or Tivoli. It issued from the gate of the same name. It was continued from Tibur, through the country of the Sabines to Adria under the name of the Via Valeria.

VI. Via Nomentana, so called from its leading to Nomentum, a Sabine town. It began originally at the Porta Collina, and afterwards from the Porta Nomentana. It crossed the Anio about three miles from Rome, and joined the Via Salaria at Eretum. This road was also called Ficulnensis, from Ficulnea, another town of the Sabines, the situation of which has been lately discovered, about seven miles from the Porta Nomentana.

VII. Via Salaria. It ran from the Porta Salaria, so called from the circumstance of the Sabines coming for salt, which gave the name to the road also. It traversed the Sabine and Picinian country to Reate and Asculum Picenum. It then proceeded towards the coast, which it followed until it merged in the Via Flaminia at Ancona.

VIII. Via Flaminia. It began from the Porta Flaminia (del Popolo). It was commenced in the censorship of C. Flaminius and S. Paulus, u.c. 533. It went by Otriculum (Otricoli), Interamna (Terni). Fanum Fortunæ (Fano), to Ariminum (Rimini). Then the Via Æmilia began, which was constructed u.c. 567, when M. Æmilius Lepidus was consul. It passed by Bononia (Bologna), Parma, Placentia, Modiolanum (Milan), Brixa (Brescia), Verona, Patavium (Padua), to Aquileia. The Via Cassia struck off from the Via Flaminia near the Pons Milvius (Ponte Molle). It passed near Veii, and then traversed Etruria, until it joined the Via Aurelia at Luna.

IX. Via Aurelia. It issued from the Porta Aurelia, and approached the sea at Alsium (Palo), and then went along the Etruscan and Ligurian coast. It extended as far as Gaul. Via Vitellia also issued from the Porta Aurelia.

X. Via Portuensis. It led from the Porta Portuensis to the Portus Trajani, near the mouth of the Tiber. A branch of this road is called the Via Campana.

XI. Via Ostiensis. It issued from the Porta Ostiensis; keeping the left bank of the Tiber, it led to Ostia, near the mouth of the Tiber. The Via Ardentina and the Via Laurentina branched off from this road at a short distance from Rome. The first led to Ardea, the second to Laurentum. The Via Severiana was a continuation of the Via Ostiensis, along the coast through Laurentum, Antium, Circei, to Terracina.

BRIDGES.—It is evident that bridges, at the early periods of Greece, were never used, as well from the smallness of the rivers as from their almost total ignorance of the use of the arch. If any bridge was used, it is probable that it was built entirely of wood, being nothing more than a wooden platform, supported upon stone piers at each extremity. An arched bridge of considerable size has been lately discovered in Greece, at Xerocampo, which Colonel Mure considers to be in a style of masonry which guarantees it a work of the remotest antiquity, probably of the heroic age itself. Several archæologists, however, who have since seen it, have declared their conviction that this bridge is of late and of Roman architecture.

Roman.—The earliest bridges of the Romans were of timber, such was that which joined the Janiculum to the Mons Aventinus, called the Pons Sublicius from the beams (sublicæ) of which it was composed. The Romans were the first people who availed themselves of their knowledge of the arch to apply it to the construction of bridges. They were thus enabled to erect structures on the grandest scale, and of such solidity that many still remain at the present day in the Roman provinces to attest their strength and utility. The passage way of the Roman bridge was divided into three parts: the centre one, for horses and carriages, was denominated agger or iter; and the raised footpaths on each side (decursoria), which were enclosed by parapet walls. We shall now mention the principal bridges in Rome, and some of the most remarkable in the provinces.

1. Pons Sublicius. This was the first bridge ever constructed in Rome. It was so called from Sublices, a Volscian term for the wooden beams of which it was built. It was erected by Ancus Martius, and became celebrated for the feat of Horatius Cocles. It was destroyed by a great flood in the reign of Augustus. It was rebuilt in stone by P. Æmilius Lepidus, hence the bridge is sometimes called Pons Æmilius or Pons Lepidi.

II. Pons Palatinus. It was begun by M. Fulvius, u.c. 574, and finished by Scipio Africanus and L. Mummius, u.c. 611. Some antiquaries have also called it Pons Senatorius. A few arches still remain, it is now called Ponte Rotto.

III. Pons Fabricius and Pons Cestius connected the Insula Tiberina with the opposite sides of the river. The Pons Fabricius was built by L. Fabricius, in the year of Rome 692. It was also called Trapeius. It is now called the Ponte Quattro Capi. It consists of two large arches and a smaller one between them, through which the water runs when it is very high. The Pons Cestius leads out of the island towards the Janiculum. Who Cestius was, from whom the bridge takes it name, is unknown.

IV. Pons Janiculensis. The date of this bridge is unknown. Some ascribe it to Trajan, some to Antoninus Pius. It is now called Ponte Sisto.

V. Pons Triumphalis, so called because the generals who had conquered in the north and west of Rome passed

over this bridge in triumphal procession on their way to the
Capitol. It was also called Pons Vaticanus. It connected the
Campus Martius and the Campus Vaticanus. It is now completely
destroyed.

VI. Pons Ælius was built by the emperor Adrian as an approach
to his mausoleum. Medals of Adrian represent it nearly as we see
it at the present day, for it has come down to the present time
nearly perfect. It consists of three large arches of equal size, and
a smaller one on each side. It is now called Ponte St. Angelo.

VII. Pons Milvius, on the Via Flaminia, of which the modern
name, Ponte Molle, is evidently a corruption. It is stated to have
been built by Æmilius Scaurus, who was censor U.C. 644. It was
repaired by Augustus. Near this bridge took place the celebrated
battle between Maxentius and Constantine, which decided the fate
of the Roman empire, A.D. 312.

VIII. The Pons Narniensis, on the Flaminian way. It is considered the noblest relic of the imperial times. It was built by
Augustus over the river Nar, near Narni, about sixty miles from
Rome. It originally consisted of four arches, three of which are
broken. The height of the arches was about 112 feet.

No modern bridge can equal the stupendous constructions built
by Trajan over the Danube. It consisted of twenty piers of stone,
60 Roman feet broad and 150 feet, without the foundations, above
the bed of the river. The width between each pier was 170 feet,
the piers were united by arches of wood. Another remarkable
Roman bridge is that at Alcantara, in Spain. It was built in the
reign of Trajan, A.D. 108, over the Tagus, by the architect Caius
Julius Lacer, who was buried near his work. The roadway is
perfectly level, and is 600 feet long by 28 feet wide. It is 245 feet
above the usual level of the river.

Etruscan.—Though the Etruscans were acquainted with the
principle of the arch, bridges are rarely met with in Etruria. The
Ponte della Badia, at Volci, is evidently a Roman arch built on
Etruscan buttresses, which were the piers of the original bridge,
and which may have been connected by an horizontal frame of
wood-work.

GATEWAYS.—The earliest and simplest form of Grecian or Etruscan
gateways, or entrances to cities, was the earliest known plan or

attempt at an arch, which was by sloping the jambs and placing a long block of stone as a lintel over them; an early instance of this style will be found in the gateway of Segni. This style of gateway is always found in connection with the polygonal style of masonry.

GATE OF SEGNI.

The next form of gateway adopted was that which was generally used in the second stage of the development of the principle of the arch, which was formed by placing horizontal courses of stones, projecting one over another, from both sides, till they met at the top, and then cutting the ends of the projecting stones in a curvilinear form,

GATEWAY AT ARPINO.

as may be seen in a gateway at Thoricus in Attica, and in the almost identical one at Arpino. This style of gateway, and other similar attempts at the principle of the arch, are always in connection with those walls which are built of blocks laid in horizontal courses, and are to be met with both in Etruria and Greece, for there was a correspondence in the sequence and development of styles in arches and walls among the Etruscans and Greeks. The more perfectly developed form, or radiating arch, is found in the gateways of Volterra, Falleri, Pæstum, and Pompeii, in connection with the regular horizontal style of masonry. The discovery of this style of arch is generally attributed to Etruria; the existence, however, of radiating arches in Egypt, Nineveh, and Ethiopia, of an ancient date, has inclined some antiquaries to contest the honour of originality with Etruria. It is not, however, inconsistent with the independent progress of development, that the principle of the arch may have been worked out independently by the Etruscans, while carrying out and following up the development of that principle of the arch. The earliest example of the arch mentioned in history, and now extant, is that of the Cloaca Maxima, at Rome, which is of undoubted Etruscan origin. Its perfection, as Mr. Dennis remarks, might lead us to suppose a long previous acquaintance with this construction. At a later date, some cities were entered by double gates, one designed for carriages entering and the other for carriages leaving the city. As at Como, Verona, and in a magnificent example at Treves. In other instances, as at Pompeii, we find only one gate for carriages, but a smaller one at each side of it for foot passengers. Of the gates of Rome, in

GATE AT POMPEII.

the wall of Servius Tullius, not a vestige now remains. Of the gates in the wall of Aurelian, the greater number have been so rebuilt at later periods as scarcely to retain a stone of the former gateway. The Porta St. Lorenzo, the ancient Porta Tiburtina, and the Porta Maggiore, alone present some remaining portion of the former gateways. *

1.   2.

3.   4.

GATES AT OENIADÆ.

AQUEDUCTS.—The supply of water in the Grecian towns was chiefly from fountains and wells. Aqueducts were scarcely known in Greece before the time of the Romans.

Aqueducts were most extensively used by the Romans. Remains

* Col. Mure in his travels in Greece gives drawings of gateways at the ruins of Oeniadæ which offer a distinct gradation of expedients for covering in such structures, from the simple flat architrave to the regularly vaulted arch. 2, 3, are the development of the principle. 4, an approximation to the perfect arch.

of those stupendous structures are to be met with not only in the
neighbourhood of Rome, but also throughout the Roman provinces
in Europe, Asia, and Africa. They were apparent or subterranean.
The latter, which sometimes traversed considerable space, and were
carried through rocks, contained pipes (fistulæ, tubuli) of lead or
terra cotta, frequently marked either with the name of the potter, or
the name of the consuls in whose time they were laid down. At convenient points, in the course of these aqueducts, as it was necessary
from the water being conveyed through pipes, there were reservoirs
(piscinæ), in which the water might deposit any sediment that it
contained. Vitruvius has given rules for the laying down of pipes,
and for forming reservoirs. The apparent aqueducts were built on
the most stupendous scale. Hills were pierced through by tunnels,
and valleys crossed either by solid substructions or arches of
masonry, according to the height required, bringing water from
sources varying from thirty to sixty miles in distance. At one

AQUEDUCT.

period of the history of Rome no less than twenty aqueducts stretched
their long line of arches, and brought as many different streams of
water, across the wide plain or Campagna in which the city stands.
For the most part they were built of brick, and consisted of nearly
square piers running up to the same height—a slight and uniform
declivity being necessarily maintained—and connected by semicircular arches, over which the conduit (specus, canalis) ran. This
conduit had a paved or tiled floor, and was enclosed laterally by
walls of brick or stone, and with a transverse arch, or by a simple

flat coping of stone. The water either ran directly through this conduit, or was carried through pipes laid along its floor. These aqueducts were either simple, double or triple, according as they were composed of a single, two or three tiers of arches. At the termination of the aqueduct, within the city, was a vast reservoir called castellum, which formed the head of the water, from which it was conducted through pipes into smaller reservoirs, and thence was distributed through the city, thus supplying the public fountains, baths, and houses. The chief castellum was, externally, a highly decorated building. The so-called trophies of Marius, at Rome, are supposed by Piranesi to have been a castellum or reservoir of the Aqua Julia. Excavations made some years ago seem to confirm his opinion. Remains of works of art found near it prove that it must have had a very ornamental exterior.

We shall begin our enumeration of the principal aqueducts by the most ancient aqueducts in Rome. Before the year of Rome, 441, the city was supplied with water from the Tiber only. In that year (B.C. 313) Appius Claudius, the censor, constructed an aqueduct which brought water from a distance of seven miles; it was called Aqua Appia, after him. It began to the left of the Via Prænestina; and, according to Frontinus, its whole course, except sixty paces near the Porta Capena, was under ground. This last portion was on arches. No traces of it remain.

The Anio Vetus was constructed by Marcus Curius Dentatus, B.C. 272, and was finished by M. Fulvius Flaccus. The water was derived from a source of the river Anio, near Augusta, twenty miles beyond Tibur, and about forty-three from Rome. It was of peperino stone. A small portion of this aqueduct is still visible outside the Porta Maggiore.

The Aqua Marcia was constructed by the prætor, Q. Marcus Rex, by command of the senate, B.C. 144. It had its source in a small stream which runs into the Anio, not far from the present town of Subiaco, about thirty-seven miles from Rome. It was repaired by Agrippa. The latter portion of this aqueduct for about six miles from Rome was on arches, the remains of which form one of the most interesting features of the Roman Campagna. It is remarkable for the excellence and wholesomeness of its water.

The Aqua Tepula was constructed by Cneus Servilius Cæpio and L. Cassius Longinus, B.C. 126. It had its source near the tenth milestone on the Via Latina.

The Aqua Julia was executed by Agrippa in his ædileship, B.C. 33, and was so called in honour of Julius Cæsar. This aqueduct was a union of three streams: the Aqua Marcia, the Aqua Tepula, and the Aqua Julia, properly so called, which had its source two miles beyond that of the Aqua Tepula. It supplied the Esquiline and Palatine hills. It was built partly on massive substructions and partly on arches. The so-called Sette Sale are supposed to have been a reservoir of the aqueduct for the use of the baths of Titus.

The Aqua Virgo was constructed by Agrippa, under Augustus, to supply his baths. Its source was between the seventh and eighth milestone, on the Via Collatina. It derives its name from the tradition that its source was pointed out by a young girl to some thirsty soldiers. It entered Rome near the Porta Pinciana, from whence it was conducted on arches to the Campus Martius. The greater portion of it was subterranean, a small portion of about 700 paces, was on arches. This aqueduct still supplies a large part of modern Rome.

The Aqua Alsietina, on the right bank of the Tiber, was brought by Augustus, from the lacus Alsietinus, to supply his naumachia. It was about thirty miles long.

The Aqua Claudia was commenced by Caligula, A.D. 36, continued and finished by the emperor Claudius, A.D. 50. The springs from which it derived its water were near the thirty-eighth milestone, on the Via Sublacensis, a few miles from Sublaqueum (Subiaco). It was more than forty-six miles long. At the present day a line of arches belonging to this aqueduct extend for about six miles across the Campagna, forming the grandest and the most picturesque vista on the plain near Rome. The arches were afterwards used by Sixtus V. to supply the city from another source, under the name of the Aqua Felice.

The Anio Novus, also built by Claudius, was the longest of all the aqueducts, being nearly fifty-nine miles long. Its source was near the forty-second milestone, on the Von Sublacensis. This aqueduct, with the Aqua Claudia, entered the city over the present Porta Maggiore, in two channels, one above the other. The upper was the Anio Novus, the lower the Aqua Claudia.

It has been calculated that these nine aqueducts furnished Rome with a supply of water equal to that carried down by a river thirty feet broad by six deep, flowing at the rate of thirty inches a second. These magnificent and useful works of the ancient Romans were not confined to the capital alone. Constructions of equal magnificence and utility, some even on a grander scale, are to be found not only in the provinces near Rome, but even in the remotest parts of the empire. Among these constructions to be met with in the provinces, the most remarkable for the scale of its magnificence and grandeur, far exceeding anything of the kind in Italy, is the so-called Pont du Gard, which supplies Nismes with water. It consists of three rows of arches one above the other: the first tier contains six arches; the second, eleven; the third, thirty-five. The whole height is 182 feet; the channel in which the water runs is three feet high. The aqueduct of Segovia, in Spain, is also a Roman work, exhibiting great perfection and solidity in its construction. It is built entirely of stone, in two ranks of arches, the piers being eight feet wide and eleven in depth; 150 arches still remain. The effect, however, is much marred by the houses and other objects that crowd their bases. In the opinion of Mr. Fergusson the aqueduct at Tarragona bears a character of lightness combined with constructive solidity and elegance unrivalled in any other work of its class. Constructions of

AQUEDUCT AT LISBON.

this kind are to be met with at Athens, Corinth, Catania, Salona, Nicomedia, Ephesus, Smyrna, Alexandria, in the Troad, Syracuse, Arcueil, Metz, Clermont, Auvergne, Lyon, Evora, Merida.

TOMBS.

Respect for the dead, and a considerate regard for the due performance of the rites of burial, have been distinctive features in man in all ages and countries. Among the Greeks and Romans great importance was attached to the burial of the dead, as, if a

corpse remained unburied, it was believed that the spirit of the
departed wandered for a hundred years on the hither side of the
Styx. Hence it became a religious duty to scatter earth over any
unburied body which any one might chance to meet. This was
considered sufficient to appease the infernal gods. The earliest
tomb was the tumulus, or mound of earth, heaped over the dead.
It is a form naturally suggested to man in the early stages of his
development. There are two classes of primitive tombs, which are
evidently of the highest antiquity. The *hyperguan*, or raised
mounds, or tumuli, and *hypogaea*, which are subterranean or excavated. The tumulus may be considered as the most simple and the
most ancient form of sepulture. Its adoption was universal among
all primitive nations. Such was the memorial raised by the Greeks
over the bodies of their heroes. These raised mounds are to be met
with in all countries. The pyramid, which is but a further development in stone of this form of sepulture, is not peculiar to Egypt
alone; it has been adopted in several other countries. Examples of
subterranean tombs are to be found in Egypt, Etruria, Greece.
Those of Egypt and Etruria afford instances of extraordinary labour
bestowed in excavating and constructing these subterranean abodes
of the dead.

Egyptian.—The pyramids were tombs (see p. 56). These monuments were the last abode of the kings and great personages of
their family or of the state. They are to be met with in Lower
Egypt alone. In Upper Egypt numerous excavations from the
living rock in the mountains of the Thebaid received their mortal
remains. Nothing can exceed the magnificence and care with
which these tombs of the kings were excavated and decorated.
Their entrance, carefully closed, was frequently indicated by a
façade cut on the side of the hill. A number of passages, sometimes intersected by deep wells and large halls, finally lead, frequently by concealed entrances, to the large chamber where was the
sarcophagus, generally of granite, basalt, or alabaster. The sides
of the entire excavation, as well as the roof, were covered with
paintings, coloured sculptures, and hieroglyphic inscriptions in
which the name of the deceased king was frequently repeated. We
generally find represented in them the funeral ceremonies, the procession, the visit of the soul of the deceased to the principal divinities, its offerings to each of them, lastly, its presentation by the god
who protected it to the supreme god of the Amenti, or Egyptian
hell. The splendour of these works, and the richness and variety
of their ornamentation, exceeds all conception : the figures, though

in great number, are sometimes of colossal size; frequently scenes
of civil life are mingled with funereal representations; the labours
of agriculture, domestic occupations, musicians, dances, and furniture of wonderful richness and elegance, are also figured on them;
on the ceiling are generally astronomical or astrological subjects.
Several tombs of the kings of the 18th dynasty and subsequent
dynasties have been found in the valley of Biban-el-Molouk, on the
western side of the plain of Thebes. One of the most splendid of
these is that opened by Belzoni, and now known as that of Osirei
Menepthah, of the 19th dynasty. A sloping passage leads to a
chamber which has been called "The Hall of Beauty." Forcing
his way further on, Belzoni found, as a termination to a series of
chambers, a large vaulted hall which contained the sarcophagus,
which held the body of the monarch, now in Sir John Soane's
Museum. The entire extent of this succession of chambers and
passages is hollowed to a length of 320 feet into the heart of the
rock, and they are profusely covered with the paintings and hieroglyphics usually found in these sepulchral chambers. The tombs
of the other kings, Rameses III. and Rameses Miamun, exhibit
similar series of passages and chambers, covered with paintings and
sculptures, in endless variety, some representing the deepest mysteries of the Egyptian religion; but, as Mr. Fergusson says, like all
the tombs, they depend for their magnificence more on the paintings that adorn the walls than on anything which can strictly be
called architecture.

Private individuals were buried according to their rank and fortune. Their tombs, also excavated from the living rock, consisted
of one or of several chambers ornamented with paintings and sculptures; the last contained the sarcophagus and the mummy. According to Sir G. Wilkinson, they were the property of the priests, and
a sufficient number being always kept ready, the purchase was
made at the shortest notice, nothing being requisite to complete
even the sculptures or inscriptions but the insertion of the deceased's name and a few statements respecting his family and profession. The numerous subjects representing agricultural scenes,
the trades of the people, in short, the various occupations of the
Egyptians, varying only in their details and the mode of their
execution, were figured in these tombs, and were intended as a
short epitome of human life, which suited equally every future
occupant. The tombs at Beni Hassan are even of an earlier date
than those of Thebes. Among these the tomb of a monarch or provincial governor is of the age of Osirtasen I. The walls of this
tomb are covered with a series of representations, setting forth the

ordinary occupations and daily avocations of the deceased, thus illustrating the manners and customs of the Egyptians of that age. These representations are a sort of epitome of life, or the career of

TOMB AT BENI HASSAN.

man, previous to his admission to the mansions of the dead. They were therefore intended to show that the deceased had carefully and duly fulfilled and performed all the duties and avocations which his situation in life and the reverence due to the gods required. Near the great pyramid are several tombs of private individuals, who were mostly priests of Memphis. Many of these tombs have false entrances, and several have pits with their mouths at the top of the tomb. The walls of these tombs are covered with the usual paintings representing the ordinary occupations of the deceased.

MUMMIES.

The origin of the process of embalming has been variously accounted for. When, however, we consider that it was a part of the religious belief of the Egyptians that, as a reward of a well-spent and virtuous life, their bodies after death should exist and remain undecayed for ever in their tombs, for we find in the "Book of the Dead" the following inscription placed over the spirits who have found favour in the eyes of the Great God: "The bodies which they have forsaken shall *sleep for ever* * in their sepulchres, while they rejoice in the presence of God most high," there will be no difficulty in seeing that with this religious creed the Egyptians should feel the necessity of embalming to ensure the eternal existence of their bodies. Some have considered that the want of ground for cemeteries, and also the excavations made in the mountains for the extraction of materials employed in the immense

* Hence it is evident the Egyptians did not believe in the resurrection of the body.

buildings of Egypt, compelled them to have recourse to the expedient of mummification. Others consider the custom arose rather from a sanitary regulation for the benefit of the living. According to Mr. Gliddon, mummification preceded, in all probability, the

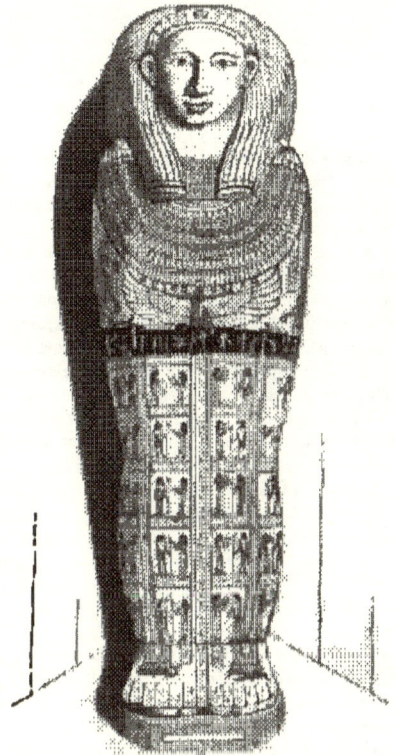

EGYPTIAN MUMMY CASE.

building of the pyramids and tombs, because vestiges of mummies have been found in the oldest of these, and, in fact, the first mummies were buried in the sand before the Egyptians possessed the necessary tools for excavating sepulchres in the rock. The earliest

mode of mummification was extremely simple; the bodies were
prepared with natron, or dried in ovens, and wrapped in woollen
cloth. At a later period every provincial temple was provided with
an establishment for the purpose of mummification. The bodies
were delivered to the priests to be embalmed, and after seventy
days restored to their friends, to be carried to the place of deposit.
The mode of embalming depended on the rank and position of the
deceased. There were three modes of embalming; the first is said
to have cost a talent of silver (about 250l.); the second, 22 minæ
(60l.); the third was extremely cheap. The process is thus described by Herodotus :—" In Egypt certain persons are appointed by
law to exercise this art as their peculiar business, and when a dead
body is brought them they produce patterns of mummies in wood,
imitated in painting. In preparing the body according to the most
expensive mode, they commence by extracting the brain from the
nostrils by a curved hook, partly cleansing the head by these means,
and partly by pouring in certain drugs; then making an incision
in the side with a sharp Ethiopian stone (black flint), they draw out
the intestines through the aperture. Having cleansed and washed
them with palm wine, they cover them with pounded aromatics,
and afterwards filling the cavity with powder of pure myrrh, cassia,
and other fragrant substances, frankincense excepted, they sew it
up again. This being done, they salt the body, keeping it in natron
during seventy days, to which period they are strictly confined.
When the seventy days are over, they wash the body, and wrap it
up entirely in bands of fine linen smeared on their inner side with
gum. The relatives then take away the body, and have a wooden
case made in the form of a man, in which they deposit it; and when
fastened up they keep it in a room in their house, placing it upright
against the wall. (This style of mummy was supposed to represent
the deceased in the form of Osiris.) This is the most costly mode
of embalming.

For those who choose the middle kind, on account of the expense,
they prepare the body as follows :—They fill syringes with oil of
cedar, and inject this into the abdomen without making any incision or removing the bowels; and taking care that the liquid shall
not escape, they keep it in salt during the specified number of days.
The cedar-oil is then taken out, and such is its strength that it
brings with it the bowels and all the inside in a state of dissolution.
The natron also dissolves the flesh, so that nothing remains but the
skin and bones. This process being over, they restore the body
without any further operation.

The third kind of embalming is only adopted for the poor. In this they merely cleanse the body by an injection of syrmæa, and salt it during seventy days, after which it is returned to the friends who brought it.

Sir G. Wilkinson gives some further information with regard to the more expensive mode of embalming. The body, having been prepared with the proper spices and drugs, was enveloped in linen bandages sometimes 1,000 yards in length. It was then enclosed in a cartonage fitting close to the mummied body, which was richly painted and covered in front with a network of beads and bugles arranged in a tasteful form, the face being laid over with a thick gold leaf, and the eyes made of enamel. The three or four cases which successively covered the cartonage were ornamented in like manner with painting and gilding, and the whole was enclosed in a sarcophagus of wood or stone, profusely charged with painting or sculpture. These cases, as well the cartonage, varied in style and richness, according to the expense incurred by the friends of the deceased. The bodies thus embalmed were generally of priests of various grades. Sometimes the skin itself was covered with gold leaf; sometimes the whole body, the face, or eyelids; sometimes the nails alone. In many instances the body or the cartonage was beautified in an expensive manner, and the outer cases wore little ornamented; but some preferred the external show of rich cases and sarcophagi. Some mummies have been found with the face covered by a mask of cloth fitting closely to it, and overlaid with a coating of composition, so painted as to resemble the deceased, and to have the appearance of flesh. These, according to Sir G. Wilkinson, are probably of a Greek epoch. Greek mummies usually differed from those of the Egyptians in the manner of disposing the bandages of the arms and legs. No Egyptian is found with the limbs bandaged separately, as those of Greek mummies. On the breast was frequently placed a scarabæus in immediate contact with the flesh. These scarabæi, when of stone, had their extended wings made of lead or silver. On the cartonage and case, in a corresponding situation above, the same emblem was also placed, to indicate the protecting influence of the Deity. The subjects painted upon the cartonage wore the four genii of Amenti, and various emblems belonging to deities connected with the dead. A long line of hieroglyphics extending down the front usually contained the name and quality of the deceased, and the offerings presented by him to the gods; and transverse bands frequently repeated the former, with similar donations to other deities. On the breast was placed the figure of Notpe, with expanded wings, protecting the deceased; sacred arks, boats, and other things were arranged in different com-

partments, and Osiris, Isis, Anubis, and other deities were fre
quently introduced. In some instances Isis was represented throwing her arms round the feet of the mummy, with this appropriate
legend: "I embrace thy feet." A plaited beard was attached to
the chin when the mummy was that of a man; the absence of this
appendage indicated the mummy of a woman.

MUMMY CASES AND SARCOPHAGI.

The outer case of the mummy was either of wood—sycamore or
cedar—or of stone. When of wood it had a flat or circular summit,
sometimes with a stout square pillar rising at each angle. The

EGYPTIAN MUMMY CASES.

whole was richly painted, and some of an older age frequently had
a door represented near one of the corners. At one end was the
figure of Isis, at the other Nepthys; and the top was painted with
bands or fancy devices. In others, the lid represented the curving

top of the ordinary Egyptian canopy. The stone coffins, usually called sarcophagi, were of oblong shape, having flat straight sides, like a box, with a curved or pointed lid. Sometimes the figure of the deceased was represented upon the latter in relief, like that of the Queen of Amasis in the British Museum; and some were in the form of a king's name or oval. Others were made in the shape of the mummied body, whether of basalt, granite, slate, or limestone, specimens of which are met with in the British Museum. These cases were deposited in the sepulchral chambers. Various offerings were placed near them, and sometimes the instruments of the profession of the deceased. Near them were also placed vases and small figures of the deceased, of wood or vitrified earthenware. The most elaborate sarcophagus is that now in the British Museum; it was formerly supposed to have been the identical sarcophagus which contained the body of Alexander the Great. The hieroglyphic name, which has been read upon the monument, proves it to be that of Nectanebo I., of the thirtieth dynasty, who reigned from B.C. 381 to 363. Its material is a breccia from a quarry near Thebes, and is remarkable for its hardness. A remarkable mummy-shaped coffin is that of Menkare, the Mycerinus of the Greeks, and the builder of the third pyramid; this interesting relic, when found by Colonel Vyse in the sepulchral chambers of the third pyramid, contained portions of a body, supposed to be that of the same king. It is now in the British Museum.

CANOPI.

The vases, generally named canopi, from their resemblance to certain vases made by the Romans to imitate the Egyptian taste, but inadmissible in its application to any Egyptian vase, were four in number, of different materials, according to the rank of the deceased, and were placed near his coffin in the tomb. Some were of common limestone, the most costly were of Oriental alabaster. These four vases form a complete series; the principal intestines of the mummy were placed in them, embalmed in spices and various substances, and rolled up in linen, each containing a separate portion. They were supposed to belong to the four genii of Amenti, whose heads and names they bore. The vase with a cover, representing the human head of Amset, held the stomach and large intestines; that with the cynocephalus head of Hapi contained the small intestines; in that belonging to the jackal-headed Smautf were the lungs and heart; and for the vase of the hawk-headed Kebhsnof

wore reserved the gall-bladder and liver. On the sides of the vases
were several columns of hieroglyphics, which expressed the adoration
of the deceased to each of the four deities whose symbols adorned
the covers, and which gave the name of the deceased.

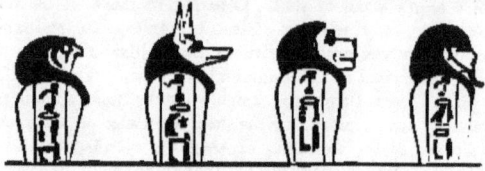

GENII OF AMENTI.

Small figures, called *shabti*, offered through respect for the dead,
are to be found in great numbers in the tombs. They were images
of the deceased under the form of Osiris, and were to the melancholy
Egyptian a reminder of mortality. They are generally of wood, or
of vitrified earthenware. The name and quality of the deceased
are found on all those in the same tomb, and thrown on the ground
round the sarcophagus. They usually bear in hieroglyphics a
chapter of the funeral ritual. Some are found with a blank space
left for the name of the deceased, which leads one to think that the
relations and friends procured these figures from dealers ; the
funeral formula, with a list of the customary presentations of
offerings for his soul to Osiris were already on them; nothing was
wanting but the name of the deceased; this being added, they were
then evidently offered as testimonies of respect by the relations and
friends of the deceased, perhaps at the funeral, and then collected
and placed in the tomb. Sometimes these small figures were placed
in painted cases divided into compartments. These cases were
about 2 feet long and 1 foot high.

PAPYRI.

Manuscripts on papyrus, of various lengths, have been found on
some mummies. These rolls of papyrus are found in the coffins, or
under the swathings of the mummies, between the legs, on the
breast, or under the arms. Some are enclosed in a cylindrical case.
The papyrus of the Museum of Turin is 66 feet long, that at Paris
is 22 feet long ; others are of different lengths, down to 2 or 3 feet.
That of Turin may be considered as complete. On all, the upper
part of the page is occupied by a line of figures of the divinities

which the soul visits in succession; the rest is filled with perpendicular columns of hieroglyphics, which are prayers which the soul
addresses to each divinity; towards the end of the manuscript is
painted the judgment scene; the great god Osiris is on his throne,
at his feet is an enormous female crocodile, its mouth open; behind,
is the divine balance, surmounted by a cynocephalus emblem of universal justice; the good and bad actions of the soul are weighed in
his presence. Horus examines the plummet, and Thoth records the
sentence; standing close by is the soul of the deceased in its cor-

JUDGMENT OF THE SOUL.

poreal form, conducted by the two goddesses, Truth and Justice, before the great judge of the dead. A papyrus of this kind is, according
to Lepsius, a history of the soul after death, and for this reason it
was placed in the tomb with the deceased. Champollion appears to
have regarded this kind of papyrus as a book of rituals—a " livre
funeraire," and that it was more or less complete according to the
expense the deceased wished to incur; perhaps, also, according as,
by his rank, he had more or less obligations and duties to fulfil
towards his god, for, in the opinion of the Egyptians, kings had to
fulfil every duty, and great personages more duties than a simple
individual. The extract, consequently, from the ritual depended
on his rank and on the extent of his duties. Many of those rituals
are also found written, not in hieroglyphics, but in hieratic characters, which are an abbreviated form of hieroglyphic signs.
Papyri with hieroglyphics are nearly always divided by ruled lines
into narrow vertical columns of an inch or less in breadth, in which
the hieroglyphic signs are arranged one under the other. Sometimes
the papyri are found written in the enchorial character. Several
manuscripts in Greek on papyrus have been also discovered in
Egypt; they are, however, of a late date, and relate to the sale of
lands; many have been discovered referring to lands and possessions
about Thebes.

TOMBS.

Greek.—The Greeks also honoured the memory of the dead by public monuments; those of founders of cities, and those of heroes, were in the interior of the city, and the others outside. At Sparta, however, a law of Lycurgus allowed of burial around the temples and in the city. The most ancient tombs of the Greeks were tumuli or mounds of earth (χώματα). Some are still to be seen in the plains of Troy, which have been described by Homer. Subterranean vaults were also used for sepulchral purposes. The so-called "Treasury of Atreus," at Mycenæ, and of Minyas at Orchomenos, are supposed to have been royal sepulchres. The structure at Mycenæ consists of a large vault, 50 feet in width and 40 in height, which was the sanctuary of the deceased; this

STELE.

gave access by a side door to a small chamber excavated in the solid rock; this was probably the burial place. At a later period, a simple cippus or truncated column, surrounded by trees, arose over the corpse, and an inscription gave the name and titles of the deceased. Those of private individuals were generally in the shape of pillars (στῆλαι) or upright stone tablets, columns (κίονες), small buildings in the form of temples (ναΐδια, or ἡρῷα): others

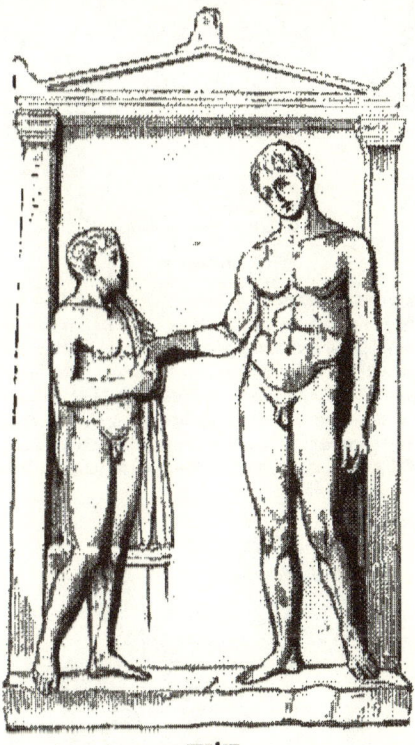

HERÖON.

were in the form of altars, but the inscription and emblems on them prevent them from being confounded. Sometimes the stone tablets were surmounted with an oval heading called ἐπίθημα. These tombs were most frequently built by the side of roads, and near the gates of the city commemorative monuments were also erected, in which architecture and sculpture have vied to enhance the splendour of these sepulchral structures. Many have been discovered in Lycia, rich with architectural and sculptural decoration. At Telmessus

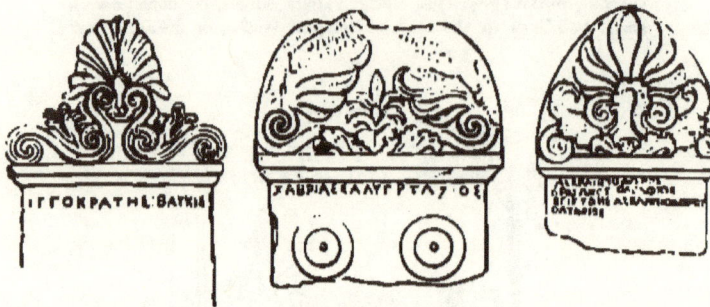

EPITHEMATA.

the rock-cut tombs assume the form of temples. The Harpy tomb, formerly in the acropolis of Xanthus, now in the British Museum, affords examples of archaic sculpture, its date being probably not later than 500 B.C.; the sculptures decorated the four sides of a rectangular solid shaft, about 17 feet high, and supported a roof inclosing a chamber 7 feet 6 inches square; the sculptures are supposed to represent the myth of Pandarus, whose daughters were carried off by harpies. Another remarkable tomb is that of a satrap

TOMB OF SOUTHERN ITALY.

of Lycia, discovered at Xanthus, now in the British Museum. It resembles a roofed house, with beams issuing forth from the gables, the arch of the roof resembling that of the early Gothic. On each side of the roof is sculptured an armed warrior, conjectured to be Glaucus or Sarpedon, in a chariot of four horses. But the most sumptuous commemorative monument of ancient times was the mausoleum of Halicarnassus, erected by Queen Artemisia, B.C. 353, in memory of her husband, Mausolus, King of Caria. The most celebrated architects and sculptors of the age were employed by the sorrowing queen, as she had resolved to raise a sepulchral monument which should surpass everything the world had yet seen.

In Magna Grecia tombs were built underground (ὑπόγαια, or ὑπόγεια); they were built with large cut stones, and rarely connected with cement, the walls inside were coated with stucco and adorned with paintings. The corpse was placed on the ground, its feet turned towards the entrance; painted vases were placed by the side of the corpse, and more were suspended on the walls by nails of bronze. Several rock-cut tombs, with frontispieces in the Ionic style, have been lately discovered at Canosa.

GROTTA CAMPANA VEII.

Etruscan.—Mr. Fergusson divides Etruscan tombs into two classes: First, those cut in the rock, and resembling dwelling houses; secondly, the circular tumuli, by far the most numerous and important class. Each of these may be again subdivided into two kinds. The rock cut tombs include, firstly, those with only a façade in the face of the rock, and a sepulchral chamber within, as at Norchia; secondly, those cut quite out of the rock, and standing free all round, as at Castel d' Asso. The second class may be divided into those tumuli erected over chambers cut in the tufaceous

rock, which is found all over Etruria, as at Tarquinii, and those
which have chambers built above ground, as in the Regolini Galassi
tomb. Besides these rock-hewn and earth-covered tombs, there are
at Saturnia, others of a most primitive character, bearing a strong
resemblance to the cromlechs of Britain ; rude graves sunk a few feet
beneath the surface, lined with rough slabs of rock, set upright, one
on each side, and roofed over with a single slab of enormous size,
covering the whole. Each tomb was evidently inclosed in a mound
of earth. In many instances, however, the earth has been washed
away, so as to leave the structure standing above the surface. They
doubtless date from the infancy of the Etruscan people, and must
be considered the first in age.

Etruscan tombs were all subterranean, and mostly hewn in the
rock ; either beneath the surface of the ground, or in the face of the
cliff, or at its foot. They were then shaped by the chisel into a monument, the interior taking the form of a cross. They evince an Oriental
character in their architectural style. A remarkable characteristic of
Etruscan tombs, according to Dennis, is that they generally show
an imitation of the abodes of the living. Some display this analogy
in the exterior, others in their interior, a few in both. Some have
more resemblance to temples, and may be the sepulchres of augurs,
or aruspices, or of families in which the sacerdotal office was
hereditary. The walls were covered with paintings representing
various scenes of every-day life, banquets, love-scenes, dancers,
horsemen, games, boar-hunts. Other paintings represent funeral
dances, and other ceremonies relative to burial. In one tomb discovered at Tarquinii, a most remarkable painting represents a procession of souls, with good and evil genii; and in another, a group
in the frieze running round the tomb, represents the good and evil
spirits in the act of drawing, on a car, the soul of the deceased to judgment.[*] The corpse was placed on the ground, and around it were

---

[*] The paintings in the tombs would seem to represent the every-day scenes of
life which the deceased passed through, and to show that he had given those
entertainments, dances, banquets, gladiatorial combats, races, hunts, which his
position in life entitled him to, and which tended to display his wealth. These
tombs being evidently of chiefs or of persons of rank and wealth, the entertainments depicted in them were evidences of the high position of the deceased.
Attributing symbolical meaning to these representations is evidently absurd, for,
as Mr. Dennis remarks, they are truthful delineations of Etruscan customs and
manners ; and thus depict, not only scenes of every-day life, but also the
common occurrences at a feast, as the cat and domestic fowls gleaning the crumbs.
They thus cannot possibly represent the bliss of souls in the other world, as is
Gerhard's opinion. Some paintings represent the last offices to the inmate of the
tomb; others represent the spirit of the deceased under the guidance of Charun,
the infernal Mercury of the Etruscans, and conducting demons, who are leading

tho painted vases which are generally found in tombs. Armour, lances, and whatever evinced the occupation of the deceased when alive, were buried with the corpse. Beautiful specimens of gold ornaments have been also found in these tombs. The other characteristic feature in the Etruscan mode of sepulture is the constant use of the tumulus, which would seem to confirm the tradition of the Lydian origin of the Etruscans; the tumulus of la Cocumella, at Vulci, bearing a striking analogy to that of Alyattes, King of Lydia, described by Herodotus. One of the most remarkable is the tumulus known as the Rogolini Galassi tomb at Corvetri, the ancient Cære. It contains two sepulchral chambers, with sides, and roof vaulted in the form of a pointed arch, with a horizontal lintel at the top, a style of vaulting which is evidence of very high antiquity. The outer chamber evidently contained the body of a warrior, from the number of beautifully embossed shields found near the bronze bier. The inner chamber is supposed to have contained the body of a priest, from the sacerdotal character of the beautifully embossed breastplate, and other articles of the purest gold found in the ashes of the corpse. The tumulus of la Cocumella, Vulci, is a vast mound of earth, about 200 feet in diameter, and must have been about 115 feet high. It is still 50 feet high. It was encircled at its base by a wall of masonry. Other tumuli are to be met with in the necropolis of Tarquinii and Cære. An Etruscan necropolis was always outside the walls of the town. The Etruscans—unlike the Greeks, who, in their colonies in Italy and Sicily, formed their cemeteries in the north of the towns—availed themselves of any site that was convenient, and frequently, as at Veii, buried their dead on several or opposite sides of their cities. Every necropolis in Etruria had its peculiar style of tomb. The tomb near Albano is now generally supposed to be of Etruscan origin, and to be the tomb of Aruns, the son of Porsenna. Mr. Fergusson, however, from the character of the mouldings with which it is adorned, would assign it to a more modern date. It is interesting from the analogy it bears to the description of the tomb of Porsenna, as given by Pliny.

Roman.—The Romans called sepulcrum, the ordinary tomb, and monumentum, the building consecrated to the memory of a person without any funeral ceremony; so that the same person could have several monuments, and in different places, but could

---

the soul to judgment. These mythical representations of life after death are generally the result of a later stage in the development of religious ideas, and consequently are evidences of these tombs being of a much later period.

have but one tomb. Roman tombs assume different forms. The tombs of the rich were commonly built of marble, and the ground enclosed with an iron railing or wall, and planted with trees. The best example of a Roman tomb, now remaining, is the well-known one of Cæcilia Metella, the wife of Crassus, and daughter of Quintus Metellus, who obtained the surname of Creticus, for his conquest of Crete, B. C. 67. It is composed of a circular tower, nearly 70 feet in diameter, resting on a quadrangular basement, about 100 feet square. The circular part of the tomb is coated with blocks of the finest travertine, fitted together with great precision; it has a beautiful frieze and cornice, over which a conical roof is supposed to have risen. On a marble panel below the frieze, on the side towards the Via Appia, is the inscription:—"Cæciliæ—Q. Cretici. F.—Metellæ Crassi." Next in age and importance is the tomb of Augustus, erected by Augustus, during his lifetime, in the Campus Martius. It was a circular building, about 300 feet in diameter, and about 60 feet in height. It is thus described by Strabo :—"It is built upon immense foundations of white marble, and covered with evergreens. On the top is a statue of Augustus in bronze, underneath are the vaults for himself, his relations, and dependents." It is now completely ruined, and so surrounded with buildings that its plan can be with difficulty made out. The most remarkable and well known

Roman tomb is the Mausoleum of Adrian. This massive edifice was erected by Adrian about A. D. 130, on the right bank of the Tiber. It is a massive circular tower, 235 feet in diameter, and 140 feet in height, standing on a square basement, each side of which is 247 feet in length, and about 75 feet high. According to Mr. Fergusson, the whole was crowned, probably by a dome, or at least by a curvilinear roof, which, with its central ornament, must have risen to a height of not less than 300 feet. In the centre of the mausoleum is the sepulchral chamber, in the form of a Greek cross, in which was the urn enclosing the ashes of Adrian.

The kind of tomb more commonly used was a cippus, or low column, frequently of a quadrangular form, but sometimes round, which bore on its principal face the Latin inscription which gave the name, titles, and the relationship of the deceased. The funeral inscriptions generally commence with the letters D M—Diis Manibus, followed by the name in the genitive case. Sometimes the letters

D M are wanting, then the name and title of the deceased are in the
dative case. We find frequently on them the age of the deceased,

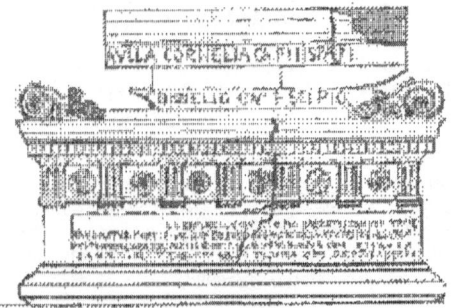

SARCOPHAGUS OF SCIPIO.

D · M
COSSVTIAE
PRIMAE
MATRI
PIENTISSIMAE
BENEMERENTI
FECIT

SEPULCHRAL URN.

in years, months, and days,—the name of the parent, freedman,
or of the friend who raised the monument over the tomb of the
deceased.

Frequently the body was placed in a sarcophagus, or marble coffin,
with similar inscriptions; a very remarkable specimen of this kind
is the celebrated sarcophagus of Scipio, found in the tomb of the
Scipios, at Rome. Under the Antonines sarcophagi were frequently
used. They were embellished with ornaments and elaborate bas
reliefs.

The ashes of the bodies were enclosed in cinerary urns, which
were composed of various materials, and were varied in form,
with or without inscriptions. The urns of the same family
were sometimes deposited in a place prepared for that purpose,
generally below the level of the ground. Its interior walls were
pierced with several stories of arched niches, in each of which one

COLUMBARIUM.

or several urns were placed. This is what the Romans called a
columbarium, a name derived from the likeness of the niches in the
walls to pigeon holes.* When the deceased, having been killed in
battle, or having died at sea, did not receive the honours of sepul-

---

* There are several of these columbaria at Rome. The most remarkable are,
the columbarium in the Vigna Codini, on the Appian way; and the columbarium
in the Villa Doria.

ture, a cenotaph, or empty tomb, was raised to him with the ceremonies regulated by law; these cenotaphs bore the same ornaments
as the sarcophagi and tombs. The place appointed for tombs was
generally by the side of roads; and though they were not allowed
to be constructed within the city, there was no restriction as to
their approaching close to the walls. Accordingly we find that most
of the roads leading out of ancient towns are lined with tombs, an
instance of which we have at Pompeii, where the street of the

STREET OF TOMBS, POMPEII.

tombs, forming an approach to the city gate, is one of the most
interesting objects in that place; and lately it has been discovered

I

that the Via Appia, and the Via Latina have been lined with tombs close to Rome. A number of these tombs, extending on the Via Appia for over eight miles beyond the tomb of Cæcilia Metella, have been discovered and brought to light by the energy and talent of the late Commendatore Canina, who has published a most interesting work on them, giving restorations of the principal monuments.

ROCK-CUT TOMB AT PETRA.

Tombs of a Roman period, exhibiting the utmost magnificence of architectural decoration, have been found at Petra. The Khasné and the Corinthian tomb, in that city of sepulchres, display most splendid architectural façades. Though all the forms of the architecture are Roman, Mr. Fergusson remarks, the details are so elegant, and generally so well designed, as almost to lead to the suspicion that there must have been some Grecian influence brought to bear upon it. Tombs of a Roman epoch are also found at Jerusalem, and at Cyrene, on the African coast.

SCULPTURE.

We do not intend to enter here on the history of sculpture in all its phases, but to give the distinctive features which characterize the different styles of Egyptian, Greek, Etruscan, and Roman sculpture, as they are visible in statues of the natural or colossal size, in statues of lesser proportion, and lastly in busts and bas reliefs.

We shall give also the styles of each separate nation which prevailed at each distinct age or epoch, styles which mark the stages of the development of the art of sculpture in all countries. For sculpture, like architecture, painting, and everything else, has its stages of development, its rise, progress, maturity, decline, and decay. The first and most important step in examining a work of ancient sculpture is to distinguish with certainty whether it is of Egyptian, Etruscan, Greek, or Roman workmanship; and this distinction rests entirely on a profound knowledge of the style peculiar to each of those nations. The next step is, from its characteristic features to distinguish what period, epoch, or stage of the development of the art of that particular nation it belongs to. We shall further give the various attributes and characteristics of the gods, goddesses, and other mythological personages, which distinguish the various statues visible in Egyptian, Etruscan, Greek, Roman sculpture. This enumeration will be found of use in the many sculpture galleries of the various museums both at home and abroad.

Egyptian.—Three great periods of art may be distinctly traced in Egypt:—1. The archaic style, reaching from the date of the earliest known monuments of the country till the close of the twelfth dynasty, in which the hair is in rude vertical curls and heavy masses, the face is broad and coarse, the nose long, and forehead receding, hands and feet large and disproportionate; the execution rude, even when details are introduced, the bas reliefs depressed. This style continued improving till the twelfth dynasty, at which period many of the monuments are finished with a purity and delicacy rivalling cameos. 2. The art from the restoration of the eighteenth dynasty till the twentieth—the hair is disposed in more elegant and vertical curls, a greater harmony is observable in the proportion of the limbs, the details are finished with greater breadth and care, has reliefs become rare, and disappear after Rameses II.; under the nineteenth dynasty, however, the arts rapidly declined. 3. The epoch of the revival of art, commencing with the twentieth dynasty, distinguished for an imitation of the archaic art. The portraiture is more distinct, the limbs freer and rounded, the muscles more developed, the details executed with great accuracy and care, and the general effect rather dependent on the minute finish than general scope and breadth. Under the Ptolemies and Romans a feeble attempt is made to engraft Greek art on Egyptian. But a rapid decay took place both in the knowledge, finish, and all the details. To these may be added a fourth period, in which a pseudo Egyptian style, not genuine Egyptian, was introduced at Rome in the time of the emperors, and principally under Adrian, an imitation of Egyptian figures. Antinous, the favourite of Adrian, is frequently represented in this style. This recurrence to the early and antiquated style being always an evidence of the exhausted and deteriorated state of art.

The general characteristics of Egyptian sculpture are extreme simplicity of lines, absence of motion, want of details; lastly, an imposing grandeur which makes the smallest Egyptian statue convey the idea of something colossal. All the statues we possess of the Egyptians, in whatever material, and of whatever dimensions they may be, are erect, seated, or on their knees, and all, in whatever position they are found, with their back to a pillar, or at least so rarely detached from some support, that this exception confirms rather than weakens the general rule. This pillar was destined to contain inscriptions.

With regard to the erect figures, whether they represent a man or a woman, they have their arms hanging down close to their sides, or crossed symmetrically on their breasts. Sometimes one of the arms is detached from its vertical position and brought forwards, while the other remains stretched down the length of the body; but whatposition they assume, their attitude is rigid and immovable. The hair was disposed in very regular masses of vertical curls, the hole of the ear was on a level with the pupil of the eye, the beard was plaited in a narrow mass of a square or recurved form. The feet are almost always parallel, but not on the same plane, one is always placed before the other, and as the one behind, being thrown further back, would appear somewhat shorter, for this reason it is generally a little longer. The extremities of the hands and feet are badly finished, the fingers of unusual length, the muscular development not expressed at all. As to the seated figures, they have uniformly

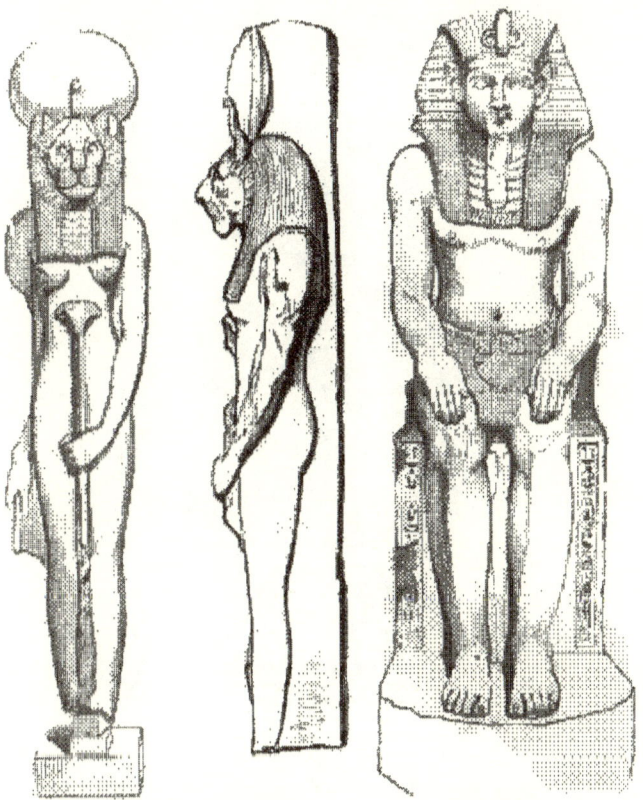

STATUE OF PASHT STANDING.   SEATED FIGURE.

their feet on the same line, and their hands placed parallel on their knees. Figures on their knees have generally a kind of chest before them, figured like a sanctuary, and enclosing some idols. These three positions are characterized by the same rigidity, the same

want of action and life. With regard to their costume, the statues
of the women are always draped, but generally with a very slight
vesture, which forms no fold, and fits so close to the figure, that

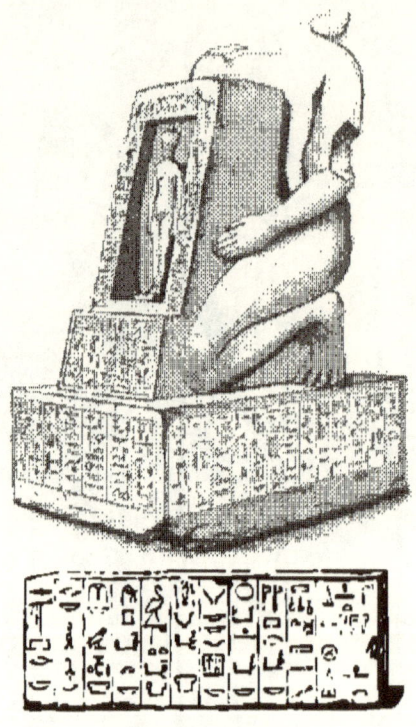

EGYPTIAN KNEELING FIGURE.

frequently one cannot distinguish the drapery from the body which
it enfolds, did one not remark exactly at the neck and at the legs a
little rim, which indicates each extremity of the drapery. The
form of the breast was sometimes indicated by a circular indented
line. The statues of men are entirely nude, with the exception of a
kind of apron falling from the hips to the knees. When we speak

of nudity in an Egyptian, we must remember that they did not exhibit the least detail of muscular development, and consequently no real nudity. Egyptian artists evidently attempted no imitation of nature, thus statues were questionless symbols of ideas alone. A statue which was a combination of a human figure with the head of a hawk or jackal, was no imitation of nature, it was a more symbolic image. They were so intimately connected with the symbolic language, that they may be considered, if we may be allowed the expression, the capital letters of that language. The Egyptian artist, in treating them as symbolic signs only, always neglected the human part, giving all his care to the head of the animal, which was the symbol of the divinity represented. This care and skill in representing the animal form has been frequently observed, a stern theocracy forbidding all study and progress in the knowledge of the anatomy of the human figure. No innovation being allowed, the same early forms were repeated and reproduced in endless varieties.

In the early period of Egyptian sculpture low relief was adopted on all large monuments, and was generally painted. At a later period the intaglio rilievato, or relieved intaglio, was introduced by Rameses II. The sides of the incavo, which are perpendicular, are cut to a considerable depth, and from that part to the centre of the figure is a gradual swell, the centre being frequently on a level with the surface of the wall. In the bas reliefs the heads were always given in profile, and the eyes elongated, with a full pupil. These features, however, are the characteristics of art, in all countries, in the early stages of its development.

A remarkable feature of Egyptian sculpture is the frequent representation of their kings in a colossal form. The two most famous colossi are the seated figures in the plain of Thebes. One is recognized to be the vocal Memnon (Amunoph III.) mentioned by Strabo. They are 47 feet high, and measure about 18 feet 3 inches across the shoulders. But the grandest and largest colossal statue was the stupendous statue of king Rameses II., of Syenite granite, on the Memnonium at Thebes. It represented the king seated on a throne, in the usual attitude of kings, the hands resting on his knees. It is now in fragments. It measured 22 feet 4 inches across the shoulders. According to Sir G. Wilkinson, the whole mass, when entire, must have weighed about 887 tons. Another well-known colossus is the statue of the so-called Memnon, now in the British Museum. It is supposed to be the statue of Rameses II. It was brought by Belzoni from the Memnonium at Thebes.

In the different epochs of Egyptian sculpture, the Egyptian artists were bound by certain fixed canons or rules of proportion to guide them in their labours, and which they were obliged to adhere to rigidly. The following are the canons of three distinct epochs: 1. The canon of the time of the pyramids, the height was reckoned

COLOSSAL FIGURE OF RAMESES II.

at 6 feet from the sole of the foot to the crown of the head, and subdivisions obtained by one-half or one-third of a foot. 2. The canon from the twelfth to the twenty-second dynasty is only an extension of the first. The whole figure was contained in a number of squares of half a foot, and the whole height divided into eighteen parts. In these two canons the height above the sixth foot is not reckoned. 3. The canon of the age of Psammetici, which is mentioned by Diodorus, reckoning the entire height at 21½ feet from the sole to the crown of the head, taken to the upper part. The proportions are different, but without any introduction of the Greek canon. The canon and the leading lines were originally traced in red, subsequently corrected by the principal artist in black, and the design then executed. In Egypt, almost every object of sculpture and architecture was painted. The colossal Egyptian statues are generally of granite, basalt, porphyry, or sandstone. The two colossi on the plain of Thebes are of coarse, hard gritstone. The Egyptians also worked in dark and red granites, breccias, serpentines, arragonite, limestones, jaspers, feldspar, cornelian, glass, gold, silver, bronze, lead, iron, the hard woods, fir or cedar, sycamore, ebony, acacia, porcelain and ivory, and terra cotta. All objects, from the most gigantic obelisk to the minute articles of private life, are found decorated with hieroglyphics.

Egyptian sculptors were also remarkable for the correct and excellent representation of animals. There may, indeed, be noticed in their representation a freedom of hand, a choice and variety of forms, a truthfulness, and even what deserves to be called imitation, which contrast with the uniformity, the rigidity, the absence of nature and life, which human figures present. Plato mentions a law which forbade the artists to depart, in the slightest degree, in the execution of statues of the human form from the type consecrated by priestly authority. The artist, therefore, not being restricted in his study of the animal form, could thus give to its image greater variety of motion, and by imitating animals in nature, indemnify himself for the constraint he experienced when he represented kings and priests. The two colossal lions in red granite, brought to England by Lord Prudhoe, may be considered as remarkably good specimens of Egyptian art, as applied to the delineation of animal forms. They evince a considerable knowledge of anatomy in the strongly marked delineation of the muscular development. The form also is natural and easy, thus admirably expressing the idea of strength in a state of repose. They were sculptured in the reign of Amunoph III. The representations of the sacred animals, the cynocephalus, the lion, the jackal, the ram, &c., are frequently to be met with in Egyptian sculpture.

Etruscan.—The principal characteristics, as visible in the most ancient monuments of this people, are, the lines rectilinear, the

attitude rigid, the moulding of the features imperfect, want of proportion in the limbs, which are generally so meagre that they give
no idea of flesh or muscles, and thus their outline exhibits no
undulation. The form of the head is an oval, narrow towards the
chin, which terminates in a point; the eyes are long or slightly
raised at the outer extremity. No Egyptian work exhibits such
shapelessness. In the small Etruscan figures the arms are pendant,
and closely adhering to the body; the feet are parallel; the folds of
the drapery are marked by a simple line. This was the first style.
Of this style were the "Opera Tuscanica," a term used by the
Romans to imply all productions which exhibited the hard and dry
manner of the earlier Etruscan school. These characteristic features,
however, which are supposed to be peculiar to early Etruscan art,
are not indicative of any particular nation; they exhibit the natural
imperfection and want of art peculiar to the first stage of the
development of art in all countries.

ETRUSCAN FIGURE.

The second style may be recognised
by some essential improvement, by a
stronger expression of the features of
the face, and by a more energetic action
of the limbs, without the rigidity and
restraint of the attitude entirely disappearing; the muscles and the bones
are indicated in a hard manner, especially in the calves of the legs; and in
general the whole expression is exaggerated, the very opposite to all
that is graceful, easy, and flowing.
These characteristics are peculiar to
all statues of the same style, and in
order to recognise the mythological
personages which they represent, recourse must be had to their attributes;
for an Apollo is made like a Hercules.
Almost all the male figures wear beards;
the hands are constrained, the fingers
rigid, the eyes monstrous and protruding, the features of a coarse nature,
and the different parts of the body badly put together; the hair
falls in tresses, and the drapery is indicated by parallel folds;
sometimes, on the statues of women, the sleeves of the tunic are
plaited very elaborately.

The third style is indebted to the influence of the Greeks, and forms a near approach to their practices, without, however, equalling their perfection. They are in this epoch amalgamated in one school, and one has frequently need of inscriptions in Etruscan characters engraved on the monuments to attribute them with certainty to their real authors; the air and form of the heads larger, rounder, more marked than those of the Greeks, serve to distinguish them. At this period, and at an earlier period also, Etruscan art was not only Greek in the choice and disposition of subjects—subjects belonging entirely to either Greek mythology or history—but also Greek in its character and style of art. There was, indeed, frequent intercommunication in the early periods between Greece and Etruria; the people of Agylla sent frequent embassies to Delphi. The Corinthian Demaratus emigrated to Tarquinii, and bringing with him a colony of artists, established schools of Greek art there. Mr. Dennis gives the following names to the three Etruscan styles according to their characteristic features. 1. The Egyptian; 2. The Etruscan, or Tyrrhene, as it is sometimes called, perhaps in compliment to its more than doubtful Greek character; 3. The Hellenic. To these three, he adds, may be added a fourth, the Decadence. This, indeed, must follow as a necessary consequence in all developments. Whatever has a rise, and reaches maturity, must have a decline.

Greek.—The stages of the development of the art of sculpture in Greece may be given in five distinct periods or epochs, naming these, for greater convenience, chiefly from the name of the principal artist whose style prevailed at that period:

  I. The Dædalean, or early   , (—580 B.C.)
  II. The Æginetan, or archaic . (580—480 B.C.)
  III. The Phidian, or the grand . (480—400 B.C.)
  IV. The Praxitelean, or the beautiful (400—250 B.C.)
  V. The Decline .   . (250—   )

Prior to the age of Dædalus, there was an earlier stage in the development of the art, in which the want of art, which is peculiar to that early stage, was exhibited in rude attempts at the representation of the human figure, for similar and almost identical rude representations are attempted in the early stages of art in all countries; as the early attempts of children are nearly identical in all ages. In this early period the first attempt at representation consisted in fashioning a block of stone or wood into some semblance

of the human form, and this rude attempt constituted a divinity.
Of this primitive form was the Cupid of Thespiæ; the Juno of Argos
was fashioned in a similar rude manner from the trunk of a wild
pear tree.   These attempts were thus nothing more than shapeless

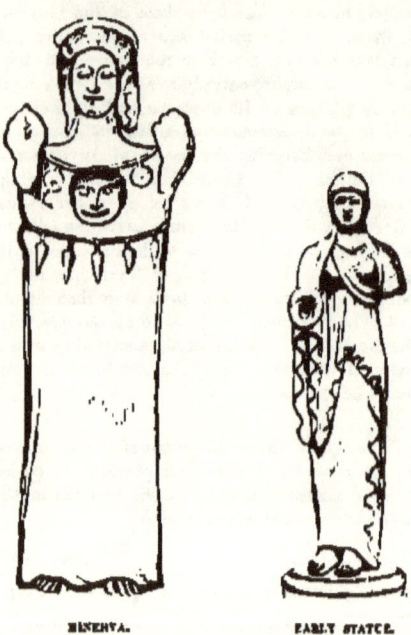

MINERVA.   EARLY STATUE.

blocks, the head, arms, and legs scarcely defined. Some of these
wooden blocks are supposed to have been, in a coarse attempt at
imitation, furnished with real hair, and to have been clothed with
real draperies in order to conceal the imperfection of the form. The
next step was to give these shapeless blocks a human form. The
upper part assumed the likeness of a head, and by degrees arms and
legs were marked out, but in these early imitations of the human
figure the arms were, doubtless, represented closely attached to the
sides; and the legs, though to a certain extent defined, were still
connected and united in a common pillar.

The age of Dædalus marks an improvement in the moulding of the human figure, and in giving it life and action. This improvement in the arts consisted in representing the human figure with the arms isolated from the body, the legs detached, and the eyes open; in fine, giving it an appearance of nature as well as of life,

STATUES OF THE DÆDALIAN STYLE.

and thus introducing a principle of imitation. This important progress in the practice of the art is the characteristic feature of the school of Dædalus, for under the name of Dædalus we must understand a school of artists, probably Athenians, who practised their art in this style. According to Flaxman, the rude efforts of this

age were intended to represent divinities and heroes only—Jupiter,
Neptune, Hercules, and several heroic characters had the self-same
face, figure, and action; the same narrow eyes, thin lips, with the

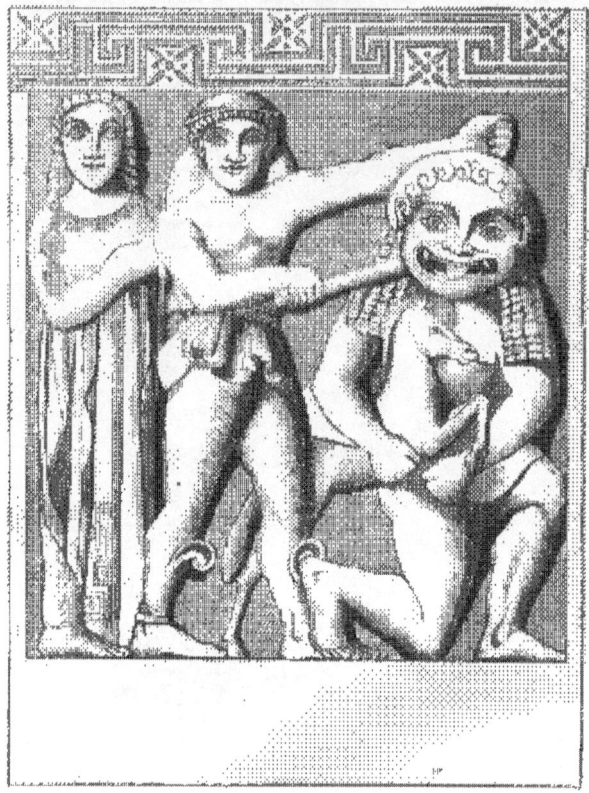

METOPE FROM SELINUS.

corners of the mouth turned upwards; the pointed chin, narrow
loins, turgid muscles; the same advancing position of the lower
limbs; the right hand raised beside the head, and the left extended.
Their only distinctions were that Jupiter held the thunderbolt,

Neptune the trident, and Hercules a palm branch or bow. The female divinities were clothed in draperies divided into few and perpendicular folds, their attitudes advancing like those of the male figures. The hair of both male and female statues of this period is arranged with great care, collected in a club behind, sometimes entirely curled.

Between the rudeness of the Dædalean and the hard and severe style of the Æginetan there was a transitional style, of which the Minerva of Dipœnus and Scyllis may afford an example. The metopes of the temple of Selinus in Sicily were of this transitional period.

Æginetan.—In the Æginetan period of sculpture there was still retained in the character of the heads, in the details of the costume, and in the manner in which the beard and the hair are treated some-

ADVANCING FIGURE FROM THE EASTERN PEDIMENT OF THE TEMPLE OF JENNA.

thing archaic and conventional, undoubtedly derived from the habits and teachings of the primitive school. But there prevails at the same time, in the execution of the human form, and the manner in which the nude is treated, a knowledge of anatomy, and an excellence of imitation carried to so high a degree of truth as to give convincing proofs of an advanced step and a higher stage in the development of the art. The following are the principal characteristics of the Æginetan style, as derived from a careful examination of the statues found in Ægina, which were the undoubted productions of the school of the Æginetan period.

The heads, either totally destitute of expression, or all reduced to a general and conventional expression, present, in the oblique position of the eyes and mouth, that forced smile which seems to have been the characteristic feature common to all productions of the ancient style; for we find it also on the most ancient medals, and on bas reliefs of the primitive period.

The hair treated likewise in a systematic manner in small curls or plaits, worked with wonderful industry, imitates not real hair, but genuine wigs, a peculiarity which may be remarked on other works in the ancient style, and of Etruscan origin. The beard is indicated on the cheek by a deep mark, and is rarely worked in relief, but, in the latter case, so as to imitate a false beard, and consequently in the same system as the hair. The costume partakes of the same conventional and hieratic taste; it consists of drapery, with straight and regular folds, falling in symmetrical and parallel masses, so as to imitate the real draperies in which the ancient statues in wood were draped. These conventional forms of the drapery and hair may, therefore, be considered as deriving their origin from

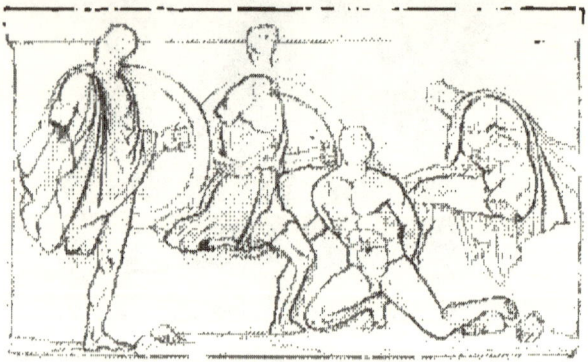

FRIEZE FROM THE THESEUM.

an imitation of the early statues in wood, the first objects of worship and of art among the Greeks, which were frequently covered with false hair, and clothed with real draperies. The muscular development observable in these figures is somewhat exaggerated, but, considering the period, is wonderfully accurate and true to nature. The genius for imitation exhibited in this style, carried as far as it is possible in the expression of the forms of the body, although still accompanied by a little meagreness and dryness, the truth of detail, the exquisite care in the execution, evince so profound a knowledge of the structure of the human body, so great a readiness of hand, in a word—an imitation of nature so skilful, and, at the same time, so simple, that one cannot but recognise in them the productions of an art which arrived at a point the nearest to perfection. Art had reached that stage when there was nothing wanting but a great man to completely emancipate it from its archaic and hieratic fetters, and lead it, by a further step onwards, to its perfect development. That man was Phidias.

Between the severity of the Æginetan school and the perfect style of the age of Phidias, there may be placed the sculptures of the Thoseum as a connecting link or a transitional style.

Phidias.—" This period (we here adopt Mr. Vaux's words) is the golden age of Greek art. During this period arose a spirit of sculpture which combined grace and majesty in the happiest manner, and by emancipating the plastic art from the fetters of antique stiffness, attained under the direction of Pericles, and by the hand of Phidias, its culminating point. It is curious to remark the gradual progress of the arts; for it is clear that it was slowly and not per saltum that the gravity of the older school was changed to the perfect style of the age of Phidias : indeed, even in his time a slight severity of manner prevailed ; a relic of the rigidity which characterized the art of the earlier ages. In the same way the true character of the style of Phidias was maintained but for a little after the death of the master himself. On his death, nay even towards the close of his life, its partial decay had commenced ; and though remarkable beauty and softness may be observed in the works of his successors, art never recovered the spiritual height she had reached under Phidias himself." In this age alone sculpture, by the grandeur and sublimity it had attained to in its style, was qualified to give a form to the sublime conceptions of the deity evolved by the mind of Phidias. He alone was considered able to embody and to render manifest to the eye the sublime images of Homer. Hence he was called " the sculptor of the gods." It is well known that in the conception of his Jupiter Olympius, Phidias wished to render manifest, and that he succeeded in realizing, the sublime image under which Homer represents the master of the gods. The sculptor embodied that image in the following manner, according to Pau-

K

sanias: " The god sat on a throne of ivory and gold, his head
crowned with a branch of olive, his left hand presented a Victory of
ivory and gold, with a crown and fillet; his right hand held a

JUPITER OLYMPIUS.   RESTORED FROM PHIDIAS BY QUATREMERE DE QUINCY.

sceptre, beautifully distinguished by all the different metals, on
which an eagle sat; the sandals of the god were gold, so was his
drapery, on which were various animals, with flowers of all kinds,
especially lilies; his throne was refulgent with gold and precious
stones.   There were also statues; four Victories, alighting, were
annexed to the feet of the throne; those in front rested each on a
sphinx that had seized a Theban youth; below the sphinxes the
children of Niobe were slain by the arrows of Apollo and Diana."

This statue, Flaxman observes, sixty feet in height, was the most renowned work of ancient sculpture, not for stupendous magnitude alone, but more for careful majesty and sublime beauty. Müller thus characterizes the distinctive features of this period: " We find overywhere a truth in the imitation of nature, which, without suppressing anything essential (such as the veins swollen from exertion) without over allowing itself to be severed from nature,

METOPE OF PARTHENON.

attained the highest nobleness and the purest beauty, a fire and a vivacity of gesture when the subject demands it, and an ease and comfort of repose when, as in the gods especially, it appeared fitting; the greatest truth and lightness in the treatment of the drapery when regularity and a certain stiffness is not requisite, a luminous projection of the leading idea and abundance of motives in subordinate groups, evincing much ingenuity of invention; and lastly, a natural dignity and grace united with a noble sublimity and unaffectedness, without any effort to allure the senses, or any aiming at dazzling effect and display of the artist's own skill, which characterized the best ages not merely of art, but of Grecian life generally." The sculptures of the Parthenon, now in the British Museum, can lead us to appreciate the manner of Phidias, and the character of his school, as observed by Flaxman; they are to be admired for their

simplicity, grandeur, elegance, and nature. The Theseus of the
pediment, the metopes, and bas reliefs, are remarkable for that

THESEUS. PARTHENON.

grandeur of style, simplicity, truth, beauty, which are the characteristics of the school of Phidias. These sculptures, however, which
emanated from the mind of Phidias, and were most certainly executed
under his eyes, and in his school, are not the works of his hands.
Phidias himself disdained, or worked but little in marble. They
were, doubtless, the works of his pupils, Alcamenes, Agoracritus, and
some other artists of his time. For, as Flaxman remarks, the
styles of different hands are sufficiently evident in the alto and
basso riliovo.

Praxitelean.—This period is characterized by a more rich and flowing style of execution, as well as by the choice of softer and more
delicate subjects than had usually been selected for representation.
In this the beautiful was sought after rather than the sublime.
Praxiteles may be considered the first sculptor who introduced this
more sensual, if it may be so called, style of art; for he was the
first who, in the unrobed Aphrodite, combined the utmost luxuriance
of personal charms with a spiritual expression in which the queen
of love herself appeared as a woman needful of love, and filled

with inward longing. He first gave a prominence to corporeal attractions, with which the deity was invested. Lysippus con-

CUPID OF PRAXITELES.

tributed to advance this style by the peculiar fulness, roundness, and harmonious general effect, by which it appears that his works were characterized.

The following are some of the more particular characteristics of the human form, adopted by the Grecian sculptors of this age :—

In the profile, the forehead and lips touch a perpendicular line

drawn between them.   In young persons, the brow and nose nearly
form a straight line, which gives an expression of grandeur and

VENUS OF CNIDAS.—PRAXITELES.

delicacy to the face.   The forehead was low, the eyes large, but not
prominent   A depth was given to the eye to give to the eyebrow a

finer arch, and by a deeper shadow, a bolder relief. To the eyes a living play of light was communicated, by a sharp projection of the upper eyelid, and a deep depression of the pupil. Small eyes were reserved for Venuses and voluptuous beauties, which gave them the languishing air called *vypor*. The upper lip was short, the lower lip fuller than the upper, as this tended to give a roundness to the chin; the short upper lip, and the round and grandly-formed chin, being the most essential signs of genuine Greek formation. The lips were generally closed, though slightly open in the statues of the gods, but the teeth were never seen. The ear was carefully modelled and finished. The hair was curly, abundant, and disposed in floating locks; in females it was tied in a knot behind the head. The face was always oval, and a cross drawn in the oval indicated the design of the face. The perpendicular line marked the position of the brow, the nose, the mouth, and the chin; the horizontal line passed through the eyes, and was parallel to the mouth. The hands of youth were beautifully rounded, and the dimples given; the fingers were tapered, but the articulations were not generally indicated. In the male form, the chest was high and prominent. In the female form, especially in that of goddesses and virgins, the breasts were in moderate relief, and generally a little higher than in nature. The abdomen was without prominence. The proportion of the limbs was longer than in the preceding period. In the male and female figure, the foot was rounded in its form; in the female the toes are delicate, and have dimples over their first joints gently marked.

The sculptors of this age avoided all violent motions and perturbations of the passions, which would have completely marred that expression of serene repose which is a prominent characteristic of the beautiful period of Greek sculpture. Indeed, the chief object of the Greek sculptor was the representation of the beautiful alone, and to this principle he made character, expression, costume, and everything else subordinate. It is evident that this type of beauty of form, adopted by the Grecian sculptors, is in unison with, and exhibits a marked analogy to the type of face and form of the Greeks themselves; for, as Sir Charles Bell observes, the Greek face is a fine oval, the forehead full and carried forward, the eyes large, the nose straight, the lips and chin finely formed; in short, the forms of the head and face have been the type of the antique, and of all which we most admire.[*]

* Tinos, Naxos, Samos, and other favoured spots in the Ægean, still furnish types of that glorious race which gave models to Phidias and Praxiteles. In the men there may still be seen beauty of form and the most ample development of

Decline.—Art having in the two previous periods reached its culminating point of perfection; as is the law of all development, when
a culminating point is reached, a downward tendency and a period of
decline begins, for the cycle of development must be completed and
the stages of rise, progress, maturity, decline and decay run through.
Müller remarks, " the creative activity, the real central point of the
entire activity of art, which fashions peculiar forms for peculiar ideas,
must have flagged in its exertions when the natural circle of ideas
among the Greeks had received complete plastic embodiment, or it
must have been morbidly driven to abnormal inventions. We find
therefore, that art, during this period, with greater or less degrees
of skill in execution, delighted now in fantastical, now in effeminate
productions, calculated merely to charm the senses. And even in
the better and nobler works of the time there was still on the whole
something—not, indeed, very striking to the eye, but which could
be felt by the natural sense, something which distinguished them
from the earlier works—the *striving after effect.*" The spirit of imitation marked the later portion of this kind of decline. The sculptors
of this age, despairing of equalling the productions of the former age,
gave themselves up completely to servile imitation. The imitation
was naturally inferior to the original, and each succeeding attempt
at imitation was but a step lower in degradation of the art. When
they ceased to study nature they thought to repair the deterioration
of the beauty of form by the finish of the parts; and in a still
later period they gave, instead of a grandeur of style, an exagge-
ration of form. Lastly, being utterly unable to cope with their
predecessors in the sculpture of statues, they had recourse to the
manufacture of busts and portraits, which they executed in countless
numbers.

Roman.—In the very early periods, the Romans imitated the
Etruscans, for, generally speaking, all the works of the first periods
of Rome were executed by Etruscan artists. Etruscan art exercised the greatest influence in Rome, for Rome was adorned with
monuments of Etruscan art, in its very infancy; it was a Tuscan
called Veturius Mamurius who made the shields (ancilia) of the
temple of Numa, and who made, in bronze, the statue of Vortumna,
a Tuscan deity, in the suburb of Rome. The most ancient monu-

---

the muscles and limbs—perfect symmetry united with manly strength. In the
women the straight brow and nose, the delicately formed mouth and chin, the
smooth and rounded neck, losing itself in the flowing curve of the shoulders, and
bearing, like a pedestal of Parian marble, the exquisitely shaped head, the graceful carriage, and the well-proportioned limbs.—*Quarterly Rev.,* Vol. 94.

ments of Rome thus corresponded with the contemporaneous style of
Etruscan art; there is thus a similarity in the figures; the attributes
alone can lead one to distinguish them, as those attributes tell if the
statue was connected with the creed or modes of belief of Etruria or
Rome. There was not, therefore, any Roman style, properly so called,
the only distinction to be remarked is that the statues of the early
periods, executed by the Romans, are characterized, like the Romans
themselves of the same period, by a beard and long hair. At a
late period all the architecture, all the sculpture of the public edifices at Rome, were in the Tuscan style, according to the testimony
of Pliny.

After the second Punic war, Greek artists took the place of Etruscan artists at Rome; the taking of Syracuse gave the Romans a
knowledge of the beautiful works of Greece, and the treasures of art
brought from Corinth chiefly contributed to awaken a taste among
them, and they soon turned into ridicule their ancient statues in
clay; Greek artists abounded in Rome, and the history of Roman
art was thenceforward confounded with that of the vicissitudes of
Greek art. It may be observed, however,
as a general remark, that the Roman statues
are of a thicker and more robust form, with
less ease and grace, more stern, and of a less
ideal expression than Greek statues, though
equally made by Greek artists. The style
of the works of sculpture under the first
emperors may be considered as a continuation of the fourth period of Greek sculpture.
Those works exhibit a great deal of force
and character, though a want of care is visible in some parts, especially in the hair.
The characters of the heads always bear out
the descriptions which historians have given
of the person they belong to, the Roman
head differing essentially from the Greek, in
having a more arched forehead, a nose more
aquiline, and features altogether of a more
decided character. Under Augustus, and the
following Roman emperors, to meet the de-

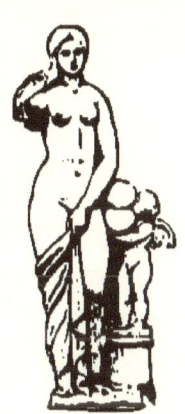

VENUS OF A ROMAN PERIOD.

mand for Greek statues, to embellish their houses and villas, several
copies and imitations of celebrated Greek works were manufactured
by the sculptors of the age. The Apollo Belvidere, the Venus de
Medici, the Venus of the Capitol, and several copies of celebrated
Greek works, in the British Museum, are supposed to be of this age.

According to Flaxman, the Venus de Medici is a deteriorated variety or repetition of a Venus of Praxiteles. Even in this age, the taste for Etruscan art still retained its influence, as the colossus of Apollo,

STATUE OF ADRIAN.

in bronze, of excellent workmanship, placed in the library of the temple of Augustus, was an Etruscan work. Under Tiberius and Claudius a limit was placed to the right of having statues exposed in public; consequently a lesser number of statues were made, and less attention was paid to the perfection of the portrait. However, some excellent works were produced in this period. The style became purer and more refined under Adrian, for a partial revival of Greek art is attributed to this emperor. The hair was carefully worked, the eyebrows were raised, the pupils were indicated by a deep cavity—an essential characteristic of this age, rare before this period, and frequently introduced afterwards; the heads acquired greater strength, without, however, increasing in character. Under the Antonines, the decay of art was still more manifest, displaying a want of simplicity, and an attention to trivial and meretricious

BUST OF A ROMAN LADY.							BUST OF CARACALLA.

accessories. Thus, in the busts, the hair and the beard luxuriate in an exaggerated profusion of curls, the careful expression of the features of the countenance being at the same time frequently neglected. This age was remarkable also for its recurrence to the style of a primitive and imperfect art in the reproduction of Egyptian statues. Like the pre-Raphaolitism of the present day, this imitation of, and recurrence to, the early and imperfect forms of art, like second childhood in man, are evident signs of the downward tendency and total decay of art. The art declined still further under Commodus and Severus. The use of perukes and false hair is exhibited in the busts. The figures were mechanical in style, and totally deficient in life. Under Alexander Severus it was degraded into a coarse and low style. Deep furrows were marked on the forehead, the hair and beard were indicated by long lines, a deeper cavity was given to the pupils of the eyes; the forms became dry and languid, the heads lost all character, and were reduced to such a low grade as to be scarcely distinguishable one from another.

MYTHOLOGY OF SCULPTURE.

When the style and period of an object of sculpture is known, a further knowledge will be required of the god, goddess, king, or hero it represents, which can only be acquired by an intimate acquaintance with their distinctive attributes. In order, therefore, to assist the student of archæology, we shall here give a brief enumeration of the distinctive attributes of the gods, goddesses, kings, heroes, which are visible in Egyptian, Etruscan, Greek, and Roman sculpture.

Egyptian.—The objects represented in sculpture by the Egyptians were deities, men, and animals.

Egyptian Deities.—The same deity among the Egyptians was represented under three different forms:—1. Pure human form, with the attributes peculiar to the god. 2. A human body bearing the head of an animal which was especially dedicated to that deity. 3. This same animal with the attributes of the god. These three classes combine the greater portion of figures of all dimensions, which are found in cabinets and museums. It is the head which bears the principal characteristic attribute of each, whether standing or seated, in a natural form or mummified. Egyptian deities are represented in every kind of material; wax, wood, baked clay and glazed, porcelain, marble, hard and soft stone, precious stones, bronze, silver, gold. Frequently the figures in wood, in stone, or in bronze, are gilt, and more frequently they are painted in various and consecrated colours, especially for the face and for the nude, nothing in this respect being left to the will of the artist. These representations being thus regulated by law or by custom in all these details, their constant uniformity is of great assistance in the study of Egyptian mythology, for it explains at once the scenes in which these gods appear, whether they are represented in the round, in relief, in intaglio, painted on linen, on papyrus, in wood, or in stone, the same attributes always indicate the deity, and the combination of these attributes, that of the divine personages, according to the ideas and creed of the Egyptians. Bunsen remarks that the system of Egyptian mythology, as presented to us in its three orders, as in the following section, would appear to have been complete at the commencement of the historical age, or reign of Menes, the founder of one united Egyptian empire, according to him, 3643 B.C.

The Egyptian system of mythology, as interpreted by Sir Gardner Wilkinson and the Chevalier Bunsen, recognised three orders of deities, of which eight were called the greater gods, twelve were considered as the lesser gods, and seven of the third order.

First Order.

Male.

AMUN,
  The concealed god,
  The god of Thebes.

KHEM,
  The generative god of nature,
  The god of Panopolis.

Female.

MAUT,
  The mother (Buto),
  The temple consort of Khem and Amun,
  The goddess of Buto in the Delta.

NEITH
  (Without descent, "I came from myself"), .
  The goddess of Sais in the Delta.

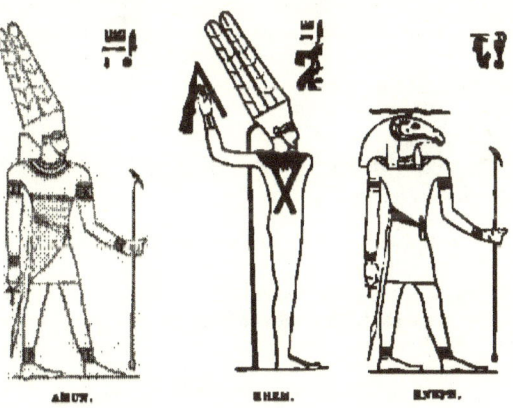

AMUN.   KHEM.   KNEPH.

KNEPH (CENUBIN),   SETI (in Coptic, SATE, "ray,
  The ram-headed god of   arrow "),
    Thebes.   The consort of Knoph.

PHTAH,
  The creator of the world.
  The god of Memphis.

RA,
  Helios, the sun god,
  The god of Heliopolis (On) in
    the Delta.

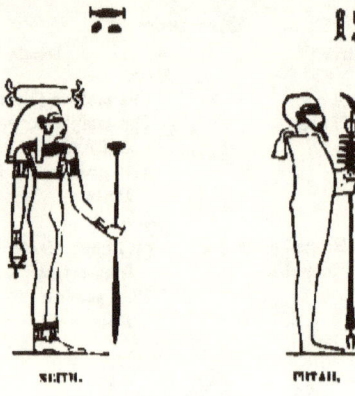

NEITH.   PHTAH.

Second Order.

A. The child of Amun.
    1. Khunsu (Chonso), Hercules.

B. The child of Knoph.
    2. Tot (Thoth), Hermes.

C. The children of Phtah.
    3. Atumu, Atmu, Atum.
    4. Pasht (Bubastis), the cat-headed goddess of Bubastis,
      Artemis.

D. The children of Ra, Helios.
    5. Hather (Athor), Aphrodite.
    6. Mau.
    7. Ma, Thmei (Truth).
    8. Tefnu, the lioness-headed goddess.

9. Muntu, Munt (Mandulis).
10. Sobak, Sevek, the crocodile-headed god.
11. Sob, Chronos.
12. Nutpe, Netpe (Rhea).

Third Order.

I. Set, Nubi, Typhon.

II. Hesiri, Osiris.

III. Hes, Isis.

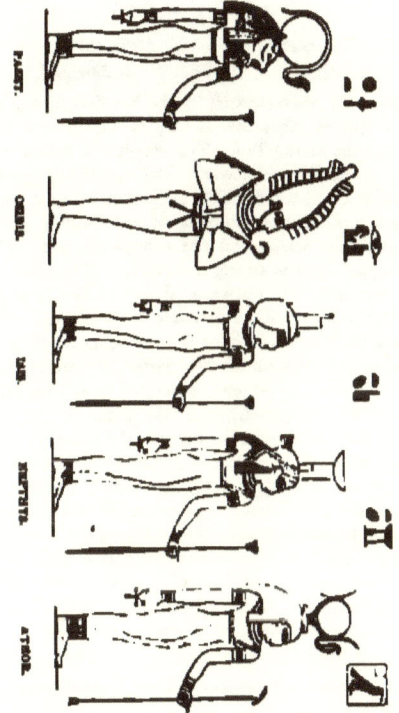

IV. Nebti, Nepthys, the sister of Isis, "the mistress of the house."

V. Her-her, Aroeris, Hor the elder, the god of Apollinopolis.

VI. Hor, Horus, child of Isis and Osiris, "Hor-pa-chrat," Harpocrates, *i.e.* Horus the child.

VII. Anupu, Anubis.

Several of these gods were represented as grouped in sets of three, and each city had its own trinity. In Thebes it was Amun-Ra, Maut, and Chonso; at Philæ the trinity was Osiris, Isis, Horus, a group the most frequently represented in most parts of Egypt.

Four Genii of the Dead.

Amset.	Smautf.
Hapi.	Kebhsnof.

All the gods are characterized by the board hanging down from the chin. In general, they hold a sceptre surmounted by the Kukufa head, and the sacred Tau. The sceptre is called "tam," and is considered the emblem of power. The sacred tau is the symbol of life, or eternal existence. The goddesses carry a sceptre surmounted by a lotus flower (emblem of sovereignty); in pictures they frequently have wings, and are always clothed. Their common hieroglyphic sign is an egg or a snake. The gods, as well as goddesses, often carry the whip and crown of the Pharaohs. The latter is called *schen;* with the article prefixed, and the nominal suffix *t,* it was pronounced in later times P-schent, and is so written by the Greeks. It consists of two parts. According to the pictures, the lower one is red, and called, on that account, *Teacher;* the upper one is white (abach), with the name of *Het.* The gods and goddesses have, moreover, the royal snake, the type of dominion (the Urœus, basilisk), as a frontlet, like the Pharaohs. Another crown is sometimes worn (generally by Osiris), the *atf.* It is composed of a conical cap, flanked by two ostrich plumes, with a disc in front, placed on the horns of a goat. The gods and goddesses were principally distinguished according to their head-dresses. The following is an enumeration of the principal Egyptian deities, as represented under three different forms, and as characterized by their head-dresses:—

I.—*Gods and Goddesses of Pure Human Form.*

1. Gods of pure human form bearing on their heads—
   Two long plumes, the nude painted
   blue　..　..　..　..　..　..　.. 　Amun.

Two long plumes, the body ityphallic   Khem.

A cap fitting tightly to the head, the
    flesh green, the body mummified,
    leaning against the emblem of sta-
    bility; in his hand the emblem of
    stability .. .. Ptah.

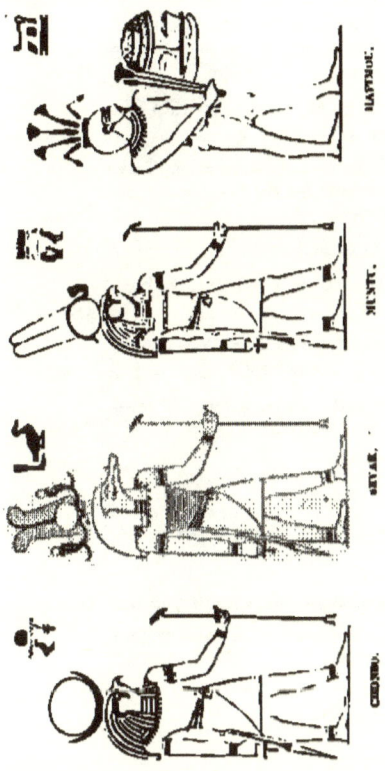

A scarabæus, the body of a bandy-
    legged dwarf   .. Ptah.

L.

The sun's disk encircled by an uræus,
the flesh coloured rod   ..   ..   ..   RA.

A goose ..   ..   SEB.

A lunar disk with a single lock of hair   CHONSO.

The lunar crescent, a disk in the midst   THOTH.

The pschent ..   ..   ,,   ,,   ..   ,,   ATMU.

The hat with two feathers, bearing in
his hands the tau, with the whip
and crook ..   ..   OSIRIS.

The atf, in his hands the whip and
crook ..   ..   ,, ...   OSIRIS.

The nilometer, or emblem of stability,
surmounted by the atf, his counte-
nance barbaric ..   ..   OSIRIS.

An ostrich feather   ..   ..   MAU.

Two tall plumes and horns, the body
of a child ..   ..   HORUS, the child.

The pschent with a single lock of hair,
his finger to his mouth   ..   ..   ..   HORUS, the child.

A disk with uræus, a body of mon-
strous proportions ..   ..   TYPHON.

Four plumes ..   ..   A form of THOTH.

The papyrus plant   ..   ..   HAPIMOU, the Nile.

The hat, in his hands a battle-axe, } RANFO, the god of
shield, and spear   ..   .. }   war.

2. Goddesses of human form bearing on their head—

The cap representing the royal vulture
surmounted by the pschent, the flesh
yellow   ..   ..   MAUT.

The teacher)
A shuttle   }   ,, ...   NEITH.
A hawk   )

The hat with a cow's horn on each
side   ..   ..   ,, ...   SATE.

The sun's disk with cow's horns and
plumes .. .. ATHOR.

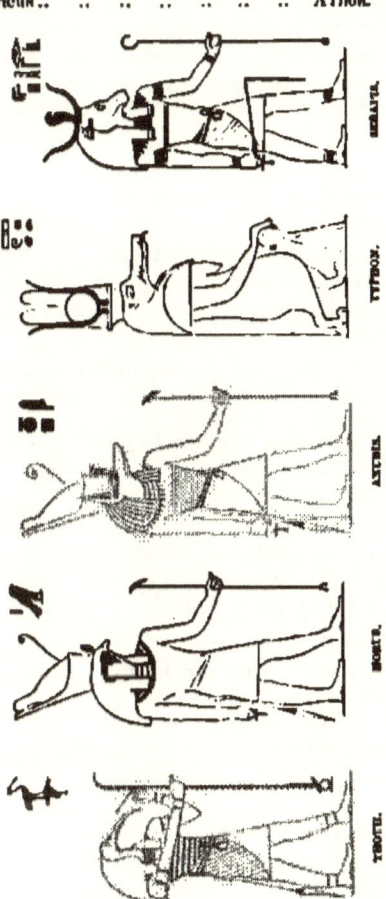

An ostrich feather .. .. MA, THMEI.
A water-vase .. .. NETPE.

Cap representing the royal vulture
surmounted by the sun's disk with
cow's horns .. ..   Isis.

A throne .. ..   Isis.

A basket on a house, hieroglyphic for
"mistress of the house" .. .. ..   Nepthys.

A number of plumes .. ..   Ank, Anouke.

A cap representing the royal vulture
surmounted by hot, or hot with
plumes .. ..   Eileythuia.

Hot with plumes, in her hands battle- ⎫ Anta, the goddess
axe, shield, and spear .. .. .. ⎭   of war.

The emblem of purity .. ..   Chemi, Egypt.

11.—*Deities of Human Form with the Head of an Animal.*

1. Gods :—

A ram's head, blue, surmounted by a
disk and two plumes .. .. ..   Amun.

A ram's head, green, two long horns
and the uræus .. ..   Kneph.

A ram's head surmounted by the atf ..   Kneph.

The head of a hawk surmounted by the
het and two plumes .. ..   Phtah, Sokkari.

A hawk's head surmounted by atf ..   Ra.

A hawk's head surmounted by disk
and uræus .. ..   Ra.

A hawk's head surmounted by lunar
crescent and disk .. ..   Chonso.

The head of the ibis surmounted by
atf .. ..   Thoth.

The head of the ibis surmounted by a
lunar crescent, a disk, and feather ..   Thoth.

A hawk's head surmounted by disk,
uræus, and two plumes .. .. ..   Mentu.

The head of a crocodile surmounted
by atf .. ..   Sevak.

The head of a bull surmounted by horns and uræus	OSIRIS-APIS, SERAPIS.
A hawk's head surmounted by pschent	HORUS.
The head of a jackal	ANUBIS.
Same, surmounted by pschent and uræus	ANUBIS.
The head of a hippopotamus with body of monstrous size	SETH, TYPHON.
The head of an ass	SET, SETH, TYPHON.

2. Goddesses:—

A cat's head surmounted by uræus ..	PASHT.
Same, surmounted by disk and uræus	PASHT.
A cow's head surmounted by disk and horns	ATHOR.
The head of a lioness surmounted by disk and uræus	TEFNE.
A cow's head surmounted by disk and uræus	ISIS.
Same, surmounted by disk, horns, and two plumes	ISIS.
Same, nursing Horus	ISIS.

The Four Genii of Amenti, or of the Lower World.

Human-headed Amset.	Jackal-headed Smautf.
Ape-headed Hapi.	Hawk-headed Kebnsnef.

These were originally names of Osiris as god of the lower world.

III. *Symbolic Animals representing those Gods whose Head-dress they sometimes bear.*

Ram with disk, horns, and two plumes on its head	AMUN.
Ram with disk and horns on its head	KNEPH.
The uræus with horns ..	KNEPH.
The uræus with tescher ..	NEITH.
The scarabæus	PTAH.
Vulture with the het crown .. .	MAUT.

Vulture, on its head the pschent		Neith.
The male sphinx, bearded, the rod disk and urœus on its head		Ra.
A hawk, on its head the disk and urœus	..	Ra.
Scarabœus with disk in its fore claws	..	Ra.
Hawk with lunar crescent and disk	..	Chonso.
Cynocephalus, a tablet in its hand ..	..	Thoth.
White ibis	..	Thoth.
Hawk in a square	..	Athor.
Cow with a disk on its head	..	Athor.
Lioness with a disk on its head	..	Tefne.
Hawk, on its head a disk and plume	..	Munt.
A crocodile	..	Sevak.
Hawk with atf	..	Osiris.
Nycticorax (heron) wearing the atf	..	Osiris.
Hawk with head-dress of Isis	..	Isis.
Hawk with pschent	..	Horus.
Jackal on an altar, with or without whip	..	Anubis.
Bull with a disk on its head	..	Apis.
Hawk hovering over a monarch	..	{ Horhat, Agatho dœmon.
An asp	..	{ Horhat, Agatho dœmon.
Serpent, bearded, with two human legs ..	..	Seth, Typhon.
An ass	..	Eileythuya.
Vulture with outspread wings	..	{ Horhat, Agatho dœmon.
The winged disk with urœi	..	Afof (Apophis).
The great serpent	..	

SPHINX.

The sphinx was an emblem of royalty, and the symbol of intellectual and physical power. The sphinx was of three kinds—the Andro-Sphinx, with the head of a man and the body of a lion, denoting the union of intellectual and physical power; the Crio-Sphinx, with the head of a ram and the body of a lion; and the Hieraco-Sphinx, with the same body and the head of a hawk. They were all types or representations of the king.

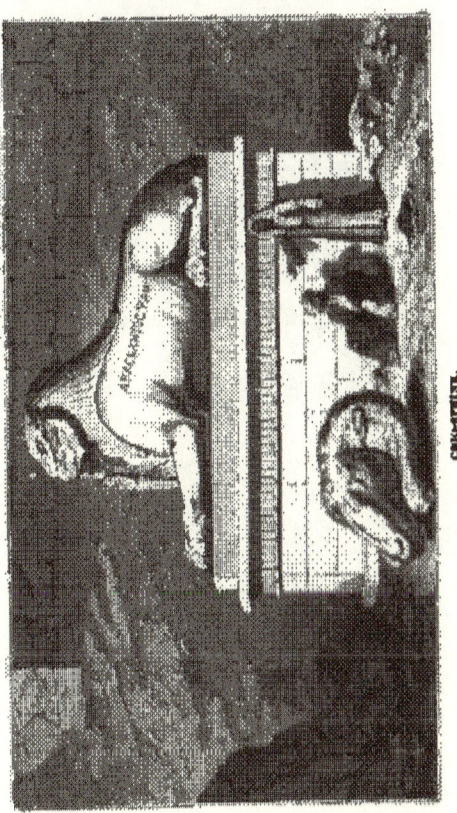

The celebrated sphinx in front of the pyramids, in its original state, presented the appearance of an enormous couchant andro-sphinx, with gigantic paws, between which was a miniature temple

with a platform, and flights of steps for approaching it, with others
leading down from the plain above, the head was formerly adorned
with the pschent.   The whole is cut out of the solid rock, with the

THE GREAT SPHINX.

exception of the forelegs. The rock was cut into this form about
the reign of Thotmes IV.   On a granite tablet in the temple is the
oval of this king.   An avenue of Sphinxes formed a usual approach
to an Egyptian temple.

The Phoenix is represented under the form of a bird, with wings partly raised, and seated upon its open claws, having at the back of its head a small tuft of feathers, and in front it raises two human arms, as if in an attitude of prayer. It is supposed to be a type of

PHOENIX.

the Sothic period, the great year of the Egyptians, at the end of which, all the planets returned to the same place they occupied at its commencement. It was a period of 1461 years, which brought round to the same seasons, their months and festivals. The story of its rising from its ashes was a later invention. according to Sir G. Wilkinson the Egyptian name seems to be III-ENES or ΦENES, signifying "sæculum," or a period of years.

The examples we have here given will be sufficient to give a general idea of the representation of the Egyptian deities under the three forms above indicated, further and more accurate information will be found in the works of Sir Gardner Wilkinson and of the Chevalier Bunsen.

Kings and Queens.—The figures of kings and queens which are found in Egyptian monuments of all kinds, are represented in a pure human form, nude, dressed, or mummified. For the kings, as for the gods, an appendage to the chin, or plaited beard, distinguished them from the queens, as from the goddesses. This plaited beard is the general mark of the male form in all figures sculptured or painted by the Egyptians. The king is recognised by two peculiar signs: 1. The serpent (ureus), which raises its head and swollen neck over his brow and in front of his crown. 2. The name engraved on his statue, or written by his side on bas-reliefs and paintings, and this name is a series of hieroglyphics enclosed in an oval or cartouche. The honours of the oval were reserved for the kings and queens alone, and for those gods who were considered as *dynasts*, or who had reigned in Egypt; but in the latter case, the gods can be recognised by their attributes, and especially by the head-dress; the kings being distinguished by their purely human forms, and by the richness of their costume.

when they are not represented as mummified.   The deceased kings
are further to be distinguished from living kings, as the dead kings,
passing into the rank of gods by their apotheosis, bear, like the gods,

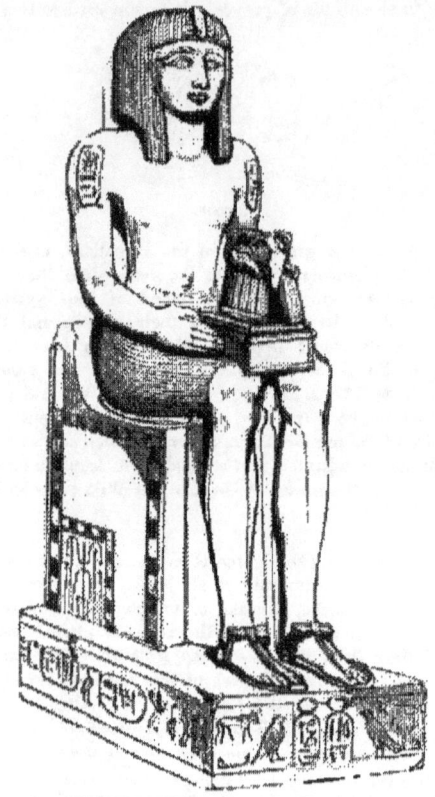

KING MENEPTHAH II., FIFTH KING OF THE NINETEENTH DYNASTY.

the sacred tau in one hand, and some other divine attribute in the
other, the uræus on their brow, and the head-dress of the god under
whose protection they had placed themselves when alive. The same
observation may be applied to the queens.

Private Individuals.—Private individuals bear no distinctive sign; men have their heads shaved, or covered with hair carefully plaited and curled, frequently wigs of a large size, a striped garment (shenti) round the loins, falls as far as the knees, and a semicircular collar

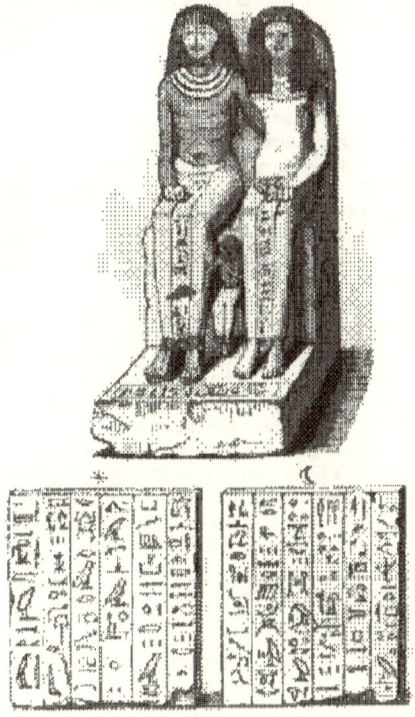

EGYPTIAN FIGURES.

(oskh) with patterns in rows, is worn round the neck and on the chest; the legs are naked, and the feet generally bare. Women wear either their own hair or a wig, and their head is covered by a kind of striped cap (claft), sloping off to allow the ears to be seen, and descending in two long, broad, and rounded masses on each side of the neck. They wear a collar round their neck, and are clothed in a tight-fitting tunic, which descends to their ankles. The head of a family is known by his long cane, which is nearly as tall as himself. If he is seated with a table before him covered with offerings, and sometimes a flame on his head, this is a representation of him when deceased, and the offerings are made by the personages of his family; and if a woman is seated by his side with the flower of a lotus in her hand, with or without the flame on her head, this is also a representation of her when deceased. In all their funereal representations, as in all those of domestic life, the name of these private individuals is always written by the side of their head, which generally is a short series of hieroglyphics; preceded, in the case of their being deceased, by the characteristic signs of the name of Osiris, all men becoming subjects of this god on their leaving life. The small statuettes (shabti) in a mummified form, without any ornament on the head, are offerings made to the deceased by their relations and friends, who had the name of the deceased placed on them. They are supposed to represent the deceased under the form of Osiris.

Animals.—The figures of animals, sculptured by the Egyptians, are remarkable for the perfection of the resemblance, the finish of the details, and minute imitation of the colours. If these animals are symbolical, their head-dress is that of the god of which they are the emblem. If they are represented only in their natural forms without any accessory, they represent the animal itself, the form of which is given—a lion, a rat, a crocodile; but it must be observed that almost all these animals partook of a symbolic character, which is the principal reason of their infinite multiplication. A bird with a human head, wearing a disk and horns, represented Athor. She was then in a character, connected with the virtuous souls who have been admitted to the regions of Amenti. The scarabæus or beetle was an emblem of the world, and was sacred to the sun and to Phtah. Scarabæi, manufactured out of almost every known material, are found in great abundance in Egyptian tombs. Of greenstone, carnelian, hæmatite, granite, serpentine, agate, lapis lazuli, plasma, amethyst, and other materials; a cheaper kind was made of limestone, stained to imitate a harder and dearer quality; and of the ordinary blue pottery. Many bear hieroglyphics, but the greater number are quite plain. Those with hieroglyphics bear on their bases the figures of deities, sacred animals, names of kings, the name of the wearer, and other symbols. A great number are funereal, and are engraved with a prayer, or formula, relative to the heart or soul of the deceased. These are found between the

folds of the interior bandages, and on the chest of the mummies.
Many, also, were used as amulets, and are found set in chains,

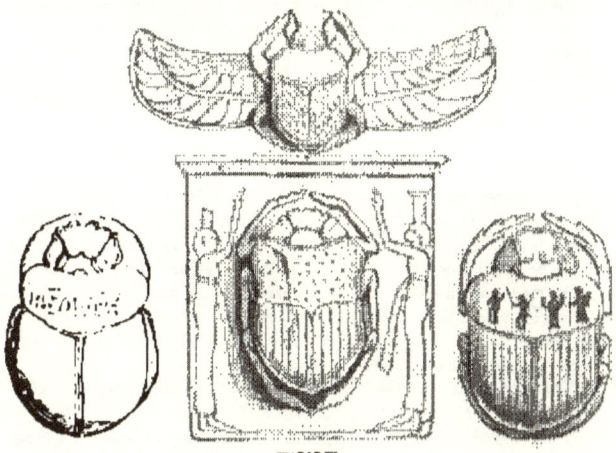

SCARABÆI.

collars, rings, etc. They may be classed as ornamental, funereal,
or historical, some of those last of great size, bearing the name of
Amunoph III., and his queen Taia, relate to his conquests, his
lion-hunts, or the public works of his reign. The real sacred
scarabæus of the Egyptians has been found living in Ethiopia.
The white ibis is frequently represented by ancient artists, though
rarely found in Egypt. It has been met with by Bruce in Abyssinia,
and has been named by Cuvier, *Ibis religiosa.* Several kinds of
serpents are found represented, but especially the uræus, with its
swollen neck, now known to be the *Naia haje,* a most venomous
snake. An asp, represented Hor-hat (the Agatho-dæmon, or protecting genius). The great serpent, Apop (Apophis), was the emblem of evil or sin. Another animal often figured in Egyptian
sculpture and painting is the cynocephalus, or dog-headed baboon.
It was the emblem of the god Thoth.

Sepulchral Tablets.—Sepulchral tablets or stelæ, are bas-reliefs of a
rough stone rounded at the top, and which represent offerings made by
one or several persons, either to the gods or to men ; the offerings to
the gods are made by the deceased persons, who in their turn receive

them from their family. They also contain invocations addressed
to the deities. These tablets, which are all funeral, have several
rows of figures; the hieroglyphic inscriptions which accompany
them explain the subject, and also give the name of the personages,
whether dead or living. These sepulchral tablets are almost all of
calcareous stone, some of wood. They vary in height from a few
inches to three, four, and six feet. They were placed in sepulchral
chambers, and in the tombs of families.

Etruscan.—To afford a key to the interpretation of the mythological personages, frequently represented in Etruscan art, we
extract the following from Dennis's "Etruria." The mythological
system of Etruria is learned partly from ancient writers, partly
from national monuments, particularly figured mirrors. It was in
some measure allied to that of Greece, though rather to the early
Pelasgic system than to that of the Hellenes; but still more nearly
to that of Rome, who in fact derived certain of her divinities and
their names from this source.

The three great deities, who had temples in every Etruscan city,
were Tina or Tinia—Cupra—Menrva or Menerva.

TINIA was the supreme deity of the Etrurans, analogous to the Zeus
of the Greeks, and the Jupiter of the Romans. He is always represented on Etruscan monuments with the thunderbolt in his hand.

CUPRA was the Etruscan Hera or Juno, and her principal shrines
seem to have been at Veil, Falerii, and Perusia. Like her counterpart among the Greeks and Romans, she appears to have been
worshipped under other forms, according to her various attributes—
as Feronia, Thalna or Thana, Ilithyia, Leucothea.

MENRVA, as she is called on Etruscan monuments, answers to the
Pallas Athene of the Greeks. It is probable that the name by
which the Romans knew her was of purely Etruscan origin. Like
her counterpart in the Greek and Roman mythology, she is represented armed, and with the ægis on her breast, but in addition has
sometimes wings.

The other gods represented on Etruscan monuments are :—

SUMMANUS, who hurled his thunderbolts by night, as Jupiter did
by day.

VEJOVIS or VEDIVS, whose thunderbolts made those they struck deaf.

ERCLE or HERCLE.—Hercules, a favourite god of the Etruscans.

SETHLANS, or Vulcan, represented with a hammer and pincers.

PHUPHLUNS, the Etruscan Bacchus, also called VERTUMNUS.

APLU, or Apollo, who often appears on Etruscan monuments as God of the Sun, being sometimes called UHL.

TURMS, or Mercury.

TURAN, or Venus.

THESAN, the goddess of the dawn—Aurora.

LOSNA, or LALA, the Etruscan Luna or Diana.

NETHUNS, or Neptune, is of rare occurrence on Etruscan monuments.

CASTOR and PULTUKE.—Castor and Pollux, are frequently represented on mirrors.

NORTIA, the Fortuna of the Etruscans.

VOLTUMNA, the great goddess, at whose shrine the confederate princes of Etruria held their councils.

HORTA, the goddess of gardens.

LASA, or MEAN.—The goddess of fate, who is represented with wings, sometimes with a hammer and nail, as if fixing unalterably her decrees, but more frequently with a bottle in one hand and a stylus in the other, with which she inscribes her decisions.

MANTUS and MANIA, the Pluto and Proserpine of the Etruscan creed. Mantus is represented as an old man wearing a crown, with wings at his shoulders, and a torch, or it may be large nails in his hands, to show the inevitable character of his decrees. Of Mania we have no decided representation, but she is probably figured in some of the female demons who were supposed to be present at scenes of death and slaughter. She was a fearful deity, who was propitiated by human sacrifices.

CHARUN, the great conductor of souls, the infernal Mercury of the Etruscans the chief minister of Mantus, is often introduced on sepulchral monuments, with his numerous attendant demons and Furies.

The Etruscans also represented mythological animals in clay and bronze. The style of these figures, which has all the defects which primitive art could not avoid, is sufficiently characteristic of them ; the most remarkable is the Chimæra, a monster having the body of a lion, a goat's head springing from its back, and a serpent for a tail. A bronze chimæra is in the Florentine Gallery, with an inscription in Etruscan characters on the fore leg. The celebrated wolf of the capitol is also an Etruscan work. Griffins, sphinxes, hippocamps, or sea monsters, Scylla, with a double fish's tail, and Typhons, with winged human bodies, terminating in serpents instead of legs, are also found on Etruscan monuments in a better style of art, being of a later period.

Greek and Roman.—As it is by the knowledge of mythology and the characteristic attributes of each deity or hero, in connexion with the creed and traditions of the Greeks and Romans, that the various sculptured representations of their deities and heroes can be known; we shall give a concise enumeration of their distinctive characteristics and attributes, from Winkelman and Müller.[*] A dictionary of mythology will afford every information with regard to the history of these deities, but we shall more particularly devote our attention to the illustration of the attributes and characteristics of the deities as visible in figured representation, and as given to them by Greek and Roman sculptors.

The forms and attributes of nearly all the Greek and Roman deities are very uncertain, and their number is considerable and various, for, as Cicero confesses, " Nos Deos omnes ea facie novimus. quâ pictores, fictoresque voluerunt." The mode of representing them depended on the caprice of painters and fabulists. We shall therefore carefully follow the authorities we have taken as our guide.

We shall first enumerate the forms adopted by the ancient sculptors in their representation of the human figure. They were the following, and were in close connexion with the spaces which they occupied and were intended to fill :

The HERMA, which was a human head on a pillar, having the proportions of the human form. It was an intermediate step between the isolated statue and the pillar from which the isolated statue was historically developed.

The BUST, a representation of the head down to the shoulders, sometimes also with the breast and waist, was derived from the Herma.

The STATUE was the complete development of the human form, and was destined to stand alone. The temple images of the gods, which are the more perfect representations of the human form, were generally isolated statues.

The GROUP was when two or more statues were combined. It was a form frequently used among the Greeks for pediments of temples. The centre figure was then rendered more prominent by greater dimensions, the other figures being arranged on both sides of it. A pyramidal form was thus given to the group, in order to adapt it to the shape of the pediment.

* We have made large extracts from Müller, but our excuse must be that he is an indispensable authority on this subject.

We shall further enumerate here the different kinds of garments adopted as drapery by the Greek and Roman sculptors, as frequent mention will be made of them in the descriptions of Greek and Roman sculpture.

GRECIAN COSTUME.

Among the Greeks their garments were divided into ἐνδύματα, those that were drawn over, and ἐπιβλήματα, those that were thrown

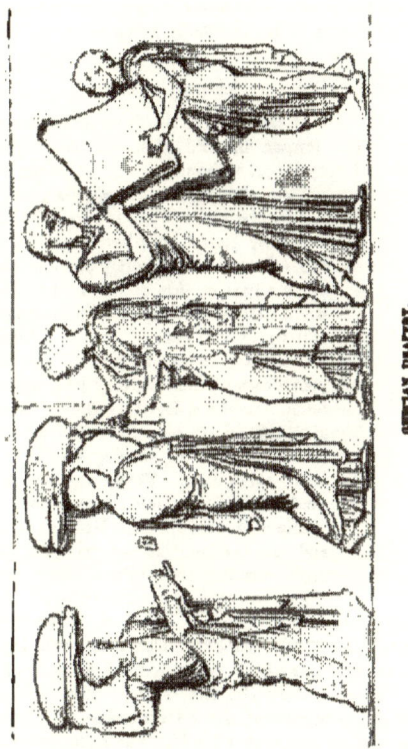

GRECIAN DRAPERY.

round the body. The male *Chiton* was a woollen shirt, originally without sleeves, which was then named the Dorian. The Ionian was a long linen garment in many folds, with sleeves. The himation was a large square garment worn over the chiton, generally drawn round from the left arm, which hold it fast, across the back, and then over the right arm, or else through beneath it towards the left arm. Essentially different from these was the Chlamys, which was adopted in Greece, especially by horsemen and ephebi. It was a mantle fastened on the right shoulder with a buckle or clasp (περόνη), and falling down along the thigh in two lengthened skirts. Covering on the head was seldom introduced in sculpture; the only coverings introduced are the petasus, which was worn by horsemen and ephebi, and the Phrygian cap, which is usually given to Paris.

GRECIAN FEMALE COSTUME.

Among the Chitons of the women, the Doric and Ionic are easily distinguished. The former, the old Hellenic, was a garment of woollen cloth, not very large, without sleeves, and fastened on the shoulders by clasps. This, also called the σχιστός χιτών, was fre-

quently so short as not to reach the knees. It was only joined together on one side, and on the other was left partly open or slit up, to allow a free motion of the limbs. Diana and the Amazons are frequently represented in this chiton. The Ionic, which the Athenians borrowed from the Ionians, was of linen, all sewed, provided with sleeves, very long and in many folds. In both, for the ordinary costume, the girdle (ζώνη) is essential; it lies around the loins, and by the gathering up of the garment forms the κόλπος. There was also a peculiar kind of dress, which seems to have been a species of double chiton, called διπλοΐς, διπλοΐδιον, and ἡμιδιπλοΐδιον. It was the upper part of the cloth forming the chiton, which was larger than was required for the ordinary chiton, and

DOUBLE CHITON.

was therefore thrown over the front and back. The himation of women had in general the same form as that worn by men: a common use, therefore, might have existed. The mode of wearing was nearly the same, only the envelopment was generally more complete and the arrangement of the folds richer.

The peplos was an ample shawl, which was worn round the body. Sometimes it was so arranged as to cover the head, while it enveloped the body. It was so worn by brides.

ROMAN COSTUME.

The Roman tunic, like the Greek chiton, was a woollen under-garment. It was sometimes girded with a belt, or girdle, round the waist, but was usually worn loose. The toga was an outer garment, of a semi-circular shape and of great length, and so worn as to let its ends fall on both sides down to the ground in considerable masses. The stola, which was a tunic with a broad border, and the palla, which was a kind of large shawl worn over the stola, were female dresses.

THE TWELVE OLYMPIAN DEITIES.

ZEUS.—JUPITER.

He was represented either standing or sitting. The sitting posture, in which the himation, which is sunk down to the loins, forms the usual drapery, is connected with the idea of tranquil power, victorious rest. The standing posture, in which the himation is often entirely discarded, or only the back is covered, carries with it the idea of activity; Zeus is then conceived as protector, patron of political activity, or as the god who punishes and guards with thunderbolts. The characteristic features of his head (as stamped by Phidias) are remarkable in the arrangement of the hair, which rose up from the centre of the forehead, and then fell down on both sides like a mane; the brow clear and bright above, but greatly arching forward beneath, mild lineaments round the upper lip and cheeks, the full rich beard descending in large wavy tresses. He was also given a noble, ample, and open chest, as well as a powerful but not an unduly enlarged muscular development of the whole body. His usual attributes are the sceptre, eagle, thunderbolt, and a figure of Victory in his hand, and sometimes a cornucopia. The Olympian Zeus sometimes wears a wreath of olive, and the Dodonean Zeus a wreath of oak leaves.

JUPITER.

In the character of Zeus Meilichios he assumed a more youthful and
softer form, with less beard and masculine vigour in the countenance. In the character of Zeus Orkios, the oath avenger at
Olympia, he appeared the most terrible, with a thunderbolt in each

JUPITER OLYMPIUS OF PHIDIAS.

hand. Sometimes he appears represented as a child, in accordance
with the Cretan myth, with the goat Amalthæ, or lying on the

ground, with the Curetes around him. He frequently also appears, especially in the later period of art, under the metamorphosed forms of a bull carrying off Europa, of a swan embracing Leda, of a satyr enclasping Antiope, of an eagle bearing away Ganymede. Under Adrian he was worshipped as Jupiter Serapis, assuming the attributes

HEAD OF SERAPIS.

of an Egyptian deity who presided over the dead. He is then usually represented with a modius on his head, and rays.

HEADS :—

> Colossal bust found at Otricoli, Vatican ; another in the Boboli Gardens, Florence ; others in the British Museum. Serapis, Vatican. British Museum.

STATUES :—

> The Verospi Jupiter.
> A seated statue in the Vatican.

HERA.—JUNO.

The principal attribute of Hera is the veil which the betrothed virgin draws around her, as the symbol of her separation from the rest of the world. Phidias characterizes her, in the frieze of the Parthenon, by the throwing back of the veil. She generally wears a sort of crown, or diadem, called *stephanos*. The countenance of Hera, as it was established, probably by Polyclitus, presents forms of unfading bloom and ripened beauty, softly rounded, without too much plumpness ; awe-inspiring, but free from ruggedness, as exemplified in the noble colossal head of the villa Ludovisi. The forehead, encompassed with hair flowing obliquely down, forms a

gently arched triangle; the rounded and open eyes look straight
forward. Winkelman remarks that she may be known, not only
by her lofty diadem, but by her large eyes, and an imperious
mouth, the line of which is so characteristic that we can say, simply
from seeing such a mouth in profile, that it is a head of Juno. Her
figure is blooming, completely developed, that of a matron who
always continues to bathe, as is related of Hera, in the fountain of

BUST OF JUNO.

virginity. Her costume is a chiton, which merely leaves the neck
and arms bare, and a himation, which lies around the middle of the
figure; in statues of improved art, the veil is for the most part
thrown towards the back of the head, or omitted altogether. By
the Romans she was frequently represented as the goddess of marriage, Juno Pronuba. The Romans had also a peculiar mode of
representing her as Juno Sospita, with a goat's skin round her body,
a double tunic, a lance and shield.

The peacock was consecrated to her.

Busts :—

    The Ludovisi bust.

Statues :—

    The Farnese Juno, Naples.
    The Barberini Juno, in the Vatican.

POSEIDON.—NEPTUNE.

Poseidon was for the most part, in earlier times especially, represented in lofty repose, and carefully draped; although, however, he

was even at that time also sculptured entirely naked, and in violent
action. The flourishing period of Greek art unfolded the idea more
charactoristically; it gave to Poseidon, with a somewhat more
slender structure of body, a stronger muscular development than to
Zeus, which is generally rendered very prominent by the posture,
and to the countenance more angular forms, and less clearness and
repose in the features; his hair also is less flowing, more bristling

NEPTUNE.

and disordered, and the pine wreath forms for it a fitting, although
not frequently used, ornament. He is frequently represented with
his spouse Amphitrite, accompanied by sea gods. His amour with
the fountain nymph Amymone, also forms a frequent subject in
figured representation. His attributes were the trident, and the
dolphin.

Bust :—

From Ostia, in the Vatican.

Statues:

In the western pediment of the Parthenon.
Torso in the British Museum.

DEMETER.—CERES.

Demeter appears more matronly and motherlike than Hera, the
expression of her countenance, the back part of which is concealed
by an upper garment, or a veil, is softer and milder; her form
appears, in completely enveloping drapery, broader and fuller, as

becomes the mother of all (παμμήτωρ). The crown of corn-ears, poppy and ears of corn in her hands, the torches, the fruit-basket, also the swine beside her, are the most frequent attributes.

The goddess is not unfrequently seen enthroned alone, or with her daughter, Persephone, Proserpine.

STATUES:

    Ceres, in the Villa Borghese. British Museum.
    Ceres. Villa Albani.
    Ceres. Louvre.

APOLLO.

Apollo was a favourite subject of the great artists who immediately preceded Phidias. At that period Apollo was formed more mature and manly than afterwards, with limbs stronger and broader, countenance rounder and shorter; the expression more serious and stern than amiable and attractive, for the most part undraped, when he was not imagined as the Pythian Citharœdus. He is shown thus in numerous statues, many vase paintings, and also coins. On these we find the older form of the head of Apollo often very gracefully developed, but still the same on the whole, until down to the time of Philip. The laurel wreath, and the hair parted at the crown, shaded to the side along the forehead, usually waving down the neck, sometimes, however, also taken up and pinned together, here serve particularly to designate the god.

The more slender shape, the more lengthened oval of the head, and the more animated expression, Apollo doubtless received especially from the younger Attic school, by which he was frequently sculptured. The god was now conceived altogether younger, without any sign of manly ripeness, as a youth not yet developed into manhood, in whose forms, however, the tenderness of youth seemed wonderfully combined with massive strength. The longish oval countenance, which the bow of the hair (crobylus) above the forehead often lengthened still more, and which served as an apex to the entire upstriving form, has at the same time a soft fulness and massive firmness; in every feature is manifested a lofty, proud, and clear intelligence, whatever the modifications may be. The forms of the body are slender and supple; the hips high, the thighs lengthy; the muscles without individual prominence, rather fused into one another, are still so marked as that agility, elasticity of form, and energy of movement, become evident. However, the configuration here inclines sometimes more to the gymnastic strength of Hermes, sometimes to the effeminate fulness of

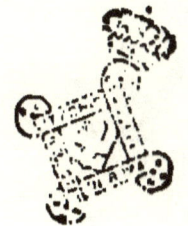

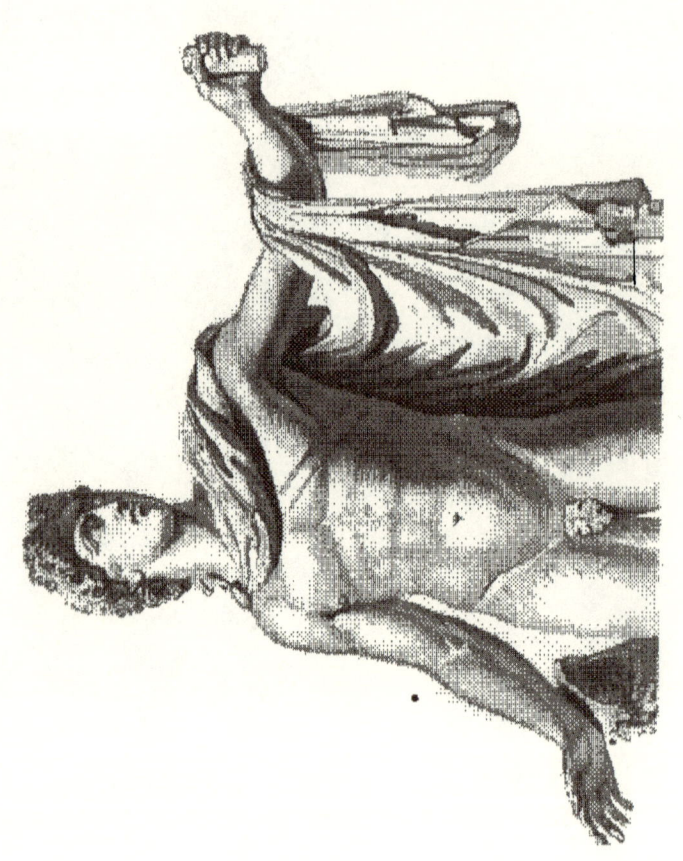

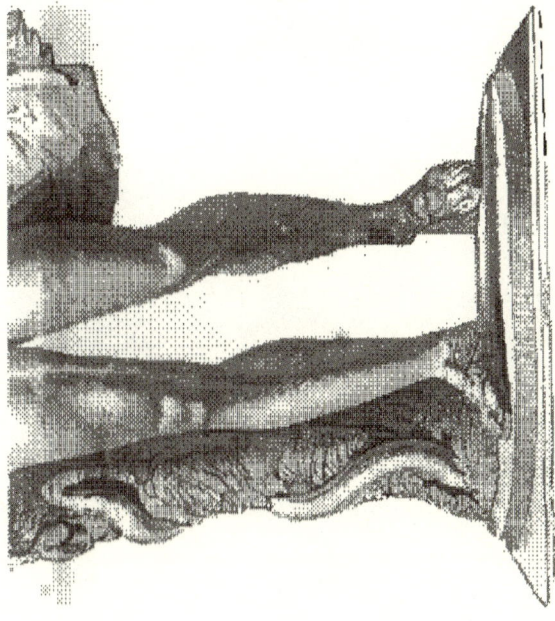

APOLLO DELVIDERE.

[To face page 185]

Dionysus. According to Winkelman, the highest conception of ideal male beauty is especially expressed in the Apollo, in whom strength of adult years is found united with the soft forms of the most beautiful spring-time of youth. The artistic representations of this deity may be given as the following:—

1. Apollo Callinicus having just slain his adversary, Python or Tityos, his countenance still expressive of anger and disdain, and noble pride of conquest; as in the Apollo Belvidere.

2. The god reposing from battle, his right arm resting on his head, and the quiver, with closed lid hanging beside him; as in the Apollino, of the Florentine Gallery.

3. The lyre-playing Apollo (Citharædus), who appears variously costumed, although a complete envelopment in the chlamys here prevails, as in the Apollo Citharædus of the Vatican.

4. The Pythian Agonistes. In this the drapery is perfected into the solemn and gorgeous costume of the Pythian Stola, exhibiting at the same time a soft, roundish, almost feminine form.

ATTRIBUTES:

The lyre, a bow and quiver, a griffin.

STATUES:

Early.—The Apollo of Canachus. Paris.

The Apollo Callinicus, or Belvidere. Vatican.
Apollo Lycius, or Apollino. Florentine Gallery.
Apollo Citharædus. Vatican.
Apollo Sauroctonos. Vatican. In bronze, in the Villa Albani.
Apollo Citharædus, seated, in porphyry. Naples.
Apollo Musagetes. Naples.
A small statue of Apollo, in bronze. Naples.

ARTEMIS.—DIANA.

In the earlier style the goddess invariably appears in long and elegant drapery (in Stola). In later times, when Scopas, Praxiteles, and others had perfected the ideal, Artemis, like Apollo, was formed slender and light-footed, her hips and breast without the fulness of womanhood; the still undeveloped forms of both sexes before puberty, here seem, as it were, arrested, and only unfolded into greater size. The countenance is that of Apollo, only with

less prominent forms, more tender and rounded; the hair is often
bound up over the forehead into a knot (crobylus), but still oftener
gathered together into a bow at the back, or on the crown of the
head.   Her dress was a Doric chiton, either girt high, or flowing

DIANA TRIFORMIS.

down to the foot.   She is often represented in statues as Artemis
the huntress, in very animated movement; sometimes in the act of
taking the arrow from the quiver in order to discharge it; sometimes on the point of shooting it.   She is generally represented
under two phases: as a slaying deity, in connection with the chase,
and as a life-giving, light-bringing goddess (Lucifera), when she

appears holding a torch. The Greeks have also given her three different characters: as the moon, she was Lucina; as the goddess of the chase, Diana; as a deity of the lower regions, Hecate. When represented under this triple form, with corresponding attributes, she was styled Triformis, or Trivia, as statues of this kind were usually placed in towns and villages where three ways met. As the Artemis of the Ephesians, she was the personification of the fructifying and all-nourishing power of nature. Her image in this character represented her with many breasts (πολυμαστος, multimamma).

Her attributes are the bow, quiver, and arrows; or a spear, stag, and dogs.

STATUES :

    Diana a la biche. Louvre.
    Diana of Gabii. Louvre.
    Diana Venatrix. Vatican.
    Diana. Florentine Gallery.
    Diana Triformis. British Museum.
    Diana, draped. British Museum.

HEPHÆSTUS.—VULCAN.

Hephæstus was represented as an industrious and vigorous man, bearded, and of a mature age. He is more clearly recognized in the few works which remain of him by his semi-oval cap, and the chiton, which leaves the right shoulder and arm uncovered. He holds a hammer or some other instrument in his hand.

ATHENA.—MINERVA.

In the statues of early Greek art, in its more advanced state, Athena always appears in martial costume, stepping forward more or less; clad over the chiton with a stiffly-folded peplos, and a ægis, which sometimes also lay over the left arm, serving as a large shield, or covered the whole back, besides the breast: in later times, on the contrary, it became more and more contracted. The outlines of the body have less feminine fulness in the hips and breast, at the same time that the forms of the legs, arms, and back are developed in a more masculine manner. The countenance has already the peculiar cast which improved art further unfolded, but at the same time very harsh and ungraceful features. Since Phidias perfected the ideal of Athena, tranquil seriousness, self-conscious power, and clearness of intellect always remained the fundamental character of Pallas. Her virginity is nothing else than exaltation above all feminine weakness; she is too masculine herself to be capable of surrendering herself to man. The pure forehead, the long and finely-shaped nose, the somewhat stern cast of the mouth and cheeks, the large and almost angular chin, the eyes not fully opened and rather downcast, the hair artlessly shaded back along the brow, and flowing down upon the neck: all features in which early hardness appears transformed into grandeur, are in complete accordance with this wonderful ideal creation. She is chiefly characterised by her helmet, either the lofty, highly-ornamented Phidian helmet, which is given to her in the gem of Aspasius, and on the coins of Athens after the time of Phidias, or the close fitting, unadorned Corinthian helmet, as on the coins of Corinth, and in the

HEAD OF PALLAS, WITH CORINTHIAN HELMET.

Pallas of Velletri. The modifications of this form stand in intimate connection with the drapery. Athena, in the first place, has, in many statues of the perfected style, a himation thrown about her, either so as that falling over in front, it lies merely around the lower part of the body, and thus heightens the majestic impression of the form, or so as to conceal the left arm and a portion of the ægis, whereby the goddess receives a peculiarly peaceful character. This Athena has always the shield resting on the ground, or wants it altogether; she is accordingly conceived as a victorious (hence also

the Nike in her hand) and peacefully-ruling goddess. Of this kind
was the celebrated chryselephantine statue by Phidias in the
Parthenon. In contrast to it stand the statues of Pallas in the
Doric chiton, with the hemidiploidion, but without the himation;

MINERVA.

a costume which is immediately adapted for combat. With this
drapery agrees very well an uplifted shield, which characterized
the Pallas Promachos of Phidias, and is probably to be restored in
many statues of Pallas executed after a sublime model, which

exhibit a somewhat more combative action than usual in the bold
sweep of the ægis, and the whole bearing of the body, and are
distinguished by the particularly powerful and athletic form of the
limbs. Where, therefore, Athena appears in smaller works of art,
hastening to battle or already engaged in combat, uplifting the
lance, or hurling the thunderbolt, she has always this drapery.
However she is also to be found in the same garb as a politically
active, as an oratorical, and without helmet or ægis, as a peace-

COIN OF ATHENS.

establishing goddess; and this more lightly clad Athena is also to
be found in small bronze statues with shield laid down, and a patera
in the hand, especially in reference to conquests just achieved.

ATTRIBUTES:

 An olive branch, a serpent, an owl, a cock, a lance, a shield
 with the Gorgon Medusa's head on it.

STATUES:

 Early.—Minerva Polias, at Athens.

 Pallas Athena, from Ægina. Munich.
 Pallas from Herculaneum. Naples.
 Pallas of Velletri. Louvre.
 The Farnese Minerva. Naples.
 Pallas Athena. Vatican.
 Pallas. Dresden.
 Minerva Medica. Vatican.
 Fragments of Statue, from the western pediment of the
 Parthenon, in the British Museum.

ARES.—MARS.

A compact and muscular development, a thick, fleshy neck, and
short, disordered hair, seem to belong universally to the conception
of the god. Ares has smaller eyes, somewhat more widely-dia-

tended nostrils, a less sereno forehead than other sons of Jupiter.
With regard to age, he appears more manly than Apollo, and even
than Hermes, the youth (ephebos) among the gods—as a youthful
man, whom, like almost all heroes, early art formed with a beard,
improved art, on the contrary, without beard; the former representation, however, was also preserved in many districts and for
many purposes.

The drapery of Ares, where he does not appear entirely undressed, is a chlamys. On reliefs in the archaic style he is seen
in armour; in later times he retained merely the helmet. He
usually stands; a vigorous stride marks the Gradivus on Roman
coins; the legionary eagle and other signs, the Stator and Ultor
(who recovered them); victories, trophies, and the olive branch,
the Victor and Pacifier. Scopas sculptured a sitting Ares, he was
doubtless conceived as reposing in a mild mood, which seems also
to be the meaning of one of the chief statues extant (the Ludovisi
Mars), in which a copy after Scopas is, perhaps, preserved to us.
In groups he is frequently represented together with Aphrodite,
symbolical of the union of war and love, which in the posture of
the bodies and disposition of the drapery, indicate a famous original.
In Roman art he is sometimes represented as descending to Rhea
Silvia, a subject pleasing to the Romans, as they considered him
their progenitor.

ATTRIBUTES:—

> Spear, helmet, and shield. The wolf and woodpecker were
> sacred to him.

STATUES:—

> The Ludovisi Mars. Villa Ludovisi, Rome.
> Borghese Mars. Louvre.
> Mars and Venus. Florentine Gallery.

APHRODITE.—VENUS.

When art, in the cycle of Aphrodite, soared above rude stones and
shapeless idols, it suggested the idea of a goddess powerfully sway-
ing, and everywhere prevailing; it was usual to represent her
enthroned, with symbols of blooming nature and luxuriant fertility;
her drapery was complete, only that, perhaps, the chiton partly disclosed her left breast, and gracefully-folded, as an affected grace in
drapery and motion belonged, of all others, to the character of Aphrodite. Art in the Phidian period also represented in Aphrodite the
sexual relation in its sacredness and dignity. Later Attic art at first

treated the idea of Aphrodite with a purely sensual enthusiasm,
and deified in her no longer a world-swaying power, but the individual embodiment of the most charming womanhood ; nay, it even
placed this ideal, released from moral relations, in decided contrast
therewith. The forms which improved art gave to Aphrodite are
mostly those natural to the sex. She is altogether a woman, in a
much fuller sense of the word, than Athena or Artemis. The
ripened bloom of the virgin is, in many modifications, the stage of
physical advancement which is adhered to in the forms of the body.
The shoulders are narrow, the bosom has a maidenly development,
the fulness of the hips tapers away into elegantly shaped feet,
which, little adapted for standing or treading firmly, seem to betray
a hurried and tender gait. The countenance of Junonian fulness,
and grand development of features in the elder representation,
appears afterwards more delicate and longthened ; the languishing
eye (ὑγρόν) and smiling mouth are combined with the general expression of grace and sweetness. The hair is arranged with elegance,
usually encircled by a diadem, and gathered into it in the earlier
representations, but knotted together into a bow (crobylos) in the
undraped statues of Venus, produced by later art. Here also, the
essential modifications of the form, are closely connected with the
drapery. The entirely draped Aphrodite, who, however, for the
most part wears only a thin chiton, which but slightly conceals the
body, and with a graceful movement of the left arm merely draws
forward a little upper garment, which is falling down behind,
is derived from the Urania of the early artists; according to
Winkelman this celestial Venus, the daughter of Jupiter and
Harmonia, is different from the other Venus, who is the daughter of
Dione ; she is distinguished, he says, by a high diadem of the kind
peculiar to Juno. She was worshipped in Roman times as mother
Aphrodite, Venus Genetrix, and honoured by numerous representations, partly as the progenitrix of the Julian family, partly as the
goddess of lawful, wedded love. The style of the period in which
this manner of representation originated, combined to give to this
class of statues of Aphrodite rounder and stronger forms, shorter
proportions of figure, and a more matronly character than was
otherwise the custom in regard to this goddess. Very clearly
distinguished from these is a second class of statues of Venus,
which, without the chiton, have only an upper garment thrown
round the lower portion of the body, and are characterized at the
same time by the placing of one foot on a slight elevation, as in the
Venus of Milo. In these the goddess approaches a heroine in
aspect ; the forms of the body are remarkably firm, and, though

slender, powerful, the bosom less rounded than in others, and the countenance furnished with more prominent features, not without the expression of pride and self-consciousness. In this class of statues, therefore, we must recognise a Venus victorious, whether she embraced Ares himself, or held in her hands his helmet and shield, or a palm, or the apple, as a sign of victory. She is also represented in a less powerful form, but of greater fulness and roundness, as ANADYOMENE, which represents her at the bath covering her bosom with a piece of drapery which hangs round behind her. Another form, over delicate and flowing, is observable in the meretricious statue of Aphrodite Callipygus. On the other hand, ancient art felt itself challenged to the observance of the purest proportions, the most fault-less representation of beautiful forms, when the goddess appeared completely unveiled. Although the bath was originally imagined as the occasion of this unveiling, here all reference to action dis-appears; the statue is entirely a symbol of female loveliness, height-ened by the manifestation of natural shame, and of womanhood in gene-ral. Of this kind was the cele-brated Venus of Cnidos, by Praxi-teles, of which the Venus de Medici, the Venus of the Capitol, and other Venuses in a similar position, are supposed to be either imitations or copies. Other attitudes which indi-cate more movement and action, notwithstanding the particular

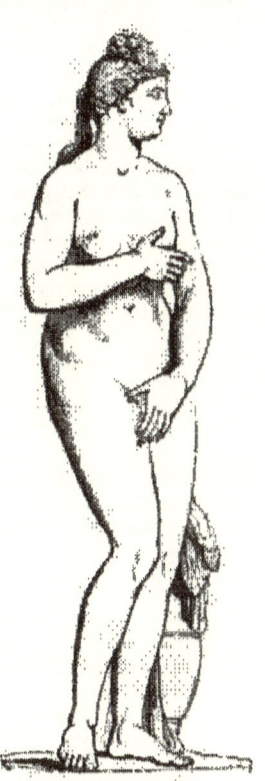

VENUS OF THE CAPITOL.

charms which they unfold, have not the same pervading and uni-form fulness of beauty as the chief statues before described. To this class belong those crouching in the bath, girding themselves with the cestus, putting on a shoulder-belt or sandals.

N

In groups Aphrodite frequently appears with her child Eros in fondling representations, and with the Charites (Graces), when also is adorned by them. There are also numerous representations of Aphrodite as a sea deity, in which the loveliest product of the watery deep is usually combined and placed in contrast with the grotesque beings which are destined to express the wild and changeable nature of the ocean. Among the proper love intrigues of Aphrodite, her amour with Ares and the legend of Adonis gave not a little occupation to Greek art in the good times. More works of art relate to the Trojan mythus; the competition for the prize of beauty gave to artists of different kinds occasion for manifold representations. A very excellent work of sculpture—Aphrodite persuading Helen to fulfil her promise to Paris—forms the basis of numerous reliefs still preserved. The goddess is frequently seen aiding lovers—for instance, Peleus in the obtainment of Thetis, especially in vase paintings, either enthroned or standing, but always completely draped, for the naked Aphrodite of later art is foreign to the vase style. Here we only recognise her by her elegant drapery and her manner of holding it, and also by her attributes.

ATTRIBUTES :—

> The dove, the swan, the swallow, the sparrow, a bird called iynx, the myrtle, the rose, the apple, a mirror.

EARLY REPRESENTATION : —

> On the triangular altar, Louvre; on the puteal, in the Capitol.

STATUES :—

> The Venus de Medici, Florentine Gallery.
> Venus Victrix, of Melos, Louvre.
> Venus of the Capitol.
> Repetition in the British Museum.
> Venus Genetrix, Louvre. According to Flaxman, a copy of the draped Venus of Cos.
> Venus of Arles, Louvre.
> Townely Venus, British Museum.
> Venus Callipygos, Naples.
> Venus Victrix, with Cupid, of Capua, Naples.
> Venus of Ostia, called also Angerona, British Museum.
> Crouching Venus, Florentine Gallery.
> Venus of Menophantus, Chigi Palace, Rome.

HERMES—MERCURY.

By the aboriginal inhabitants of Greece, Hermes was represented as the giver of all good, in the form of a stake provided with a bearded head and a phallus. In the further advance of civilization, gain and traffic being the chief object of men's wishes, he was converted into an economical and mercantile deity, and received the form of an active powerful man with thick pointed beard, and long tresses, in a chlamys thrown back—the dress best adapted for rapid movement—with a travelling hat, talaria, and the kerykeion (caduceus) in his hand, which is often like a sceptre. He is thus exhibited universally in works of early art.

The higher development of the form of Hermes originated with the Gymnasia, over which the god had presided from early times, as he from whom flows corporeal vigour.

It is probably to be ascribed to the later Attic school, after the Peloponnesian war. He now became the gymnastically perfected ephebos, with large expanded chest, slender but powerful limbs, which had received their development especially through the exercises of the Pentathlon (running, leaping, and the discus); his dress that of the Attic ephebi, a chlamys, which appears for the most part much abridged, and not unfrequently the petasos as a covering for the head, the hair of which, according to the custom of young men at that age, appears cut short away, and not much curled. The features indicated a calm and acute intellect, and a friendly, benevolent disposition, which is also expressed in the gentle inclination of the head; they do not pretend to the noble and proud

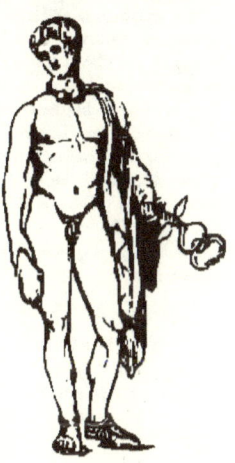

MERCURY.

look of Apollo, but with broader and flatter forms, have still something uncommonly fine and graceful. Winkelman remarks: "The youth which is so beautiful in Apollo, advances to mature years in other youthful gods, and becomes manly in Mercury and Mars. Mercury is distinguished by a particular delicacy of countenance, which Aristophanes would have called Ἀστεῖον βλέπος, an Attic look, and his hair is short and curly." Among the statues we distinguish,

N 2

first, a class in which the Hermes ideal evidently soared to its highest point : figures of ripened youth, and full of solid strength, the expression of whose countenance melts into a gentle smile, in firm tranquil posture, the chlamys thrown back from the beautifully turned limbs, and wrapped round the left arm ; in these, Hermes was evidently conceived as patron of gymnic exercises and bestower of bodily strength, as the palm-tree beside him also indicates, as exemplified in the Belvidere Mercury. This was formerly styled an Antinous and a Moleager, but its resemblance to the Farnese Mercury and to a gem in the Florentine Gallery have proved it to be a Mercury. Next to these come statues similarly draped, in which, however, the gesture of the uplifted right hand shows that Hermes is to be conceived as the god of eloquence, as Hermes Logios : a conception which was very easily and naturally formed out of that of the god of gain and herald of the gods. As executor of the commands of Zeus, we see him half sitting and already half springing up again, in order to hasten away ; sometimes in bronzes, winging his flight gaily through the air ; also reposing after a long journey, when he leans his arm merely on a pillar, and does not double it over his head—an attitude which would be too effeminate and careless for Hermes. Hermes, the performer of sacrifices ; the protector of cattle, and especially of sheep ; the inventor of the lyre, to whom therefore the tortoise is sacred ; lastly, the guide of souls and restorer of the dead to life, is seen chiefly in works of slighter compass. He is also represented as a thievish child, illustrating the Homeric myth. The purse was an attribute of Hermes in later times.

ATTRIBUTES :—

> The Petasus, a travelling hat with a broad brim, which in later times was adorned with two small wings. The herald's staff (ραβδος). The winged sandals (πέδιλα). The enduceus, the palm-tree, the tortoise.

BUST :—

> In the possession of the Duke of Buccleuch.

STATUES :—

> The Belvidere Mercury, Vatican.
> Mercury, in the Villa Albani.
> The Farnese Mercury, British Museum.
> Mercury, Lansdowne House.
> Mercury reposing, in bronze, Naples.

HESTIA—VESTA.

The form of this goddess is that of a woman in matronly costume, yet without the character of motherliness, standing at rest or enthroned, with broad powerful forms, and a serious expression in her clear and simple features.

STATUE:—

Vesta, formerly in the Giustiniani Palace.

DIONYSUS—BACCHUS.

The elder Dionysus, commonly called the Indian Bacchus, was represented under a stately and majestic form, with a magnificent luxuriance of curling hair restrained by the mitra, gently flowing beard, clear and blooming features, and the oriental richness of an almost feminine drapery, with usually, at the same time, the drinking cup, or karchesion, and a vine-shoot in his hand. It was not till afterwards,—at the time of Praxiteles, that the youthful Dionysus, conceived as at the age of the ephebus, was modified therefrom; in him also the corporeal forms, which flow softly into one another without any prominent muscular development, bespeak the half-feminine nature of the god, and the features of the countenance present a peculiar blending of happy intoxication, with a dark and undefined longing, in which the Bacchian frame of feeling appears in its most refined form.

BUST OF INDIAN BACCHUS.

Winkelman thus characterizes him: "In the most beautiful statues, he always appears with delicate, round limbs, and the full expanded hips of the female sex, for, according to the fable, he was brought up as a maiden. The forms of his limbs are soft and flowing, as though inflated by a gentle breath, and with scarcely any indication of the bones and cartilages of the knees, just as these are found in youths of the most beautiful shape. The type of Bacchus is a lovely boy, who is treading the boundaries of the spring-time of life and adolescence, in whom emotions of voluptuousness, like the tender shoots of a plant, are budding, and who, as if between sleeping and waking, half in a dream of exquisite delight, is beginning to

collect and verify the pictures of his fancy; his features are full of
sweetness, but the joyousness of his soul is not manifested wholly in
his countenance." Yet even these forms and features admit of a

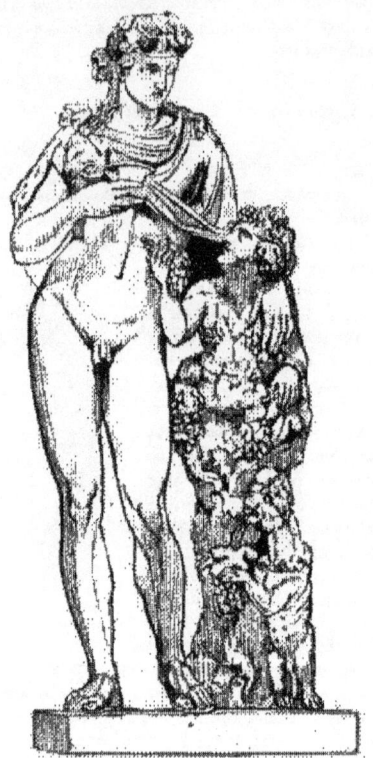

BACCHUS AND AMPELUS.

grand and powerfully impressive development, in which Dionysus is
revealed as son of the lightning, as the god of irresistible power.
The mitra around the forehead, and the vine or ivy crown throwing
its shade from above, produce a very advantageous effect in the
Bacchian expression; the hair flows down softly and in long ringlets
on the shoulders; the body, with the exception of a roe-skin, νεβρίς,

thrown around it, is usually quite naked, only the feet are sometimes covered with high, ornamented boots, the Dionysian cothurni;
the light ivy-entwined staff with the pine cone (narthex, thyrsus)
serves as a supporting sceptre. However, a himation falling down
to the loins is also suitable to the character of Dionysus; sometimes,
too, in later art he is dressed completely in female fashion. The
posture of the statues of Dionysus is generally that of reclining
comfortably, or lying; he is seldom enthroned; in gems and in
pictures we see him walking with tottering steps, and riding on his
favourite animals, or drawn by them. A favoured satyr is often
given him as a support, Methe is his cupbearer. Many other representations of Dionysus are found in works of art in connection with
the various myths related of him. His being carried by Hermes as
a child, and consigned to the care of nymphs and satyrs, his finding
his bride Ariadne, the Naxian solemnization of his nuptials, are
frequent subjects in works of art. He is also represented in the
circle of frenzied mænads, subduing and punishing Pentheus and
Lycurgus, the insulters and foes of his worship, and also the piratical
Tyrrhonians, by means of his bold satyrs, and in rich relievo representations, celebrating the triumphs of the conquest of India.

ATTRIBUTES :—
  The thyrsus, the vine, laurel, the dolphin, the tiger, a
  serpent, lynx, panther, and the ass.

ELDER OR INDIAN.
BUST :—
  Indian Bacchus, Louvre, British Museum.

STATUE :—
  Indian Bacchus, Vatican; on the border of the mantle is
  inscribed Sardanapolus.

YOUTHFUL DIONYSUS.
BUSTS :—
  Vatican, British Museum.

STATUES :—
  The Ludovisi Bacchus.
  Bacchus, Villa Albani.
  Bacchus, Louvre.
  Bacchus handing bunch of grapes to panther, Vatican.
  Bacchus pouring wine from Karchesion, Florentine Gallery.
  Farnese Bacchus, Naples.
  Richelieu Bacchus, Louvre.
  Bacchus and Ampelus, British Museum.

DEITIES IN CONNECTION WITH DIONYSUS.

SATYRS, FAUNS.

Their characteristics are limbs powerfully built, but not ennobled by gymnastics, sometimes flabby, sometimes firm ; snub-nosed, and otherwise unnobly formed countenances, with pointed goat-like

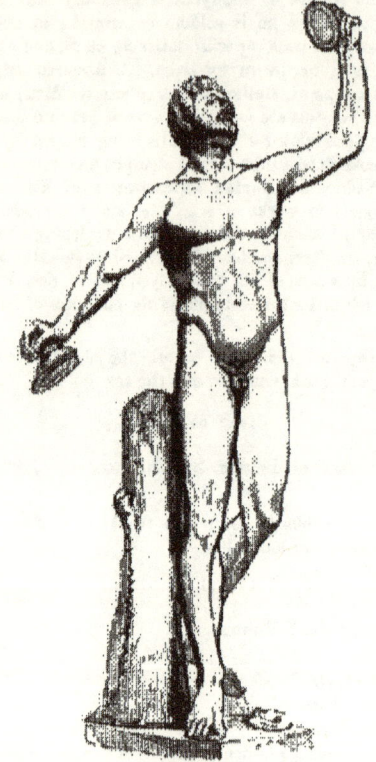

BARBERINI FAUN.

ears ; sometimes also protuberances on the neck, and in old figures baldness of the forehead ; the hair bristly and often erect ; moreover, a scanty tail ; these are the marks, in very manifold gradations, how-

ever, of the figures which were called satyrs in the genuine language
of Greek poetry and art, from which the Roman poets first ventured
to depart, who identified them with the Roman fauni, who are
described as half men, half goats, and with horns. Sometimes, however, the satyrs rise into very noble, slender shapes, which are
scarcely betrayed by anything but the pointed ears. Winkelman
says, "The most beautiful statues of fauns present to us an image of
ripe beautiful youth, in perfect proportion. Several statues of young
satyrs and fauns, resembling each other in attitude and feature,
have been found in Rome, the original of which, it is possible, was
the celebrated satyr of Praxiteles, which was regarded by the artist
himself as his best work."

The more decided satyrs' forms may be classified as follows: 1.
The gracefully reclining flute-players, with indolence, and a slight
dash of petulance, but without rudeness in the expression. 2. The
sturdy and joyous figure of the cymbalista. 3. Dancers. 4. The
wild enthusiastic, inspired by Bacchus. 5. Slender and powerfully-
built hunters. 6. Satyrs lying at ease, often with pretension to the
completion of some great work. 7. Sleepers stretched out comfortably, also in a coarse and indecent manner, exhaling the perfumes of
wine. 8. Lascivious satyrs, drawing the garments from the persons
of Bacchantes and Hermaphrodites, and struggling with them. 9.
Satyrs occupied with the processes of preparing wine in the earliest
and simplest manner, and exhibiting their rude efforts with a sort of
pride. 10. Carousing figures pouring out wine for themselves. 11. The
combatants of the Tyrrhenians, amid whose wildness there gleams
through, nevertheless, an insolent joviality. Earlier antiquity formed
satyrs more as bugbears and caricatures; the more tender and
youthful forms, in which there is combined with the satyric
character an exceedingly graceful figure and an amiable roguishness,
first made their appearance in the later Attic school. Flaxman thus
characterizes them: "The fauns are youthful, sprightly, and
tendinous, their faces round, expressive of merriment, not without
an occasional mixture of mischief."

STATUES:—

The satyr or faun, Capitol, Vatican; ancient copies of the
  Satyr of Praxiteles,
The Barberini Faun, Munich.
The Faun, *in rosso antico*, Capitol.
Rondanini Faun, British Museum.
Drunken Faun, Vatican.
The Dancing Faun, Florentine Gallery.
Young Faun playing the pipe, Louvre.

SILENI.

The older satyrs were generally named Sileni, but one of these Sileni is commonly known as the Silenus, who always accompanies Dionysus. He is usually represented as a jovial old man, with a bald head, a puck nose, fat and round, and generally intoxicated. He is generally represented riding on an ass, or supported by other satyrs.

Statues:—Silenus, with infant Bacchus in his arms, Louvre.

Ditto, Vatican.

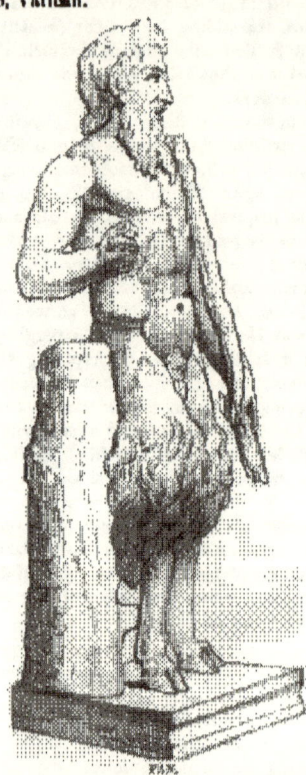

PAN.

PAN.—Before the age of Praxiteles he was usually represented in a human form, and was characterized by the shepherd's pipe, the pastoral crook, the disordered hair, and also sprouting horns. The goat-footed, horned and hook-nose form became afterwards the rule probably through the Praxitelean art. In it Pan appears as an active leaper and dancer, and the amusing buffoon in the cycle of Dionysus. As a peaceful syrinx-player, he inhabits the grottoes consecrated to him, where his figure is not unfrequently found, amid graceful nymphs, hewn out of the living rock.

STATUE:—Pan, British Museum.

MÆNADES (BACCHANTES). BACCHÆ.

The female companions of Dionysus, in his wanderings through the east, are represented as crowned with vine-leaves, clothed with

BACCHANTE.

fawn-skins, carrying in their hands the thyrsus.   They are distinguished by their revelling enthusiasm, dishevelled hair, and head thrown back, with thyrsi, swords, serpents, dismembered roe-calves, tympana, and fluttering, loose flying garments.

BAS-RELIEF :—

    Bacchante, attributed to Scopas, British Museum.

CENTAURS.

In earlier times they were represented in front entirely as men, with the body of a horse growing on to them behind ; but afterwards, perhaps from the time of Phidias, the forms were blended much

CENTAUR.

more happily, by the joining of the belly and breast of a horse to the upper part of a human body, the forms of whose countenance, pointed ears, and bristly hair betray an affinity to the satyr.

STATUES :—

    Borghese Centaur with Eros on its back, Louvre.

    Centaurs, with names of sculptors, Aristeas and Paphias, Capitol.

BAS-RELIEFS :—

    Metopes of the Parthenon.

    Phigaleian Marbles.

Eros.—Cupid.

At first Eros was represented in temple statues as a boy of developed beauty and tender grace of mien, and this mode of representation prevails throughout in the different statues of the god still

CUPID.

extant. A later art, however, after the time of Alexander, which was allied to the toying poetry of the Anacreontica, preferred the childish form for such purposes. In the imitations of the famous statue of Praxiteles, he is represented as a slender, undeveloped boy, full of liveliness and activity, earnestly endeavouring to fasten the strings to his bow. He is also frequently represented with Psyche.

STATUES:—

> Copies of the Cupid of Praxiteles, Vatican, Capitol, British Museum, Louvre, Villa Albani.
> Cupid and Psyche, Florentine Gallery.

HERMAPHRODITUS.

Hermaphroditus was a favourite subject of later art, being an artistic creation of fancy. He combines the form of the female sex, with the characteristics of the male. He is usually represented reclining in gentle slumber on a couch, or fanned while asleep by cupids.

STATUES:—

> Florentine Gallery.
> Villa Borghese.

PSYCHE.

Psyche, as the soul, appears as a virgin with butterfly wings. At a later period, after the myth of Apuleius, there are frequent representations of the loves of Eros and Psyche.

STATUE:—

> Psyche, Naples.

CHARITES. (The Graces.)

They were the attendants of Venus. In early times, they were represented draped. In later times, they were figured completely undraped, and are characterized by the joining of hands, or mutual embracing.

EARLY REPRESENTATION:—

> On triangular altar, Louvre.

STATUES:—

> In the sacristy of the Cathedral of Siena.

THE MUSES.

In the most ancient works of art we find only three muses, and their attributes are musical instruments, such as the flute, the lyre, or the barbiton; it was not until the more modern ideal of Apollo Musagetes, in the garb of the Pythian musicians, was developed,

THE MUSE.

that the number nine was established by several famous artists in regard to these virgins, who were in like manner clad for the most part in theatrical drapery, with fine intellectual countenances, distinguished from one another by expression, attributes, and sometimes also by attitudes. 1. Calliope, the muse of epic poetry, is characterized by a tablet and stylus, and sometimes by a roll of papers. 2. Clio, the muse of history, is represented either with an open roll of paper, or an open chest of books. 3. Euterpe, the muse of lyric poetry, is given a flute, and sometimes two flutes. 4. Melpomene, the muse of tragedy, is characterized by a tragic mask, the club of Hercules, or a sword, her head is surrounded with vine leaves, and she wears the cothurnus. 5. Terpsichore, the muse of choral dance and song, appears with the lyre and the plectrum. 6. Erato, the muse of erotic poetry and mimic imitation, is also characterized by a lyre. 7. Polymnia, the muse of the sublime hymn, is usually represented leaning in a pensive or meditating attitude. 8. Urania, the muse of astronomy, bears a globe in her hand. 9. Thalia, the muse of comedy, and idyllic poetry, is characterized by a comic mask, a shepherd's staff, and a wreath of ivy. They are sometimes represented with plumes on their head, supposed to typify their victory over the Sirens.

STATUES :—

   In the Vatican.
   In the Museum, Naples.
   In the Villa Borghese.

BAS-RELIEF :—

   Front of Sarcophagus, British Museum.

ÆSCULAPIUS.

Æsculapius was represented as a man of mature age, of Zeus-like but less sublime countenance, with mild benevolent expression, his copious hair encircled with a fillet, standing in the attitude of one ready to help, the himation taken about the left arm, round under the breast, and drawn tight, and the staff enwreathed with a serpent in his right hand.

STATUES :—

   Æsculapius, Vatican.
   Æsculapius, Louvre.

HYGIEIA.

The goddess of health was represented as a virgin of remarkably blooming form, who generally gives drink to a serpent from a patera in her left hand.

RHEA.—CYBELE.

HEAD OF CYBELE.

Rhea is recognised by a crown of towers, the tympanum as a symbol of her enthusiastic worship, and her car yoked with lions.

HADES.—PLUTO.

Hades, the ruler of the shadowy realm, is distinguished from his brothers, Zeus and Poseidon, by his heavier drapery, by his hair hanging down upon his forehead, and his sombre aspect.

Bust:—
    Vatican.

Statue:—
    Pluto, Vatican.

PERSEPHONE.—PROSERPINE.

She is usually represented enthroned by the side of her husband Hades, and sometimes in the act of being carried off by Pluto.

Statue:—
    Proserpine, Vatican.

MOIRÆ. (The Fates.)

They were three, Clotho, Lachesis, and Atropos. In later times, Clotho was represented as spinning; Lachesis, marking out the destiny on a globe; Atropos, sitting. Lachesis is also to be found writing, or holding a roll; Atropos showing the hour on a sundial, or holding scales.

TYCHE.—FORTUNE.

She is usually represented with a rudder, as guiding the affairs of the world, and a cornucopia as a symbol of the plentiful gifts of nature, and also with a ball at her feet, showing the varying un-

o

steadiness of fortune. Sometimes she wears a diadem, and a veil
hanging over the back of her head to indicate her mysterious
origin.

FORTUNE.

STATUES :—

    Fortune, Vatican.
    Fortune, British Museum.

NEMESIS.

In the earlier times, Nemesis was scarcely to be distinguished
from the representations of Aphrodite. So slight was the distinction
between the representations of Nemesis and Aphrodite, that Agoracritus, the sculptor, in losing the prize in competition with Alcamenes, for making an Aphrodite, by a slight change (supposed to be

by the addition of some attribute) transformed his Aphrodite into a Nemesis, afterwards called the Nemesis Rhamnusia. A fragment of this statue is now in the British Museum. In later art she is distinguished by the characteristic posture of the right arm; the arm being half raised, so as to form an angle, and the robe partly withdrawn from the breast. Sometimes a wheel lies at her feet.

IRIS.

Iris, the light-winged messenger of the gods, is sometimes represented in a long and wide tunic, over which hangs a light upper garment; sometimes in a short tunic, with wings to her shoulders and wings to her feet, carrying the herald's staff in her left hand, and in her right hand a vase (επρχους).

FLORA,

The goddess of flowers and spring, is usually represented with flowers in her hand.

STATUE:—

Farnese Flora, Naples.

NIKE.—VICTORY.

Victory is represented in a short tunic, with wings, and usually carries a palm. She is also represented writing on a shield, and frequently sacrificing a bull.

STATUE:—

Victory, bronze, Museum, Brescia.

BAS-RELIEF of Victory sacrificing a bull:—

British Museum.

HEBE.

Hebe is generally represented completely draped, and with wings, pouring nectar from a vase.

HERCULES.

The heroic ideal is expressed with the highest force in Hercules, who was pre-eminently an Hellenic national hero. Strength, steeled and proved by exertion, is the main feature, which early Greek art already indicated in its creations, but Myron and Lysippus especially unfolded into a form which could not again be outdone. Even in the statues of the youthful Hercules, which are often extremely noble and graceful, this concentrated energy is displayed in the enormous strength of the muscles of his neck, the thickly-set short curls of his small head, the comparatively small eyes, the great size and prominence of the lower portion of the forehead, and the form

o 2

of the entire limbs. But the character of the victorious combatant
of monsters, of the toil-laden hero, is exhibited more clearly by the
matured figure, such as it was perfected by Lysippus, with especial
predilection, in the protuberant layers of muscle developed by
infinite labour, the huge thighs, shoulders, arms, breast, and back,
and also in the earnest features of his compressed countenance, in

HEAD OF HERCULES.

which the impression produced by exertion and fatigue has not been
effaced by transient repose. Both forms can still be pointed out in
an almost unlimited cycle of adventures and combats; and the
development of the hero can be traced from the serpent-quelling
child throughout all the events of his life, his twelve labours
forming the most frequent subjects of representation. In earliest
art, as well as at a later period, the lion's hide, the club and the bow,
were the ordinary accoutrements of the hero. Other phases of his
character are disclosed by his relation to Omphale—the hero spinning
in transparent female drapery, and the voluptuous woman in heroic
nudity, with club and lion's hide. He is supposed to be represented
in the famous masterpiece, the Torso Belvidere, whose posture
entirely agrees with that of the hero reposing among satyrs.
Hercules here rested on his right arm, in which he probably held a
cup (skyphos), and had the left doubled over his head. The most
celebrated statue of Hercules is the so-called Hercules Farnese,
which bears the name of the sculptor inscribed on it—Glycon, the
Athenian. From its frequent repetition in bronze and marble, on
gems and coins, it must have been universally admired in ancient
times. It represents Hercules resting on his club. It is chiefly

remarkable for the anatomical detail displayed in the body and the limbs. Flaxman remarks that statues of a much earlier date have the proportions of common men, and that a series of them may be

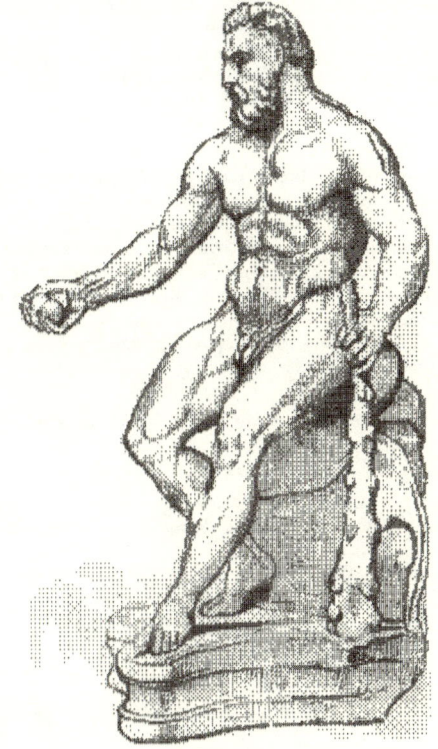

HERCULES.

found in various collections, gradually increasing to the terrific strength of the Glyconic statue.

YOUNG HERCULES.

BUSTS:—
      British Museum.
STATUE:—
      Lansdown Collection.

ELDER HERCULES.

Busts:—

  In the British Museum.

Statues:—

  The Farnese Hercules, Naples.
  The Torso Belvidere, Vatican.
  Hercules and Anteus, Pitti Palace, Florence.
  Small statues in the British Museum.

THESEUS.

In sculpture, not less than mythology, the heroic form of Theseus was, as early as the Phidian school, fashioned after that of Hercules; he received, however, a less compact structure of body, one which especially indicated activity in wrestling, a less compressed and more graceful form of countenance, and short but less crisped hair; his costume is usually the lion's hide and club, sometimes also the chlamys and petasus, after the manner of Attic ephebi. His contest with the Amazons, and his vanquishing the Minotaur, form the chief subjects of his myth.

Statues:—

  Theseus, Pediment of Parthenon, British Museum.

AMAZONS.

In statues and reliefs they were represented in simple light drapery, and with strong rounded forms of the limbs, which were

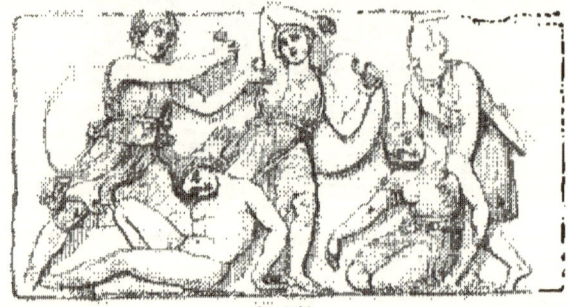

AMAZONS.

given to them at the Polyclitan period. They are usually represented in the Doric chiton.

STATUES :—

    Amazon, with arm uplifted, Vatican, Capitol.

BAS RELIEF :—

    Phigaleian Frieze.
    Front of Sarcophagus, Capitol.

ACHILLES.

The hair reared up like a mane, the nostrils swollen with courage and pride, a slender pillared neck, and thoroughly noble and powerful forms of body belong to the character of Achilles, according to ancient testimonies, with which such at least of the monuments as are authentic and more carefully handled, are in accordance ; a certain heroic attitude, in which the one leg is quickly advanced, and the himation falls negligently over the thigh of that limb, is also at least frequently introduced in Achilles ; when he is seated, the himation is drawn, in the same way as in Zeus, around the lower portions of the figure.

BUSTS :—

    Munich. Dresden. Louvre.

STATUES :—

    Borghese Achilles.

MELEAGER.

Meleager appears in a celebrated statue as a slender but powerful youth, with broad chest, active limbs, curling hair, and a chlamys thrown back and wrapped round the left arm, after the manner of hunters ; he is a huntsman among heroes ; the boar's head, on which he leans, points him out unmistakeably.

STATUE :—

    Meleager, Vatican.

ORPHEUS.

The Thracian Orpheus appears as an inspired Citharœdus, with a certain effeminacy of conformation, in tolerably pure Hellenic costume in earlier art ; it was at a later period that he received the Phrygian garb.

PERSEUS.

Perseus appears very like Hermes in configuration and costume. He is frequently represented with talaria, and sometimes holds the head of Medusa in his hand.

THE DIOSCURI.—CASTOR.—POLLUX.

To the Dioscuri, who always retained very much of their divine nature, belong a perfectly unblemished youthful beauty, an equally slender and powerful shape, and, as an almost never-failing attribute, the half-oval form of the hat, or at least hair lying close at the back of the head, but projecting in thick curls around the forehead and temples. The distinction between Polydeuces the boxer, and Castor, in his equestrian costume, is only to be found where they are represented in heroic circumstances, not where they are exhibited as objects of worship, as the Athenian Anakes and as genii of light in its rising and setting. The most celebrated statues of these horse-tamers are the two on the Quirinal Hill at Rome; though

CASTOR MANAGING A HORSE.

styled the works of Phidias and Praxiteles, they are supposed to have been executed at Rome, probably after the time of Augustus, from Greek originals; they are of colossal proportions, being 18 feet high.

STATUES:—

    Castor and Pollux, Quirinal Hill, Rome.

BAS-RELIEFS.

BAS-RELIEFS are works of sculpture in which the objects are not isolated, but are attached to a background, or to a plane surface, on which sometimes the sculptured figures were placed, or as is more generally the case, the entire background and figures were formed of the same material. The term alto-rilievo is used when the figures seem almost entirely detached from the background: mezzo-rilievo when the figure projects from the background by about a half. Basso-rilievo, or bas-relief, when the figures project slightly from the background, and seem, so to say, flattened on the background; but common use has given to all these works of sculpture the general name of bas-reliefs, or basso-rilievo. By the Greeks the term anaglypta was applied to all works in relief in general. The "ectypa sculptura" of Pliny also means works in relief.

The work of the sculptor in bas-reliefs presents greater difficulty in proportion as the projection of the figure is less; for it requires consummate art to give size and natural proportions to a figure slightly relieved.

In bas-reliefs the composition, the picturesque arrangement, and the grouping of the figures, are principally studied, and here another difficulty presents itself, as the sculptor has but one background, and not several, each distant from the other, as is the case in painting. In bas-reliefs the study of the light it receives is of the greatest importance, for the shadows are real shadows, not artificial or imitated, and consequently the effect ought to be carefully calculated. The alto-rilievo is calculated for a high light, and the basso-rilievo for a subdued light.

Egyptian.—Bas-relief was in general use among the Egyptians. It was employed to decorate the front of the propyla of their temples and of their tombs. The style of relief peculiar to the Egyptians was the intaglio rilievato, or koilanaglypha, as termed by the Greeks. The flat surface of the stone was cut into, and thus formed the outline of the object to be represented. Within this sunk space the Egyptian artist contrived to raise the figure by cutting it deepest all round the edge, and allowing it to rise in a curved form towards the central parts, so that there was no salient point beyond the original plane. The degree of elevation given to this sunk relief is very different in various specimens: in some it is scarcely perceptible, while in others the central parts of the relief are almost on a level with the tablet. The figures were always sculptured in profile. The sepulchral tablets frequently afford examples of bas-reliefs. An

EGYPTIAN ALTO-RILIEVO.

example of alto-rilievo will be found in a stele, or sculptured monument, in the British Museum, which represents the monarch, Thotmes III., supported by the god Munta, and the goddess Athor.

Etruscan.—The earliest known examples of Etruscan bas-reliefs are the cippi, or so-called "altars" of fetid limestone, from Chiusi and its neighbourhood. They show an archaic style of art. Bas-reliefs also of an archaic style are found on the façades of the rock-hewn sepulchres, but chiefly on sarcophagi and cinerary urns. The cinerary urns of Volterra and Perugia are of a later period, and have more of a Roman than a Greek character.

Greek and Roman.—Bas-reliefs were executed by the Greeks from the earliest period of art, and by the Romans especially in the early period of the Empire. The same diversity of style will be

ALTO-RILIEVO.

found in these, according to the period of their execution; the same attributes, the same traditions in connection with gods and men; what has been said with regard to the characteristics and distinctive styles of statues and busts, can be equally applied to bas-reliefs. Bas-reliefs were generally used for the purpose of adorning temples, altars, the bases of statues, and also sarcophagi and tombs. In general, some well-known myth of a god, or hero, was traced on them.

MEZZO-RILIEVO.

The finest existing examples of alto-rilievo are those metopes which adorned the temple of the Parthenon. As they were destined to receive the open light, they were executed in bolder relief, to insure the masses of shadow which make them conspicuous. They represent the contests between the Centaurs and the Athenians.

sculptured metopes of the temples of Selinus, in Sicily, afford examples of the earliest styles of alto-rilievo.

Mezzo-rilievo was generally used to adorn sculptured vases and arms. These sculptured vases probably ornamented interiors, where any indistinctness in their distant effect, or in unfavourable light, might be obviated by closer inspection. The celebrated Medicean and Borghesan vases, the finest known examples, are ornamented with mezzi-rilievi. The frieze encircling the choragic monument of Lysicrates is also in mezzo-rilievo. Mezzo-rilievo was also employed (as well as alto-rilievo, when in situations not exposed to accidents) to ornament tombs and sarcophagi.

Bas-relief, or basso-rilievo, may be fully exemplified in the most perfect examples of that art in the celebrated Panathenaic frieze of the Parthenon. It was executed under the direction of Phidias

BAS-RELIEF.

himself; it was one uninterrupted series of bas-reliefs, which occupied the upper part of the Parthenon within the colonnade, and which was continued entirely around the building. By its position it only obtained a secondary light. Being placed immediately below the soffit, it received all its light from between the columns, and by reflection from the pavement below. The flatness of the sculpture is thus sufficiently accounted for; had the relief been prominent, the upper parts could not have been seen; the shade projected by the sculpture would have rendered it dark, and the parts would have been reduced by their shadows. The subject represents the sacred

procession, which was celebrated every fifth year at Athens, in
honour of Minerva, conveying in solemn pomp to the temple of the
Parthenon the πέπλος, or sacred veil, which was to be suspended before the statue of the goddess within the temple.   Mr. Westmacott

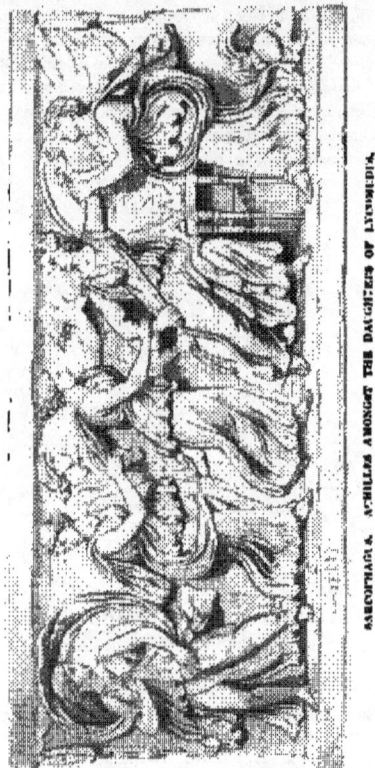

SARCOPHAGUS. ACHILLES AMONGST THE DAUGHTERS OF LYCOMEDES.

remarks that these works are unquestionably the finest specimens of
the art that exist, and they illustrate, fully and admirably, the progress, and it may be said, the consummation, of sculpture. They
exhibit in a remarkable degree all the qualities that constitute fine
art,—truth, beauty, and perfect execution. In the forms, the most

perfect, the most appropriate, and the most graceful, have been
selected. The earliest known example of bas-relief is that in the
Louvre representing Agamemnon and Talthybius. It is in very low
relief. In style it corresponds with that of the early vase painting.
In the decline of art in Greece, bas-reliefs were erected in memory
of illustrious men instead of statues. In Rome bas-reliefs were
more particularly employed in adorning arches of triumph, triumphal
columns, and especially sarcophagi. The subjects which decorated

GREEK VASE.

the front of these funereal monuments were various, though sometimes repeated when a subject was composed by a celebrated artist.
In general the bas-reliefs of sarcophagi are of inferior workmanship;
sometimes the last farewell of the deceased is represented; sometimes two figures only, and the one which is the object of the atten-
tions of the other, is the figure of the deceased. Others represent
mythological subjects. One in the Capitol presents a bas-relief
which Flaxman considers one of the finest specimens of bas-relief.
It represents the battle of Theseus and Amazons. An excellent example, in the British Museum, forming the front of a sarcophagus,
represents Achilles amongst the daughters of Lycomedes. It has
been remarked with regard to some sarcophagi that the head of the
principal figure is not finished: it has been inferred from this that
the sculptors preparing these monuments as objects for sale, did not

terminate the head until the sarcophagus was sold, endeavouring then to give, as well as he was able, the portrait of the deceased. Funereal urns are also frequently ornamented with bas-reliefs, several examples of which will be found in the British Museum. Sepulchral stelæ are sometimes ornamented with bas-reliefs. They are generally in low relief, and usually represent some scene in connection with the memory of the deceased.

MATERIALS OF SCULPTURE.

We extract the following excellent summary of the materials of sculpture from Professor Westmacott's "Handbook of Sculpture:" — " Every substance that could by possibility be used for carved works has been employed by sculptors. Among the Egyptians especially the hardest were preferred, as basalt, porphyry, and granite, though they also worked extensively in other materials. Marble, various kinds of alabaster, stone, ivory, bone, and wood of all kinds, were used according to circumstances. The variety of marbles both found and recorded is almost infinite. Pliny supplies an interesting catalogue of those most generally employed in ancient times. The chief Greek marbles were the Parian and the Pentelic. The former was found in the island of Paros, whence its general name; but it is also alluded to as the marble of Marpessus, from the particular mountain where it abounded. Its colour is a warm or creamy white, and it is remarkable for a sparkling quality in its crystals, from which it is supposed it received its epithet of 'lychnoum.' The Pentelic marble came from Mount Pentelicus, in the neighbourhood of Athens. Its colour also is white, but it often has blue or grey, and even light green streaks running through it, which gave it a cold tone compared with the Parian marble. The ancients also much esteemed a marble procured from Mount Hymettus in Attica. It bore in many respects a close resemblance to the Pentelic. A great quantity of this marble was imported into Italy after the conquest of Greece by the Romans. A marble of Thasus was also much used, but more for architecture than for sculpture. It was in this way employed for baths, fishponds, and for encasing buildings. Italy produces marble of a very fine quality. That spoken of as the marble of Luni was procured from the range of mountains near which are situated the modern towns of Massa and Carrara. It does not appear that it was known, or its quarries worked before the time of Julius Cæsar, in the century before the birth of Christ. Remains of the former working in the quarries of Luni may still be traced; and it is thought the material found here was of a somewhat finer texture than the more modern produce. In many respects the Italian is superior to the Parian and Pentelic marbles. The grain of the Carrara marble is much closer and finer than that of Greece, and its general colour is a rich white. It must, however, be admitted that the Carrara marble, now so generally used by sculptors, is not often found quite pure in very large blocks. Veins and spots of grey and blue-black, and red and yellow streaks (the latter probably oxides of iron) occur in it, and the quality or texture of the material varies also in different parts of the quarries. Occasionally large crystals are found which resist the chisel. The Romans formerly procured a white marble from some quarries they worked in Africa. Marble is no longer procured, as a rule, from Greece, though occasionally blocks of it are used. This, however, is exceptional, and the only supply for general purposes of sculpture in modern times is from the above named source—the mountain quarries in the former duchy of Massa and Carrara, on the west coast of Italy. Different kinds of marble were frequently employed by the later Romans in the same piece of sculpture, which was then termed polylithic.

The composition which was so extensively used by the ancients for statues, called by the Greeks *chalcos* (χαλκός) the Romans *æs*, and the moderns *bronze*, from the Italian *bronzo*, a name derived from its colour—a rich brown—is a mixture of copper and tin, with sometimes small portions of other metals. The composition of this material, so extensively used by the artists of antiquity, appears to have been a subject of the greatest care. The mere list of titles of the different kinds of bronze known to and used by the ancients is astonishing from its extent, and the refinements it suggests in their practice. A few of the most important only need be mentioned to show the student how profoundly all subjects connected with their art were considered by the great masters of sculpture. There were even rival schools for its preparation. Pliny especially records those of Ægina and Delos; and says the highest honour was given to the Delian and the next to the Æginetan bronze. It has been supposed from a passage in Plutarch that this famous bronze of Delos was of a pale colour; but it appears that in the time of this writer the secret of its composition was unknown. Pliny says that there was rivalry between two of the greatest sculptors of the best period of the art in the material each employed. Myron used the bronze of Delos, Polycletus that of Ægina. Besides these more especially celebrated bronzes of Delos and Ægina, there were at least three, if not more, varieties of the Corinthian. That which

P

was called *æs Candidum* is supposed to have had a portion of silver mixed with it, which gave it a white or light tint. There was also the famous *æs Corinthium*, which it was pretended was accidentally produced by the melting and running together of various metals (especially gold and bronze), at the burning of Corinth by L. Mummius, about 146 B.C. A third was a composition of equal portions of different metals. The composition of what is now known as bronze, an alloy of tin with copper, gives, on analysis, very nearly the same results in all the examples which have been subjected to examination. From 10 to 12 parts of tin occur in 100 parts, the remainder being copper.

Among the varieties of wood used by the ancients for sculpture, the oak, cypress, cedar, box, sycamore, pine, fig, the vine, and ebony occur. Pausanias mentions numerous statues made of wood, ξόανα, but all these works have perished.

Figures of wood, usually of small dimensions, have constantly been found in Egypt, preserved in the most ancient tombs; but there are also examples of Egyptian statues on a larger scale, and even of life size, made of wood. The wood of which they are made is usually sycamore.

The ancients also used clay (terra cotta) extensively as a material for sculpture, as may be seen from the countless number of figures, reliefs, lamps, architectural ornaments, vases, domestic utensils, and other objects, which are preserved in museums and in similar collections. Usually such works are of small size; but there are statues in the Museum at Naples, which prove it was also used for statues of large dimensions.

PAINTING.

Egyptian.—The Egyptians cultivated painting from the highest antiquity; the most ancient monuments of this people afford examples of it, such as the temples, tombs, mummies, and papyri. It seems to have originated among them from their fashion of colouring bas-reliefs and statues. The colours they usually employed on the painted reliefs and on the stuccoes are black, blue, red, green, and yellow. These are always kept distinct, and never blended. Of blue, they used both a darker and a lighter shade. Red was used to represent the human flesh. Most objects in Egyptian painting had a distinct and conventional colour. The Egyptian colours have been analyzed by Professor John of Berlin. All the blues appear to be oxides of copper, with a small intermixture of iron; the result of the analysis never showed any cobalt in any of the blues. The reds may be divided into brown reds, and brick coloured reds, and are composed of a brown-red oxide of iron mixed with lime. The greens are a mixture of a yellow vegetable pigment with a copper blue. The bluesh-green colour sometimes observed on Egyptian antiquities is a faded copper-blue. The yellows appear to be vegetable colours; they are often very pure, and of a bright sulphur colour. The blacks might be from wine lees, burnt pitch, charcoal, or soot. The whites were generally, no doubt, preparations of lime

AN ARTIST SEATED.

or gypsum. Madder also appears to have been used, at least for the reddish coloured dye of the mummy cloths. These colours were used on the hardest and softest stones, on wood, linen, and papyrus. The sculptures of the most ancient temples were coloured. The tombs of the kings exhibit endless paintings on their walls. Three

classes of paintings have been discovered in Egypt; those on the
walls, those on the cases and cloths of mummies, and those on
papyrus rolls. The coloured bas-reliefs may be classed among the
paintings. The Egyptians painted detached statues also, examples
of which will be found in the British Museum. No 31 has received
several coats of paint. They painted also architectural decorations
and columns. Egyptian painting was imbued with one common
character, and the same conventional style always prevailed. It
was not an imitation of nature, but merely the harmonious combination of certain hues, which they well understood, as Sir
Gardner Wilkinson remarks. The Egyptian artists had no idea
of perspective; objects on the same plane, instead of being shown
one behind another, were placed in succession one above another,
on the perpendicular wall.

The following description of the mode in which the painted
bas-reliefs were executed is from Belzoni's account of the great
tomb which he opened in the Biban el Molouk, or valley of the
tombs of the kings, at Thebes. In this instance, the reliefs are cut
out of the natural rock in which the excavation was made; but a
similar process must have been adopted with bas reliefs cut on any
surface of stone. All the figures and hieroglyphics in this tomb are
in bas-relief, and painted, with the exception of one chamber, which
Belzoni called the outline chamber, from its not being finished, but
only prepared for the sculptor. The first process was to make the
wall quite smooth, filling up the interstices, if any, with plaster.
The outline of the figures was then drawn by some apprentice or
inferior hand, in red lines, and corrected by the principal workman
in black. Then the sculptor chiselled out the form, cutting away
the stone all round the outline, which would leave the figure
standing out above the rest of the stone to the height of half an
inch, or less if the figure were a small one. The angles of the
bas-relief were afterwards rounded, so as to diminish the prominence
of the object, the dress and the limbs were marked by narrow lines,
not more than the thickness of a half-crown in depth, but exact
enough to produce the desired effect. The next process was to lay
on a coat of lime white work, which in these tombs is so beautiful
and clear as to surpass the finest paper. The painter then completed his work, using the colours already described. When the
figures were finished, a coat of varnish was laid on; or, perhaps, in
some cases it was incorporated.

The process for painting on the walls, both of the natural rock and
constructed edifices, where there were no bas-reliefs, was pretty
nearly the same. The ground was covered with a thick layer of fine

plaster, consisting of lime and gypsum, which was carefully smoothed and polished. Upon this a thin coat of lime whitewash was laid, and on it the colours were painted, which were bound fast either by animal glue, or occasionally with wax.

The Egyptians painted also on wood. The process adopted was the following:—First a thin layer of whitewash or fine lime was laid immediately on the wood, and on this the colours, being first mixed with glue water, were placed by means of a brush. Sometimes a more costly process was adopted in the case of sarcophagi of wood. An almost similar process was adopted in painting on mummy cloths and mummy cases. The paintings on the papyrus are scarcely more than coloured hieroglyphics.

The variety of paintings, or exact representation of natural objects, or of objects used in the arts, is very considerable, and it is in the tombs that this endless variety is found represented. Besides religious or funereal ceremonies, we find represented there a number of scenes derived from civil, military, and domestic life, agricultural works, fishing, the chase, dances, gymnastic games, instruments of music, furniture of the greatest elegance; lastly, views of extensive gardens, with ponds containing fish and birds, and surrounded by fruit-trees.

The Egyptians painted portraits also. Rosellini gives a series of portraits of Egyptian kings, some from painted bas-reliefs, others from paintings on the walls of tombs. They go as far back as Amunoph I. of the eighteenth dynasty. They are all in profile; and though drawn with strict regard to certain conventions, still the outline of the face, from the forehead to the chin, has a marked individual character, and indicates that it is intended to designate a particular individual.

Etruscan.—The Etruscans, it is said, cultivated painting before the Greeks, and Pliny attributes to the former a certain degree of perfection before the Greeks had emerged from the infancy of the art. Ancient paintings at Ardea, in Etruria, and at Lanuvium still retained, in the time of Pliny, all their primitive freshness. According to Pliny, paintings of a still earlier date were to be seen at Cære, another Etruscan city. These paintings mentioned by Pliny were commonly believed to be earlier than the foundation of Rome. At the present day the tombs of Etruria afford examples of Etruscan painting in every stage of its development, from the rudeness and conventionality of early art in the tomb of Veii to the correctness and ease of design, and the more perfect development of the art exhibited in the painted scenes in the tombs of Tarquinii. In one of these tombs the pilasters

are profusely adorned with arabesques, and a frieze which runs round
the side of the tomb is composed of painted figures draped, winged,
armed, fighting, or borne in chariots. The subjects of these paintings
are various; in them we find the ideas of the Etruscans on the state
of the soul after death, combats of warriors, banquets, funereal scenes.
The Etruscans painted also bas-reliefs and statues.

Greek.—The Greeks carried painting to the highest degree of perfection; their first attempts were long posterior to those of the Egyptians; they do not even date as far back as the epoch of the siege of
Troy; and Pliny remarks that Homer does not mention painting.
The Greeks always cultivated sculpture in preference. Pausanias
enumerates only 88 paintings, and 43 portraits; he describes on the
other hand 2827 statues. These were, in fact, more suitable ornaments to public places, and the gods were always represented in the
temple by sculpture. In Greece painting followed the invariable
law of development. Its cycle was run through. Painting passed
through the successive stages of rise, progress, maturity, decline, and
decay. Painting in Greece is said to have had its origin in Sicyon,
and to have been originally more outline, or monogrammon. After
this the outlines were filled in, and light and shade introduced of
one colour, and hence were styled monochromes. Cimon of Cleonæ
is the first who is mentioned as having advanced the art of painting
in Greece, and to have emancipated it from its archaic rigidity. He
is also supposed to have been the first who used a variety of colours,
and to have introduced foreshortening. The first painter of great
renown was Polygnotus. Accurate drawing, and a noble and distinct
manner of characterizing the most different mythological forms was
his great merit; his female figures also possessed charms and grace.
His large tabular pictures were conceived with great knowledge of
legends and in an earnest religious spirit. A more advanced stage
of improved painting began with Zeuxis, in which art aimed at
illusion of the senses and external charms. He appears to have been
equally distinguished in the representation of female charms (his
Helena of Crotona), and of the sublime majesty of Zeus on his throne.
His rival Parrhasius excelled in giving a roundness and a beautiful
contour to his figures, and was remarkable for the richness and
variety of his creations. His numerous pictures of gods and heroes
attained the highest consideration in art. He was overcome, however, in a pictorial contest by the ingenious Timanthes, in whose
Sacrifice of Iphigenia the ancients admired the expression of grief
carried to that pitch of intensity at which art had only dared to
hint. The most striking feature in the picture was the concealment

of the face of Agamemnon in his mantle.* Before all, however,
ranks the great Apelles, who united the advantages of his native
Ionia—grace, sensual charms, and rich colouring—with the scientific
serenity of the Sicyonian school. To his highly endowed mind was
imparted grace (charis), a quality which he himself avowed as
peculiarly his, and which serves to unite all the other gifts and
faculties which the painter requires; perhaps in none of his pictures
was it exhibited in such perfection as in his famous Anadyomene.
But heroic subjects were likewise adapted to his genius, especially
grandly-conceived portraits, such as the numerous likenesses of
Alexander, his father, and his generals. He not only represented
Alexander with the thunderbolt in his hand, but he even attempted,
as the master in light and shade, to paint thunderstorms, probably
at the same time as natural scenes and mythological personifications.
The Anadyomene was transferred from Cos by Augustus to the
temple of D. Julius at Rome, where, however, it was in a decayed
state even at the time of Nero. Contemporaneously with him
flourished Protogenes and Nicias; Protogenes was both a painter
and a statuary, and was celebrated for the high finish of his works.
Nicias of Athens was celebrated for the delicacy with which he
painted females. He was also famous as an encaustic painter, and
was employed by Praxiteles to apply his art to his statues. The
glorious art of these masters, as far as regards light, tone, and local
colours, is lost to us, and we know nothing of it except from obscure
notices and later imitations. It is not thus necessary to speak at
length of the various schools of painting in Greece, their works being
all lost, the knowledge of the characteristics peculiar to each school
would be at the present day perfectly useless. Painting had to follow
the invariable law of all development; having reached a period of
maturity, it followed, as a necessary consequence, that the period of
decline should begin. The tendencies which are peculiar to this
period gave birth sometimes to pictures which ministered to a low
sensuality; sometimes to works which attracted by their effects
of light, and also to caricatures and travesties of mythological
subjects.

We shall now make a few extracts from Mr. Wornum's excellent

* The concealment of the face of Agamemnon in this picture has been generally
considered as a " trick," or ingenious invention of Timanthes; when it was the
result of a fundamental law in Greek art—to represent alone what was beautiful,
and never to present to the eye anything repulsive or disagreeable: the features of
a father convulsed with grief would not have been a pleasing object to gaze on,
hence the painter, fully conscious of the laws of his art, concealed the countenance
of Agamemnon.

article on the vehicles, materials, colours, and methods of painting used by the Greeks.

The Greeks painted with wax, rosin, and in water-colours, to which they gave a proper consistency, according to the material upon which they painted, with gum, glue, and the white of egg; gum and glue were the most common.

They painted upon wood, clay, plaster, stone, parchment, and canvas. They generally painted upon panels or tablets (πίνακες, tabulæ), and very rarely upon walls; and an easel, similar to what is now used, was common among the ancients. These panels when finished were fixed into frames of various descriptions and materials, and encased in walls. The ancients used also a palette very similar to that used by the moderns, as is sufficiently attested by a fresco painting from Pompeii, which represents a female painting a copy of a Hermes, for a votive tablet, with a palette in her left hand.

The earlier Grecian masters used only four colours: the earth of Melos for white; Attic ochre for yellow; Sinopis, an earth from Pontus, for red; and lampblack; and it was with these simple elements that Zeuxis, Polygnotus, and others of that age, executed their celebrated works. By degrees new colouring substances were found, such as were used by Apelles and Protogenes.

So great, indeed, is the number of pigments mentioned by ancient authors, and such the beauty of them, that it is very doubtful whether, with all the help of modern science, modern artists possess any advantage in this respect over their predecessors.

We now give the following list of colours, known to be generally used by ancient painters :—

Red.—The ancient reds were very numerous, κιννάβαρι, μίλτος, cinnabaris, cinnabar, vermilion, bisulphuret of mercury, called also by Pliny and Vitruvius, minium. The κιννάβαρι Ἰνδικός, cinnabaris Indica, mentioned by Pliny and Dioscorides, was what is vulgarly called dragon's blood, the resin obtained from various species of the calamus palm. Μίλτος seems to have had various significations; it was used for cinnabaris, minium, red lead, and rubrica, red ochre. There were various kinds of rubrica; all were, however, red oxides, of which the best were the Lemnian, from the Isle of Lemnos, and the Cappadocian, called by the Romans rubrica sinopica, by the Greeks, Σινωπίς, from Sinope in Paphlagonia. Minium, red oxide of lead, red lead, was called by the Romans cerussa usta, and, according to Vitruvius, sandaracha; by the Greeks μίλτος, and according to Dioscorides, σανδαράχη. It was the colour which we now call vermilion.

The Roman sandaracha seems to have had various significations. Pliny speaks of different shades of sandaracha; there was also a compound colour of equal parts of sandaracha and rubrica calcined, called sandyx, which Sir H. Davy supposed to approach our crimson in tint; in painting it was frequently glazed with purple to give it additional lustre.

Yellow.—Yellow-ochre, hydrated peroxide of iron, the *sil* of the Romans, the *ὤχρα* of the Greeks, formed the base of many other yellows, mixed with various colours and carbonate of lime. Ochre was procured from different parts—the Attic was considered the best; sometimes the paler sort of sandaracha was used for yellow.

Green.—Chrysocolla, which appears to have been green carbonate of copper, or malachite (green verditer), was the green most approved of by the ancients; there was also an artificial kind which was made from clay impregnated with sulphate of copper (blue vitriol) rendered green by a yellow die. The commonest and cheapest colours were the Appianum, which was a clay, and the creta viridis, the common green earth of Verona.

Blue.—The ancient blues were very numerous; the principal of these was coeruleum, *κύανος*, azure, a species of verditer, or blue carbonate of copper, of which there were many varieties. The Alexandrian was the most valued, as approaching the nearest to ultramarine. It was also manufactured at Pozzuoli. This imitation was called coelon. Armenium was a metallic colour, and was prepared by being ground to an impalpable powder. It was of a light blue colour, and cost 30 sesterces a pound, about 4s. 11d. It has been conjectured that ultramarine (lapis lazuli) was known to the ancients under the name of armonium, from Armenia, whence it was procured. It is evident, however, from Pliny's description, that the 'sapphirus' of the ancients was the lapis lazuli of the present day. It came from Media.

Indigo, indicum, was well known to the ancients.

Purple.—The ancients had several kinds of purple, purpurissimum, ostrum, hysginum, and various compound colours. Purpurissimum was made from creta argentaria, a fine chalk or clay, steeped in a purple dye, obtained from the murex (πορφύρα). In colour it ranged between minium and blue, and included every degree in the scale of purple shades. The best sort came from Pozzuoli. Purpurissimum indicum was brought from India. It was of a deep blue, and probably was the same as indigo. Ostrum was a liquid colour, to which the proper consistence was given by adding honey. It was produced from the secretion of a fish called ostrum, οστρον, and differed in tint according to the country from whence it came; being deeper and more violet when brought from the northern, redder when from the southern coasts, of the Mediterranean. The Roman ostrum was a compound of red ochre and blue oxide of copper. Hysginum, according to Vitruvius, is a colour between scarlet and purple. The celebrated Tyrian dye was a dark, rich purple, of the colour of coagulated blood, but, when held against the light, showed a crimson hue. It was produced by a combination of the secretions of the murex and buccinum. In preparing the dye the buccinum was used last, the dye of the murex being necessary to render the colours fast, while the buccinum enlivened by its tint of red the dark hue of the murex. Sir H. Davy, on examining a rose-coloured substance, found in the baths of Titus, which in its interior had a lustre approaching to that of carmine, considered it a specimen of the best Tyrian purple.

Brown.—Ochra usta, burnt ochre.—The browns were ochres calcined, oxides of iron and manganese, and compounds of ochres and blacks.

Black.—Atramentum, or black, was of two sorts, natural and artificial. The natural was made from a black earth, or from the secretion of the cuttle-fish, sepia. The artificial was made of the dregs of wine carbonized, calcined ivory, or lamp-black. The atramentum indicum, mentioned by Pliny, was probably the Chinese Indian ink.

White.—The ordinary Greek white was melinum, an earth from the Isle of Melos; for fresco-painting the best was the African paraetonium. There was also a white earth of Eretria, and the annularian white. Carbonate of lead, or white-lead, cerussa, was apparently not much used by the ancient painters. It has not been found in any of the remains of painting in Roman ruins.

Methods of Painting.—There were two distinct classes of painting practised by the ancients—in water-colours, and in wax; both of which were practised in various ways. Of the former the principal were fresco, al fresco; and the various kinds of distemper (a tempera), with glue, with the white of egg, or with gums (a guazzo); and with wax or rosins when those were rendered by any means vehicles that could be worked with water. Of this latter the principle was through fire (διὰ πυρός), turned encaustic (ἐγκαυστική ονομαστικα).

Fresco was probably little employed by the ancients for works of imitative art, but it appears to have been the ordinary method of simply colouring walls, especially amongst the Romans. Colouring al fresco, in which the colours were mixed simply in water, as the term implies, was applied when the composition of the stucco on the walls was still wet (udo tectorio), and on that account was limited to certain colours, for no colours except earths can be employed in this way.

The fresco walls, when painted, were covered with an encaustic varnish, both to heighten the colours and to preserve them from the injurious effects of the sun or the weather. Vitruvius describes the process as a Greek practice, which they term καυσις. When the wall was coloured and dry, Punic wax, melted and tempered with a little oil, was rubbed over it with a hard brush (seta) ; this was made smooth and even by applying a cauterium, or an iron pan, filled with live coals, over the surface, as near to it as was just necessary to melt the wax; it was then rubbed with a candle (wax) and a clean cloth. In encaustic painting the wax colours were *burnt into* the ground by means of a hot iron (called cauterium) or pan of hot coals being held near the surface of the picture. The mere process of burning in, constitutes the whole difference between encaustic and the ordinary method of painting with wax colours.

POLYCHROMY.—We shall now say a few words with regard to the much canvassed question of painting or colouring statues. Its antiquity and universality admit of no doubt. Indeed, the practice of painting statues is a characteristic of a primitive and barbarous style of art. Though it must be admitted that the early Greek artists painted their wooden, clay, and sometimes their marble, statues, we must positively refuse credence to what some would wish us to believe, that the Greek sculptors of the best period coloured the nude parts of their marble statues.* This mistake has arisen from

---

* The application of colour to statues and temples I would consider to belong to a late or Roman period of art. As Nero had the statue of Alexander, by Lysippus, gilt, so we may suppose the colour, the traces of which are found on some Greek statues of the fine period of art, was applied at a much later period to please the false taste of that age. Virgil mentions a Cupid with coloured wings; the three Corinthian columns of the temple of Minerva Chalcidica, in the Forum, were painted red, and the Trajan column still retains traces of colour and gilding used at that period; this practice was thus evidently in accordance with the taste then prevailing in Roman art, the extravagance of which has been deplored by Pliny and Vitruvius. The following remarkable passage of Vitruvius is to the purpose:—" The ancients laboured to accomplish and render pleasing by dint of art, that which in the present day is obtained by means of strong and gaudy colouring, and for the effect which was formerly obtained only by the skill of the artist, a prodigal expense is now substituted. Who, in former times, used minium other-

a misconception of the word *circumlitio*, mentioned by Pliny, which expresses a painting round (περιχρισις), a framing of the borders of the drapery, the hair; and sometimes border ornaments variously executed (of which the archaic Minerva in the Museum of Naples is a valuable instance); a painting of the ground round the figures, in order to separate and make them stand out, as Quinctilian VIII., s. 2, shows : a "circumductio colorum in extremitatibus figurarum, quâ ipsa figura aptius finiuntor et eminentius extant." This practice was confined alone to the metopes, bas-reliefs, and the background of statues in pediments, and all such objects as were placed high up, and were to be seen from a distance. The effect was calculated for height and distance; the most ancient instances of which are the metopes from the temple of Selinus. This mode of colouring was practised only at an archaic period, for Plutarch tells that the ancient statues (τα παλαια των αγαλματων) were daubed with vermilion, and no stronger evidence can be adduced of the imperfection, antiquity, and, we may add, barbarism of the art in any nation, than this custom of painting sculpture, as may be seen in the early sculptures of Assyria, India, and Mexico. The καυσις applied by the so-called painters of statues, αγαλματων εγκαυσται, to the nude parts, was not paint or colouring, but white wax melted with oil, which was laid on with a thick brush, and rubbed dry : "ita signa marmorea nuda curantur," Vitruvius says—a practice adapted by Canova. On the other hand, we have no proof that the Greeks coloured the nude parts of their statues; on the contrary, we have positive evidence that the masterpiece of antiquity, the Cnidian Venus of Praxiteles, was colourless. That the Venus de Medici had her hair gilt, cannot be adduced as any evidence, for in the opinion of Flaxman, to whose correct taste this fashion was totally repugnant, it is a deteriorated variety of the Venus of Praxiteles, and consequently of a later period, when art was in a declining and degraded state. We may, therefore, be led to this conclusion, that the custom of colouring sculpture was only practised

wise than as a medicine? In the present age, however, walls are everywhere covered with it. To this may be added the use of chrysocolla (green), purple, and sacro decorations, which, without the aid of real art, produce a splendid effect." In this passage it is quite evident that Vitruvius places art—that is, beauty of form and proportion, and absence of colour, adopted by the sculptors and architects of the last period—in opposition to the gaudy colouring used by the artists of his day. Further, we have here evidence that red (minium) could not have been applied in sculpture or architecture by the artists of the best period, as in those times it was used only as a 'medicamentum.' If colour had been applied to sculpture and architecture by artists of the age of Phidias, Praxiteles, or Lysippus, Vitruvius would doubtless have referred to that practice in this passage.

at the worst periods of art, at the archaic period, and when it was in its decline.

That Plato mentions that the artists of his age adopted the practice of painting statues, is no proof that the eminent sculptors of his age coloured their marble statues, no more than the modern custom in Italy of painting statues of the Virgin and saints, proves that Michael Angelo or Canova coloured their statues. It was evidently a practice of inferior artists in inferior workmanship of clay or wood. It was a continuation of the old religious practices of daubing the early statues of the gods with vermilion, and was done to meet the superstitious tastes of the uneducated. Statues for religious purposes may have been painted in obedience to a formula prescribed by religion, but statues as objects of art, on which the sculptor exhibited all his genius and taste, were unquestionably executed in the pure and uncoloured marble alone. In the chrysolophantine, or ivory statues of Jove and Minerva, by Phidias, art was made a handmaid to religion. Phidias himself would have preferred to have executed them in marble. We may further remark that form, in its purest ideal, being the chief aim of sculpture, any application of colour, which would detract from the purity and ideality of this purest of the arts, could never be agreeable to refined taste. We must also consider that sculpture in marble, by its whiteness, is calculated for the display of light and shade. For this reason statues and bas-reliefs were placed either in the open light to receive the direct rays of the sun, or in underground places, or thermæ, where they received their light either from an upper window, or, by night, from the strong light of a lamp; the sculptor having for that purpose studied the effects of the shadows. It must be also remembered that the statues in Greek and Roman temples received their light from the upper part of the building, many of the temples being hypæthral, thus having the benefit of a top light, the sculptor's chief aim. Colour in these statues or bas-reliefs would have tended to mar the contrasts of light and shade, and blended them too much; for example, colour a photograph of a statue, of a statue which exhibits a marked contrast of light and shade, and it will tend to confuse and blend the two. The taste for polychrome sculpture in the period of the decline of art, was obviously but a returning to the primitive imperfection of art, when an attempt was made to produce illusion, in order to please the uneducated taste of the vulgar.*

* We may remark here a curious analogy in the development of art to the development of the individual man. As man in his declining years resumes the childishness of his earliest days, so we find in the decline of art, a recurrence to its

On the colouring of temples we have already spoken under the head of temples.

Roman.—The Romans derived their knowledge of painting from the Etruscans, their ancestors and neighbours. Tradition attributes to them the first works which were used to adorn the temples of Rome; and, according to Pliny, not much consideration was bestowed either on the arts or on the artists. Fabius, the first among the Romans, had some paintings executed in the temple of Salus, from which he received the name of Pictor. Julius Cæsar, Agrippa, Augustus, were among the earliest great patrons of artists. Under Augustus, Marcus Ludius painted marine subjects, landscape decorations, and historic landscape as ornamentation for the apartments of villas and country houses.* At this time, also, a passion for portrait painting prevailed; an art which flattered their vanity was more suited to the tastes of the Romans than the art which could produce beautiful and refined works, similar to those of Greece. Portraits must have been exceedingly numerous; Varro made a collection of the portraits of 700 eminent men. Portraits, decorative and scene painting seem to have engrossed the art. The example, or rather the pretensions, of Nero, must also have contributed to encourage painting in Rome; but Roman artists were, however, but few in number; the victories of the consuls, and the rapine of the prætors, were sufficient to adorn Rome with all the masterpieces of Greece and Italy. They introduced the fashion of having a taste for the beautiful works of Greek art. Roman artists

---

earliest, simplest, and consequently most imperfect forms, when in its infancy. In the age of the Antonines, when Roman art was in its decline, this tendency was conspicuously evident in its predilection for the earlier forms of art and in its reproduction of Egyptian statues. In the last stage of the decline of vase-painting a similar tendency is visible. We find the artists recurring to the ancient forms, and imitating the subjects of the earlier vases. The whole field of art being thoroughly exhausted, artists were obliged to have recourse, as a novelty, to the reproduction and imitation of the antique and earlier forms of art. The Pre-Raphaelite tendency of the present day, which is also a recurrence to the early forms of art, is an evident sign of the decline of painting.

* One of the latest discoveries near Rome is that of the Villa Livia, alluded to by Pliny as Villa Cæsarum. It is about eight miles from the city. In it has been discovered an apartment most exquisitely ornamented. The lower portions of the walls, to the height of about five feet from the floor, represent a trellis work, from which spring the most exquisitely painted trees, shrubs, plants. These are loaded with fruit and flowers, among which a variety of birds and insects are feeding, fluttering, or reposing. As these paintings are in a villa built for Livia by Augustus, the Roman antiquaries have concluded that they are of that period; and consequently may be with good reason attributed to the hand of Ludius.

were the pupils of the Greeks; what we said of the paintings of the Greeks can be equally applied to those of the Romans.

The remains of paintings found at Pompeii, Herculaneum, and in the baths of Titus at Rome, are the only paintings which can

DANCING FIGURE, POMPEII.

give us any idea of the colouring and painting of the ancients, which, though they exhibit many beauties, particularly in composition, are evidently the works of inferior artists in a period of decline. At Pompeii there is scarcely a house the walls of which are not decorated with fresco paintings. The smallest apartments were lined with stucco, painted in the most brilliant and endless variety of colours, in compartments, simply tinted with a light ground, surrounded by an ornamental margin, and sometimes embellished with a single figure or subject in the centre, or at equal distances. These paintings are very frequently historical or mythological, but embrace every variety of subject, some of the most exquisite beauty. Landscape painting was never a favourite

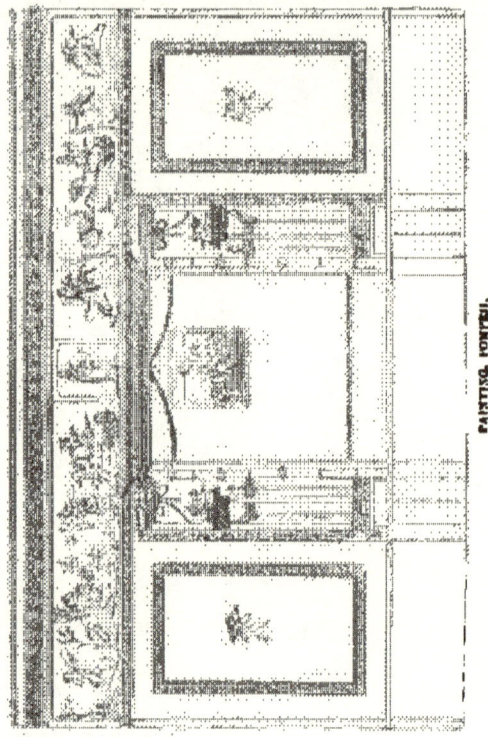

PAINTING POMPEII.

with the ancients, and if ever introduced in a painting, was subordinate. The end and aim of painting among the ancients was to represent and illustrate the myths of the gods, the deeds of heroes, and important historical events, hence giving all prominence to the delineation of the human form. Landscape, on the other hand, illustrated nothing, represented no important event deserving of record, and was thus totally without significance in a Grecian temple or pinacotheca. In an age of decline, as at Pompeii, it was employed for mere decorative purposes. Many architectural subjects are continually found, in which it is easy to trace the true

PAINTING, POMPEII.

principles of perspective; but they are rather indicated than minutely expressed or accurately displayed; whereas in most instances a total want of the knowledge of this art is but too evident. Greek artists seem to have been employed: indeed native painters were few, while the former everywhere abounded, and their superiority in design must have always ensured them the preference.

Sir W. Gell thus remarks on the painting of the ancients: " In grandeur and facility of drawing they warrant all that can be said in their praise; with that feeling for simplicity which distinguishes the ancients from the moderns, many are quite in the taste of the finest bas-reliefs, which, like their tragedies, admitted no under plot to heighten or embarrass. In colouring they are said to be deficient; want of transparency in the shadows exhibits little knowledge of chiaro-oscuro; each figure has its own light and shade, while none are obscured by the interposition of its neighbour. But if we are called upon to make allowance in some of these points for the lapse of centuries, when viewing the works of a later age, how much more indulgence may be claimed when two thousand years might reasonably have been expected to leave no traces at all."

The walls at Pompeii were carefully prepared for the reception of the fresco painting. They appear to have been prepared in the

q

manner prescribed by Vitruvius, who directs that, after the first
rough coat was applied, a second was to be added of arenatnm,
composed principally of sand and lime; this was afterwards to be
covered with *marmoratum*, in the composition of which the place
of sand of the *arenatum* was supplied by pounded marble. The last
coat at Pompeii was put on very thin, and seems to have been well
worked and rubbed upon the rough exterior of the arenatnm, until
a perfect level, smooth, and at length polished surface was obtained,
nearly as hard as marble. While the last coat was still wet, the
colours were laid on, and so done, having, according to Vitruvius,
incorporated with the incrustation, were not liable to fade, but
retained their full beauty and splendour to a great age. According
to Mr. Wornum, the majority of the walls in Pompeii are in common
distemper; but those of the better houses, not only in Pompeii, but
in Rome and elsewhere, especially those which constitute the grounds
of pictures, are in fresco. All the pictures, however, are apparently
in distemper of a superior kind, called by the Italians a *guazzo*; it
is a species of distemper, but the vehicle or medium, made of egg
gum, or glue, completely resists water. He further remarks, "It
appears that no veritable fresco painting has been yet discovered,
though the plain walls in many cases are coloured in fresco. The
paintings upon the walls appear sometimes to have been varnished
by an encaustic process; many specimens bearing a polish, or gloss,
to which water does not readily adhere."

The Romans divided colours into two classes—florid and grave
(floridi, austori)—the former, on account of their high price, were
usually provided for the artist by his employer. These were again
divided into natural and artificial or factitious. The florid colours
appear to have been six—minium, red; ohrysocolla, green; armonium; purpurissimum; indicum; cinnabaris; ostrum; the rest
were the austeri.

The natural colours were those obtained immediately from the
earth; the others were called artificial on account of their requiring
some particular preparation to render them fit for use.

It is the opinion of Sir Humphry Davy, that the ancient painters,
like the best masters of the Roman and Venetian schools, were
sparing in the use of the more florid colours, and produced their
effects, like them, by contrast and tone.

MOSAIC.—Mosaic, *opus musivum*, is a kind of painting made with
minute pieces of coloured substances, generally either marble, or
natural stones, or else glass, more or less opaque, and of every
variety of hue which the subject may require, set in very fine

cement, and which thus forms pictures of different kinds, rivalling in colour and hue those painted by the brush.

Early nations knew the art of mosaic, and it is supposed to derive its origin from Asia, where paintings of this kind were composed, in imitation of the beautiful carpets manufactured at all periods in those countries. The Egyptians employed it very probably for different purposes; no traces of it have, however, been found in the temples or palaces, the ruins of which remain. There is in the

MOSAIC PAVEMENT, POMPEII.

Egyptian collection at Turin a fragment of a mummy case, the paintings of which are executed in Mosaic with wonderful precision and truth. The material is enamel, the colours are of different hues, and their variety renders with perfect truth the plumage of birds. It is believed to be the only example of Egyptian mosaic.

The Greeks carried the art of mosaic to the highest perfection. Skilfully managing the hues, and giving to the figures in their composition an exquisite harmony, they resembled at a slight distance real paintings. Different names were given to the mosaics, according as they were executed in pieces of marble of a certain size; it was then *lithostroton*, *opus sectile*; or in small cubes, in this case it was called *opus tesselatum*, or *vermiculatum*. The name of *asaroton* was given to a mosaic destined to adorn the pavement of a dining hall. It was supposed to represent an unswept hall, on the pavement of which the crumbs and remains of the repast which fell from the table still remained.

Mosaic was used to adorn the pavements, walls, and ceilings of public and private edifices. The Greeks in general preferred marble to every other material. A bed of mortar was prepared, which served as a base, which was covered with a very fine cement. The artist, having before him the coloured design which he was to execute, fixed the coloured cubes in the cement, and polished the entire surface when it had hardened, taking care, however, that too great a polish, by its reflection, might not mar the general effect of his work. The great advantage of mosaic is that it resists humidity, and all which could change the colours and the beauty of painting. Painting could not be employed in the pavement of buildings, and mosaics gave them an appearance of great elegance. The mosaic of the Capitol, found in Adrian's Villa, may give an idea of the perfection which the Greeks attained to in that art. It represents a vase full of water, on the sides of which are four doves, one of which is in the act of drinking. It is supposed by some to be the mosaic of Pergamus mentioned by Pliny. It is entirely composed of cubes of marble, without any admixture of coloured glass. Mosaics of this kind may be considered as the most ancient; it was only by degrees that the art of colouring marble, enamel, and glass, multiplied the materials suited for mosaics, and rendered their execution much more easy. It was then carried to a very high degree of perfection. The mosaic found at Pompeii, which represents three masked figures playing on different instruments, with a child near them, is of the

MOSAIC OF DIOSCORIDES.

most exquisite workmanship. It is formed of very small pieces of glass, of the most beautiful colours, and of various shades. The hair, the small leaves which ornament the masks, and the eyebrows, are most delicately expressed. What enhances the value of this mosaic is the name of the artist worked in it—Dioscorides of Samos. The subjects represented in mosaics are in endless variety, and generally are derived from mythology or heroic myths. Landscapes and ornaments in borders, in frets, in compartments, intermingled with tritons, nereids, centaurs, are to be found on them. The principal subject is in the centre, the rest serves as a bordering or framework.

MOSAIC PAVEMENT.

The Romans brought the art of mosaic to the highest perfection, not with regard to taste and composition, but by adding new materials to those which had been employed by the Greeks. They obtained their knowledge of this art by their conquests; and towards the end of the republic they transported to Rome the most beautiful pavements of this kind found in the Greek cities which they had conquered. The first mosaic of Roman origin was executed in the temple of Fortune at Palestrina, which was restored by Sylla, where it was discovered in 1640. The subject of it has given rise to much controversy. The subject is now supposed to be Egyptian, and it is generally considered to represent a popular fête at the inundation of the Nile.

Mosaics from this period came into general use, and some were made small enough to be carried about in the tents of generals in their campaigns. Cæsar carried one with him in his military expeditions. In the time of Augustus, coloured glass was generally employed, and under Claudius the artists succeeded in staining marble, and giving it different colours.

The most interesting and valuable of all ancient mosaics is the one found at Pompeii, in the house of Pansa. It is supposed to have represented the Battle of Issus.* It is remarkable for the beauty of

* See plate.

its design and composition, and is composed entirely of very small cubes of coloured marble; no glass has been used. It has been calculated that the entire composition, when perfect, was composed of 1,384,000 cubes of marble, for 7000 can be counted in each square palm. In order to know the age of a mosaic, particular regard must be paid to the nature of the materials of which it is composed. Its antiquity will depend on whether it exhibits artificial compositions or not. The stained marbles and artificial compositions will be proofs of later date.

The common Roman pavements are made of cubes of common stones, and form borders more or less wide, of different colours, and rather coarsely put together, examples of which may be seen in the baths of Caracalla at Rome.

The number of Roman mosaics which have come down to us, sometimes in an excellent state of preservation, are considerable. Some excellent specimens have been found in the villa of Adrian, near Tivoli. They have been also found in the various Roman colonies. Some very valuable specimens have been lately discovered at Carthage; several have been also found in the Island of Sardinia, now in the Museum of Turin. Some have been discovered in the south of France. That of Vienne represents Achilles recognised by Ulysses among the daughters of Lycomedes. A very fine specimen is in the Museum of Lyons. It represents the Circensian games. The Romans carried their luxurious tastes as far as Britain, for several mosaics have been found in many parts of England.

In the Lower Empire mosaics were made at Constantinople of pearls and precious stones. The richness of the material was substituted for the beauties of an art which had degenerated.

PAINTED VASES.

Painted Vases may be considered as the most curious, the most graceful, and the most instructive remains that have come down to us from ancient times. The beauty of the forms, the fineness of the material, the perfection of the varnish, the variety of the subjects, and their interest in an historical point of view, give painted vases a very important place among the productions of the arts of the ancients. Painted vases have been collected with great eagerness ever since they have been known, and the most remarkable have been engraved by celebrated artists, and explained by profound archæologists. Modern art and archæology have obtained from them beautiful models and important information. They

were known for the first time in the seventeenth century; La-
chausse published some of them in his Museum Romanum, in
1690; Beger and Montfaucon imitated his example; Dempster
subsequently wrote on them more fully; Gori, Buonarotti, and
Caylus, added some general observations to those of Dempster;
Winckelman could not omit them in his immortal work on the
history of Ancient Art, and modified, by the accuracy of his
observations, the theories of his predecessors. Lastly, the beautiful
collection of Sir William Hamilton, published by Hancarville in
1766, brought them more fully into public notice; Passeri still
supported after him the Italian opinion in regard to the origin of
these vases; Tischbein, Boettiger, and Millin, declared themselves
of the same opinion as Winckelman; and 'the study of these
beautiful objects confirms it at the present day in every respect.

Painted Vases received at first the denomination of *Etruscan
Vases*; Dempster, a great abettor of what was called Etrusco-
mania, gave them this denomination, and Tuscan antiquaries have
defended it as a title of glory for their country. The impartial
comparison of remains of antiquity had not as yet established
any fundamental distinction between the Etruscan style, properly
so called, and the ancient Greek style. Every composition
characterised by the stiffness of the features, the straight folds
of the drapery, and long braided hair, was attributed to the
Etruscans. Painted vases which presented those characteristics
were therefore attributed to them, and in spite of the evidence
of the subjects borrowed from the mythic ideas of the Greeks,
in spite of the inscriptions, all Greek, which were read on them,
general opinion, too readily followed, recognised in them every
thing that could explain the manners, customs, creed, and even
the history of the Etruscans. It was further generally believed
that these vases had issued from the manufactures of Arezzo,
because Martial praises the potteries of that town; and, that
those which were found in Campania, Puglia, and even in Sicily,
had been carried there by the Etruscans themselves. This theory
could not be maintained, even after a slight examination, especially
as painted vases have been found at Athens, Megara, Milo, in Aulis,
in Tauris, at Corfu, and in the Isles of Greece. The greater
number, indeed, are found even at the present day in Magna
Graecia, Nola, Capua, Paestum, and in Sicily, but they are found
in every country where Greek domination prevailed. The extent
of the domination of the Tyrrhenians in Italy was not sufficiently
extensive to attribute to them all the painted vases. Eucheir and
Eugrammus came, according to Pliny, into Etruria, and taught

there the plastic arts, but this does not prove that they invented there the art of making painted vases, for these two artists who worked in clay, being from Corinth, might have brought this art from Greece. Everything leads us to conclude that we must attribute their origin to Greece. In their forms they bear a great resemblance to the vases which we see on the medals and some of the sculpture of the Greeks; the style of the figures which ornament them entirely corresponds with that of the figures of the ancient Greek style; lastly, the myths which are represented on them, the inscriptions in Greek characters which frequently accompany the figures, are sufficient to establish this opinion. But we must acknowledge that Greek myths are always expressed with peculiar circumstances, which probably are derived from the alterations which Greek traditions had experienced in ancient Italy.

Painted vases were, to a considerable extent, objects of traffic and of export from one country to another. They may be generally traced to Athens as the original place of exportation. Corinth also exported vases, for the products of Corinthian pottery have been found in Sicily and Italy, and there can be no doubt that Corinth had established an active trade in works of art with the Greek colonies all over the Mediterranean. Athenian vases were carried by the Phœnicians, the commercial traders of the ancient world, as objects of traffic to the remotest parts of the then known world. In the Periplus of Scylax, the Phœnicians are mentioned as exchanging the pottery of Athens for the ivory of Africa. They were, in fact, the ornamental china of the ancient world.

The variety of opinions with regard to the origin of these vases, has produced a similar diversity with regard to their denomination. To that of Etruscan Vases succeeded that of Greek Vases, still too general; Visconti wished to name them Græco-Italian; Arditi, Italo-Greek; Lanzi, Campanian, Sicilian, Athenian, according as they were found in Campania, Sicily, or at Athens; Quatremère de Quincy, Cerano-graphic Vases (of painted clay); and Millin, Painted Vases in general, adding the name of the place where they were discovered. We may, however, be able to class them more systematically, on considering, in the first place, that painted vases form a class apart among the remains of antiquity; secondly, that it is recognised at the present day, that the Etruscans manufactured them also, as well as the Greeks; thirdly, that the subject itself of the painting is the most certain type of their origin, especially with regard to Etruscan vases, for we cannot suppose that the Greeks, who cultivated the arts after the Etruscans, would have painted on the vases the myths, creed, and the history of Etruria, though the

Etruscans might have done so for the Greeks: lastly, that vases which bear subjects purely Greek are found in many countries, and in different places, without, however, their bearing any local characteristic, all belonging alike to Greek art, and without any other distinction than that which results from the style itself, according to the greater or less antiquity of the execution. We may, therefore, adopt the general denomination of Painted Vases, distinguished into *Etruscan*, for those which are the work of that people, and into *Greek* for those, in far greater number, which can have no other origin; while those can be classed according to their relative antiquity, proved by the style of the figures, the characters, the form and the orthography of the inscriptions when they accompany the painting. We adopt this division which appears to us as the most simple and most natural, which can be equally applied to the painted vases of every other country, if any should happen to be discovered.

We shall further observe on this subject, that there is no passage of any ancient author which could serve to throw any light on the uncertainty produced by the various opinions published with regard to painted vases: nothing relative to them has been hitherto found in Greek or Latin writers; and this singularity, when we consider the beauty, the variety, and the number of these remains of antiquity, has been very justly remarked.

Etruscan.—Vases, the Etruscan origin of which cannot be disputed, have been found at Volterra, Tarquinii, Perugia, Orvieto, Vitorbo, Acquapendente, Corneto, and other towns of ancient Etruria. The clay of which they are made is of a pale or reddish yellow, the varnish is dull, the workmanship rather rude, the ornaments are devoid of taste and elegance, and the style of the figures possesses all those characteristics already assigned to that of the Etruscans. The figures are drawn in black on the natural colour of the clay: sometimes a little red is introduced on the black ground of the drapery. It is by the subject chiefly that the Etruscan vases are distinguished from the Greek vases. On the former, the figures are in the costume peculiar to ancient Italy; the men and the heroes are represented with their beards and hair very thick; the gods and godi have large wings; we may also observe divinities, religious customs, attributes, manners, arms, and symbols, different from those of Greece. If an inscription in Etruscan characters, traced invariably from right to left, accompanies the painting, certainly with regard to their origin may be considered as complete. It is true that the greater number of the letters of the ancient Greek

alphabet are of the same form as those of the Etruscan alphabet;
but there are in the latter some particular characters which will
prevent any confusion. We must also observe, that Etruscan painted
vases are very rare, and are but few in number, compared with
those for which we are indebted to the arts of Greece. Dennis, in
his work on Etruria, gives a specimen of a vase of undoubted
Etruscan manufacture, as it bears an Etruscan subject and an
Etruscan inscription. It is an amphora, with a Bacchic dance on
one side; on the other side, the parting of Admetus and Alcestis,
whose names are attached, between the figures of Charun and
another demon. Of late years vases are found in great numbers in
Etruria, more particularly at Vulci; but most of these painted vases
are imitations of those of Athens.

Greek.—They are made of a very fine and light clay; their
exterior coating is composed of a particular kind of clay, which
seems to be a kind of yellow or red ochre, reduced to a very fine
paste, mixed with some glutinous or oily substance, and laid on with
a brush; the parts which are painted black have all the brilliancy
of enamel. The colours being laid on in a different manner in the
earlier and later vases has caused them to be distinguished into two
general classes. In the earlier the ground is yellow or red, and the
figures are traced on it in black, so as to form kinds of silhouettes.
These are called the black or archaic vases, they are generally in an
ancient style; their subjects belong to the most ancient mythological
traditions, and their inscriptions to the most ancient forms of the
Greek alphabet, written from right to left, or in boustrophedon.
The drapery, the accessories, the harness of the horses, and the
wheels of the chariots, are touched with white. At a later period,
the whole vase was painted black, with the exception of the figures,
which were then of the colour of the clay of the vase; the contours
of the figures, the hair, drapery, &c., being previously traced in
black. There are then two general classes of Greek vases, distinguished by the figures, which are black or yellow. They are in
general remarkable for the beauty and elegance of their forms.
There is a great variety in their sizes; some being several feet
high, and broad in proportion; others being not higher than an
inch. The subject is on one side of the vase; sometimes it occupies
the entire circumference, but more generally it is one side alone
(called in Italy the *parte nobile*), and then there is on the reverse
some insignificant subject, generally two or three of old men leaning
on a stick, instructing a young man, or presenting him with some
instrument or utensil; a bacchanalian scene is sometimes represented

on the reverse. Some vases have been found with two subjects on
the sides of the vase. On some of the finest vases, the subject goes
round the entire circumference of the vase. On the foot, neck, and
other parts are the usual Greek ornaments, the Vitruvian scroll, the
Meander, Palmetto, the honeysuckle. A garland sometimes adorns
the neck, or, in its stead, a woman's head issuing from a flower.
These ornaments are in general treated with the greatest taste and
elegance. Besides the obvious difference in the style of the vases,
there is a remarkable difference in the execution of the paintings.
They are not all of the highest merit, but the boldness of the outlines is generally remarkable on them. They could be executed
only with the greatest rapidity, the clay absorbing the colours very
quickly, so that if a line was interrupted, the joining would be perceptible. Some thought that the figures were executed by the means
of patterns cut out, which being laid on the vase, preserved on the
black ground the principal masses in yellow, which were finished
afterwards with a brush. But this opinion of Sir William Hamilton
has been abandoned by himself, particularly since the traces of a
point have been recognised, with which the artist had at first
sketched on the soft clay the principal outlines, which he finished
afterwards with a brush dipped in the black pigment, without, however, strictly following the lines traced by the point. The traces of
the point are rarely observed; all depended on the skill and talent
of the artists. They must have been very numerous, as these vases
are found in such numbers, and the greater number may be considered as models for the excellence of their design and the taste of
their composition. Not unfrequently, the artists, by whom the
designs have been painted, have placed their names on them; the
principal names known are those of Lasimon, Taleides, Asteas, and
Calliphon. Taleides is the most ancient; his designs evince the
infancy of art, those of the other artists display greater progress in
the art; the name can be recognised from the words ΕΠΟΙΕΙ or
ΕΠΟΙΕΣΕΝ, and ΕΓΡΑΨΕ, made or painted, which follow them
immediately; the two former being united with the name of the
potter, and the latter with the name of the painter. Other inscriptions are sometimes found on vases, which enhance their value
greatly. They are generally the names of gods, heroes and other
mythological personages, which are represented in the paintings.
These inscriptions are of great interest for two reasons: in the first
place, from the form of the letters and the order according to which
they are traced, the greater or less antiquity of the vase can be
recognised, these inscriptions necessarily following all the changes
of the Greek alphabet; care must be taken to examine whether the

inscription goes from right to left, whether the long vowels ΗΩ, the
double letters Ψ Ξ are replaced by the silent vowels, or single letters;
these are in general signs of relative antiquity which prove that of
the vase itself; secondly, because the names invariably explain the
subject of the painting, and even indicate by a name hitherto unknown, either some personage who sometimes bore another name, or
a person whose real name was unknown, in fine, some mythic beings
of whom ancient writers give us no information. The information derived from vases is of great importance for the study of
Greek mythology, viewed in its different epochs, and for the interpretation and understanding of ancient tragic or lyric poets. Moral
or historical inscriptions, in prose and in verse, have been also found
on vases. The letters of those inscriptions are capital or cursive;
they are very delicately traced, and often require a great deal of
attention to perceive. They are traced in black or white with a
brush, sometimes they are incised with a very sharp point. The
word ΚΑΛΟΣ is very frequently found on vases which bear inscriptions, almost always accompanied by a proper name.* It seems to
be nothing more than an epithet, expressive of admiration, applied
to the most remarkable and conspicuous personage represented on
the vase, as on a vase in the Vatican Museum we see a painting
representing Priam, Hector, and Andromache, with their names over
each; over Hector is the inscription Εκτωρ καλος, "The noble
Hector."† In the form καλοκαγαθος, it signified brave and beautiful,
the very acme of praise given to a person. On some which had
been gifts to some "beautiful youths," we find the inscription η ο
παις καλος. On others, salutatory expressions are sometimes found,
such as ΧΑΙΡΕ ΣΥ, "Hail to thee"; or, ΠΟΣΟΝ ΔΕΠΟΤΕ ΕΥΦΡΟΝ,
"Happy as possible."

The subjects represented on painted vases, although of infinite
variety, may be reduced to three classes,‡ which include them all:

* Some suppose that the painter wrote it at first on executing the vase, and that
afterwards the name of the person who was to possess it was added to it, for many
vases are found on which no name follows this Greek word, which means
"beautiful."

† Similar inscriptions are to be found on vases in the British Museum. The same
custom has been retained on some Majolica ewers of modern Italy; on one is the
portrait of a lady, with the inscription around it "La bella Laura," the beautiful
Laura.

‡ Millingen divides them into the following seven classes, according to their
subjects:—

1. Those subjects which refer to the Divinities, their wars with the giants, their
amours, the sacrifices which are offered to them.

2. Those relative to the Heroic Times. This class, the most numerous, as well

— 1. Mythological subjects; 2. Heroic subjects; 3. Historical subjects. The *Mythological* subjects relate to the history of all the gods, and their adventures in human form are reproduced on them in a thousand shapes. It requires a deep and intimate knowledge of Greek mythology, in order to explain the different subjects. The greater part of the paintings of the vases are relative to Bacchus, his festivals and mysteries. On them we see depicted his birth, childhood, education, all his exploits, his banquets, and his games; his habitual companions, his religious ceremonies, the lampadophoræ brandishing the long torches, the dendrophoræ raising branches of trees, adorned with garlands and tablets; the initiated preparing for the mysteries; lastly, the ceremonies peculiar to those great institutions, and the circumstances relative to their dogmas and their aim.

The *Heroical* subjects, which are far more numerous than the mythological, represent the deeds of the heroes of ancient Greece: Hercules, Bellerophon, Cadmus, Perseus and Andromeda, Actæon,

as the most interesting, embraces all the mythological period, from the arrival of Cadmus to the return of Ulysses to Ithaca; it includes the Heracleid, the Theseid, the two wars of Thebes, that of the Amazons, the expedition of the Argonauts, and the war of Troy.

3. The Dionysiac subjects: Bacchus—The Satyrs, the Sileni, the Nymphs, and his other attendants. Dionysiac festivals and processions, with the dances and amusements which accompany them. As these festivals were the most celebrated and the most popular, the ancients were naturally anxious to multiply representations of them.

4. Subjects of Civil Life, such as marriages, amorous scenes, repasts, sacrifices, hunts, military dances, warriors setting out for the war, or returning victorious to their country. This class is of the greatest use in giving information with regard to the manners, customs, and dresses of the ancients.

5. Those which represent Funeral Ceremonies. On these we see depicted the representations of tombs, around which the relations and friends of the deceased bring offerings and libations; among the offerings we sometimes observe objects symbolical of initiation into the mysteries. This class, a very numerous one, seems to have been particularly destined to be placed in the tombs.

6. Subjects relating to the Gymnasia: ephebi occupied in different exercises, who are conversing with one another, or with the gymnast. As vases were frequently given as prizes to the conquerors in the games, it has been supposed that those on which similar subjects are represented were destined for that purpose.

7. Subjects which have reference to the Mysteries, and which represent ceremonies preparatory to the initiations. Similar subjects are only to be met with on vases of the period of the decline of art, and which are found in that part of Italy formerly occupied by the Lucani, Brutili, and the Samnites, where Greek ideas and customs were corrupted by the mixture of those of those barbarous nations.

Danaus, Medea, the Centaurs, the Amazons, etc.; the myth of
Theseus was also the constant theme of the artist.

The *Historical* subjects begin with the war of Troy. Painters, as
well as poets, found in this event a vast field to exercise their
talents and their imagination. The principal actors in this memorable drama appear on the vases. The principal scenes of the
Trojan war are depicted; but wo must remark, that the historical
subjects do not extend to a later period than that of the Heraclidæ.
We may consider, as belonging to the class of historical vases, those
with paintings relative to public and private customs; those representing games, repasts, scenic representations of combats of animals,
hunting and funereal subjects. Millingen remarks that the subjects
of the paintings vary according to the period and the places in which
they have been executed; on the most ancient vases Dionysiac scenes
are frequently seen. As, originally, the greater number were destined
to contain wine, they were adorned with analogous subjects. Those
of the beautiful period of the art, especially of the manufacture of
Nola, a town in which Greek institutions were observed with extreme
care, present the ancient traditions of mythological episodes in all
their purity. Those of a later period represent subjects taken from
the tragic writers. Lastly, on those of the decline wo see depicted
the new ceremonies and superstitions which were mingled with the
ancient and simple religion of the Greek. Painted vases are, therefore, of the greatest interest for the study of the manners and customs
of ancient Greece, and of those which the Romans adopted from her
in imitation.

We must introduce an important remark here, relative to the
variety of mythological, heroical, and even historical subjects.
These subjects, especially the first and second, seem to form a
mythology and heroic history distinct from those of the Greek poets
and prose writers. We find on the vases persons not mentioned in
ancient writers; entire scenes, also, which cannot be explained by
any written tradition, or which are represented with circumstances
which history has not handed down to us. We must further remark,
that the mythology of the poets is not always in harmony with that
of the prose writers; and among the poets themselves, that of the
lyric writers is frequently different from that of the tragic poets.
Traditions must have changed; and, perhaps, at the period of the
great writers of Greece, there was established, amidst this confusion,
a kind of eclecticism, which left the poet, the mythograph, etc., the
liberty of choosing among those traditions whatever suited best the
aim and nature of the poem, or whatever appeared most likely.
Painted vases, especially the most ancient, which are anterior to

these writers, give us information which we do not receive from ancient writers: this gives to their study a great degree of importance and interest: further, they represent, in the most authentic manner, the genuine history of art among the Greeks from its origin until it reached perfection.

As to the uses of these vases, there have been a variety of opinions; but a careful examination of a great number of vases would lead us to suppose that many were, doubtless, articles of household furniture, for use and adornment, such as the larger vases, destined, by their size, weight, and form, to remain in the same place, while others, of different sizes and shapes, were made to hold wine and other liquids, unguents, and perfumes. It is evident that they were more for ornament than use, and that they were considered as objects of art, for the paintings seem to have been executed by the best artists of the period. Those with Panathenaic subjects were probably given, full of oil, as prizes at the national games. Others may have been given at the palaestric festivals, or as nuptial presents, or as pledges of love and friendship; and these are marked by some appropriate inscription. We find that they were also used in the ceremonies of the Mysteries, for we see their forms represented on the vases themselves: Bacchus frequently holds a cantharus, Satyrs carry a diota. A few seem to have been expressly for sepulchral purposes. Some have supposed that these vases were intended to hold the ashes of the dead; but this could not have been their use, for they are only found in tombs in which the bodies have been buried without being burnt. The piety of the relations adorned the tomb of the deceased with those vases, together with his armour and jewellery, which they had prized most in life, which were associated with their habits, or recalled circumstances the memory of which they cherished.* The origin of the custom of placing objects belonging

* That it was the custom in ancient times to place in tombs the vases that were dear to the deceased, we find from the following passage of Vitruvius:—" Virgo civis Corinthia jam matura nuptiis, implicita morbo decessit: post sepulturam ejus, quibus ea viva poculis delectabatur, nutrix collecta et composita in calatho portavit ad monumentum et in summo collocavit; et uti ea permanerent diutius sub divo, tegula texit."—Vitruvius, lib. iv, cap. 1. The same custom, and the same feelings which lead to that custom, we find in the funeral rites of an Indian tribe, as thus beautifully embodied in a poetic dirge by Schiller:

" Here bring the last gifts! and with these
The last lament be said—
Let all that pleased, and yet may please,
Be buried with the dead."—Sir E. B. Lytton.

In a passage of an ancient author, quoted by Athenæus, lib. xi, c. 1, we find a

to the deceased with him in his tomb would seem to be the superstitious objection of the relatives of the deceased to use anything
belonging to, or connected with the memory of, the dead. These
objects were consequently placed with the deceased in his tomb.
This superstitious objection, prevalent among all uncivilized
nations, has given rise to this custom, which is found to be adopted
by all the early and primitive races of the world. This custom has
handed them down to our times. It is supposed to have ceased
when Roman sovereignty was established throughout Italy and
Sicily. The Romans, burning their dead, and never adopting the
custom of burying vases in tombs, by their influence must have
brought them into disuse, and, consequently, their manufacture
ceased. Kramer thinks that there are no painted vases of a later
date than the Second Punic War.

It is very remarkable, that no ancient author, not even Pliny, has
noticed painted vases, although they seem to have been in such
general use : nor is there any passage known expressly relative to
these vases. Suetonius, indeed, tells us that the colonies established
at Capua by Julius Cæsar, destroyed, when building country houses,
the most ancient tombs, especially as they found in them ancient
vases (aliquantum vasculorum operis antiqui reteriobant). In the
opinion of Boettiger, vascula can only be applied to vases of bronze;
however, as Suetonius speaks of the tombs of Capua in particular,
and as there are still painted vases found there, and that no bronze
vases are ever found in the tombs, it is very likely that the phrase
of Suetonius can be applied to the painted vases which are still
found there in such numbers. The Romans might then have known
them ; and this opinion seems to be justified by the following observation. The Greeks of Italy buried their dead without burning
them ; for this reason, human ashes have never been found in vases
in Greek tombs, the vases were placed by the side of the corpse
stretched out on the ground. However, some vases have been
discovered full of ashes and half-burnt bones ; and, as it was the
custom of the Romans to burn the dead, it has been inferred that

similar custom mentioned :—Νεκυν χαμαιστρωτον επι τυποι ευρεσηι στιβαδος προ-
θησεν αυτοις θαλειαν τε τα ποτερα τε στεφανους τ'επικρασιν εθηκεν. "The corpse
being stretched on the ground, and placed on a thick bed of leaves, they placed
near it meats, drinking cups, and they placed a chaplet on its head." In the
early periods of Chinese history a similar custom seems to have prevailed of
interring with the dead, vases, which reprend with them for ages. These vases
were conferred as marks of honour by the prince, and other illustrious personages,
for services rendered to the state.— *Vide Thoms on Ancient Chinese Vases of the
Shang Dynasty, from 1743 to 1196, B.C.*

the vase at first deposited empty in a Greek tomb, had been taken out of it, and that afterwards it was used as a cinerary urn for a Roman. These substitutions were not rare in ancient times; there is, in the museum of the Louvre, a vase in Oriental alabaster, executed in Egypt, which bears the name of Xerxes in hieroglyphic and cuneiform characters, which was at a later period employed as a cinerary urn for a member of the Roman family Claudia, as the Latin inscription shows engraved on the side of the vase, the other side bearing the Egyptian and Persian inscription.

We could not but feel astonished at the perfect preservation of such fragile objects, did we not know that they were found in tombs. The tombs in which they are found, are placed near the walls, but outside the town, at a slight depth, except those of Nola, where the eruptions of Vesuvius have considerably raised the soil since the period when the tombs were made, so that some of the tombs of Nola are about twenty-one feet under ground. The common tombs are built of brick, or of rough stones, and are exactly of sufficient size to contain a corpse and five or six vases; a small one is placed near the head, and the others between the legs of the body, or they are ranged on each side, frequently on the left side alone. The number and beauty of the vases vary, probably, according to the rank and fortune of the owner of the tomb. The tombs of the first class are larger, and have been built with large cut stones, and rarely connected with cement; the walls inside are coated with stucco, and adorned with paintings; these tombs resemble a small chamber; the corpse is laid out in the middle, the vases are placed round it, frequently some others are hung up to the walls on nails of bronze.* The number of vases is always greater in these tombs; they are also of a more elegant form. Several other articles are sometimes found in the tombs, such as gold and silver fibulæ, swords, spears, armour, and several ornaments. The objects buried with the corpse generally bespeak the tastes and occupation of the deceased. Warriors are found with their armour, women with ornaments for the toilet, priests with their sacerdotal ornaments, as in the tomb at Cervetri. When the vases are taken out of the excavations, they are covered with a coating of whitish earth, something like tartar, and of a calcareous nature; it disappears on the application of aqua fortis. This operation ought to be done with great caution; for though the aqua fortis does not injure the black varnish, it might destroy some of the other colours.. Some of these vases are as well preserved as if they had just issued from the hands of the potter, others have been greatly injured by the earthy salts

* See page 107.

R

with which they have come in contact; many are found broken,
these have been put together and restored with great skill. But
this work of restoration, especially if the artist adds any details
which are not visible on the original, might alter or metamorphose
a subject, and the archæologist ought to set little value on these
modern additions, in the study of a painted vase.

The first manufactories of these vases are supposed to have been
established not far from the shores of the sea, as in Sicily, Calabria,
Campania, and Etruria. The vases of more ancient style, with
black figures, are more frequently found at these places. At a
later period manufactories were established more in the interior of
the country, on plains and on hills, as at St. Agata de Goti, in la
Puglia, in Basilicata, and near Naples. Among judges, the vases
most to be preferred are those which are of the manufacture of
Locri in Calabria, of Agrigentum in Sicily; those of Cuma, of
Capua, and of Nola in Campania; and those of Vulci and Canino
in the Roman states. In those places, where manufactories were
established at a later period, many excellent vases with beautiful
compositions have been frequently found, but not in that simple
and elegant style which was peculiar to the Greeks. Several
imitations have been made of ancient vases, either through a love
of art or for the purpose of deceit. The first may be considered
praiseworthy, as it has contributed considerably to bring to perfection modern pottery; the second as highly censurable, for even
experienced connoisseurs have been deceived. Pietro Fondi, who
had established his manufactories at Venice and at Corfu, was
remarkable for his success in this kind of deceit. The family
Vavari, at Arezzo, manufactured vases of this kind; there are
several of them in the gallery at Florence. Of this kind of de-
ception there are several kinds. Sometimes the vase is ancient
but the painting is modern, frequently details and inscriptions are
added to the ancient painting; but the difference of the style of
drawing, the multiplicity of details, the nails indicated on the
hands and feet, betray the fraud, as well as the coarseness of the
earth (which makes the vases heavier), and the metallic lustre of
the varnish. The test which the colours of the false vases are made
to undergo is also decisive. If colours mixed with water or alcohol
have been employed, it is sufficient to pass a little water or spirits
of wine over them to make them disappear; the ancient colours
having been baked with the vases resist this test. In modern
times, imitations have been made by the celebrated Wedgwood,
remarkable alike for their elegance and taste.

Several collections have been formed of these vases. The British

Museum contains the finest collections, purchased by government from Sir William Hamilton and others. The Museum at Naples, and the Gregorian Museum in the Vatican, also contain many beautiful specimens from Magna Græcia and Etruria. Several amateurs have also formed collections in England, France, and Italy. We may mention those of Rogers, Hope, Sir Harry Englefield, in England : those of the Duc de Blacas, the Comte Pourtales, in France; and that of the Marquis Campana, in Rome. Some of these collections have been published, such as the first collection of Sir William Hamilton, explained by d'Hancarville; the second by Tischbein. Several works have also been published, giving detailed accounts of painted vases in general. We shall only give the principal :—

Passori, "Picturæ Etruscorum in Vasculis," Rome, 1767, 3 vols. fol.; "Collection of Engravings from Ancient Vases, in the possession of Sir William Hamilton," by Tischbein, Naples, 1798—1803, 4 vols.; C. Böttiger, "Griechische Vasengemälde," Weimar, 1797, 1800; "Peintures de Vases Antiques," A. Millin, publié par Dubois Maisonneuve, l'aris, 1808, 2 vols., fol.; Millingen, "Peintures de Vases Grecques," Rome, 1813, fol.; Panofka, "Raccolta di Vasi Scolti," Rome, 1826; Dubois Maisonneuve, "Introduction à l'Etude de Vases Antiques," Paris, 1817, fol.; Gerhard, "Berlins Antike Bildwerke;" Kramer's work, "Ueber den Styl und die Herkunft der vermahlten Griech.," Berlin, 1827, 8vo.; and Mr. Birch's valuable work on "Ancient Pottery."

Epochs of Painted Vases.

We shall now give descriptions of these painted vases according to their several styles or epochs, illustrations of which we have given.

Early or *Egyptian.*[*]—The ground is of a pale yellow, on which the figures are painted in black or brown. These consist chiefly of animals, such as lions, rams, stags, swans, cocks, sphinxes, and other chimæras, arranged in several bands around the vase. Borders of flowers, also, and other ornaments, run round them. Human figures are rarely met with. This style has been termed Egyptian, in consequence of its obvious resemblance to that rigid style of art

---

[*] Specimens of this style we give in Plate 1—I. Earlier than this style was a ruder style found at Athens with plain bands, or zones disposed round the axis of the vase, sometimes displaying ornaments of mæander, zigzag, which were the earliest attempts at decoration.

peculiar to Egypt. The inner outlines of the figures are traced in the clay with a pointed instrument. In consequence of these vases exhibiting animals not natives of Italy, and as the clay of which they are made has been in vain sought for in Italy, some have been led to infer that the vases of this epoch found in Italy have been imported by the Greeks. The date generally assigned to them is between B.C. 600 and 520.

Archaic Greek.[*]—In this style, the figures are black on a red ground. The design is stiff, hard, and severe; yet at times there is a degree of spirit evinced, evidently indicating a progress in the development of the art. The scenes represented are taken from the Hellenic Mythology. The class of subjects is, however, numerous, for we find some of Dionysiac character. Another is Panathenaic, of which there is a remarkable specimen, representing Minerva brandishing her lance, which, from the inscription it bears, is supposed to have been given as a prize in the public games. They are generally supposed to have been made previous to the year B.C. 430.

Severe or *Transitional.*[†]—In the vases of this class, the figures are red on a black ground. White is seldom used. Although the colour of these vases and their figures present a striking contrast to those of the first two classes, yet the character of their designs vanishes and gives way to the beautiful, so that they might be ranked in the fourth class. The harshness and violence of movement so striking in the archaic vases gradually disappear, and make way for a calm and severe dignity. The artists, however, did not yet work with perfect freedom, and the designs are rather stiff. The subjects represented are the same as those on the vases of the second class. The forms of the vases have something more elegant than those of the second class, although they present great variations in style and size. They occur most frequently in Etruria and at Nola; they contain inscriptions in characters of a middle kind between the archaic mode of writing and the later one. The period commonly assigned to works of this class, is from B.C. 460 to 420.

The Beautiful, or *Greek.*[‡]—This style is the more perfect development of the former, all severity and conventionality which dis-

---

[*] See Plate 1—II.
[†] Named by Mr. Birch " The strong style."
[‡] See Plate 2.

THE BEAUTIFUL OR GREEK STYLE.

tinguishes the earlier styles, having entirely disappeared. The distinguishing characteristics of this style are elegance of form, fineness of material, brilliancy of varnish, and exquisite beauty of design. The predominating subjects are Greek myths, or representations of Greek manners; but scenes connected with the worship of Demeter and Dionysus are of frequent occurrence. The most common form of the vases of this kind, is that of the slender amphora, the round hydria, and the crater. Vases of this style appear to belong to the period beginning with the year B.C. 400. They are seldom found in Etruria, and the most frequently in Nola, Sicily, and Attica.

Florid.[*]—This class of vases is rarely found in Etruria, but abundant in the Greek colonies of Italy, especially in the districts of Puglia and Basilicata. Like the last class, it has yellow figures on a black ground, but differs widely in style. The vases are often of enormous size, and exaggerated proportions. The multitude of figures introduced, the complexity of the composition, the inferiority and carelessness of the design, the flourish and lavishment of decoration, in a word, the absence of that chasteness and purity which gave the perfect style its chief charm, indicate these vases to belong, if not always to the period of Decadence, at least to the verge of it. Polychrome vases are also frequently found in this style. The draperies being coloured blue, vermilion, green.

Decadence.—At a later period,[†] we may remark a still greater deterioration in the arts of design, while more capricious forms were invented. We must also remark the latest period of the art; for at that epoch several imitations of the vases of earlier epochs were made. Among these, we frequently find imitations of the first epoch, but the clay is coarse, and different from that of the genuine. We also find imitations of the second and third epochs; but their forms are ill-proportioned, and destitute of taste.

SHAPES OF PAINTED VASES.

We first give Mr. Dennis' arrangement, after the nomenclature of Gerhard, of these vases in classes, according to the purposes they served. We then give a list of their several shapes, with the names by which they are known in England, and also with the names they are given in Italian Museums:

[*] See Plate 3—IV., named by Mr Birch "The florid style."
[†] See Plate 3—V.

THE FLAMED STILL.

CLASS I.—Vases for holding wine, oil, or water—amphora, police, stamnos.

II.—Vases for carrying water—hydria, calpis.

III.—Vases for mixing wine and water—crater, colobo, oxybaphon.

IV.—Vases for pouring wine, etc., jugs—œnochoe, olpe, prochous.

V.—Vases for drinking-cups and goblets—cantharus, cyathus, carchesion, holoion, scyphus, cylix, lepaste, phiale, ceras, rhyton.

VI.—Vases for ointments or perfumes—lecythus, alabastron, ascos, bombylios, aryballos, cotylisoos.

English Nomenclature.		Italian Nomenclature.*
1 Amphora. Egyptian.		1 Langella.
2 " Tyrrhenian.		2 "
3 " Panathenaic.		3 "
4 " Bacchic.		4 "
5, 6 " of Nola.		5, 6 "
7 " Apulian.		7 "
8 " with handles, with circular ornaments.		8 Olla con manichi a girelle.
9 " with handles as volutes.		9 Olla con manichi a volute.
10 " with handles with faces on them.		10 Olla con manichi a mascheroni.
11 Thymaterion.		11 Ingensiera.
12 Hydria.		12 Olla o vaso vinario.
13 Calpis.		13 Olla o canopo.
14 Pelike.		14 Idria.
15 Stamnos.		15 Olla.
16 Crater.		16 Calice.
17 Oxybaphon.		17 Campana.
18 Stamnos (Apulian).		18
19 Celebe.		19 Olla con manichi annodati.
20 Lepaste.		20 Patera.
21 Lekane.		21 Patera col coperchio.
22 Cylix.		22 Patera.
23 Carchesion.		23 Tazza co manichi inarcati.
24, 30, 31 Cantharus.		24 Tazza co manichi inarcati.
25, 26 Cyathus.		25 Sendella.
27 Holmos.		27
29 Holcion.		28

* See Plate 4.

J.Dobbins

V. DÉCADENCE.

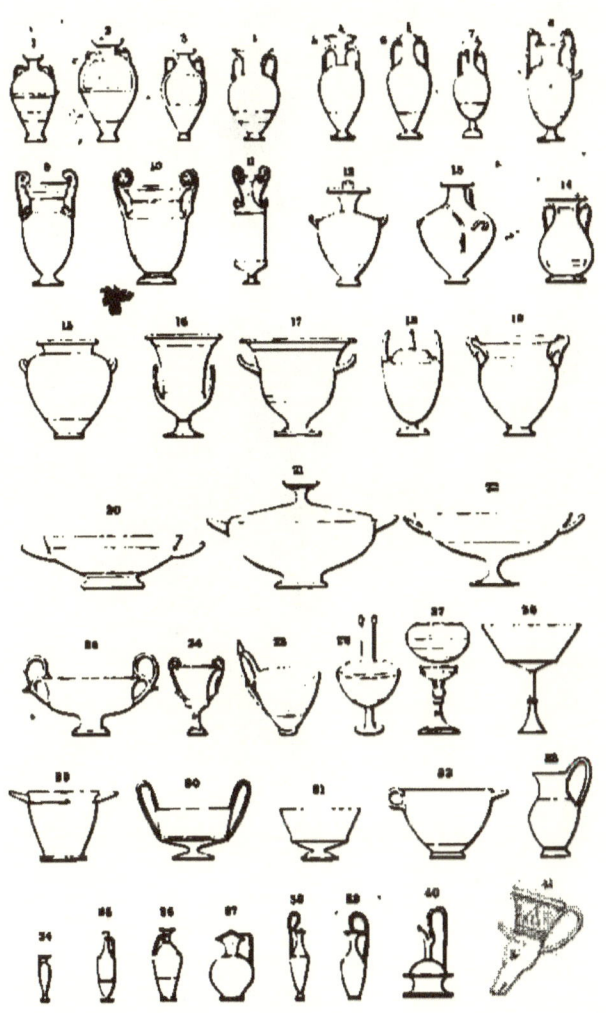

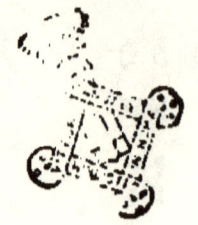

English Nomenclature.	Italian Nomenclature.
29 Scyphus.	29 Bicchiere.
30 } Cantharus.	30 Tazza con manichi orizzontali.
31	
32 Scyphus.	32
33 Olpe.	33 Uroeolo.
34 Cotyliskos.	34
35, 36 Lecythus.	35, 36 Lagrimale.
37 Oenochoe.	37 Preferieolo.
38, 39, 40, 42 Prochous.	38 Prefericolo a becco.
41, 43 Rhyton.	41 Riton.
44, 45 Ascus	44 Unguentario.
46 Bombylios.	46 Balsamario.
47, 48 Alabastron.	47 Unguentario.
49, 50 Aryballos.	49 Balsamario con manico.

ALCIBIADES. *Cornelian.*

Second Division.

GLYPTOGRAPHY, OR ENGRAVED STONES.

INTRODUCTION.

The Art of engraving on precious stones and gems is styled "glyptic," and the description of these engraved stones which have come down to us from ancient times, glyptography, from γλυφειν, to engrave, and γραφειν, to describe.

Among those objects of ancient art which have reached us through the lapse of ages, engraved stones may be considered among the number of the most elegant and refined by their form, their lustre, and their use, the most precious from their material and their workmanship, the most sought for from the facility with which they can be mixed with other ornaments, and set in connection with the most precious jewels. The luxury of the ancients led them to adopt a style of workmanship which was agreeable to the most exquisite taste, whether it adorned diadems, collars, bracelets, earrings, waistbands, portions of dress, shoes, or even valuable pieces of furniture, or whether, set in a ring of gold, it served both as a finger ring and a signet.

The most beautiful engraved stones were offered to the gods, and deposited in temples. For princes, they were as an ensign of supreme power and the seal of the state: for private individuals they gave authenticity to their public and private acts. Alexander, after he had conquered Darius, used the signet of that king for his letters and acts relative to Asia. Augustus adopted at first a stone bearing a sphinx, and substituted for it afterwards a head of Alexander, and then his own head; his successors adopted this latter, but Galba changed it for his family signet, on which was represented a dog on the prow of a vessel. At a later period some of the Roman emperors adopted the head of Alexander.

The use of signets of this kind was very general in Greece; cities, corporations, and families, had signets of their own. Rings were in general use in Rome; and it was by that ornament that Cicero assures us that he recognised a statue of Scipio Africanus; doubtless because that ring bore the signet of the family of the Scipios. The engraved stones which have come down to us from ancient times have not changed their destination: the same taste employs them for the same purposes; they are not the less sought after at the present day than they were formerly in all parts of the world by the Greeks and Romans. The abettors of modern luxury have inherited the passion of the Cyrenian for engraved stones, and perhaps we might still find musicians who, following the example of the Ismenias of Pliny, wear a valuable engraved emerald which by its value evinced his high artistic merit, and, like that flute player, are annoyed at not being able to purchase it at the highest price.

But considering here engraved stones in a more important and useful view, in the interest of the study of the arts and customs of antiquity, we may truly say that their importance in that respect is not surpassed by any other kind of monument. Besides being witnesses to the progress and history of the arts, we find on these engraved gems, the religion, the history, the opinions, the customs, even to the very amusements, of ancient nations; the portraits of their great men; the reproductions, in much smaller proportions, of some of the masterpieces of their architecture, their sculpture, or of their painting, which have come down to us; certain indications, with regard to their progress in the knowledge of nature, and a number of examples of their graceful, singular, or fantastic compositions which the taste or caprice of Greek artists multiplied in infinite numbers. It was by the study of engraved stones that Raphael and Michael Angelo received ideas which purified their taste. Other celebrated painters have found in them compositions

which they have not disdained to imitate, and modern glyptics
still work after the beautiful models which antiquity furnishes us
with, and which they have not equalled. We here adopt the words
of Dr. Croly. "The importance of these relics to learned investi-
gation, to the artist and the amateur, to the natural and elevating
indulgence felt in looking on the features of the mighty dead,
deserves to make them a favourite study with the accomplished mind
of England. Gems illustrate the attributes and tales of mythology,
the costumes of antiquity, the fine romances of the poets, the
characters of the early languages, the great historic events, and the
progress of the arts; the countenances of Virgil and Mæcenas, of
Cicero and Alexander, live only on gems; the Venus of Praxiteles,
the head of the Phidian Minerva, the Apoxuomenos of Polycleitus,
that triumph of ancient statuary, are to be found only on gems;
the restorations of the Venus de Medici and the Laocoon have been
made from gems; they offer an endless treasure of the brilliant
thoughts, and buried wisdom, the forgotten skill, and the vanished
beauty, of a time when the mind and form of man reached their
perfection."

TABLE. *Beryl.*

ORIGIN AND HISTORY.

The period of the invention of the art of engraving on precious
stones is unknown. The art is evidently of the highest antiquity.
Some seem to consider that all evidence tends to prove the oriental
origin of this art. Stones have been discovered with inscriptions in
Sanscrit, the earliest language of India; some attribute its invention
to Assyria, as many engraved stones have been found there in the
form of cylinders; but in the practice of this art, as well as others,

Egypt still maintains over all other nations its high antiquity, demonstrated not only by historical data, but also by monuments which have come down to the present time. The king of Egypt, who chose Joseph for his minister, gave him his signet ring as a testimony of his delegated authority, and Joseph lived about 1700, B.C. Engraved gems adorned the ephod and pectoral of the high priest of the Hebrews, and were probably the work of Egyptian artists, B.C. 1490. According to Herodotus, the treasure cell of Rhampsinitus, whom Sir Gardner Wilkinson identifies with Rameses III., B.C. 1219, was secured by his seal. The collections of engraved stones, called scarabæi, exhibit in the inscriptions engraved on them the names of kings of a very early date. Egyptian cylinders have been also found of the earliest periods; one bears the name of Osirtasen I., B.C. 2020. The study of these monuments of the glyptic art prove that the most ancient productions of the art are the works of the Egyptians. Mr. King attributes the invention of the art of engraving on "hard stones," crystal, onyx, agate, to the seal engravers of Nineveh, shortly before the reign of Sargon, B.C. 722, as before that period the material used was comparatively soft; the earliest Assyrian cylinders being of serpentine, and the Egyptian scarabæi being of clay or soft stone (steaschist). But squares used for the bezels of rings of hard stone engraved by the Egyptians, are to be met with of a much earlier date than that of Sargon. A remarkable one may be cited, bearing the name and title of a king of the 18th dynasty (15th century B.C.) of yellow jasper.* There are also others known of cornelian. The engraving of these is, indeed, generally bad, as if the workman was not master of his craft. From there being scarabæi, engraved with Assyrian emblems and sculptural ornaments of undoubted Egyptian origin, not unfrequently found in Assyrian ruins, it is evident that there must have been a close connection between Assyria and Egypt, as is conjectured about the time of the 18th (15th century B.C.) and the four subsequent dynasties. The mode of engraving may therefore have been introduced from Egypt. The knowledge of the art of engraving on hard stones is supposed to have been diffused by the Phœnicians among the Asiatic and Insular Greeks.

The Etruscans, the Greeks, and the Romans, practised the art also, and it was preserved among them, like all other arts, until the impetuous irruption of barbarism on the degenerate remains of ancient civilization. It is conjectured that the Etruscans learnt the art from the Egyptians through the Phœnicians, whose merchant

* There is an engraved agate cylinder of the time of Amenem Ha II. (B.C. 2070) in the British Museum.

ships trafficked in ornaments and jewellery at an early period, for
the most ancient Etruscan engraved stones are also in the form of a
scarabæus. Sicily and Magna Græcia preceded Greece in the knowledge of the glyptic art, as in that of all other arts which depend on
design. The Greeks, however, carried that art to the highest degree
of excellence, and it is to their genius that we are indebted for the
wonderful perfection it attained to. The art reached a culminating
point in the age after Alexander the Great, who gave it a fresh im-
pulse by his patronage, for he gave the privilege of engraving his
sacred portrait to Pyrgoteles, the first artist of the day. It thence
became the fashion for princes to adopt their own engraved portrait
as their signet. Portraits in cameo were introduced by the successors of Alexander, the earliest known being the beautiful portraits,
in sardonyx, of Ptolemy and Berenice.

The Romans imitated the Greeks in employing engraved gems
for signets, though at an early period they adopted the scarab signet
of the Etruscans. Under Augustus, gem engraving was brought to
a high perfection by the Greek artists of his time. At this period
flourished the celebrated engravers, Dioscorides, Solon, Aulus, Gnæus,
who introduced the practice of engraving their names on their best
works. At this period also a taste for cameo and works in relief
began to prevail, to which the arrival of pieces of sardonyx from
Asia, remarkable for their size and beauty, greatly contributed.
These were generally worked into cameei, vases, or cups, with subjects
in relief on them. Portraits in cameo became the prevailing taste of
the age. As is usually the case where there is a large demand for
any object, and there is not enough of the genuine material to supply
the demand, imitations were made to make up the deficiency. To
supply the large demand for these objects, and to please the taste of
those who could not afford the more expensive kinds, paste imitations
were made to an enormous extent. Numberless examples of these
paste intagli have come down to us. Camei were also imitated with
wonderful accuracy, the imitation too of the material itself being
admirably carried out. Some wonderful examples of camei in sardonyx have been produced in this age. The celebrated sardonyx
cameo of the apotheosis of Augustus, now in Paris, is considered a
masterpiece of the glyptic art. Some very fine camei are attributed
to the age of Hadrian, which has been considered the most flourishing period of Roman art. The glyptic art maintained a tolerable
degree of excellence till the time of Septimius Severus, when, together with the other arts, it began gradually to decay. From Rome
it spread almost over the whole west of Europe; but at the time of
the last emperors nothing remained except the mechanical part: the

genius and spirit of the art, the correctness of design and taste, the nobleness of expression, and even many of the practical advantages of which the ancient masters had availed themselves for conveying their grand ideas on stone, had all vanished together. The last expiring attempts at the art were the rude and ill-drawn Gnostic amulets.

VENUS MARINA. *Sard.*

MATERIALS OF THE ART.

THE mechanical process of the glyptic art has not been described in any work which has come down to us from ancient times; a few scanty remarks are found in Pliny. It is generally believed that the ancients used the same process as the moderns, in employing the drill (terebra), the punch (ferrum retusum), the wheel, diamond powder, and the diamond point, for cutting into the stone. The artist engraved the stone partly with iron instruments, smeared with Naxium, or emery and oil, which were sometimes round, sometimes pointed and drill-formed, but partly also with a diamond point set in iron. The adjustment of the wheel, by which the instruments were set in motion, whilst the stone was held to them, was probably similar in antiquity to what it is now. For polishing the stone, naxium, or emery powder, which was also called smyrris, was used.

It seems that the ancient artists performed that operation themselves, for the careful polishing of all parts of the engraved figures was a great aim with the ancient stone engravers, and is therefore a criterion of genuineness. These artists were generally designated under the denomination of "lithoglyphi," engravers on stone, a Greek word to which the Latin, sculptor or cavator, seems synonymous. The art of setting stones was styled among Greeks, lithocolleais, and among the Romans the setters of stones were named "compositores gemmarum." The name of "dactyloglyphi" was given to the engravers of rings, and from the Greek word for ring, δακτυλον, was derived the terms, "dactylogia," the science of engraved stones in general, but more particularly of finger rings; "dactylography," the science of their description; and "dactylotheca," a cabinet or collection of this kind of ornament.

The materials employed by the ancients in the glyptic art were various and numerous; they were animal, vegetable, mineral, or artificial. Among the first we may count coral and ivory; among the second, citron wood, box, ebony, sycamore, etc.; the mineral substances were clay, metals, and stones. Mineral substances, from their hardness, and other useful qualities, are more fit for the purposes of the engraver; and none more so than those belonging to the siliceous genus of the earthy class of minerals. That assemblage of stones, however, which is distinguished by the name of precious stones or gems, has scarcely ever been employed by the ancients for the purpose of engraving upon. These scarce and splendid substances were considered sufficiently valuable in themselves, and the art of engraving was more judiciously employed to enhance the value of other less expensive stones, which moreover possessed, in a superior degree, all the properties requisite for the nicest execution. Lessing and the Count de Clarac altogether deny the existence of any really antique intagli in the harder gems; but as Mr. King remarks, the instances that can be adduced of engraved emeralds, sapphires, and rubies, sufficiently prove that this rule, though generally true, yet admits of some, though rare, exceptions. He adds, however, that engravings on any of the precious stones are always to be examined with the greatest suspicion.

Stones may be classed according as they are transparent, semi-transparent, or opaque, and in those three classes may be mentioned: 1st, the diamond, the hyacinth, the sapphire of the present day, the emerald, the ruby, the topaz, the chrysolite, the jacynth, the amethyst, the beryl, the garnet, and rock crystal. 2nd, the opal, plasma, chalcedony, sard, onyx, sardonyx, agate. 3rd, green, yellow, brown, black jasper; lapis-lazuli, the sapphire of the ancients; hæmatite, obsidian, steatite, basalt, granite, serpentine. Turquoise has also been employed by the Romans.

The artificial substance generally employed by the ancients was a paste composed of coloured glass. The ancients excelled in colouring glass and porcelain. In order to imitate camei, they joined strata of different colours, which were fused together by the action of fire. The Egyptians used coloured glass in the earliest times, and the number of their scarabæi in porcelain, and other baked materials, is very considerable. The ancients manufactured also green, blue, and white pastes imitating precious stones.

The nature of the engraving on stones has led them to be divided into two principal divisions. Intaglio, or engraving in a concave form (Gr. διαγλυπτική, Lat. cœlatura); cameo, or engraving in relief. (Gr. γλυπτική, Lat. sculptura). The Egyptians, the Greeks, and the Romans practised both methods. The scarabæus, figured in relief and in all its details in Egyptian stones, constitutes a kind of cameo, while the flat part of the stone generally bears a subject or inscription in intaglio; several Egyptian stones are in existence, the flat part of which is engraved in cameo, the relief being, however, within the intaglio, or concave portion. Similar Etruscan stones have been also found.

The ordinary style of relief used for gems was mezzo-relievo, a style which was usually adopted for all works which required a close inspection. A flat style of relief was sometimes adopted in cameo, only for the sake of displaying a subject on a different coloured ground; the layers of colour in the stone employed, generally the sardonyx, being very thin. The difference of colour in the ground has, however, the effect of giving roundness to the figures relieved on it. The impressions from intagli are never in the flat style of relief, but however slightly mixed, are on the principle of mezzo-relievo (see Bas-reliefs). The gems of Dioscorides, the finest of antiquity, are in mezzo-relievo, and often of the fullest kind; as for instance the heads of Demosthenes and Io, and the figures of Mercury and Perseus. The same may be observed of other celebrated gems, such as the Medusa of Solon, the Hercules of Cneus.

Besides the two principal divisions we have just pointed out, engraved stones have received other characteristic denominations, derived from their form, or from the nature of their subjects. Scarabæi are oval engraved stones, with the upper surface cut in the shape of a beetle, or scarabæus, the flat lower surface being usually engraved. Cabochons, stones which are curved on one side, called by jewellers "tallow drop." Grylli, caricature heads, so called from

s

an Athenian of the name of Gryllus, famous for his ugliness.
Caprices or Symplegmata, heads grouped together in a fantastic
manner. Chimeras are imaginary beings, produced by the monstrous
union of the members of several creatures into one. Astriferi, those
in which astrological subjects and the stars are represented; *joined*
(conjugata) are heads represented together on the same profile; and
opposite, heads which face each other.

MINERVA WITH ÆGIS. *Sard.*

KNOWLEDGE AND TESTS OF ENGRAVED STONES.

THE art of distinguishing ancient stones from modern imitations,
or compositions, is the most difficult part of the study; the most
skilful judges are sometimes deceived in them, as Mr. King remarks:
" No definite rules can indeed be given, as nothing but long experience, and the careful examination of large numbers of gems
belonging to every period, can supply that almost intuitive percep-
tion in the art, so impossible to be acquired in any other manner.
We ought to examine, in the first place, if the material of the stone
was known to or worked by the ancients, and if it was employed by
the first artists. The harder gems were hardly ever used by
ancient artists. There is such scanty evidence of the celebrated
ancient artists engraving on precious stones, that precious stones
with an engraving on them are to be looked on with suspicion.

Lessing and the Count de Clavac, indeed, deny the existence of any really antique intaglio in the harder gems. The ancient artists preferred the sard and such stones as were best suited for the execution of the work, and for giving the most perfect impression of it."

The perfect finish of the work, the ease and freedom of the design, the fidelity of the costume, the interior of the engraving well polished, and very pure, are almost certain indications of antiquity. According to Mr. King, the truest test of antiquity appears to be a certain degree of dulness, like the mist produced by breathing on a polished surface, which the lapse of ages have cast upon the high lustre of the interior of the intaglio.* A slight incorrectness, or even a slight fault in the design, need not, however, awaken suspicion ; a very slight relief, or even when almost flat, is not a proof of a modern work ; the ancient engraving is generally very deep, and the relief very high. The employment of perspective renders a stone very suspicious, as the ancients were unacquainted with the application of that science; their chief aim was to engrave the principal figure as deeply as possible, in order that it might stand out more in relief. One of the principal characteristics of the engraving of ancient stones is what is termed in French the méplat, a flattening of the round parts of the human body in the figure. An important consideration also in regard to intagli is their size, as it must always be kept in view that engraved stones were used for signets and rings, and consequently their size could not be very large.

Camei, a great number of which have been manufactured in modern times, are in general more to be suspected than intagli. A careful examination of the material of the stones, of their hardness, their weight, their taste, their opaqueness, and their touch, is particularly required. They ought also to be exposed to the sun in order to be certain that their layers are natural, and the inscriptions should be carefully examined to see that they were not added by forgers. It must also be remarked here, that modern work has been frequently executed on ancient stones, which have been found unengraved. The appearance of ancient stones is generally duller, and less brilliant than those of modern stones. The subject and the

* Mr. King adds, a very satisfactory proof of antiquity is found when the engraving appears to have been executed almost entirely with the diamond point. According to the observations of Natter, the famous gem engraver, the extensive use of the diamond point is the great distinction between the antique and the modern art. The use of the diamond point has, however, been much questioned by some authorities, as its use would tend more to scratch the stone than to give that exquisite polish, which is one of the chief characteristics of a genuine stone.

inscriptions are a great assistance in lending their aid to an accurate knowledge of distinguishing them, while a comparative study of ancient and modern works, and a great practice of the eyes and the judgment, will lead to more certain results.

It has been said that wax attaches itself more readily to modern stones than to ancient stones, but this rule is not to be depended on ; wax will attach itself the more readily to a stone, the less perfect is its polish, whether it is ancient or modern. Further, ancient stones are in existence which have been repolished, which sensibly alters the features of the composition, and deteriorates their value.

Inscriptions are important tests of the antiquity of engraved stones, they are generally very short. They are either mottoes or proper names. Thus, on a cornelian representing Hercules reposing after his labours, this sentence in Greek is engraved, " Labour is the source of an honourable repose." As to proper names, three rules may be laid down : on Etruscan stones, it is the name of the person represented ; on Greek stones it is the name of the artist ; on Roman stones it is the name of the proprietor, or of the artist.   Inscriptions are of the greatest assistance in the examination of the authenticity of a stone ; the greatest importance should be attached to the inscription ; the shape of the letters should be examined ; if it is such as is indicated by the ancient alphabets, their variation and their forms in accordance with the period to which the stone may be assigned ; if it is Etruscan, the letters ought to be so also. In the old Greek style the letters should belong to the alphabet of that period, and the same for the later periods. In general, Greek artists wrote their name in the genitive case, when the word εργον is to be supplied, i.e., the work of ——. If the name be in the nominative case, it is the verb which is omitted, thus Διοσκουρίδης implies the word εποιει : Dioscorides made it. An inscription adds to the value of a stone, but forgers have particularly applied themselves to this mode of deceit. The stone should be carefully examined, if the beauty of the work answers to the reputation of the ancient artist to whom it has been attributed, and whose style is known by other works ; if the material, by its beauty and by its value, is in conformity with the rule adopted by the best engravers, to work only on the most beautiful of stones. The manner in which the letters are engraved is also an excellent test ; on the more ancient stones they are not very carefully done, and sometimes are very uncertain. The interior, however, is well finished, and the polish is in harmony with that of the stone itself ; here the magnifying glass is indispensable. The incriptions on stones of the age of Augustus are remarkable for the beauty of the letters, and their perfect execution, though very small. The great artists never left it to others to engrave their name on the stone; they wished that everything should be perfect in their work. These inscriptions, particularly those of the age of Augustus, are generally terminated by small round dots, very equal in their proportions, intervals, and depth. It is generally supposed that these dots were destined to mark the distances of the letters and to give greater regularity to them.

The forms of the letters may likewise serve to discover fraud. The mixture of Greek with Latin letters is an evident sign of forgery. The same may be said of a letter expressed in two different ways in the same word; for instance, the *sigma*, written as C, and as Σ in the word ΚΟΣΤΡΑΤΟΣ. Such errors are commonly committed by modern artists, who undertake to add names of ancient masters to their works. They are generally indifferent grammarians; and therefore liable to commit errors that no artist of antiquity could have fallen into. Thus, also, deceived by the pronunciation of the name, they have written Διοσκοριδου, instead of Διοσκουριδου. When two names occur in the same case, one is the name and the other the surname; but when the first name is put in the nominative case, and the second in the genitive, this indicates that the artist was the son or pupil of him whose name is put in the genitive case. Thus ΕΥΤΥΧΗΣ ΔΙΟΣΚΟΥΡΙΔΟΥ, signifies that Eutyches was the son or pupil of Dioscorides. If we read two proper names united by the conjunctive ΣΥΝ, it implies that these two artists worked on the same stone, as ΑΛΦΗΙΟΣ ΣΥΝ ΑΡΕΘΩΝΙ: Alpheus with Arethon. We have but one single instance of an engraver who, with his name, has indicated his profession on his gem, and this is Apollodotus; by the side of the head of Minerva we read: ΑΠΟΛΛΟΔΩΤ · ΑΙΘΟ. Απολλοδοτου λιθογλυπτου: εργον—the work of Apollodotus, the engraver. The greater number of the names of engravers are Greek. The names of Roman engravers are, for the most part, written in Greek letters. It is almost useless to add that a stone bearing the name of an artist whose age is known, and a subject derived from a period posterior to that artist, is a palpable forgery.

The most skilful imitators of antique inscriptions among modern artists, were Flavisno Sirleti, Natter, and Pichler, engravers of the 18th century. The first signed his own works to give them an appearance of antiquity, with the initials of his name in Greek letters ΦΣ, Phlabiou tou Sirletou. Pichler engraved his entire name ΠΙΧΛΗΡ. Natter translated his name into the Greek word ΥΑΡΟΣ, which deceived Winkelman and others.

Some amateurs of the last two centuries, following the example of Lorenzo de Medici, have had their name engraved on ancient stones as a mark that it is their property. It is said that the celebrated Maffei found some difficulty in interpreting the letters LAUR MED., which he found on some engraved stones which belonged to Lorenzo de Medici.

We may also in some measure determine the period in which the engraver of a particular gem lived, by finding out the time when his name was most common: thus, for instance, the name of Zosimus, more common in the Lower Empire than in any other period, will, with some probability, indicate that period to be the date of the work in question.

PAIN. *Sardonyx. Florence.*

SUBJECTS OF ENGRAVED STONES.

The subjects of engraved stones, excepting portraits and fantastic compositions, are derived from mythology, from the heroic periods, or from historic events. Careful attention should be given in order to see whether the subject is in conformity with the rites, myths, and traditions which have been handed down to us; whether the attributes and the character of the figures are in exact accord-

ance, as well as the accessory symbols. It must be remarked, however, that mythological subjects, unknown or difficult to explain,
prove rather in favour of the antiquity of the stone than otherwise.
The Egyptians have strictly adhered in their works to the creed and
religious ideas of their nation; and their scarabæi are in such endless
numbers as to preclude imitation, except in rare materials; but in
this case the incongruity and want of connection in the symbols
traced in the inscription will quickly betray the forgery. As to the
Etruscans, the style of their works is a type of authenticity which
it is not easy to imitate. The Greeks treated only subjects taken from
their mythology or their heroic history, and rarely from events
contemporaneous with the practice of the art. At Rome, the artists
still continued to adopt Greek subjects, and if they represented a
subject from Roman history, they always mingled allegory with
history; and the absence of allegorical figures in subjects of that
kind always makes the stone very suspicious.

We here take advantage of the extensive experience and profound critical knowledge of Mr. King, in extracting from his work
on Antique Gems, a portion of his summary of the subjects
generally found on engraved stones. First, beyond all dispute, are
the figures of Victory, executed in every style, from that of the best
epoch to the rude scratches of expiring art. Almost as frequent are
the figures of Nemesis, only to be distinguished from Victory by her
being always helmeted and holding a bridle or a measuring rod in
her hand. Venus comes next in point of frequency. Cupids, as a
necessary consequence, also abound in gems, and give scope for the
most elegant fancy, on the part of the artist, in his representation
of their various groups and attitudes, as engaged in various sports
and occupations. Minerva takes the next place, and, as may be
deduced from the style of the intagli, was the goddess who chiefly
occupied the engravers under the Flavian family. Roma, distinguished from the preceding by being seated on a throne and
holding an orb, is very frequent, especially in the gems of a later
period. Next follows, in frequent representation, Bacchus, old,
young, bearded, beardless; the Dionysus, the Indian, the Liber
Pater of the Romans, with all his train of Silenus, Fauns, and
Bacchantes, who disport themselves as full figures, busts, and heads,
on all kinds of gems. Mercury has been also frequently figured on
gems, the god of gain being probably the favourite deity of all times.
Hercules, as the deity whose protection assured good luck, was a
special favourite, particularly of the Romans, under the Middle
Empire. The bust of Jove, usually given as a front face, also is
tolerably frequent, but much less so in the full figure of this deity

seated on a throne. Serapis, however, whose worship was so universal under the later emperors, claims by far the largest share of the intagli representing Jupiter. Apollo is next to Serapis in point of popularity, together with his attributes, especially lyres, represented in a great variety of shapes. Mars is by no means uncommon upon Roman gems. Diana is more unfrequent, still more so Juno. Ceres is not seen very frequently. Neptune is still more rare; still more so Saturn and Vulcan. Pluto has been never represented. Miflin has remarked a kind of connection between the colour of the stones used and the subjects represented; for instance, for the sea-born Venus the artists adopted the sea-green colour of the plasma; for Bacchus, the amethyst; for Neptune and the Tritons, the beryl, or acqua marine; for Proserpine, a black stone; for Marsyas, flayed, a red jasper. This rule is not, however, strictly carried out in its application.

An infinite variety of masks, chimeræ, and caprices, are also frequently found represented. They all belong to the second century.

Animals make up the majority of Etruscan intagli, especially in that rude class the origin of which can be distinctly assigned to the engravers of that nation. Of Roman date, the lion and the bull are the most common subjects, then the various kinds of dogs, and the wild boar. Among birds, eagles, with various emblems, are the most frequently engraved. But of all subjects, portraits seem to have been most in favour. The Greek period gives us some magnificent portraits, but they are rare, and were most probably engraved only for the use of the person himself as his private signet. In the Roman period it seems to have been held a mark of loyalty to wear the portrait of the reigning emperor, which accounts for the vast number of such down to the time of Caracalla, and many of which, even of the early Cæsars, are of the most inferior execution, clearly manufactured at a cheap rate for the wear of the military and the poorer classes.

APOLLO. *Carl.*

GLYPTOGRAPHIC COLLECTIONS AMONG THE ANCIENTS,

ENGRAVED STONES, besides being used as signets, were also employed for ornamenting the most precious works of art, and religious utensils. A Greek inscription, published by Chandler, and which was the public inventory of the treasure deposited in the opisthodomos of the Parthenon, distinctly shows that engraved stones formed a portion of it. A horn of abundance, of gold, and adorned with similar stones, was given by Augustus to the Temple of Concord at Rome; and the eloquence of Cicero against Verres has rendered famous a candelabrum adorned with intagli and camei, destined by king Antiochus for the temple of Jupiter Capitolinus. According to Pliny and Suetonius, Cæsar and Marcellus consecrated collections of engraved stones in the temples of Venus and of the Palatine Apollo at Rome. Another collection, formed by king Mithridates, was celebrated for its magnificence, even in ancient times. Pompey and Scaurus had also rich collections at Rome. Pliny remarks that Scaurus was the first who possessed a collection of precious stones in Rome. In the Lower Empire, engraved stones and precious stones were profusely used to ornament the dresses of princes, of ladies, and of rich private individuals; in the middle ages, they were still much sought after, when other ancient monu-

ments were despised or unknown. The seal of king Pepin was
an ancient stone bearing the figure of a Bacchus, and that of
Charlemagne, a Serapis. The church jewellory, the reliquaries,
the shrines of saints, the covers of missals, were adorned with them ;
and these profane monuments, the subjects of which were at times
anything but pious, added to the splendour of religious worship. The
preservation of a great number of engraved stones, some indeed of
the finest, is indebted to that custom. In the 15th century, an
attempt was made to restore the glyptic art in the west. This art,
which was not completely forgotten at Constantinople, passed on
the revival of letters into Italy, where the Medici received it with
a munificence which is one of their fairest titles to the gratitude of
mankind. They evinced a particular taste for engraved stones, and
their courtiers propagated that taste, while their object was to flatter
that of their masters. Giovanni and Domenico excelled in the
practice of an art which was then the object of the greatest en-
couragement. The first engraved in intaglio, the second in relief,
both with such success, that they are known in the history of the
art under the names Giovanni de Cornaline, and Domenico de
Camoi.

ZEUS OVERCOMING THE GIANTS. *Cameo.* *By Athenion.* *Naples.*

ANCIENT ARTISTS.

THE number of ancient artists who have signed their works is
rather considerable, and we shall give here a concise list of them,

according to their epochs. It will be of some use, as well for the
history of the art as for the study of those monuments themselves,
especially by the indication of the principal works of each artist,
and of their special signatures.—The name of any Egyptian or
Etruscan artist has not been known. The list opens with Greek
artists, and history places at their head Theodorus of Samos, who
engraved the ring of Polycrates. We shall place an asterisk before
the names of those engravers of whom no work has come down
to us.

I. Greek Engravers anterior to the Age of Alexander.

*Theodorus of Samos; the ring of Polycrates.

*Mnesarchus, father of Pythagoras.

Lysander; a warrior armed (early style), with the name of the
engraver in retrograde letters of the ancient Greek alphabet.
Lanzi thinks this name is rather that of the warrior himself.

Heius; ΗΕΙΟΥ. A Diana venatrix (archaic style), supposed to be the
most ancient gem known, bearing the artist's name.—Sard.
Stosch.

Phrygillus; ΦΡΥΓΙΛΛΟΥ. Cupid issuing from an egg : one of the
earliest inscribed intagli.—Sard. Blacas.

Thamyrus; ΘΑΜΥΡΟΥ. A sphinx scratching her ear.—Sard.
Vienna.

II. From the Age of Alexander to the Age of Augustus.

Admon; ΑΔΜΩΝ. Hercules drinking.—Sard. Marlborough.
Head of Hercules, advanced in life. ΑΔ.

Apollonides; ΑΠΟΛΛΩΝΙΔΟΥ. Cow lying down.—Cameo fragment.—Duke of Devonshire.

Polycleitus: ΠΟΛΥΚΛΕΙΤΟΥ. Diomedes carrying off the Palladium.—Sard. Florence.
A subject frequently reproduced. According to Millin, the
name of the celebrated sculptor Polycleitus has been added
only to indicate that this engraving is only a copy of one
of his statues.

Pyrgoteles; ΠΥΡΓΟΤΕΛΗΣ ΕΠΟΙΕΙ.
Head of Alexander.—Blacas.
Head of Medusa.—Blacas.
Both doubtful.
Dispute between Neptune and Minerva, ΠΥ.—Cameo. Naples.
The head of Phocion (the work of Alessandro Cesati).

Tryphon; ΤΡΥΦΩΝ. The marriage of Cupid and Psyche.—Cameo.
    Marlborough, Naples.
    Cupid riding a lion.—Sard. The Hague.
Chronius; ΧΡΟΝΙΟΥ. Terpsichore standing (doubtful), repeated
    by Onesas and Allion.

III. Age of Augustus.

Acmon; ΑΚΜΩΝ. The Head of Augustus.—Cameo. Blacas.
Quintus Alexa; ΙΝΤΟΣ ΑΛΕΞΑ ΕΠΟΙΕΙ. Legs of a warrior.—Cameo
    fragment. Florence.
    Supposed to be the work of Alessandro Cesati.
Cœmus, or Cænus; ΚΟΙΜΟΥ. ΚΟΙΝΟΥ. Adonis, nude.—Onyx,
    Prince Lichtenstein; a faun, celebrating the bacchanalia.—
    Nicolo.
Agathopus; ΑΓΑΘΟΠΟΥΣ ΕΠΟΙΕΙ. The head of Sextus Pom-
    peius.—Beryl. Florence.
Aulus; ΑΥΛΟΥ. Æsculapius.—Sard. Strozzi.
    Horseman in armour.—Sard. Florence.
    Cupid tied to a trophy.—Sard. Carlisle.
    Cupid in fetters, leaning on a hoe.—Cameo.
    Head of Diana.—Sard.
    Head of Ptolemy Philopator.—Sard. Bibliothèque, Paris.
    It is supposed that there were several engravers of this name.
    Visconti is of opinion that the difference of style in the
    works attributed to Aulus is owing to his name having
    been frequently put on engraved stones that were nothing
    but copies of his work.
Cnaius or Cnæus; ΓΝΑΙΟC. Athlete rubbing himself with oil.—
    Nicolo. Bibliothèque, Paris.
    Athlete holding a Strigil.—Sard. Hendorp.
    Diomede carrying off the Palladium.—Sard. Denham.
    A female head, supposed by Bracci to be of Cleopatra.—Sard.
    Collegio Romano.
    Head of Theseus covered with a bull's hide.—The name added
    by Pichler. Amsterdam.
    Head of the young Hercules.—Beryl. Strozzi.
Dioscorides (of Ægea in Asia Minor); ΔΙΟΣΚΟΥΡΙΔΟΥ. Head of
    Augustus.—Amethyst. Blacas.
    Bust of Augustus.—Amethyst. Thoms.
    Head of Demosthenes.—Amethyst. Ludovisi.
    Head of Io.—Sard. Poniatowsky.

Mercury Criophorus, carrying a ram's head.—Sard. Devonshire.

Mercury, as god of travellers.—Sard. Lord Holdernew.

Perseus, resting his hand on a shield with Medusa's head.—Sard. Naples.

Diomede carrying off the Palladium.—Sard. Devonshire.

Epitynchanus; ΕΠΙΤΥΓΧΑ. Portrait of Germanicus, or Marcellus.—Sard. Blacas.

Bellerophon or Pegasus; ΕΠΙ.—Sard. Azara.
Attributed to Epitynchanus by Visconti.

Eutyches, son or pupil of Dioscorides; ΕΥΤΥΧΙΙΟ ΔΙΟCΚΟΥΡΙΔΟΥ ΑΙΓΕΛΟC ΕΠ.

Bust of Pallas.—Amethyst. Marlborough.

Solon; CΟΛΩΝ ΕΠΟΙΕΙ. ΣΟΛΩΝΟΣ.

Head of Medusa.—Chalcedony. Blacas.

Diomede, master of the Palladium.—Sard. Blacas.

Portrait of a bald man.—Sard. Ludovisi.

Head of Mæcenas.—Topaz. Florence.

Bust of a Bacchante.—Sard. Storch.

Livia, as Ceres.—Sard. Gori.

Victory, apteros, sacrificing a bull, fragment.—Sard. Storch.

Victory, with wings, flying, fragment.—Sard. H. Westropp.

GREEK ENGRAVERS POSTERIOR TO AUGUSTUS.

AGE OF TIBERIUS.

Ælius; ΑΕΛΙΟΥ. Head of Tiberius.—Sard. Corsini.
Head of Homer.—Nicolo. The Hague.

AGE OF CALIGULA.

Alpheus and Arethon; ΑΛΦΙΟΣ ΣΥΝ ΑΡΕΘΟΝΙ. Head of the young Caligula.—Cameo.
Germanicus and Agrippina.—Cameo.
Alpheus alone; Ajax seated on a rock.—Sard.
Dying warrior (doubtful).—Cameo.

AGE OF TITUS.

Evodus; ΕΥΟΔΟC ΕΠΟΙΕΙ. Head of Julia, daughter of Titus.—Amethyst. Marlborough.

AGE OF HADRIAN.

Antiochus; ANTIOXOY. Head of Pallas.—Sard.
    Head of Sabina (doubtful).
Anteros; ANTEPSTOC. Hercules carrying a bull.—Sard. Devonshire.
Hollen; EAAHN. Bust of Antinous as Harpocraton.—Sard. Starch.

AGE OF MARCUS AURELIUS.

Æpolian; AEPOLIANI. Head of Marcus Aurelius.—Paste. Stosch.

DECLINE OF THE ART.

Gnurnnus Anicetus; combat between a dog and a boar.—Bloxolstone.
    Millin supposes that the name may be that of the dog, Gnurnnus the invincible.

GREEK ENGRAVERS WHOSE AGE IS UNCERTAIN.

Ætion; AETIONOC. Head of Priam.—Sard. Devonshire.
Agathemerus; ΑΓΑΘΗΜΕΡΟC. Head of Socrates.—Sard. Blacas.
Allion; AAAIΩNOC. AAAYΩN. The muse Terpsichore.—Sard. Strozzi.
    The signature of Gio. Mar. da Pescia, according to some.
    Head of Apollo.—Sard. Florence.
    Bacchante.—Chalcedony. Desburough.
    Marietto attributes the Seal of Michael Angelo to this artist.
Ammonius; AMMONIOY. Head of laughing Faun.—Jacynth, B.M.
Apollodotus; AΠOAAOΔOTOY AIΘO. The only artist who added his profession to his name.
    The Head of Pallas armed.—Sard, Barberini.
    The dying Othryades.—Sard. Lucatelli.
Apollonius; AΠOAAΩNIOY. Diana Montana, leaning against a pillar.—Amethyst. Naples.
    Head of Mæcenas.—Jacynth. Rhodes.
Aspasius. ACΠACIOY; From his engraving on an inferior stone he is supposed to be of a later date than the flourishing period of Augustus.
    Head of Pallas.—Red jasper. Vienna.
    Supposed to represent the Pallas of Phidias.
    Head of Indian Bacchus.—Red jasper.
    Head of Jupiter.—Red jasper. Florence.
Athenion; AΘENIΩN. Jupiter hurling his thunderbolts at two giants with serpent legs.—Cameo. Naples.

Axeochus; ΑΞΕΟΧ. Faun playing on a lyre before a child.—
Stosch.

Carpus; ΚΑΡΠΟΥ. Bacchus and Ariadne.—Red jasper. Florence.
Head of Hercules and Iole.—Chalcedony.

Euplus; ΕΥΠΛΟΥ. Cupid on a Dolphin.

Euthus; ΕΥΘΟΥ. Silenus seated between two Cupids.

Hyllus; ΥΛΛΟΥ. Dionysiac bull.—Chalcedony. Stosch.
Head of a female.—Sard. St. Petersburg.
Young Hercules.—Onyx. Stosch.
Head of Philosopher.—Sard. Florence.
Triton, Nereid and two Cupids.—Sard. Marlborough.
From the resemblance of the Dionysiac bull to the bull
on the coins of Sybaris, he may be placed before the age
of Augustus.

Mithranes or Mithridates; ΜΙΘ. Head of a horse.—Sard. Berlin.

Mycon; ΜΥΚΩΝ. Head of an old man.—Jasper. Stosch.

Myron; ΜΥΡΩΝ. Head of a Muse.—Sard. Berlin.
Lion.—Sard. Blacas.

Myrton; ΜΥΡΤΩΝ. Leda.—Blacas.

Nicomachus, Faun sitting on tigor's skin.—Black jasper. Marlborough.

Nisus; ΝΕΙΟΟΥ. Jupiter holding a thunderbolt in his right hand.
Sard. St. Petersburgh.

Nymphoros; Standing warrior.—Sard. Florence.

Oneras; ΟΝΗCΑC ΕΠΟΙΕΙ. Muse.—Paste. Florence.
Leda. | Head of Hercules.—Sard. Blacas.

Pamphilus; ΠΑΜΦΙΛΟΥ. Cupid rescuing Pysche.—Sard. B.M.
Achilles playing the lyre.—Amethyst. Paris.
Achilles.—Sard. Devonshire.

Pergamos; ΠΕΡΓΑΜΟΥ. Faun dancing.—Stosch.
Hercules carrying a bull.—Stosch.
A young Bacchante.

Philemon; ΦΙΛΗΜΟΝΟC, ΦΙΛΗΜΩΝ'ΕΠΟΙ. Theseus gazing on
the body of the Minotaur.—Sard. Venice.
Head of a Faun.—Paste. Strozzi.

Plotarchus, or Protarchus; ΠΛΩΤΑΡΧΟΣ ΕΠΟΙΕΙ. Cupid riding
on a lion.—Cameo. Florence.
He is supposed to have lived before Augustus.

Scopas; ΣΚΩΠΑΣ. Œdipus and the Sphinx.—Stosch.
Young woman at her toilette.—Caylus.

Scylax; CΚΥΛΑΚΟΥ. The head of an eagle.—Sard. Percy.
Hercules Musagetes.—Sard. Baron Roger.
Head of Pan.—Amethyst. Blacas.

Scymnus; ΣΚΥΜΝΟΥ. Bacchus followed by a Panther.
Seleucus; CΈΛΕΥΚ. Head of Silenus.—Sard. Florence.
    Head of Hercules.—Blacas.
Socrates; ΣΩΚΡΑΤΗΣ. A comic actor.—Onyx. Roger.
Sostheues; CΩCΘΗΝ; formerly read CΩCΟΚΛΕ.—Sosocles.
    Head of Medusa.—Chalcedony. Carlisle.
Sostratus; CΩCΤΡΑΤΟΥ. Victory in a car.—Cameo. Naples.
    Genius in a car, drawn by two Panthers.—Devonshire.
    Victory sacrificing a bull.—Sard. Devonshire.
Sotratus; CΩΤΡΑΤΟΥ.
    Winkelman supposes this and the preceding name to be the
    same, with the accidental omission of the letter C.
    Meleager and Atalanta.—Cameo. Devonshire.
Teucer. ΤΕΥΚΡΟΥ.
    Hercules and Iole.—Amethyst. Florence.
    Faun holding a wreath.—Sard. Carlisle.

ROMAN ENGRAVERS.

Aquilas; ΑΚΥΙΛΛC. Venus bathing, Cupid by her.—Raspe.
Felix; ΚΑΛΠΟΥΡΝΙΟΥ CΕΟΥΕΡΟΥ ΦΙΛΙΞ ΕΠΟΙΕΙ. Diomedes
    and Ulysses carrying off the Palladium.—Sard. Marl-
    borough.
    Head of Mercury.—Red jasper. Paris.
Quintillus; ΚΥΙΝΤΙΑ. Neptune in a car.—Beryl. Ludovisi.
    Mercury.—Sard. Poniatowsky.
Rufus; ΡΟΥΦΟΥ, ΡΟΥΦΟC ΕΠΟΙΕΙ. Aurora guiding the solar
    car.—Cameo. St. Petersburg.
    Head of Ptolemy Physcon.—Sard. Raspo.
    A number of engraved stones bear Roman proper names,
    but they are supposed to be the names of the proprietors
    of the stones, and not of the engraver.

ENGRAVERS OF THE LOWER EMPIRE.

Chæremon; ΧΑΙΡΗΜΩΝ. The head of a Faun.
Nicephorus; ΝΙΚΗΦΟΡΟC. Mercury.—Onyx.
    Man seated, forging a helmet.—Sard. Thoms.
Phocas; ΦΟΚΑC. An Athlete holding a palm.—Jacynth. Caylus.
    One of the most remarkable works of this period is the
    stone called the Sapphire of Constantine, in the Rinuccini
    Cabinet, Florence. It represents the Emperor Constan-
    tine attacking a wild boar, near Cæsarea, in Cappadocia.

CAMEO OF THE STE. CHAPELLE.

CELEBRATED ENGRAVED STONES.

SOME ancient engraved stones have acquired celebrity from the perfection of the workmanship, from the beauty or size of the material. Among Camei the most celebrated are

1. The Cameo called that of the Sainte Chapelle in the Bibliotheque, at Paris. It is a Sardonyx composed of two brown and two white layers, and is an oval of 13 inches by 9. It was brought from

the East by king Baldwin and given to the Sainte Chapelle by
king Charles V. It presents three scenes. In the upper portion is
the Apotheosis of Augustus. In the middle portion, are Tiberius
under the figure of Jupiter, and Livia, his mother, under the
figure of Ceres. They receive Germanicus on his triumphal
return to Rome A.D. 17. Agrippina, his wife, assists him in taking
off his helmet, and his son, Caligula, stands behind him. The young
man who carries a trophy, is Drusus, son of Tiberius. In the
lower portion are vanquished nations personified under the figures
of warriors dressed in the costume of eastern and western nations.

GEMMA AUGUSTEA, OF VIENNA.

11. The Cameo of Vienna, or the Gemma Augustea, is not so
large as that of Paris, and presents but two scenes. It is superior as a work of art, and is in better preservation. It passed
from the Abbey of Poissy to Germany, having been purchased by
Rudolph 11. for 1200 ducats. It is considered the finest work in
relief extant. It has but two layers. Its shape is elliptical, 9 by
8 inches. The subject is the reception of Drusus (father of Germanicus) after his victory over the Rhæti and Vindelici, B.C. 17.
Augustus as Jove, and Livia as Rome, seated on thrones, welcome
the hero and his brother Tiberius. Behind Augustus are Neptune
and Cybele, who seem to be symbols of his powers over land
and sea.

TAZZA FARNESE.

III. The Tazza Farnese, at Naples. It is composed of a single piece of sardonyx, and is nearly a foot in diameter. The subject of the sculpture has given rise to much learned and elaborate disquisition. It is generally supposed to represent the apotheosis of the first Ptolemy. According to Professor Quaranta, it represents Ptolemy Philadelphus, consecrating the festival of the harvest instituted by Alexander the Great, at the time of the foundation of Alexandria. The outside is ornamented with the head of Medusa. The place of its discovery is uncertain. It is supposed to have been found in the Villa Adriana, near Rome.

IV. The portraits of Ptolemy Philadelphus, and his first wife Arsinoe. According to Visconti, the head of Ptolemy Energetes, and Berenice. This cameo is of sardonyx, but is composed of

T 2

several pieces. The collars and ornaments given to each head
conceal the joinings. It is in the Imperial collection of Russia.

PTOLEMY AND BERENICE.   Cameo.

JUPITER ÆGIOCHUS

V. The head of Jupiter Ægiochus. This cameo was found at
Ephesus, and is now in Venice.

VI. The Carpogna cameo in the Vatican. It represents the triumph of Bacchus and Ceres in a car drawn by Centaurs. This cameo is remarkable as being the largest slab of sardonyx known, being 16 inches long by 12 deep. It is composed of five layers.

The Museum of Venice possesses several other magnificent camei, especially those which represent Orestes, the car of Neptune, Rome and Augustus, Claudius and his family. In Paris, in the Bibliotheque, there are many remarkable camei. The apotheosis of Germanicus, Agrippina and Germanicus under the figures of Ceres and Triptolemus, Ulysses, portraits of Tiberius, Claudius, Marcus Aurelius, Faustina, Adrian, Antinous. In the British Museum and in the Devonshire collection are some smaller, yet beautiful specimens of Greek and Roman work. In the collection at Naples is the cameo by Athenion, representing Jupiter hurling his thunderbolts against the Titans.

Among the most celebrated intagli are

Of Dioscorides, the Io, considered by Visconti as one of the finest engravings in existence. It cannot be reproduced exactly in the plaster cast on account of the under cutting of the nose, the intaglio being a three quarter face. It is far superior, both in delicacy and correctness, to the Demosthenes by the same artist.

The Demosthenes. This is on a splendid amethyst, but shows somewhat of stiffness and hardness of manner. Both these intagli are much more deeply cut than is usual with antique gems, and differ in this respect from his Diomede, master of the Palladium, which is in flat relief. It may be set down as one of his earliest productions. (C. W. King.)

Diomede, master of the Palladium. The hero appears seated, with one leg extended, and contemplating the statue placed on a cippus before him. It is on a red sard in very flat relief.

Mercury Criophorus. A naked and wingless figure holding a ram's head in his left hand, and in his right a caduceus. The head presents a full face. A sard in the Devonshire collection.

Perseus resting his hand on a shield with a Medusa's head, and a sword. A sard in the Museum at Naples.

The head of Augustus.

The Medusa, of Solon. Following the invariable rule of Greek art never to represent anything hideous or repulsive, Medusa is here represented with features of exquisite beauty. Eleven serpents are twined in her hair. It was found in a vineyard on the Monte Celio, near St. Giovanni e Paolo. It is engraved in chalcedony. It was formerly in the Strozzi collection, and is now in that of the Duc de Blacas.

The Pallas, of Aspasius. The richly ornamented helmet is surmounted by a lofty crest, and by a sphinx, the emblem of celestial intelligence; two griffins, placed in the lateral parts, present an analogous emblem; and over the visor, eight horses in front, in full gallop, present a sublime image of the power and the rapidity with which the divine mind acts. It is supposed to represent the head of the Pallas of Phidias.

The Julia, of Evodus. It is the portrait of Julia, the daughter of Titus and Marcia, with diadem, curled hair, necklace, earrings. It is engraved on a beryl or pale sapphire, of extraordinary magnitude. The size and beauty of the stone and the high finish of the work, render this gem very remarkable. It is in the collection of the Imperial Library at Paris.

The young Hercules, of Cnæus. An exquisite example of the Greek type of head, and a most perfect specimen of Greek work.

The Esculapius, of Aulus. It is a bust of Esculapius. The name of the artist is engraved on a tablet. This is considered the finest of the works of Aulus. There are several other engraved stones bearing the name of this artist, but from their inferior workmanship, are evidently not by the same engraver.

The Pallas, of Eutyches. It is a bust of Pallas, by Eutyches, the son or pupil of Dioscorides. She wears the Corinthian helmet, such as is worn by the Pallas of Velletri, and as she is represented on the coins of Corinth. She holds her robe on her breast. The stone is a pale amethyst, deeply engraved.

The Dionysiac Bull, of Hyllus. The bull is girt with ivy, and over him a thyrsus. It is almost similar in style to the bull on the coins of Sybaris. There are several antique copies of this intaglio.

The Achilles Citharædus, of Pamphilus. It represents Achilles seated on a rock playing the lyre. It is engraved in amethyst, and is now in the Bibliotheque in Paris.

The signet of Michael Angelo. The subject is a vintage, and Bacchic festival, and in the exergue is a boy fishing. It is a sard, and has given rise to many opposite opinions with regard to the representation of the subject, as also with re-

THE MOST CELEBRATED INTAGLI.

(The same size as originals.)

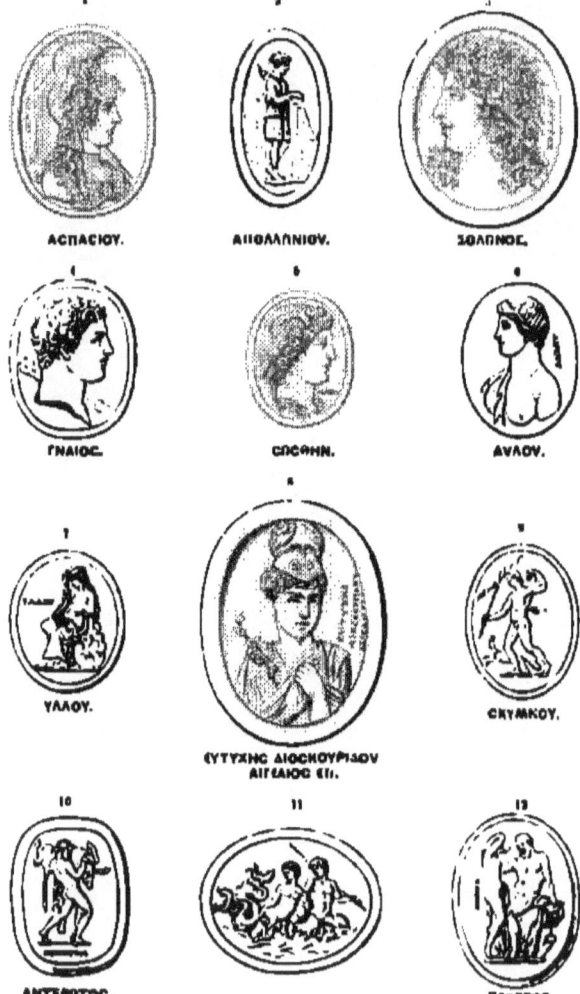

1. ACΠACIOV.
2. AΠΟΛΛΩΝΙΟV.
3. ΣΟΛΠΝΟΣ.
4. ΓΝΑΙΟΣ.
5. CΩCΩHN.
6. AVΛOV.
7. VΛΛΟΥ.
8. ΕΥΤΥΧΗC ΔΙΟCΚΟΥΡΙΔΟV ΑΙΓΕΛΙΟC ΕΙΙ.
9. CKYMKOY.
10. ANTEPΩTOC.
11.
12. TEVKΡΟΥ.

ΔIOCKOΥPIΔOΥ.   ΔIOCKOΥPIΔOΥ.

ΔIOCKOΥPIΔOΥ.

1. The Head of Pallas . . By Aspasius. . . . Red Jasper . . Vienna.
2. Diana Montana . . . By Apollonius . . . Amethyst . . . Naples.
3. Head of Medusa . . . By Sosos . . . . Calcedony . . . Blacas.
4. Head of the Young } By Gnaeus . . . . . Beryl . . . . . Strozzi.
   Hercules . . . . . . }
5. Head of Medusa . . . By Sosthenes . . . Calcedony . . . Carlisle.
6. Bacchus . . . . . . By Aulus . . . Jacynth . . . Pichler.
7. Ariadne abandoned . . By Hyllus . . . Sard . . . . British Museum.
8. Bust of Pallas . . . { By Euticles, son of } Pale Amethyst . Marlborough.
                         { Dioscorides . . . }
9. Bacchus with a Pan- } By Sostratus . . . Sard. . . . . — —
   ther . . . . }
10. Hercules carting a } By Antaeus . . . Sard . . . . Devonshire.
    Bull . . . . }
11. Nereus and Boreas . . — — Amethyst . . Florence.
12. Hercules and Iole . . By Teucer . . . . Amethyst . . . Florence.
13. Head of Medusa . . . — Amethyst . . . Blacas.
14. Mercury Criophoros . . By Dioscorides . . Sard . . . . Devonshire.
15. Head of Io . . . . By Dioscorides . . Sard. . . . Poniatowski.
16. Victory leading Four } — — Sard. . . . . Blacas.
    Horses . . . . . . }
17. Drunken . . . . . . By Dioscorides . . Sard. . . . . Devonshire.
18. Hermaphrodite re- } By Dioscorides . . Amethyst . . . Wardley.
    clining . . . . . }

[Between pages 310 and 311.]

gard to its antiquity. Those who believe it to be antique,
consider the boy fishing as the symbol of the Greek engraver
ΛΛΛΙΩΝ; others, on the other hand, deem it a rebus upon the
name of the artist Gio Maria da Pescia, the celebrated
engraver, and friend of Michael Angelo.

CAR OF BACCHUS. *Sard.*

CUPS.

Though, strictly speaking, not included under the head of engraved
gems, we must not omit to notice drinking cups and vases, particularly as they are sometimes found ornamented with mythic subjects
in relief, and, as Mr. King remarks, may be considered as huge
cameoi. They are generally of the same stone as used for cameoi,
sardonyx. The ancients were fond also of decorating their drinking
cups with precious stones and cameoi. They called such vessels
" gemmæ potoriæ." The most splendid agate vase of this kind is
the two-handled cup or carchesium of St. Denys, usually styled
the cup of the Ptolemies. Its sculptures represent masks,
vases, and other Bacchic emblems. It is supposed to have been
executed for Ptolemy Dionysus. But Mr. King considers it to be
from its style of the time of Nero. It was presented by Charles
the Bald,* in the ninth century, to the Abbey of St. Denys, and
was always used to hold the wine at the coronation of the kings

---

* M. Labarte says it was given by Charles III. (the Simple).

of France. It is now in the collection of antiquities at Paris.
Another celebrated vase, is the Brunswick vase, of sardonyx, which
represents the myth of Ceres in search of Proserpine, and that
of Triptolemus. It is an *alabastron*, or tall perfume jar, with narrow
neck, five inches high by two in the greatest diameter. Its style
is supposed to indicate the age of the Antonines. It originally
belonged to the Gonzaga family but was stolen at the sacking of
Mantua, in 1630, by a soldier, who sold it for 100 ducats to the
Duke of Brunswick. It is now in Paris. We must not omit also to
mention the celebrated murrhine vases of antiquity, upon which
such high value was set by the ancients. They are thus men-

THE TWO-HANDLED CUP OF ST. DENYS.

tioned by Pliny: "Pompey was the first who introduced murrhine
vases at Rome. He being the first to dedicate, at the conclusion
of his triumph, vases and cups made of this material, in the temple
of Jupiter Capitolinus, a circumstance which soon brought them
into private use; small dishes even, and eating utensils made of
murrhine being in great request. This species of luxury, too, is

daily on the increase; a simple cup, which would hold no more than three sextani (pints) having been purchased at the price of 70,000 sesterces." He thus describes the material of which these vases were made: "The East sends us murrhina* (the pieces in the rough). For they are found there in several places, in not very remarkable parts of the Parthian dominions, principally however in Carmania. They are supposed to be formed of a moist substance solidified by subterraneous heat. In superficial extent they never exceed that required for small dishes (abaci). In thickness, they are rarely large enough for a drinking cup, such as already mentioned. The polish they take is without strength, being rather a gloss or lustre than a brilliant polish. But their value lies in the variety of their colours—the spots, or strata, winding around, here and there, presenting hues of purple and white, and a third colour made of both, which assumes a fiery tint, as if by the passage of the colour through the purple, or that the milky white colour assumes a ruddy glow. Some especially admire in them the ends or boundaries of the colours, and a certain play of colours, such as is seen in the rainbow. To others the opaque spots, or strata, are more agreeable; any transparency or paleness in them is considered a defect. Murrhine exhibits also crystals and warts, not prominent, but frequently as if imbedded in the substance itself. There is some recommendation also in the agreeable odour."

The material that answers best to this description of Pliny, is the piece of "murra" found under the ruins of a house by a dealer in antiquities in Rome. It was purchased by the Jesuits, was cut up into thin slices, and now forms the front of the altar in the Chiesa del Gesu, at Rome. It fully answers the description of Pliny. It is purple in colour, with strata of dull white through it; on the edges of the white layer there is a slight iridescence. In some parts it has a reddish hue. It exhibits crystals also.† The specimens of it shown to Mr. Tennant and Mr. Davis of the British Museum have been pronounced by them to be fluor spar, the white stratum being a layer of hornstone, sometimes, but rarely found

---

* Here Pliny is evidently speaking of the material itself, pieces in the rough, and not of vases or vessels as generally understood.

† If the word "salex," is to be translated crystals, as in Mr. Bostock's translation of Pliny, it would confirm the view of the murrhine being of fluor spar, as fluor is characterised by crystallising in regular cubes. Agate exhibits no crystallisation.

In further confirmation of the murrhine vases being of fluor spar, we may adduce Pliny's statement of a person of consular rank, who used to drink out of a murrhine vase, and grew so passionately fond of it, as to gnaw its edges; this could be done to fluor spar, as it is of a very brittle nature, and could be easily abraded by the teeth, but could not be done to agate or any other siliceous stone.

running through fluor spar, the crystals also being those of true fluor spar. Mr. King's remark, that the material itself was brought to Rome in the rough, and there wrought up into dishes and flat bowls, would seem to confirm the supposition that this piece in the rough found at Rome is a piece of the true "murrhina." Some have considered the "murrhina" to be agate, but this could not be, as numerous specimens of agate cups have been found, and no specimens of agate answering to the "murrhina" of Pliny have been found in a cup or bowl, or in any of the broken portions frequently to be met with; besides, the murrhine vases were exceedingly rare, while the agate cups were, in comparison, rather common. Further, the agate was well known as a distinct class of stone, originally coming from a river in Sicily, Achates, whence it derives its name, whereas the "murrhina" came only from the East. It has also been conjectured that the murrhine vases were made of Oriental alabaster. In the passage, however, of Lampridius "in murrhinis et onychinis minxit," it is clearly distinguished from Oriental alabaster, for judging from Pliny's description "onychina and onyx" were terms applied to Oriental alabaster.[*] The name onyx was afterwards exclusively appropriated to the gem still called by that name. The murra and the onyx (Oriental alabaster), however, bear a resemblance to one another, as they are striped, and exhibit zones and bands of various strata. Pliny also mentions varieties of coloured glass imitating the murrhine. The portions of coloured glass belonging to cups, found at Rome, bear a closer resemblance to the striped or zoned appearance of the murra and onyx (Oriental alabaster) than the agate.

As a result we may come to this conclusion, that the "murrhina" were pieces of fluor spar, with a stratum of hornstone, of which the piece found at Rome (called murra) is a specimen. The onyx, or onychina, were Oriental alabaster, and the Achates was the agate as commonly understood at the present day.

---

[*] Seneca also distinguishes the murrhine vases from sardonyx; for he speaks of the wealthy having mules to carry their vases of crystal, murrhine, and those engraved by the hands of famous artists, evidently meaning by them last, vases of sardonyx carved in relief by celebrated artists.

MERCURY AND FORTUNE. *Sard.*

MODERN COLLECTIONS.

The example given in Italy by the Medici, found imitators in other parts of Europe; collections of ancient engraved stones were formed in different places by princes, rich private individuals, learned men, and artists. The Crusaders brought several from the East; Peiresc collected engraved stones at the same time that he collected inscriptions, manuscripts, and medals; he propagated that taste by his example. The kings of France gave some very valuable stones to churches and abbeys; these precious objects became afterwards the property of the crown, and were placed in the royal cabinets, and those of princes; and after the sixteenth century. several collections enjoyed great celebrity. Time has dispersed some and increased others. At the present day the most remarkable among public collections are those of the Florence Gallery, the stones of which are considered to be over four thousand in number; of the Vatican, at Rome, of the Museum at Naples, of the King of Prussia, of the Emperor of Austria, of the King of Denmark, at the castle of Rosenburg at Copenhagen, of the Emperor of Russia, which contains the Natter and d'Orleans cabinets; and among the cabinets which do not belong to sovereigns, the most celebrated are the Strozzi and Ludovisi collections in Rome, the Poniatowsky in Russia, the Devonshire, Marlborough, Besborough, Carlisle, and Bedford collections

in England; and the collections of the Duc de Blacas, the Count
Pourtales, and the Baron Rogers at Paris. Some very beautiful
works, both ancient and modern, are to be found in these collections.

Many learned men have devoted themselves to the interpretation
of engraved stones. Leonardo Agostini published, in the beginning
of the seventeenth century, a collection of them, several editions of
which have been published. The collection of La Chausse appeared
at Rome in 1700, that of Gorlæus was printed several times in Leyden,
and the collection of Ebermayer, at Nuremberg, in 1720. Some
antiquarians devoted especial attention to a particular class of those
stones, as Chifflet to abraxas, Passori to astrological stones, Ficoroni
to those which bore inscriptions. Afterwards there appeared particular descriptions of the most celebrated cabinets; such are the
great works known under the title of Pierres gravées, by Gori, by
Bassi, the Museum Florentinum of Gori, the "Galérie de Florence,"
by Wicar and Mongé, the Museum Odescalchum, by Galeotti; the
description of intagli of the cabinet of the King of France, by
Mariette, that of the engraved stones of the Duke of Orleans, by
Leblond and Lachaux, of the cabinet of Vienna by Eckhel, of the cabinets of Gravelles, Crassier, and Stosch, by Winkelman; the description of the cabinet of the Duke of Marlborough, and that of the
Imperial Cabinet of St. Petersburg, by M. Koehler. A valuable
work has been published by Millin, entitled, "Pierres gravées inédites
tirées des plus célébres cabinets de l'Europe." Other archæologists
have also devoted their attention to engraved gems, in particular,
or in works containing different branches of archæology. Among
these are Montfaucon in his "Antiquité Expliquée;" the Count de
Caylus, in his important "Recueil," and also Amaduzzi, Raspoui,
Vivenzio, Lippert, and Raspè. Several other archæologists have
published works, laying down rules for the study of engraved
stones; works for this purpose have been published by Millin,
Marcelli, Murr (Dresden, 1606), and by the senator Vettori (Rome,
1739), Busching (Hamburg, 1781), Aldini (Cesena, 1789), Eschem-
burg (Berlin, 1787), M. de Koehler (St. Petersburg, 1810). The
most important work of the present day is that of Mr. King, on
"Antique Gems," which displays an extensive critical knowledge of
engraved stones, combined with exquisite taste.

BELLONARIUS. *Illustration*

GLYPTOGRAPHY OF ANCIENT NATIONS.

AFTER making those few general remarks on Glyptography, it will be necessary to enter into some particular details on the productions of that art which have come down to us from each of the ancient nations, the antiquities of which we have undertaken to illustrate. In the paragraphs of this section will be found some special observations on the engraved stones of the Egyptians, the Etruscans, the Greeks, and Romans; some particulars which ought to be especially observed, so as not to be misled with regard to their authenticity, the genuine expression of the subject, the characteristics of the workmanship, and their classification.

EGYPTIAN GLYPTIC ART.

The most general form of Egyptian engraved stones is that of the scarabæus or beetle, with an oval flat base; the surface of which received the engraving in flat intaglio. This base is pierced in its length. The insect is more or less in relief over the base, according to the

finish of the workmanship. Egyptian scarabæi may be considered at one
and the same time as camei and intagli. Sometimes the execution in
relief of the figure of the insect is so carefully finished, as to leave
no doubt that it is an accurate representation of the scarabæus sacer,
at the present day found in Barbary and all along the coast of
Africa. It was sacred to the sun, and to Pthah, and was adopted as
a sacred emblem of the God who made all things out of clay. Its
Egyptian name was Cheper, Creator. The elytra or upper wings
of the stone scarabæi are generally united, and sometimes marked
with furrows. They were generally used for ornamental, funereal,
and historical purposes, and were usually worn as seals and amulets.

EGYPTIAN SCARABÆI.

The greater number of scarabæi were mounted in rings, which frequently bore the name of the wearer, the name of the monarch in
whose reign he lived, and also the emblems of certain deities: they
were so set in the gold ring so as to allow the scarabæus to revolve
on its centre, it being pierced for that purpose. They were also
strung in necklaces. Scarabæi are of various sizes, and were made
of different substances, of green stone, cornelian, hæmatite, granite,
serpentine, agate, lapis lazuli, plasma, amethyst, and other materials; a cheaper kind was made of limestone, stained to imitate a
harder and dearer quality, or of the ordinary blue pottery. Scarabæi

have been used at all periods of Egyptian history. According to Mr. Birch, they are of all ages, from the fourth dynasty down to the Roman Empire. The principal period of their manufacture was, however, the reign of Thotmes III. of the eighteenth dynasty, one tenth of these amulets bearing his name. A great number of others are referable, from their style, to the eighteenth, nineteenth, and twentieth dynasties.

The large and small scarabæi form two separate classes, distinguished by the use each class was put to. Those from one to three inches in length belong to the larger class, and from the study of their inscriptions, it is now proved that the large scarabæi were for

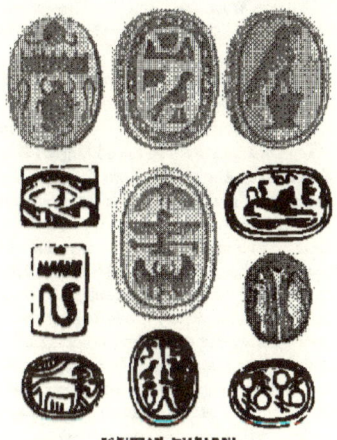

EGYPTIAN SCARABÆI.

the most part funereal. The representation of these large scarabæi may be seen in papyri taken from mummies, among the different objects traced on their mortuary rituals. They have been also found on mummies, either in the centre of their necklaces, or placed on their breast. A scarabæus was also placed on the outer case of the mummy, between other symbolical images. The inscription on their face is generally a formula or prayer for the deceased, such as is found traced or repeated on mummies, papyri, and other funereal objects. The only difference being that the name of the deceased is changed. Sometimes a royal oval gives the date of the scarabæus, but large scarabæi of this kind are of very rare occurrence. Many scarabæi are found uninscribed. Some have a blank left in the inscriptions, which was for the name of the deceased, which proves the universality of the use of scarabæi for funereal purposes, and further, that they were prepared beforehand with the usual formula from the consecrated type, to which the name of the deceased was afterwards added. Some of these large scarabæi are very carefully finished; on some the elytra and corslet of the insect are ornamented with figures. Some rare examples are found with human heads. Others were historical. Some of three inches long, belonging to the reign of Amunoph III, of the eighteenth dynasty, have been found, recording the marriage of the King Amunoph with Taia; the name of the queen's parents, and the limits of the Egyptian Empire; the number of lions killed by the king, and other statements.

The smaller scarabæi are more numerous than the larger kind, and more interesting also · for the study of the periods of Egyptian history. They are valuable documents for the annals and chronology of Egypt. On them will be found engraved representations of Egyptian deities, under their three forms, religious symbols, funereal formulæ, sacred and civil emblems, the names of kings, of queens, of private individuals, various ornaments, animals, plants; dates and numbers expressed in cyphers have also been recognised on the inscriptions. Others have been found inscribed with mottos, such as "A happy life," "Sacred to Amun," "Good luck," being probably used as seals in epistolary correspondence. The variety of subjects leads to the following classification of small scarabæi; they may be distinguished as: *mythological*, for all subjects, figures or inscriptions which are connected with religion; *historical*, for those which bear ovals or royal names, names of private individuals, or figures relating to civil customs; *physiographical*, those on which have been engraved animals or plants, which are connected with consecrated symbols; *various*, or those which bear alone ornamental designs to which no special meaning can be assigned. Those ought to be particularly observed which bear ovals containing the name of a king or queen. Sometimes the elliptical shape of the stone forms itself the oval which contains the name. These royal names give especial interest to the small scarabæi. Some ascend to the highest period of Egyptian history. These scarabæi are found made of every kind of material. The most ancient are almost all of common materials, and the hieroglyphics exhibit a want of finish. A collection of scarabæi might be formed displaying a chronological series of the names of the kings of Egypt, ranging from the highest antiquity down to the second century of the Christian era.

Some beautiful examples of Greco-Egyptian art in intaglio were executed in the age of the Ptolemies, of which we may instance the wonderful portrait of one of the Ptolemies, in dark sard, formerly in the Herz collection. Some good intagli were also executed in the earlier style, under Hadrian, when the Egyptian religion was again revived.

We must also notice here a class of engraved stones, which bear an analogy to engraved gems, though they differ in their form, yet were probably used for the same purpose, for seals. We would speak of cylinders. They are of a cylindrical form and are made of hard materials, of basalt, jasper, hæmatite, agate, and also of blue pottery, ranging in their lengths from one to three inches. They are perforated in their entire length, and their surface is covered with figures and inscriptions. They were evidently intended for signets. These cylinders have been generally supposed to be peculiar to the Persians and Assyrians, and cylinders have been found in Egypt bearing Egyptian figures and Persian inscriptions. This did not tend to contradict the general opinion on their origin, these objects having possibly been manufactured in Egypt under the domination of the Persians. But of late cylinders have been found which are undoubtedly of pure Egyptian origin, of materials worked by Egyptians, covered with Egyptian figures and inscriptions, and bearing the names of Egyptian kings anterior by many centuries to the Persian invasion of Egypt. One in the Imperial Library at Paris bears the titles and name of Shafra, a monarch of the fourth dynasty; an agate cylinder in the British Museum is of the time of Amenem Ha II. of the twelfth dynasty. Sir G. Wilkinson mentions one in the Alnwick Museum bearing the name of Osirtasen I., B.C. 2020, thus proving them to have been of the earliest date in Egypt, and the origin, rather than derived from, the cylinders of Assyria. These monuments appear, therefore, to be of Egyptian origin, and they may have passed to other countries, like the scarabæi, through the Phœnicians, to whom also some cylinders are attributed. The Egyptian cylinders bear the figures of gods, with their names in hieroglyphics, and are also found inscribed with ovals containing royal names. Assyrian and Persian cylinders present subjects derived from the religious myths of the Assyrians and Persians, sometimes accompanied by inscriptions in cuneiform characters.

FAUNS SACRIFICING A GOAT.　*Scarf.*

ETRUSCAN GLYPTIC ART.

Numerous as are Etruscan gems, none of them are cameos, or
with figures cut in relief; all are intagli, and all are cut into the
form of the scarabæus, or beetle. Nothing seems to indicate a closer
analogy between Etruria and Egypt than the multitude of these
curious gems found in this part of Italy. The use of them was,
doubtless, derived from the banks of the Nile. They appear to
have served the same purpose as in Egypt, to have been worn as
charms, or amulets, generally in rings.* The Etruscan scarabæi
have a marked difference from the Egyptian in material, form, and
decoration. The Etruscan are of cornelian, sardonyx, and agate,
rarely of chalcedony. The Egyptian are truthful representations of the insect; the Etruscan are exaggerated resemblances,
especially in the back, which is set up to an extravagant height.
The flat, or under part of the stone, which is always the side
engraved, in the Egyptian bears hieroglyphics, or representations
of deities; in the Etruscan, though sometimes with imitations of
Egyptian subjects, it has generally figures or groups taken from

---

* The greater number of these scarabæi have been found on a slope called
Campo degli Orefici, at Chiusi. They are found in greater abundance there than
in any other Etruscan site.

the Greek mythology, of which the deeds of Hercules, or of the heroes of the Theban and Trojan wars, were favourite subjects. More rare are figures of the gods, and of the chimæra and other symbols of the Etruscan creed. The frequent representations from the Greek mythology prove them to have no very early date. From the heroic or palæstric subjects on these scarabæi it is thought that they were symbols of valour and manly energy, and were worn only by the male sex (Dennis, vol. i. p. 73). Etruscan intagli may be recognised by the following distinctive marks:—1. The form of the scarabæus, which is the form usually adopted. 2. The milled border, formed of small strokes set close together: the granulated border, resembling a string of beads; and the guilloche, resembling a loosely-twisted cable. Etruscan scarabæi are all perforated in their length, and were usually worn set in rings, or introduced as ornaments or amulets, entwined with beads, in necklaces. A peculiarity must be remarked in the development of the glyptic art among the Etruscans, the absence of a transitional style between the extremely rude designs of the earlier style, almost entirely executed by the drill, and the engravings of the utmost finish in low relief, as Mr. King remarks: " While the first class offers caricatures of men and animals, the favourite subjects being figures throwing the discus, fawns with amphoræ, cows with sucking calves, or the latter alone, the second gives us subjects from the Greek mythology, especially scenes from Homer and the tragedians, among which the stories of Philoctetes and Bellerophon occur with remarkable frequency," thus leading to the natural inference that the rude are of Etruscan manufacture, and the fine of Greek.

The inscriptions on Etruscan stones are always the names of the persons represented on the stones, and there are few exceptions to this general rule. It is certainly deserving of remark that the works of Etruscan glyptic art for the most part represent Greek subjects, derived from the religious system, the heroic history of the Greeks, and from events which preceded or followed the war of Troy. We may, therefore, make the following classification of stones of Etruscan workmanship by distinguishing them as, Etruscan stones: Etruscan subjects. Etruscan stones: Greek subjects. Those of the first class are less numerous than the others. Among the most remarkable we may mention—1. An agate of the Florentine Gallery, on which are represented two men standing, bearded, a veil covers their heads and descends over their shoulders. On the robe of one is a hippocampus, on that of the other a triton; they bear on their right shoulders a rod, to which are suspended six

U 2

shields. They have been recognised as two Salii, or priests of Mars, or probably their servants. On the upper part is an inscription in Etruscan letters, which reads from right to left, ALLIUS,

in the lower part ALCE. 2. A scarabæus of cornelian, in the King of Prussia's collection, a man standing, his head covered with a cap, having a rod by his side, holds in his left hand a sack or kind of vase, from which he seems to draw lots; behind him is inscribed NATIS. Winkelman would consider this to represent Nautes, the companion of Æneas. 3. A warrior, half man, half dolphin; a helmet on his head, a shield in one hand, a spear in the other, with the inscription MILALAS .. A. By some it is supposed to represent one of the Tyrrhenians, who were changed into dolphins by Bacchus at Naxos. In the opinion of Lanzi it represents Glaucus. 4. The beautiful stone in the Bibliotheque at Paris, representing a man seated on a stool before a three-legged table, on which are three small round objects, which he seems to move with his right hand, while he holds in his left a tablet covered with two columns of signs, which are letters of the Etruscan alphabet. Signor Orioli, of Bologna, recognises in the inscription, which he reads ABUAIL, the word "abacus" with an Etruscan termination. He would consider it as representing a man making calculations by the means of an abacus.

Subjects from the mythical and heroical periods of Greece are more frequently met with. The Greek subjects most known among Etruscan engraved stones relate to Hercules, his name in Etruscan characters from right to left, being HRKLE; to Perseus, PERSE; to Tydeus, TVTE; to Theseus, THESE; to Pelous, PELE; to Ulysses, VTVSSE; to Achilles, AXELE, AXILE; to Ajax, AIVAS. Other stones bear unknown names. The most beautiful among Etruscan works, which Winkelman considers one of the most ancient speci-

mens of the glyptic art, is the celebrated cornelian formerly in the
Stosch collection, now at Berlin, which represents a council held by

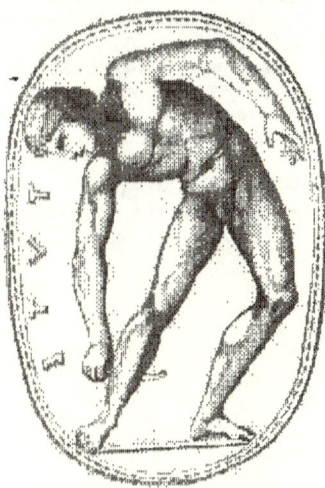

TYPES. SCARABEUS. *Sard. Paris.*

five of the Greek heroes who besieged Thebes; three without arms
and seated; two, armed at all points, are standing; the names of the

heroes, written by their side, leaves no doubt on the subject of this
magnificent intaglio. They are Amphiaraus, AMPHTIARE; Poly-

nicæ, PHVLNICES ; Tydeus, TVTE ; Adrastus, ATRESTHE ;
and Parthenopæus, PARTHANAPAE. Some Roman names are
also found on stones attributed to the Etruscans by their style and
workmanship. A cornelian published by Caylus, bears the letters
VIBIASF, written from right to left round the figure of a dying
warrior Lanzi reads it thus: VIBIA SEXTI FILIA, and considers that the dying warrior represents the father of Vibia, and
that the daughter wore the gem as a seal. A careful examination of its workmanship can alone decide if it really belongs to
Etruscan art, and if the inscription is of the same period. The
forms of early letters have been so frequently forged that one cannot
be too much on their guard against such fraudulent practices.

BELLEROPHON TRAINING PEGASUS.   *From a Gem.*

GREEK GLYPTIC ART.

PLINY remarks that rings used for signets were unknown to the
Greeks at the period of the Trojan war, as Homer nowhere makes
mention of them. Plutarch gives an opposite opinion, as, according to him, Polygnotus painted Ulysses with a ring ; but the opinion
of Polygnotus does not decide the question with regard to a fact
anterior by seven centuries to the period of that painter, and as we

do not intend to enter here on the origin of the glyptic art among the Greeks, who might have received a knowledge of that art before the siege of Troy, from the Phœnicians, or from colonies coming from Egypt where that art was practised from the earliest periods, we shall only say that the most ancient Greek engraved stone mentioned in history is that in the celebrated ring of Polycrates, the work of Theodorus of Samos. According to Herodotus it was an emerald, the device engraved on it being a lyre. Pliny says, it was a sardonyx; and that in his time there existed one in the Temple of Concord, the gift of Augustus, affirmed to be this of Polycrates. Some consider the most ancient engraved stone in existence of Greek workmanship to be the Sard in the Berlin Cabinet, in which is represented the death of the Spartan hero, Othryades, which took place in the sixth century B.C. The inscription engraved on the shield is in Greek characters, traced from right to left. The design is hard and flat, the attitude forced, and without grace. It is in the old Greek style. The Diana the huntress, of Ileius, is supposed to be the most ancient gem known bearing the artist's name. Its stiff archaic style evinces an early period of the art.

Glyptics followed among the Greeks the progress and decline of art. The Greek school has been divided into three periods:— From the time of Theodorus of Samos (B.C. 560), to that of Alexander the Great; from Alexander to Augustus; and from Augustus to the fall of the Empire. The number of Greek engraved stones is very numerous, and some are justly celebrated for their excellence in style and finish. Their period may be deduced from their style and execution. The characteristics of Greek gems are grace and vigour; the figure is drawn with remarkable precision, the attitude is elegant, and the auxiliaries are finely composed; the emblems and attributes exhibit an accuracy which implies an extraordinary degree of historical and mythological information in the artists who engraved them. Greek engraved stones are in general of an oval form, and the stone itself is of little thickness. The work is in the height or breadth, according to the space the subject requires. Sometimes the surface of the intaglio is slightly convex. In the early periods of gem engraving, the design is invariably so arranged as to fill up the entire field of the surface. Extreme simplicity of design, and that repose which is the essential feature in all Greek art, are the distinguishing characteristics of gem engraving of the finest period. The dull polish in the interior of the intaglio, which does not reflect like the brilliant polish of the moderns, is also an essential characteristic of Greek workmanship. As we have already remarked, a name engraved on a Greek stone ought to be generally considered as that of the artist who executed it, as may be observed on the stones of the beautiful period of the art in Greece, and on stones executed by Greek artists among the Romans. This name is more usually in the genitive than in the nominative case; at least it is rare that the same artist should sometimes put his name in the first case, and sometimes in the second. That which he adopted for his finest work, he almost always retained in all his other works. There is but one example of the name of a Greek artist written in Latin letters; that of Diphilus. All the productions of Greek engraving were not perfect works of art; indeed we possess several of very inferior workmanship. An artist could excel only in one especial style; one was most successful in the drapery; another in the representation of the nude; one excelled in the art of giving expression and strength, another in giving gracefulness to his figures. The great artists alone reached that perfection which combined them all. Sometimes they engraved their figures very deeply, and sometimes in very low relief. Dioscorides excelled in giving a very slight relief to his figures; this difficulty overcome is one of the greatest merits of this engraver. In general the Greeks applied themselves more to intaglio than to cameo engraving. They were unacquainted with perspective, the place of which, however, they supplied, in some measure, by the greater or less depth they gave to the different parts. The engravers avoided multiplying their figures, or crowding them in a small space. The Greek artists were remarkable for their skill in representing animals; they preferred also representing their figures nude, and, indeed, most of the masterpieces of art produced in Greece are figures without drapery; while those executed at Rome are generally draped: with the exception, however, of those of Dioscorides who followed the taste of his own nation in this respect, for nearly all his figures are nude. The works of the great engravers of Greece are all stamped with a peculiar national character, which is better felt than described. Mythological and heroical subjects were adopted by Greek artists, in preference to those of contemporaneous history. We must remark here that the artists of later times, frequently imitated the forms of the primitive style, and also the so-called Etruscan border, especially in representing deities; the severity of these forms, according to Demetrius Phalereus, giving more grandeur and gravity to these representations. If the stone imitating the ancient style bears an inscription, it will be a means of ascertaining the date by the form of the letters; and if this inscription is the name of the engraver, the known period of the latter will be a sufficient proof that the work is only an imitation of the ancient style.

BY BRAMEL.   *Engraved Gem.*

ROMAN GLYPTIC ART.

THE knowledge of the glyptic art must have been derived by the Romans, in the first place, from the Etruscans, and afterwards from the Greeks. There was no Roman school properly so called, and it seems that, at all periods of that ruling people, its martial propensities made it consider the culture of the arts as a profession worthy only of slaves, freedmen, or of strangers whom it had subdued. But when it became acquainted with the beautiful works of Greece and Asia, a taste for them was developed, and they were eagerly sought for.

Greek engravers were attracted to Rome, where they usually represented subjects of Greek history, in which the Romans began to take an interest; and when they treated in their works any scene of Roman history they usually added to the purely historical composition some allegorical figures, which evinced the genius of the artist in that kind of invention, and which raised his work above a simple imitation of nature. But, though produced in Rome, these works of Greek engravers do not the less belong to the Greek school, which continued to the fall of the Western Empire, keeping pace with the vicissitudes and the decline of art.

Some Roman artists devoted themselves also to the glyptic art,

and we have already mentioned the most celebrated names ; the
taste which was very generally evinced for engraved stones among
the highest persons of the empire, the collections formed by some
rich citizens, the general use of signets in rings, excited the emula-
tion of the Roman artists, who succeeded in producing some very
beautiful works. It may be supposed, however, that the works of
Greek artists met more favour in the opinion of amateurs, as Roman
artists affected to give a Greek character to their productions by
engraving their names in Greek letters. Some authors think that,
from the time of Marcus Aurelius, the best works are due to Roman
artists.

As the Greeks evinced a predilection for the nude, the Romans
exhibited a decided taste for draped figures. The stones engraved
in Rome exhibit in general proofs of this preference ; and Dioscorides, otherwise so devoted to the taste of his own nation, engraved
a draped Mercury.

This requirement of Roman taste was very unfavourable to the
development of the beauty of the art, and engraved stones executed
at Rome evince this influence. The figures seldom trespass against
the rules of design, but they are deficient in elegance ; they seldom
bespeak either genius or elevation of mind in the artist. The ideal,
which is the soul of Greek composition, is never perceived in that
of the Romans ; and the art sensibly declined into a servile imitation.

The taste for engraved stones was introduced into Rome with
that for other monuments of art ; it maintained itself till the time
of Septimius Severus, when it began gradually to decline. We may
trace the gradual decline of the art in the various engraved portraits of Antoninus Pius, Marcus Aurelius, Lucius Verus, Gordian,
Maximian, Philip, Probus, and Constantine II.

Engraved stones bearing inscriptions are more common among
Roman works than among those of the Greeks. Roman inscriptions
are of five kinds :—1. The name of artist. 2. The name of the person
represented. 3. The name of the owner of the stone. This is more
usually the case. 4. The name of the person who made a present
of it. 5. Good wishes, affectionate expressions which accompany
the gift, as " multis annis " (vivas understood), " ave," " amor meus,"
and acclamations relative to the Circensian games. The Etruscan
milled border is sometimes found on Roman intagli of very late
times, but may be readily distinguished by its carelessness and irregularity.

MITHRAIC AND GNOSTIC ENGRAVED STONES.

Before noticing the Gnostic gems which were so extensively used in the latest stage of the decline of the art, we must mention an earlier class of intagli, which are connected with the worship of Mithras. According to Mr. King, from their good execution many of these intagli date from the early Empire. They are evidences of the prevalence of those Oriental doctrines which were widely diffused through the Roman world during the Middle Empire. Mithras was the Persian type of the sun. He is usually represented as a young man plunging his sword into the throat of a bull, while a dog licks up the blood which falls. The bull is the earth, which Mithras, or the sun, is fertilizing with heat, and penetrating with his influence in the sign of Taurus. The dog denotes that all things are nourished by the sun's influence upon the earth. The bull's tail terminates in ears of corn, to denote fecundity. On the engraved gems this central figure is frequently surrounded with a number of allegorical figures. Numerous intagli of the time of Hadrian representing the head of Serapis, with the legend, ΕΙΣ ΘΕΟΣ ΣΕΡΑΠΙΣ (There is but one god Serapis), are also frequently to be met with, as the worship of the god Serapis was greatly in vogue in that age.

We come now to the period when the glyptic art, following the necessary stages of the development of art, reached its latest stage of decline, and was at the lowest ebb. We would speak here of a particular class of engraved stones, bearing the name of Abraxas, or Basilidan stones. This name has been given to those on which are represented, in a very rude and inferior style of workmanship, Egyptian deities and others, combined with symbols derived from the religious ideas of the Indians and Persians, and accompanied by inscriptions in Greek, Coptic, Hebrew, or Latin, and by cabalistic signs mixed together. These stones were usually worn as amulets or talismans. The engraving of these gems is generally of very rude workmanship, and the stones used are of a very inferior kind. They are frequently engraved on both sides. Sometimes also a more ancient stone, and of superior work, has received an inscription which has made of it a sacred amulet. Those two periods must be, therefore, carefully distinguished on the same stone. According to Mr. King the earliest are doubtless those which offer purely Egyptian types; a very frequent one being a serpent, erect, and with a lion's head surrounded by seven rays, and usually accompanied by the inscription, ΧΝΟΥΦΙΣ or ΧΝΟΥΜΙΣ. This is Kneph, the good genius, or Agatho dæmon, the creative spirit and the type of the sun, of the Egyptians, one of the characteristics of whom was the serpent, probably the uræus or basilisk, the sign of power. According to Plutarch and Diodorus the name of the Egyptian Zeus signified spirit (πνεῦμα), which of course can only apply to Kneph. Champollion derives it from the Egyptian root *nf* (Coptic *nef*) to breathe. The word Chnubis differs from Kneph only in the accidental admission of the inherent vowel *v* instead of *e*, and of *b* instead of *p*, as spelled in the Gnostic monuments of the Basilidans, it would sound like Chnumis (Bunsen). A common inscription around this figure, or on the back of the stone, is the Hebrew-

KNEPH OR CHNUBIS.　　　　ABRAXAS.　　　　SETH.

Greek ΣΕΜΕΣ ΕΙΛΑΜ, the eternal sun, and also another legend, ΑΝΑΘΑΝΑΒΡΑ, "Thou art our father."[*]　Another frequent type is Seth, the Egyptian Typhon or evil deity, the ass-headed god of the Semitic tribes,[†] which gave rise to the calumny against the Christians that they worshipped the head of an ass.[‡]　As

---

[*] Whence the famous talisman or charm "Abracadabra" has been derived.

[†] Mr. King considers this to represent Anubis, the jackal-headed god. A single glance at the gem will be enough to convince any one that it is an ass-headed god.

[‡] The graffito found in a room of the Palatine Hill, evidently a προσκύνημα, or act of worship, by some Gnostic Christian, represents the crucified Seth, the father of Judaism and Palestinus, the ass-god of the Semitic tribes, for, as Mr. Sharpe observes, the creator of the world, the author of evil, in the Gnostic creed, was looked upon by the Gnostics as the god of the Jews, and the author of the Mosaic law. Valentinus, a native of Pharbethium, who had studied in Alexandria, carried his Gnostic opinions to Italy, in the reign of Antoninus Pius, where the mystic superstitions of this sect were eagerly embraced. This

Mr. Sharp remarks, Basilides, the founder of the Egyptian sect of Christian Gnostics, being puzzled, as so many inquirers have been, with the origin of evil, and with the difficulty of believing that the Giver of all Good was himself the author of sin, he made a second god of the Devil, or the personification of evil, consequently we find the same Typhon, or god of evil, also figured as Nubi, the lord of the world, who is represented under the form of a griffin. On some of the coins of Hadrian we see also exhibited the Gnostic spirit of that age, in the representation of the antagonism of good and evil, as figured in the opposition of the serpent of good (Horhat, the Agatho dæmon), and the serpent of evil (Apophis). The figure which is most frequently found on these stones is that which has given its name to this entire class. The god Abraxas, or, as it reads on the gems, ΑΒΡΑΣΑΞ, the letters of which, taken numerically, according to the Greek alphabet, give, when summed up, the number 365 (A 1, B 2, P 100, A 1, Σ 200, A 1, Ξ 60), being the number of days in the sun's annual course. He is supposed to be the sun god, or the supreme deity, whose physical representative the sun is. He is figured with the head of a cock, sacred to the sun, with a human body, clad in a cuirass, terminating in serpents instead of legs. By the side of the god, besides the word Abraxas, is also engraved the name Ino, which would seem, as well as the names Adonai, Sabaoth, frequently engraved on these gems, to be other titles of the sun god. Abraxas, the supreme deity or good spirit, and Seth, or the god of evil, are the representatives of the two antagonistic principles in nature, according to the Gnostic doctrines. In the Gnostic creed, the author of evil was regarded as the creator of the world, and was considered as the being with whom men have chiefly to do, either in this world or in the next. According to the Gnostic view, matter was essentially evil, consequently the supreme deity, or author of good, could not be its author.

graffito may, therefore, be of that period. These proskunemata are frequently found in Egypt. They usually were votive sentences, and were inscribed on walls by the worshipper to indicate his respects for the deity and to solicit his protection.

CUPID AND BUTTERFLY. *Gem.*

RINGS.

SIGNET-RINGS may be considered as the earliest kind of useful ornament known to the ancients. Their use dates from the earliest
periods. Originally rings bore the signet or seal of the owner, but
in later times they were worn more as ornaments than articles of
use; and to such a pitch was passion for ornament carried by the
ancients, that it is recorded of some that they loaded their hands
with rings.

The earliest mention of signet-rings is in the Bible, when Tamar
receives a signet-ring from Judah as a token of recognition; and
when Pharaoh " took off the ring from his hand and put it upon
Joseph's hand," thereby investing him with delegated authority.
The most ancient known ring is supposed to be that in the possession of Dr. Abbot, of Cairo. It is thus described by him: " This
remarkable piece of antiquity is in the highest state of preservation,
and was found at Ghizeh, in a tomb near the excavation of Colonel
Vyse's, called Campbell's tomb. It is of fine gold, and weighs
nearly three sovereigns. The style of the hieroglyphics is in
perfect accordance with those in the tombs about the Great Pyramid,

and the hieroglyphics within the oval make the name of that Pharaoh (Cheops, Shofo) of whom the pyramid was the tomb." Another

ring of great historical importance is the bronze one which bears the name of Amunoph III. engraved on the oval face of the ring.

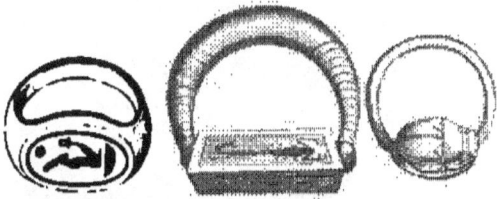

It was probably worn by some official in the king's household. It is now in the collection of Lord Londesborough. Sir G. Wilkinson mentions an Egyptian ring, remarkable for its size; it contained twenty pounds' worth of gold. It consisted of a massive ring, half an inch in its largest diameter, bearing an oblong plinth, on which devices were engraved, an inch long. One one face was the name of King Horus, of the eighteenth dynasty, B.C. 1337; on the other, a lion, with the legend, "Lord of strength," referring to the monarch; on one side, a scorpion, and, on the other, a crocodile. The favourite form for signets set in the ring among the Egyptians was the scarabæus. It was perforated in its length, and was so set as to revolve in the ring. Engraved on the under surface of the scarabæus was the name of the owner, the name of the monarch in whose reign he lived, and sometimes the emblems of certain deities. Some Egyptian rings were occasionally in the form of a shell, a knot, a snake, or some fancy device. They were mostly of gold. Silver rings, however, are occasionally met with; two in the possession of Sir G. Wilkinson, found in a temple at Thebes, are engraved with hieroglyphics containing the name of the royal city. Sir G. Wilkinson states that bronze was seldom used for rings, though frequently for signets. Some have been discovered of brass and iron, the latter of a Roman period; but ivory and blue porcelain were the materials of which those worn by the lower class were usually made. From the example of the crossed hands of the figure of a woman on a mummy case in the British Museum, Egyptian ladies seem to have indulged extensively in their passion for loading their fingers with rings. According to Sir G. Wilkinson, they wore many rings; sometimes two or three on the same finger. The left was considered the hand peculiarly privileged to bear those ornaments, and it is remarkable that its third finger was decorated

with a greater number than any other, and was considered by
them, as by us, *par excellence*, the ring finger. They even wore a
ring on the thumb.

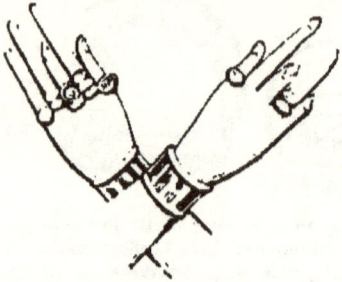

Among the Greeks, judging from the silence of Homer, signets
were not in use in the early periods. It is supposed the fashion of
wearing them was introduced from Asia. In the age of Alexander,
the perfection of workmanship attained to by the gem-engravers of
that age contributed greatly to the taste for wearing signet-rings.
Alexander permitted none but the celebrated artist Pyrgoteles to
engrave his head on a signet-ring. After conquering Darius, he is
reported to have sealed his first acts with that monarch's ring. On
his death-bed, Alexander drew off his signet-ring, and delivered it
in silence to Perdiccas, thus declaring him his successor. The most
celebrated ring of antiquity was that of Polycrates, the tyrant of
Samos. According to Pliny, the stone in this ring was a sardonyx,
and was said to be still shown in Rome in his day. According to
Herodotus, the stone was an emerald, the engraving on it (which
represented a lyre) was by Theodorus, of Samos. Like the Egyptian
ladies, the Grecian ladies displayed upon their fingers a profusion
of rings, of which some were set with signets, others with jewels
remarkable for their colour and brilliance. Seal rings were styled
by the Greeks σφραγίδες, and rings without precious stones were
termed ἄψηφοι.

The general form of the stone used by the Etruscans in their
rings was the scarabæus, supposed to have been imitated from the
Egyptian signets of that form. The Etruscan scarabæus was
usually so set that it revolved round its centre, and thus exposed
alternately either surface to view. From the number of heroic
subjects found on them, it is supposed that they were symbols of

valour and manly energy, and were worn only by the male sex.
Some very rare Etruscan rings are found made of very thin pure
gold, filled up in the centre with some composition. One of this
kind is in the possession of the author, the bezel of the ring being a
piece of amber.

The fashion of wearing rings among the Romans dates from an
early period, as the gemmed fingers of the statues of the two immediate successors of Romulus, Numa and Servius Tullius, cited by
Pliny, sufficiently attest. The use of signet-rings was evidently
derived from their neighbours, the Etruscans, who were famous for
the beauty of their signet-rings and their jewellery. The Sabines,
too, as we learn from Livy, were distinguished, even from the
infancy of Rome, for the size and beauty of their rings. In the
period of republican simplicity in Rome, an iron ring was usually
worn, and was considered to be the right of freemen. The right of
wearing a gold ring became for several centuries the exclusive privilege of senators, magistrates, and equites. As luxury increased, and
a more general taste for these ornaments prevailed, each person
adopted a separate subject to be engraved on his signet-ring. On
that of Pompey was engraved three trophies. Julius Cæsar took
Venus Victrix as his tutelar deity. Augustus at first sealed with a
sphinx, afterwards with a head of Alexander the Great, and at last
with his own portrait, in which he was imitated by some of his
successors. Mæcenas adopted a frog. Nero wore a ring given him
by his infamous favourite, Sporus, with the rape of Proserpine for
subject. Galba adopted a dog for the family seal. Under Claudius
it became the fashion to engrave the device upon the gold of the
ring itself, now made solid; the portrait of the emperor was engraved on it, and was only worn by courtiers: but other subjects
are found engraved on solid gold rings of an earlier date than the
age of Claudius. One in the possession of Mr. M. Taylor bears an
exquisite engraving of Ceres, evidently of Greek workmanship.
These signet-rings were usually employed for sealing the legal acts
of public, and much of the business of private life. They were also
used to seal up such parts of the house as contained stores or
valuable things, in order to secure them from thieves. Wine jars
were usually sealed with them. Sometimes, but very rarely, the
ring was adorned with two gems. The Emperor Valerian mentions
one of these under the name of "annulus bigemmeus." The wood-
cut presents a specimen of this kind of ring, the larger gem representing a figure of Mars; the smaller, a dove on a myrtle branch.
Beside it are placed two examples of the emblematic devices and
inscriptions adopted for rings when used as memorial gifts. The

first is inscribed, " You have a love pledge;" the second, " Proteus
[to] Ugia," between conjoined hands—a type of concord.   To some

rings a key has been attached, and is supposed to have been worn
by housekeepers.   The passion for rings and other ornaments

reached a high pitch among the Romans. We here quote Pliny's
words on rings, and on the extravagance the passion for them led to
in his day :—" It was the custom at first to wear rings on a single
finger only—the one, namely, that is next to the little finger ; and
thus we see the case in the statues of Numa and Servius Tullius.
In later times, it became the practice to put rings on the finger next
to the thumb, even in the case of the statues of the gods ; and more
recently, again, it has been the fashion to wear them upon the little
finger as well. Among the peoples of Gallia and Britannia, the
middle finger, it is said, is used for this purpose.   At the present
day, however, among us, this is the only finger that is excepted, all
others being loaded with rings ; smaller rings even being separately
adapted for the smaller joints of the fingers.   Some there are who
heap several rings on the little finger alone ; while others, again,
wear but one ring on this finger, the ring that sets a seal on the
signet-ring itself ; this last being carefully shut up as an object of
rarity, too precious to be worn in common use, and only to be
taken from the cabinet [dactyliotheca] as from a sanctuary.   And
thus is the wearing of a single ring upon the little finger no more
than an ostentatious advertisement that the owner has property of a
more precious nature under seal at home ! Some, too, make a parade of

the weight of their rings, while to others it is quite a labour to wear more than one at a time; some, in their solicitude for the safety of their gems, make the hoop of gold tinsel, and fill it with a lighter material than gold, thinking thereby to diminish the risk of a fall. Others, again, are in the habit of inclosing poisons beneath the stones of their rings, and so wear them as instruments of death. And then, besides, how many of the crimes that are stimulated by cupidity are committed through the instrumentality of rings! How happy the times—how truly innocent—in which no seal was put to anything! At the present day, on the contrary, our very food even and our drink have to be preserved from theft through the agency of the ring; and so far is it from being sufficient to have the very keys sealed, that the signet-ring is often taken from off the owner's fingers while he is overpowered with sleep, or lying on his death-bed." As an instance of one of those rings worn by some who

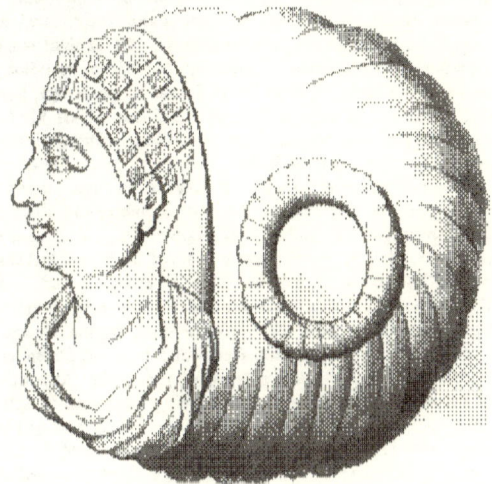

"made a parade of the weight of their rings," we may mention the ring figured in Montfaucon. It is a thumb ring of unusual magnitude, and of costly material. It bears the bust in high relief of the Empress Plotina, the consort of Trajan: she is represented with the Imperial diadem. It is supposed to have decorated the hand of some member of the Imperial family. Mr. King mentions one now

in the Fould collection, the weight of which, though intended for
the little finger, was three ounces. It was set with a large Oriental
onyx, not engraved. The wealthy expended enormous sums on
their rings: the ring of the Empress Faustina cost £40,000, and
of Domitia £60,000.

The subjects engraved on rings were in endless variety; among
those which are more frequently found are the Olympic divinities.
Jupiter, Mercury, Bacchus, Apollo, Mars, are the more frequently
chosen for subjects. The Cupids and Neptunes, Plutos and Vul-
cans are less frequent. Harpocrates, with his finger on his lip, was
fashionable at Rome in Pliny's day. Of the goddesses, in bust or in
whole length, there are more Minervas than Dianas; more Dianas
than Junos; of Venus the effigies are numerous. Heroes were also
frequently chosen. Achilles dragging Hector round the walls of
Troy, the return of Ulysses, the parting of Hector and Andromache,
Æneas escaping from Troy, Tydous, are favourite subjects. The
sages, poets, orators, statesmen, of Greece and Italy, furnished a
large supply of heads as subjects for signets. Of ancient sages the
most popular was Epicurus. According to Cicero, the image of
Epicurus was not only represented at Rome in paintings, but also
engraved on drinking cups and rings. Animals of all kinds also
occur on rings—lions, horses, dogs, sphinxes. Among birds the
eagle was a favourite seal at Rome. Silver rings are by no means
rare. They are either solid with devices cut on them, or set with
intagli. From the rudeness of the workmanship, and their small
size, they are supposed to belong to the Lower Empire. Bronze rings
are numerous, as they were frequently worn at Rome, but the engraving on the stones set in the rings is generally rude. Paste
intagli are also found in bronze setting. These rings were sometimes gilt. Small rings of bronze were worn by the Roman soldiers. Several of these rings are frequently found at Rome, and in
the Roman colonies, with the number of the legion to which the
soldier belonged engraved on it. Lead rings, set with intagli, are
sometimes to be met with, but they are exceedingly rare. Though
iron rings were in frequent use, few have come down to us, iron
being so extremely liable to corrode. Rings entirely carved out of
crystal, agate, or chalcedony, with subjects engraved on them, occur
only in the period of the Lower Empire. The other materials used
for this purpose were ivory, bone, amber, jet, glass, and porcelain.

AUCTUMNUS. *From a gem.*

STONES USED FOR ENGRAVING KNOWN TO THE ANCIENTS.

Transparent.

ADAMAS—DIAMOND.

The ancients were ignorant of the art of cutting this gem. They set the diamonds in their rough state, preferring those which nature had cut for them in an octohedral form. In the Herz collection was a diamond of this form, of about one carat, set upon in a massy gold ring of indubitable antiquity. The Waterton collection furnishes a yet finer example of the diamond in its original setting. It is supposed to date from the Lower Empire. The four diamonds in the clasp which belonged to the dress of Charlemagne, and which was preserved at St. Denis, were of this description. According to Pliny, six different varieties of diamond were known in his time, of these the largest came from India. From its extreme hardness it was known to the ancients by the word "adamas." Fragments of diamonds were made use of by ancient engravers for engraving and finishing their work. For, according to Pliny, "when, by good fortune, this stone does happen to be broken, it divides into fragments so minute as to be almost imperceptible. These particles are held in great request by engravers, who enclose them in iron, and are enabled thereby, with the greatest facility, to cut the very hardest substances known." The art of cutting and polishing this precious stone was only discovered in 1496, by Louis de Berquem. Jacolo da Trezzo appears to have been the first who engraved on diamond. Ambrose Cardossa is also mentioned as having, in 1500, engraved the portrait of a father of the church on a diamond, and sold it for 22,800 crowns to Pope Julius II. Natter and Costanzi have likewise engraved on diamonds.

SMARAGDUS—EMERALD.

It is evident that the true emerald was known to the ancients, both from the description of Pliny, and as several engraved emeralds have been found. It was long supposed that the true emerald only came from Peru. According to Herodotus the signet of Polycrates was an emerald. Pliny also mentions an engraved emerald, with an Amymone, which the musician Ismenias was anxious to purchase at the highest price. It is thus described by Pliny : " There is no stone, the colour of which is more delightful to the eye : for whereas the sight fixes itself with avidity upon green grass, and the foliage of trees, we have all the more pleasure in looking upon the smaragdus (emerald), there being no green in existence of a more intense colour than this. It has always a softened and graduated brilliancy ; and transmitting the light with facility, they allow the vision to penetrate its interior." Pliny adds, further, that it was universally agreed upon among mankind to respect these stones, and to forbid their surface to be engraved. Hence engraved emeralds are found to be the rarest of the rare. Of the varieties known to the ancients the Scythian smaragdus was considered the finest (by some supposed to be the Oriental emerald or green sapphire). It was more free from flaws, which almost invariably are found in the other varieties. Next in esteem to this were the Bactrian and Egyptian. The inferior varieties of emerald mentioned by Pliny are regarded as prasus or jaspers. The Romans derived their principal supply of emeralds from the mines in the vicinity of Coptos, in Egypt. In the opinion of some this was probably the only locality of the genuine stone that was known to the ancients. Extensive traces of the working of these mines have been found by Sir Gardner Wilkinson, at Mount Zebara, near the Red Sea. In the possession of the author is a small emerald, with a lotus flower engraved on it. It is considered to be a specimen of a genuine emerald from the mines near Coptos. Pliny remarks when the surface of the smaragdus is flat, it reflects the image of objects in the same manner as a mirror. It is told of the emperor Nero that he viewed the combats of the gladiators upon a smaragdus. By holding the flat surface of the emerald, in possession of the author, close to the eye, distant objects can be distinctly seen reflected on it. It thus confirms Pliny's statement, as the distinct reflection of distant objects in the flat surface of the emerald must have been of great importance to a near-sighted person, as Nero was. [*]

Mr. King enumerates the following antique intagli in the possession of L. Fould, of Paris, as true emeralds, some of considerable size and beauty of colour, and the work of which, as far as his judgment goes, bears every mark of authenticity. A bull butting with his head, of the Roman period; the busts of Hadrian and Sabina, facing each other; a lion's head, full face, crowned with the person. This last gem, in his opinion, was a miracle of the glyptic art, while the stone was of the finest colour, purity and lustre, and in itself of considerable value as a first-rate emerald.

HYACINTHUS—SAPPHIRE.

The hyacinthus of the ancients is now generally considered to be the sapphire of the present day. It is pure crystallised alumina. The most valuable sapphire is a deep indigo blue (the male sapphire of the lapidaries). The pale blue sapphires are sometimes called female or water sapphires. It is inferior in hardness only to the diamond, and consequently has been seldom engraved on. Mr. King mentions a magnificent head of Jupiter, inscribed ΠΥ, supposed to be the signature of Pyrgoteles himself, but more probably the owner's name, engraved on a pale sapphire. But the most celebrated engraved sapphire is the signet of Constantius II., in the Rinuccini collection in Florence. It represents the emperor spearing a wild boar near Cæsarea, in Cappodocia.

LYCHNIS—RUBY.

The ruby is identically the same stone as the sapphire, differing only in colour. Its colour varies from the richest red (known as the

---

[*] The highly-polished flat surface of any stone will reflect in a similar way, but the power of reflection on a polished flat surface of a gem was known to the ancients only through the emerald, as it is the only stone cut in that form, all other stones being usually of a convex shape.

pigeon's blood tint) to the lightest rose tint. The stones called
spinel and balas rubies belong to another class of stones. They
consist principally of alumina combined with magnesia, and are
rather less hard than the true ruby. Jewellers give the name spinel
to those stones which have a colour approaching to scarlet, they call
those of a delicate rose colour, the balas ruby.

With the class of carbunculi (a term applied by the ancients to
all red or fiery-coloured stones), Pliny associates the *lychnis* (so called
from its lustre being heightened by the light of the lamp). It was
of two kinds; the Indian was the best, the Ionian was the next best.
This latter sort was of two varieties; one with a crimson (purpura),
the other with a scarlet (cocco) colour. Pliny also speaks of the
lychnis as sometimes called a more languid or paler (remission)
carbuncle. This, and the divisions into which he groups it, would
seem to indicate that here we have the true ruby in the Indian
lychnis, as distinct from the spinels (the spinel and balas ruby),
which we exactly recognize in the Ionian lychnis.* Engravings
on this precious stone are exceedingly rare. Mr. King mentions
an intaglio on a pale (balas) ruby, which has been pronounced
antique by the best judges in Paris, it represents the full face of a
Bacchante crowned with ivy, on it is the name EΛΛΙΝ, in very
minute characters. In spinel, a most spirited Gorgon's Head in the
Rhodes Gems.

TOPAZOS—CHRYSOLITE.

Under the name of topazos, Pliny evidently speaks of the stone
known to us as chrysolite, while, on the other hand, the chrysolitos
of the ancients is the present topaz.

The topazos (chrysolite) came from the Red Sea, and was a bright
greenish yellow; according to Pliny, it was the largest of all the
precious stones, and is the only one among those of high value that
yields to the action of the file, the rest being polished by the aid of
stone of Naxos. It admits, too, of being worn by use. The chry-
sopleron of Pliny is supposed to be the Oriental chrysolite.

CHRYSOLITOS—ORIENTAL TOPAZ.

The chrysolitos (Oriental topaz) was, according to Pliny, a transparent stone, with a refulgence like that of gold. The most highly
esteemed came from India. No genuine ancient intagli on this
stone have been met with.

"Edinburgh Review," No. 258, p. 255.

TOPAZOS PRASOIDES—PERIDOT.

The topazos prasoides of Pliny is supposed to be our peridot, which is of an olive-green colour; it is so soft that it will scarcely scratch glass. It comes from India. Some Greek intagli occur in this stone, but are exceedingly rare. It seems not to have been used for engraving by the Romans in consequence of its softness.

LYNCURIUM—HYACINTH OR JACINTH.

The lyncurium of the ancients was probably the jacinth of the present day. Pliny describes its colour as being like that of some kind of amber, of a fiery hue, and adds that it admits of being engraved. At the present day, it is termed zircon (it being a silicate of zirconia) or jargoon. It resembles amber in colour and electricity, and is remarkable for excessive hardness. Mr. King mentions two kinds; one a dark orange, extremely agreeable in tint (the male), and another a pale yellow of extraordinary lustre (the female). These have been frequently used by the ancients for intagli in the earliest times, and by the Romans for camei also. For the latter purpose the darker kind was preferred.

The "mormorio" mentioned by Pliny, as being a stone adapted for engraving in relief (ad ectypos sculpturas aptantur), is supposed by Mr. King to be the deep-coloured jacinth, of the richest orange brown.

AMETHYSTOS—AMETHYST.

Of all transparent stones, the amethyst was the most frequently used for engraving, numberless examples of Roman intagli in this stone, of all dates and in every style, have been found. Egyptian and Etruscan scarabæi of this stone are not uncommon. Pliny thus describes its several varieties: "In the first rank belongs the amethystos of India, having in perfection the very richest shades of purple, and it is to attain this colour that the dyers in purple direct all their endeavours; this stone is also found in the part of Arabia that adjoins Syria, and is known as Petra; as also in Lesser Armenia, Egypt, and Galatia; the very worst of all and the least valued, being those of Thasos and Cyprus. Another variety approaches more nearly the hyacinthus (sapphire) in colour: the people of India call this tint 'socon,' and the stone itself 'socon-dian.' Another was in colour like that of wine, and a last variety, but little valued, bordering very closely upon that of crystal, the purple gradually passing off into white. A fine amethyst should

always have, when viewed sideways (in *suspectu*) and held up to
the light, a certain purple effulgence, like that of the carbuncular,
slightly inclining to a tint of rose. To these stones the names of
'*paderos*' and '*Venus*' eyelid' (*Veneris gena*, ἀφροδίτης βλέφαρον)
was given, being considered as particularly appropriate to the
colour and general appearance of the gem.

"The name which these stones bear originates, it is said, in the
peculiar tint of their brilliancy, which, after closely approaching the
colour of wine, passes off into a violet without being fully pronounced." He adds, "all these stones are transparent, and of an
agreeable violet colour, and are easy to engrave."

According to some authorities, the word amethystos is derived
from ἀ, not, μεθύω, to intoxicate, on account of its being a supposed preservative against inebriety.

The common amethyst is but a variety of rock crystal, coloured
violet. The paler variety was generally adopted by ancient
engravers.

The Oriental amethyst is a ruby or sapphire of a dark rich violet
colour; it may be distinguished from the ordinary amethyst by its
superior brilliancy, as well as by its hardness. It is a gem of rare
occurrence. Some intagli of this stone are said to be in the Vatican.

BERYLLUS—BERYL, OR AQUAMARINE.

Pliny thus mentions beryls: "Beryls, it is thought, are of the
same nature as the emerald, or at least closely analogous. India
produces them, and they are rarely to be found elsewhere. The
most esteemed beryls are those which in colour resemble the pure
green of the sea."

The beryl, or modern aquamarine, is essentially the same substance (silicate of alumina, with glucina) as the emerald (as Pliny
correctly surmised), differing only in the colouring matter, which in
the emerald is oxide of chrome, and in the beryl oxide of iron.

The beryl was seldom engraved on, and consequently genuine
antique intagli on beryl are rarely to be met with. The most remarkable example of an intaglio in this stone is the bust of Julia,
the daughter of Titus, by Evodus. It is of extraordinary size, being
2½ by 2½ inches. The Praun collection affords another example of
an intaglio in beryl, it represents Tarus on the dolphin.

CHRYSOBERYLLUS—YELLOW BERYL.

Pliny describes as next in value to the beryl, the Chrysoberyllus, a stone of a somewhat paler colour, but approaching a golden tint. From his associating this stone with the beryl, it is evidently only a yellowish beryl. It is supposed by some to be the modern chrysoberyl (called by jewellers the Oriental chrysolite), a much harder and more brilliant gem of a greenish yellow.

CARBUNCULUS—GARNET.

The term Carbunculus being indiscriminately applied by the ancients to all red and fiery-coloured stones, comprises the several varieties of the garnet as well as of the Ruby. The Greek synonymous word is *anthrax*. There are several kinds of Garnet, differing from each other in their colour and transparency, and even in their constituents, yet having the same crystalline forms and nearly the same hardness. The precious garnet is a silicate of aluminium, magnesium, and iron. This gem varies greatly in colour. It is sometimes of a deep blood red, and frequently "of the colour of Burgundy wine, more or less diluted according to its goodness." The name garnet is supposed to be derived from granaticus, a pomegranate (from the red colour of the seeds and juice).

The Pyrope, or Bohemian garnet, is of a deep blood red. The Almandine of a crimson red inclining to violet. It is found in India, Ceylon, Brazil. The Sirium is of a carmine tint with an admixture of blue. It is so called because it comes from Sirium, the old capital of Pegu. The garnet in which yellow predominates, or as Mr. King distinguishes it "of a vinous yellow," combining the orange of the jacinth and the wine colour of the garnet, is styled by the Italians guarnaccino. The hyacinthine garnet and essonite (cinnamon stone) are characterised by different tones of orange and yellow, mingled with the reds of the other varieties. The finest of these is that with a hyacinthine hue, often called by the jewellers "hyacinthe la belle." The carbuncle is a name given to the garnet in jewellery, when cut "en cabochon," or into a very convex form on the upper surface.

Pliny thus describes the several varieties of the carbunculus or garnet known in his day: "There are various kinds of carbunculus, the Indian and the Garamantic, which last has been also called the Carchedonian. To these are added the Æthiopian and the Alabandic stones, the latter of which are found at Orthosia in Caria, but are cut and polished at Alabanda. The most highly esteemed, however, is the amethyst-coloured stone, the fire at the extremity of which closely approaches the violet tint of amethystos." This is undoubtedly the Almandine garnet.

Garnets seem to have been little employed by the Greeks for engraving upon, but were largely in favour with the Romans of the Empire. Some excellent intagli occur in the Almandine garnet, but no certain Greek or early Græco-Roman work is recorded on the blood-red garnet. Fine Roman intagli frequently, and sometimes imperial portraits, are to be met with on the guarnaccino.

CRYSTALLUS—ROCK CRYSTAL.

Rock Crystal (pure silica) was never used for intagli by the Greeks, or in the Roman period. It was exclusively employed for vases and cups. Intagli on finger rings of a solid piece of crystal, are of the time of the Lower Empire. In Italy, during the Renaissance period, some important intagli on crystal have been executed. Valerio Vicentino was famous for this style of work. In the Cinque Cento collection in the museum at Naples, is a magnificent casket of silver gilt, with engraved plaques of crystal, representing mythological subjects, and various events in the history of Alexander the Great, in complimentary allusion to the achievements of Alessandro Farnese, to whom it belonged. It bears the name of Joannes dé Bernardi. A casket of rock crystal, on which are engraved the events of the Passion, by Valerio Vicentino, is in the cabinet of gems in the Florentine Gallery. It was a present from Pope Clement VII. to Francis I., on the marriage of his niece Catherine de Medici.

Crystal has been often used both in ancient and modern times for the purposes of fraud. In Pliny's time the art was well known how to stain crystal so as to pass for emerald or any other transparent precious stone. At the present day by placing a piece of coloured glass under crystal cut to the proper form, it is made to pass for a real gem, so as to deceive the best judges. This kind of stone has been termed "doublet" by jewellers.

Semi-Transparent.

OPALUS—OPAL.

Pliny thus describes the opal: " Of all precious stones it is the opal that presents the greatest difficulties of description, it displaying at once the piercing fire of carbunculus, the purple brilliancy of amethyst, and the sea-green of smaragdus, the whole blended together, and refulgent with a brightness that is quite incredible. This stone, in consequence of its extraordinary beauty, has been called 'pæderos' (lovely youth)." India, Pliny says, is the sole parent of this precious stone, but he adds afterwards, that some inferior stones are found in Egypt, Arabia, and, of a very inferior quality, in Pontus. At the present day the finest opals come from Hungary. Few antique intagli are found on opals, and those of a rude description, the opal used being of an inferior kind. The noble opal was too highly esteemed by the ancients as a precious stone, to find its way into the hands of the engraver.

ASTERIA—STAR SAPPHIRE.

According to Pliny, "Asteria is a gem which holds its rank on account of a certain peculiarity in its nature, it having a light enclosed within, in the pupil of an eye as it were. This light, which has all the appearance of moving within the stone, it transmits according to the angle of inclination at which it is held; now in one direction and now in another. When hold facing the sun, it emits white rays like those of a star, and to this, in fact, it owes its name. The stones of India are very difficult to engrave, those of Carmania being preferred." The asteriated sapphire is still called by this name.

PRASIUS—PLASMA.

Plasma, or as called by the Italians, plasma di smeraldo, and prasina, are corruptions of praso, or prasius. It is a chalcedony of a leek-green colour, with a waxy lustre. By Pliny it is considered the commonest among the numerous kinds of green stones. It was extensively used for intagli among the Romans at a later period, the subjects engraved being mythological figures of a late epoch of Rome.

The stone now known as "praso" is a dull but hard green impure translucent quartz.

HELIOTROPIUM.

Heliotropium, Pliny says, is found in Æthiopia, Africa, and Cyprus. It is of a leek-green colour, streaked with blood-red veins. It is a praso, or semi-transparent green quartz, interspersed with small patches of opaque, bright red jasper.

CHRYSOPRASIUS—YELLOW-GREEN JADE.

The chrysoprasius is mentioned by Pliny as being similar to the colouring matter of the leek, but varying in tint between topazos (chrysolite) and gold. Pliny says this stone is found of so large a size as to admit of drinking vessels even being made of it, and is cut into cylinders very frequently. This was most likely the yellowish-green jade so often used in India as the material for the well-known elegant cups and vases that are among the most beautiful of the products of the artisans of that country.[*]

The modern chrysoprase is a chalcedony of a light apple-green colour. The green colour is given by a trace of oxide of nickel. It has been frequently confounded with plasma, but is distinguished from it by its brightness of tint, and its hardness.

It is doubtful if any intagli are to be met with on the true chrysoprase, as it has been hitherto found only in Silesia. According to Mr. King a stone much resembling it is found sometimes set in old Egyptian jewellery.

JASPIS—CHALCEDONY.

In the opinion of Mr. King the jaspis of Pliny answers to our chalcedony. It is a species of quartz of a bluish milky colour. When tinged with yellow it is named the opaline. The kind with a pale bluish tint is termed sapphirine. It was extensively used by the ancients in all ages for intagli. There are many masterpieces of ancient glyptic art in chalcedony extant, for instance, the celebrated Dionysiac bull by Hyllus.

The chalcedonius of Pliny was an inferior kind of emerald, so called from being found in the copper mines near Chalcedon, which, however, were exhausted in Pliny's time.

SARDA—SARD, OR ORIENTAL CORNELIAN.

The sard is a red chalcedony. It varies in colour from deep cherry, and even blood red, to reddish white, and passes on one side into dark brown, and on the other into yellow of several degrees of intensity. It has obtained various names, according to the tints it exhibits. A general term for the superior variety of this stone with the ancients appears to have been sarda. According to Pliny, " it is a common stone, and was first found at Sardis ; but the most esteemed kind is that of the vicinity of Babylon. In India there are three varieties of this stone : the red sarda ; the one known as 'pionia,' from its thickness ; and a third one, beneath which they place a ground of silver tinsel. The Indian stones are transparent, those of Arabia being more opaque. Among the ancients there was no precious

* " Edinburgh Review," No. 253, p. 258.

stone in more common use than this. Other stones, which are like
honey in colour, are generally disapproved of, and still more so
when they have the complexion of earthenware." The sard is the
stone which was commonly employed by the greatest artists of antiquity, and even by inferior artists, to a late period of the Roman
Empire, and, indeed, its moderate hardness, combined with the exquisite delicacy of its texture, which makes it susceptible of the
finest polish, which it retains longer than any other gem, will ever
secure it a distinguished rank among the stones most desirable to
the engraver of gems.

SARD ACHATES—CORNELIAN.

The common cornelian is a dull red variety of the sard. Egyptian
and Etruscan scarabæi of an early period are to be met with in this
stone. It is the sard achates of Pliny. The white cornelian of
lapidaries is the leucachates of Pliny.

ONYX—NICOLO—SARDONYX.

When chalcedony occurs with opaque stripes or layers of black
and white, dark red and white, in strong contrast to each other, it
is termed onyx. It was so called from ὄνυξ, a finger-nail. Pliny
mentions several kinds of onyx, which seem to include the several
varieties of striped chalcedony. The name onyx, or onyohites, has
been also applied by the ancients to Oriental alabaster.

When an onyx occurs with two layers, the upper of a bluish
colour and the lower black, an intaglio is frequently made by cutting
through the upper layer until the lower black zone appears. This
style of intaglio is termed nicolo, a corruption of the word oniculus,
which is derived from onyx. It was peculiar to Roman art after the
time of Nero.

According to Mr. King, " the sardonyx is defined by Pliny as
' candor in Sarda,' that is to say, a white opaque layer superimposed
upon a red transparent stratum of the true red sard," for as Pliny
says, as the name itself indicates Σαρδ́ον, sard, ὄνυξ, finger-nail, it
was like the flesh beneath the human finger-nail. Such, he adds, is
the sardonyx of India.

Three strata or coloured zones are generally considered essential
to the idea of a sardonyx.

Pliny relates that " in his time these stones were not held by the
people of India in any high esteem, although they were found there
of so large a size as to admit of the hilts of swords being made of

them. It is well known, too, that in that country they are exposed to view by the mountain streams, and that in our part of the world they were formerly valued from the fact that they are nearly the only ones among engraved precious stones that do not bring away the wax when an impression is made. The consequence is, that our example has at last taught the public of India to set a value upon them, and the lower classes there now pierce them even, to wear as ornaments for the neck; the great proof, in fact, at the present day, of a sardonyx being of Indian origin." Pliny also mentions that the first Roman who wore a sardonyx, according to Demostratus, was the elder Africanus, since whose time this stone has been held in very high esteem in Rome.

Both onyx and sardonyx, and other striped chalcedonic substances, have been employed by ancient and modern artists for executing those gems in relief, called camei; and it is wonderful to see with what dexterity they have frequently availed themselves of the different colours of the alternating zones to express the different parts of a figure, such as the hair, the garments. Some of the most celebrated productions of the glyptic art among the ancients have been executed in these stones, among which we may mention the apotheosis of Augustus, of two brown and two white layers; the apotheosis of Germanicus, of four zones; the head of Augustus, of three layers; the Jupiter Ægiochus, of white and black stones.

The most valuable stones are from India. Some of the pieces of sardonyx used by the ancient engravers for their most important works were of enormous dimensions.

At the present day onyxes and sardonyxes are imported from Germany, but their colours are produced artificially by boiling the stone, a kind of flint, for several days in honey and water, and then soaking it in sulphuric acid to bring out the black and white, and in nitric to give the red and white layers. They are, however, considered of little value.

ACHATES—AGATE.

Agate is a variegated siliceous stone; the colours in clouds, spots, or bands; the banded consisting of parallel or concentric layers, and either in straight, circular, or zigzag forms. The name is applied to many combinations of chalcedony, quartz, cornelian, amethyst, and even flint and jasper. Mr. King remarks that the agate and onyx are the same substance, only differing in the arrangement of the layers, which in agate are wavy and often concentric, whilst in onyx they are placed parallel to each other.

Pliny thus mentions it: "Achates was a stone formerly in high esteem, but now held in none. It was first found in Sicily, near a river of that name (now the Drillo, in the Val di Noto) but has since been discovered in numerous other localities. In size it exceeds any other stones of this class, and the varieties of it are numerous, the name varying accordingly, thus, for example, we have iaspachates (jasper agate), cerachates (the modern orange agate probably), smaragdachates (emerald-coloured agate), hæmachates (agate sprinkled with spots of red jasper), leucachates (white cornelian), dendrachates (marked with shrubs as it were, moss agate). The stones too that are found in India present the appearance in them of rivers (the river agate), woods (the moss agate), beasts of burden, and forms even, like ivy, and the trappings of horses. Agate was generally used by the ancients for cups and dishes. The term "Achates" among the ancients was of wide application, as it included not only several varieties of chalcedony, but also those now called jaspers. Several Etruscan scarabæi, and some Greek intagli of an early period, are of agate, cut across the layers or bands. This has been termed tricoloured, or banded agate. In modern times agates are coloured by artificial processes, such as boiling them in honey, and subsequently treating them with sulphuric acid. This artificial treatment in an agate may thus be considered as a proof of its modern origin.

MURRHINA—FLUOR SPAR.

The only stone which answers with any probability to Pliny's description of the "murrhina," used for cups and vessels, which were so highly prized by the ancient Romans, is the piece of fluor spar (murra) found in Rome, and employed by the Jesuits for the front of the altar of the Chiesu del Gesu (see page 281).

The "Murrhina in Parthis pocula coata fociis" of Propertius, is, as Mr. King justly supposes, a mode of expression which is nothing more than one of his favourite poetical conceits for conveying the same idea as Pliny, when he says "Some consider it to be a liquid substance solidified by subterranean heat."

Some take this literally, that it was "baked in ovens," as at the present day, in the neighbourhood of Broach, nodules of onyx are baked in earthen pots. This treatment is, however, only applied to small stones, and could never have been applied to the large pieces of "murrhina" of which the cups and vases were made, and which were dedicated by Pompey in the Temple of Jupiter Capitolinus.

MOLOCHITES—NEPHRITE.

Nephrite, or Jade, is a semi-opaque stone, which varies in colour
from a milky white to a dark olive-green. It is sometimes found
beautifully transparent. It is remarkable for its extreme hardness.
The name is from νεφρος (kidney), for it was used in the middle ages
as an amulet against diseases of the kidney. Vases and figures of this
material are to be met with in collections, and it has been worked into
images and ornaments in China and New Zealand. In the opinion
of some this stone never found its way to Rome. In the possession
of the author is a piece of dark green jade found on the Palatine Hill.
It is known to Roman antiquaries by the name of "Verde di Tar-
quinia." It may be the molochites of Pliny, which he describes as
not transparent, being of a deeper green, and more opaque than
smaragdus (emerald); it is highly esteemed for making seals.

Opaque.

JASPER.

Jasper is a siliceous stone, of a variety of colours—red, yellow,
brown, green, sometimes blue or black. It is nearly or quite
opaque, and presents little beauty until polished. The dark green
jasper is often seen in the form of Egyptian scarabæi. Yellow
jasper has been sometimes found with Egyptian engravings. Red
jasper takes a very fine polish, and has been most generally used by
the ancients. Of this there are two kinds, one of a vermilion colour,
the other of a very rich crimson; the latter is by far the rarest.
Marsyas flayed by Apollo, symbolical combinations, chimæra, and
other subjects, have been frequently represented on it. One of the
finest examples of ancient intagli, the head of Minerva, after
Phidias, by Aspasius, has been engraved on this stone. Red jasper
came into use long after Pliny's time, consequently he has left
no particular description, though it seems to be intended by his
vermilion-coloured Achates. Some intagli have been also found in
black jasper. Besides these, we now and then find striped, and
even party-coloured jaspers with intagli, which sometimes appear
so confused that the subject of the engraving can scarcely be distinguished on the stone. The "jaspis" of the ancients was properly
a green transparent chalcedony, evidently a kind of plasma. Pliny
distinguishes several varieties of jasper, from his description, being
doubtless various coloured semi-transparent chalcedonies. The
modern jasper is an opaque stone, answering more to the "achates"

of the ancients. Pliny thus enumerates the several varieties of jasper: "Many countries produce this stone; that of India is like smaragdus (emerald) in colour, that of Cyprus is hard, and of a full sea-green; and that of Persia is sky-blue, whence its name 'aërizum.' Similar to this last is the Caspian iaspis. On the banks of the river Thermodon, the iaspis is of an azure colour; in Phrygia, it is purple, and in Cappadocia of an azure purple, sombre and not refulgent. Amisos sends us an iaspis like that of India in colour, and Chalcedon, a stone of turbid hue. The best kind is that which has a shade of purple, the next best being the rose-coloured, and the next with the green colour of the amaragdus, to each of which the Greeks have given names, according to their respective tints. A fourth kind, which is called by them "boria," resembles in colour the sky of a morning in autumn. There is an iaspis also which resembles sarda in appearance, and another with a violet hue. To this class also belongs the stone called "sphragis," from the circumstance that it is best of all for making signets. According to Mr. King, the iaspis "stained with red spots," mentioned by Pliny, is not the heliotrope, but a white chalcedony full of red spots.

PRASIUS—HELIOTROPE, OR BLOODSTONE.

The variety of "prasius" mentioned by Pliny, as disfigured with spots like blood, is our heliotrope or bloodstone. It is a deep green chalcedony or jasper with red spots. Antique intagli in this stone are rarely to be met with. Bloodstone is at present much used for seal stones.

SAPPHIRUS—LAPIS LAZULI.

Lapis Lazuli is the Sapphirus of the ancients. It is thus described by Pliny: "Sapphirus is refulgent with spots like gold (particles of iron pyrites). It is of an azure colour, though sometimes, but rarely, it is purple. The best kind comes from Media. In no case is the stone diaphanous; in addition to which it is not suited for engraving when intersected with hard particles of crystalline nature (probably quartz)." Inferior intagli of a Roman period are frequently to be met with in lapis lazuli.

SMARAGDUS MEDICUS—MALACHITE.

Malachite (green carbonate of copper) was sometimes, but very rarely, used by the ancients for cameos. The Pulsky collection, affords an example of a cameo in malachite, representing the bust of a Bacchante. It is generally understood to answer to the smaragdus medicus of Pliny.

SANDARESOS—AVANTURINE.

The sandaresos of Pliny, which he describes as "having all the appearance of fire placed behind a transparent substance, it burning with star-like scintillations within, that resemble drops of gold, and are always to be seen in the body of the stone and never upon the surface," is doubtless the stone termed avanturine, a brownish semi-transparent quartz, full of specks of yellow mica. The common avanturine is a Venetian glass imitation. The name is usually derived from its discovery by accident "per avantura.' This name is more probably, however, of older origin. In the Targum of the pseudo Jonathan-ben-Uzziel, referred by Mr. Deutsch to the middle of the seventh century, a stone, translated jasper in our version, is called the margniath apanturin, or panthor gem. The step from *apanturin to avanturine is* a short one." A green variety is found in India, which corresponds with the green sandaresos which Pliny describes as a native of India, and of an apple green, but which was considered of no value.

CALLAIS—TURQUOISE.

The callais of Pliny is supposed to answer to the turquoise of the present day. He thus describes it: "Callais is like sapphire (lapis lazuli) in colour, only that it is paler and more closely resembles the tint of the water near the sea shore in appearance." The Oriental or mineral turquoise comes from Persia and Arabia, and is composed of phosphate of alumina, coloured by a compound of copper. It is met with in Persia in narrow cracks in aluminous ironstone, and in veins in siliceous rocks. Stones of great size and beauty, some being not less than four and five inches in circumference, have been lately brought from Arabia Petræa. They were found in lofty precipitous mountains of iron sandstone. The occidental, or bone turquoise, is said to be composed of fossil bones or teeth coloured with oxyde of copper. Intagli and camei in turquoise are of very doubtful antiquity.

The green variety of turquoise, on which the Romans set the highest value, was the callaina of Pliny.

TANOS—AMAZON STONE.

Pliny includes tanos among the smaragli. It came from Persia

* "Edinburgh Review," No. 233.

and was of an unsightly green and a soiled colour within. Mr. King, with every probability, considers this stone to bear certain analogies to the amazon stone, a very compact felspar of an emerald green colour, but opaque and with nacrous reflections, extremely hard, and taking a high polish. The cylinder or signet of Sennacherib, discovered by Mr. Layard, is of amazon stone.

HÆMATITES—HÆMATITE.

Hæmatite is a red iron stone. According to Pliny it is found in Ethiopia. It has been also called bloodstone, and has often been used for scarabæi and intagli by the Egyptians.

MAGNES—MAGNETITE.

Magnetite is a magnetic iron ore, commonly termed "loadstone." It has a dark iron-grey colour and metallic lustre. "It varies in colour, according to Pliny; that of Magnesia, bordering on Macedonia, being of reddish black; that of Bœotia being more red than black. The kind found in Troas is black. The most inferior, however, of all," he says, "is that of Magnesia, in Asia. It has been frequently made use of by ancient engravers, especially by those of Egypt and Persia." Babylonian cylinders are frequently found of this material. Rude intagli, with Gnostic subjects, used as amulets, have been largely manufactured in this stone.

OBSIDIANUM—OBSIDIAN.

Obsidian is a volcanic glass of a blackish greenish colour, consisting of lava suddenly cooled. It is opaque, or slightly translucent on the edges of fragments. It is thus noticed by Pliny: "This stone is of a very dark colour, and sometimes transparent; but it is dull to the sight, and reflects, when attached as a mirror to a wall, the shadow of the object, rather than the image. Many persons use it for jewellery, and I myself have seen solid statues in this material of the late Emperor Augustus, of very considerable thickness." Intagli of this material are very rare.

BASALTES—BASALT.

Basalt is an igneous rock, usually of a dark green or brownish black colour, and of a very fine grain. Intagli and scarabæi of a very late period among the Egyptians are only to be met with of this material. There are also some Gnostic amulets of this stone.

It was frequently employed for statues by the Egyptians, and by the Romans of the age of Adrian. It is the "basanites" of Pliny.

PORPHYRITES—PORPHYRY.

Porphyry is a stone of a beautiful red colour, thickly disseminated with white crystals of feldspar. It receives a fine polish, and has been chiefly used for columns, vases, and bas-reliefs. A few intagli of an early imperial date occur in this material. It was also employed by Italian artists at the Revival.

OPHITES—SERPENTINE.

' The serpentine met with in Italy, which is called serpentino antico, is of a dark dull green colour, with long whitish spots. It was called by the ancients marmor, "ophites," or momphites, and was obtained, as its name imports, from the neighbourhood of Memphis.

GRANITE.

Granite is a primitive rock, whose constituent parts are feldspar, quartz, and mica. The red or Egyptian variety (the red feldspar predominating) was principally used by the ancients. The variety of granite called syenite is composed of feldspar, quartz, and hornblende. Though deriving its name from Syene, in Egypt, but little of it is met with in that place, the rock there being chiefly granite. The syenite of antiquity, used for statues, was really granite.

The Egyptians were the only people who engraved small objects on serpentine and granite. Scarabæi, bearing hieroglyphics, of these materials frequently occur.

IMITATIONS.

The art of imitating gems or precious stones was well known to the ancients. The Egyptians were undoubtedly in possession of this art, as several valuable examples sufficiently prove. Pliny tells us that the Greeks and Romans were equally skilful in imitating emeralds and other transparent stones, by colouring crystals; they also manufactured onyx and sardonyx by cementing red and dark-coloured chalcedony to a white layer. Camei have been also imitated by fusing together coloured layers of glass, which when cooling was made to receive the impression of the relieved figure it was intended to imitate. In the possession of the author is a paste head of Omphale, imitating a cameo of sardonyx, so exquisitely done as to almost deceive an experienced judge. Pastes, or imitations of engraved gems in intaglio, are to be seen in many collections. Ancient objects of this kind are much prized, their value being independent of the material, for we have become acquainted by the means of these imitations with several admirable works, the originals of which have not come down to us. Countless modern imitations of these are also to be frequently met with.

IMPRESSIONS.

The finest order of gems being seldom within the means of private purchasers, the prevailing taste for engraved gems, and the impossibility for amateurs and artists to visit every cabinet and collection, has led to the necessity of making collections of impressions of engraved gems, in plaster, sulphur, and other materials. Excepting the nature of the stone itself, these impressions are a complete image of the gem, and serve, as well as the original, for the researches of the historian, the artist, and the archæologist. The art of making these impressions and imitations, places all that constitutes the true value of the original within the most moderate expenditure. These impressions have been multiplied, and systematic collections have been formed most useful for the study of engraved gems. Pickler made a large collection of impressions of the most beautiful stones, but did not publish the catalogue, which he intended to compile. Lippert made a very extensive collection of impressions, and the learned catalogue which he drew up is most useful for their study; but the best imitations of the antique are the pastes executed by Tassio. The engraving and tint of the gem are copied with extraordinary fidelity. Tassio's collection, perhaps the most complete in Europe, amounts to about 15,000, and comprises fac-similes of all the most celebrated gems. Raspé published a catalogue of them. Collections of these impressions would be of the greatest advantage and utility, if their selection was made with some care, if particular attention was paid not to mix modern works with ancient works, and also if the nature of the material, the form and dimensions of the stone, and the cabinet in which it was to be found, were carefully indicated. Collections of impressions in sulphur and in scagliola are frequent in Italy. Those of Paoletti, and particularly those of Cades at Rome, are remarkable for their careful finish.

Ancient impressions of intagli in fine clay (γῆ σημαντρὶς the sealing earth of the Greeks), are frequently found, sometimes with the impress of a monogram on the reverse. They are supposed to be tesseræ, or tokens given by the owner of the impressed seal.

PALÆOGRAPHY, OR INSCRIPTIONS.

I.

Aim and Utility of its Study.

The study of ancient inscriptions is termed palæography. These inscriptions are isolated, or traced on some monument of architecture, sculpture, &c., or on vases or paintings. We shall here treat alone of inscriptions, properly so called, giving the text of laws, decrees, public accounts, dedications, votive and laudatory inscriptions, historical narratives and documents, epitaphs, &c. The Greeks generally gave to inscriptions the name of epigraph, or epigram, ἐπιγραφή, ἐπίγραμμα. The Romans termed them inscriptio, titulus, marmor, lapis, monumentum, memoria, tabula, mensa, epitaphium, &c., according to their distinction, and the nature of the text they present. The importance of the study of ancient inscriptions need not be dwelt on here. Inscriptions are the real archives of the annals of ancient nations. They are the contemporaneous witnesses of the event and of the men whose memory they hand down. They bear unquestionable evidences of authenticity, and are consequently deserving of every confidence. Their public exhibition during centuries to the eyes of numerous people who might find an interest in contradicting them, give them a character of truth and a general sanction which the narratives of historians do not always inspire, who may have had opposing interests in the same historical fact.

The study of palæography, or at least the knowledge of its results, is therefore the first duty of the historian of ancient nations. He will find in them important data regarding the chronology, the geography, the religious systems, the civil government, the laws and administration of affairs, the state of individuals, the affiliations of illustrious families, the customs, manners, even the very prejudices of ancient societies; and in regard to everything which is connected with the organization of the societies, the magistrates, the public revenue and its employment, with military organization, wars and alliances, lastly with their mode of intellectual life, their progress in knowledge, their languages, their dialects, and their system of writing. It is to inscriptions that history is mainly indebted for the greater number of the corrections, which have cast their light on obscure passages of the great writers of antiquity, or have rectified their erroneous assertions. " A great number of inscriptions, especially those recording great events, laws, or decrees of the government, which it was important for every citizen to know, supplied to some extent the want of the art of printing. When, for example, the laws of the twelve tables at Rome were set up in public, their public exhibition was equivalent to their publication by means of the art of printing, for every Roman might go and read them, and if he liked, take a copy of them for his private use. Previous to the invention of the art of printing, inscriptions set up in a public place were the most convenient means of giving publicity to that which it was necessary or useful for every citizen of the State to know. Inscriptions therefore are, next to the literature of the ancients, the most important sources from which we derive our knowledge of their public, religious, social, and private life, and their study is indispensable for every one who desires to become intimately acquainted with the history of antiquity. For the history of the languages they are of paramount importance, since in most cases, they show us the different modes of writing in the different periods, and exhibit to us the languages in their grand progress and development; though it is manifest that the ancients did not bestow that care upon the accuracy of the language and orthography which we might expect, and in many cases they seem to have left those things to the artisan who executed the inscription. After the overthrow of the Roman Empire in the west, inscriptions continued to be made very frequently; but as the ignorance of the middle classes increased, and as all knowledge became more and more confined to the priesthood, the custom of making certain things known by means of inscriptions gradually fell into disuse, until the art of printing did away with it almost entirely."[*]

II.

MATERIALS WHICH BEAR INSCRIPTIONS, AND VARIETIES OF INSCRIPTIONS.

All solid materials known to the ancients were employed by them for the purpose of inscribing or engraving inscriptions, wood, clay, stones, rocks, marble, metals, ivory, and artificial materials, but especially bronze in Greece and in the Roman Empire for inscriptions of general interest. Inscriptions are usually —1. *Inscribed*, that is to say, simply traced with a brush on hard materials. The greater number of this description has been found

* " Penny Cyclopædia."

in Egypt on parts of the temples, on rough stones, and on fragments
of pottery. 2. *Engraved*, the letters of which are traced in a
concave form or in intaglio, on stone, marble, or metal ; all Greek,
Etruscan, and Roman inscriptions are done in this manner ; the
Egyptians alone engraved their inscriptions in relief. 3. *Laid on*,
being composed of bronze letters, wrought separately, and afterwards attached by cramps to the monument which they ornamented. These have almost all disappeared, either from the effects
of time or cupidity, but the holes for the cramps partly, however,
take their place. It was thus the learned Seguier, by means of an
exact cast of those holes, which are seen on the façade of the
Maison Carrée, at Nismes, succeeded in establishing the form of
each letter, and in restoring the inscription in bronze of that
temple. By these ingenious means, applied to other buildings, the
same success has been obtained.

III.

RELATIVE IMPORTANCE OF INSCRIPTIONS.

Travellers in ancient countries have furnished us with a number
of inscriptions, and many are now known belonging to the great
nations of antiquity : India, Phœnicia, Persia, Babylonia, Palmyra,
Carthage, Spain. We shall, however, treat only of the inscriptions
belonging to the four nations which we have chosen as the chief
objects of our inquiries. First, in relative importance, may be
placed the more extended inscriptions, as from the number of words
a number of facts may be elicited, and because it is rare that a text
of several lines should not be something more than a matter of
private interest, or the narrative of an unimportant action. Almost
equally important are *bilingual* or *trilingual* inscriptions, the texts of
which are expressed in two or several languages at once, one being
a translation of the other. Such are—1. The inscription found at
Eugubium, which is in Etruscan and in Latin. 2. The celebrated
inscription of Rosetta, in Egyptian hieroglyphics and in Greek.
The great importance of this kind is sufficiently evident, the text
of which, in a known language, is the translation of the neighbouring text, written in a language and in an alphabet which is
not known. To such inscriptions we are indebted for the discovery
of several ancient alphabets.

A great number of ancient inscriptions have been brought to
Europe, travellers have seen a still greater number in the countries
they have passed through, and not being able to remove them, they
have taken copies of them ; but very few of these are strictly

faithful, as copies of the same inscription made by different travellers, have frequently proved their incorrectness. When these copies are carefully compared they are sometimes sufficient for a skilful critical scholar to re-establish the text in its purity; but it were to be wished for, that the exercise of this critical ingenuity was not necessary. A fac-simile of the inscription, taken with a sheet of damp paper pressed against it, and then allowed to dry, would obviate all these inconveniences. A fac-simile of that kind cannot contain any error, or the substitution of one letter for another. It has this merit also, that it retains the style of the letters in all its purity and exactness, an undeniable advantage, as the characters of that style afford a certain indication to determine the epoch and age of a monument. This mode of taking an impression is strongly recommended to all travellers.

IV.

CRITICAL KNOWLEDGE OF INSCRIPTIONS.

The text of inscriptions is generally remarkable for its conciseness, energy, and precision; these with the ancients were the three essential characteristics, which constitute what has been termed "the lapidary style." Abbreviations abound in them. These consequently require a particular study, and the best Latin scholar might fail in reading even a short inscription, if he had not devoted himself to their study. Besides the abbreviations, Greek and Latin inscriptions present a number of peculiarities opposed to the usual syntax of their language, peculiarities which critics have characterized by terms, which they name—1. *Anacoluthon*, a want of connection between the verb and the nominative case, as CIVITAS ... CO-OPTAVERUNT. 2. *Antiptosis*, when one case is put for another, as PATRONO FRATRI for PATRONI FRATRIS. 3. *Protousteron*, when a word or phrase is not in its place. 4. *Ellipsis*, or suppression of words essential to the clearness of the sentence, such as conjunctions; words relative to relationship, to the nation, to ceremonies, &c. 5. *Tautology*, or useless repetition of the same idea. In regard to Greek inscriptions, we must also add to their difficulties the use of different dialects and local modes of expression, the variations of inflections through the effects of time, the habits which vitiate the regular termination of words, the use of certain words, verbs, modes of speech, &c. The ignorance of the engraver adds sometimes to those difficulties, careful discrimination and great practice will, however, be sufficient to guard against being led into error in the interpretation of inscriptions by mistakes of that kind.

In general Greek and Latin inscriptions are in prose; a great
number, however, are in verse, and are styled " metric inscriptions."
Some are found in which verse is conjoined with prose, especially
in sepulchral inscriptions. There are also some which are composed at the same time of a few lines of Latin, and of a few lines of
Greek. A Roman funereal cippus in this style was lately discovered at Lyons. The Latin portion informs us that this cippus
had been placed on the tomb of Lucretia Valeria, by Sextus Avius
Hermerus, her husband. Four lines in Greek are placed beneath.
They are two verses which contain a moral reflection against envious
persons, and are a bad copy of an epigram on that subject in the
Greek Anthology.

V.

Classification of Inscriptions.

It is the subject which ought to regulate the classification of
inscriptions. There is a variety of opinions with regard to the
most convenient and proper plan of classifying inscriptions, for
in a large collection of inscriptions, divisions and subdivisions might
be carried out to a large extent. Large classes or divisions will
be found more useful, as they will be sufficient to make out with
sufficient completeness the nature of an inscription lately discovered ; and to connect it, by its interpretation, with monuments
of the same kind. We may therefore adopt the following classification of ancient inscriptions :—

I. RELIGIOUS.—Honours paid to the gods, demigods, and to
heroes : vows, dedications, religious ceremonies, foundations, altars,
sacrifices, taurobolia, suovetaurilia, libations, invocations, imprecations, moral precepts.

II. HISTORICAL.—Laws, decrees, treaties of peace, of alliance,
of hospitality, public acts of all kinds, accounts and public inven-
tories, lists of priests, magistrates, warriors who died in the service
of the State, services rendered to the State by citizens, honours
decreed to a private individual in his lifetime, marbles bearing
the indication of an epoch, chronological facts, calendars, inscriptions not belonging to any other class, but bearing a date, acts of
cities and of corporations, texts containing the names of places and
other geographical information, such as military columns ; the dedications of public monuments, not religious edifices ; the allocutions
of kings, magistrates, and all inscriptions indicating a public
observance, a fact relative to the manners and customs, to the state
of individuals, to social organization, &c.

III. SCIENTIFIC.—Expressing some principles of the science, some processes of the arts, bearing the names of artists or writers; the causes and periods of disease and death; the names of trades.

IV. FUNEREAL.—Traced on cippi, stelæ, sarcophagi, cenotaphs, &c., and relative to whatever concerns the tombs and funerals of the ancients, if the quality of the deceased does not make him an historic personage, or the text of the inscription, a geographical or a chronological monument.

V. CHRISTIAN.—The four divisions we have given may be followed by this important class of inscriptions, as they, for the most part, belong to the Roman period, and are written in the same language with those of Rome.

In general, it is the principal subject which marks out the inscription as belonging to one class or the other; the cippus of an obscure private individual, without titles and without office, shall be considered as belonging to the funereal class, if it does not present any indication relative to subjects which belong to one of the former classes. The invocation to the *Gods Manes* will not change its attribution, for these gods preside alone over funereal ceremonies.

VI.

HISTORY OF PALÆOGRAPHY.

The importance of inscriptions has been recognised by learned men of all ages. Even in ancient times great importance was attached to these monuments as the most authentic archives of nations, to which were entrusted their public and private rights; treaties of all kinds, laws, and the memories of great deeds, as well as of great citizens, were consigned to them by the order or by the approbation of the grateful city. There were collectors of inscriptions even in ancient times. The historian Euhemerus was the first, according to Eusebius and Lactantius. Athenæus relates that Philochorus collected also, in a special work, the inscriptions which he saw in the different states of Greece. The historians Herodotus, Pausanias, and others, mention several of them, not indeed for the same purpose as Philochorus, who set an example in that respect to the palæographist of modern times. Cosmas Indicopleustes, who wrote in Greek a Christian Topography in 545 A.D., introduced several inscriptions in it. It is through his work that we have become acquainted with the celebrated Greek inscription of Adulis (the monumentum Adulitanum) relative to the conquests of Ptolemy Euergetes, King of Egypt, in Asia. The original marble has perished, with many others, the text of which the manuscript of Cosmas has preserved. At the revival of letters, Petrarch sought inscriptions, as well as manuscripts and medals, but his chief interest was in studying them, without uniting them in a systematic collection. In the fifteenth century, the study assumed great importance, and among the travellers of that age, Cyriacus of Ancona was the first who transcribed in his itinerary the inscriptions which he met with in Europe and the Levant. At the same period Felix Feliciano, Joannes Marcanova, and Fra Giocondo, were remarkable for their zeal in their researches for ancient inscriptions; the latter especially, two volumes in manuscript of whom still exist in the library of the Chapter of Verona, his native city. In the sixteenth century collections of inscriptions were published. Peutinger brought out the first at Augsburg, in 1505; then followed those of John Huttich, Mayence, 1520 to 1525, of Fulvio Orsini, or Colocci, which has been wrongly attributed to Mazzochi, who was only the printer of it. Works of this kind were soon multiplied; inscribed monuments, collected in all parts of the Roman dominions, were engraved or transcribed, and the collection of Smetius, increased by Justus Lipsius (Leyden, 1588), is considered the first which has been arranged in methodic order, and is remarkable also for its fidelity and the excellent criticisms on the texts. It served as a model to the numerous works of that kind which appeared in Europe in the following centuries. Besides general collections, particular collections of a province or of a single city engaged the attention of the learned. Inscriptions of a particular kind were also collected. Some particular collections contained metric inscriptions, in Greek and Latin verses; others, those which were connected with a special subject. The Doctor Annibal Mariotti, of Perugia, has left an unedited collection of epigraphs relating to physicians and medicine. Public and private collections of original marbles were formed in many places, and interpreters were also found to describe and publish them. Gruter undertook an universal collection of all known inscriptions; Grævius and Gronovius published an edition of it revised and augmented in 1707. Muratori published a similar collection in 1739. These two works form, with the supplement of Donati, a complete body of inscriptions, which exhibit all the riches and all the interest attached to the authentic documents which constitute the science of palæography. In 1628 the learned Selden published his "Marmora Arundelliana," in which the Greek inscriptions brought from Smyrna, and purchased by the Earl of Arundel, are deciphered and illustrated. These inscriptions, with several others collected by Sir George Wheler, Dawkins, Bouverie, and Wood, were again published in a new and splendid form in

1763 by Dr. Richard Chandlor, under the title of "Marmora Oxoniensia."

The study of inscriptions became more extended every day. Maffei published his Arte Critica Lapidaria, an unfinished work, exhibiting great learning, but too extensive to be of general use. Padre Zaccheria published a work with that aim, but in his Instituzioni Lapidarie he deviates too frequently from his subject, and devotes more attention to teaching the art of composing inscriptions than that of deciphering ancient inscriptions. Morcelli attempted both in his treatise "De Stilo Inscriptionum." It is the best elementary work on that subject. A more convenient and less extensive work has been compiled by M. Spotorno, in his "Trattato dell'Arte Epigrafica," published at Savona, 1813. An extremely useful, though not very accurate, collection of inscriptions is that published by J. C. Orelli, Zurich, 1828. The most complete collection of Greek inscriptions is the great work in two large folios, of which A. Boeck undertook the editorship. It bears the title of "Corpus Inscriptionum Græcarum," the first vol. was published in 1828, the second in 1843. The inscriptions in this work have been arranged according to the countries and localities in which they were found, and have been most judiciously classified. This work has exercised an important influence on the scholars of our time, and has been the cause of a prodigious number of inscriptions having been brought to light by travellers which were before unknown. Col. Leake, Sir Charles Fellowes, and Mr. Hamilton, have copied and reproduced in their travels a large number of inscriptions from Greece and Asia Minor. In France a most important work has been published by Mr. Letronne, 1842, entitled "Recueil des inscriptions Grecques et Latines de l'Egypte." Mr. Rangabé of Athens has published in his "Antiquités Helléniques," a number of inscriptions discovered in Greece since its freedom. Dr. Henzen, of Rome, is at present devoting much time to collecting and editing Greek and Roman inscriptions.

The discovery of an ancient Christian cemetery or catacomb in 1578, extending like a vast subterranean city, far and wide, beneath and along the Via Salaria, near Rome, forms an epoch in the science of Christian Archæology. The inscriptions found in them excited the enthusiasm and piety of the most celebrated antiquarians of the day. Bosio devoted his time to collecting and deciphering the inscriptions with an earnestness and enthusiasm unparalleled. He however did not live to enjoy the reward of his labours. They were published in Italian in 1632, under the title of Roma Sotterranea, and the work was afterwards reproduced in Latin, with considerable additions, by Aringhi. Boldetti and Marangoni, spent

more than thirty years in the exploration of the catacombs and other
sacred antiquities of Rome. A portion of the results was published
by Boldetti in 1720, but by far the greater part still remained in
manuscript, which was unfortunately destroyed by fire in 1737. A
collection of Christian inscriptions is included in Muratori's " Novus
Thesaurus Veterum Inscriptionum," though the great body of them
is of course profane. The most critical and scholarly work on these
inscriptions is the publication of the Cavalier de Rossi, undertaken at
the express solicitation of Card Mai. Sr. de Rossi's first volume as
the title implies, " Inscriptiones Christianæ Urbis Romæ, Septimo
Sæculo Antiquiores," 1857 to 1863, contains only the Christian
inscriptions of the city of Rome, and of these only the inscriptions
which are anterior to the sixth century, and of whose genui. oness,
as well as age, no reasonable doubt can be entertained.

Collections of ancient inscriptions have been formed in the principal museums of Europe. In the British Museum are several important inscriptions from the Elgin and Townly collections, among
which are the well known Potidœan inscriptions, the Sigean
inscriptions, and several other valuable engraved marbles. At
Oxford are the Arundel marbles, or inscriptions, the most important of which is the celebrated Parian chronicle, so called from the
supposition of its having been made in the island of Paros, B.C. 263.
At the Vatican, the long gallery, " Galleria Lapidaria," leading to the
Museum, presents on its walls the finest known collection of ancient
sepulchral inscriptions in Latin and in Greek, amounting to
upwards of 8000 examples. In the Florentine Gallery is a hall of
inscriptions arranged in classes by Lanzi. The museum at Naples
contains a most interesting collection of inscribed monuments
from Herculaneum, Pompeii, Stabiæ, Pozzuoli, Baiæ, Cuma.
Within the last few years all the inscriptions found in Greece are
placed in the Thæsoum, within the walls of the Propylæa, or in the
Acropolis of Athens.

It remains for us now to speak of what is most essential in the
separate study of those inscriptions which have come down to us,
belonging to those nations whose monuments we have undertaken
to illustrate in this work. We shall endeavour to give some general
hints with regard to the principal characteristics of each kind of
inscription, the variations in the form of the letters, and in the
orthography of words, the sigla or numerous abbreviations, and to
the means of discovering the period of an inscription which bears
no precise date. Our chief aim shall be to give in the following
chapters the most important hints on these various subjects which
must, however, necessarily be very brief and elementary.

THE PALÆOGRAPHY OF DIFFERENT NATIONS.

EGYPTIAN.[*]

No nation has left so many inscriptions as the Egyptian. All its monuments are covered with them. Its temples, palaces, tombs, isolated monuments, present an infinite number of inscriptions in hieroglyphic, hieratic, and demotic characters. The Egyptians rarely executed a statue, or figured representation, without inscribing by its side its name or subject. This name is invariably found by the side of each divinity, personage, or individual. In each painted scene, on each sculptured figure, an inscription, more or less extensive, explains its subject.

The characters used by the Egyptians were of three kinds—hieroglyphic, hieratic, and demotic. The latter has been also termed enchorial, or popular. The first was doubtless a system of representational signs, or picture writing—the earliest form of writing, in the first stage of its development; the hieratic is an abbreviated form of the hieroglyphic; the demotic, a simplified form of the hieratic, and a near approach towards the alphabetic system.

Hieroglyphics (styled by the Egyptians skai n ntr tnr—writing of sacred words) are composed of signs representing objects of the physical world, as animals, plants, stars, man and his different members, and various objects. They are pure or linear, the latter being a reduction of the former. The pure were always sculptured or painted. The linear were generally used in the earlier papyri, containing funereal rituals.

They have been divided into four classes:—1, representational or ikonographic; 2, symbolic or tropical; 3, enigmatic; 4, phonetic. From the examination of hieroglyphic inscriptions of different ages, it is evident that these four classes of symbols were used promiscuously, according to the pleasure and convenience of the artist.

* In this chapter we are much indebted to Sir G. Wilkinson's treatise on Hieratic and Demotic writing, in Rawlinson's Herodotus.

z

1. Ikonographic, representational, or imitative hieroglyphics, are those that present the images of the things expressed, as the sun's disc to signify the sun, the crescent to signify the moon. These may be styled pure hieroglyphics. This class is the κυριολογικη κατα μιμησιν of Clemens Alexandrinus.

2. The symbolical, or tropical (by Bunsen termed ideographic), substituted one object for another, to which it bore an analogy, as heaven and a star expressed night; a leg in a trap, deceit; two arms stretched towards heaven expresses the word offering; a censor with some grains of incense, adoration; a bee was made to signify an obedient people; the fore-quarters of a lion, strength; a crocodile, rapacity. This kind of character appears to have been particularly invented for the expression of abstract ideas, especially belonging to religion or the royal power. These are the characters generally alluded to by the ancients when they speak of hieroglyphics, and are the most difficult of interpretation.

3. Enigmatic are those in which an emblematic figure is put in lieu of the one intended to be represented, as a hawk for the sun; a seated figure, with a carved beard, for a god. These three kinds were either used alone, or in company with the phonetically written word they represented. Thus: 1. The word Re, sun, might be written in letters only, or be also followed by the ikonograph, the solar disc (which if alone would still have the same meaning—Re, the sun). So too the moon, Aah, or Ioh, was followed by the crescent. In these cases the sign so following the phonetic word has been called a determinative, from its serving to determine the meaning of what preceded it. 2. In the same manner, the tropical hieroglyphics might be alone or in company with the word written phonetically; and the expression "to write," skhai, might be followed or not by its tropical hieroglyphic, the "pen and inkstand," as its determinative sign. 3. The emblematic figure, a hawk, signifying the "sun," might also be alone, or after the name "Re" written phonetically, as a determinative sign; and as a general rule the determinative followed, instead of preceding the names. Determinatives are therefore of three kinds—ikonographic, tropical, and enigmatic.[*]

---

[*] Champollion (Palæographie Universelle) ascribes the necessity of the determinative sign to the custom, as among Oriental nations, of omitting the middle vowels of words in Egyptian writing; this would produce confusion in respect to words unlike each other in meaning, but written with the same consonants. Thus, the words Nib, an ibis, and Nebi, a plough, were traced in the same manner by two hieroglyphical characters, expressing only N and B. All confusion of ideas and words, however, was avoided, by placing at the end of each phonetic word an additional determinative character, which determined the meaning of the word, and its real pronunciation.

4. Phonetic. Phonetic characters or signs were those expressive of sounds. They were formed by taking the first letter of the name of those objects selected to be the representative of each sound; thus, the name of an eagle, in the Coptic or Egyptian language—akhóm—began with the sound A, and that bird was taken as a sign for that letter; a *lion* stood for the letter L, as it was the initial letter of *labo*, or lion, in the Coptic; a *mouth* was selected to represent R, it being the initial letter of ro, or mouth, in Coptic. This phonetic principle being admitted, the numbers of figures used to represent a sound might have been increased almost without limit, and any hieroglyphic might stand for the first letter of its name. So copious an alphabet would have been a continual source of error. The characters, therefore, thus applied, were soon fixed, and the Egyptians confined themselves to particular hieroglyphics in writing certain words.

Hieroglyphic writing was employed on monuments of all kinds, on temples as well as on the smallest figures, and on bricks used for building purposes. On the most ancient monuments this writing is absolutely the same as on the most recent Egyptian work. Out of Egypt there is scarcely a single example of a graphic system identically the same during a period of over two thousand years. The hieroglyphic figures were arranged in vertical columns, or horizontal lines, and grouped together as circumstances required, so as to leave no spaces unnecessarily vacant. They were written from right to left, or from left to right. The order in which the characters were to be read, was shown by the direction in which the figures are placed, as their heads are invariably turned towards the reader. A single line of hieroglyphics—the dedication of a temple or of any other monument, for example—proceeds sometimes one half from left to right, and the other half from right to left; but in this case a sign, such as the sacred *tau*, an obelisk, which has no particular direction, is placed in the middle of the inscription, and it is from that sign that the two halves of the inscription take each an opposite direction.

The period when hieroglyphics—the oldest Egyptian characters —were first used, is uncertain. They are found in the Great Pyramid of the time of the fourth dynasty, and had evidently been invented long before, having already assumed a cursive style. This shows them to be far older than any other known writing; and the written documents of the ancient languages of Asia, the Sanscrit and the Zend, are of a recent time compared with those of Egypt, even if the date of the Rig-Veda in the fifteenth century B.C. be proved. Manetho shows that the invention of writing was known in the

reign of Atôhthis (the son and successor of Menes), the second king
of Egypt, when he ascribes to him the writing of the anatomical
books; and tradition assigned to it a still earlier origin.   At all
events hieroglyphics, and the use of the papyrus, with the usual
reed pen, are shown to have been common when the pyramids were
built; and their style in the sculptures proves that they were then
a very old invention.   In hieroglyphics of the earliest periods there
were fewer phonetic characters than in after ages, being nearer to
the original picture writing.   The number of signs also varied at
different times; but they may be reckoned at from 900 to 1000.
Various new characters were added at subsequent periods, and a
still greater number were introduced under the Ptolemies and
Cæsars, which are not found in the early monuments; some, again,
of the older times, fell into disuse.

Hieratic is an abbreviated form of the hieroglyphic; thus each
hieroglyphic sign—ikonographic, symbolic, or phonetic—has its
abridged hieratic form, and this abridged form has the same import
as the sign itself of which it is a reduced copy.   It was written from
right to left, and was the character used by the priests and sacred
scribes, whence its name.   It was invented at least as early as the
ninth dynasty (2240 B.C.), and fell into disuse when the demotic
had been introduced.   The hieratic writing was generally used
for manuscripts, and is also found on the cases of mummies, and on
isolated stones and tablets.   Long inscriptions have been written
on them with a brush.   Inscriptions of this kind are also found
on buildings, written or engraved by ancient travellers.   But its
most important use was in the historical papyri, and the registers
of the temples.   Most valuable information respecting the chronology and numeric systems of the Egyptians has been derived from
them.

Demotic, or enchorial, is composed of signs derived from the
hieratic, and is a simplified form of it, but from which figurative or
ikonographic signs are generally excluded, and but few symbolical
signs, relative to religion alone, are retained ; signs nearly approaching the alphabetic are chiefly met with in this third kind of writing.
It was invariably written, like the hieratic, from right to left.   It is
thus evident that the Egyptians, strictly speaking, had but one system
of writing, composed of three kinds of signs, the second and third
being regularly deduced from the first, and all three governed by
the same fundamental principles.   The demotic was reserved for
general use among the Egyptians : decrees and other public acts,
contracts, some funereal stelæ, and private transactions, were written
in demotic.   The intermediate text of the Rosetta inscription is of

this kind. It is not quite certain when the demotic first came into use, but it was at least as early as the reign of Psammotichus II., of the twenty-sixth dynasty (604 B.C.); and it had therefore long been employed when Herodotus visited Egypt. Soon after its invention it was adopted for all ordinary purposes.

The chief objects of interest in the study of an Egyptian inscription are its historical indications. These are found in the names of kings or of chief officers, and in the dates they contain. The names of kings are always enclosed in an oval called *cartouche*. An oval contains either the royal title or prenomen, or the proper name or nomen of the king. The royal title is more frequently found, and though there are a great many of them which bear a great resemblance to one another, yet none are exactly similar, each of these ovals containing a title, belongs to a separate king, whom it designates particularly. An accurate study of these ovals having led to the knowledge of connecting the ovals containing titles with the kings who bore them, and thereby forming a list of these, founded on and confirmed by monuments, this oval containing the title or prenomen, though alone, has thus become a most important historical indication, and we are thus able to attribute, with every certainty, the monuments bearing this oval to the reign of the king designated by the oval, or to the reign of the king who was latest in date of the two or more which are sometimes found on the same monument. The greatest attention ought to be paid to these ovals; their presence adds to the value of any inscription, which contains one or more in its text. The oval containing the proper name, or nomen, frequently follows the oval containing the title, a group of two signs, a semicircle and a bee, meaning "Lord of an obedient People," is placed over the pronomen; and another group of two signs, a goose and a solar disc, is placed over the nomen, and in this case the royal legend is complete. This latter group which reads *Phra* or *Ra, &c.* ("Son of the Sun") is a title common to all the kings of Egypt, and we have thus the complete designation of each king. For example, "Lord of an obedient people (first group of two signs). Sun, guardian of justice and truth, approved by Ra (oval containing title or prenomen). Son of the Sun (second group of two signs). Beloved of Amun. Rameses (oval

RAMESES II.

proper name)." Such is the royal legend of Rameses II. The kings of the eighteenth dynasty assumed the additional title of "Lord of the Upper and Lower Country," which was placed over their prenomen. The first sign of the oval, containing the title, is always the disc of the sun, and this sign, as well as all the others of ovals of this kind, is ikonographic or symbolic. In the ovals containing proper names, on the contrary, the signs are either entirely phonetic, or ikonographic and phonetic mixed together. The names of Egyptian gods sometimes forming a portion of the proper names of kings and individuals, frequently the figure itself of the god, or his animal representative, was placed instead of the phonetic signs which would have represented that part of his name in the oval : thus the name of the king Thotmes is spelt by an ibis (Thoth), and the usual signs of M and S. The semicircle at the end of an oval denotes the name to be that of a female.

The dates which are found with these royal legends are also of great importance in an historical point of view, and monuments which bear any numerical indications are exceedingly rare. These numerical indications are either the age of the deceased on a funereal tablet, or the number of different consecrated objects which he has offered to the gods, or the date of an event mentioned in the inscription. Dates, properly so called, are the most interesting to collect ; they are expressed in hieroglyphic cyphers, single lines expressing the number of units up to nine, when an arbitrary sign represents 10, another 100, and another 10,000.

The most celebrated Egyptian Inscriptions are those of the Rosetta stone. This stone, a tablet of black basalt, contains three inscriptions, one in hieroglyphics, another in demotic or enchorial, and a third in the Greek language. The inscriptions are to the same purport in each, and are a decree of the priesthood of Memphis, in honour of Ptolemy Epiphanes, about the year B.C. 190. "Ptolemy is there styled King of Upper and Lower Egypt, Son of the gods Philopatores, approved by Pthah, to whom Ra has given victory, a living image of Amun, son of Ra, Ptolemy Immortal, beloved by Pthah, God Epiphanes, most gracious. In the date of the decree we are told the names of the priests of Alexander, of the gods Soteres, of the gods Adelphi, of the gods Euergetæ, of the gods Philopatores, of the god Epiphanes himself, of Berenice Euergetis, of Arsinoë Philadelphus, and of Arsinoë Philopator. The preamble mentions with gratitude the services of the king, or rather of his wise minister Aristomenes ; and the enactment orders that the statue of the king shall be worshipped in every temple of Egypt, and be carried out in the processions with those of the gods of the country ; and lastly that the decree is to be curved at the foot of every statue of the king in sacred, in common, and in

Greek writing."* (Sharpe.) It is now in the British Museum. This stone is remarkable for having led to the discovery of the system pursued by the Egyptians in their monumental writing, and for having furnished a key to its interpretation, Dr. Young giving the first hints by establishing the phonetic value of the hieroglyphic signs, which were followed up and carried out by Champollion.

Another important and much more ancient inscription is the tablet of Abydos in the British Museum. It was discovered by Mr. Banks in a chamber of the temple at Abydos, in 1818. It is now greatly disfigured, but when perfect it represented an offering made by Rameses II., of the nineteenth dynasty, to his predecessors on the throne of Egypt. The tablet is of fine limestone, and originally contained the names of fifty-two kings disposed in the two upper lines, twenty-six in each line, and a third or lower line with the name and prenomen of Rameses II. or III. repeated twenty-six times. On the upper line, beginning from the right hand, are the names of monarchs anterior to the twelfth dynasty. The names in the second line are those of monarchs of the twelfth, and the eighteenth or nineteenth dynasties. The King Rameses II. probably stood on the right hand of the tablet, and on the other is the lower part of a figure of Osiris. The lateral inscription is the speech of the deceased kings to "their son" Rameses II.

The tablet of Karnak, now in one of the halls of the Royal Library at Paris, was discovered by Burton in a chamber situated in the south-east angle of the temple-palace of Thebes, and was published by its discoverer in his "Excerpta Hieroglyphica." The chamber itself was fully described by Rosellini in his "Monumenti Storici." The kings are in two rows, overlooked each of them by a large figure of Thotmes III., the fifth king of the eighteenth dynasty. In the row to the left of the entrance are thirty-one names, and in that to the right are thirty, all of them predecessors of Thotmes. The Theban kings who ruled in Upper Egypt during the usurpation of the Hyksos invaders are also exhibited among the lists. Over the head of each king is his oval, containing his royal titles.

A most valuable tablet of kings has been lately discovered by Mr. Marriotte in a tomb near Memphis. It contains two rows of kings' names, each twenty-nine in number. Six have been wholly obliterated out of the upper row, and five out of the lower row. The upper row contains the names of Rameses II. and his predecessors, who seem all meant for kings of Upper Egypt, or kings of Memphis who ruled

* A second copy of this inscription, in hieroglyphic and demotic characters, has been found by Professor Lepsius in the court of the great temple of Isis, at Philæ.

over Upper Egypt, while the names in the lower row seem meant for contemporaneous High Priests of Memphis, some or all of whom may have called themselves kings of Lower Egypt. The result of the comparison of this tablet with other authorities, namely Manetho, Eratosthous, and the tablet of Abydos, is supposed by some to contradict the longer views of chronology held by Bunsen, Lepsius and others. Thus, reading the list of names backwards from Ramoses II. to Amrmis, the first of the eighteenth dynasty, this tablet, like the tablet of Abydos, immediately jumps to the kings of Manetho's twelfth dynasty; thus arguing that the intermediate five dynasties mentioned by Manetho must have been reigning contemporaneously with the others, and add no length of time to a table of chronology. There is also a further omission in this tablet of four more dynasties. This tablet would thus seem to confirm the views of the opponents of the longer chronology of Bunsen and others, by striking out from the long chronology two periods amounting together to 1530 years. But a complete counterpart of the tablet of Memphis has been recently found at Abydos by Mr. Mariette, fully confirming the chronology of Manetho, and bearing out the views of Bunsen and Lepsius. The *Moniteur* publishes a letter from Mr. Mariette, containing the following statement:—"At Abydos I have discovered a magnificent counterpart of the tablet of Sakharah (Memphis), Seti I., accompanied by his son, subsequently Ramoses II. (Sesostris), presents an offering to seventy-six kings drawn up in line before him. Menes (the first king of the first dynasty on Manetho's list) is at their head. From Menes to Seti I., this formidable list passes through nearly all the dynasties. The first six are represented therein. We are next introduced to sovereigns still unknown to us, belonging to the obscure period which extends from the end of the sixth to the beginning of the eleventh. From the eleventh to the eighteenth the new table follows the beaten track, which it does not quit again during the reign of Thotmes, Amenophis, and the first Ramoses. If in this new list everything is not absolutely new, we at least find in it a valuable confirmation of Manetho's list, and in the present state of science we can hardly expect more. Whatever confirms Manetho gives us confidence in our own efforts, even as whatever contradicts it weakens the results we obtain. The new tablet of Abydos is, moreover, the completest and best preserved monument we possess in this respect. Its style is splendid, and there is not a single cartouche or oval wanting. It has been found engraved on one of the walls of a small chamber in the large Temple of Abydos."

An important stone bearing a Greek inscription with equivalent

Egyptian hieroglyphics has been discovered this year (1866) by Professor Lepsius, at San, the former Tanis, the chief scene of the grand architectural undertakings of Rameses II. The Greek inscription consists of seventy-six lines, in the most perfect preservation, dating from the time of Ptolemy Euergetes I. (238 B.C.) The hieroglyphical inscription has thirty-seven lines. It was also found that a demotic inscription was ordered to be added by the priests, on a stone or brass stele, in the sacred writing of the Egyptians and in Greek characters; this is unfortunately wanting. The contents of the inscription are of great interest. It is dated the 9th year the 7th Apellaeus—17 Tybi, of the reign of Euergetes I. The priests of Egypt came together in Canopus to celebrate the birthday of Euergetes, on the 5th Dios, and his assumption of the royal honour on the 28th of the same month, when they passed the decree here published. They enumerate all the good deeds of the king, amongst them the merit of having recovered in a military expedition the sacred images, carried off in former times by the Persians, and order great honours to be paid in reward for his services. The stone is twenty two centimètres high and seventy-six centimètres wide, and is completely covered by the inscriptions. The discovery of this stone is of the greatest importance for hieroglyphical studies.

We may mention here another inscribed tablet, the celebrated Isiac table in the Museum at Turin. It is a tablet in bronze, covered with Egyptian figures or hieroglyphics engraved or sunk, the outlines being filled with silvering, forming a kind of niello. It was one of the first objects that excited an interest in the interpretation of hieroglyphics, and elicited learned solutions from Kircher and others. It is now considered to be one of those pseudo-Egyptian productions so extensively fabricated during the reign of Hadrian, and it has been ascertained that its hieroglyphics have no meaning at all.

The Egyptian obelisks also present important inscriptions. Of these the most ancient is that of Heliopolis: it reads thus, "The Horus; Living of men; Lord of an obedient people; Sun presented to the world; Lord of Upper and Lower Egypt; The living of men; Son of the sun; Osirtasen; Lord of Spirits in Pone; Ever-living; Life of men; Resplendant Horus; Good God; Sun presented to the world: Who has begun the celebration of his two assemblies to his Creator; Life-giver for ever."

We have selected these few examples of Egyptian inscriptions from their celebrity. Almost every Egyptian monument, of whatever period, temples, statues, tablets, small statues, were inscribed with hieroglyphic inscriptions, all generally executed with great

care and finish. The Egyptian edifices were also covered with
religious or historical tableaux, sculptured and painted on all the
walls; it has been estimated that in one single temple there existed
not less than 30,000 square feet of sculpture, and at the sides of
these tableaux were innumerable inscriptions, equally composed of
ingeniously grouped figurative signs, in explanation of the subjects,
and combining with them far more happily than if they had been
the finest alphabetical characters in the world.

Their study would require more than a lifetime, and we have only
space to give a few general hints.

GREEK.

We have a much more accurate knowledge of Greek inscriptions
than we have of Egyptian palæography. The Greek alphabet, and
all its variations, as well as the language, customs, and history of
that illustrious people, are better known to us. Greek inscriptions
lead us back to those glorious periods of the Greek people when
their heroes and writers made themselves immortal by their illustrious deeds and writings. What emotions must arise in the breast
of the archæologist who finds in a marble worn by time the funereal monument placed by Athens, twenty-three centuries ago, over
the grave of its warriors who died before Potidæa.

> "Their souls high heaven received; their bodies gain'd,
> In Potidæa's plains, this hallowed tomb.
> Their foes unnumbered fell; a few remained
> Saved by their ramparts from the general doom.
> The victor city mourns her heroes slain,
> Foremost in fight, they for her glory died.
> 'Tis yours, ye sons of Athens, to sustain,
> By martial deeds like theirs, your country's pride."

Our chief and principal aim in the examination of a Greek inscription ought to be the discovery of its period. The subject, if it
belongs to history, indicates in the first place that period, within
certain limits; but it is more accurately recognised, 1, in the chronological signs, if it has any; 2, in their absence, in the forms of the
letters belonging to a certain period, in the arrangement of the lines
of the inscription; lastly, in certain grammatical forms peculiar to
the more ancient Greek inscriptions. The dialect which is employed
is also an indication, at least topographical, with regard to the
country in which the inscription was engraved.

The usual chronological signs are—1. The names of the magistrates by whose authority the monument was executed, or who were

in office at the time it was erected. 2. Dates derived from some era adopted in each state of Greece, and expressed according to the calendar peculiar to each of these states. Dates of this kind are only found in Greek inscriptions of a later period; on the more ancient —on those of Greece anterior to the invasion of the Romans—the names of kings or magistrates generally mark the period. The length of the time of office of the latter, prescribed by law, and the order of their succession inscribed in the public archives, left, in those times, no uncertainty with regard to the expression of these dates. Modern critical scholars, combining the authority of inscriptions with the statements of historians, have succeeded in establishing lists of the succession of Greek magistrates in chronological order, and in connecting them with the years before the Christian era, and in thus forming useful tables for the establishing of epochs of ancient history, and the determination of the precise date of a monument. A Greek inscription bearing the name of an archon (Eponymus) is undoubtedly of the self-same year in which that archon was in office, and the same may be said with regard to the inscriptions of other towns or countries of which lists of kings or magistrates have been established. With regard to dates, properly so called, in years, months, or days, we must remark that the ancients never employed a general era. When a period was established by a city or state, its origin was derived from some important event peculiar to it, such as the Olympiads, hence arise a diversity of modes in the notation of epochs, whence spring a great number of difficulties. Chronologists have endeavoured to explain the nature of these numerous and variable eras, and to discover a means of making them harmonise, and of connecting them with the years before the Christian era. Chronological tables will therefore supply the interpretation of these dates. The principal towns of Greece adopted their own dates, but in every state where royal authority was established, the dates were taken from the year of the reign of the king who then occupied the throne, and the succession of their kings is sufficiently well known, as well as the period of their reigns, for one to arrive at every certainty on that subject. Chronological tables will give the necessary information with regard to the date of their reigns.

The forms of the letters of a Greek inscription are also an approximate indication of its date. It is evident that it is impossible to find in an inscription of a certain date the use of a letter which was not as yet in the Greek alphabet at that same period. The Greek alphabet, like that of all the ancient nations of Europe, was at first composed only of sixteen letters, A B Γ Δ Ε Ι Κ Α Μ Ν Ο Π Ρ Σ Τ Υ,

which were said to have been introduced by Cadmus from Phœnicia.
At a later period Palamedes is supposed to have added the four
double letters, Θ Ξ Φ X, representing TH, KΣ, ΠΛ, KΓ: to these
twenty Simonides is stated to have made the further addition of
Z Η Ψ Ω; * before the adoption of which two omicrons (O O) were
used instead of Ω, and two epsilons (EE) for H, and as this alphabet
came generally into use at Athens after the archonship of Euclides,
403 B.C., it follows as a necessary result that an inscription in which
one or several of these letters are found, must be, with every
certainty, considered as posterior to Euclides, and to the year
403 B.C. The first twenty letters of the Greek alphabet are to be
met with in earlier inscriptions. The digamma, or double gamma,
corresponding to the Vau of the Hebrew, and the F of the Latin
alphabet, is found in some early inscriptions—it is seen on the Elean
tablet. It prevailed more particularly in the Æolic dialect of the
Greek tongue. The koppa ρ, derived from the Phœnician koph,
is found in many of the older Greek inscriptions, and on the coins of
Croton and Corinth. It was only used when the following vowel
was O. The Ω appears rarely before the 403 B.C. The long O, on
the early inscriptions, was represented by an O with a dot in the
centre, as in a Greek inscription found at Aboosimbel, dating from
the reign of Psammitichus, B.C. 600. The size and form of these
letters thus furnish important data for determining the approximate
period of an inscription. The direction of the lines of an inscription
is also an indication of the period. The Greeks, following the
mode used by Eastern nations of Semitic origin (the languages of the
Aryan race are read from left to right), at first wrote from right to
left; no monument, however, has come down to us that can with
certainty be attributed to the period in which this method was exclusively in use. Inscriptions of a single line are, it is true, written
in this manner, as, for instance, the inscription found by Colonel

* This is the usually accepted tradition with regard to the origin of Greek
letters. Mr. Champollion (Paléographie Universelle) is of opinion that the
Greeks already possessed an alphabet before the arrival of Cadmus; that Cadmus
taught them certain letters or signs of sounds, which their alphabet did not
previously contain, and that these new letters, adopted by the Greeks, were
introduced in time into general use. But the distinction between the two alphabets
was not lost by this adoption; the learned Greeks still distinguished between the
ancient national alphabet, the *Pelasgic*, and the new alphabet, augmented by the
Phœnician letters, which assumed the name of the Phœnician or Cadmian alphabet.
The Pelasgic or primitive alphabet was composed of sixteen letters, representing
only the simple and primitive sounds. To Cadmus, the Greek alphabet was
indebted for four new signs, nearly all aspirated, Z, Θ, Φ, X; the sounds of which
exist in the Phœnician alphabet, these signs becoming necessary for the few
Phœnician words which the Greeks adopted.

Leake on a small votive helmet at Olympia, and the inscription on an early vase of Athens, ΙΜΕΝΟΙΟΑΝΘΕΝΕΘΑΝΟΤ, but the first line of an inscription which belongs to the second mode of writing adopted at a later period by the Greeks, is always inscribed from right to left. A remarkable feature of this very early period is the great irregularity of size in the letters, the O being generally very small. The second mode is termed Boustrophedon, βου-στροφη-δον, or ox turning-wise, in which the direction of the lines alternated, as in the course of a plough, so that the first line began on the right, the second on the left, immediately beneath the end of the first. The most ancient inscriptions are written in this manner, which is thus a certain indication of antiquity—when, however, the primitive form of the letters is in harmony with this peculiar arrangement of the lines; for the Boustrophedon has been imitated at a period when it was no longer in use, so as to give the inscription the appearance of an antiquity which it did not in reality possess. An inscription, therefore, written in Boustrophedon, should be carefully examined to see if the form of the letters and the spelling of the words concur in proving its authenticity, as belonging to the ancient Greek style. In the course of time, and about the eighth century B.C., the Boustrophedon was abandoned, and the uniform direction of the lines from left to right generally adopted. An inscription will be thus: 1. In the first style, and in the most ancient, if it is traced from right to left, and if the letters have the forms of the early alphabet: no inscription is known of this first period. 2. In the second style, and anterior to the seventh century B.C., if it presents the forms of the alphabet of that period, and if its lines are traced in the manner termed Boustrophedon. 3. In the third style, and anterior to the end of the fifth century, B.C., if not being traced in the Boustrophedon, it does not present any of the four double letters, Z, Ψ, Η, Ω, and if the forms of the letters still preserve the traces of the old style. (It must be stated here that the presence of the H in inscriptions of this period will not invalidate their antiquity, as it is introduced as an aspirate, as HEKATON, εκατον, and not as a long E, which was expressed in inscriptions of that period by two E's, as MAIEEP for MATHP). 4. In the fourth style, and posterior to the end of the fifth century B.C., if the twenty-four letters of the Greek alphabet are found in an inscription. Inscriptions of this kind are the most usual. These may be also divided into a number of different epochs, comprising a period of nine centuries, almost to the time of the Lower Empire. A vertical mode of engraving inscriptions was sometimes used by the Greeks, termed kionedon, or columnar. In this mode of engraving monumental inscriptions, the letters were ranged perpendicularly, and the greatest care was taken to preserve an equal number of letters in each line. A Greek inscription in this style, containing an inventory of valuable articles kept in the opisthodomos, or treasury of the Parthenon, is in the British Museum. From its orthography, however, Visconti affirms that it is posterior to the archonship of Euclides, that is, after the year 403 B.C.

In the plate will be found the Greek alphabet of the most ancient inscription, taken from the monuments themselves. By these the forms of the letters can be distinguished from those which are observed in Greek inscriptions of the Roman period, which bear a great resemblance to the forms of the capital letters of the Greek alphabet as used at the present day. We must, however, remark that the forms ϲ ε ω of the letters Σ Ε Ω, do not prove the late period of an inscription; these forms are common to the period of the Lower Empire, but they are also found on several monuments of an early date. The study of original monuments will furnish a number of data for distinguishing the relative antiquity of inscriptions, which it would be impossible to give in this short treatise.

After these few general observations on Greek inscriptions, on the forms of the letters, on the direction of the lines, it remains for us to make a few remarks on their subjects, on the signs peculiar to each of them, on the numerous abreviations observable on them, and on the numerous signs employed at different periods. The accurate interpretation of the text will alone lead one to fully recognise the object and usefulness of a Greek inscription in an historical point of view. This interpretation will require not only a profound knowledge of the Greek language of its period, but also an accurate acquaintance with the style called *lapidary*, which is found in the Greek texts traced on monuments, and if we consider in how many different countries the Greek language has been that of public monuments, how variable has been the introduction of certain modes of expression, according to the different places, and sometimes also according to different periods in the same place, we may form an idea of what the study of inscriptions requires to make it productive of important results. But this profound critical knowledge will not be required by the general scholar or archæologist. Thus there will not be expected from us here more than some few general hints, with regard to the prominent signs which are characteristic of their different epochs, which will lead to a brief knowledge of a monument, and such as will be sufficient to class it conveniently in a collection.

The decrees and public acts of cities and of corporations, treaties and conventions of general interest, are generally preceded by an invocation to good fortune; ΑΓΑΘΙΙΙ ΤΥΧΙΙΙ. Sometimes ΚΑΙ ΕΙΙΙ ΣΙΥΤΙΙΡΙΙΙ, 'and for safety' was added, then came the designation of the city or corporation, the names of the magistrates or priests in office, and the subject of the monument; frequently a date is at the end of the text, as well as the name, either of the person who drew up the inscription, or who presided at its execution, or of the artist who engraved it; the name of the magistrates or of the priests are sometimes placed only after the subject of the monument. In the short honorary inscriptions to kings or citizens, the verb of the sentence is generally understood; the name of the person honoured, either by a statue, or by any other public testimony, is written in the first line in the accusative; it is followed by the name of the town or of the corporation who voted the monument, and the names of the magistrate, or of the priest, and of the artist, are at the end; a decree frequently bears the word ΨΙΡΦΙΣΜΑ, and when it is in favour of a citizen who has rendered some important service, the usual reward being a crown decreed by the city, the crown is represented over the decree, and the name of the citizen is inscribed within it.

The most important monumental inscriptions which present Greek records, illustrating and establishing the chronology of Greek history is the Parian chronicle, now preserved among the Arundelian marbles at Oxford. It was so called from the supposition of its having been made in the island of Paros, B.C. 263. In its perfect state it was a square tablet, of coarse marble, five inches thick; and when Selden first inspected it it measured three feet seven inches, by two feet seven inches. On this alone were engraved some of the principal events in the history of ancient Greece, forming a compendium of chronology during a series of 1318 years, which commenced with the reign of Cecrops, the first king of Athens, B.C. 1582, and ended with the archonship of Diognetus. It was deciphered and published by the learned Selden in 1628. They make no mention of Olympiads, and reckon backwards from the time then present by years.*

* The first era, or computation, of time, from an epoch made use of among the Greeks, was that of the Olympiads. The reckoning was made to commence from the games at which Corœbus was the victor, being the first at which the name of the victor was recorded. The Olympiad of Corœbus, accordingly, is considered in chronology as the first Olympiad. Its date is placed 108 years after the restoration of the games by Iphitus, and is calculated to correspond with the year B.C. 776. Timæus, of Sicily, who flourished in the reign of Ptolemy Philadelphus (B.C. 283-29.5), was the first who attempted to establish an era, by comparing and correcting the dates of the Olympiads, the Spartan kings, the archons of Athens, and the

The date on an inscription when derived from a local era, is sometimes found at the beginning. Of these dates there are a great many
varieties. The most easily to be distinguished date is that taken
from the years of the reign of a king. It is expressed in Greek
letters or in ciphers; in the first case they present no difficulty, but
in the latter, the variations which existed among the Greeks in the
mode of noting numbers, may prove embarrassing. It was only at a
late period that the twenty-four letters of the alphabet were adopted
as signs for numbers, according to their order in the alphabet. This
numerical alphabet being the most usual, we must here state that the
signs which were in use before this application of letters to the
expression of numbers, were signs taken in general from the initial
letters of the words expressive of those numbers. In the following
list the usual number precedes its equivalent in Greek. 1—I; 2—II
and Δ; 3—III; 4—IIII; 5—Π; 6—Σ and ⊏; 7—EΠΔM; 8—ΠIII;
9—ΠIIII; 10—Δ or Γ; 11—ΔI, Λ; 12—ΔII, B; 13—ΔIII or
TPIΣΔ; 14—ΔIIII, or E; 15—ΔΠ or EK-|; 20—ΔΔ or ΔΓ; 25—
ΚΟ or ΔVII; 30—ΔΓΔ or ΓΓΓ; 40—ΔΔΔΔ or TEΣΣAPA; 50—
ΔΔΔΔΔ or Δ̄; 100—H.P.; 200—ΟΚΝ; 500—Π̄; 1000—X; 5000
—X; 10,000—M. When the numbers are expressed by letters of
the alphabet, the letter L, which precedes them, indicates that they
are used for this purpose, when the word ETOYΣ or ETΩN is not
found on the inscription; this L, of a Roman form derived from the
ancient Greek alphabet, is the initial letter of the word Λιαβδατος,
genitive of Λιαβδας, which means year. These words and these
number of dates are in the genitive in Greek, as they are in the
ablative in Latin, on account of a preposition being understood.

Particular attention should be paid, in the interpretation of Greek
inscriptions, to distinguish the numerous titles of magistrates of
every order, of public officers of different ranks, the names of gods
and of nations, those of towns, and the tribes of a city; the prescribed formulas for different kinds of monuments; the text of
decrees, letters, &c., which are given or cited in analogous texts;
the names of monuments, such as stelæ, tablets, cippi, &c.; the indication of places, or parts belonging to those places, where they
ought to be set up or deposited, such as a temple or vestibule, a
court or peristyle, public square, &c.; those at whose cost it was set

priestess of Juno. This Olympiad era was chiefly used by historians, and is
scarcely ever found on inscriptions The Olympiad era met with on inscriptions
is another, or a new Olympiad, which came into use under the Roman emperors.
It began in Ol. 227.3 (A.D. 131), in which year Hadrian dedicated the Olympieion
at Athens; and accordingly we find Ol. 227.3 spoken of as the first Olympiad,
Ol. 228.3 (A.D. 135, as the second Olympiad Böckh, Corp. Inscr. .

up, the entire city or a curia, the public treasure, or a private fund, the names and surnames of public or private individuals; preroga-tives or favours granted, such as the right of asylum, of hospitality, of citizenship; the punishments pronounced against those who should destroy or mutilate the monument; the conditions of treaties and alliances; the indications of weights, moneys, and measures.

An act of piety or of adoration to a divinity, and in a particular temple devoted to that purpose, either by a legal privilege, or through the effect of the general opinion of devotees, is termed a ΠΡΟΣΚΥΝΗΜΑ. Private individuals performed this act of devotion either for themselves or in the name of their parents, and of their friends at the same time, and they included their own names in the commemorative inscription which they had engraved or written on some part of the temple; kings appointed for these religious duties certain functionaries, who received this especial mission, and who never neglected to introduce in the inscription that they had fulfilled this mission in the name of the king men-tioned in the first lines. It appears also that the same king gave the same mission several times during his reign, and that the general use of this religious homage was peculiar to Egypt during the Greek and Roman period. In the temple of Isis at Philæ many of these προσκυνηματα are to be seen. A great number occur also in the temples of Nubia, in honour of Isis and Serapis, and of the other gods worshipped in the same building. Sir Gardner Wilkinson gives the following as a complete formula of one of these pros-kunémata: "The adoration of Caius Capitolinus, son of Flavius Julius, of the fifth troop of Theban horse, to the goddess Isis, with ten thousand names. And I have been mindful of (or have made an adoration for) all those who love me, and my consort, and children, and all my household, and for him who reads this. In the year 12 of the Emperor Tiberius Cæsar, the 15 of Paüni."

Votive or dedicatory inscriptions always contain the names of the gods or kings to whom a monument is dedicated, and the names of the town, corporation, of the tribes, functionaries, or private indivi-duals who erected the monument; public works executed at the expense of the tribes or of private individuals, bear also inscriptions commemorative of their munificence, and the very portion of the building, built or repaired through their generosity, is expressly designated in the text of the inscription, the ancients allowing this competition of individual zeal for public utility.

Funereal monuments usually bear an inscription which gives the names and titles of the deceased, his country, his age, the names of his father and of his mother, his titles and his services, his

2 A

distinguished qualities, and his virtues. Frequently a funereal
inscription contains only the names of the deceased, that of his
country, and acclamations and votivo formulæ generally terminate it. A few examples will better explain these rules:—
ΧΡΗΣΤΟΣ ΠΡΩΤΟΥ ΘΕΣΣΑΛΟΣ ΛΑΡΕΙΣΑΙΟΣ ΠΕΛΑΣΓΙΟΤΗΣ
ΕΤΩΝ·ΙΗ. ΗΡΩΣ ΧΡΗΣΤΕ ΧΑΙΡΕ. The first word is the name of
the deceased Chrestus; the second word is the name of his father
Protos, the word υιος being understood, as is generally the case in
Greek inscriptions. The three words which follow are the designation of the country of Chrestus, a Thessalian, and born in the town
of Larissa, which was styled Pelasgian to distinguish it from other
towns of the same name. The words ΕΤΩΝ ΙΗ, mean *of eighteen
years*; the age of the deceased. The rest is an acclamation: " *Hero
Chrestus! farewell!*" These words ΧΑΙΡΕ, ΕΥΨΥΧΕΙ, ΘΑΡΣΕΙ, which
express similar good wishes, frequently terminate, alone, funereal
inscriptions. Other inscriptions read: ΦΙΛΩΝ ΚΑΛΛΙΠΠΟΥ
ΑΙΞΩΝΕΥΣ;—ΛΑΚΙΜΑΚΗ ΚΑΛΛΙΜΑΧΟΥ ΑΝΑΓΥΡΑΣΙΟΥ. The
first two words of each of these inscriptions are proper names.
1. Philo, the son of Callipus. 2. Alcimache, daughter of Callimachus, and the words ΑΙΞΩΝΕΥΣ and ΑΝΑΓΥΡΑΣΙΟΥ, are the names
of two of the 174 demi or townships of Attica. The towns,
boroughs, and villages of Attica, and the divisions of Athens,
which formed each a community inscribed in one of the thirteen
tribes (φυλαι) of Athens, were so called. The community or town
of the Æxoni was part of the Cecropian tribe, and Anagyrus of the
Erectheid tribe. These names of places should be carefully noted
in an inscription, in order to prevent any mistake, and to give an
accurate and complete interpretation of the words. The following
should be also carefully noted. 1. The honorary titles of kings;
they serve sometimes to distinguish those who have borne the same
name. 2. The names of places and titles; they are frequently
written in an abbreviated form, and with the first letters alone.
Punctuation is never observable in Greek inscriptions on marble,
the words themselves are seldom or over separated, and it is the
sense and grammatical construction alone which determine the
arrangement of the words which form the sentence. On some inscriptions there have been observed, principally upon funereal
monuments of a late date, separate signs, mingled with the words,
such as a leaf, a triangle, a straight or bent line, but these signs
have rarely any meaning; sometimes they are symbols connected
with the subject of the inscription.

The abbreviations or sigla, which abound in all Greek inscriptions, are the source of many difficulties: celebrated scholars have

occupied themselves in collecting and interpreting them, and the learned Corsini has written on this subject a folio volume (Notæ Græcorum), published in Florence in 1708. The study of Greek palæography has, however, furnished several additions to that work; the following list contains the most usual abbreviations which are found in Greek inscriptions, and which is necessarily very short in his compendious treatise:

SIGLA; OR, ABBREVIATIONS IN GREEK INSCRIPTIONS.

Α. πρῶτος, first; ἀπό (preposition); Αὐτοκράτωρ, emperor.

ΑΓΑ. Τ. ἀγαθῇ τυχῇ, to good fortune.

ΑΔΕΛΦ. ἀδελφος, a brother.

ΑΝΕΘ. ἀνέθηκε, placed, dedicated.

ΑΠΕΛ., ΑΠΕΛΕΥΘΕΡ. ἀπελεύθερος, freedman.

ΑΡΙΣ. ἄριστος, the best.

ΑΡΧ. ἄρχων, archon.

ΑΥΤ. αὐτοκράτωρ, emperor.

Β. δεύτερος, the second; βουλή, council.

ΒΑΣΙΛ. βασιλεὺς, king.

Β. Δ. βουλῆς δόγματι, by a decree of the council.

ΒΙΣ. βώμιον, sepulchre, tomb.

ΒΩ. βωμὸς, base, altar.

ΓΟΝΕ. γονεὺς, father, ancestor.

ΓΡΑ. γραφεὺς, scribe, writer.

ΓΥΜ. γυμνικος, gymnastic, public games.

Δ. Ε. δημαρχικῆς ἐξουσίας, of the tribuneship of the people (title of the Roman emperors).

ΔΕΣΠ. δεσπότης, master, lord.

ΔΗΜΟΣ. δημοσίᾳ, publicly.

Δ. Μ. Diis Manibus; Δ. Μ. Σ Diis Manibus Sacrum (Latin funeral formulæ).

Δ. Τ. Διὶ τῷ, to Jupiter.

ΕΒΔ. ἔβδομος, seventh.

ΕΔ. ΕΙ. εἰδῶν, of the Ides.

ΕΖΗ. ἔζησεν, he lived.

Ε. Θ. εὔνοια θεῶν, the protection of the gods.

ΕΛΕΥ. ἐλεύθερος, free.

ΕΝ., ΕΝΘ. ἐνθάδε, here; or ἐν θεῷ, in God.

ΕΤ. ἐτῶν, years, age.

ΕΤΕ., ΕΤΕΛ. ἐτελεύτησεν, he died.

ΕΝΤΟ. ἐχώρησατο, was received.

ΖΗ., ΣΗΣΑΝ, ζήσας ζήσαντι, having lived (age).

ΗΖΗΣ. ἔζησεν, he lived.

ΗΜ. ἡμέρα, day; ΗΜΕΡΩ. ἡμέρας ὀκτὼ, eight days.

ΘΕ. θεᾶς, to the gods.

Θ. Ε θεοῖς ἐπιχωρίοις, to the gods of the country.

Θ. Η. θεοῖς ἥρωσιν, to the gods heroes.

Θ. Κ., Θ. ΚΑ., Θ. ΚΑΤ., Θ. ΚΥ., ΘΣ., ΚΑ. θεοῖς καταχθονίοις, to the infernal gods.

ΘΥ., ΘΣ., ΘΠ. θεοῦ, θεος, θεῷ, of God, God, to God.

ΘΥ., ΘΥΓΡΙ. θυγατηρ, θυγατρι, daughter, to the daughter.

ΙΜΡ. ἰμπερατωρ, emperor.

ΙΡ. ἱερεὺς priest.

ΙΣΙ. ισιδι, to Isis.

Κ. και, and.

ΚΛ. καλανδῶν, of the calends.

ΚΑΙ. καίσαρ, Cæsar.

Κ. Β. κελεύσματι βουλῆς, by the order of the council.

2 A 2

K. Θ. καταχθωνιοις θεοις, to the infernal gods.

ΚΙ. κιται, he lies.

ΚΟΣ., ΚΩΣ. κωνσυλ, consul.

K. II. κελευσματι πολεως, by the order of the city.

ΚΡΑΤ. κράτιστος, excellent.

ΚΣ. κυριος, lord, master.

K. Φ. κελευσματι φρατριας, by the permission of the tribe.

K. X. κοινοις χρημασιν, at the public expense.

ΛΑΜ. λαμπροτατος, most splendid.

ΛΕΓ. λεγιωνος, of the legion.

ΛΙΘ. λιθος, stone, inscription, stele.

M., ΜΗ. μηνος, month.

M. μνημειων, monument, tomb.

ΜΑ. μάτηρ, mother.

ΜΑΙ. μαιων, of the calends of May.

ΜΑΡ. μαρτων, of the calends of March.

ΜΕ. μηνων, of the months.

ΜΗ., ΜΡ. μητηρ, mother.

M. X. μνημης χαριν, in memory.

N., ΝΙ). νωνων, of the nones.

ΝΕΡΤΕ. ἐνέρτεροι, dead.

ΞΥΣΤΑΡΧ. Ξυσταρχος, superintendent of the gymnasia.

ΟΙΚΑΤ. οἱ κατοικοι, the inhabitants.

ΟΚΤΒ. οκτωβριων, of the calends of October.

ΠΑΡΑΚΑΤΙ. παρακατατεθειται, has been deposited, entrusted.

ΠΑΡΘ. παρθικος, Parthian.

ΠΛΑ. πλάτυς, breadth.

ΠΟΣ. ποσιδεων, Athenian month.

Π. Η. πατηρ πατριδος, father of his country.

ΠΡ. πρεσβυτερος, priest.

ΠΡΕΣΒ. πρεσβευτης, ambassador, delegato.

ΡΩ. ρωμαιων, Roman.

Σ., ΣΕΒ., ΣΕΒΒ., ΣΕΒΗΒ., Σεβαστος, Angustus, and Augusti, when two or three. Sometimes OY is written instead of B.

ΣΙ. σου, of himself.

ΣΠΕΙΡ. σπειρα, cohort, legion.

Σρί. σωτηρι, to the Saviour.

ΣΣ. συγκλητου συγχωρησει, by the consent of the assembly.

ΣΩ. σωμα, the body.

T. τάλαντον, a talent (money).

T. Δ, B, K, Δ. E. τω δόγματι βουλης, και δογματι εκκλεσιας, by a decree of the Senate, and by a decree of the Assembly.

ΤΕΙΜ. τειμάς, for τιμας, honours.

TK. ἐκ των, part of.

Y. υπερ, νος, υπατεια, consulship, ὑπάτος, consul.

Y. B. υπομνημα βουλης, monument by order of the Senate.

YIIII. υπάτων, of the consuls, being consuls.

ΦΙΛΑΙ. Φηλιξ, Felix, name.

ΦΛΑΜ. φλάμην, flamen.

X., ΧΑΡ. χάριν, favour, gift, or for ἕνεκα.

ΧΕΙΡ. χειρουργος, workman, surgeon.

Ψ. B., Ψηφίσματι βουλης, by a decree of the Senate.

Ω. ὡραι, hours (in the indication of the age of deceased).

Ω. οκτωβριας, calends of October.

In this short list we have not included proper names, the titles of magistrates of different kinds, and the names of places. For these we must refer the reader to the more complete lists published by critical scholars.

EXAMPLES OF GREEK INSCRIPTIONS.

The Sigean Inscription.

The Sigean marble is one of the most celebrated palæographical monuments in existence. It is written in the most ancient Greek characters, and in the Boustrophedon manner. The purport of the inscription, which in sense is twice repeated, on the upper and lower part of the stone, is to record the presentation of three vessels for the use of the Prytaneum, or Town Hall of the Sigeans. The upper and lower inscriptions, in common letters, read thus:

φανοδικο
εμι τωρμον
ρητεος τo
τρωκοιτη
σιν᾽ κρητηρ
αδε και υπος
ρητηριον κ
αι ηθμον ες Π
ρυτανηιον
εδωκεν Σινε
εισιν.

φανοδικο ειμι το Π
ερμοκρατος το προκο
νεσιο καγο κρατερα
καπιστατον και Ηθμ
ον ες πριτανειον κ
δοκα ρνεμα Συγει
ευτε᾽ εαν δε τι πασχ
ομελεδαινν εο
Σιγαιες · και μ᾽ επο
ιεσεν Ηαισσπος και
Ηαδελφοι.

The first inscription is thus translated : " I am the gift of Phanodicus, the son of Hermocrates, of Proconnesus; he gave a vase
(crater), a stand or support for it, and a strainer, to the Sigeans
for the Prytaneum." The second, which says, " I also am the gift
of Phanodicus," repeating the substance of the former inscription,
adds, " if any mischance happens to me, the Sigeans are to mend
me. Æsop and his brethren made me." The lower inscription is
the more ancient. It is now nearly obliterated.

The Potidæan Inscription.

This ancient inscription served as an epitaph on the tomb of the
Athenian warriors, who lost their lives under the walls of Potidæa
in the year 432 B.C. It originally consisted of twelve elegiac
verses, but has suffered considerable injury. Thiersch's restoration
of this inscription is here presented for the use of such readers as
may desire to compare it with the original. The brackets show
the words which Thiersch has supplied.

Ἀθανατ [ον κλεος οἱδε φιλῃ περι πατριδι θειναι
σημαινειν [τ'ἀρετὴν ἱεμενοι σφετερην,
και προγόνω [ν τον θυμον ἐπι στηθεσσι φεμοντες
νικην ευπολεμοι [μαρναμενοι καθελον.
αιθηρ μὲμ ψυχας υπεδεξατο, σω[ματα δὲ χθων
τῶν δε Ποτειδαιας δαμφι πυλας ἐ[πεσον
ἐχθρῶν δ'αι μεν ἐχουσι ταφου μερος, οἱ δὲ φυγοντες
τειχος πιστοτάτην ἐλπιδ' ἰθεντο [βιου
ανδρας μεμ πολις ἥδι παθει και δ[ημος Ἐρεχθειος,
προσθε Ποτειδαιας οἱ θανον ἐμ π[ρομαχοις
παιδες Ἀθηναιων ψυχας δ'αντιρρε[πα θαντες
ἠ[λλ]αξαντ' ἀρετὴν και πατ[ριδ'] ευκλ[εισαν.] *

This most interesting inscription not only commemorates an
historical event which is minutely described by Thucydides, but
is also curious in a palæographical point of view. It only contains one form of the letter ε, viz., ε which serves both for the short
and long ε. The letter H is used as a mark of aspiration, and no
double letters are employed; Ξ, for instance, is represented by χς
and ψ in ψυχας by φς. The o is used both for the ω and the ου of
a later day.

* A metrical translation of this is given at page 346.

Inscription on the base of an Honorary Statue on the Acropolis.

Ο ΔΗΜΟΣ
ΣΩΚΡΑΤΗ ΣΩΚΡΑΤΟΥΣ ΘΟΡΙΚΙΟΝ
ΟΥΝΕΚΑΣΑΣ ΕΔΑΗΣΑΝΑΠΟ ΦΡΕΝΟΣ ΑΞΙΑΜΟΙΣΑΝ
ΣΩΚΡΑΤΕΣ ΩΙΥΙΩΝ ΥΙΕΣ ΕΡΙΧΘΟΝΙΙΑΝ
ΤΟΥΝΕΚΑ ΣΟΙ ΣΟΦΙΑΣ ΕΔΟΣΑΝ ΓΕΡΑΣ ΑΙΓΑΡΑΘΑΝΑΙ
ΟΙΑΙ ΙΣΑΝΤΟΙΩΙΔ ΑΝΔΡΙ ΤΕΚΕΙΝΧΑΡΙΤΑ

*The Athenian People erects this Statue of Socrates, the Son of Socrates
of Thoricus.*

"The Sons of Athens, Socrates, from thee
Imbibed the lessons of the Muse divine;
Hence this thy meed of wisdom: prompt are we
To render grace for grace, our love for thine."

Wordsworth's Athens.

ΨΗΦΙΣΜΑ ΤΗΣ
ΒΟΥΛΗΣ
ΚΑΙ ΤΟΥ ΔΗΜΟΥ ΤΩΝ
ΡΑΜΝΟΥΣΙΩΝ ΗΡΩΔΗΣ ΒΙΒΟΥΛ
ΔΙΟΝ ΠΟΛΥΔΕΥΚΙΩΝΑ ΙΩΗΕΑ ΑΝΕΘΗΚΕΝ
ΕΚ ΤΩΝ ΙΔΙΩΝ Ο ΘΡΕΨΑΣ ΚΑΙ ΦΙΛ
ΗΣΑΣ ΩΣ ΥΙΟΝ ΤΗ ΝΕΜΕ
ΣΕΙΗ ΜΕΤ ΑΥΤΟΥ ΕΘΥΕΝ ΕΥΜΕ
ΝΗ ΚΑΙ ΑΙΜΝΗΣΤΟΝ ΤΟΝ
ΕΑΥΤΟΥ ΤΡΟΦΙΜΟΝ

This inscription, found by Dr. Wordsworth at Rhamnos, records
the dedication by Herodes Atticus, who had a villa in the neighbourhood, of a statue of one of his adopted children, Polydeucion,
to the goddess Nemesia.

ΑΓΑΘΙΙΙ ΤΥΧΙΙΙ
ΑΠΟΛΛΩΝΙΟΣ
ΑΦΙΔΝΑΙΟΣ ΤΗΝ
ΘΥΓΑΤΕΡΑ ΑΝΘΕΜΙΑΝ
ΚΑΙ Ο ΘΕΙΟΣ ΟΥΛΠΙΑΝΟΣ
ΚΑΙ Η ΜΗΤΗΡ ΔΙΦΙΛΩΝΙΙ
ΚΑΝΗΦΟΡΗΣΑΣΑΝ
ΑΝΕΘΗΚΑΝ
ΕΠΙ ΙΕΡΕΙΑΣ ΠΕΝΤΕΤΗΡΙΔΟΣ
ΙΕΡΟΚΛΕΟΥΣ ΦΛΥΕΩΣ
ΚΑΙΚΟΣΘΕΝΗΣ
ΚΑΙ   ΕΠΟΙΗΣΑΝ

With good auspices; Apollonius of Aphidnæ dedicates a statue of his daughter Anthenia, having been a canephoros; her uncle, Ulpianus, and her mother, Diphilone, dedicate it with him. In the quinquennial priesthood of Hierocles of Phlya, Caeosthenes and . . . sculptured the statue.

This inscription, found in the Acropolis at Athens, is on the pedestal of a statue erected by relatives to an Athenian virgin, who had performed the honourable office of canephoros in the sacred processions in the Acropolis.

———

ΟΝΠΣΙΜΟΣΟΠΑΤΗΡ
ΚΑΙΧΡΥΣΛΙΕΙΣΗΜΗΤΗΡ
ΠΟΛΥΧΡΟΝΙΩΤΩΓΛΥΚΥ
ΤΑΤΩΤΕΚΝΩΜΝΕΙΑΣΧΑ
ΡΙΝΕΠΟΙΗΣΑΝΚΑΙΕ
ΑΥΤΟΙΣ

The translation is as follows:—" Onesimus, the father, and Chryseis, the mother, made (this tomb) for their sweetest child, Polychronius, for the sake of remembrance, and for themselves."

———

A Greek inscription found in front of the great Sphinx. It records the merits of Balbillus, who, as we learn from Tacitus and Seneca, was appointed Governor of Egypt by Nero about A.D. 56.

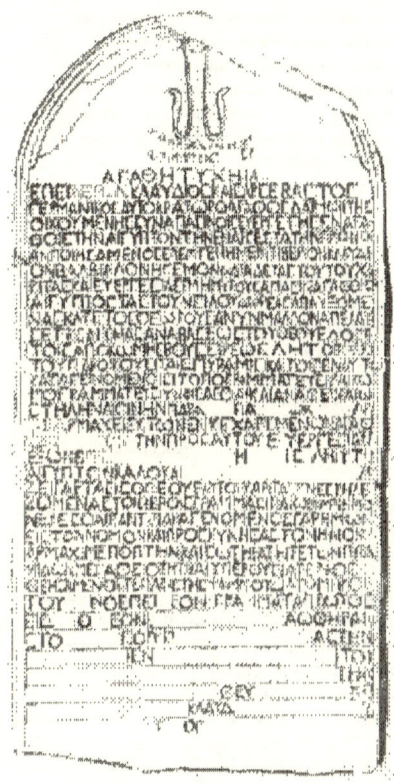

Ἀγαθῆ τυχη.

1. επι Νερων Κλαυδιος Καισαρ Σεβαστος

2. Γερμανικος αυτοκρατωρ ὁ αγαθὸς δαιμων της

3. οικουμενης συν απασιν οἱς ευεργετησεν αγα

4. θοις την Αιγυπτον την εναργεστατην προνια

5. αν ποιησαμενος επεμψεν ἡμειν Τιβεριον Κλαυδι-

6. ον Βαλβιλλον ἡγεμονα δια δε τας τουτου χα-

7. ριτας και ευεργεσιας πλημυρης απασιν αγαθοις ἡ

8. Αιγυπτος τας του Νειλου δωρεας απαιξομε-
9. νας κατ' ετος θεωρουσα την μαλλον απελαυ-
10. σε της διπλιας αναβασεως του θεου εδοξε
11. τας απο κωμης Βουσιριεως Λητο πολει-
12. του παροικουσι ταις πυραμισι και τοις εν αυτη
13. κατα γεινομενοισι τοπογραμματευσι και κω
14. μογραμματευσι ψηφισασθαι και αναθειναι
15. στηλην λιθινην παρα   αρ
16. εκ Αρμαχει εκ των ενκεχαρισμενων αγαθ-
17. ων   *   την προς αυτον ενεργησιαν
18. εξ ων επισ
19. Αιγυπτον καλοεαι
20. ζει γαρ τας ισοθεου εαυτου χαριτας επι στηλει
21. ζωμενας τοις ιεροις γραμμασιν αιωνι μνημο-
22. νευσθαι παντι παραγενομενος γαρ ημων.
23. εις τον νομον και προσκυνησας τον ηλιον
24. Αρμαχιμ εποπτην και σωτηρα τη τε των πυρα-
25. μιδων μεγαθειοτητι και υπερπατια τερφθεις
26. θεησαμενος τε πλειστης ψαμμου δια το μηκος
27. του   γραμματα πρωτη.

Translation of the Inscription to T. Claudius Balbillus.

To Good Fortune.

Since Nero Claudius Cæsar Augustus Germanicus, Autocrat, the good deity of the world, in addition to all the favours he has shown to Egypt, has demonstrated his care for the country most manifestly, by sending to us Tiberius Claudius Balbillus as governor; and through his favours and acts of kindness abounding in all good things, Egypt seeing the gifts of the Nilo yearly increasing, now more (than ever) enjoys the proper rising of the deity (i.e., the river). It has been determined by the inhabitants of the village of Busiris, in the nome of Letopolis, who live near the Pyramids, and the local clerks or collectors, and the village collectors in it, to vote and dedicate a stele of stone (15) (20) Preserves? his godlike favours on a stele living in sacred characters to be remembered for ever, for having come to our nome, and having adored the Sun Armachis inspector and saviour, and with the magnitude of the Pyramids and their surpassingness delighted, &c.

On a Gateway at Nicæa.

ΑΥΤΟΚΡΑΤΟΡΙΚΑΙΣΑΡΙΜΑΥΡΚΑΑΥΔΙΟΕΥΣΕΔΕΙ
ΕΥΤΥΧΕΙΣΕΒΔΗΜΑΡΧΙΚΗΣΕΞΟΥΣΙΑΣΤΟΔΕΥΤΕΡΟΝ
ΑΝΘΥΠΑΤΩΠΑΤΡΙΠΑΤΡΙΔΟΣΚΑΙΤΗΙΕΡΑΣΥΝΚΑΗΤΩ
ΚΑΙΤΩΔΗΜΩΤΩΝΡΩΜΑΙΩΝΠΛΑΜΗΡΟΤΑΤΗΚΑΙΜΕΓΙΣΤΗ
ΚΑΤΑΡΙΣΤΗΝΕΙΚΑΙΕΩΝΗΟΛΙΣΤΟΤΕΙΧΟΣΕΠΙΤΟΥΛΑΜΠΡ
ΥΠΑΤΙΚΟΥΟΥΕΛΛΕΙΟΥΜΑΚΡΕΙΝΟΥΠΡΕΣΒΕΥΤΟΥΚΑΙ
ΑΝΤΙΣΡΑΤΗΓΟΥΤΟΥΣΕΠΚΑΙΣΑΡΙΟΥΑΝΤΩΝΙΝΟΥΤΟΥ
ΛΑΜΠΡΑΟΓΙΣΤΟΥ

Translation.

"The very splendid, and large, and good city of the Nicæans [erects] this wall for the autocrat Cæsar Marcus Aurelius Claudius, the pious, the fortunate, august, of Tribunitial authority, second time Proconsul, father of his country, and for the Sacred Senate, and the people of the Romans, in the time of the illustrious Consular Velleius Macrinus, Legate and Lieutenant of the august Cæsar Antoninus, the splendid orator."—A.D. 269.

ETRUSCAN.

Etruscan palæography includes, 1, the inscriptions of the Etruscans properly so called, inhabiting the territory termed Etruria proper, which was bounded by the Magra and the Tiber; 2, those of the Sabines, Volsci, and Samnites (Lower Etruria), nations who dwelt to the east of the Tiber; 3, those of the northern Etruscans (Etruria Circumpadana), who occupied the banks of the Po. The monuments which have come down to us of those nations are not very numerous; their alphabets and formulæ bear such marked analogy as not to require those minute distinctions, which would be rather difficult to establish.

The Etruscan people, or Rasena as they call themselves, present a striking contrast to the other peoples of Italy. Their manners and customs also point to the conclusion that this nation was originally quite distinct from the Græco-Italian stock. The Etruscan nation was the most powerful of all the Italian peoples; its written monuments are most known, and are those on which learned scholars have most occupied themselves. From their researches a great variety of opinion has arisen, not only with regard to the origin of the Etruscan alphabet, to the period of its invention, or its introduction into

Italy, but also with regard to the date which may be assigned to the most ancient inscribed monuments of that nation. The remains of the Etruscan tongue which have reached us, numerous as they are, and presenting so many data to aid in deciphering it, occupy a position of isolation so complete, that not only has no one hitherto succeeded in its interpretation, but no one has been able even to determine precisely its proper place in the classification of languages.[*]

There is an historical tradition that Demaratus of Corinth introduced the Greek alphabet into Etruria. Dr. Mommsen, however, remarks on the origin of the Etruscan alphabet, that it cannot have been brought to Etruria from Corcyra or Corinth, or even from the Sicilian Dorians; the most probable hypothesis is that it was derived from the old Attic alphabet, which appears to have dropped the koppa earlier than other in Greece; and further, that there is a probability it was spread over Etruria from Cære, the most ancient emporium of civilization in that country. In the opinion of Dr. Mommsen, the Greek alphabet which reached Etruria is essentially different from that communicated to the Latins. While the former is so primitive, that for that very reason its special origin can no longer be ascertained, the latter exhibits exactly the signs and forms which were used by the Chalcidic and Doric colonies of Italy and Sicily. Hence we infer that two different Greek alphabets reached Italy, one with a double sign for s (sigma s, and san sh), and a single sign for k, and with the earlier form of the r (P) coming to Etruria; the second with a single sign for s, and a double for k (kappa k, and koppa q), and the more recent form of the r (R) coming to Latium. Others suppose that the Etruscan characters came directly from Phœnicia into Etruria. Mr. Daniel Sharpe, who had many opportunities of deriving important information in the recent discoveries in Lycia, declares that " it may be proved, from a comparison of alphabets, that the Etruscans derived their characters from Asia Minor, and not from Greece." Mr. Dennis also remarks the striking resemblance of the Etruscan alphabet to the Lycian, and still more so that which it bears to the Phrygian.

Our object is not here to engage in those important questions; we intend only giving a few observations on that portion of Etruscan palæography on which critical scholars have arrived at some certainty.

The subject of the greater number of these inscriptions presenting many uncertainties, the order in which we treat of them shall be made dependent on their greater or less extent : funereal inscrip-

* Mommsen.

tious are the only inscriptions the nature of which can be recognised with any certainty.

We shall first give a few remarks on the reading of the Etruscan inscriptions. 1. The inscriptions are always read from right to left. 2. The vowels are frequently suppressed, and the consonants are the only letters invariably expressed. This mode of suppressing the vowels presents a close Oriental analogy, and their absence is generally considered a proof of the high antiquity of an Etruscan inscription. They must therefore be supplied, and this is no easy matter in the words of a language which is lost: it is therefore only by analogy, and by finding in another inscription the same word with the vowels which are wanting, that we can hope to supply these vowels with any certainty. 3. The words of an inscription are sometimes separated by a point or two, or by an irregular perpendicular line, but frequently by no sign at all. 4. An Etruscan inscription, especially if it is funereal, is frequently bilingual, that is to say, in Etruscan above, and in Latin below, or sometimes the reverse; as these contain only names written according to the two alphabets, they have been of great assistance in restoring the Etruscan alphabet. 5. If the inscription is on a plaque of bronze or of lead, it is frequently traced on both sides of the plaque. Some inscriptions, though in the Etruscan character, are, however, pure Roman.

The large Etruscan inscriptions are few, and the most celebrated are—those found at Gubbio, the ancient Iguvium, in 1444, known under the name of the Eugubian Tables;—the large quadrangular cippus, three feet and a half high, presenting forty-five lines, discovered in 1822, near Perugia.

The Eugubian tables are seven in number, and were found among the ruins of the ancient theatre near Gubbio. They are now preserved in that city. The tables are of bronze, covered with inscriptions, four in Umbrian, two in Latin, and one in Etruscan letters. The inscriptions, facsimiles of which were first published by Dempster, have exercised the critical ingenuity of several scholars. Buonarotti considers them as articles of treaties between the states of Umbria; Bousquet, Gori, thought that they were forms of prayer among the Pelasgi, after the decline of their power; Maffei and Passeri that they were statutes or donations to the temple of Jupiter. In the opinion of Lanzi the inscriptions related solely to the sacrificial rites of the various towns of Umbria, and are the fragments of what the ancients named *pontificales et rituales libri*, an opinion in which most subsequent antiquaries have been disposed to concur.

There was a particular order of priests, named *fratres atherii* or *atheriates*, who were bound to perform the ceremonies prescribed by this ritual. These priests belonged to a tribe named Ikuvina, which afterwards formed an alliance with Rome. Some of these priests are mentioned in the inscriptions, as well as many towns of that part of Italy, and also several families known by historical records. Some names of local deities are also found in them. Then follow the formulæ of prayers which were to precede the sacrifices, the designation of the animals and fruits to be offered in the sacrifices, the indication of the parts of the victims consecrated to the gods, directions with regard to the dressing of the meats; lastly, the rites which were to follow the sacrifice.

In order to give an idea of Lanzi's method of interpretation, we shall cite here a single passage, and we have chosen one of those in which the celebrated interpreter had to supply a lesser number of letters and words; they are the lines 28, 29, 30 of the first and second table, according to Dempster. The reader must recollect that these lines here given from left to right are in the original Etruscan characters traced from right to left. Lanzi's Latin version is placed beneath each word in order to show the corresponding words in both languages:

IVIKA : MERSUVA : UVIIKUM : GADETU :
jecora μηρία (femora) ovium babuto ò
PUPATRUSTE : ATIIERIE : AIITISPEII :
fratribus Atheriatibus pro
EIIKVASATIS : TUTATES : IIUVINA
vadatis tota jovina
TREPIIITER IICVINA SAIKRE.
tribu pro jovina sacrum.

It will be observed here that the principal analogies of the Etruscan words are with the Latin, and that in this passage Lanzi had recourse to but one Greek word, but he is surely so moderate in deriving assistance from that language. Lepsius' opinion on the Latin inscription we shall notice farther on.

The inscription of Perugia occupies two sides of the cippus, and the letters are coloured red. M. Vermiglioli conjectures that it relates to agrarian matters, to rural laws, and to the limitation of lands. This learned scholar has undertaken a conjectural interpretation, according to the principles laid down and practised by Lanzi. He has analyzed the inscription word by word, and has recognised some names of persons and of places, as proved by some funereal inscriptions, and has sought to interpret others by analogous words in Greek or Latin.[*]

Opposite opinions on the interpretation of the Etruscan language and inscriptions are held by some of the most celebrated German writers. " Disgusted (we here quote Bunsen's words) with the unscrupulous and rambling method of Lanzi and his followers, who had ransacked the Greek dictionary and drawn largely upon their own imaginations and the credulity of their readers, in order to make the Etruscan language, what its alphabet evidently is, an archaic form of the Hellenic, Niebuhr maintained that the Etruscan was a purely barbarous language; that it was wholly distinct from the other more or less Latinizing tongues of Italy proper, of the Apennines, and even of the Alps; that the ruling nations of Etruria came from the north; and that the roots of the language must be looked for in Ræstia." This verdict of Niebuhr is however shaken by the researches of Dr. Freund, who, after travelling through the country (Tyrol, or the Grisons) supposed to be the original home of the Rasenas or Etruscans, and after having studied the language of the district, lays down as the result of his researches that the statement of Pliny is more probable, that the Rœti are the descendants of the Etruscans, who were expelled by the Gauls, and migrated thither under the command of their chief Ræetius, the open Alpine side valleys on the north of the wide plains of Upper Italy offering themselves as places of refuge to the conquered and dispossessed Etruscans. There is also a remarkable tradition in the Grisons of the immigration of the Etruscans into the country.

---

[*] Sir William Betham has founded a fanciful theory on these two inscriptions, that, from the identity of the Etruscan with the Celtic (as he proves), the Etruscans were Celts, and that both were Phœnicians. The inscriptions, according to him, relate to Etrusco-Phœnician, or Iberno-Celtic, the night voyage of the Phœnicians or Etruscans to Carne, in Ireland (Carnsore Point, county Wicklow). The following affords an example of his comparison of texts :

Etruscan.	Irish.	Literal.
PUNE	PUNE	Phœnician
CAR NE	CAR NA	to Carne
S PE TUR I E	IS BE TUR I E	it is night voyage in from
AT I I EII I E	AT I I ER I E	also in knowledge great in it
A BI E CA TE	ABII E CA TA	the being away how it is
NA RA C LU M.	NA RA AC LU AM.	the going by water on the ocean.

Free translation :

O Phœnicians, this communicates the excellent knowledge in what manner the waters of the ocean were passed over in the night voyage to Carne.

Bunsen adopts Niebuhr's view of the Rætian origin of the Etruscans, and advances the theory that the Etruscan bears strong marks of a mixed language, from the circumstance of such grammatical forms as have been ascertained being evidently analogous to what we know of Indo-Germanic flexions, whereas the greater part of the words which occur in the inscriptions prove most heterogeneous. On the other hand, the Tyrrhenic glosses in Hesychius, and the inscription found about 1836 at Agylla, contain words much more akin to the Greco-Latin stock. A mixed language of this kind would be the natural consequence of a non-Italic tribe having taken possession of Tyrrhenia or the Mediterranean part of Central Italy, subdued the Italic indigenous population, and finally adopted their language, as the Norman conquerors did that of the Saxon, or the Arabs that of Persia. The intrinsic nature of the language, as we find it on the monuments, leads also to the conclusion that the Greek words were a foreign element, received but not understood. Making every allowance for a different system of vocalization, such changes as Pultuke for Polynikes,* Akhmiem for Agamemnon, are unmistakably barbarous, and betray an absolute ignorance of the elements of which the Greek name is composed.

In the opinion of Müller, the Etruscans were a race which, judging from the evidence of the language, was originally very foreign to the Grecian, but nevertheless had adopted more of the Hellenic civilization and art than any other race not of the Greek family, in these early times. The principal reason, according to him, is probably furnished by the colony of the Pelasgo-Tyrrhenians, which was driven from Southern Lydia, and established itself chiefly around Cære (Agylla) and Tarquinii. The latter city maintained for a while the dignity of a leading member among the confederate cities of Etruria, and always remained the chief point from which Greek civilization radiated over the rest of the country.

It is not compatible with the object of this short treatise to notice more fully the different views of these authors. We now return to our subject.

Votive inscriptions and others, which are found on vases, scals, pedestals, small statues, utensils, are in general very short. Small statues seldom bear inscriptions, the attributes and symbols which they present being enough to characterise them. Small figures of animals, pigs, wolves and even chimæræ, bear a short inscription, which is usually the name of a divinity to which the figure was

* Here Bonsen is incorrect. Pultuke is the Etruscan form of "Pollux," not of Polynikes.

dedicated, or the name of the person who made an offering of it, and this inscription is almost always written on a part of the body of the figure. Inscriptions of this latter kind are formulæ frequently found repeated on monuments. The most usual are the following: MI : CANA *has given me* (on the most ancient monuments); TECE, for the Greek *έθηκε, has placed, has dedicated;* TURUCE, TURCE, *has given, has dedicated,* the most common formula; PHLERES, *gift, consecration.* SUTHI, SUTHIL, from Σωτηρια, *for the safety of* or *for.* Some names of divinities have been also recognised in these inscriptions, the names of which will be found in the portion on the mythology of sculpture. Other inscriptions, not funereal, are connected with the domestic customs of the Etruscans: they wrote on the principal door of their house ARSE VERSE, which was an invocation against fire, these two words meaning, according to Sextus, *averte ignem.* In the fields, cippi bore these words: MARE HURIE, to *Mars Terminalis.* On altars, candelabra, &c., we find engraved the nomen and prenomen of the person who offered them to the gods with or without the formula MI CANA. The names of magistrates, families, places, religious colleges, have been recognised in the votive inscriptions. The inscription on the statue of bronze of the orator in the Florentine Gallery, informs us that it was erected in honour of Anlus Metellus, son of Velius, by a lady of the family of Vesius.

Etruscan funereal inscriptions are the most numerous. They are found, inscribed or engraved, on isolated stones, on cinerary urns, on bas reliefs painted or sculptured, on small columns, on bricks or plaques of metal, on tombs, sepulchral chambers, or buried in the ground. Sometimes the letters engraved on stone have been afterwards coloured red. The inscriptions on urns bearing bas reliefs have rarely any connection with the subject of the sculpture; for the same sculptured figures are repeated on several urns, each of which bears a different inscription. It is simply relative to the deceased, of whom it contains the nomen and pronomen; a cognomen is sometimes, but very rarely, found. The name of the father is given, and that of the mother after that of the father, following a custom evidently derived from the East, as it was not practised by the Greeks and Romans. The singular custom of tracing descent by the maternal line was peculiar to the Lycians. This custom was retained even under Roman domination, for some sarcophagi bear similar epitaphs in Latin, with *satus* affixed to the mother's name in the genitive or ablative. To the woman's name was added the name of her husband or of the family to which she was allied. A funereal inscription was sometimes terminated by the indication

2 B

of the age of the deceased, but of this there are few examples. Etruscan funereal inscriptions are remarkable for their extreme simplicity as well as for their briefness. Proper names in the inscriptions are usually in the nominative case, sometimes in the genitive, and then they are preceded by the monosyllable MI, I am, as MI LARTHIAS, sum Larthiæ, I am (the tomb) of Larthia. If the inscription presents only the name of the deceased without his prenomen, this is an indication that the monument is of great antiquity, if the form of the letters confirm it, or that it is of a person of very little importance.

Proper names and family names are numerous, and the greater number have passed to the Romans. They are sometimes abridged, but have the usual terminations, E for the name of men, A for those of women; S, at the end of a name, is the genitive termination. The termination AL was employed as a designation of descent, frequently of descent from the mother; as CAINAL, which on a bilingual inscription of China is translated by CAINNIA NATUS. The termination sa, in the name of women, was used to indicate the clan into which they have married—LECNESA denotes the spouse of a Licinius; CLAN, with the inflection clansi, means son, SEC. daughter. Proper names are formed after the general Italian system. The frequent gentile termination ENAS or ENA, recurs in the termination ENUS, which is of frequent occurrence in Italian clan names. Thus the Etruscan names Vivenas and Spurinna correspond closely to the Roman Vibius or Vibienus, and Spurius. The age of the deceased is sometimes indicated in funereal inscriptions, and the numeral signs are preceded by the words RIL, AVIL, AVILS, AIVIL, which Lanzi considers as analogous to the Latin ævum, from which is derived æritas in the ancient Latin, and subsequently ætas. Some translate these two words RIL AVIL vixit annos. Some words, which seem to have no connection with the names of the deceased, are frequently found repeated on several inscriptions, such as LEINE, TULAR, or THILAR. The first is considered to be a kind of acclamation or wish, analogous to the Latin word lenis and leniter, and corresponding with the common Latin formula, SIT TIBI TERRA LEVIS. The other two words are supposed to be applied to the urn, or whatever enclosed the ashes of the deceased, the olla or ollarium of the Romans. Another word, ECASUTHINESI, the recurrence of which on tombs shows it to be a formula, has given rise to much conjecture. Professor Migliarini connects it with analogous Latin formulæ ecce situs, or hic situs est.

We now give a few of the most celebrated Etruscan funereal

inscriptions, as examples. The reader must remember that the
original Etruscan inscriptions read from right to left.

In the tomb of the Tarquinii, Cercetri.

AVLE : TARCHNAS : LARTHAL : CLAN
AULUS   TARQUINLÆ   LABTHIA NATA   FILIUS

In the tomb of the Volumnii, Perugia.

PVP : VELIMNA : AV : CAPHATIAL
PUBLIUS   VOLUMNIVS   AULUS   CAPHATIA NATUS

With the corresponding Latin inscription.

P. VOLVMNIVS. A. F. VIOLENS
CAFATIA. NATVS

THEPHRI : VELIMNAS : TARCHS : CLAN
TIBERIUS   VOLUMNLÆ   TARQUINII   FILIUS

AVLE : VELIMNAS : THEPHRISA : NVPHRVNAL : CLAN
AULUS   VOLUMNLÆ   TIBERII CONJUX   NUFRUNA NATA   FILIUS

LARTH : VELIMNAS : AVLES
LARH   VOLUMNLÆ   AVLI (filius)

ARNTH : VELIMNAS : AVLES
ARUNS   VOLUMNLÆ   AULI (filius)

Bilingual sepulchral inscription on a slab in the Museo Paolozzi, Chiusi.

Etruscan.   Latin.
VL. ALPHNI. NVVI | C. ALFIVS. A. F.
CAINAL | CAINNIA. NATVS.

In the deposito delle Monache, Chiusi.

ARNTH : CAVLE : VIPINA
ARUNS   CÆLIUS   VIPENNA

In the deposito del Granduca, Chiusi.

AV : PVRSNA : PERIS : PVMPVAL
AULUS   FORSENNA   PERI FELICIS   POMPEIA NATUS

PEPNA : RVIPHE : ARTHAL : AFILS : XVIII
PERPENNA   RVFIVS   ARUNTIA NATVS   ANNIS   XVIII

2 B 2

ROMAN.

The most ancient Roman inscriptions date from the first centuries of Rome, but they are very rare. The following conclusions may be deduced from their examination : 1. That the first Latin alphabet was composed of sixteen letters alone, like that of the Greeks, and that of the Etruscans ; 2. That the forms of the letters of these three alphabets were, it may be said, almost identical.

Demaratus of Corinth is said to have brought the Greek letters to Tarquinii, and to have taught the Etruscans alphabetical writing ; and his son Tarquinius Priscus is supposed to have introduced these letters into Rome, about 500 B.C. Pliny and Tacitus confirm this tradition that the Latin letters were derived from the Greek. Dr. Mommsen is of opinion that the derivation of the Latin alphabet from that of the Cumæan and Sicilian Greeks is quite evident, as it exhibits exactly the signs and forms which were used by the Chalcidic and Doric colonies of Italy and Sicily ; and, he adds, it is even very probable that the Latins did not receive the alphabet once for all, as was the case in Etruria, but in consequence of their lively intercourse with Sicily kept pace for a considerable period with the alphabet in use there, and followed its variations. The most striking improvement upon the Greek system effected in the Roman alphabet was the complete elimination of all composite characters, thereby forming a most strictly literal alphabet. Thus, the sound of PH, represented by the Greeks Φ, was exhibited by two distinct letters, which were available in their separate form for many other combinations. The same may be said of the Ψ, PS, the X, CH, and other characters of the Greeks. In the early Roman inscriptions, the characters used being few, the same letter represented different sounds. C was employed at the same time for G Q and for X, as acna for aqua ; culidie for quotidie, facit for faxit, roes for rox. After G was added, C was used for K. The short vowels were frequently omitted, as lebro for leboro (libero), bne for bono, krus for curus, cante for conoto, pœlum for poculum ; i was also frequently suppressed, and are was written for aries, erennt instead of erenint. The dipthong ei for i frequently occurs in proper names, and in words terminating in that vowel, as Caprius for Caprius, certutei for certuti. M N S were sometimes also omitted even in the middle of words, as Popeius for Pompeius, cosul, cesor, for cosol, censor. The long vowels were represented by double short vowels, as feelix for felix, juus for jus. The conjunction of two consonants was prevented by the introduction of a vowel between them, as in aucetum, sinistrum, materi, in lieu of auctum, sinistrum, and matri.

And the conjunction of two vowels, by the insertion of D, as *antedae* for *antehae*, and this took place occasionally even between two words, whence we have *med, alled, marid* for *me, allo, mari*, when these words were followed by a vowel. The aspirate H is rarely found on the most ancient inscriptions, it came into general use after the 7th century of Rome, when its use was carried to excess; it is found in the epitaph of Lucius, son of L. Scipio Barbatus, who was consul in the year 259 B.C. F was a comparatively late addition. Q was originally represented by a double letter, CV, it is found for the first time in the inscription on the tomb of Scipio Barbatus. Y and Z were first adopted from the Greeks in the time of Augustus, before which they wrote CS, GS, SS for Z, and I for Y. X which was originally written CS, as *macsimus*, instead of maximus, was added about the same period. It is found in the Duilian Column, but according to Cicconius, the inscription is not the original one, the orthography being too modern. The F or Æolic digamma was sometimes used to express the sound of the consonant V, as FOTVM, FIRGO for *votum, virgo*. The Latin, in ancient times, had no sound for the V, but that of a vowel: they supplied the Greek Y by their V, when they wrote Greek words in Latin characters. The consonant V was the Æolic digamma, and answered in power to the Phœnician *rau*.

The most ancient inscriptions of the Romans, those from which we can deduce the history of the variations of their written and spoken language, are 1. The hymn of the Fratres Arvales. It is preserved, in an inscription, which was written in the first year of the Emperor Elagabalus (A.D. 218) who was elected a member of the College of the Fratres Arvales. This inscription contains the hymn, which appears to have been sung at their festivals from the most ancient times. It was found in digging for the foundations of the Sacristy of St. Peter's, at Rome, where a leaden copy of the inscription may still be seen, the original, according to Ritschel, being hidden away or, very probably, lost. A facsimile of the inscription will be found in Ritschel's "Prisco Latinitatis Monumenta Epigraphica." The following passage from this ancient hymn we give as an example of the ancient Latin, and its ancient orthography:—ENOS LA-SES IVVATE NEVELVERVEMARMARSININCVRRERE IN PLEORES SATVR FV FERE MARS LIMEN SALI STA BER-BER SEMVNIS ALTERNIS ADVOCAPIT CONCTOS ENOS MARMOR IVVATO TRVMPE.—Enos, Lases, Juvate! Nevo Ine ruo, Marmar, Sins, incurrero in pleores; Satnr fn, fere Mars I limen sali! Sta! berber! Semunis alternis advocapit conctos! Enos, Marmar, Juvato I Triumpe! This dance-chant of the Arval brethren in honour of Mars, probably composed to be sung in alternate parts, is thus arranged by Dr. Mommsen :

To the Gods	Nos, Lares, juvate Ne luem ruem (ruinam) mamers, sinas Incurrere in plures! Satur este, fere Mars.
To the individual brethren	In limon insili! sta! verbers (limen ?)
To all the brethren	Semones alterni advocate conctos.
To the God	Nos, Mamers, juvate!
To the individual brethren	Tripudia!

The Latin of this chant, and of kindred fragments of the Salian song, Dr. Mommsen remarks, which were regarded even by philologists of the Augustan age as the oldest documents of their mother tongue, is related to the Latin of the Twelve Tables somewhat as the language of the Nibelungen is related to the language of Luther.

2. The inscription on the Duilian Column erected by C. Duilius after his first naval victory over the Carthaginians U.C. 493 (261 B.C.). It is now in the museum of the capitol. In the opinion of P. Ciacconus it is not that which was erected in the time of Duilius, as the carving of the letters is too good for those rude times, and the orthography of some of the words is too modern. The original inscription, defaced by time, is supposed to have been replaced by this copy in the reign of Claudius. At the end we give the inscription as it is now, with the restoration of the entire inscription by Ciacconus.

3. The inscription on the Sarcophagus of L. Scipio Barbatus, great-grandfather of Scipio Africanus, who was consul U.C. 456 (298 B.C.). It was found in the tomb of the Scipios, which was discovered in 1760. It is now in the Vatican. A number of other inscriptions in the same tomb belonging to the Scipio family, exhibit the state of the Roman alphabet and Latin orthography during the fifth and sixth centuries of Rome.

4. The Latin tablets of Eugubium. The date of which Lanzi brings down as low as the seventh century of Rome. Dr. Aufrecht considers them to be of the sixth century, two centuries later than

the Umbrian tablets. Dr. Lepsius, of Berlin, struck by the assertion of Lanzi that the language of the tables is full of archaisms, and bears great affinity to the Etruscan dialect, visited Gubbio for the purpose of examining them as philological illustrations of the formation of Latin. From a careful comparison of these tablets he arrives at the conclusion, now universally admitted, that the Latin language, both among the people of Italy generally and among the Umbri, was much more recent than the Etruscan, and that the Etruscan literature was common to the Umbri. He might also have added that these inscriptions leave little doubt that the Latin language was mainly derived from the Umbrian. The tables present, moreover, many peculiarities deserving the attention of the archæologist. The lines, like the Etruscan and other ancient languages, run from right to left; the letters show that there is little difference between the Umbrian character, and that form of ancient Greek which we call Pelasgic.* The Umbrian inscriptions of the Eugubian tablets are highly interesting to the philological student; the letter O is used in place of V; G, a letter supposed to have been unknown B.C. 353, is also to be recognised: *pir* (πυρ) is used for fire, *pani* for bread, and *rins* for wine. Niebuhr supposed the Latin to have been a mixed language, possessing a Greek element imported by the Pelasgi, and another originally Italic tribe. He supported this assertion by a very acute and essentially true observation. He remarks that, whereas the words belonging to the sphere of peaceable rural life agree in Greek and Latin, the Latin expressions for everything belonging to warfare, arms, and hunting, have no words corresponding to them in Greek.

We might point out here other monuments not less useful for the study of Roman palæography, but the examples we have here given will be sufficient for our purpose in this concise treatise.

Roman inscriptions become less rare during the seventh and following centuries of Rome, according as they approach the time of the emperors. Inscriptions are common enough during the period of the emperors. Inscribed monuments of this period are found, not only in Italy, but also in France, Spain, Germany, and England; as Gibbon remarks, if all our historians were lost, inscriptions would be sufficient to record the travels of Hadrian. These inscriptions ought to be carefully collected, as their interpretation frequently throws some important lights on the history and customs of nations. The text of these inscriptions is connected either with the worship of the gods, the ceremonies of religion, with history, as they contain public acts, the names of priests and magistrates, indications of epochs and of places, facts of general importance, such as the con-

* Murray's Central Italy.

struction and dedication of public buildings, honours decreed to citizens. Funeral inscriptions are the most numerous, and the most frequently found in many countries. Altars, statues, temples, were dedicated to the gods by inscriptions; vows were made to them, the accomplishment of which was acknowledged by an inscription on the object itself which had been vowed to them. The names and surnames of the gods are usually in the first lines of the inscription in the dative case, as IOVI SERENO, MARTI AVGVSTO. Then follows the name of the person who dedicated, and this name is followed by the titles and qualities of the devotee, and sometimes by the motives of the vow, and its accomplishment (voto suscepto), and by the formula EX. VOTO, which indicates the object of the monument. This formula is also frequently expressed by EX VOTO. S. L. M. or V. S. L. M. votum solvit libens merito; or again UT VOVERAT. D. D. ut voverat dedit, dedicavit. If the inscription is terminated by the word, SACRUM, or a simple S, which is its abbreviated form, it is not the result of a vow, but only proceeding from the piety of the person at whose cost it was erected.

Among religious inscriptions we must also class the acts of the colleges of priests, sacrifices, such as the tauribolia (the sacrifice of a bull), suovetaurilia (the sacrifice of a pig, a sheep, and a bull). Their object always was the health of the emperor, or his success in some difficult undertaking. The inscription names the person at whose cost the sacrifice was performed, the magistrate who presided, the priest who made the invocation, the singers, the flute-player, the decorator, and the indication of the date terminates it.

Historical inscriptions comprise the Senatus consulti, plebisciti, the decrees, letters, and addresses of the civil colleges of the emperors, agreements with regard to hospitality, clientela, and patronage between towns, colonies, municipi, or corporations, and between citizens, military commissions, and all which concerns civil and political rights. In the same class may be comprised the inscriptions on public monuments, buildings, which usually indicate the date of the construction of the buildings, the object proposed, at whose cost it was built, and sometimes also the partial repairs rendered necessary by decay. Such are the inscriptions which are read on arches of triumph, columns, theatres, amphitheatres, basilicæ, on baths, bridges, aqueducts, gates, walls of towns, and on milliary columns, which mark the distances on public roads. These columns usually present only the names, titles, and surnames (in the ablative if the nominative is not expressed) of the emperor in whose reign the road was constructed or repaired, followed by the indication of the number of thousand Roman paces from the place which has been taken as a point of departure. The name of this place is generally found on the column. (See page 52.)

In these inscriptions, as in all those which belong to the class of historical monuments, the abbreviations are the portion which usually present the greatest difficulty in their interpretation. The titles of the emperors are sometimes very numerous, and those of the magistrates are almost always indicated by the single initial letter of the word. Not to enter too much at length on the usual method of interpretation, we shall here cite an example, as in all teaching examples are better than rules. In the following inscription, discovered at Narbonne, we shall find almost all the formulæ relative to the titles of the Roman emperors:—IMP. CAESARI. DIVI. ANTONINI. PII. FIL. DIVI. HADRIANI. NEPOTI. DIVI. TRAJANI. PARTHICI. PRONEPOTI. DIVI. NERVAE. ABNEPOTI. L. AVRELIO. VERO. AVG. ARMENIACO. PONT. MAXIM. TRIBVNIC. POTESTAT. IIII. IMP. II. COS. II. PROCOS. DECVMANI. NARBONENSES.

This inscription has few abbreviations, but the nearly complete words will be of great assistance in recognising them more easily in inscriptions where they will be found more abridged. In every case we should endeavour to comprehend the construction of the sentence, by taking as a guide the verb, if it is expressed, or the cases of the names, if they are understood. The following is the grammatical construction of the sentence in this inscription :— Decumani Narbonenses (didicaverunt hoc monumentum) imperatori Cæsari Lucio Aurelio Vero Augusto Armeniaco, pontifici Maximo (ex) tribunicia potestate quartum, imperatori secundum, consuli secundum, proconsuli ; filio divi Antonini Pii, nepoti divi Hadriani, pronepoti divi Trajani Parthici abnepoti divi Nervæ.

It may be thus translated :—" The decumans of Narbonne (have dedicated this monument) to the Emperor Cæsar Lucius Aurelius Verus Augustus Armeniacus, chief pontiff, exercising the tribunicial power for the fourth time, emperor for the second time, consul for the second time, proconsul : son of the divine Antoninus Pius, grandson of the divine Hadrian, great-grandson of the divine Trajan, surnamed the Parthian, great-great-grandson of the divine Nerva." We may remark in this inscription—1. The words decumani Narbonenses, as a geographical indication. 2. The titles, prenomina, and names of the emperor to whom the monument is dedicated, Lucius Aurelius Verus Augustus, at first the colleague and afterwards the successor of Marcus Aurelius. 3. The surname of Armeniacus, because he made war in Syria and in Armenia. 4. The title of chief pontiff, common to all the emperors, who combined

in their persons priestly and imperial authority. 5. The fourth
tribuneship, the emperors assuming also the office of tribune, which
was renewed every year, and as the emperors renewed this office of
tribune from the first year of their accession, the indication of the
number of the tribuneship is also the indication of the years of the
emperor's reign ; the inscription of Narbonne is therefore of the fourth
year of the reign of Lucius Verus, and of the year 164 A.D., L. Verus
having been associated in empire by M. Aurelius in the month of
March, 161 A.D. 6. The words emperor for the second time. This title
of emperor followed by a number must not be confounded with the
same title in the beginning of the sentence, where it is indicative
of his sovereign power ; here it relates to two victories gained by
the emperor, and was decreed by the army twice. 7. The words
consul for the second time; the emperors were sometimes consuls
before their accession to the throne, and also during their reign.
8. The title of proconsul which he assumed with all the others. 9. The
words son, grandson, great-grandson, and great-great-grandson,
which indicate his real or adopted genealogy, each of his predecessors being styled DIVUS, a title which was given to the emperors
only after their death. The successive examination of the words
of this inscription thus leads one to recognise the subject, the
period, its authors, and the emperor who was the object of it. For
this kind of monument it is extremely useful to become familiar
with the text of imperial legends, in which the prenomina, surnames, titles, and qualities of the emperors are usually written in
an abbreviated form.

With regard to the precise date of an historical or any other inscription, it may be deduced from indications analogous to those we
have just remarked. 1. By the number of the tribuneships of an
emperor, which invariably answers to the number of the years of his
reign, counted from the year of his accession. 2. Sometimes by
the consulships, but the consulships were not borne year after year
by the same person ; and thus an emperor may have been only once
or twice consul, though he may have reached the fourth or tenth
year of his reign. In this case, and if the number of tribuneships
is not expressed, attention ought to be directed to some other event
of the reign given in the inscription, either to the very number of
the consulships, for it is certain that the inscription could not be
anterior to the year in which the emperor exercised the last consulship mentioned in the inscription ; or to the surnames derived from
his victories, for the time in which he obtained them is recorded in
history. 3. By the means of the date itself of the monument
expressed by the names of the consuls in office, as : T. SEXTIO.

LATERANO L. CUSPIO, RUFINO, COS.—Tito Sextio Laterano, Lucio Cuspio Rufino consulibus. It may be seen by the list of the Roman consuls, given by chronologists, that Titus Sextius Lateranus and Lucius Cuspius Rufinus were consuls in the year 197 A.D. 4. If all other indications fail, particular attention should be given to the form of the titles and to the orthography of the words.

Among historical inscriptions the fasti consulares or Capitoline marbles may be considered first in importance. They contain a list of the consuls and all public officers from U.C. 272 to the reign of Augustus. After the year 610, the account is not kept so accurate as before. Only one tribune of the people is named out of the ten, and several other magistrates are omitted. These inscriptions were found in 1545, in the Forum not far from the Church of Santa Maria Liberatrice. They are in several fragments and sadly mutilated, but are very legible. They were collected and arranged under the inspection of Cardinal Farnese, and deposited in the Capitol. Another portion was found in 1815, which supplies some names which were not known before. A facsimile of these was published by Borghesi, with learned illustrations. In the fire which consumed the Capitol in the time of Vitellius, all the records preserved there were burnt. Vespasian, who rebuilt the temple, had the loss repaired by copies from the most authentic documents; and it is not improbable that these fragments are of that date. Another inscription of historical importance is the Kalendarium Prænestinum, or Fasti Verriani, an inscription, according to Suetonius, set up by Verrius Flaccus, at Præneste, arranged by himself, and engraved on marble slabs. Fragments of the marble slabs of this ancient calendar were found near Palestrina by an Italian antiquary, Foggini. The months of January, March, April, and December, were recovered by him. They contain information concerning the festivals, and a careful detail of the honours bestowed upon, and the triumphs achieved by, Julius, Augustus, and Tiberius.

Another important Inscription presents us with one of the most interesting records of antiquity. The celebrated *Monumentum Ancyranum*, which may still be read on the portico of a temple at Ancyra, in Galatia, is a Latin inscription in parallel columns, covering the walls of the pronaos, or exterior porch of a temple of Augustus at Ancyra. It attests the energy, sagacity and fortune of the second Cæsar in a detailed register of all his public undertakings through a period of fifty-eight years. Commencing with his nineteenth year, it bears witness to his filial piety in prosecuting his father's murderers; it touches lightly on the proscriptions, and vaunts the unanimity of all good citizens in his favour, when

500,000 Romans arrayed themselves under the banner of the triumvir. It records his assignments of lands to the veterans, and the triumphs and ovations decreed him by the senate. It signalises his prudence in civil affairs, in revising the senate, in multiplying the patricians, and in thrice performing the lustrum of the people. It enumerates the magistracies and priesthoods conferred upon him and boasts of his three times closing the temple of Janus. His liberality is commemorated in his various largesses both of corn and money, and the contributions he made from his private treasures to relieve the burdens of his subjects. His magnificence is made to appear in the temples and public structures he built or caused to be built; in his halls and forums, his colonnades and aqueducts; nor less in the glorious spectacles he exhibited, and the multitude of beasts he hunted in the circus. The patriotism of Octavius shone conspicuously in the overthrow of the pirate Sextus, with his crew of fugitive slaves. Italy, it was added, swore allegiance to him of her own accord, and every province in succession followed her example. Under his auspices the empire had reached the Elbe, a Roman fleet had navigated the Northern Ocean, the Pannonians and Illyrians had been reduced, the Cimbric Chersonese had sought his friendship and alliance. No nation had been attacked by him without provocation. He had added Egypt to the dominions of Rome; Armenia, with dignified moderation, he had refrained from adding. He had planted Roman colonies in every province. He had recovered from the Parthians the captured standards of Crassus. For all these merits, and others not less particularly enumerated, he had been honoured with the laurel wreath and the civic crown; he had received from the senate the title of Augustus, and been hailed by acclamation as father of his country.

This record purports to be a copy from the original statement of Augustus himself, engraved on two brazen pillars, at Rome :— "Rerum gestarum divi Augusti . . . . exemplar subjectum." It runs throughout in the first person: "Annos undeviginti natus exercitum privato consilio et privata impensa comparavi," etc.

It was first copied by Busbequius, in 1544, and has been transcribed often since. The traces of the letters have become fainter, but the greater care of recent explorers has more than balanced this misfortune. In the present century fragments of the Greek text of the same inscription have been discovered at Apollonia in Pisidia, which have served to supply some defects and verify some corrections.*

Funereal inscriptions are the most commonly found in all

* Merivale, "The Romans under the Empire," vol. iv. p. 329.

countries under the Roman domination. They are specially
characterized by their first words and sigla D M. Diis Manibus
Sacrum, QVIETI, or MEMORIAE AETERNAE, or PER PETVAE,
these invocations are then followed by the names of the deceased in
the genitive. Sometimes their names are in the dative or nominative,
the invocation to the 'Gods manes' is then unconnected with the rest
of the sentence. Examples of these styles of inscriptions are found
in the following taken from urns in the British Museum :

D M

SERVLLIAE ZOSIMENI
QVAE VIXIT ANN XXVI
BENE MEREN FECIT
PROSDECIVS FILIVS

DIS. MAN.

COMICVS. ET
AVRIOLA . . PARENTES
INFELICISSIMI
LICINIO SVCCESSO
V.A. XIII. M.I.D XIX

Frequently the inscription begins with the names in the nominative,
it is then a *titulus*, or indication of the person buried in the tomb
to which the cippus or marble tablet belongs. To the names of the
deceased are added his civil or military titles, if he had any during
his lifetime, his age, and the names, qualities and relationship of the
persons who consecrated the monument ; if the deceased was a
Roman citizen, the name of the tribe in which he was enrolled precedes his surname. It sometimes happened on the death of a head
of a family that the surviving members, in consecrating the tomb to
him, destined it also for themselves, and took care to mention it in
the inscription. A few examples will illustrate these rules. The
following is an inscription found at Lyons:—D. M. AEMILI
VENVSTI MIL. LEG. XXX. V. P. F. INTERFECTI. AEMILI
GAIVS ET VENVSTA FIL. ET. AEMILIA. AFRODISIA.
LIBERTA. MATER EORVM. INFELICISSIMA. PONENDVM.
CVRAVERVNT. ET SIBI. VIVI. FECER. ET. SVB ASCIA
DEDICAVER. ADITVS. LIBER EXCEPTVS. EST. LIBRARIVS
EJVSD. LEG. The names of Æmilius being here in the genitive
we must read Diis manibus Æmilii Vonusti; the six abridged
words or sigla which follow indicate the profession of Æmilius; and
are to be read thus: *militis legionis tricesimæ victricis piæ felicis*, and
we learn that he was a soldier of the 30th legion, surnamed the
victorious, the pious, the happy ; and the word *interfecti* informs us
that he was killed in the service. The nominatives Gaius and
Venusta show that another sentence commences. All following the
word *interfecti* may be construed thus : *Æmilius Gaius et Venusta filia
(ejus) et Æmilia Afrodisia liberta Mater eorum infelicissima, ponendum
curaverunt et sibi vivi fecerunt et sub ascia dedicaverunt :*" Æmilius

Gaius and Venusta his children, and Æmilia Afrodisia, a freedwoman, their unhappy mother, took care to erect this monument, and during their lifetime destined it for themselves, and dedicated it *sub ascia.*" The words *aditus liber exceptus est,* inform us that when the place of the tomb was concealed by public authority, the path which led to it was expressly reserved. The words librarius ejusdem legiones were added to show that the deceased held the office of librarian or accountant in the 30th legion. We may remark further in this inscription—1. That Venustus has no surname. 2. That his prenomen is the name of one of the chief families of Rome, whence it follows that this soldier, at first a slave under the name of Venustus, was freed by the Æmilia family, and according to the general custom, he took the name of that family for his prenomen. It was the same in regard to his wife; a slave at first under the name of Afrodisia, and also made a freedwoman, *liberta,* by the Æmilia family. She took this same name for her prenomen. The words *sub ascia* are variously interpreted; ascia is the name of a kind of chisel, used by stonecutters, the figure of which is often found represented on sepulchral marbles. They are generally supposed to indicate that the monument was erected according to the wish of the children or relatives of the deceased, and that it was dedicated as soon as finished by the stonecutter (sub ascia).

The following inscription shows us how the name of a tribe to which a deceased citizen had belonged was placed: M. TITIO. M. F. VOLT. GRATO. The words M. (Marco) Titio Grato, were the prenomen, nomen, and surname (cognomen) of the deceased ; the letters M. F. read Marci filio. The abbreviation VOLT is explained by the word voltinia (tribus), and thus we see the monument was consecrated to Marcus Titius Gratus, son of Marcus, a citizen of the Voltinian tribe at Rome. Another inscription presents, L. LICINIVS. L. F. QUIR. PATERNVS. and reads Lucius Licinius, son of Lucius, (of the tribe) Quirina, (surnamed) Paternus. When the heirs of the deceased built a tomb for him at their own expense (do suo) they frequently recorded it in the inscription on the funereal monument, as in the following example taken from an urn in the British Museum :

DIIS MANIBVS
L. LEPIDI EPAPHRAE
PATRIS OPTIMI
L. LEPIDIVS
MAXIMVS F.
DE SVO.

Magistracies, priesthoods, military grades and functions are very frequently indicated in funereal inscriptions, but it would bo impossible to give their nomenclature in this concise treatise. For their interpretation, recourse must be had to the large collections of inscriptions. It will be sufficient for us to place before the reader a list of the most difficult abbreviations, or those most usually found on Roman monuments. In this list we shall not include either pronomina or cognomina, as these words will not be likely to present any difficulty to the archæologist.

SIGLA; OR, ABBREVIATIONS IN ROMAN INSCRIPTIONS.

A. agor, annis, augustales, augustalis.

A. A. apud agrum.

AB. AC. SEN. ab actis senatus.

AE. CVR. ædilis curulis.

A. FRVM. a frumento.

A. H. D. M. amico hoc dedit monumentum.

A. K. ante kalendas.

A. O. F. C. amico optimo faciendum curavit.

A. P. ædilitia potestate, amico posuit.

A. S. L. animo solvit libens, a signis legionis.

A. T. V. aram testamento vovit.

A. XX. H. EST. annorum viginti hic est.

B. A. bixit, pro vixit annis.

B. DE. SE, M. bene de so meritæ, rel merito.

B. M. D. S. bene morenti, bene merito de so.

B. P. D. bono publico datum.

B. Q. bene quiescat.

B. V. bene vale.

BX. ANOS. VII. ME. VI. DI. XVII. vixit annos septem, menses sex, dies docem septem.

C. B. M. conjugi bono merenti.

C. B. MF. conjugi bono merenti fecit.

CENS. PERP. P. P., rel CENS. P. P. P. censor perpetuus, pater patriæ.

COH. I. AFR. C. R. cohors prima africanorum romanorum.

C. I. O. N. B. M. F. civium illius omnium nomine bene merenti fecit.

C. K. L. C. S. L. F. C. conjugi carissimo loco concesso sibi libenter fieri curavit.

C. P. T. curavit poni titulum.

C. R. civis romanus; civium romanorum; curaverunt rofici.

C. S. H. S. T. T. L. communi sumpto hæredum, sit tibi terra levis

D. decimus, decuria, decurio, dedicavit, dedit, devotus, dies, diis, divus, dominus, domo, domus, quinquagenta

D. C. D. P. decuriones coloniæ dederunt publice.

D. D. D. S. decreto decurionum datum sibi, dono dedit de suo.

D. K. OCT. dedicatum kalendis octobris.

D. M. ET. M. diis manibus et memoriæ.

D. N. M. E. devotus numini majestati ejus.

D. O. S. Deo optimo sacrum ; diis omnibus sacrum.

D. P. P. D. D. de propria pecunia dedicaverunt, de pecunia publica dono dedit.

D. S. F. C. H. S. E. de suo faciundum curavit, hic situs est.

D. T. S. P. dedit tumulum sumptu proprio.

E. CVR. erigi curavit.

EDV. P. D. edulium populo dedit.

E. R. ex edicto, ejus ætas.

E. H. T. N. N. S. externi hæredem titulus nostri non sequitur.

E. I. M. C. V. ex jure maniam consertum voco.

E. S. ET LID. M. E. et sibi et libertis monumentum erexit.

E. T. F. I. S. ex testamento fieri jussit sibi.

E. V. L. S. ei votum libens solvit.

FAC. C. faciundum curavit.

F. C. facere curavit, faciundum curavit, fecit conditorium, felix constans, fidei commissum, fieri curavit.

F. H. F. fieri hæres fecit, fieri hæredes fecerunt.

F. I. D. P. S. fieri jussit de pecunia sua.

F. M. D. D. D. fecit monumentum datum decreto decurionum.

F. P. D. D. L. M. fecit publice decreto decurionum locum monumenti.

F. Q. Flamen Quirinalis. ·

F. T. C. fieri testamento curavit.

F. V. F. fieri vivens fecit.

G. L. genio loci.

G. M. genio malo.

G. P. R. genio, seu gloria populi Romani.

G. D. gratis datus, vel dedit.

G.S. genio sacrum, genio senatus.

G. V. S. genio urbis sacrum, gratia votum solvit.

H. habet, hâc, hastatus, hæres, hic, homo, honesta, honor, hora, horis, hostis.

H. B. M. F. hæres bene merenti fecit, re. faciundum curavit.

H. C. CV. hic condi curavit; hoc cinerarium constituit.

H. DD. hæredes dono dedêro; honori domûs divinæ.

HE. M. F. S. P. hæres monumentum fecit sua pecunia.

HIC. LOC. HER. N. S.

HIC. LOC. HER. NON. SEQ. hic locus hæredem non sequitur.

H. L. H. N. T. hunc locum hæres non teneat.

H. M. AD. H. N. T. .

H. M. AD. H. N. TRAN. hoc monumentum ad hæredem non transit.

H. N. S. N. L. S. hæres non sequitur nostrum locum sepulturæ.

HOC. M. H. N. F. P. hoc monumentum hæredes nostri fecerunt ponere.

H. P. C. hæres ponendum curavit, hic ponendum curavit.

H. P. C. L. D. D. D. hæres pon-eadem curavit loco, dato decreto decurionum.

H. S. C. P. S. hic curavit poni sepulchrum, hoc sepulohrum condidit sua pocunia, hoc sibi condidit proprio sumptu.

H. T. V. P. haeres titulum vivus posuit, hunc titulum vivus posuit.

I. AG. in agro.

I. C. Judex cognitionum.

I. D. M. inferis diis maledictis, Jovi deo magno.

I. F. P. LAT. in fronte pedes latum.

II. V. DD. duumviris dedicantibus.

II. VIR. AVG. duumviris Augustalis.

II. VIR. COL. duumvir coloniæ.

II. VIR. I. D. duumvor juri dicundo.

II. VIR. QQ. Q. RP. O. PEC. ALIMENT. duumviro quinquennali quæstori reipublicæ operum pecuniæ alimentariæ.

III. VIR. AED. CER. trinmvir ædilis cerealis.

IIII. V. quatuor virum.

IIII. VIR. A. P. F. quatuor viri argento, ærf auro, publico feriundo.

IIII. VIREL. IOVR. DEIC. quattuor viri juri dicundo.

IIIIII. VIR. QQ. I. D. sex vir quinquennalis juri dicundo.

IX. AGP. PXV. IX. F. P. XXV. in agro pedes quindecim in fronte pedes viginti quinque.

I. O. M. D. D. SAC. Jovi optimo maximo diis deabus sacrum.

I. P. indulgentissimo patrono, innocentissimo puero, in pace, junxit poni.

I. S. V. P. impensa sua vivus posuit, seu viri ponêre.

K. B. M. carissimæ, vel carissimo bene merenti.

K. CON. O. carissimæ conjugi defunctæ (Θανουσα).

K.D. calendis decembris, capite diminutus.

L. liberta.

L. B. D. M. libonæ bene merito dicavit, locum bene merenti dedit.

L. F. C. libens fieri curavit, libertis faciendum curavit, libertis fieri curavit, locum fieri curavit, lugens fieri curavit.

LIB. ANIM. VOT. libero animo votum.

L. L. FA. Q. L. libertis libertabus familiisque libertorum.

L. M. T. F. J. locum monumenti testamento fieri jussit.

LOC. D. EX. D. D. locus datus ex decreto decurionum.

L. P. C. D. D. D. locus publicè concessus datus decreto decurionum.

L. Q. ET. LIB. libertisque et libertabus.

L. XX. N. P. sestertiis viginti nummum pendit.

MAN. IRAT. H. manes iratos habeat.

M. B. memoriæ bonæ, merenti bene, mulier bona,

M. D. M. SACR. magnæ doûm matri sacrum.

MIL. K. PR. milites cohortis prætoriæ.

M. P. V. millia passus quinque, monumentum posuit vivens.

NAT. ALEX. natione alexandrinus.

NB. G. nobili genere.

N. D. F. E. ne de familiâ exeat.

N. H. V. N. AVG. nuncupavit hoc votum numini Augusto.

N. N. AVGG. IMPP. nostri Augusti imperatores.

NON. TRAS. II. L. non transilias hunc locum.

N. T. M. numini tutelari muncipii.

N. V. N. D. N. P. O. neque vendetur neque donabitur neque pignori obligabitur.

OB. HON. AVGVR. ob honorem anguratûs.

.... II. VIR. duumviratûs.

O. C. ordo clarissimus.

O. E. B. Q. C. ossa ejus bene quiescant condita.

O. II. I. N. R. S. F. omnibus honoribus in republica sua functus.

O. LIB. LIB. omnibus libertis libertabus.

O. O. ordo optimus.

OP. DOL. opus doliare, seu doliatum.

P. D. M. patri, seu patrono, seu posuit bone merenti.

P. C. ET. S. AS. D. ponendum curavit et sub asciâ dedicavit.

PED. Q. BIN. pedes quadrati bini.

P. GAL. prefectus Galliarum.

PIA. M. H. S. E. S. T. T. L. pia mater hic sita est, sit tibi terra lovis.

P. M. passus mille, patronus municipii, pedes mille, plus minus, pontifex maximus, post mortem, posuit merenti, posuit merores, posuit monumentum.

P. P. pater patriæ, pater patratus, pater patrum, patrono posuit, pecuniâ publicâ, perpetuus populus, posuit præfectus, prætorio præpositus, propria pecunia, pro portione, pro prætor, publico posuit, publice propositum.

P. Q. E. vel P. Q. EOR. posteris que eorum.

P. S. D. N. pro salute domini nostri.

P. V. S. T. L. M. posuit voto suscepto titulum libens merito.

Q. K. quæstor candidatus.

Q. PR. vel Q. PROV. quæstor provinciæ.

Q. R. vel Q. RP. quæstor rei publicæ.

Q. V. A. III. M. II. D. V. qui vel quæ vixit annos tres, menses duos, dies quinque.

Q. V. A. P. M. qui vixit annos plus minus.

R. C. romana civitas ; romani cives.

R. N. LONG. P. X. retro non longe pedes docem.

ROM. ET AVG. COM. ASI.

Romæ et Augusto communi-
tates Asiæ.

R. P. C. republicæ cauaa, republicæ consorvator, republicæ constituendæ, retro
podes centum.

R. R. PROX. CIPP. P. CLXXIIII
rejectis rudoribus proxime
cippum podes centum sep-
tuaginta quatuor.

R. S. P. requiotorium sibi posuit.

S. macollum, sacrum, scriptus,
somis, senatus, sepulchrum,
scquitur, serva, sibi, sin-
guli, situs, solvit, stipen-
dium.

S. uncia.

S. centuria.

S. semuncia.

SB. sibi, sub.

S. D. D. simul dederunt, rel
dedicaverunt.

S. ET. I. L. P. E. sibi et libertis
libertabus posteris ejus.

S. F. S. sine frande sua.

SGN. signum.

S. M. P. I. sibi monumentum
poni jussit.

SOLO. PVB. S. P. D. D. D. solo
publico sibi posuit dato
decroto decurionum.

S. P. C. sua pecunia constituit,
sumptu proprio curavit.

S. T. T. L. sit tibi terra levia.

S. V. L. D. sibi vivens locum
dedit.

TABVL. P. II. C. tabalarius provinciæ Hispaniæ citorioris.

T. C. testamento constituit, rel
curavit.

T. T. F. V. titulum testamentum
fiori voluit.

V. C. P. V. vir clarissimus præ-
foetus urbi.

V. D. P. S. vivens dodit propria
sumptu, vivens de pecunia
sua.

V. E. D. N. M. Q. E. vir ogregius
devotus numini majestati
que ejus.

VI. ID. SEP. sexto idus septem-
bris.

VII. VIR. EPUL. soptem vir
epulonum.

V. L. A. S. votum libens animo
solvit.

VO. DE. vota decennalia.

V. S. A. L. P. voto suscepto animo
libens posuit.

V. V. C. C. viri clarissimi.

VX. B. M. F. II. S. E. S. T. T. L.
uxor bene merenti fecit, hic
situs est, sit tibi terra lovis.

X. mille.

X. ANNALIB. decennalibus.

X. IIII. K. F. decimo quarto
kalendis februarii.

X. VIII. AGR. DAND. ADTR.
IVO. decem vir agris dandis
attribuendis judicandis.

XV. VIR. SAC. FAC. quindecem-
vir sacris faciendis.

XXX. P. IN. F. triginta pedes
in fronte.

XXX. S. S. trigesimo stipendio
sepultus.

EXAMPLES OF ROMAN INSCRIPTIONS OF DIFFERENT PERIODS.

Inscription on Duilian Column.   U.C. 493.   B.C. 261.

C. BILIOS. M. F. COS. ADVORSOM. CARTACINIENSEIS. EN. SICELIAD.
REM. CERENS. ETESTANOS. COGNATOS. POPLI. ROMANI. ARTISVMAD
OBSEDEONED. EXEMET. LECIONEIS. CARTACINIENSEIS. OMNEIS.
MAXIMOSQVE. MACISTRATOS. LVCAES. BOVEROS. RELICTEIS
NOVEM. CASTREIS. EXFOCIONT. MACELAM. MOENITAM. VRBEM
PVCNANDOD. CEPET. ENQVE. EODEM. MACESTRATOD. PROSPERE
REM. NAVEBOS. MARID CONSOL. PRIMOS. CESET. RESMECOSQVE
CLASESQVE. NAVALES PRIMOS. ORNAVET. PARAETQVE DIEROS. LX
CVMQVE EIS. NAVEBVS CLASEIS. POENICAS. OMNIS. PARATASQVE
SVMAS. COPIAS CARTACINIENSIR. PRAESENTED. MAXVMOD
DICTATORED. OLOROM. IN ALTOD MARID. PVCNANDOD. VICET
XXXQVE: NAVEIS. CEPET. CVM. SOCIEIS. SEPTEMRESMOMQVE DVCIS
QVINRESMOSQVE. THIRESMOSQVE. NAVEIS. XX. DEPRESET
AVROM. CAPTOM. NVMEI. ꓷꓷ ꓷꓷ ꓷ DCC.
ARCENTOM. CAPTOM. PRAEDA. NVMEI. CCꓶ.LXI) C.

CRAVECAPTOM.AIS cccꓶɔɔɔ cccꓶɔɔɔ cccꓶɔɔ cccꓶɔɔɔ cccꓶɔɔɔ cccꓶɔɔɔ
cccꓶɔɔɔ cccꓶɔɔɔ cccꓶɔɔɔ cccꓶɔɔɔ cccꓶɔɔɔ cccꓶɔɔɔ cccꓶɔɔɔ cccꓶɔɔɔ
cccꓶɔɔɔ cccꓶɔɔɔ cccꓶɔɔɔ cccꓶɔɔɔ cccꓶɔɔɔ cccꓶɔɔɔ cccꓶɔɔɔ PONDOD
THIOMPOQVE NAVALED. PRAEDAD. POPLOM. ROMANOM. DONAVET
CAPTIVOS. CARTACINIENSEIS, INCENVOS. DVXET. ANTE. CVROM
PRIMOSQVE. CONSOL. DE. SICELEIS. CLASEQVE CARTACINIENSEOM
TRIOMPAVET. EAROM. REROM. ERCO. S. P. Q. R. EI. HANCE. COLVMNAM. P.

In more modern orthography.

C. DVILIVS. M. F. COS. ADVERSVS. CARTHAGINIENSES.
IN. SICILIA. REM. GERENS. EGESTANOS. GOGNATOS.
POPVLI. ROMANI ARCTISSIMA OBSIDIONE. EXEMIT.
LEGIONES. CARTHAGINIENSES. OMNES. MAXIMOSQVE
MAGISTRATVS ELEPHANTIS RELICTIS NOVEM. CAS-
TRIS. EFFVGERVNT. MACELLAM MVNITAM VRBEM.
PVGNANDO. CEPIT. INQVE. EODEM. MAGISTRATV. PROS-
PERE REM. NAVIDVS. MARI. CONSVL. PRIMVS. GESSIT.
REMIGISQVE CLASSESQVE. NAVALES. PRIMVS. ORNA-
VIT. PARAVITQVE DIEBVS. LX. CVMQVE. IIS. NAVIDVS
CLASSES. PVNICAS OMNES PARATASQVE SVMMAS.
COPIAS. CARTHAGINIENSES. PRAESENTE. MAXIMO. DIC-
TATORE ILLORVM. IN. ALTO. MARI. PVGNANDO VICIT
XXXQVE NAVES. CEPIT. CVM. SOCIIS. SEPTIREMEMQVE.
DVCIS. QVINQVEREMEMQVE. TRIREMESQVE. NAVES. XX.
DEPRESSIT.

AVRVM. CAPTVM. NVMMI. III. M. DCC.
ARGENTVM. CAPTVM. PRAEDA. NVMMI. C. M. C.
GRAVE CAPTVM, AES. XXI. C. M. PONDO.
TRIVMPHOQVE. NAVALI. PRAEDA. POPVLVM. ROMANVM.
DONAVIT. CAPTIVOS. CARTHAGINIENSES. INGENVOS
DVXIT. ANTE. CVRRVM PRIMVSQVE. CONSVL. DE.
SICVLIS. CLASSEQ. CARTHAGINIENSIVM. TRIVMPHAVIT.
EARVM. RERVM. ERGO. S. P. Q. R. EI. HANCE. COLVM-
NAM. P.

Capitol.

---

*Inscription on the Sarcophagus of L. Scipio Barbatus, great-grandfather
of Scipio Africanus. Consul V.C. 455. B.C. 297.*

CORNELIVS. LVCIVS. SCIPIO. BARBATVS. GNAIVOD.
PATRE
PROGNATVS. FORTIS. VIR. SAPIENSQVE. QVOIVS. FORMA.
VIRTVTEI. PARISVMA
FVIT. CONSOL. CENSOR. AIDILIS. QVEI. FVIT. APVD.
VOS. TAVRASIA. CISAVNA.
SAMNIO. CEPIT. SVBIGIT. OMNE. LOVCANA. OPSIDESQV.
ABDOVCIT.

Vatican.

---

*On the tomb of Lucius Scipio, son of Sc. Barbatus. Consul V.C.
B.C. 250.*

HONC. OINO. PLOIRVME. CONSENTIONT. R
DVONORO. OPTVMO. FVISE. VIRO
LVCIOM. SCIPIONE. FILIOS. BARBATI.
CONSOL. CENSOR. AIDILIS. HIC. FVET. A.
HEC. CEPIT. CORSICA. ALERIAQVE VRBE
DEDET. TEMPESTATIBVS. AIDE. MERETO.

According to the Augustan orthography.

HVNC. VNVM. PLVRIMI. CONSENTIVNT ROMÆ
BONORVM OPTIMVM. FVISSE. VIRVM
LVCIVM. SCIPIONEM. FILIVS. BARBATI.
CONSVL. CENSOR. .EDILIS. HIC. FVIT.
HIC. CEPIT CORSICAM. ALERIAMQVEVRBEM
DEDIT TEMPESTATIBVS. ÆDEM. MERITO.

Epitaph of Syphax, king of Numidia, who was brought to Italy by Scipio
Africanus, to grace his triumph, B.C. 203.

SYPHAX. NVMIDIAE. REX.
A. SC. PIONE. AFRC. IVR. BEL. CAVSA.
ROM. IN. RIVMPH. SVMORNV.
CAPTIVS. PERDVCTVS.
INTIBVRTINO. TERRI. RELEGATV.
SVAMQSERVIT-V-INANIREVOL
SVPREM. D. CLAVSIT
ETATIS, ANN. XLVIII. M. VI. D. XI
CAPTIVITS. V. OBRVT
P. C. SCPIO. CONDITOSEPVL.

It may be written at length in the following manner :

SYPHAX. NVMIDIAE. REX.
A. SCIPIONE. AFRICANO. IVRIS. BELLI. CAVSA.
ROMAM. IN. TRIVMPHVM. SVVM. ORNANDVM.
CAPTIVVS. PERDVCTVS
IN. TIBVRTINORVM. TERRIS. RELEGATVS
SVAMQVE. SERVITVTEM. IN. ANIMO. REVOLVENS.
SVPREMAM. DIEM. CLAVSIT.
ÆTATIS. ANNO. XLVIII. MENSE. VI. DIE XI
CAPTIVITATIS. VI. OBRVTVS
P. C. SCIPIONE. CONDITORE. SEPVLCRI.

Vatican.

Epitaph on the tomb of C. Publicius Bibulus.   According to Burton he
was probably grandson of the C. Publ. Bibulus, who was tribune in v.c. 544.
This would fix the date of the monument about 630 v.c., 123 B.C.

C. POBLICIO. L. F. BIBVLO. AED. PL. HONORIS
VIRTVTISQVE. CAVSSA. SENATVS
CONSVLTO. POPVLIQVE. IVSSV. LOCVS.
MONVMENTO. QVO. IPSE. POSTERIQVE
EIVS. INFERRENTVR. PVBLICE. DATVS. EST.

At the foot of the Capitoline Hill.

Inscription of Augustus, on his restoration of the Aqua Julia, B.C. 34.

IMP. CAESAR. DIVI. IVLI. F. AVGVSTVS.
PONTIFEX MAXIMVS. COS. XII.
TRIBVNIC. POTEST. XIX. IMP. XIIII.
RIVOS. AQVARVM. OMNIVM. REFECIT.

On the Porta St. Lorenzo.   Rome.

On the arch of Titus. A.D. 82.

SENATVS. POPVLVSQVE. ROMANVS
DIVO. TITO. DIVI. VESPASIANI. F.
VESPASIANO. AVGVSTO.

Another inscription supposed to have been on the other side of the arch.

IMP. TITO. CAESARI. DIVI. VESPASIANI. F.
VESPASIANO. AVG. PONTIFICI. MAXIMO
TRIB. POT. X. IMP. XVII. COS. VIII. P. P.
PRINCIPI. SVO. S. P. Q. R.
QVOD. PRAECEPTIS. PATRIS. CONSILIISQVE. ET.
AVSPICIIS. GENTEM. IVDAEORVM. DOMVIT. ET.
VRBEM. HIEROSOLYMAM. OMNIBVS. ANTE. SE
DVCIBVS. REGIBVS. GENTIBVSQVE. AVT. FRVSTRA
PETITAM. AVT. OMNINO. INTENTATAM. DELEVIT.

On the column of Trajan. A.D. 115.

SENATVS. POPVLVSQVE. ROMANVS.
IMP. CAES. DIVI. NERVAE. F.
TRAIANO. AVG. GERM. DACICO. PONT
MAXIMO. TRIB. POT. XVII. IMP. VI. COS. VI. P. P.
AD. DECLARANDVM. QVANTAE. ALTITVDINIS
MONS. ET. LOCVS. TANTIS. OPERIBVS. SIT. EGESTVS.

On the arch of Septimius Severus. A.D. 205.

IMP. CAES. LVCIO. SEPTIMIO. M. FIL. SEVERO. PIO.
PERTINACI. AVG. PATRI. PATRIAE. PARTHICO. ARA-
BICO. ET
PARTHICO. ADIABENICO. PONTIFIC. MAXIMO. TRIBVNIC.
POTEST. XI. IMP. XI. COS. III. PROCOS. ET
IMP. CAES. M. AVRELIO. L. FIL. ANTONINO. AVG. PIO.
FELICI. TRIBVNIC. POTEST. VI. COS. PROCOS. P. P.
OPTIMIS. FORTISSIMISQVE. PRINCIPIBVS.
OB. REM. PVBLICAM. RESTITVTAM. IMPERIVMQVE. PO-
PVLI. ROMANI. PROPAGATVM
INSIGNIBVS. VIRTVTIBVS. EORVM. DOMI. FORISQVE.
SENATVS. POPVLVSQVE. ROMANVS.

The words OPTIMIS FORTISSIMISQVE PRINCIPIBVS were substituted by
Caracalla, after he had put his brother Geta to death A.D. 213, for
the original words P. SEPT. LVC. FIL. GETAE. NOBILISS. CAESARI.

On the arch of Gallienus. A.D. 260.

GALLIENO. CLEMENTISSIMO. PRINCIPI.
CVIVS. INVICTA. VIRTVS.
SOLA. PIETATE. SVPERATA. EST.
ET. SALONINAE. SANCTISSIMAE. AVG.
M. AVRELIVS. VICTOR.
DEDICATISSIMVS.
NVMINI. MAIESTATIQVE
EORVM.

On the arch of Constantine, erected on his victory over Maxentius.
A.D. 312.

IMP. CAES. FL. CONSTANTINO. MAXIMO.
P. F. AVGVSTO. S. P. Q. R.
QVOD. INSTINCTV. DIVINITATIS. MENTIS. _
MAGNITVDINE. CVM. EXERCITV. SVO
TAM. DE. TYRANNO. QVAM. DE. OMNI. EIVS
FACTIONE. VNO. TEMPORE. JVSTIS.
REMPVBLICAM. VLTVS. EST. ARMIS.
ARCVM. TRIVMPHIS. INSIGNEM. DICAVIT.

Epitaphs.

M. ARRIVS. DIOMEDES
SIBI. SVIS. MEMORIAE.
MAGISTER. PAG. AVG. FELIC. SVBVRB.

Pompeii.

M. ALLEIO. LVCCIO. LIBELLAE. PATRI. AEDILI
II. VIR. PRAEFECTO. QVINQ. ET. M. ALLEIO. LIBELLAE. F.
DECVRIONI. VIXIT. ANNIS. XVII. LOCVS. MONVMENTI
PVBLICE. DATVS. EST. ALLEIA. M. F. DECIMILLA. SA-
CERDOS
PVBLICA. CERERIS. FACIENDVM. CVRAVIT. VIRO. ET.
FILIO.   *Pompeii.*

NAEVOLEIA. J. LIB. TYCHE. SIBI. ET
C. MVNATIO. FAVSTO. AVG. ET. PAGANO.
CVI. DECVRIONES. CONSENSV. POPVLI
BISELLIVM. OB. MERITA. EIVS. DECREVERVNT
HOC. MONIMENTVM. NAEVOLEIA. TYCHE. LIBERTIS.
SVIS.
LIBERTABVSQ. ET. C. MVNATI. FAVSTI. VIVA. FECIT.

Pompeii.

M. PORC. M. F.
EX. DEC. DECRETO.
IN. FRONTEM. P. XXV.
IN. AGRO. PED. XXV.   *Pompeii.*

IVLIA. ALPINVLA
HIC. IACEO
INFELICIS PATRIS INFELIX. PROLES
DEAE. AVENTIAE. SACERDOS
EXORARE PATRIS. NECEM. NON. POTVI
MALE. MORI. IN. FATIS. ILLE. ERAT
VIXI. ANNOS. XXIII

"I know of no human composition so affecting as this, nor a history of deeper interest."—*Byron.*

D. M.
DASVMIAE. SOTERIDI. LI
BERTAE. OPTIMAE. ET. CON
IVGI. SANCTISSIMAE. BENE
MER. FEC. L. DASVMIVS. CAL
LISTVS. CVM. QVA. VIX. AN
XXXV. SINE. VLLA. QVE
RELLA. OPTANS. VT. IPSA
SIBI. POTIVS. SVPERSTES. FV.
ISSET. QVAM. SE. SIBI. SVPER
STITEM. RELIQVISSET.

On a cippus in the British Museum.

DIIS. MANIBVS
CLAVDIAE. PISTES.
PRIMVS. CONIVGI
OPTVMAE. SANCTAE
ET. PIAE. BENEMERITAE
NON. AEQVOS. PARCAE. STATVISTIS. STAMINA. VITAE
TAM. BENE. COMPOSITOS. POTVISTIS. SEDE. TENERE
AMISSA. EST. CONIVNX. CVR. EGO. ET. IPSE. MOROR.
SI. FELIX. ESSEM. PISTE. MEA. VIVERE. DEBVIT
TRISTIA. CONTIGERVS. QVI. AMISSO. CONIVGE. VIVO
NIL. EST. TAM. MISERVM. QVAM. TOTAM. PERDERE.
      VITAM.
NEC. VITAE. NASCI. DVRA. PEREGISTIS. CRVDELIA.
      PENSA. SORORES.
RVPTAQVE. DEFICIVNT. IN. PRIMO. MVNERE. FVSI
O. NIMIS. INIVSTAE. TER. DENOS. DARE. MVNVS. IN.
      ANNOS
DECEPTVS. GRAVIVS. FATVM. SIC. PRESSIT. EGESTAS.
DVM. VITAM. TVLERO PRIMVS. PISTES. LVGEA. CONIV-
      GIVM.

                                Galleria Lapidaria. Vatican.

                        —

                        D. M.
OTTEDIAE. ZMYRNAE. CONIVG. B. M. Q. V. ANN XVI
M. VIII. C. SALVIVS. ADASCANTVS. FECIT. ET. SIBI. ET
      SVIS. POSTERISQVE. EORVM
HIC. IACEO INFELIX ZMYRNA. PVELLA. TENEBRIS
QVAE. ANNOS. AETATIS. AGENS. SEX. ET. DECEMENSI-
      BVS. OCTO
AMISI. LVCEM. ANIMAM. ET. RAPVERVNT FATA INIQVA.
CASTIOR VT PROBIOR SERVATIOR VLLA MARITO
TE PRECOR HOC. QVI RELEGES. SI PIETAS HADETVLLA.
      LOCVM.
SIC. SIMILE TITVLVM.....TIS NON SCRIBERET OSSIS
DISCEDENS DIC ZMYRNA....E ITERVM TERET
            IN...
                                Galleria Lapidaria. Vatican.

                        — ———

VITRIA. PHRYNE. VIXIT. TERSEXOS. ANNOS
CARA MEIS. VIXI SVBITO FATALE. RAPINA
FLORENTEM. VITA. SVSTVLIT. ATRA. DIES
OC. TVMVLO. NVNC. SVM. CINERES. SIMVL. NAMQVE.
 SACRATI
PER. MATREM. CARAM. SVNT. POSITIQVE. MEI
QVOS. PIVS. SAEPE. COLIT. FRATER. CONIVNXQVE.
 PVELLAE
ATQVE. OBITVM. NOSTRVM. FLETIBVS. VSQVE. LVGENT
DI. MANES. ME. VNVM. RETINETE. VT. VIVERE. POSSINT
QVOS. SEMPER. COLVI. VIVA. LIBENTE. ANIMO
VT. SINT. QVI. CINERES. NOSTROS. BENE. FLORIBVS.
 SERTI
SAEPE. ORNENT. DICAT. SIT. MIHI. TERRA. LEVIS.

Galleria Lapidaria. Vatican.

CHRISTIAN INSCRIPTIONS.

As Christian inscriptions form a portion of Roman inscriptions,
being contemporaneous and in the same language, we have thought
fit to introduce here a short notice of them.

Christian inscriptions form a separate class. They are all funereal,
and are for the most part found in the catacombs, or subterranean
cemeteries* of the early Christians in Rome. They are character-

---

* The word cemetery is derived from κοιμητηριον, "a sleeping place," hence
the frequent formula in the Christian epitaphs, "dormit in pace." he sleeps in
peace; "dormitio Elpidis," the sleeping place of Elpis; "cubiculum Aureliæ,"
the sleeping chamber of Aurelia. The term catacomb was applied to these subterranean cemeteries at a much later period. The practice of subterranean burial
among the early Christians was evidently derived from the Jewish custom of
burying the dead in excavated sepulchres, and thus may have been adopted by the
early Jewish converts. The Roman Jews had a very early catacomb of their own,
in the Monte Verde. contiguous to their place of abode, in the Trastevrine quarter
of Rome. This subterranean mode of sepulture is undoubtedly of Egyptian origin.
It is generally supposed that the early Christians used for their burial places the
excavations made by the Romans for procuring stone and cement for building
purposes. This is an erroneous view. Recent geological observations on the soil
of the Agro-Romano have shown that the surface of the Campagna consists of
volcanic rocks of different natures and ages. The earliest of the series, the tufa
lithoide, was constantly employed from the earliest ages in the buildings of the
city, as attested by the massive blocks of the Cloaca Maxima, the tabularium of the
Capitol, and the walls of Romulus; the second, or tufa granolare, which though it
has just consistency enough to retain the form given to it by the excavator, cannot
be hewn or extracted in blocks; and the pozzolana, which has been extensively
used in all ages for mortar or Roman cement. The tufa lithoide and the pozzolana

ised by symbols and formulæ peculiar to the Christian creed; the idea of another life, a life beyond the grave, usually prevails in them.

The symbols found in connection with the funeral inscriptions are of three kinds; the larger proportion of these refer to the profession of Christianity, its doctrines and its graces. A second class, of a partly secular description, only indicate the trades of the deceased; and the remainder represent proper names: thus a lion must be read as a proper name, *Leo*, an ass, *Onager*, a dragon—*Dracontius*. Of the first kind the most usually met with is the monogram of Christ.[*] The other symbols generally in use are the ship, the emblem of the church, the fish (ιχθυς, containing the initials of Ιησους Χριστος Θεου Υιος Σωτηρ) the emblem of Christ. The palm, the symbol of martyrdom. The anchor represented hope in immortality; the dove, peace; the stag reminded the faithful of the pious aspiration of the Psalmist; the horse was the emblem of strength in the faith; the hunted hare, of persecution; the peacock and the phœnix stood for signs of the resurrection. Christ as the good pastor and the A—Ω of the Apocalypse were also introduced in the epitaphs. Even personages of the pagan mythology were introduced, which the Christians employed in a concealed sense, as Orpheus, enchanting the wild beasts with the music of his lyre, was the secret symbol of Christ as the civilizer of men leading all nations to the faith. Ulysses, fastened to the mast of his ship, was supposed to present some faint resemblance to the crucifixion.

The most usual written formulæ are H. H. I. P. hic requiescat in

were thus alone used for building purposes by the Romans, and the catacombs are never found excavated in these. The catacombs were hewn only in the tufa granolare, and were consequently excavated expressly for burials by the early Christians. The Christian architects carefully avoided the massive strata of the tufa lithoide, and we believe it is ascertained that all the known catacombs are driven exclusively along the course of the tufa granolare. With equal care these subterranean engineers avoided the layers of puzzolana, which would have rendered their work insecure, and in which no permanent rock tomb could have been constructed. Thus we arrive at the curious fact, that in making the catacombs the excavators carefully avoided the strata of hard stone and the strata of soft stone, used respectively for building and for mortar, and selected that course of medium hardness which was best adapted to their peculiar purpose.—Edinburgh Review, CXX.

* This monogram is not of Christian origin. It was probably only adopted by the Christians, as it occurs on coins of Probus, who was not a Christian, and in inscriptions anterior to Christianity. It was not in received use among the Christians until the time of Constantine. The cross also, is found as an ornamental device in Egyptian paintings, fifteen centuries before the Christian era.

pace, BONAE MEMORIAE. The following are also sometimes met with; anima sancta salve, bibas (vivas) in Christo, and all those in which the name of Christ or the idea of a resurrection are expressed: gratia plena; innox et dulcis, nobile decus; Kere, Xero (for the Greek Χαῖρε); lux vivas in Deo; pax tecum sit; pudicæ feminæ, quiescas in pace; qui in menm Deum credidit: recessit in somno pacis; recorditur illius Dena; Spiritus tuus in pace; servus Dei fidelis; vive in æterno; zezca (vivas) pie zezos (pie vivas). The pagan D. M. was also retained by the Christians in the earlier ages. When Christianity was established on securer foundations, imprecations and anathemas against any person who should violate the tombs, were also employed in the inscriptions. There formulæ are sometimes found—male pereat insepultus; jaceat non resurgat, cum Juda partem habeat, so quis sepulchrum hunc violaverit; set malidictus et in perpetuum anathemate constrictus.

In classifying the Roman inscriptions, M. de Rossi has adopted the following divisions: The first comprises those inscriptions only which contain some express note of time, and are therefore susceptible of exact chronological arrangement. The second comprises the select inscriptions, viz.: first, sacred and historical ones, and next those which, either by testimony, by forms, or by symbols, illustrate the doctrines, the worship, or the morals of the Christians. The third, the purely topographical, assigning each inscription its proper place among the ancient localities of Rome. This comprises also inscriptions of unknown or uncertain locality, as well as inscriptions of spurious origin or doubtful authenticity.[*]

In considering the chronological arrangements of Christian inscriptions, it is important to keep in view that in the earlier centuries the Christians kept note of time either by the years of the bishop, or by some of the civil forms which prevailed in the various countries in which they resided. In Rome the common date was that of the consular year. The common use of the Christian era as a note of time began, as is well known, later than the sixth century, at which M. de Rossi's series terminates. In M. de Rossi's collection one inscription bears date from the year 107 A.D., and another from 111. Of the period from the year 204, in which the next inscription with a date occurs, till the peace of the church in 312, twenty-eight dated inscriptions have been found; after the peace of the church the number of dated inscriptions increases rapidly. Between the accession of Constantine and the close of the fourth century, his collection contains 450 dated inscriptions, and the fifth century presents about the same number; but in the sixth,

[*] *Edinburgh Review, CXX.*

the number again declines, that century producing little more than 200.

In those cases where no note of time is marked, M. de Rossi has availed himself of other chronological indications and tests, founded on the language, on the style, on the names, and on the material execution of the inscription, in determining the date. Out of the 11,000 extant Roman inscriptions anterior to the seventh century, M. de Rossi finds chronological evidence of the date of no fewer than 1374.

One of the leading peculiarities of these inscriptions is the frequent disregard of the usual rules of grammar, and the tendency to the corruption of words, as "cum uxorem suam," "cum quem," "pro caritatem," "santa" for "sancta," "soxes" for "sexies," "posuele" for "posuit," "iscribit" for "scribit." We find also the cockney aspirate and its contrary anticipated in their inscriptions; as Hossa (ossa), Horiane, Hoctobres, Hetebna, and oo for hoc, ic for hic. The letters also of these inscriptions are usually very irregular. They are from half an inch to four inches in height, coloured in the incision with a pigment resembling Venetian red. The sense, too, of the inscriptions is not always very obvious. An extreme simplicity of language and sentiment is the prevailing characteristic of the earlier inscriptions. But on the other hand, exaggerated examples of the opposite style are occasionally met with.

Another peculiarity in these Christian inscriptions is the disuse of the three names usually assumed by the Romans. M. de Rossi has given twenty inscriptions with the names complete, prior to Constantine. Of these, no fewer than seventeen have pronomina, whereas after Constantine pronomina may be said entirely to disappear. The gentile name was displaced by new forms terminating in sius, as Inclantantius, Crescentius. The names of the fourth, fifth, and later centuries are usually fanciful appellations, as πιστις, ελπις, αγαπη, Decontia, Prudentia, Dignitas, Idonius, Renatus, Redemptus, Projocius; or self-abasing appellations, as Stercorius, Contumeliosus. Compound names are also found, Deus dedit, Servus Dei, Adeodatus, Quod Deus vult. In general, the Christians took the names of their saints, sometimes they retained their pagan names, such as Afrodisius, Mercurius. They assumed also the names of animals, as Leo, Onager, Ursa, Ursula.

At the date of the discovery of the Roman catacombs, the whole body of known Christian inscriptions collected from all parts of Italy, fell far short of a thousand in number. Of these, too, not a single one was of subterranean origin, and not dated earlier than

553 A.D. At present the Christian inscriptions of Rome alone, and anterior to the sixth century, considerably exceed 11,000. They have been carefully removed from the cemeteries, and are now classified by Cavalier de Rossi, previous to their being fixed in the walls of the Christian museum, recently formed by order of Pius IX., in the Lateran Palace. A large number of these inscriptions are also inserted in the walls of the Galleria Lapidaria in the Vatican.

SIGLA; OR, CHRISTIAN ABBREVIATIONS.

A. ave, anima, aulus, &c.

A. B. M. animæ bene merenti.

A. D. anima dulcis.

B. F. bonæ feminæ, bonæ fidei.

B. M. bene merenti.

BVS. V. bonus vir.

CL. F. clarissima femina, *vel* filia.

C. R. corpus requiescit, *vel* repositum.

D. depositus, dormit, dulcis, &c.

D. B. Q. dulcis bene quiescas!

D. D. S. decessit de sæculo.

D. I. P. decessit in pace.

DM. Dominus.

DIS. depositus, depositio.

H. R. I. P. hic requiescit in pace.

IN. D. in Deo, indictione.

IN. P. D. in pace Domini.

IN. X. in Christo.

M. monumentum, memoria, martyr.

N. DEVS. nobile decus.

P. pax, ponendus, posuit.

P. M. plus, minus.

PPS. probus.

P. Z. pie zazca.

Q. quiescat.

Q. FV. AP. N. qui fuit apud nos

R. recessit, requiescit.

R. I. PA. requiescat in pace.

S. salvo, spiritus, suos.

SAC. VG. sacra virgo.

S. I. D. spiritus in Deo.

SC. M. sanctæ memoriæ.

S. T. T. C. sit tibi testis cœlum.

Θ. θανατος, defuncta.

TT. titulum.

V. vixit, virgo, vivas.

V. B. vir bonus.

V. C. vir clarissimus.

VV. F. vivo felix.

V. S. vale, salvo.

V. X. vivas charissimo.

X. Christus, decem.

Z. Zeses, Ζανο (Jesus).

EXAMPLES OF CHRISTIAN INSCRIPTIONS OF
DIFFERENT PERIODS.

D. M.
P. LIBERIO VICXIT
ANI N. II MENSES N. III
DIES N. VIII. R. ANICIO
FAVSTO ET VIRIO GALLO
COSS.

Publius Liberio lived two years, three months, and eight days.
Anicius Faustus and Virius Gallus being consuls. A.D. 102.

SERVILIA. ANNORVM. XIII
PIS. ET ROL. COSS

Servilia, aged thirteen, died in the consulate of Piso Rolanus.
A.D. 111.

TEMPORE. ADRIANI. IMPERATORIS. MARIVS. ADOLES-
CENS DVX
MILITVM. QVI. SATIS. VIXIT DVM VITAM PRO CHO CVM.
SANGVINE
CONSVNSIT. IN. PACE. TANDEM QUIEVIT. BENE MEREN-
TES CVM
LACRIMIS. ET. METV. POSVERVNT. I. D. VI.

In Christ. In the time of the Emperor Adrian, Marius, a young
military officer who had lived long enough, when with blood he
gave up his life for Christ. At length he rested in peace. The well-
deserving set up this with tears and in fear, on the 6th before the
ides. A.D. 130.

ALEXANDER MORTVVS NON EST SED VIVIT SVPER
 ASTRA ET CORPVS
IN HOC TVMVLO QVIESCIT VITAM EXPLEVIT SVB AN-
 TONINO IMP°
QVIVBI MVLTVM BENE FITII ANTEVENIRE PRAEVI-
 DERET PROGRATIA
ODIVM REDDIDIT GENVA ENIM FLECTENS VERO DEO
 SACRIFICATVRVS
AD SVPPLICIA DVCITVRO TEMPORA INFAVSTA QVIBVS
 INTER SACRA
ET VOTA NE IN CAVERNIS QVIDEM SALVARI POSSIMVS
 QVID MISERIVS
VITA SED QVID MISERIVS IN MORTE CVM AB AMICIS
 ET PARENTIBVS
SEPELIRI NEQVEANT TANDEM IN COELO CORVSCANT
 PARVM VIXIT QVI
VIXIT IV. X. TEM.

In Christ, Alexander is not dead, but lives beyond the stars, and his body rests in this tomb. He lived under the Emperor Antoninus, who, foreseeing that great benefit would result from his services, returned evil for good. For, while on his knees, and about to sacrifice to the true God, he was led away to execution. O, sad times! in which sacred rites and prayers, even in caverns, afford no protection to us. What can be more wretched than such life? and what than such a death? when they could not be buried by their friends and relations.—At length they sparkle in heaven. He has scarcely lived who has lived in Christian times. A.D. 160.

From the cemetery of St. Callisto.

AVRELIA DVLCISSIMA FILIA QVAE
DE SAECVLO RECESSIT VIXIT ANN. XV. M. IIII.
SEVERO ET QVINTIN COSS.

Aurelia; our sweetest daughter, who departed from the world. She lived fifteen years and four months. Severus and Quintinus being consuls. A.D. 235.

D. M.
CVBICVLVM. AVRELIAE. MARTINAE. CASTISSIMAE
ADQVE. PVDI.
CISSIMAE FEMINAE QVE FECIT. IN. COIVGIO. ANN.
XXIII. D. XIIII.
BENE MERENTI. QVE VIXIT. ANN. XL. M. XI. D. XIII.
DEPOSITIO EIS
DIE III. NONAS. OCT. NEPOTIANO. ET FACVNDO. CONNS.
IN PACE.

To the well deserving.

The chamber of Aurelia Martina, my wife, most chaste and modest, who lived in wedlock twenty-three years and fourteen days. To the well-deserving one, who lived forty years, eleven months, and thirteen days. Her burial was on the third nones of October. Nepotianus and Facundus being consuls. In peace. A.D. 336.

Galleria Lapidaria, Vatican.

ROMANO. NEOFITO
BENEMERENTI QVI VI
XIT. ANNOS. VIII. DXV.
REQVIESCIT IN PACE DN
FL. GRATIANO. AVG. II. ET.
PETRONIO PROBO. CS.

To Romanus, the neophyte, the well-deserving, who lived eight years, fifteen days. He rests in the peace of the Lord. Flavius Gratianus and Petronius Probus being consuls. A.D. 371.

HIC QVIESCIT ANCILLA DEI QVE DE
SVA OMNIO POSSIDIT DOMVM ISTA
QVEM AMICE DEFLEN SOLACIVMQ REQVIRVNT.
PRO HVNC VNVM ORA SVBOLEM QVEM SVPERIS.
TITEM REQVISTI ETERNA REQVIEM FELICITA.
S. CAVSA MANBIS IIIIX. KILENDAS OTOBRIS
CVCVRBITINVS ET ABVMDANTIVS HIC SIMVL QVIESCIT
DD. NN. GRATIANO V. ET TEODOSIO. AAGG.

Thus read by M. de Rossi :

Hic quiescit ancilla Dei, quæ de suis omnibus possidet domum istam, quam amici deflent solaciumque requirunt.   Pro hac una

orn subolo, quam superstitem roliquisti. Æterna in requie felici-
tatis causa manobis, XIV. kalendis Octobris, Cucurbitinus et Abumdantius hic simul quiescunti. DDNN Gratiano v et Theodosio
Augustis (Consulibus).

Here rests a handmaid of God, who out of all her riches now possesses but this one house, whom her friends bewail, and seek in vain
for consolation. Oh pray for this one remaining daughter, whom
thou hast left behind! Thou wilt remain in the eternal repose of
happiness. On the 14 of the Calends of October. Cucurbitinus
and Abumdantius rest here together. In the consulship of our
Lords Gratian (V.) and Theodosius Emperors. A.D. 380.

PERPETVAM SEDEM NVTRITOR POSSIDES IPSE
HIC MERITVS FINEM MAGNIS DEFVNCTE PERICLIS
HIC REQVIEM FELIX SVMIS COGENTIBVS ANNIS
HIC POSITVS PAPAS ANTIMIOO VIXIT ANNIS LXX
DEPOSITVS DOMINO NOSTRO ARCADIO II ET FL. RVFINO
VVCCSS NONAS NOBEMR.

You, our nursing father, occupy a perpetual seat, being dead, and
deserving an end of your great dangers. Here happy, you find rest,
bowed down with years. Here lies the tutor Antimio, who lived
70 years. Buried on the nones of November; our Lords Arcadius
for the second time, and Flavius Rufinus being consuls. A.D. 392.

Galleria Lapidaria.

LEVITAE CONIVNX PETRONIA FORMA PVDORIS
HIS MEA DEPONENS SEDIBVS OSSA LOCO
PARCITE VOS LACRIMIS DVLCES CVM CONIVGE NATAE
VIVENTEMQVE DEO CREDITE FLERE NEFAS
DP IN PACE III NON OCTOBRIS FESTO VC. CONSS

Petronia, a priest's wife, the type of modesty. In this place I lay
my bones; spare your tears, dear husband and daughters, and believe that it is forbidden to weep for one who lives in God. Buried
in peace on the 3rd nones of October, in the consulate of Festus.
A.D. 472.

IRENE IN PACE.   ARETVSA IN DEO.

Irene sleeps in peace.   Aretusa sleeps in God.

———

Valeria sleeps in peace.

———

ZOTICVS HIC AD DORMIENDVM.

Zoticus laid here to sleep.

———

DOMITIANVS ANIMA SIMPLEX
DORMIT IN PACE.

Domitianus, a simple soul, sleeps in peace.

———

NICEFORVS ANIMA
DVLCIS IN REFRIGERIO.

Nicephorus, a sweet soul, in a place of refreshment.

———

IN PACE
AVRELIO. FELICI QVI DIXIT CVM COIVCE
ANNOS X. VIII DVLCIS. IN COIVGIO
BONE MEMORIE BIXIT. ANNOS. L. V
RAPTVS ETERNE DOMVS. XII KAL. IENVARIAS.

In peace

To Aurelius Felix, who lived with his wife eighteen years in
sweetest wedlock. Of good memory. He lived fifty-five years.
Snatched away eternally on the twelfth kalend of January.

PRIMITIVS IN PACE QVI POST
MVLTAS, ANGVSTIAS FORTISSIMVS MARTYR
ET. VIXIT. ANNOS P.M. XXXVIII CONIVG. SVO
PERDVLCISSIMO BENEMERENTI FECIT.

Primitius in peace : a most valiant martyr after many torments.
Aged 38. His wife raised this to her dearest well-deserving
husband.

LANNVS XPI. MARTIR HIC REQVIESCIT.
SVB DIOCLIZIANO PASSVS.

Lannus, a martyr of Christ, rests here. He suffered under Diocletian.

NABIRA IN PACE ANIMADVLCIS
QVI BIXIT ANNOS XVI. M.V
ANIMA MELEIEA
TITVLV FACTV
A PARENTES.

Navira in peace ; a sweet soul who lived 16 years and 5 months ;
a soul sweet as honey : this epitaph was made by her parents.

SEVERO FILIO DVL
CISSIMO LAVRENTIVS
PATER BENEMERENTI QVI BI
XIT ANN. IIII. ME. VIII. DIES. V.
ACCERSITVS AB ANGELIS VII. IDVS. IANVA.

Laurence to his sweetest son Severus, borne away by angels on
the 7th ides of January.

MACVS PVER INNOCENS
ESSE IAMINTER INNOCNTIS COEPISTI.
QVAM STAVILES TIVI HAEC VITA EST
QVAM TELETVM EXCIP ET MATER ECLESIAE DEOC
MVNDO REVERTENTEM COMPREMATVR PECTORVM.
GEMITVS STRVATVR FLETVS OCVLORVM.

Macus (or Marcus) an innocent boy. You have already begun to
be among the innocent ones. How enduring is such a life to you !

How gladly will your mother, the church of God, receive you, returning to this world. Let us restrain our sighs and cease from weeping.

Galleria Lapidaria.

PAX

HIC MIHI SEMPER DOLOR ERIT IN AEVO
ET TVVM BENERABILEM DVLTVM LICEAT VIDERE
    SOPORE
CONIVNX ALBANAQVE MIHI SEMPER CASTA PVDICA
RELICTVM ME TVO GREMIO QVEROR.
QVOD MIHI SANCTVM TE DEDERAT DIVINITVS AVTOR
·RELICTIS TVIS IACES IN PACE SOPORE
MERITA RESVRGIS TEMPORALIS TIBI DATA REQVETIO
QVEVIXIT ANNIS XLV. MENV. DIES XIII
DEPOSITA IN PACE FECIT PLACVS MARITVS

Peace

This grief will always weigh upon me; may it be granted me to behold in sleep your revered countenance. My wife Albana, always chaste and modest, I grieve, deprived of your support, for our Divine Author gave you to me as a sacred (boon). You, well-deserving one, having left your (relations), lie in peace—in sleep—you will arise—a temporary rest is granted you. She lived 45 years, 5 months, and 13 days. Buried in peace. Placus, her husband, made this.

Galleria Lapidaria.

APPENDIX.

APPENDIX.

TABLE OF EGYPTIAN CHRONOLOGY.

Dynasty.	Wilkinson.	Bunsen.	Lepsius.	Events.
I.—THINITE.				
Menes	2700	3645	3893	Founded the temple of Phtah at Memphis.
II.—THINITE.				
Kenkenes				Introduction of the worship of the bull Apis at Memphis, Mnevis at Heliopolis.
III.—MEMPHITE.				
		3643	3816	Building of the pyramids of Sakkara and Dashour (Lepsius).
IV.—MEMPHITE.				
Saufu	..	..	..	Builder of the pyramid of Abooseer.
Shufu { Suphis } { Cheops }	2450	3229	3426	Builders of the great Pyramid.
Non-shufu (Suphis II.)[*]				
Menkaru (Mycerinus) . .				Builder of the third Pyramid.
V.—ELEPHANTINE.				
Shafre (Cephren)				Builder of the second Pyramid.
VI.—MEMPHITE.				
Papi { Phiops } { Apappus } Nophre-ka Nofercere (Qerlus).	2210	3044		Was the first who added a royal prenomen to his phonetic names, calling himself Mai-ra-Papi. The Moeris of the Greeks, according to Bunsen. Tombs of this period at Beni Muhammed et Kebeer.
VII.—MEMPHITE.				
VIII. MEMPHITE.				
IX.—HERACLEOPITAN.				
X.—HERACLEOPITAN.				
XI.—THEBAN.				
Schorshahar. Auten-ra	2021	2801	2530	The last king of the XIth dynasty.

[*] Mr. Birch reads these two names as Khufu, and Ratat Khufu, and regards them as two names of the same monarch, which opinion has been confirmed by the new tablet of Abydos, found by Mr. Dümichen, and by the tables of Sakkara, discovered by Mariette. Shaafra he considers to be the Suphis II. of Manetho.

Dynasty.	Wilkinson.	Bunsen.	Lepsius.	Events.
XII.—THEBAN.				
Osirtasen I. . .	2020	2554	2120	The Branchidæ of Miletus, and the original Semmites of the Greeks. Built the original sanctuary of the temple of Amun-Ra at Karnak. Erected the obelisk, and built the temple of the Sun (Ra) at Heliopolis. Tomb of his age at Beni-Hassan.
Amen-emhe II.				
Osirtasen II.				
Osirtasen III.				
Amenemhe III.				The Mœris of the Labyrinth and of the Lake (Wilkinson).
Amenemhe IV.				
Sebeknofru.				
XIII.—THEBAN.				
XIV.—XOITE.				
XV. XVI. XVII. } THE HYKSOS OR SHEPHERD KINGS.				
XVIII.—THEBAN.				
Amosis	1520	1638	..	The shepherds driven out by Amosis, who assumes the title of Lord of Upper and Lower Egypt.
Amenoph I.	1499	1613		Added some new chambers to the great temple of Karnak. Crude brick arches used in Egypt. The sandstone quarries of Silsilis begun to be generally used for building.
Thotmes I.	1478			Made additions to the great temple of Karnak, and erected two obelisks, one still standing. The granite quarries of Syene used for obelisks and statues.
Amun-nou-het	1464			A queen who reigned with Thotmes II. and III. She erected the great obelisks at Karnak.
Thotmes II. } Thotmes III. }	1464 1463			Erected numerous buildings in Thebes, and throughout Egypt, built the sanctuary of the temple of Amun, at Karnak; made great additions to Karnak, and built the chamber "of the kings." Monuments at Memphis, Heliopolis, Coptos, Ombos, bear his name. The obelisks of Alexandria, Constantinople, and St. John Lateran, bear his name. The Sporis Arsinoiden begun. A great conqueror. Reigned 47 years.
Amenoph II.	1414	..	..	Added the small edifice attached to the first area of the temple of Karnak.
Thotmes IV.	1410		..	The great Sphinx at the pyramids bears his name, and was cut out of the rock by his order. His name is on the obelisk of St. John Lateran.
Amenoph III.	1403			Added to the great temple of Karnak, built the principal part of that of Luxor. Erected the two sitting colossi at Thebes, one of which has been known as the "vocal Memnon." The temple of Elethyia (El Kab) bears his name. The name of his queen, Taia, was usually

Dynasty.	Wilkinson.	Bunsen.	Lepsius.	Events.
				introduced with his own in his records.
				Sesostris used as example. Great progress in the arts of sculpture and painting.
Abth Town.				Stranger kings, who introduced sun worship. Tel-el-Amarna their capital. Tombs of this period at Tel-el-Amarna.
Athea—Bassan	..			Made additions to the great temple of Amun, at Karnak. Restored the worship of Amun.
Horus	1331			
XIX.—DIOSPOLITES or THEBANS				
Rameses I.	1324	1408	1440	Built the hypostyle hall of Karnak; commenced Memnonium at Abydus; dedicated Temple of Amun at Kurneh (Thebes). His tomb in the valley of the kings.
Sethi I.	1322	..	..	
Osiri-Meneptmah.				
Rameses II.	1311			Rameses the Great, styled Miamun, or Amunmai, The Sesostris of the Greeks. A great conqueror. Built the Rameseum or palace-temple (called Memnonium) at Thebes. Added to the temples of Luxor and Karnak, and his victories were displayed on the walls; restored the sculptured Temple of Kurneh; erected a hundred statues of himself in red granite at the Rameseum; and additions to temples at Memphis. Completed Memnonium and temple of Osiris at Abydus. Tablet of Abydus on one of the walls of this apartment, sculptured by his order; made considerable additions to the temple of Phtah, at Memphis. Set up a tablet commemorative of his victories on the rocks near Berytus.
Pthammes	1315	1322		The rock temple of Aboosimbel.
Pthasues-Ptmah . . .	1277			A splendid age of Egypt. The exodus, according to Sir G. Wilkinson. Not admitted in the Theban lists.
XX.—DIOSPOLITES.				
Seti, Osiris II.	1273			Added avenue of Sphinxes to the great temple of Karnak.
Sethi, Osiris III.	1232	1267	1270	Called also Miamun and Amunmai. Built temple at Medeenet Haboo. A great conqueror. Art beginning to show decline.
Rameses III.	1215	..	..	
Rameses IV.	1148			
Rameses V.	1148			
Rameses VI.	1146	..		These four were sons of Rameses III.
Rameses VII.	1176			
Rameses VIII.	1172			
Rameses IX.	1161			Made additions to the temple of Karnak.
Rameses X.	1142			
Rameses XI.	1136	..	..	
Rameses XII.				Decline of Thebes.
Rameses XIII.				
XXI.—TANITE.				
Sesonns	1046	1119		
Amun-Pisum	1019			

Dynasty.	Wilkinson.	Bunsen.	Lepsius.	Remarks.
Pesoe	1013 }			{ High priests, according to Sir G. Wil-
Pisham	1004 }			{ kinson.
XXII.—BUBASTITE.				
Sheshonk I	990	982		The Shishak of Scripture, and the contemporary of Solomon. The first king of lower Egypt. King of Bubastis. Took Jerusalem; and recorded his campaigns on the outside of the great temple of Karnak. Adorned the temple of Pasht at Bubastis
Osorkon	969			
Sheshonk II	952			
Osorkon II	952			
Sesonchis II	929			
Takelot I	924			
Osorkon III	899			
Sheshonk III	872			
Takelot, Takelothis II	812			
XXIII.—TANITE.				
Petubates	818	672		
Osorkon IV	815			
Psammus	777			
XXIV.—SAITE.				
Bocchoris	737	743		Called "The Wise." Sole king of this dynasty
XXV.—ETHIOPIAN.				
Sabaco, or Sevechus I	714	737		So or Sava of Scripture.
Sabacon				
Sabaco, or Sevechus II	7.2			
Tirhakah	690			The Tirhakah of Scripture, and the contemporary of Hezekiah, added court to the temple of Medeenet Haboo, Thebes.
XXVI.—SAITE.				
Psametik (Psammetichus I)	664			Accepted the services of the Greeks; made additions to the temples in Thebes, and to the temple of Ptah at Memphis. Rise of Sais. Revival of Egyptian art.
Nero	610			Africa circumnavigated by his orders.
Psammetichus II	594			Made additions to the temple at Karnak.
Apries	589			The Hophra of Scripture. The school of Heliopolis flourished. New gods found in the sculptures.
Amasis (Ames)	570			His name was the same as that of the first king of the 18th dynasty (called by way of distinction, Amosis); made several additions to the Temple of Neith, at Sais; erected temple to Isis at Memphis. Solon, Thales, Pythagoras visited Egypt.
Psammenitus	526			His short reign of six months was cut short by the Persian conquest, B.C. 525.
XXVII.—PERSIAN.				
Cambyses	525			Egypt conquered by Cambyses. The monuments of Egypt injured and destroyed by the Persians.
Darius Hystaspes	519			The Persians expelled from Egypt.
Xerxes	485			In the second year of Xerxes, the Egyptians were again reduced to subjection, and Artabanus, his brother, made governor.

Dynasty.	Wilkinson.	Bunsen	Lepsius.	Events.
Artabanus	463			
Artaxerxes	462			The Egyptians again revolted, and are assisted by the Greeks.
Xerxes II.	425			
Sogdianus	424			In his tenth year, the Egyptians revolted again, and succeeded in freeing their country from the Persians; Amyrtæus became king.
Darius Nothus	424			
XXVIII.—SAITE.				
Amyrtæus	414			Reigned six years. Herodotus visited Egypt.
XXIX.—MENDESIAN.				
Nepherites	4-3			
Achoris	399	..		Added to the temples of Thebes.
Psammuthis	384			
XXX.—SEBENNYTE.				
Nectanebo	381			The Nectabis of Pliny. Dedicated a small chapel to Athor, and built a temple of Isis at Philæ. Plinæ visited Egypt. His sarcophagus in the British Museum, formerly supposed to be that of Alexander.
Teos, or Tachos . . .	3-3			
Nectanebo II.	361			Defeated by the Persians. The last of the Pharaohs.
XXXI.—PERSIAN.				
Ochus	342			
Arses	371			
Darius	336			Conquest of Egypt by Alexander, B.C. 332.
MACEDONIAN.				
Philip Aridæus	323	..		Alexandria founded, B.C. 332. The sanctuary at Karnak rebuilt.
Alexander . . . . . (Son of Alexander the Great)		..		Ptolemy made governor of Egypt, B.C. 323.
PTOLEMIES, or LAGIDÆ.				
Lagus, or Soter	3-3		..	Married 1. Eurydice; 2. Berenice; Serapeum. Library and Museum built at Alexandria.
Philadelphus . .	284		..	Mus. Aridæus. Commenced to rebuild the temples of Isis at Philæ. Pharos of Alexandria built. Berenice founded.
Euergetes	246			Mus. Hermoine; erected Pylon of Karnak; founded small temple at El Pages, near Esne.
Philopator	221			Mus. Andrea. Temple at Alexandria (Now, at Kalneh) erected.
Epiphanes	204			Mus. Cleopatra. A decree of the priesthood of Memphis (the Rosetta stone) set up in his honour.
Philometor	180			Mus. Cleopatra. Temple of Apollinopolis Magna (Edfou) founded. Enterior of Gend-decorated.
Euergetes II. or Physcon .	145			Mus.—1. Cleopatra 2. 1. of his sister; considerable small temples to Athor at Philæ. Small temple of Edfou erected. Greek inscription containing a petition of the priests set up at Philæ.
Soter II. or Lathyrus . .	116			Mus.—1. Cleopatra; 2. Selene. Temple erected at Contra Latopolis. Expelled 106.

Dynasty.	Wilkinson.	Poole.	Lepsius.	Events.
Alexander I.	196			With his mother, Mat. Cleopatra, Lathyrus restored, his. Her his reign, after three years' reign, and the inscriptions raised.
Berenice	81			Daughter of Lathyrus.
Alexander II.	80			Bequeaths his kingdom to the Romans.
Neus Dionysius, or Auletes.	65			Mar. Cleopatra ; expelled 58 ; restored 55. Temple of Ombos completed. Roderick Scaurus visited Egypt.
Ptolemy, the elder son of Auletes	51			With Cleopatra, his sister and wife. Temple of Edfou completed. Temple of Isis at Philæ continued.
Ptolemy, the younger . .	47			Mar. Cleopatra also.
Cleopatra	44			Also, and then with Cæsarion, her son, by J. Cæsar. Back temple at Hermonthis (Erment).
	20	..	..	Egypt becomes a Roman province.

A.D.	EVENTS.
173	Visit of Adrian to Egypt, and again A.D. 130.
291	Taking of Alexandria by Diocletian.
325	Council of Nicæa in the reign of Constantine ; Athanasius ; Arius.
379	Edict of Theodosius ; destruction of the temple of Serapis.
672	Conquest of Egypt by Amrou.

TABLE OF GREEK AND ROMAN ARTISTS.

The following list and dates of eminent artists of Ancient Greece and Italy has been taken from Julius Sillig's Dictionary of the Artists of Antiquity.

Olymp.	B.C.	Names of Artists, &c.	Contemporary Events.
		Pericles of Athens. Smilis of Ægina. Endœus I. discovers the art of painting. Dibutades of Corinth, and his daughter Cora, first make plastic works. Philocles the Egyptian, or Cleanthes the Corinthian, invent painting in outline. Their contemporaries are Aregon, Deato of Mycena, and Saurias of Samos. Ardices the Corinthian, and Telephanes of the Sicyonia, exercise the art of painting. (The precise dates of the above facts are uncertain.)	Iphitus of Elis and Cleosthenes of Pisa re-establish the Olympian games.
I.	776	About this period Bathyclef of Chersiphron of Cnossus, the architect, and Theodotus and Theodorus I., sons of Rhœcus. In a earlier but r period Metagenes L. Son of Chersiphron. Praxias I. of Epimenes ; and Learchus of Rhegium.	Coroebus of Elis is victorious in running. The Era of the Olympiads begins.
VI. 3.	753	..	..	Rome built.
XVIII.	704	Shortly before this time Bularchus, the painter, appeared in Asia.	Pentathlon and wrestling introduced at the Olympic games.

Olymp.	B.C.	Names of Artists, &c.	Contemporary Events.
XXV.	680	Glaucus I, invents the soldering of iron ...	Chariot races **established at** Olympia.
XXIX.	664	Rhoecus II, and Eugrammus, Corinthian modellers, exercise their art in Italy.	
XXX.	660	Cleophantus, the Corinthian, flourishes.	
XXXV.	640	Malas of Chios appears as a sculptor.	
XLIX.	612	Mnesides, the Chian, practises sculpture ...	Age of Solon.
XLVIII.	588	Mnesarchus, the Etruscan, the father of Pythagoras, becomes eminent as an engraver of precious stones.	
L.	580	Dipoenus and Scyllis, natives of Crete, attain great eminence in sculpturing marble. About this period flourished also Anthermus of Archagemus of Chios, Byres of Naxos, and Endoeus the Athenian.	
LII.		... ...	Polycrates, tyrant of Samos.
LIV.	564	Aristocles, the Cydonian, flourishes.	
LV.	560	Perillus, probably of Agrigentum, flourishes.	Pisistratus usurps **sovereign** power at Athens.
LVIII.	548	Tectaeus and Angelio make the statue of the Delian Apollo. About this time flourished also Bupalus and Athenis of Chios, and Theocles the Laconian, sculptors; Dontas, Dorycleidas, and Medo, all of Laconia, statuaries; and Theodorus II, the Samian, an engraver.	
LIX.	544	Syadras and Chartas, Lacedaemonian statuaries, flourish probably about this period.	
LX.	540	Bathycles the Magnesian, statuary, and Spintharus, an architect of Corinth, flourish. About this time Antimaches, Callaeschrus, Antimachides, and Pothaeus, architects, lay the foundation of the Temple of Jupiter Olympius at Athens.	
LXI.	536	Cimon, of Cleonae, the **statuary**	Thespis begins to have his plays exhibited.
LXII.	532	Dameas I, of Crotona, statuary, flourishes.	
LXV.	520	Ageladas of Argos, statuary, makes a statue of Anochus, a victor in the Olympic games.	
LXVI.	516	Ageladas makes a chariot in honour of the victory of Cleosthenes at Olympia, and about the same period executes a victory obtained by Timasitheus. Callon I, of Aegina, Chrysothemis and Eutelidas of Argos, and Glaucias the Lacedaemonian, flourish as statuaries.	
LXVII. 2	510	... ...	Pisistratidae **expelled from** Athens. Chrysilaus obtains his first prize as a dramatic poet.
LXVIII.	508	Amphicrates, the statuary, makes the figure of a lioness. Antenor makes statues of Harmodius and Aristogeiton. Aristocles I and his brother Canachus I, both of Sicyon, flourish as statuaries. This was the age also of Chersilaus of Rhegium.	
LXX.	500	Hegesias and Hegias of Athens, Menaechmus and Soidas of Naupactus, Telephanes II, of Phocis, and Aristenus I flourish as statuaries. Aeschylus I, of Thasos, father of Polygnotus and Aristophon, exercises the art of painting. Nikas of Rhegium, the painter, flourishes.	Aeschylus produces his first tragedies.

Olymp.	B.C.	Names of Artists, &c.	Cotemporary Events.
LXXI. 4.	493	Demophilus I. and Gorgasus practise the arts of painting and making plaster-casts at Rome.	
LXXII.	492	Simmias, statuary, flourishes.	
— 3	490		Battle of Marathon.
LXXIII.	488	Glaucias of Ægina, statuary, flourishes. Pythagoras I. of Rhegium, begins to exercise the art of statuary. About this time Praxiteles in Sparta.	
LXXIV.	484	Ascarus, the Theban, forms for the Thessalians a statue of Jupiter out of the spoils of the Phocians. Ampelius, Dytius, and Chionis produce several statues out of the spoils taken from the Thessalians by the Phocians, which are dedicated by the latter at Delphi. Aristomedes is also engaged in this undertaking.	Epicharmus flourishes.
LXXV.	480	Simon of Ægina, statuary, flourishes. Aristocles and Ptolichus, two Theban statuaries, flourish. Critias Nesiotes makes statues of Harmodius and Aristogeiton, which are almost immediately erected.	Battles of Thermopylæ and Salamis.
LXXVI.	476	Anaxagoras of Ægina makes a statue of Jupiter at the request of several states of Greece, which participated in the victory over Xerxes at Salamis. Dionysius I. and Glaucus of Argos, and Simon of Ægina, flourish. Hippodamus, an architect of Miletus, fortifies the Piræeus at Athens.	Æschylus produces his Perse, and obtains a prize.
LXXVII.			Sophocles produces his first tragedy.
LXXVIII.	468	Onatas of Ægina and Calamis make a chariot in honour of Hiero, lately deposited, which is afterwards dedicated at Olympia. Their cotemporaries are Anchlaos of Argos, Hegias of Athens, Callicles, Colyntehus, Hippias, Stomicrates, and Praxiteles I. Ascelaos and Hippias here mentioned were instructors of Phradmon.	
LXXIX.	464	Teleephanes II. of Rhegium, and Simon of Chios, flourish as painters.	Pericles appears as a public character.
LXXX.	460	Panænus I., statuary; Bathyeles of Athens, statuary and painter; and probably Olympus, statuary, flourish. To this period likewise belong Pantænus and Aristophon, painters of Thasos, and Panægenes of Colophon, a painter, and probably Aimas of Cleonæ, together with Ageladas II. and Nicanor of Paros, who practised the same art.	Death of Æschylus. Euripides appears as a tragic poet.
LXXXI.	456	Policletus of Sicyon, statuary, flourishes. Soon after this year Ageladas II. of Argos prepares a statue of Jupiter for the Messenians occupying Naupactus.	
LXXXII.	452	Acestor of Cnossus, and Panælus of Sicyon, flourish as statuaries; the former as a statuary and engraver, and Dædalus as a sculptor.	
— 3	451		Decemviri first created at Rome.
		Polydates of Athens, statues exist undraused.	
LXXXIII.	448	Alcamenes, an Athenian, and Agoracritus the Parian, both pupils of Phidias, flourish as statuaries and sculptors. In this period likewise the Cretan Nesiotes is still living, and the following artists are engaged in their several professions: Crito and Nicostiphus as statuaries; Xenophon the Athenian, a statuary; Praxias the Athenian, scholar of Polidates by the father's side; Thrasymedes, the brother of Praxias, and Pyromachus of Cholcis, painters.	

Olymp.	B.C.	Names of Artists, &c.	Contemporary Events.
LXXXIV.	444	Libo, the Elean, builds the Temple of Zeus Olympius. Mys, the engraver, flourishes.	Herodotus completes his history at Thurii.
LXXXV. 3.	434	Phidias dedicates his statue of Athene, made of ivory and gold, in the Parthenon. The Vestibule of the Acropolis commenced.	
LXXXV. 4.	437	Phidias commences his statue of Zeus Olympius, with the assistance of Colotes of Paros. About this time Ictinus, Callicrates, Metagenes II. of Athens, Scopas of Cyprus, architects, and, probably, Carpio.	
LXXXVI.	436	Corcebus and Menecles, architects; Cleœtas, a statuary, and probably Democritus III., a statuary, flourish. This appears to have been the period when Socrates, the philosopher, bestowed attention on sculpture.	
—— 4.	433	Phidias dedicates his statue of Zeus Olympius.	
LXXXVII.	432	Phidias dies.	Euripides produces his Medea.
		Myro of Eleuthera, and Polycrates I. of Argos, attain great eminence as statuaries. About this time flourished also the following statuaries; Callo I. of Elis, Gorgias of Laconia, Pleisidas of Argos, Sognas of Elis, and Theocosmus of Megara.	Commencement of the Peloponnesian war.
—— 3.	430	Calamis makes his statue of Apollo, the Averter of evil.	Pericles dies.
LXXXVIII.	428	Agoladas of Corinth, statuary, and Peisidas II. of Mende in Thrace, statuary and sculptor, flourish.	
LXXXIX.	424	Contelmas of Rhegium flourished as a statuary.	Aristophanes produces his Knights.
XC.	420	Polycrates I. of Argos makes his statue of Hera.	
		Apellas, Dionysiodorus, Nicerates of Athens, Nicodamus of Mænalus, Patrocles and Kanachus of Chios, flourish as statuaries. Praxias and Androsthenes, two Athenian sculptors, decorate with their productions the temple at Delphi. Cleoblikus, the architect, Eucrates, Eupalinus, the Argive, rebuilds the altar in the temple of Mycene. To this period we should in all probability refer Callimachus κατατηξίτεχνος.	
XCI.	416		Expedition of the Athenians against Sicily. Alcibiades eminent as a statesman.
XCII.	412	Lyrius, the son of Myro, flourishes as a statuary. To this period we should probably refer Theocles.	
XCIII.	408	Phryne, the statuary, flourishes.	Euripides dies.
XCIV.	404	Antiphanes of Argos and Aristander of Paros flourish as statuaries. A large group of statues is dedicated at Delphi by the Lacedæmonians, in commemoration of their victory at Ægospotami, made by the following artists; Alypus, Patrocles I. and Canachus II. of Sicyon, Pragon II. of Thebes, Pison of Calauria, Samolas of Arcadia, Theocosmus of Megara, and Pleander. Aristander makes statues of Athene and Heracles, which are dedicated in acknowledgment of the overthrow of the Thirty Tyrants.	Sophocles dies.
XCV. 3.	398	Aristocles IV. flourishes as a sculptor.	
XCV. 4.			Socrates put to death.

2 K

Olymp.	B.C.	Names of Artists, &c.	Cotemporary Events.
XCV. 4.	397	Zeuxis of Heraclea, the distinguished painter, flourishes. To this period we must refer, also, Androcydes of Cyzicus, and Eupompus of Sicyon, painters; Naucydes the Argive, brother and instructor of Polycletus II., who was also engaged as an artist about this time; Patroclus, Canachus of Megara, and Dædalus II. of Sicyon, all statuaries.	
XCVI.	396	Parrhasius of Ephesus, Timotheus of Sicyon, Timon, and Colotes II. flourish as painters. Pamphilus of Chios, a statuary, flourishes.	Veii taken by the Romans.
XCVII.	393	Scopas, the celebrated Parian sculptor, builds the temple of Pallas at Tegea. Aristodemus I., a painter, flourishes.	
— 3.	390		The Gauls take and burn the city of Rome.
XCVIII.	388	To this period belong Ctesidemus, the painter, and the following statuaries, all of whom were pupils of Polycletus I.: Alexis, Aristodemus, Asopodorus, Athenodorus, and Dæmon II.	
C.	380	Polycletus II. of Argos, Cleon of Sicyon, Deiniomenes I. of Sicyon, Daïppus as statuaries, and Pamphilus I. of Amphipolis and Euphranor, as painters.	Plato and Xenophon flourish.
CII.	372	The following statuaries flourish: Aristogiton of Thebes, Cephisodotus I. of Athens, Leochares II. of Sicyon, Hypatodorus, Pausanias I. of Apollonia, Polycles I., Xenophon the Athenian, Callistratus the Theban, and probably Olympiosthenes and Strongylio. Demophilus the Himeræan, and Euclides II. the Athenian, practise sculpture; and Mnasis, and Ephorus the Ephesian. The instructor of Arcesaus, flourish as painters.	
— 7.	371	.. ..	Battle of Leuctra.
CIII.	367	Lysippus, the Sicyonian, first appears as an artist.	
CIV.	364	Euphranor, the distinguished statuary and painter, and Praxiteles, eminent in the arts of statuary and sculpture, flourish. To this period, also, belong Cephisodotus and Herodotus the Olympian statuaries, Cydias of Cythnus and Nicias I., painters. The date of these artists rests on Praxiteles in the description of his statues.	
— 3.	362	.. .. ..	The battle of Mantinea.
CV.	360	Nicomachus I., a Theban painter, flourishes.	Philip reigns in Macedon.
CVI.	356	Scopas, the Parian, engaged with other artists in building the Temple of Diana at Ephesus. Pythes of Sicyon, the father of Pausias, flourishes as a painter. Pamphilus I., of Amphipolis, is still living.	The sacred war.
— 4.	353	..	Mausolus, king of Caria, dies.
CVII.	352	Apelles just appears as a painter. Aristides II. of Thebes, Echio, and Theriomachus, all painters, now flourish. The Mausoleum of Halicarnassus, built by Pithous and Satyrus, is about this time decorated with figures by Scopas, Praxiteles, Leochares, Timotheus, Bryaxis, and Pythis. This was probably the age of the statuary Chares.	
— 1.	349		Olympian war. Demosthenes delivers his Olynthiac orations.

Olymp.	B.C.	Names of Artists, &c.	Contemporary Events.
CVIII.	348	Ocybas, the painter, flourishes.	
— 4.	345	... ...	Timoleon undertakes the expedition to Syracuse.
CIX.	344	Philochares, the Athenian, appears as a painter.	
CX.	340	Antorides and Leontion flourish as painters. Leochares is still living.	
— 3.	338	... ...	Battle of Chæronea.
CXI.	336	Antiphilus the pupil of Euphranor, Ctesidemus, and Leonidas of Anthedon, flourish as painters.	Alexander ascends the throne of Macedonia.
CXII.	332	Apelles flourishes. The painters, contemporary with him are, Amphio, Asclepiodorus the Egyptian, Nicophanes, Anaxidemus, Theon of Samos, Melanthius, Pausias of Sicyon, The-omnestus, Nicias II. of Athens, and Chorilus also the pupil, and perhaps the brother, of Apelles. Pyrasicrates the engraver on precious stones flourishes. To this period also belong Philo the statuary, Ctesiphon II. the sculptor, and Dinocrates, an architect of Macedonia.	
— 3.	329	Asiclepiodorus, Aglaophon V., and Philoxenus (the last two scholars of Erexius), flourish as painters; and Amphistratus as a statuary and sculptor.	The battle of Arbela. Aristotle flourishes.
CXIII.	328		
CXIV.	324	Leucippus still living. In this period the subjoined artists flourish: Lysistratus the brother of Lysippus, Apollodorus, Io, Py-rgoteles Silanio the Athenian, Boedas of Sicyon, and sculptors; Ctistias of Chios, Arcia and his brother Nicetas, both of Thebes, painters; and probably Mnestorus II. sculptor.	Alexander dies.
— 2.	322		Demosthenes dies. Menander.
CXV.	320	Protogenes the Sicyonian, flourishes as a statuary.	
— 2.	318		Demetrius Phalereus governs Athens.
CXVII.	312	Bryaxis still exercises the arts of statuary and sculpture.	Epicurus begins to flourish.
CXVIII.	308	Aristolaus and Nicias II. the Athenian, still living; Dionysius, Perseus, and Aristodemus were painters, flourish as painters, and Cahles of Arados as an architect. To this period we should also refer Metrodorus the Stoic.	Antigonus, Lysimachus, Seleucus, Ptolemy, assume the name of kings.
CXIX. 3.	304	Protogenes of Caunus paints in the island of Rhodes the figure of Ialysus. Fames to him decorates with his paintings the Temple of the Goddess Athena at Rome. This was probably the age of Praxiteles II. the character.	
CXX.	300	Cephisodotus II. a statuary, sculptor, and painter, and Timarchus a statuary, both sons of Praxiteles, now flourish. Euphranor, Euthycrates, Eutychides of Sicyon, Phanias, Pyromachus, and Tisicrates of Sicyon, flourish as statuaries; and Athenio of Maronea, and Mechopanes as painters.	The celebrated Alexandrian library collected and arranged.
CXXII.	292	Bedas, son of Lysippus, Chares of Lindus, and Xenocrates, flourish as statuaries.	

Olymp.	B.C.	Names of Artists, &c.	Contemporary Events.
CXXV.	286	Omphalio, a painter, flourishes.	
— 3.	278		The Gauls attack Greece.
CXXVI.	276	Plato and Xenocrates flourish as statuaries.	
CXXVIII.	268	Cantharus, the Sicyonian, practises the art of statuary; and Mydo of Soli, and Arcesilaus III., probably of Sicyon, that of painting.	The Romans become masters of all Italy.
CXXIX.	264		The Parian marbles engraved.
CXXXIII.	248	Nealces and Arigontis flourish as painters.	
CXXXV.	240	Thomnthes II., painter, flourishes.	
CXXXVI.	236	Isigonus, Pyromachus, Stratonicus, and Antigonus, flourish as statuaries, and Leontiscus as a painter.	
CXL.	220	Anaxandra, the daughter of Nealces, practises the art of painting. Ætineta, a modeller, and his brother Pasias, a painter, flourish.	
CXLII.	212	Mico III., of Syracuse, flourishes as a statuary.	
CXLVII.	192	Stadions, Athenian statuary, flourishes.	
CL.			Library of Pergamos formed.
CLI.	180	Cossutius, Roman architect, flourishes.	
CLIII.	176	Heraclides I., a Macedonian, and Metrodorus, probably an Athenian, flourish as painters.	P. Terentius flourishes.
CLV.	168	Antheus, Polycles II., Callistratus, Callixenus, Pythias, Pythocles, Timocles, and Timarchides, flourish as statuaries and sculptors. To this period we should probably refer Philo of Byzantium.	
CLVII.	140	Pacuvius, the tragic poet and painter, flourishes.	
CLVIII. 3.	146		Corinth destroyed. Greece subjected to the Romans.
CLXXVI. 3.	74	Arcesilaus IV., sculptor, the intimate friend of L. Lucullus, flourishes.	
CLXXIX. 3.	63	Valerius of Ostia flourishes as an architect. The following artists flourished about this period: Pasiteles, statuary, sculptor, and engraver; Timomachus of Byzantium, and Arellius, painters; Cyrus, architect; Posidonius of Ephesus, statuary and engraver; Leosthides, and Pythees I., engravers; Coponius, Roman sculptor; and Epitynchanus, engraver on precious stones.	Cicero, Caesar, Varro, and Sallust flourish.
	48		Battle of Pharsalia.
	42		Battle of Philippi.
	31		Battle of Actium.
CLXXXVII. 3	30	In this period Pasiteles still practises the arts of sculpture and engraving, and the following artists also flourish: Nearus, Barmetus, Dionysus, Lysias, and, probably, Stephanus, sculptors; Arisimius Evander, Athenian sculptor and engraver; Diovsitus, Sopolis, Ludius, Pedius a youth, and Lala, a female born at Cyzicus, painters; Dioscorides and Aulmo, engravers on gems; and Posis, a Roman modeller.	Augustus constituted emperor. Horace, Virgil, Livy, Tibullus, and Vitruvius flourish.
	28		Palatine library of Augustus formed.

Olymp.	B.C.	Names of Artists, &c.	Contemporary Events.
70		Chimarus, a statuary, flourishes; probably, Menelaus, a sculptor.	
	14	Diogenes and Fabullus flourish as painters; Attica the Athenian, as a statuary, and sculptor; and Zenodorus as a statuary.	Nero emperor. Seneca, Persius, and Lucan flourish.
	69	Agesander, Athenodorus his son, and Polydorus, make for Titus, who afterwards became emperor, the celebrated group of the Laocoon.	Vespasian emperor.
		To this period also belong Craterus, the two Pythodori, Polydeuces, Hermolaus, Artemas, and Aphrodisias of Tralles, sculptors; Cornelius Pinus, Attius Priscus, Turpilius the Venetian, and Artemidorus, painters; and Evodus, an engraver on precious stones.	
	79	. . . .	Titus emperor. Eruption of Mount Vesuvius. Pliny the elder dies.

LIST OF THE PRINCIPAL GREEK AND ROMAN ARCHITECTS.

(From Gwilt's Encyclopædia of Architecture.)

BEFORE CHRIST.

Name of Architect.	Country.	Principal Works.
Theodorus of Samos	7th	Labyrinth at Lemnos; some buildings of Sparta; and the temple of Jupiter at Samos.
Hermogenes of Alabanda	"	Temple of Bacchus at Teos, and that of Diana at Magnesia.
Agamedes and Trophonius of Delphi	"	Temple of Apollo at Delphi; a temple dedicated to Neptune, near Mantinea.
Demetrius of Ephesus	6th	Continuation of the temple of Diana, which had been begun by Chersiphron.
Eupalinus of Megara	"	Aqueducts, with many other edifices at Samos.
Mandrocles of Samos	"	Wooden bridge over the Thracian Bosphorus, erected by the command of Darius.
Chirosophus of Crete	"	Temple of Ceres and Proserpine; another of the Paphian Venus; and one of Apollo at Tegea.
Pytheus of Priene	4th	Mausoleum of Artemisia in Caria; design for the temple of Pallas at Priene. In the former he was assisted by Satirus.
Spintharus of Corinth	"	Rebuilds the temple of Apollo at Delphi, which had been destroyed by fire.
Agaptos of Elis	"	Portico at Elis.
Libon of Elis	"	Temple of Jupiter Olympius at Olympia.
Ictinus of Athens	"	Parthenon at Athens; temple of Ceres and Proserpine at Eleusis; temple of Apollo Epicurius in Arcadia.
Callicrates of Athens	"	Assisted Ictinus in the erection of the Parthenon.
Mnesicles of Athens	"	Propylæa of the Parthenon.
Antistates of Athens	"	A temple of Jupiter at Athens.
Scopas of Greece	"	One side of the tomb of Mausolus; a column of the temple at Ephesus.
Archias of Corinth	5th	Many temples, and other edifices, at Syracuse.
Callias of Arados	"	Temples, &c., at Rhodes.
Ayclus of Arados	"	Temple of the Indian Æsculapius.

BEFORE CHRIST.

Name of Architect.	Century.	Principal Works.
Mandrus . . .		Temple of Apollo at Magnesia.
Clerocrates of Athens .	4th	Plan of the city of Alexandria.
Idmacrates of Macedonia .	..	Rebuilt the temple of Diana at Ephesus; engaged on works at Alicarnassus; was author of the proposition to transform Mount Athos into a colossal figure.
Andronicus of Athens .	..	Tower of the Winds at Athens.
Callimachus of Corinth .	..	Reputed inventor of the Corinthian order.
Sostratus of Cnidus .	..	The Pharos of Alexandria.
Philo of Athens .	..	Enlarged the arsenal and the Piræus at Athens; erected the great theatre, finished by order of Adrian.
Eupolemus of Argos .	3rd	Several temples, and a theatre at Argos.
Theon of Agrigentum .		Various buildings at Agrigentum.
Cossutius of Rome .	2nd	Design for the temple of Jupiter Olympius at Athens.
Hermodorus of Salamis .	..	Temple of Jupiter Stator (Meravit. Christopolis) in the Forum at Rome; temple of Mars in the Circus Flaminius.
Caius Mutius of Rome .	..	Temple of Honour and Virtue, near the trophies of Marius at Rome.
Valerius of Ostia .		Several magnificent rooms, with roofs.
Batrachus of Lacunia .	1st	Three two architects built several temples at Rome. The name of the first (βατραχος) signifies a frog; and that of the latter (σαυρος) a lizard; and they perpetuated their names on some of their works by the allegorical representation of these two animals sculptured upon them. The churches of St. Lorenzo and of St. Lorenzo fuori le Mura, at Rome, still contain some columns whose pedestals are sculptured with a lizard and a frog.
Saurus of Lacunia .		
Deiphanes of Cyprus .		Rebuilt the Pharos of Alexandria, at the command of Cleopatra, the other having fallen down.
Cyrus of Rome .		Architect to Cicero.
Posthumius of Rome .		Many works at Baiæ and Naples.
Coccius Auctus .		Baths at Pozzuoli; grotto of Avium.
Funditus of Rome .		Several buildings at Rome; like this, Rome, who wrote on architecture.

AFTER CHRIST.

Name of Architect.	Century.	Principal Works.
Vitruvius Pollio of Fano .	1st	Basilica Justitiæ at Fano; a great writer on architecture.
Vitruvius Cerdo of Verona .	..	Triumphal arch at Verona.
Celer and Severus of Rome .	..	Golden House of Nero.
Rabirius of Rome .	..	Palace of Domitian on Mt Palatine.
Musitus of Rome .	..	Temple of Ceres at Rome.
Frontinus of Rome .	2nd	He has left a work on aqueducts.
Apollodorus of Damascus .	..	Forum Trajani at Rome; a bridge over the Danube, in Lower Hungary.
Lacer of Rome .	..	A bridge over the Tagus, in Spain; a temple, now dedicated to San Giuliano.
Detrianus of Rome .		Moles Hadriani, and the Pons Ælius, now called the Castello and Ponte Sant' Angelo.
Antoninus, the Senator of Rome .		Pantheon at Epidaurus; baths of Æsculapius.
Nicon of Pergamus .	..	Several fine works at Pergamus.

LIST OF ROMAN EMPERORS, EMPRESSES, AND THEIR RELATIONS.

CAIUS JULIUS CÆSAR,
Son of C. Cæsar and of Aurelia, born 100, pontifex maximus 63, prætor 62, consul 59, dictator 48, assassinated 44 B.C.

CORNELIA, wife of Cæsar, daughter of L. Cinna, died 68 B.C.

JULIA, daughter of Cæsar and Cornelia, married to Pompey 59 B.C., died 54 B.C.

JULIA, sister of Cæsar and wife of M. Atius Balbus.

ATIA, daughter of M. A. Balbus and Julia, wife of Caius Octavius, mother of Augustus.

C. OCTAVIUS, father of Augustus, died 58 B.C.

CAIUS OCTAVIUS CÆSAR AUGUSTUS,
Son of C. Octavius and Atia, niece of Julius Cæsar, born 63 B.C., declared emperor 29 B.C., obtained the name of Augustus 27 B.C., died 14 A.D.

CLODIA, daughter of Clodius and Fulvia, first wife of Octavius.

SCRIBONIA, second wife of Octavius, married 40 B.C., was divorced by him in order to marry Livia.

LIVIA DRUSILLA, was married first to Tib. Claudius, and afterwards became third wife of Augustus, born 57 B.C., died 29 A.D.

OCTAVIA, sister of Augustus, married first to C. Marcellus 50 B.C., and subsequently to Antony 40 B.C., died 11 B.C.

MARCELLUS, son of C. Marcellus and Octavia, married to Julia, daughter of Augustus, was adopted by him, and was destined to be his successor, but died in 23 B.C.

MARCELLA, daughter of C. Marcellus and Octavia, was thrice married—first, to M. Agrippa; second, to Julius Antonius; third, to Sextus Appuleius.

MARCUS AGRIPPA, son-in-law of Augustus, born 63 B.C., died 12 A.D.

JULIA, daughter of Augustus and Scribonia; wife of M. Marcellus, Marcus Agrippa, and lastly of Tiberius, born 39 B.C., died 14 A.D.

CAIUS and LUCIUS, sons of M. Agrippa and Julia—Caius, born 20 B.C., Cæsar 17 B.C., died 4 B.C.; Lucius, born 17 B.C., Cæsar same year, died 2 A.D.

AGRIPPA POSTHUMUS, son of M. Agrippa and Julia, born 12 B.C., Cæsar 4 A.D., killed 14 A.D.

JULIA, daughter of M. Agrippa and Julia; wife of L. (Æmilius Paulus, banished by her grandfather, Augustus, to the island Tremerus, died 28 A.D.

TIBERIUS CLAUDIUS NERO, married to Livia Drusilla, father of the Emperor Tiberius.

TIBERIUS CLAUDIUS NERO CÆSAR,
Son-in-law of Augustus, born 42 B.C., Cæsar 4 A.D., emperor 14 A.D., smothered 37 A.D.

DRUSUS SENIOR, brother of Tiberius, born 38 B.C., died 9 A.D.

ANTONIA, wife of Drusus senior, born 38 B.C., poisoned 38 A.D.

DRUSUS JUNIOR, son of Tiberius, born 13 B.C., poisoned 23 A.D.

LIVIA, or LIVILLA, daughter of Drusus senior and Antonia, and wife of Drusus junior, starved 32 A.D.

JULIA, daughter of Drusus junior and Livia, married to Nero, son of Germanicus; afterwards to Rubellius Blandus.

GERMANICUS, son of Drusus senior, born 15 B.C., Cæsar 4 A.D., poisoned 19 A.D.

AGRIPPINA SENIOR, daughter of M. Agrippa and of Julia, daughter of Augustus; wife of Germanicus, born 15 B.C., starved 33 A.D.

NERO and DRUSUS, sons of Germanicus and Agrippina. Nero born 7 A.D., starved 31 A.D.; Drusus born 8 A.D., died of hunger 33 A.D.

CAIUS CÆSAR CALIGULA,
Son of Germanicus and Agrippina, born 12 A.D., emperor 37 A.D., killed 41 A.D.

CLAUDIA, first wife of Caligula, married 33 A.D., died 36 A.D.

ORESTILLA, consort of Cn. Piso, second wife of Caligula.

LOLLIA PAULINA, espoused and shortly after repudiated by Caligula, 38 A.D.

CÆSONIA, fourth wife of Caligula, married 39 A.D., killed 41 A.D.

DRUSILLA, daughter of Cæsonia, killed 41 A.D.

DRUSILLA, sister of Caligula, born 17 A.D., died 38 A.D.

JULIA LIVILLA, sister of Caligula, youngest daughter of Germanicus and Agrippina, married to M. Vinicius, born 18 A.D., killed 41 A.D.

TIB. CLAUDIUS DRUSUS NERO GERMANICUS,
Son of Drusus senior (brother of Tiberius) and Antonia, born 10 B.C., emperor 41 A.D., poisoned 54 A.D.

PLAUTIA URGULANILLA, first wife of Claudius.

AELIA PETINA, second wife of Claudius.

VALERIA MESSALINA, third wife of Claudius, killed 48 A.D.

AGRIPPINA JUNIOR, daughter of Germanicus and Agrippina, was married first to Cn. Domitius Ahenobarbus 28 A.D., by whom she had a son, afterwards the Emperor Nero; next to Crispus Passienus; and thirdly to the Emperor Claudius (44 A.D.), although she was his niece. Murdered 59 A.D.

DRUSUS, son of Tiberius and Plautia Urgulanilla, died in infancy.

CLAUDIA, daughter of Tiberius and Plautia Urgulanilla, killed 63 A.D.

ANTONIA, daughter of Claudius and Ælia Petina.

BRITANNICUS, son of Claudius and Messalina, born 42 A.D., poisoned 55 A.D.

NERO CLAUDIUS CÆSAR DRUSUS GERMANICUS,
Son of Cn. Domitius Ahenobarbus and Agrippina, son-in-law of Claudius, born 37 A.D., Cæsar 50 A.D., emperor 54 A.D., killed himself 68 A.D.

OCTAVIA, first wife of Nero, daughter of the Emperor Claudius and Messalina, married to Nero 53 A.D., killed herself 62 A.D.

POPPÆA SABINA, second wife of Nero, died 66 A.D.

STATILIA MESSALINA, third wife of Nero, married 66 A.D.

CLAUDIA, daughter of Nero and Poppæa, born 64 A.D., died same year.

SER. SULPICIUS GALBA,
Born 3 B.C., emperor 68 A.D., killed 69 A.D.

M. SALVIUS OTHO,
Born 32 A.D., emperor 68 A.D., killed same year.

A. VITELLIUS,
  Born 15 A.D., emperor 69 A.D.,
  put to death same year.
  L. VITELLIUS, father of the emperor,
  died 49 A.D.
  L. VITELLIUS, son of the preceding,
  and brother of the emperor.

T. FLAVIUS SABINUS VESPA-
SIANUS,
  Born 9 A.D., emperor 69 A.D.,
  died 79 A.D.
  FLAVIA DOMITILLA, wife of Vespa-
  sian.
  DOMITILLA, daughter of Vespasian
  and Flavia Domitilla.

TITUS FLAVIUS SABINUS VES-
PASIANUS,
  Son of Vespasian and Flavia
  Domitilla, born 41 A.D., Cæsar 69,
  emperor with his father 71, sole
  emperor 79, died 81 A.D.
  ARRICIDIA, first wife of Titus.
  MARCIA FURNILLA, second wife of
  Titus.
  JULIA, daughter of Titus and Fur-
  nilla, married Flavius Sabinus,
  nephew of Vespasian.

T. FLAVIUS DOMITIANUS AU-
GUSTUS,
  Son of Vespasian and Flavia
  Domitilla, born 51 A.D., Cæsar 69,
  emperor 81 A.D., assassinated 96
  A.D.
  DOMITIA, wife of Domitian, died
  110 A.D.
  ANONYMUS, son of Domitian and
  Domitia.

M. COCCEIUS NERVA,
  Born 32 A.D., emperor 96 A.D.,
  died 98 A.D.

M. ULPIUS TRAJANUS,
  Born 53, associated in the empire
  with Nerva 97 A.D., sole emperor
  98, died 117 A.D.

POMPEIA PLOTINA, wife of the Em-
  peror Trajan, died 120 A.D.
  TRAJANUS PATER, father of the
  Emperor Trajan, died 100 A.D.
  MARCIANA, sister of Trajan, died
  144 A.D.
  MATIDIA, daughter of Marciana.

P. ÆLIUS HADRIANUS,
  Son-in-law of Matidia, Trajan's
  niece, born 76 A.D., adopted by
  Trajan 117, emperor same year,
  died 138 A.D.
  JULIA SABINA, wife of Hadrian,
  grandniece of Trajan, being
  daughter of Matidia, who was
  daughter of Marciana, Trajan's
  sister; killed herself 137 A.D.
  PAULINA, sister of Hadrian, married
  to Servianus.

T. ÆLIUS HADRIANUS ANTO-
NINUS PIUS,
  Born 86 A.D., adopted by Ha-
  drian 138 A.D., emperor same
  year, died 161 A.D.
  ANNIA GALERIA-FAUSTINA senior,
  wife of Antoninus Pius, born 105
  A.D., died 141 A.D.
  GALERIUS ANTONINUS, son of Anto-
  ninus and Faustina.

M. AURELIUS ANTONINUS,
  Son-in-law of Antoninus Pius,
  and son of Hadrian's sister Paulina, born 121 A.D., adopted by
  Antoninus 138, emperor 161, died
  180 A.D.
  ANNIA-FAUSTINA JUNIOR, wife of
  M. Aurelius, daughter of Antoninus Pius and the elder Faustina, died 175 A.D.
  ANNIUS VERUS, youngest son of Marcus Aurelius and Faustina, born
  169 A.D., Cæsar 166, died 170
  A.D.

LUCIUS AURELIUS VERUS,
  Son of L. Ceionius Commodus,
  who had been adopted by Ha-

drian in 136. On the death
of his father in 138, he was
adopted, along with M. Aurelius,
by M. Antoninus; associated in
the empire by M. Aurelius 151,
died 169 A.D.

ANNIA LUCILLA, daughter of M.
Aurelius and the younger Faustina, and wife of Lucius Verus,
banished to Capreæ 183 A.D.

L. AURELIUS COMMODUS,
Elder son of Marcus Aurelius
and Faustina the younger, born
161 A.D., Cæsar 166, emperor
176, sole emperor 180, strangled
192 A.D.

CRISPINA, wife of Commodus, died
183 A.D.

HELVIUS PERTINAX,
Born 126 A.D., emperor 192,
assassinated after a reign of 87
days.

TITIANA, wife of Pertinax.

M. DIDIUS SALVIUS JULIANUS,
Born 133 A.D., emperor 198, put
to death after a reign of 66
days.

MANLIA SCANTILLA, wife of Didius
Julianus.

DIDIA CLARA, daughter of Didius
Julianus and Scantilla.

C. PESCENNIUS NIGER,
Saluted emperor by the legions
in the East 193 A.D., killed 194
A.D.

CLODIUS ALBINUS,
Named Cæsar by Septimius Severus 193 A.D., took title of
emperor 196, defeated and killed
by Septimius Severus 197 A.D.

L. SEPTIMIUS SEVERUS,
Born 146 A.D., emperor 193,
master of the whole empire 197,
died 211 A.D.

JULIA DOMNA, wife of Septimius

Severus, starved herself 217
A.D.

MARCUS AURELIUS ANTONI-
NUS CARACALLA,
Son of Septimius Severus and
Julia, born 188 A.D., Cæsar 196,
Augustus 198, emperor with his
brother Geta 211, sole emperor
212, assassinated 217.

FULVIA PLAUTILLA, wife of Caracalla, put to death 212.

SEPTIMIUS GETA,
Second son of Septimius Severus
and Julia Domna, born 189 A.D.,
Cæsar 198, emperor with his
brother Caracalla 211, assassinated by him 212 A.D.

MACRINUS,
Born 164, emperor 217, killed
218 A.D.

DIADUMENIANUS, son of Macrinus,
Cæsar 217, killed 218.

MARCUS AURELIUS ANTONI-
NUS—ELAGABALUS,
(Priest of Baal, the Sun-god),
son of Varius Marcellus and
Julia Sœmias, born 205 A.D.,
emperor 218, put to death 222
A.D.

JULIA CORNELIA PAULA, first wife
of Elagabalus, divorced 200 A.D.

AQUILIA SEVERA, second wife of
Elagabalus.

ANNIA FAUSTINA, third wife of
Elagabalus.

JULIA SŒMIAS, mother of Elagabalus, killed 222 A.D.

JULIA MÆSA, sister-in-law of Septimius Severus, aunt of Caracalla,
and grandmother of Elagabalus
and A. Severus, died 223 A.D.

M. AURELIUS ALEXANDER
SEVERUS,
Son of Gessius Marcianus and
Julia Mamæa, was first cousin of
Elagabalus, born 205, adopted

by Elagabalus with the name of
Cæsar 221, emperor 222, assassinated 235 A.D.

MEMMIA, second wife of Alexander
Severus.

BARBIA ORBIANA, third wife of
Alexander Severus.

JULIA MAMÆA, daughter of Julia
Mœsa, and mother of Alexander
Severus, put to death 235 A.D.

URANIUS ANTONINUS, emperor in
Asia during the reign of Alexander Severus.

MAXIMINUS I.,
Born 173, emperor 235, assassinated 238 A.D.

PAULINA, wife of Maximinus.

MAXIMUS, son of Maximinus, Cæsar
235, killed 238 A.D.

JULIA FADILLA, wife of Maximus.

TITUS QUARTINUS, emperor in Germany during the reign of Maximinus.

M. ANTONIUS GORDIANUS
AFRICANUS I., PATER,
Son of Metius Marullus and
Ulpia Gordiana, born 158 A.D.
emperor in Africa 238 A.D., puts
an end to his life after reigning
40 days.

FABIA ORESTILLA, wife of Gordianus pater.

GORDIANUS AFRICANUS II.,
FILIUS,
Son of Gordianus Af. I. and
Fabia Orestilla, born 192 A.D.,
emperor with his father 238,
killed 40 days afterwards.

D. CÆLIUS BALBINUS,
Born 178, emperor with Pupienus 238, massacred after a reign
of three months.

M. CLODIUS PUPIENUS MAXI-
MUS,
Born 161 A.D., emperor with

Balbinus 238 A.D., massacred
about three months afterwards.

GORDIANUS PIUS III.,
Grandson of Gordianus the elder,
born 222, Cæsar 238, emperor
same year, assassinated 244 A.D.

TRANQUILLINA, wife of Gordian III.

M. JULIUS PHILIPPUS, I.,
Born 204 A.D., emperor 244,
killed 249 A.D.

MARCIA OTACILIA SEVERA, wife of
Philip the elder.

M. JULIUS PHILIPPUS II.,
Son of Philip the elder, born
237, Cæsar 244, Augustus 247,
killed 249 A.D.

MARINUS, emperor in Mœsia and
Pannonia, 249 A.D.

JOTAPIANUS, emperor in Syria 248
A.D.

PACATIANUS } only known on coins.
SPONSIANUS }

C. MESSIUS QUINTUS TRAJA-
NUS DECIUS,
Born 201 A.D., emperor 249,
drowned in a bog 251.

ETRUSCILLA, wife of Decius.

HERENNIUS ETRUSCUS, son of Decius, Cæsar 249, Augustus 251,
killed same year.

HOSTILIANUS, son of Decius, Cæsar
249, emperor with Gallus 251,
died same year.

C. VIBIUS TREBONIANUS GAL-
LUS,
Emperor 251, put to death 251
A.D.

VOLUSIANUS, son of Gallus, Cæsar
251, emperor 252, killed 251.

ÆMILIUS ÆMILIANUS, born 208 A.D.,
emperor in Mœsia 253, killed
254.

CORNELIA SUPERA, wife of Æmilianus.

P. LICINIUS VALERIANUS, SENIOR, born 190, emperor 253, taken prisoner by the Persians 260, died 261.

MARINIANA, second wife of Valerian.

P. LICINIUS VALERIANUS EGNATIUS GALLIENUS, Son of Valerian by his first wife, emperor 253, assassinated 268.

SALONINA, wife of Gallienus.

SALONINUS, son of Gallienus, born 242 A.D., cæsar 253, put to death 259 A.D.

QUINTUS JULIUS GALLIENUS, youngest son of Gallienus.

VALERIANUS JUNIOR, son of Valerian and Mariniana, killed 268 A.D.

LICINIA GALLIENA, aunt of Gallienus.

POSTUMUS PATER, emperor in Gaul 258, killed 267.

JULIA DONATA, wife of Postumus.

POSTUMUS FILIUS, Augustus in Gaul 258, killed 267.

LAELIANUS.

LOLLIANUS.

QUINTUS VALENS AELIANUS.

VICTORINUS PATER, associated in the empire of Gaul by Postumus 265, killed 267.

VICTORINUS FILIUS, Cæsar in Gaul 267.

VICTORINA, mother of Victorinus senior.

MARIUS, emperor in Gaul 267, killed after a reign of three days.

TETRICUS PATER, emperor in Gaul 267, defeated by Aurelian 274 A.D.

TETRICUS FILIUS, son of the above, Cæsar in Gaul 267.

CYRIADES, emperor in Asia 257, killed 258.

MACRIANUS PATER, emperor in the East 261, killed by his soldiers 262.

MACRIANUS FILIUS, son of Macrianus pater.

QUIETUS, brother of Macrianus filius.

BALISTA, emperor in Syria 262, killed 264.

INGENUUS, emperor in Mœsia and Pannonia 262.

REGALIANUS, emperor in Mœsia 261, killed 263.

DRYANTILLA, wife of Regalianus.

VALENS, emperor in Achaia 261.

PISO FRUGI, emperor in Thessalia 261.

ALEXANDER ÆMILIANUS, emperor in Egypt 262.

SATURNINUS I., emperor 263.

TREBELLIANUS, emperor in Isauria 264.

CELSUS, emperor of Carthage 265.

AUREOLUS, emperor in Illyria and Rhætia 267, killed 268.

SULPICIUS ANTONINUS, emperor in Syria 267.

M. AURELIUS CLAUDIUS II. GOTHICUS,
Born 214 A.D., emperor 268, died 270.

CENSORINUS, emperor at Boulogne 270.

QUINTILLUS, brother of Claudius Gothicus, emperor at Aquileia 270.

AURELIANUS,
Born 207 A.D., emperor 270, assassinated 275.

SEVERINA, wife of Aurelian.

SEPTIMIUS ODENATHUS, king of Palmyra 261, associated in the empire by Gallienus 264, assassinated 266.

Zenobia, last wife of Odenathus, queen of Palmyra 261.

Herodes, son of Odenathus by his first wife, Augustus 264, killed 267.

Timolaus, son of Odenathus and Zenobia, Augustus 260, taken prisoner by Aurelian 273.

Vabalathus Athenodorus, son of Zenobia, emperor in Syria 266, taken prisoner by Aurelian 273.

Maeonius, emperor 267.

Firmus, emperor in Egypt 273.

M. CLAUDIUS TACITUS,
Emperor 275, assassinated 276 A.D.

M. ANNIUS FLORIANUS,
Brother of the emperor Tacitus, born 232, emperor 276, killed same year.

M. AURELIUS PROBUS,
Born 232, emperor 276, murdered 282 A.D.

Bonosus, emperor of Gaul 280.

Saturninus, emperor of Egypt and Palestine 280.

Proculus, emperor of Cologne 280.

M. AURELIUS CARUS,
Born 230 A.D., emperor 282, killed by lightning 283.

M. AURELIUS CARINUS,
Eldest son of Carus, born 249 A.D., Cæsar 282, emperor 283, killed 284 A.D.

Magnia Urbica, wife of Carinus.

M. AURELIUS NUMERIANUS,
Youngest son of Carus, born 254 A.D., Cæsar 282, Augustus 283, died 284 A.D.

Nigrinianus, son of Carus.

Marcus Aurelianus Julianus, emperor in Pannonia 284, killed 285.

VALERIUS DIOCLETIANUS,
Born 245, emperor 284, adopted Galerius 292, abdicated 305, died 313 A.D.

Prisca, wife of Diocletian, executed by order of Licinius 313 A.D.

M. AURELIUS VALERIUS MAXIMIANUS I.,
Styled Herculius and Jovius, associated in the empire with Diocletian 286, abdicated 305, retook the empire 306, abdicated again 308, emperor a second time 309, strangled himself 310 A.D.

Eutropia, wife of Maximian.

Amandus, emperor in Gaul 285, killed 287.

Ælianus, emperor in Gaul 285, killed 287.

Carausius, emperor in Britain 287, assassinated 289 A.D.

Allectus, emperor in Britain 293, killed 296 A.D.

Achilleus, emperor in Egypt 292.

Domitius Domitianus, emperor in Egypt 305.

CONSTANTIUS I. CHLORUS,
Born 250, Cæsar 292, emperor 305, died 306.

Helena, first wife of Constantius Chlorus, died 328.

Theodora, second wife of Constantius Chlorus.

GALERIUS VALERIUS MAXIMIANUS,
Adopted and named Cæsar by Diocletian in 292, Augustus and emperor 305, died 311.

Galeria Valeria, daughter of Diocletian and Prisca, and second wife of Galerius Maximianus, executed by order of Licinius 315 A.D.

Flavius Valerius Severus, named Cæsar by Maximianus I. 305,

Augustus and emperor 306, put to death 307.

GALERIUS VALERIUS MAXIMIANUS II., DAZA, son of Galerius, named Cæsar by Diocletian 305, son of the Augusti 307, emperor 308, poisoned himself 313 A.D.

CANDIDIANUS, natural son of Galerius Maximianus, put to death by Licinius 313.

M. AURELIUS VALERIUS MAXENTIUS, son of Maximianus I. and Eutropia, born 282, emperor of Rome 306, drowned in the Tiber 312 A.D.

ROMULUS, son of Maxentius, born 306, Cæsar 307, died 309.

ALEXANDER, emperor of Carthage 306, put to death 311 A.D.

LICINIUS SENIOR, son-in-law of Constantius Chlorus, born 263, associated in the empire with Galerius Maximianus 307, put to death by his brother-in-law Constantine 323.

CONSTANTIA, daughter of Constantius Chlorus, wife of the elder Licinius, died 330 A.D.

LICINIUS JUNIOR, son of the elder Licinius, born 315, named Cæsar 317, put to death 320.

AURELIUS VALERIUS VALENS, named Cæsar by Licinius 314.

MARTINIANUS, Cæsar and Augustus at Byzantium by Licinius 323.

EUTROPIA, daughter of Constantius I. and sister of Constantine.

JULIUS CONSTANTIUS, son of Constantius Chlorus, and brother of Constantine.

GALLA, first wife of J. Constantius.

BASILINA, second wife of J. Constantius.

CONSTANTINUS I. MAGNUS,
Son of Constantius Chlorus and Helena, born 274, named Cæsar

and Augustus 306, converted to the Christian religion 311, sole emperor 311, changed the seat of government to Byzantium, which he called Constantinople, 336, died 337 A.D.

MINERVINA, first wife of Constantine.

FAUSTA, second wife of Constantine, daughter of Maximian; smothered by her husband's order 326 A.D.

FLAVIUS JULIUS CRISPUS, son of Constantine and Minervina, born 300, Cæsar 317, put to death by order of his father 326.

HELENA, wife of Crispus.

DALMATIUS, brother of Constantine, Cæsar 335, killed 337 A.D.

HANNIBALIANUS, brother of Constantine and of Dalmatius, died 337 A.D.

CONSTANTINUS II.,
Eldest son of Constantine and Fausta, born 316, Cæsar 317; emperor and Augustus 337, killed in 340 A.D.

CONSTANS I.,
Youngest son of Constantine and Fausta, born 320 A.D., Cæsar 333, emperor of the East 340, assassinated 350 A.D.

SATURNINUS, emperor in the reign of Constans.

CONSTANTIUS II.,
Second son of Constantine and Fausta, born 317, Cæsar 323, Augustus 337, master of all the empire 350, died 361 A.D.

EUSEBIA, wife of Constantius, married 352.

FAUSTINA, wife of Constantius; favours the cause of Procopius 365 A.D.

NEPOTIANUS, son of Eutropia, sister of Constantine, emperor at Rome

350, killed after a reign of 28
days.

VETRANIO, emperor in Pannonia
350, died 350.

NONIUS.

FLAVIUS POPILIUS MAGNENTIUS,
born 303, emperor at Autun
350, killed himself 353 A.D.

DECENTIUS, brother of Magnentius,
Cæsar, 351.

DESIDERIUS, brother of Magnentius,
Cæsar, 351.

CONSTANTIUS GALLUS,
Son of Julius Constantius and
Gallus, nephew of Constantine,
born 325, Cæsar 351, executed
354.

CONSTANTINA, wife first of Hannibalianus, and secondly of Constantius Gallus, died 354 A.D.

SYLVANUS, emperor at Cologne, 355
A.D.

FLAVIUS CLAUDIUS JULIANUS,
Surnamed the Apostate, son of
Julius Constantius, brother of
Constantine, by his second wife
(Basilina), and nephew of Con-
stantine, born 331, Cæsar 355, em-
peror at Paris 360, sole emperor
361, killed in battle against the
Persians 363 A.D.

HELENA, daughter of Constantine
and wife of Julian, died 360 A.D.

FLAVIUS CLAUDIUS JOVIANUS,
Born 331, emperor 363, died
364 A.D.

VALENTINIANUS I.,
Son of Gratianus, born 321, emperor 364, died 375.

VALERIA SEVERA, first wife of Valentinian I.

JUSTINA, second wife of Valentinian, died 387.

FLAVIUS VALENS,
Brother of Valentinian, born 328,

associated in the empire and
Augustus 364, burnt alive 378.

DOMINICA, wife of Valens.

PROCOPIUS, born 334, emperor at
Constantinople 365, put to
death by order of Valens 366
A.D.

GRATIANUS,
Son of Valentinian I. and Severa,
born 359, Augustus at Amiens
367, emperor 375, slain 383 A.D.

CONSTANTIA, daughter of Constantine and Faustina, grand-daugh-
ter of Constantine, and wife of
Gratian, died 383 A.D.

VALENTINIANUS II.,
Son of Valentinian I. and Justina, born 371, Augustus 375,
emperor of the Western Empire
383, assassinated 392 A.D.

THEODOSIUS MAGNUS I.,
Born 316, Augustus and associated in the empire by Gratian
379, entered Rome in triumph
389, died 395 A.D.

FLACCILLA, first wife of Theodosius,
died 388.

GALLA, daughter of the Emperor
Valentinian I., and second wife
of Theodosius.

MAGNUS CLEMENS MAXIMUS, Augustus in Britain 383, acknowledged emperor in Britain and
Gaul 387, put to death 388.

FLAVIUS VICTOR MAXIMUS, son of
Magnus Maximus, Augustus 383,
put to death 388.

EUGENIUS, a rhetorician, proclaimed
emperor by Arbogastes 392, defeated and slain by Theodosius
394.

ARCADIUS, elder son of Theodosius,
born 377, Augustus 383, emperor of the East 395, died 408
A.D.

EUDOXIA, wife of Arcadius, died
404.

FLAVIUS HONORIUS,
  Youngest son of Theodosius and
  Flacilla, born 384, Augustus
  393, emperor of the West 395,
  died 423.

CONSTANTINUS III., Augustus in
  England and Gaul 407, put to
  death 411 A.D.

CONSTANS, son of Constantinus III.,
  Augustus in Gaul 408, assassinated 411 A.D.

CONSTANTIUS III.,
  Augustus and associated in the
  empire of the West 421 A.D.,
  died same year.

GALLA PLACIDIA, daughter of
  Theodosius and Galla, sister of
  Honorius, widow of Ataulf, king
  of the Goths, 414, wife of Constantius 417, died in 423.

MAXIMUS, emperor in Spain 409,
  abdicated 411.

JOVINUS, emperor of Mayence 411,
  beheaded 413.

SEBASTIANUS, brother of Jovinus,
  associated in the sovereign power
  by his brother 412, beheaded
  413 A.D.

PRIEST ATTALUS, made emperor
  by Alaric at Rome 409, deprived
  of that title, reassumed it in
  Gaul 410, died in the island of
  Lipari.

THEODOSIUS II., son of Arcadius
  born 401, Augustus 402, emperor of the East 418, died 450
  A.D.

EUDOCIA (ATHENAIS, daughter of
  Leontius), wife of Theodosius II.,
  died 460.

JOHANNES, born 383, emperor at
  Rome 423, died 425.

VALENTINIANUS III.,
  Son of Constantius III. and Galla
  Placidia, born at Rome 419, em-
  peror 425, slain by Petronius
  Maximus 455 A.D.

LICINIA EUDOXIA, daughter of

Theodosius II. and Eudoria,
  wife of Valentinian III., married
  to the Emperor Maximus 455
  A.D.

HONORIA, daughter of Constantius III. and Galla Placidia, and
  sister of Valentinian III., born
  417, Augusta 433, died 454.

EUDOXIA, eldest daughter of Valentinian III. and Eudoxia, married to Hunneric, son of Genseric
  king of the Vandals.

PETRONIUS MAXIMUS,
  Born 395, emperor at Rome 455,
  slain after a reign of three months.

MARCIANUS, a Roman senator, born
  391, married the Empress Pulcheria and acknowledged emperor of the East 450, died 457.

PULCHERIA, sister of Theodosius II.,
  born 399, proclaimed empress
  on the death of Theodosius,
  married the Senator Marcian
  450, died 453 A.D.

AVITUS, emperor 455, deposed 456.

  LEO I., emperor of the East 457,
  died 474 A.D.

  VERINA, wife of Leo I., died 484
  A.D.

MAJORIANUS, emperor 457, compelled to abdicate 461, died five
  days after.

LIBIUS SEVERUS emperor 461, died
  465.

ANTHEMIUS, son of Procopius, emperor 467, slain by his son-in-
  law Ricimer 472.

EUPHEMIA, daughter of the Emperor Marcian, and wife of Anthemius.

OLYBRIUS, a Roman senator, emperor
  of the West 472, died same year.

  PLACIDIA, youngest daughter of
  Valentinian III. and Eudoxia,
  and wife of Olybrius.

GLYCERIUS, Augustus at Ravenna, 473, permitted to exchange the Roman sceptre for bishopric of Salona 474, died 480.

LEO II., born 495, emperor of the East 474.

ZENO, son-in-law of Leo I., and father of Leo II., born 426, associated in the Eastern empire by his son, Leo II., 474, sole emperor same year, deposed 476, re-established 477, died 491.

BASILISCUS, brother of Verina, emperor of the East 476, dethroned by Zeno 477.

AELIA ZENONIS, wife of Basiliscus.

MARCUS, son of Basiliscus.

ANASTASIUS, emperor 491.

ARIADNE, daughter of Verina, and wife of Anastasius.

JULIUS NEPOS.
Married to a niece of the Empress Verina, emperor of the West 474, retires to Dalmatia 475, assassinated by Glycerius 480.

ROMULUS AUGUSTULUS,
Son of the patrician Orestes, emperor of the West 475, dethroned by Odoacer, king of the Heruli, 476, extinction of the Western empire.

ODOACER assumes the title of king of Italy.

GLOSSARY OF TERMS USED IN GREEK AND ROMAN ARCHITECTURE.

ABACUS. The flat and quadrangular stone which constitutes the highest member of a column, being interposed between the capital and the architrave.

ACROTERIA. Bases or low pedestals resting on the angles and vertex of a pediment, and intended for the reception of statues, or their ornaments.

ADITUS. The approach or entrance to a building.

ADYTUM. The chamber in a temple to which none but priests had access.

ÆTOMA. The tympanum of a pediment, so called from being decorated with the figure of an eagle.

AMBITUS. A space which surrounded a tomb.

AMPHIPROSTYLE. Having a portico at both extremities.

ANTÆ. Pilasters terminating the side walls of a temple.

ANTIFIXÆ. Ornaments of lions' heads, and other heads, below the eaves of the temple, through the perforation in which the water from the roof was carried off.

APODYTERIUM. The apartment at the entrance of the baths, where a person took off his dress.

APOTHECA. A storehouse or cellar, for oil or wine.

APSIS. The semicircular and vaulted end of a basilica.

ARÆOSTYLE. An intercolumniation of four or more diameters.

ARCHITRAVE. The lowest horizontal member of the entablature, and which rests immediately on the columns.

ARCHIVOLT. A collection of mouldings on the face of an arch, resting on the imposts.

ARENA. The central space in a Roman amphitheatre.

ARENATUM. A plaster used on walls, formed of sand and lime.

ASTRAGAL. A narrow moulding, the profile of which is semicircular. It is also a moulding composed of beads and berries.

ATRIUM. An open court surrounded by porticos.

ATTIC-BASE. The base of a column consisting of an upper and lower torus, a Scotia, and fillets between them.

BASE. A general term for the lowest member of any construction. The base of a column is the ornamental portion on which the shaft is placed.

BASILICA. A court of justice, with a semicircular vaulted end, apsis.

BELL. That portion of a column around which the foliage and volutes are arranged.

CALDARIUM. A room for hot baths.

CANEPHORÆ. Figures of females, bearing a basket on their heads.

CAPITAL. The head or upper part of a column or pilaster.

CARYATID. A female figure supporting an entablature.

CASTELLUM AQUÆ. A reservoir in the city, which formed the head of water, received by the aqueduct, and thence conducted through leaden pipes to the several parts of the city.

CAULICOLÆ. The twisted stalks in a Corinthian capital.

CAVÆDIUM. An open court within a house.

CAVEA. The place for spectators in a theatre, so called as it was often a real excavation from the side of a hill.

CAVEA. Subterranean cells in amphitheatres where wild beasts were confined.

CAVETTO. A hollowed moulding, whose profile is the quadrant of a circle.

CELLA (ναος). The central chamber of a temple, supposed to be the peculiar habitation of the deity, whose statue it usually contained.

CENOTAPH. A monument erected to the memory of a person buried in another place.

CEROMA. An apartment in the baths, where the bathers were anointed with oil thickened by wax.

CHALCIDICUM. A chamber attached to a basilica, for the convenience of the judges and lawyers.

CHORAGIC MONUMENT. A monument erected in honour of the choragus who gained a prize at the festivals of Bacchus.

CIPPUS. A small low column, frequently bearing an inscription, generally for sepulchral purposes.

CLOACÆ. The common sewers at Rome.

CÆNACULUM. A supper room.

COLONNADE. A range of columns.

COLUMN. A cylindrical pillar, which serves either for support or ornament of a building.

COMITIUM. A building in the Roman forum, where assemblies of the people were held.

COMPLUVIUM. An area in the centre of a Roman house, for the purpose of receiving the water from the roof.

CONCAMERATA SUDATIO. The vapour bath in Roman Thermæ.

CONISTERIUM. A room in a gymnasium, where the wrestlers, having been anointed with oil, were sprinkled over with dust.

CORNICE. The crowning projection of the entablature.

COROMA. A broad flat member, below the cymatium, in a cornice.

CRYPTO PORTICUS. A subterranean or dark gallery in a Roman villa, used as a cool sitting room.

CUBICULUM. A bedchamber.

CUNEUS. That part of the Roman theatre where the spectators sat, so called from its wedge-like shape.

CURIA. A Roman council house.

CYMA. A moulding, so called from its contour resembling that of a wave, being hollow in its upper part, and swelling below. This is distinguished as the cyma recta; the cyma reversa is where the upper part swells, whilst the lower is hollow.

CYMATIUM. The upper moulding of a cornice, of an undulating form.

CYZICENUM. A large hall decorated with sculpture.

DADO. The die, or that part in the middle of the pedestal of a column between its base and cornice.

DECASTYLE. A temple with ten columns in front.

DIASTYLE. An intercolumniation of three diameters.

DIATONI (διάτονοι). Bond stones of a single piece crossing the wall, from one face to the other.

DIAZOMA. Landings, or resting places, encircling the amphitheatre at different heights.

DICASTERICUM. A tribunal, or hall of justice.

DICTYOTHETON. Masonry worked in courses like the meshes of a net.

DIGLYPH. A projecting face, with two panels or channels sunk thereon.

DIPTERAL. A temple surrounded by a double range of columns.

DISPLUVIATUM. An open court, its roof so inclined as to throw the water off to the outside of the house, instead of carrying it into the impluvium.

ECHEA. Vessels of bronze, in the form of a bell, placed under the seats of spectators in a theatre, to give resonance to the voices of the actors. Earthenware jars are often found in the walls of Roman buildings, and have been supposed to be for similar purposes. They were for the purpose of lightening the building, and it is supposed used to expedite the work. They are generally found in Roman buildings of a later date, in the walls of a circus, or such buildings where no conveyance of sound was required. Examples may be seen at the circus of Caracalla, at Rome.

ECHINUS. The ovolo or quarter round; it is usually carved with the egg and tongue moulding.

ELÆOTHESIUM. An apartment in the baths, where the bathers, after leaving the bath, anointed themselves.

EMPLECTON. A term employed in masonry by Vitruvius, in which the front stones were wrought, and the interior left rough and filled in with stones of various sizes.

ENCARPUS. Festoon on a frieze.

ENTABLATURE. The horizontal portion of a temple, supported on the columns, and including the architrave, frieze, and cornice.

ENTASIS. The swelling of the shaft of a column.

EPHEBEIUM. A building for the exercise and wrestling of the youth.

EPISCENIUM. The upper order of the scene in a theatre.

EPISTYLIUM. The same as architrave.

ERGASTULUM. A prison house for slaves.

EUSTYLE. An intercolumniation of two diameters and a half.

EXEDRA. A recess, or small room, in the Thermæ and other buildings, appropriated for conversation.

FASCIA. A band or broad fillet on an architrave.

FASTIGIUM. See pediment.

FLUTING. The vertical channelling of the shafts of the columns.

FORUM. A public place in Rome, and the leading Italian towns, where the causes were tried, public business transacted, and political speeches made by the great orators of the state ; also a market place.

FRET. An ornament consisting of one or more small fillets, meeting in vertical and horizonal directions.

FRIEZE. The central course of the entablature between the cornice and the architrave.

FRIGIDARIUM. The apartment in which the cold bath was placed.

GRÆCOSTASIS. A wall or portico adjoining the Roman comitia, in which foreign ambassadors waited before entering the senate.

GUILLOCHE. An ornament composed of a series of bands twisting over each other.

GUTTÆ. Drops or ornaments, introduced under the triglyphs, in the Doric order.

GYMNASIUM. A building used for the exercise of athletic games.

GYNÆCEUM. A portion of a Greek house, set apart for females.

HECATOMPEDON. A term applied to the Parthenon, from the use of 100 feet in one of its leading dimensions, probably the breadth.

HELIOCAMINUS. A chamber in the Roman houses, which depended on the rays of the sun for warming it.

HELIX. A small volute under the abacus of the Corinthian capital.

HEMICYLE. A semicircular building, with an arched roof.

HEXASTYLE. A temple having six columns in front.

HIPPODROME. A place appropriated by the Greeks to equestrian exercises.

HYPÆTHRAL. A temple without a roof, and open to the sky, as the cella of the temple often was.

HYPERTHYRUM. The upper member or lintel of a doorway.

HYPOCAUSTUM. A vaulted apartment under the baths, which served to distribute the heat from the furnace.

HYPOGÆUM. A building below the level of the ground.

HYPOSCENIUM. The front wall of the theatre, facing the orchestra.

Hypotrachelium. The slenderest part of the shaft of a column, being that immediately below the neck of the capital.

Impluvium. The open portion of a court in a Roman house, into which the rainwater was carried.

Impost. The capital of a pier or pilaster which receives an arch.

Incertum. A style of masonry used in walls, consisting of very small rough rough stones, not laid in courses.

Intercolumniation. The space between two columns.

Isodomum. Masonry employed by the Greeks. It was executed in courses of equal heights.

Koilon. The Greek term for the cavea.

Laconicum. A kind of stove in the vapour bath which served to heat the room.

Lacunae, Lacunaria. Ornamental compartments in ceilings.

Laquear. Ornamental compartments with bands between them.

Lararium. The apartment in which the lares or household gods were kept.

Lysis. A plinth above the cornice of the podium of ancient temples, which surrounded the stylobate.

Mæander. An ornamental border, like the fret, on the different members of buildings.

Marmoratum. Plaster composed of lime and pounded marble, used in the last coat on ancient walls.

Mausoleum. A sepulchral building, the term derived from the celebrated one erected to the memory of Mausolus, king of Caria, by his wife Artemisia, about 353 B.C.

Metocha. A term used by Vitruvius, to denote the space or interval between the dentils of the Ionic, or triglyphs of the Doric order.

Metope. The square space or interval between the Doric triglyphs.

Minute. Sixtieth part of the lower diameter of a column.

Modillion. An ornament resembling a bracket in the Ionic, Corinthian and Composite orders.

Module. A certain measure, either a diameter, or semidiameter, by which the proportions of columns are regulated.

Mæniana. Divisions of seats in a Roman amphitheatre.

Monolith. A work consisting of a single stone.

Monopteral. A temple of a round form, without walls or cells, but only one range of columns.

Monotriglyph. The space of one triglyph and two metopes, between two Doric columns.

Mutule. A projecting ornament in the Doric cornice, corresponding to the modillion in the Ionic and Corinthian entablatures.

Naos. The central chamber of a temple.

Naumachia. A place where mock sea engagements were exhibited.

NECK, or NECKING. The space between the astragal of the shaft and the annulet of the capital.

NYMPHÆUM. An artificial grotto dedicated to the nymphs.

OCTASTYLE. A temple having eight columns in front.

ODEUM. A kind of theatre among the Greeks, wherein poets and musicians rehearsed their compositions.

ŒCUS. A hall or saloon, in a Roman house, used for extensive banquets.

OPISTHODOMUS. The chamber behind the cella, often used as a treasury.

ORCHESTRA. A level space in a theatre, set apart for the chorus.

OVA. Ornaments in the shape of an egg, on the echinus.

OVOLO. A moulding, the section of which is usually the quarter of a circle.

PALÆSTRA. A Grecian building, appropriated to wrestling and gymnastic exercises.

PARASCENIUM. Another name for the postscenium in the theatre.

PEDIMENT. The triangular termination of the roof of a temple, resting upon the entablature which surrounds the building, and enclosing the tympanum.

PENETRALE. The most sacred part of the temple.

PENETRALIA. Small chapels dedicated to the Penates, in the innermost part of Roman houses.

PERIBOLOS. Enclosure within a wall, surrounding a temple.

PERIDROMOS. The space between the columns of a temple and the walls enclosing the cells.

PERIPTERAL. A temple encompassed by columns.

PERISTYLE. A court which had a colonnade around it; also a range of columns within a court or temple.

PILASTER. A square engaged pillar, i.e. attached to a wall.

PISCINA. A reservoir in the Roman baths for practising swimming.

PLINTH. The low square step on which a column is placed.

PODIUM. A continued pedestal; a parapet surrounding the arena of an amphitheatre.

POLYSTYLE. Of many columns.

PORTICO. The covered space in front of a temple, supported by columns.

PORTICUS. The covered space behind a temple.

POSTSCENIUM. The back part of a theatre.

PRÆCINCTIO. The landing which separated and gave access to the ranges of seats in theatres.

PRODROMOS. The portico before the entrance to the cell of a temple.

PRONAOS. The part of a temple in front of the nave.

PROPYLÆUM. A vestibule before a building or temple.

PROSCENIUM. The stage in a Grecian theatre.

PROSTYLE. A temple with four columns in front.

PROTHYRUM. An entrance door.

PSEUDISODOMUM. A style of masonry in which the stones are arranged in regular courses of unequal heights.

PSEUDODIPTERAL. A temple with eight columns in front, and only one range round the cell.

PSEUDOPERIPTERAL. A temple with a range of columns in front, and the columns on the sides engaged in the wall.

PTERA. Colonnades which surrounded the cell of the temple.

PTEROMA. The space between the wall of the cell of a temple and the columns of the peristyle, called also ambulatio.

PULPITON. The stage in a Roman theatre.

PULVINAR. The emperor's seat in the circus.

PULVINARIA. Couches provided for the statues of the gods in the temple.

PUTEAL. The marginal stone of a well.

PYCNOSTYLE. An intercolumniation of a diameter and a half.

PYRAMID. A solid square massy edifice, constructed in the form of a pyramid.

PYRAMIDION. The small pyramid which terminates the top of an obelisk.

REGULA. A band below the tenia in the Doric architrave.

RETICULATUM. A style of masonry in which the stones were placed diagonally, so as to resemble network.

ROSTRUM. The platform in the Roman forum whence the orators addressed the people, so called from its basement being decorated with prows of ships.

ROTUNDA. A circular building.

RUDERATIO. Applied to a floor paved with pieces of bricks, tiles, stones, &c.

SACELLUM. A small enclosure without a roof, consecrated to a god, containing an altar, and sometimes a statue of a god.

SACRARIUM. A term applied to any place in which sacred things were deposited or kept, whether in a temple or a private house.

SCHOLA. The margin or platform surrounding a bath.

SCOTIA. The hollow moulding in the base of an Ionic column.

SCROLL. A spiral ornament.

SECOS. The secret chamber in a temple, to which none but the priests had access.

SOFFIT. A ceiling; the under side of arches, and other architectural members.

SPECUS. The conduit or covered channel, through which the water flowed in aqueducts.

SPHÆRISTERIUM. A building for the exercise of the ball.

SPINA. A low wall running down the centre of a circus, so called from its resemblance to the position of the dorsal bone in the human frame.

STADIUM. A place for foot races.

STEREOBATE. The same as stylobate.

STOA. A porch, used as a public walk.

STRIÆ. The fillets between the flutes of columns.

STRIGES. The channels of a fluted column.

STYLAGALMATIC. Supported by figure-columns.

STYLOBATE. The basis on which a colonnade is placed.

SUBPLINTH. A second or lower plinth placed under the principal one in columns and pedestals.

SUDATIO } A vapour bath.
SUDATORIUM }

SYSTYLE. An intercolumniation of two diameters.

TABLINUM. A hall or chamber at the further end of the atrium, in a Roman house, and separate from it by an aulæum or curtain. In summer it was used as a dining room.

TÆNIA. The fillet which separates the Doric frieze from the architrave.

TECTORIUM OPUS. The smooth finishing coat of plaster on a wall.

TELAMONES. Figures of men used in the same manner as Caryatides, sometimes called Atlantes.

TEMONES. Places in a temple where statues were placed.

TEPIDARIUM. The temperate hall in a Roman bath.

TESTUDO. An arched roof.

TETRASTYLE. A temple with four columns in front.

THERMÆ. A term applied to Roman buildings for public baths, but strictly meaning only warm baths.

TORUS. A large semicircular moulding, used in the bases of columns.

TRICLINIUM. A Roman dining room, in which were three couches, lectus imus, lectus medius, lectus summus, on which the guests reclined at dinner. The table was placed in the centre, and the fourth side was left open for the servants to place on or remove the dishes.

TRIGLYPH. A tablet fluted with upright grooves, in the Doric frieze.

TRIPOD. A table or seat with three legs.

TROCHILUS. An annular moulding whose section is concave.

TYMPANUM. The triangular space within the cornices of a pediment.

VELARIUM. The awning covering a theatre or an amphitheatre.

VESTIBULUM. The entrance to a Roman house.

VISORIUM. The audience part of an amphitheatre.

VOLUTE. A spiral scroll, which forms the principal feature of the Ionic and Composite capitals.

VOMITORIA. Passages facilitating entrance to and egress from a theatre or amphitheatre.

XENODOCHIUM. A building for the reception of strangers.

XYSTUS. A spacious portico in which athletes exercised themselves during winter; also the garden at the further end of a Roman house.

ZIGZAG. The most primitive style of ornament, and generally indicative of a very early stage in art.

ZOPHORUS. The frieze of an entablature.

ZOTHECA. A small room or alcove, which might be added to, or separated from, the room to which it adjoined.

TABLE OF SOME OF THE PRINCIPAL GREEK AND ROMAN TEMPLES.

Athens	Theseion	Doric	Hexastyle, peripteral, with 13 intercolumns on sides, 45 feet by 108 feet.
"	Parthenon	Doric	Octastyle, peripteral, hyperthral, 100 feet by 226 feet; Ictinus and Callicrates, architects.
"	Propylæa	Doric	Hexastyle on both fronts, with wings of a smaller order, at right angles to west front. Mnesicles, architect, 437-432 B.C.
"	Erechtheion	Ionic	Hexastyle, prostyle at east end, with a tetrastyle, Aprostyle on north side.
"	Pandrosos	Ionic	Tetrastyle, amphiprostyle. A well-known example, though no longer extant, having been destroyed by the Turks since Stuart's time.
"	Nike Apteros	Ionic	Tetrastyle, amphiprostyle. Recently explored, and since rebuilt.
"	Jupiter Olympius	Corinthian	Decastyle, peripteral, columns 60 feet high, 96 feet by 259 feet. Enclosed by a peribolus. A Roman work, originally begun in the time of Pisistratus, continued by Antiochus Epiphanes, and completed by Hadrian.
Eleusis	Ceres	Doric	A square building of about 180 feet on each side, with a dodecastyle columnaie forming the west front. This temple, begun by Ictinus; colonnade added by Philo, architect, about 318 B.C.
"	Propylæum	Doric	Hexastyle on both fronts, with inner Ionic order at Athens, 56 feet by 40 feet. A second and smaller propylæum within the peribolus, dietyle in antis. See "Unedited Antiquities of Attica." None of these buildings now remain.
Thoricus		Doric	Epistyle, peripteral, or with seven columns at each end, and fourteen on each side. No cella remaining; but supposed to have been a double temple, with a passage through the centre, from the sides, dividing the cella into two.
Rhamnus	Nemesis	Doric	Hexastyle, peripteral, eleven intercolumns on sides, 35 feet by 70 feet.
"	Themis, or Lesser Temp. of Nemesis	Doric	Distyle in antis.
Ægina	Jupiter Panhellenius	Doric	Hexastyle, peripteral, hyperthral, 41 feet by 90 feet. This structure is celebrated for its polychromy and sculpture (the Æginetan Marbles).
Olympia	Jupiter Olympius	Doric	Hexastyle, peripteral, hyperthral, 95 feet by 230 feet. Completed about 435 B.C. Libon, architect.
Bassæ	Apollo Epicurius	Doric	Hexastyle, peripteral, hyperthral, 47 feet by 125 feet. Date, about 430 B.C. Ictinus, architect. In interior, Ionic columns.
Tegea	Athena Alea	Ionic	Peripteral, hyperthral. Doric internally; with upper Corinthian order. Scopas, architect.
Nemea	Jupiter	Doric	Hexastyle, peripteral.

MAGNA GRÆCIA AND SICILY.

Pæstum	Neptune	Doric	Hexastyle, peripteral, hyperthral, 79 feet by 195 feet.
	Ceres	Doric	Hexastyle, peripteral, 47 feet by 107 feet.
Agrigentum	Jupiter Olympius	Doric	Apteral, or with engaged columns, eptastyle, 182 feet by 369 feet. Wilkins, in his restoration of it, makes this temple hexastyle amphiprostyle.
"	Juno Lucina	Doric	Hexastyle, peripteral, 61 feet by 124 feet.
"	Concord	Doric	Hexastyle, peripteral, 31 feet by 93 feet. Deep pronaos and opisthodomos.
Segesta	"	Doric	Hexastyle, peripteral, 76 feet by 190 feet. All the external columns (unfluted) standing, but no remains of cella.
Selinus	Great Temple	Doric	Octastyle, dipteral, 180 feet by 330 feet. There are remains of five other temples, two of which appear to have been hexastyle peripteral.
Syracuse	Minerva	Doric	Hexastyle, 13 intercolumns on sides; now converted into a church with a modern Italian Corinthian façade.

TABLE OF SOME OF THE PRINCIPAL GREEK AND ROMAN
TEMPLES—*continued.*

ASIATIC GREEK.

Ephesus	Diana	Ionic	Decastyle, dipteral, hypæthral; columns 60 feet high; one of the largest Grecian temples, being 700 feet by 450 feet. Ctesiphon and Metagenes architects. Took about 340 B.C.
Miletus	Apollo Didymæus	Ionic	Decastyle, dipteral, hypæthral. 164 feet by 303 feet. Columns, 9½ diameters. Proclus, architect. A peribolus.
Magnesia	Diana	Ionic	Octostyle, pseudo-dipteral, 108 feet by 189 feet. Hermogenes, architect.
Priene	Minerva Polias	Ionic	Hexastyle, peripteral, 64 feet by 114 feet. Pytheos, architect, about 340 B.C. The order the best example of Asiatic Ionic. This temple had a peribolus and propylæum; the inner octastyle, with two rows of square pillars within.
Teos	Bacchus	Ionic	Hexastyle, peripteral. Hermogenes, architect; about the time of Alexander the Great.
Samos	Juno	Ionic	Decastyle, dipteral; 149 feet by 346 feet.

ROMAN.

Rome	Quirinal	Ionic	Hexastyle. Appears to have been a dipterale, but nothing of the cella remains.
"	Fortuna Virilis	Ionic	Tetrastyle, dipterastyle, cella pseudo-peripteral; about 34 feet by 44 feet.
"	Jupiter and Juno	Corinthian	Two separate temples, alongside each other, in centre of a colonnaded peribolus. Similar in dimensions, but the one octastyle, peripteral; the other octastyle, dipterastyle. Erected by Metellus Macedonicus, about 146 B.C. No remains; but the authority in the ancient plan of Rome in the capitol.
"	Jupiter Stator	Corinthian	Supposed to have been octastyle, peripteral. The celebrated "Three Columns" in the Forum, are all that now remain of this very fine example.
"	Jupiter Tonans	Corinthian	Octastyle, dipteral; 92 feet by 110 feet. Columns 42 feet high.
"	Mars Ultor	Corinthian	Of this temple, sometimes called that of Nerva, only three columns remaining; but it is said to have been octastyle, peripteral.
"	Venus and Roma	Corinthian	Decastyle, pseudo-peripteral, enclosed within a peribolus formed by double colonnades of a lesser order.
"	Antoninus and Faustina	Corinthian	Hexastyle, triprostyle; 33 feet by 95 feet.
"	Pantheon	Corinthian	An octastyle, triprostyle, attached to a rotunda.
"	Vesta	Corinthian	A circular peripteral of 20 columns.
Tivoli	Vesta, or the Sibyl	Corinthian	A circular peripteral, of 18 columns around cella. The order a very peculiar and fine example.
Præneste	Fortuna		No remains of this celebrated temple itself; but mosaics of the suites of terraces and flights of steps on which it was elevated.
Pompeii	Jupiter	Corinthian	Hexastyle, tetraprostyle; about 60 feet by 110 feet.
Nismes	Maison Carrée, or Temple of Caius and Lucius	Corinthian	Hexastyle, triprostyle; order continued along the cella, making it a pseudo-peripteral; 39 feet by 77 feet.
Baalbec	Great Temple	Corinthian	Decastyle, peripteral; 160 feet by 290 feet.
"	Lesser Temple	Corinthian	Octastyle, peripteral; 119 feet by 225 feet.
Palmyra	Helios, or the Sun	Corinthian	Octastyle, peripteral; 95 feet by 180 feet. Enclosed within a peribolus about 740 feet square, formed by an outer wall and two ranges of Corinthian columns, making a double colonnade.

SYNOPSIS OF THE PROPORTIONS OF THE DORIC, IONIC, CORINTHIAN, AND COMPOSITE ORDERS.

COMPILED BY W. H. LEEDS.

Names of Orders.	Base.		Column.		Capital.		Architrave.		Frieze.		Cornice.		Entablature.		Inter-columniation.		Diameter of Column.	
	Dia. Mod.	Ft.	Dia. Mod.	Ft.	Dia. Mod.	Ft.	Dia. Mod.	Ft.	Dia. Mod.	Ft.	Dia. Mod.	Ft.	Dia. Mod.	Ft.	Dia. Mod.	Ft.	Ft.	In.
DORIC.																		
Parthenon at Athens																		
Temple of Theseus, Athens																		
Great Temple of Paestum																		
Temple of Apollo, at Delos																		
Portico of Philip, &c.																		
Temple at Corinth																		
Propylaea at Athens																		
Portico of Augustus, Athens																		
Theatre of Marcellus, Rome																		
IONIC.																		
Temple on the Ilissus																		
Temple of Minerva Polias																		
Temple of Erechtheus, Athens																		
Temple of Fortuna Virilis, Rome																		
Theatre of Marcellus																		
CORINTHIAN.																		
Choragic Monument of Lysicrates																		
Temple of Jupiter Olympius, Athens																		
Incantada, at Salonica																		
Arch of Theseus, Athens																		
Temple of Jupiter Stator, Rome																		
Temple of Vespasian																		
Portico of Pantheon																		
Interior of Pantheon																		
Temple of Antoninus and Faustina																		
Arch of Constantine																		
Temple of Mars Ultor																		
Temple of the Sibyl, Tivoli																		
COMPOSITE.																		
Arch of Titus																		
Arch of Septimius Severus																		

LIST OF OBELISKS.

Situation.	Height.	Thickness.	
		At top.	Below.
	ft. in.	ft. in.	ft. in.
EGYPT.			
Obelisk of Heliopolis Hieroglyphics. It bears the oval of Ostragen I. of the XII th dynasty. (2022 B.C.)	{ 64 2 above the pedestal. }	. .	{ 6 1 N. & S. face. 6 3 E. & W. face. }
The Great Obelisk of Karnak Hieroglyphics. Erected by the Queen Amen-nou-hei. (1444 B.C.)	92 6	. .	8 0
The Smaller Obelisk of Karnak Hieroglyphics. Erected by Thotmes I. (1476 B.C.)	63 5	4 9	6 1
Obelisks of Luxor. Larger Smaller, taken to Paris Hieroglyphics. Erected by Ramses II. (1311 B.C.)	67 0 / 76 0	8 5 / 8 5	8 0 / 8 0
Obelisks of Alexandria (Cleopatra's Needles) Hieroglyphics. In the central line they bear the oval of Thotmes III., and in the lateral lines are the ovals of Ramses II.	70 0	. .	7 7
Obelisks of Paris. They are about ten in number, and are all of the time of Ramses II.; some with only one, others with two lines of hieroglyphics. They vary in size, some have a mean diameter of about 6 feet, and when entire, may have been from 60 to 80 feet high. Those at the lower extremity of the avenue, measure about 35 feet.			
Obelisk of Begig Hieroglyphics. It bears the oval of Ostragen I.	43 5		{ 6 94 Sides. 4 9 }
ROME.			
Obelisk of the Vatican Without hieroglyphics. It was erected by Sixtus V. in 1586. It was brought from Heliopolis to Rome in the reign of Caligula, and was found in the Circus of Nero.	82 6		8 10
Obelisk of S. Maria Maggiore Without hieroglyphics. Was erected in 1587 by Fontana, during the pontificate of Sixtus V. It was one of a pair which originally flanked the entrance of the mausoleum of Augustus.	48 5	2 9	6 5
Obelisk of the Lateran Hieroglyphics. Was erected by Fontana, in the pontificate of Sixtus V., in 1588. It was brought from Heliopolis to Alexandria by Constantine, and was removed to Rome by his son Constantius, who placed it on the spina of the Circus Maximus. It bears the ovals of Thotmes III. and Thotmes IV.	106 9	8 3	{ 9 94 9 0 }
Obelisk of the Piazza del Popolo, or Flaminian Hieroglyphics. Was erected by Fontana in 1589, during the pontificate of Sixtus V. It stood originally before the temple of the Sun at Heliopolis. It was removed to Rome by Augustus, and placed in the Circus Maximus. According to Lepsius it bears the oval of Seti I. (Menepthah.)	109 0	6 6	7 4
Obelisk of the Piazza Navona, or Pamphilian Hieroglyphics. Erected by Bernini in 1651, during the pontificate of Innocent X. A Roman work of the time of Domitian. It was found in the Circus of Romulus.	61 5	3 0	4 5
Obelisk of the Piazza della Minerva Hieroglyphics. Erected in 1667 by Bernini. Of the time of Apries (3rd B.C.)	17 6	2 0	2 6

Situation.	Height.	Thickness.	
		At top.	Below.
	ft. in.	ft. in.	ft. in.
Obelisk of the Pantheon	17 0	2 1	2 4
Hieroglyphics. Erected in 1711 by Clement XI. Of the time of Psammeticus II.			
Obelisk of the Monte Cavallo	45 0	. .	
Hieroglyphics. Erected in 1786 by Antinori. It formerly stood with that of St. Maria Maggiore, in front of the mausoleum of Augustus.			
Obelisk of the Trinita de Monte, or Sallustiano	49 0	3 0	4 0
Hieroglyphics. Erected by Antinori, in 1789. A Roman imitation of that of the Piazza del Popolo.			
Obelisk of Monte Citorio	72 0	4 0	5 9
Hieroglyphics. Erected by Antinori in 1792. It was brought to Rome by Augustus from Heliopolis, and placed in the Campus Martius, where it was used as a gnomon. According to Lepsius, it was erected in honour of Psammeticus I.			
Obelisk of Monte Pincio, or Barberini . .	30 0	2 2	3 0
Hieroglyphics. It was erected in honour of Antinous, by the name of Hadrian and Sabina.			
Obelisk of the Villa Matei	25 4	2 2	2 7
Hieroglyphics. It bears the oval of Psammeticus II.			
CONSTANTINOPLE.			
Obelisk in the Hippodrome, or Atmeidan . .	50 0	4 6	7 2
Hieroglyphics on two faces. Erected by the Emperor Theodosius. An imitation of an earlier work.			
Small Obelisk.	26 0	3 0	5 0
Hieroglyphics. In the Sultan's garden.			
Obelisk at Arles	54 1	6 0	7 0
Without hieroglyphics. It was discovered in 1389, and erected in 1675.			
Obelisk at Benevento.			
Hieroglyphics. A Roman imitation of the time of Domitian.			
The Borgian Obelisk.			
In the Egyptian Museum at Naples. A fragment found at Palestrina. An imitation.			
The Obelisk of Philæ	22 1½	1 5½	2 2
It is now erected at Kingston Hall, Dorset, and is the property of Mr. W. J. Banks.			
Obelisk of Cumae.			
It is polygonal. A Roman imitation.			
The Obelisks in the British Museum.			
These two obelisks are fragments. They are of black basalt.			

SHORT GRECIAN MEASURES OF LENGTH.

												—	Decimals of a Foot.	Feet.	Inches.
												Δάκτυλος	·0632	–	·7584375
2												Κόνδυλος	·1264	–	1·516875
4	2											Παλαιστή, Δῶρον, Δοχμή, or Δακτυλοδοχμή	·2528	–	3·03375
8	4	2										Διχάς, or Ἡμιπόδιον	·5056	–	6·0675
10	5	2½	1¼									Λιχάς	·6320	–	7·584375
11	5½	2¾	1⅜	1 1/10								Ὀρθόδωρον	·6952	–	8·3428125
12	6	3	1½	1⅕	1 1/11							Σπιθαμή	·7584	–	9·10125
16	8	4	2	1⅗	1 5/11	1⅓						ΠΟΥ͂Σ	1·01125	1	0·135
18	9	4½	2¼	1⅘	1 7/11	1½	1⅛					Πυγμή	1·13706	1	1·631875
20	10	5	2½	2	1 9/11	1⅔	1¼	1⅑				Πυγών	1·264	1	3·16875
24	12	6	3	2⅖	2 2/11	2	1½	1⅓	1⅕			ΠΗΧΥΣ	1·5169	1	6·2025
72	36	18	9	7⅕	6 6/11	6	4½	4	3⅗	3		Ξύλον	4·5506	4	6·6075
96	48	24	12	9⅗	8 8/11	8	6	5⅓	4⅘	4	1⅓	ὈΡΓΥΙΑ	6·0675	6	0·81

SHORT ROMAN MEASURES OF LENGTH.

						Decimals of a Foot.	Feet.	Inches.
Digitus						·060675		·7281
1¼	Uncia or Pollex					·0809		·9708
4	3	Palmus				·2427		2·9124
12	9	8	Palmus Major (of late times)			·7281		8·7372
16	12	4	1⅓	Pes		·9708		11·6496
20	15	5	1⅔	1¼	Palmipes	1·2135	1	2·563
24	18	6	2	1½	1¼ Cubitus	1·4562	1	5·4744

APPROXIMATE VALUES.—The Greek foot, cubit, and orguia only exceed the English foot, foot and a half, and fathom, by about 1-10th, 2-10ths, and 6-10ths of an inch respectively. The Roman uncia, pes, and cubitus only fall short of our inch, foot, and foot and a half, by less than 1-10th, 4-10ths, and 6-10ths of an inch respectively.

INDEX.